Peter Robinson grew up in Yorkshire, but now lives in Toronto.

His Inspector Banks series has won numerous awards in Britain, Europe, the United States and Canada.

PETER
ROBINSON

WEDNESDAY'S CHILD

&

DEAD RIGHT

INSPECTOR BANKS MYSTERIES

PAN BOOKS

Wednesday's Child first published in Great Britain 1994 by Chivers Press.
First published in paperback 2001 by Pan Books.
Dead Right first published in Great Britain 1997 by Constable.
First published in paperback 2001 by Pan Books.

This omnibus first published 2006 by Pan Books
an imprint of Pan Macmillan Ltd
Pan Macmillan, 20 New Wharf Road, London N1 9RR
Basingstoke and Oxford
Associated companies throughout the world
www.panmacmillan.com

ISBN-13: 978-0-330-44677-8
ISBN-10: 0-330--44677-0

1 3 5 7 9 8 6 4 2

A CIP catalogue record for this book is available from
the British Library.

Typeset by SX Composing DTP, Rayleigh, Essex
Printed and bound in Great Britain by
Mackays of Chatham plc, Chatham, Kent

WEDNESDAY'S CHILD

For Sheila

'Lost in the desart wild
Is your little child.
How can Lyca sleep
If her mother weep?'

. . .

Sleeping Lyca lay
While the beasts of prey,
Come from caverns deep,
View'd the maid asleep.

William Blake
'The Little Girl Lost'

1

ONE

The room was a tip, the woman was a slattern. On the floor, near the door to the kitchen, a child's doll with one eye missing lay naked on its back, right arm raised above its head. The carpet around it was so stained with ground-in mud and food, it was hard to tell what shade of brown it had been originally. High in one corner, by the front window, pale flowered wallpaper had peeled away from a damp patch. The windows were streaked with grime, and the flimsy orange curtains needed washing.

When Detective Chief Inspector Alan Banks perched at the edge of the scuffed olive-green armchair, he felt a spring dig into the back of his left thigh. He noticed Detective Constable Susan Gay turn up her nose as she looked at a garish oil painting of Elvis Presley above the mantelpiece. 'The King' was wearing a jewelled white cape with a high collar and held a microphone in his ringed hand.

In contrast to the shabby decor, a compact music centre in mint condition stood against one wall, a green and yellow budgie in a cage nonchalantly sharpened its bill on a cuttlefish, and an enormous matt black colour television blared out from one corner. *Blockbusters* was on, and Banks heard Bob Holness ask, 'What "B" is the name of an African country bordering on South Africa?'

'Could you turn the sound down, please, Mrs Scupham?' Banks asked the woman.

She looked at him blankly at first, as if she didn't understand his request, then she walked over and turned off the TV altogether. 'You can call me Brenda,' she said when she sat down again.

Banks took a closer look at her. In her late twenties, with long dirty-blonde hair showing dark roots, she possessed a kind of blowzy sexuality that hinted at concupiscent pleasure in bed. It was evident in the languor of her movements, the way she walked as if she were in a hot and humid climate.

She was a few pounds overweight, and her pink poloneck sweater and black miniskirt looked a size too small. Her full, pouty lips were liberally coated in scarlet lipstick, which matched her long, painted fingernails, and her vacuous, pale blue eyes, surrounded by matching eyeshadow, made Banks feel he had to repeat every question he asked.

Seeing the ashtray on the scratched coffee table in front of him, Banks took out his cigarettes and offered the woman one. She accepted, leaning forward and holding back her hair with one hand as he lit it for her. She blew the smoke out through her nose, emulating some star she had seen in a film. He lit a cigarette himself, mostly to mask the peculiar smell, redolent of boiled cabbage and nail-polish remover, that permeated the room.

'When did you first get the feeling something was wrong?' he asked her.

She paused and frowned, then answered in a low voice, husky from too many cigarettes. 'Just this afternoon. I phoned them, and they said they'd never heard of Mr Brown and Miss Peterson.'

'And you got worried?'

'Yes.'

'Why did you wait so long before checking up?'

Brenda paused to draw on her cigarette. 'I don't know,' she said. 'I thought she'd be all right, you know . . .'

'But you could have called this morning. That's when they said they'd bring her back, isn't it?'

'Yes. I don't know. I suppose so. I just . . . Besides, I'd got things to do.'

'Did the visitors show you any identification?'

'They had cards, like, all official.'

'What did the cards say?'

Mrs Scupham turned her head to one side, showing only her profile. 'I didn't really get a good look. It all happened so fast.'

'Did the cards have photographs on them?'

'No, I don't think so. I'm sure I would have noticed.'

'What exactly did they say to you?' Banks asked.

'They told me their names and said they was from the social, like, and then they showed their cards . . .'

'This was at the door, before you let them in?'

'Yes. And then they said they'd come to see me about my Gemma. Well, I had to let them in, didn't I? They were from the authorities.'

Her voice cracked a little when she mentioned her daughter's name, and she sucked her lower lip. Banks nodded. 'What happened next?'

'When I let them in, they said they'd had reports of Gemma being . . . well, being abused . . .'

'Did they say where they'd heard this?'

She shook her head.

'Didn't you ask them?'

'I didn't think to. They seemed so . . . I mean, he was

wearing a nice suit and his hair was all short and neatly brushed down, and she was dressed proper smart, too. They just seemed so sure of themselves. I didn't think to ask anything.'

'Was there any truth in what they said?'

Mrs Scupham flushed. 'Of course not. I love my Gemma. I wouldn't harm her.'

'Go on,' Banks said. 'What did they say next?'

'That's about it really. They said they had to take her in, just overnight, for some tests and examinations, and if everything was all right they'd bring her back this morning, just like I told you on the phone. When they didn't come, I got so worried . . . I . . . How could anyone do something like that, steal someone else's child?'

Banks could see the tears forming in her eyes. He knew there was nothing he could say to console her. In fact, the best thing he could do was keep quiet about how bloody stupid she'd been, and not ask her if she hadn't heard about the cases, just a few years ago, when bogus social workers had visited homes all around England with stories just like the one they'd given her. No, best keep quiet.

She had a fear of authority, probably bred into her, that meant she would believe just about anything that someone in a suit with a card, a nice haircut and an educated accent told her. She wasn't unique in that. Most often, the phoney social workers had simply asked to examine the children in the home, not to remove them. For all the mothers who had sent them packing, Banks wondered how many had allowed the examination and had then been too afraid or ashamed to admit it.

'How old is Gemma?' Banks asked.

'Seven. Just seven.'

'Where's your husband?'

Mrs Scupham crossed her legs and folded her hands on her lap. 'I'm not married,' she said. 'You might as well know. Well, there's no shame in it these days, is there, what with so much divorce about.'

'What about Gemma's father?'

'Terry?' She curled her upper lip in disgust. 'He's long gone.'

'Do you know where he is?'

Mrs Scupham shook her head. 'He left when Gemma was three. I haven't seen or heard from him since. And good riddance.'

'We need to contact him,' Banks pressed. 'Can you give us any information at all that might help?'

'Why? You don't . . . surely you don't think Terry could have had anything to do with it?'

'We don't think anything yet. At the very least he deserves to know what's happened to his daughter.'

'I don't see why. He never cared when he was around. Why should he care now?'

'Where is he, Brenda?'

'I've told you, I don't know.'

'What's his full name?'

'Garswood. Terry Garswood. Terence, I suppose, but everyone called him Terry.'

'What was his job?'

'He was in the army. Hardly ever around.'

'Is there anyone else? A man, I mean.'

'There's Les. We've been together nearly a year now.'

'Where is he?'

She jerked her head. 'Where he always is, the Barley-corn round the corner.'

'Does he know what's happened?'

'Oh, aye, he knows. We had a row.'

Banks saw Susan Gay look up from her notebook and shake her head slowly in disbelief.

'Can I have another fag?' Brenda Scupham asked. 'I meant to get some more, but it just slipped my mind.'

'Of course.' Banks gave her a Silk Cut. 'Where do you work, Brenda?'

'I don't . . . I . . . I stay home.' He lit the cigarette for her, and she coughed when she took her first drag. Patting her chest, she said, 'Must stop.'

Banks nodded. 'Me, too. Look, Brenda, do you think you could give us a description of this Mr Brown and Miss Peterson?'

She frowned. 'I'll try. I'm not very good with faces, though. Like I said, he had a nice suit on, Mr Brown, navy blue it was, with narrow white stripes. And he had a white shirt and a plain tie. I'm not sure what colour that was, dark anyways.'

'How tall was he?'

'About average.'

'What's that?' Banks stood up. 'Taller or shorter than me?' At around five foot nine, Banks was small for a policeman, hardly above regulation height.

'About the same.'

'Hair?'

'Black, sort of like yours, but longer, and combed straight back. And he was going a bit thin at the sides.'

'How old would you say he was?'

'I don't know. He had a boyish look about him, but he was probably around thirty, I'd say.'

'Is there anything else you can tell us about him? His voice, mannerisms?'

'Not really.' Brenda flicked some ash at the ashtray and

missed. 'Like I said, he had a posh accent. Oh, there was one thing, though I don't suppose it'd be any help.'

'What's that?'

'He had a nice smile.'

And so it went. When they had finished, Banks had a description of Mr Brown that would match at least half the young businessmen in Eastvale, or in the entire country, for that matter, and one of Miss Peterson – brunette, hair coiled up at the back, well-spoken, nice figure, expensive clothes – that would fit a good number of young professional women.

'Did you recognize either of them?' he asked. 'Had you seen them around before?' Banks didn't expect much to come from this – Eastvale was a fair-sized town – but it was worth a try.

She shook her head.

'Did they touch anything while they were here?'

'I don't think so.'

'Did you offer them tea or anything?'

'No. Of course I didn't.'

Banks was thinking of fingerprints. There was a slight chance that if they had drunk tea or coffee, Mrs Scupham might not have washed the cups yet. Certainly any prints on the door handles, if they hadn't been too blurred in the first place, would have been obscured by now.

Banks asked for, and got, a fairly recent school photograph of Gemma Scupham. She was a pretty child, with the same long hair as her mother – her blonde colouring was natural, though – and a sad, pensive expression on her face that belied her seven years.

'Where could she be?' Brenda Scupham asked. 'What have they done to her?'

'Don't worry. We'll find her.' Banks knew how empty

the words sounded as soon as he had spoken them. 'Is there anything else you can tell us?'

'No, I don't think so.'

'What was Gemma wearing?'

'Wearing? Oh, those yellow overall things, what do you call them?'

'Dungarees?'

'Yes, that's right. Yellow dungarees over a white T-shirt: it had some cartoon animal on the front. Donald Duck, I think. She loved cartoons.'

'Did the visitors mention any name other than Brown or Peterson?'

'No.'

'Did you see their car?'

'No, I didn't look. You don't, do you? I just let them in and we talked, then they went off with Gemma. They were so nice, I . . . I just can't believe it.' Her lower lip trembled and she started to cry, but it turned into another coughing fit.

Banks stood up and gestured for Susan to follow him out into the hall. 'You'd better stay with her,' he whispered.

'But, sir—'

Banks held his hand up. 'It's procedure, Susan. And she might remember something else, something important. I'd also like you to get something with Gemma's fingerprints on it. But first I want you to radio in and tell Sergeant Rowe to phone Superintendent Gristhorpe and let him know what's going on. You'd better get someone to contact all the Yorkshire social services, too. You never know, someone might have made a cock-up of the paperwork and we'd look right wallies if we didn't check. Ask Phil to organize a house-to-house of the neighbourhood.' He handed her the photograph. 'And arrange to get some copies of this made.'

Susan went out to the unmarked police Rover, and Banks turned back into the living room, where Brenda Scupham seemed lost in her own world of grief. He touched her lightly on the shoulder. 'I have to go,' he said. 'DC Gay will be back in a moment. She'll stay with you. And don't worry. We're doing all we can.'

He walked down the short path to the patrol car and tapped on the window. 'You told me you searched the place, right?' he said to the constable behind the wheel, pointing back up the path with his thumb.

'Yes, sir, first thing.'

'Well, do it again, just to be certain. And send someone to get Mrs Scupham a packet of fags, too. Silk Cut'll do. I'm off to the pub.' He headed down the street leaving a puzzled young PC behind him.

TWO

Detective Superintendent Gristhorpe squatted by his dry-stone wall in the back garden of his house above the village of Lyndgarth and contemplated retirement. He would be sixty in November, and while retirement was not mandatory, surely after more than forty years on the job it was time to move aside and devote himself to his books and his garden, as the wise old Roman, Virgil, had recommended.

He placed a stone, then stood up, acutely aware of the creak in his knees and the ache in his lower back as he did so. He had been working at the wall for too long. Why he bothered, the Lord only knew. After all, it went nowhere and closed in nothing. His grandfather had been a master waller in the dale, but the skill had not been passed down the generations. He supposed he liked it for the same reason he liked fishing: mindless relaxation. In an age of technocratic utilitarianism, Gristhorpe thought, a man needs as much purposeless activity as he can find.

The sun had set a short while ago, and the sharp line of Aldington Edge cut high on the horizon to the north, underlining a dark mauve and purple sky. As Gristhorpe walked towards the back door, he felt the chill in the light breeze that ruffled his thatch of unruly grey hair. Mid-September, and autumn was coming to the dale.

Inside the house, he brewed a pot of strong black tea, threw together a Wensleydale cheese and pickle sandwich, then went into his living room. The eighteenth-century farmhouse was sturdily built, with walls thick enough to withstand the worst a Yorkshire winter could throw at them, and since his wife's death Gristhorpe had transformed the living room into a library. He had placed his favourite armchair close to the stone hearth and spent so many an off-duty hour reading there that the heat from the fire had cracked the leather upholstery on one side.

Gristhorpe had given the television his wife had enjoyed so much to Mrs Hawkins, the lady who 'did' for him, but he kept the old walnut-cabinet wireless so he could listen to the news, *My Word*, cricket and the plays that sometimes came on in the evenings. Two walls were lined with floor-to-ceiling bookshelves, and a series of framed prints from Hogarth's *A Rake's Progress* hung over the fireplace.

Gristhorpe set his tea and sandwich beside the books on the small round table, within easy reach, and settled back with a sigh into his chair. The only sounds that broke the silence were the wind soughing through the elms and the ticking of the grandfather clock in the hall.

To retire or not to retire, that was the question that kept him from immediately picking up *The Way of All Flesh*. Over the past few years he had delegated most of the investigative work to his team and spent his time on administrative and co-ordinating duties. He had absolute trust in Alan Banks, his protégé, and both DS Richmond and the recently appointed DC Gay were coming along well. Should he move aside and clear the space for Banks's promotion? Certainly Alan showed an enthusiasm for work and learning that reminded Gristhorpe of himself as a young lad. Both lacked formal education beyond the local grammar school, but neither let it hold them back. Banks was a good detective, despite his anti-authoritarian tendencies, occasional rashness and a loathing for the politics that were now becoming so much a part of the job. But Gristhorpe admired him for that. He, himself, hated police politics. Banks, though twenty years younger, was a real copper, a man who had come from the street. He also had imagination and curiosity, two qualities that Gristhorpe thought essential.

And what would he do with his time if he did retire? There was the drystone wall, of course, but that was hardly a full-time occupation. Nor was reading, especially with the way his eyesight had been declining of late. He was at an age when every odd ache or pain brought a little more fear than it had before, when colds lingered and settled on the chest. But he was no hypochondriac. The Gristhorpes were robust, always had been.

He would like to travel, he decided, to revisit Venice, Florence, Paris, Madrid, and go somewhere he had never been before – the Far East, perhaps, or Russia. But travel cost money, and a policeman's pension wouldn't stretch that far. Gristhorpe sighed and picked up Samuel Butler. He didn't have to make his decision tonight; best wait for a while.

He had hardly got through the first paragraph when the phone rang. Marking the page with a leather strip and putting the book aside, he got up and walked into the hall. It was Sergeant Rowe from the station. He had received a message from Susan Gay about a child gone missing from the East Side Estate. Could the superintendent come in as soon as possible? Gristhorpe could get few more details over the phone, except that the child had been taken by a man and a woman pretending to be social workers and that she had been gone over a day. As he listened to Sergeant Rowe deliver the message in his flat, emotionless voice, Gristhorpe felt a shiver go up his spine.

Grimly, he put on his tweed jacket and went outside to the car. It was completely dark now, and the lights of Lyndgarth twinkled below on the daleside. Gristhorpe drove through the village, past the squat St Mary's, and onto the main Eastvale Road. It was a journey he had made hundreds of times, and he drove automatically, without even having to think about the dips and turns. Normally, even in the dark, he would glance at certain landmarks – the lights of the old Lister house way up on the opposite slopes of the valley; the six trees bent over by the wind on the drumlin to the west – but this time he was too distracted to notice the landscape.

As he drove towards the lights of Eastvale, he remembered that long Saturday in October 1965, when he and dozens of other young policemen had stood in the drizzle and the biting wind 1,600 feet up the Pennines listening to their orders. There they all stood, in anoraks and wellington boots, shivering in the late autumn cold on the top of Saddleworth Moor, complaining about the Saturday afternoon football they were missing. It was eerie enough just being up there in the banshee wind, the rain and inky light, with those outcrops of rocks like decayed teeth on the skyline. All day they had searched, dragging their feet through the mud and peat, from nine thirty a.m. until well after three o'clock. The rain had stopped by then, and the weather was a little warmer, the moor shrouded in a slight mist.

Suddenly Gristhorpe had heard the shout from a searcher in the distance: a young lad, he remembered, just out of training college, who had taken a break to answer a call of nature. Those nearby, Gristhorpe included, hurried towards him, and watched in horror as Detective Sergeant Eckersley came and scraped away the clinging peat from a child's arm bone. A little more digging revealed a head. Eckersley stopped at that. He sent for the scene-of-crime officers, and soon they all arrived, out of nowhere, the Assistant Chief Constable, police surgeons, photographers, Joe Mounsey, the lot.

They put up canvas screens and everyone but the brass and the SOCOs had to stand back. As the doctor scraped off the dirt and the flash camera popped, the whole gruesome discovery finally lay revealed. Gristhorpe caught only a glimpse of the body through a gap in the canvas, but it was enough.

They had been looking for a boy called John Kilbride, but what they had found was the near-skeletal body of a girl lying on her side with her right arm raised above her head. Close to her feet, her clothes lay bundled – a blue coat, a pink cardigan, a red and green tartan skirt. Instead of John Kilbride, they had found the body of Lesley Ann

Downey, aged ten, another victim of the couple who came to be called the 'Moors Murderers', Ian Brady and Myra Hindley.

Somehow, that day stood engraved in Gristhorpe's memory more than any other day in his life. Months, even years, might go by and he wouldn't even think of that October day in 1965, but when something like this happened, there it was, every bit as real and as horrifying as if he were back there on the moor seeing that arm sticking up through the quagmire as if it were waving or pointing.

He had thought of it only once in the past few years, and that was when a sixteen-year-old girl had gone missing from one of the Swainsdale villages. And now two people, a man and a woman – just as Brady and Hindley had been – had walked bold as brass into a house on the East Side Estate and abducted a seven-year-old girl.

As Gristhorpe drove down narrow North Market Street past the Town Hall, the lit window displays of the tourist shops and the community centre, he gripped the wheel so hard his knuckles turned white as he once again heard the girl's voice in his head from the tape Brady and Hindley recorded before they murdered her: Lesley Ann whimpering and begging for her mummy and daddy to help her; Brady telling her to put something in her mouth and saying he wants to photograph her. And that damn music, that damn music, 'The Little Drummer Boy'. Gristhorpe had never been able to listen comfortably to any music since then without hearing the girl screaming and begging for mercy in his head, and he let everyone believe he was tone deaf to avoid awkward explanations.

He turned his car into the parking area at the back of the station, an old Tudor-fronted building, the front of which faced Eastvale's market square, and sat for a few moments to calm himself down and rid himself of the memory. And before he went inside, he delivered a silent prayer – not without some embarrassment, for he wasn't a religious man – that there should be nothing, *nothing* to compare between this affair and the Moors Murders. No time for thoughts of retirement now.

THREE

As Banks walked down the street towards the Barleycorn, he glanced at the rows of identical red-brick houses. There was no doubt about it, the East Side Estate was a disaster. True, some tenants had bought the houses when the Thatcher government sold them off, and many had added a white fence here, a lick of paint there, or even a dormer window. But it was a shabby area, with junk-littered lawns, children's tricycles left in the street, and mangy dogs running free, fouling the pavements, barking and snapping at passers-by.

And the Barleycorn was a typical estate pub, right from its unimaginative name and its squat, flat-roofed exterior to its jukebox, video games and poorly kept keg beer.

Banks pushed open the door and glanced around. Little Richard's 'Good Golly Miss Molly' was playing too loudly on the jukebox. The cash register rang up another sale. Most of the tables were empty, and only a few diehard drinkers stood at the bar.

As the door shut behind him, Banks noticed the people look in his direction, and suddenly one man took off towards the back. Banks dashed after him, bumping his knee on a chair and knocking it over as he went. He caught the man by the shoulder just before he had reached the exit. The man tried to pull free, but Banks kept his grip, spun him around and hit him hard, just once, in the solar plexus. The man groaned and doubled up. Banks took him by the elbow and helped him to a table the way one escorts an elderly relative.

As soon as they had sat down, the barman rushed over.

'Look, mister, I don't want no trouble,' he said.

'Good,' Banks answered. 'Neither do I. But I'd like a small brandy for my friend here, just to settle his stomach.'

'What do you think I am, a bloody waitress?'

Banks looked at the man. He was about six feet tall and gone to fat. His nose looked as if it had been broken a few times, and old scar tissue hooded his left eye.

'Just bring the drink,' Banks said. 'I won't have anything myself. Not while I'm on duty.'

The barman stared at Banks, then his jaw dropped. He shrugged and turned back to the bar. In a few seconds he came back with the brandy. 'It's on the house,' he mumbled.

Banks thanked him and passed the glass over to his companion, who sat rubbing his stomach and gasping for breath. 'Here's to your health, Les.'

The man glared at him through teary eyes, knocked back the brandy in one and banged the glass down hard on the table. 'You didn't need to have done that,' he said. 'I was only off for a piss.'

'Bollocks, Les,' said Banks. 'The only time 've seen anyone run as fast as that to the bog they had dysentery. Why were you running?'

'I told you.'

'I know, but I want you to tell me the truth.'

Les Poole was well known to the Eastvale police and had been a frequent guest at the station. He had congenitally sticky fingers and couldn't stand the idea of anything belonging to anyone else but him. Consequently, he had been in and out of jail since Borstal, mostly for burglary. No doubt, Banks thought, had he the intelligence, he might also have risen to the dizzy heights of fraud and blackmail. Les had never held a job, though rumour had it that he had, in fact, once worked as a dustbin man for six weeks but got the sack for wasting too much time rummaging through people's rubbish looking for things he could keep or sell. In short, Banks thought, Les Poole was little more than a doodle in the margin of life. At least until now.

Les was an odd-looking character, too, like someone who had fallen through a time warp from the 1950s. He had greased-back hair, complete with quiff, sideboards and duck's arse, a triangular face with a Kirk Douglas dimple on his chin, a long, thin nose, and eyes as flat and grey as slate. About Banks's height, he was wearing a black leather jacket, red T-shirt and jeans. His beer belly bulged over the belt. He looked as if he should be playing stand-up bass in a rockabilly band. Why he had always been so attractive to women, Banks couldn't fathom. Maybe it was his long dark eyelashes.

'Well?' prompted Banks.

'Well what?'

Banks sighed. 'Let's start this again, Les. What we'll do is we'll back up and lead nice and slowly to the question. Maybe that way you'll be able to understand it, all right?'

Les Poole just glared at him. Banks lit a cigarette and went on. 'I came down here to ask if you know anything about young Gemma's disappearance. Do you?'

'She was taken away, that's all I know. Brenda told me.'

'Where were you when it happened?'

'Eh?'

'Where were you yesterday afternoon?'

'Out and about.'

'Doing what?'

'Oh, this and that.'

'Right. So while you were out and about doing this and that, a man and a woman, both well dressed and official-looking, called at your house, said they were child-care workers, talked their way inside and persuaded Brenda to hand over her daughter for tests and further examination. Now what I want to know, Les, is do you know anything about that?'

Les shrugged. 'It's not my kid, is it? I can't help it if she's so fucking daft she'll give her kid away.'

The barman appeared at Banks's shoulder and asked if they wanted anything else.

'I'll have a pint, Sid,' Les said.

'Bring me one too, this time,' Banks added. 'I feel like I bloody well need it.'

After the barman had brought the beer, which tasted more like cold dishwater than real ale, Banks carried on.

'Right,' he said, 'so we've established you don't give a damn about the child one way or another. That still doesn't answer my questions. Where were you, and do you know anything about it?'

'Now come on, Mr Banks. I know I've been in a bit of bother now and then, but surely even you can't suspect me of doing a thing like that? This is what they call persecution, this is. Just because I've got a record you think you can pin everything on me.'

'Don't be a silly bugger, Les. I'm not trying to pin anything on you yet. For a start, I couldn't picture you in a suit, and even if you'd managed to nick one from somewhere, I think Brenda might still have recognized you, don't you?'

'You don't have to take the piss, you know.'

'Let's make it simple, then. Do you know *anything* about what happened?'

'No.'

'Right. Another one: what were you doing?'

'What's that got to do with anything? I don't see what that's got to do with anything. I mean, if you don't suspect me, why does it matter where I was?'

'Got a job, Les?'

'Me? Nah.'

'I don't suppose you'd want me to know if you did have, would you? I might tell the social and they'd cut off your benefits, wouldn't they?'

'I don't have a job, Mr Banks. You know what it's like these days, all that unemployment and all.'

'Join the rest of us in the 90s, Les. Maggie's gone. The three million unemployed are a thing of the past.'

'Still . . .'

'Okay. So you don't have a job. What were you doing?'

'Just helping a mate move some junk, that's all.'

'That's better. His name?'

'John.'

'And where does he live, this John?'

'He's got a shop, second-hand stuff, down Rampart Street, over by the Oak . . .'

'I know it. So you spent the afternoon with this bloke John, helping him in his shop?'

'Yeah.'

'I suppose he'd confirm that?'

'Come again?'

'If I asked him, he'd tell me you were with him.'

'Course he would.'

'Where'd you get the nice new television and stereo, Les?'

'What do you mean? They're Brenda's. She had them before she met me. Ask her.'

'Oh, I'm sure she'll back you up. The thing is, they don't look that old. And Fletcher's electronics warehouse got broken into last Friday night. Someone took off with a van full of stereos and televisions. Did you know that?'

'Can't say as I did. Anyway, what's all this in aid of? I thought you were after the kid.'

'I cast a wide net, Les. A wide net. Why did Brenda wait so long before calling us?'

'How should I know? Because she's a stupid cow, I suppose.'

'Sure it was nothing to do with you?'

'What do you mean?'

'She said you had a row. Maybe you didn't want the police coming to the house and seeing that television, or the new music centre.'

'Look, I told you—'

'I know what you told me, Les. Why don't you answer the question? Was it you persuaded Brenda to wait so long before calling us?'

Poole looked away and said nothing.

'Do you know Gemma could be dead?'

Poole shrugged.

'For Christ's sake, don't you care?'

'I told you, she's not my kid. Bloody nuisance, if you ask me.'

'You ever hit her, Les?'

'Me? Course I didn't. That's not my style.'

'Ever see Brenda do it?'

Poole shook his head. Banks stood up, glanced at the beer in his glass and decided to leave it.

'I'm off now, Les,' he said, 'but I'll be around. You'll be seeing so much of the police in the next few days you'll think you've died and gone to hell. And I want you to stick around, too. Know what I mean? Be seeing you.'

Banks left the Barleycorn for the dark autumn evening. He was wearing only his sports jacket over his shirt, and he felt the chill in the air as he walked back to Brenda Scupham's with a terrier yapping at his heels. Television screens flickered behind curtains, some pulled back just an inch or two so the neighbours could watch all the excitement at number twenty-four.

As he turned up the path, he thought of Brenda and the enormity of what she had allowed. He could have told her about the recent Children's Act, designed to protect parents from overzealous social workers, but he knew he would only get a blank stare in return. Besides, telling her that was as clear an example as you can get of bolting the stable door after the horse has gone.

He thought again about Les Poole and wondered what he was hiding. Maybe it had just been the criminal's typical nervousness at an encounter with the police. Whatever it was, it had been evident in his clipped answers, his evasions, his nervous body language, and most of all in the guilty thoughts Banks could see skittering about like tiny insects behind the slate eyes.

FOUR

Gristhorpe tried to recall whether he had left anything undone. He had informed the ACC, made sure the press had all the information they needed, set up a mobile unit on a patch of waste ground at the end of Brenda Scupham's street, drawn up a search plan, arranged to draft in extra personnel, and got someone working on a list of all known local child-molesters. Also, he had faxed the bare details and a copy of Gemma's photograph to the paedophile squad, which operated out of Vine Street police station, in London. Soon, every policeman in the county would be on the alert. In the morning, the searchers would begin. For now, though, there was nothing more he could do until he had discussed developments with Banks.

His stomach rumbled, and he remembered the cheese and pickle sandwich left uneaten on the table at home, the tea going cold. Leaving a message for Banks, he went across the street to the Queen's Arms and persuaded Cyril, the landlord, to make him a ham sandwich, which he washed down with a half-pint of bitter.

He had been sitting hunched over his beer at a dimpled, copper-topped table for about ten minutes, oblivious to the buzz of conversation around him, when a voice startled him out of his dark thoughts.

'Sir?'

Gristhorpe looked up and saw Banks standing over him. 'Everything all right, Alan?' Gristhorpe asked. 'You look knackered.'

'I am,' said Banks, sitting down and reaching for his cigarettes. 'This Gemma Scupham business . . .'

'Aye,' said Gristhorpe. 'Get yourself a drink and we'll see what we can come up with.'

Banks bought a packet of cheese and onion crisps and a pint, then told Gristhorpe about his suspicions of Les Poole.

Gristhorpe rubbed his chin and frowned. 'We'll keep an

eye on him, then,' he said. 'Give him a bit of slack. If we bring him in over that Fletcher's warehouse job it'll do us no good. Besides, we can hardly cart off the poor woman's telly when someone's just abducted her child, can we?'

'Agreed,' said Banks. 'OK. So far we've got six men working on the house-to-house, questioning the neighbours. Phil and Susan are with them. At least there's a chance someone might have seen the car.'

'What about the mother? Who's with her?'

'Susan stayed for a while, then she offered to get a WPC to come in, but Mrs Scupham didn't want one. I don't think either she or Les feel comfortable with the police around. Anyway, she's got a friend in.'

'I suppose we'd better start with the obvious, hadn't we?' Gristhorpe said. 'Do you believe the mother's story?'

Banks took a sip of beer. 'I think so. She seemed genuinely shocked, and I don't think she's bright enough to make up a story like that.'

'Oh, come on, Alan. It doesn't take much imagination. She could have hurt the child, gone too far and killed her – or Poole could have – then they dumped the body and made up this cock and bull story.'

'Yes, she could have. All I'm saying is the story seems a bit over-elaborate. It would have been a hell of a lot easier just to say that Gemma had been snatched while she was out playing, wouldn't it, rather than having to make up descriptions of two people and risk us finding it odd that no one in the street saw them. They're a nosy lot down on the East Side Estate. Anyway, I had the officers on the scene search the house thoroughly twice and they didn't come up with anything. We've got a SOCO team there now doing their bit. If there's any sign Gemma was harmed in the house, then taken somewhere else, they'll find it.'

Gristhorpe sighed. 'I suppose we can rule out kidnapping?'

'Brenda Scupham's got no money. She might be fiddling the social, making a bit on the side, but that hardly makes her Mrs Rothschild.'

'What about the father? Custody battle? Maybe he hired someone to snatch Gemma for him?'

Banks shook his head. 'According to Brenda, he's not interested, hasn't been for years. We're tracking him down anyway.'

Gristhorpe waved a plume of smoke aside. 'I don't like the alternatives,' he said.

'Me neither, but we've got to face them. Remember those stories a while back? Paedophiles posing as social workers and asking to examine people's kids for evidence of abuse?'

Gristhorpe nodded.

'Luckily most parents sent them away,' Banks went on. 'But suppose this time they succeeded?'

'I've checked on the descriptions with the divisions involved,' Gristhorpe said, 'and they don't match. But you're right. It's something we have to consider. Someone else could have got the idea from reading the papers. Then there's the ritual stuff to consider, too.'

Not long ago, the press had been rife with stories of children used for ritual abuse, often with satanic overtones. In Cleveland, Nottingham, Rochdale and the Orkneys, children were taken into care after allegations of just such abuse involving torture, starvation, humiliation and sexual molestation. Nobody had come up with any hard evidence – in fact, most people thought it was more likely that the children needed to be protected from the social workers – but the rumours were disturbing enough.

And Gristhorpe didn't fool himself that such a thing couldn't happen in Eastvale. It could.

That Satanists now existed out in the dale was beyond doubt. There had been trouble with them recently, when local farmers had complained of finding sheep ritually slaughtered in copses and hollows. There was a big difference between sheep and children, of course, as there was between Satanism and witchcraft. Gristhorpe had been aware of local witch covens for years. They consisted mostly of meek husbands and bored housewives in search of an evening's naughtiness dancing naked in the woods. But the Satanists were a different breed. If they could go as far as killing sheep and draining their blood, what would they stop at?

'But you know what I'm thinking about most of all, don't you, Alan?' Banks was one of the few people Gristhorpe had talked to about his small role in the Moors Murders and the lasting effect it had on him.

Banks nodded.

'Different way of operating, of course. Brady and Hindley snatched their victims. But there could be reasons for that. It's the couple aspect that bothers me. A man *and* a woman. I know there's been a lot of argument about Myra Hindley's degree of involvement, but there's no doubt they acted together. Call it what you will – maybe some kind of psychotic symbiosis – but without the other, it's a good bet neither would have committed those crimes. Alone, they were nothing, nobodies living in fantasy worlds, but together they progressed from Hitler-worship and pornography to murder. Hindley acted as a catalyst to turn Brady's fantasies into reality, and he acted them out to impress her and exercise his power over her. Christ, Alan, if a couple like that's got hold of little Gemma

Scupham, God have mercy on her soul.' Again, Gristhorpe remembered the tape, Lesley Ann begging, 'Please don't undress me!' Brady telling her, 'If you don't keep that hand down I'll slit your neck.' And that other gruesome touch, the children's choir singing carols in the background.

'We don't know,' said Banks. 'We know bugger-all so far.'

Gristhorpe rubbed his brow. 'Aye, you're right. No sense jumping to conclusions. On the bright side, let's hope it was some poor young childless couple who just went too far to get themselves a kiddie.' He shook his head. 'It doesn't make sense, though, does it? If they took the child out of love, how could they reconcile themselves to the mother's pain? There'd be too much guilt to allow them any happiness. And I doubt they'd be able to keep a secret like that for very long.'

'I've asked Phil if he can tie in with HOLMES on this,' Banks said. 'Remember that course he went on?'

Gristhorpe nodded. HOLMES stood for Home Office Large Major Enquiry System. Developed during the hunt for the Yorkshire Ripper, HOLMES basically allows all reports coming out of an investigation to be entered and organized into a relational database. That way, a key word or phrase can be tracked more accurately than before, through previously unrelated data.

And that was as far as Gristhorpe could follow. The rest, like most computer talk, was gobbledegook to him. In fact, the mere mention of megabytes and DOS brought out the latent Luddite in him. Still, he didn't underestimate their value. An inquiry like this would generate a lot of paperwork, and every statement, every report, no matter how minor or negative, would be entered, and cross-checks would be made. He wanted no cock-ups along the lines of the Yorkshire Ripper investigation, where the left hand hadn't seemed to know what the right hand was doing.

'Phil says he'd like computers in the mobile unit,' Banks added. 'That way the officers can put everything on disk and pass it on to him without any retyping.'

'I'll see what I can do. Any more ideas?'

'Just a couple. I'd like a chat with the girl's teacher, see what I can find out about her. I'm damn sure there's been some abuse involved. Both Poole and Brenda Scupham deny it, but not convincingly enough.'

Gristhorpe nodded. 'Go on.'

'And I think we should consider bringing Jenny Fuller in. She might at least be able to give us some idea of what kind of people we're looking for.'

'I couldn't agree more,' Gristhorpe said. He liked Jenny Fuller. Not only was she a competent psychologist who had helped them before in unusual cases, but she was a pleasure to have around. A right bonny lass, as Gristhorpe's father would have said.

'Should we bring Jim Hatchley back from the seaside?' Banks asked.

Gristhorpe scowled. 'I suppose there might come a time we'll need him. Leave it for now, though.' Detective Sergeant Jim Hatchley had been transferred to a CID outpost on the Yorkshire coast, largely to make way for Philip Richmond's promotion. Gristhorpe had never much liked Hatchley, but grudgingly admitted he had his uses. As far as Gristhorpe was concerned, he was an idle, foul-mouthed, prejudiced slob, but his brain worked well enough when he took the trouble to use it, and he had a list of dirty tricks as long as your arm that often got results without compromising procedure.

Banks drained his glass. 'Anything else?'

'Not tonight. We'll have a meeting first thing in the morning, see what's turned up. You'd better get home and get some sleep.'

Banks grunted. 'I might as well have another pint first. There never seems to be anyone in these days.'

'Where's Sandra?'

'Community Centre, still organizing that local artists' exhibition. I'll swear she spends more time there than she does at home. And Tracy's out at the pictures with that boyfriend of hers.'

Gristhorpe caught the anxiety in Banks's tone. 'Don't worry about her, Alan,' he said. 'Tracy's a sensible lass. She can take care of herself.'

Banks sighed. 'I hope so.' He gestured towards Gristhorpe's empty glass. 'What about you?'

'Aye, why not? It might help me sleep.'

While Banks went to the bar, Gristhorpe considered the night ahead. He knew he wouldn't be going home. For years, he had kept a camp bed in the station storeroom for emergencies like this. Tonight, and perhaps for the next two or three nights, he would stay in his office. But he doubted that he would get much sleep. Not until he found out what had happened to Gemma Scupham, one way or the other.

2

ONE

Early the next morning, Banks stood on his doorstep holding the milk bottles and breathed in the clear air. It was a magnificent day: not a cloud in the light blue sky, and hardly any wind. He could smell peat-smoke in the air, and it seemed to accentuate the chill autumn edge, the advancing touch of winter. More than anything, it was a day for walking out in the dale, and it would bring dozens of tourists to the Eastvale area.

He went inside and put the milk in the fridge. He could hear Tracy taking her morning shower and Sandra moving about in the bedroom, getting dressed. It had been a good night when he got back from the Queen's Arms. Sandra had got home before him, and before bed they enjoyed a nightcap and some Ella Fitzgerald on the CD player she had bought him for his fortieth birthday. Tracy came home on time, cheerful enough, and Banks couldn't detect any change for the worse in her that he could attribute to her boyfriend, Keith Harrison. Still, he thought as he poured himself a cup of coffee, domestic life had changed a lot over the summer.

For one thing, Brian had left home for Portsmouth Polytechnic, where he intended to study architecture. Much as they had locked horns the past few years – especially over music and staying out too late – Banks missed him. He was left with Tracy, now so grown-up he hardly knew her: blonde hair chopped short and layered raggedly, mad about boys, make-up, clothes, pop music.

They never seemed to talk any more, and he missed those chats about history – her former passion – especially when he had been able to educate her on a point or two. Banks had always felt insecure about his lack of a good formal education, so Tracy's questions had often made him feel useful. But he knew nothing about the latest pop groups, fashion or cosmetics.

And Sandra had become absorbed in her work. He told himself, as he buttered his toast, not to be so damned selfish and to stop feeling sorry for himself. She was doing what she wanted – getting involved in the arts – after so many years of sacrifice for the sake of the family and for his career. And if he hadn't wanted an independent, spirited, creative woman, then he shouldn't have married her. Still, he worried. She was late so often, and some of these local artists were handsome young devils with the reputation of being ladies' men. They were more free-spirited than he was, too, with Bohemian attitudes about sex, no doubt.

Perhaps Sandra found him boring now and was looking for excitement elsewhere. At thirty-eight, she was a fine-looking woman, with an unusual mix of long blonde hair and dark eyebrows over intelligent blue eyes. The slim, shapely figure she had worked hard to maintain always turned heads. Again he told himself not to be such a fool. It was the work that was taking up her time, not another man.

Sandra and Tracy were still upstairs when he had finished his coffee and toast. He called out goodbye, put on his charcoal sports jacket, patting the side pocket for cigarettes and lighter, and set off. It was such a fine morning – and he knew how quickly the day could turn to misery – that he decided to walk the mile or so to Eastvale Regional Headquarters rather than drive. He could always sign a car out of the pool if he needed one.

He stuck the Walkman in his pocket and turned it on. Ivor Gurney's setting of 'In Flanders' started: 'I'm homesick for my hills again – My hills again!' Banks had come to Gurney first through some of his poems in an anthology of First World War poetry, then, learning he had been a composer too, went in search of the music. There wasn't much available, just a handful of songs – settings of other people's poems – and some piano music, but Banks found the spareness and simplicity intensely moving.

As he walked along Market Street, he said hello to the shopkeepers winding out their awnings and called in at the newsagent's for his copy of the *Independent*. Glancing at the front page as he walked, he spotted Gemma Scupham's photograph and a brief request for information. Good, they'd been quick off the mark.

When he got to the market square, the first car was disgorging its family of tourists, dad with a camera slung around his neck, and the children in orange and yellow cagoules. It was hard to believe on such a day that a seven-year-old girl probably lay dead somewhere in the dale.

Banks went straight to the conference room upstairs in the station. It was their largest room, with a well-polished oval table at its centre, around which stood ten stiff-backed chairs. It was rare that ten people actually sat there, though, and this morning, in addition to Banks, only Superintendent Gristhorpe, Susan Gay and Phil Richmond occupied chairs. Banks helped himself to a black coffee from the urn by the window and sat down. He was a few minutes early, and the others were chatting informally, pads and pencils in front of them.

First, Gristhorpe tossed a pile of newspapers onto the table and bade everyone have a look. Gemma Scupham's disappearance had made it into all the national dailies as well as the *Yorkshire Post*. In some of the tabloids, she even made the headline: the photo of the melancholy-looking little girl with the straggly blonde hair appeared under captions such as HAVE YOU SEEN THIS GIRL? in 'Jesus type'. The stories gave few details, which hardly surprised Banks as there were scant few to give. A couple of pieces implied criticism of Brenda Scupham, but nothing libellous. Most were sympathetic to the mother.

'That might help us a bit,' Gristhorpe said. 'But I wouldn't count on it. And remember, the press boys will be around here in droves as soon as the London trains come in this morning. Let's be careful what we say, eh, or before we know it we'll be up to our necks in tales of satanic rituals.' Gristhorpe stood up, grimaced and put his hand to the small of his back. 'Anyway, let's get on. We've circulated Gemma's picture, and Susan managed to lift a set of her prints from a paint-box, so we've got them on file for comparison. Nothing new came up during the night. We did about as well as can be expected on the house-to-house. Four people say they remembered seeing a car parked outside Brenda Scupham's house on Tuesday afternoon. Of these, two say it was black, one dark brown and one dark blue.' Gristhorpe paused. 'I think, therefore, that we can be certain it was a dark car.' He refilled his coffee cup and sat down again. 'As far as the make is concerned we got even less. They all agreed it was a pretty small car, but not as small as a Mini, and it looked quite new. It wasn't an estate car or a van of any kind, so we're looking at a compact. One said it reminded him of those Japanese jobbies he's seen advertised on television, so it may be an import. Needless to say, no one got the number.'

'Did anyone see the couple?' Banks asked.

'Yes.' Gristhorpe looked at the file in front of him. 'The woman at number eleven said she was washing her windows and she saw a well-dressed couple going up the path. Said they looked official, that's all. She thought maybe Mrs Scupham or her friend had got in trouble with DHSS.'

'Hmm,' said Banks. 'Hardly surprising. I don't suppose anybody saw them leaving with the child?'

Gristhorpe shook his head.

'Well,' Banks said, 'at least it helps confirm Brenda Scupham's story.'

'Aye.' Gristhorpe looked over at Susan Gay, who had done most of the questioning. 'Who would you say was our most reliable witness?'

'Mr Carter at number sixteen, sir. It wasn't so much that he'd seen more than the others, but he seemed to be thinking very seriously about what he *had* seen, and he told me he had a strong visual memory – not quite photographic, but he could close his eyes and picture scenes. He seemed careful not to make anything up. You know, sir, how a lot of them embroider the truth.'

'What colour did he say the car was?' Banks asked.

'Dark blue, and he thought it was a Japanese design, too. But he didn't see this Peterson and Brown couple, just the car.'

'Shame,' said Gristhorpe. 'Had he seen it around before?'

'No, sir.'

'Think it would do any good talking to him again?'

'It might,' said Susan. 'I'll drop by sometime today. He's a pensioner and I get the impression he's lonely. He seemed pleased to have a bit of company. It took me a while to get him round to what he'd seen.'

Gristhorpe smiled. 'Let him ramble a while, if it helps. Indulge him. And we'd better organize a house-to-house of the entire estate. I want to know if anything like this has happened there before, people posing as social workers after children. No one's likely to admit to it, but if you get the feeling that anyone's being particularly evasive, for whatever reason, make a note and we'll get back to them. Can you handle that, Susan?'

Susan Gay nodded.

'Take as many PCs as you can find, and make sure you give them a damn good briefing first. Most of the lads are out on the search, but we've been promised extra manpower on this.' He turned to Richmond. 'We've got to check with all the garages in the area and see if they remember anyone matching the description stopping for petrol. And I want to see all the police traffic reports – parking or speeding tickets – for Tuesday. In fact, make it for the past week. I want to know if anyone remembers a smartly dressed couple with a little girl in a dark blue compact. Better check with the car-rental agencies, too. Phil, can you handle all that?'

Richmond nodded. 'Yes, sir. I've already got a computer printout of locals with any kind of history of child molestation. None of the descriptions match. Do you want me to start on that too?'

'How many?'

'Six, sir – that's four in the Swainsdale area and two in Sergeant Hatchley's patch. But we've no way of telling where our couple started out from.'

'I know,' said Gristhorpe. 'I'll get onto DS Hatchley, and you just do the best you can. We'll see if we can't pay a couple of visits ourselves. But I want priority on tracking down that car. Someone must have noticed it. By the way, those computers you wanted have been delivered to the mobile unit. Do you think you can take a trip out there and give the lads a quick lesson?'

'No problem.'

'Any questions?' Gristhorpe asked.

'Did forensics find anything at the house?' Banks asked.

Gristhorpe shook his head. 'Not a sausage. The SOCO team did a thorough job, and they couldn't find any traces of a struggle – no blood, nothing – or any indications that Gemma had been harmed on the premises. I think we can assume that Mrs Scupham is telling the truth and this couple really did abduct the lass.'

'Anything new on Les Poole?' Banks asked.

'Nothing,' Gristhorpe answered. 'According to the PCs on the night shift, he got back from the pub about ten o'clock and hasn't been out since. Anything else?'

'What about Gemma's father?' Susan asked.

'As far as we know, he's serving with the army in Belfast, poor sod. We'll arrange to get the locals to interview him today, if possible, just to make sure he's got nothing to do with it.' Gristhorpe clapped his hands. 'Right. If there's nothing else, we'd better get cracking.' As they left, he touched Banks on the shoulder. 'Alan, a moment?'

'Of course.'

Gristhorpe poured more coffee for himself and Banks. He didn't look too bad for someone who hadn't had much sleep, Banks thought. Perhaps the bags under his eyes were heavier than usual, but he seemed alert and full of drive.

'I'm getting involved in this one, Alan,' he said. 'At every level. I'll not be content just to sit in my office and co-ordinate, though I'll be doing that, of course. I'll be spending a fair amount of time at the mobile unit and I'll be conducting some interviews myself. I want you to know that, and I want you to know so you don't let it interfere with your usual way of working. I've always given you a pretty free hand, and it's usually got results. I don't want to change that. What I *do* want is to be present when we get the breaks. Know what I mean?'

Banks nodded.

'And there's something else,' Gristhorpe said. 'Something the ACC made very clear as a priority concern.'

Banks thought he could guess what was coming, but kept silent while Gristhorpe went on.

'Gemma Scupham might be the first,' he said, 'but she might not be the last. Let's bear that in mind.'

Banks carried his coffee through to his office, where he lit a cigarette, then stood by the venetian blind and looked down on the market square. The façade of the Norman church and the cobbles of the market square shone pale gold in the pure light. Two more cars had arrived, and yet another was just pulling in. Banks watched the young couple get out and stand hand in hand gazing around them at the ancient square with its weathered stone cross. Honeymooners, by the look of them. The church clock rang nine.

He thought about Brenda Scupham, with her aura of sexuality, and of the sly, weasly Les Poole, and he tried to imagine what kind of parents they must have made. They can't have had much time for Gemma, with Les always at the pub or the bookie's and Brenda at home doing God knows what. Watching television, most likely. Did they talk to her? Play with her? And did they abuse her?

Then he thought of Gemma herself: that haunted face, those eyes that had seen much more and much worse than her young mind could comprehend, possibly lying dead out there right now in some ditch, or buried in a makeshift grave. And he thought of what Gristhorpe had just said. He stubbed out his cigarette and reached for the telephone. No time for brooding. Time to get to work.

TWO

A desolate, stunned air pervaded the East Side Estate that morning, Banks sensed, as he walked from the mobile unit to the school. Even the dogs seemed to be indoors, and those people he did see going on errands or pushing babies in prams had their heads bowed and seemed drawn in on themselves. He passed the maisonettes with their obscene messages scrawled on the cracked paintwork, and the two blocks of flats – each fourteen storeys high – where he knew the lifts, when they worked, smelled of urine and glue. Hardly anyone was out on the street.

The school itself was a square red-brick building with only a few small windows. A high chain-link fence bordered the asphalt playground. Banks looked at his watch. Eleven o'clock. Gemma's teacher should be waiting for him in the staffroom.

He walked through the front doors, noting that one of the glass panes was cracked in a spider-web pattern, and asked the first adult he saw the way to the staffroom. As he walked along the corridor, he was struck by the bright-ness of the place, so much in contrast with its ugly exterior. Most of it, he thought, was due to the children's paintings tacked along the walls. These weren't skilled, professional efforts, but the gaudy outbursts of untrained minds – yellow sunbursts with rays shooting in all directions, bright golden angels, red and green stick figures of mummy and daddy and cats and dogs.

There was a funny smell about the place, too, that transported him back to his own infants' school, but it took him some moments to identify it. When he did, he smiled to himself, remembering for the first time in ages those blissful, carefree days before school became a matter of learning facts and studying for exams. It was Plasticine, that coloured putty-like stuff he had tried in vain to mould into the shapes of hippos and crocodiles.

He walked straight into the staffroom, and a woman, who looked hardly older than a schoolgirl herself, came forward to greet him. 'Chief Inspector Banks?' she asked, holding out her hand. 'I'm Peggy Graham.'

It was a big room with well-spaced tables and chairs, a noticeboard full of mimeographed memos, handwritten notes and printed flyers for concerts, courses and package holidays. A couple of other teachers, sitting over newspapers, glanced up at his entry, then looked down again. One corner of the room had been converted into a mini-kitchen, complete with a fridge, microwave and coffee-maker. Here and there on the rough, orange-painted walls hung more examples of untrammelled art.

'A bit overwhelming, isn't it?' Peggy Graham asked, noticing him looking around. 'I could do without the orange walls myself, but it was a playroom before we got it, so . . . Sit down. Can I get you some coffee or something?'

'If it's no trouble,' Banks said.

She went to get it. Peggy Graham, Banks noticed, was a small, bird-like woman, perhaps fresh out of teachers' training school. Her grey pleated skirt covered her knees, and a dark blue cardigan hung over her white cotton blouse. She wore her mousy hair in a ponytail, and large glasses made her nose look tiny. Her eyes, behind them, were big, pale and milky blue, and they seemed charged with worry and sincerity. Her lips were thin and curved slightly downwards at the corners. She wore no make-up.

'Well,' she said, sitting down beside him with the coffee. It came in a mug with a picture of Big Bird on it. 'This is just dreadful about Gemma, isn't it? Just dreadful.'

She spoke, he thought, as if she were talking to a class of five-year-olds, and her mouth was so mobile she looked as if she were miming. Banks nodded.

'What could have happened?' she asked. 'Have you got *any* idea?'

'I'm afraid not,' Banks said.

'I don't suppose you could say anything even if you did have, could you?'

'We have to be very careful.'

'Of course.' She sat back in her chair, crossed her legs and rested her hands on her lap. Banks noticed the thin gold wedding band. 'How can I help you?' she asked.

'I'm not really sure. In cases like this it helps to find out as much as you can about the child. What was Gemma like?'

Peggy Graham pursed her lips. 'Well, that's a hard one. Gemma's a very quiet child. She always seems a bit withdrawn.'

'In what way?'

'Just . . . quiet. Oh, she's bright, very bright. She's an excellent reader, and I think, given the opportunity, she could be very creative. That's one of hers on the wall.'

Banks walked over to the crayon sketch Peggy had

pointed at. It showed a girl with pigtails standing beside a tree on a carpet of grass under a bright sun. The leaves were individually defined in bright green, and the grass was dotted with yellow flowers – buttercups, perhaps, or dandelions. The girl, a stick figure, just stood there with her arms stretched out. Banks found something disturbing about it, and he realized that the girl's round face had no features. He went back to his chair.

'Very good,' he said. 'Did you ever get the feeling that there was something bothering her?'

'She always seems . . . well, preoccupied.' Peggy gave a nervous laugh. 'I call her Wednesday's child. You know, "Wednesday's child is full of woe." She seemed woeful. Of course, I tried to talk to her, but she never said much. Mostly she was attentive in class. Once or twice I noticed she was weeping, just quietly, to herself.'

'What did you do?'

'I didn't want to embarrass her in front of the others. I asked her afterwards what was wrong, but she wouldn't say. Gemma's always been a very secretive child. What goes on in that imagination of hers I've no idea. Half the time she seems to be in another world.'

'A better one?'

Peggy Graham twisted her ring. 'I don't know. I like to think so.'

'What was your impression?'

'I think she was lonely and she felt unloved.'

Her first use of the past tense in reference to Gemma wasn't lost on Banks. 'Lonely? Didn't she have any friends?'

'Oh yes. She was quite popular here, even though she was quiet. Don't get the wrong impression. She liked playing games with the other girls. Sometimes she seemed quite gay – oops, I shouldn't have said that, should I, now they've censored it from all the Noddy books – cheerful, I suppose. It's just that she was moody. She had these woeful, silent moods, when you just couldn't reach her. Sometimes they'd last for days.'

'And you don't know why?'

'I can only guess. And you mustn't tell anyone I said this. I think it was her home life.'

'What about it?'

'I think she was neglected. I don't mean she wasn't well fed or clothed, or abused in any way. Though she did look a bit . . . well, shabby . . . sometimes. You know, she was wearing the same dress and socks day after day. And sometimes I just felt like picking her up and dumping her in a bath. It wasn't that she smelled or anything. She was just a bit grubby. I don't think her parents spent enough time with her, encouraging her, that sort of thing. I think that was the root of her loneliness. It happens a lot, and there isn't much you can do about it. A supportive home environment is perhaps even more important than school for a child's development, but we can't be parents as well as teachers, can we? And we can't tell parents how to bring up their children.'

'You mentioned abuse,' Banks said. 'Did you ever notice any signs of physical abuse?'

'Oh, no. I couldn't . . . I mean, if I had I would certainly have reported it. We did have a case here a year or so ago. It was dreadful, just dreadful what some parents can sink to.'

'But you saw no signs with Gemma? No bruises, cuts, anything like that?'

'No. Well, there was one time. About a week or so ago, I think it was. It was quite warm, like now. Gemma was wearing a short-sleeved dress and I noticed a bruise on her upper arm, the left one, I think. Naturally, I asked her about it, but she said she'd got it playing games.'

'Did you believe her?'

'Yes. I had no reason to doubt her word.'

'So you didn't report it?'

'No. I mean, one wouldn't want to be alarmist. Not after that business with the Cleveland social workers and everything. Look, maybe I should have done something. Lord knows, if I'm in any way responsible . . . But if you brought in the authorities every time a child had a bruise there'd be no time for anything else, would there?'

'It's all right,' Banks said. 'Nobody's blaming you. Everybody's a bit sensitive about things like that these days. I picked up plenty of bruises when I was a lad, believe me, and my mum and dad wouldn't have appreciated being accused of abusing me. And I got a good hiding when I deserved it, too.'

Peggy smiled at him over her glasses. 'As I said,' she went on, 'Gemma's explanation seemed perfectly reasonable to me. Children can play pretty rough sometimes. They're a lot more resilient than we give them credit for.'

'Was that the only mark you ever saw on her?'

'Oh, yes. I mean, if it had been a regular occurrence I'd have said something for certain. We do have to keep an eye open for these things.'

'And she never seemed in pain of any kind?'

'Not physical pain, no. She just sometimes seemed withdrawn, lost in her own world. But children often create their own imaginary worlds. They can be very complex beings, Chief Inspector. They're not all the same. Just because a child is quiet, it doesn't mean there's anything wrong with them.'

'I understand. Please believe me, I'm not criticizing. I'm just trying to find out something about her.'

'How could it help?'

'I honestly don't know.'

'You think she's dead, don't you?'

'I wouldn't say that.'

'She's been gone nearly two days now. That's what the papers say. Not in so many words, perhaps, but . . .'

'She could still be alive.'

'Then she might be better off dead,' Peggy Graham whispered. She felt up the sleeve of her cardigan for a tissue, lifted her glasses and wiped her moist eyes. They looked small and shy without the lenses to magnify them. 'I'm sorry. It's just . . . we're all so upset.'

'Did you, or anyone else on the staff, notice any strangers hanging around the school recently?'

'No. And I'm sure anything like that would have been reported. We have very strict guidelines to follow.'

'Nobody saw a dark blue car? Are you sure?'

She shook her head. 'I'm sure.'

'Did you ever see Gemma talking to any strangers nearby? Male or female?'

'No. She always came and left with her friends, the ones from the same street. She didn't live far away.'

Banks stood up. 'Thank you very much,' he said. 'If you do remember anything, here's my card. Please call.'

Peggy Graham took the card. 'Of course. But I don't see how there could be anything else.'

'Just in case.'

'All right.' She got to her feet. 'I'll walk to the door with you.'

As they walked, a host of children came out of one of the classrooms. Some were laughing and scrapping, but many of them seemed subdued. Perhaps they were too young to understand the enormity of what had happened, Banks thought, but they were old enough to sense the mood of tension and fear. One little girl with glossy dark curls and brown spaniel eyes tugged at Banks's sleeve.

'Are you the policeman?' she asked.

'Yes,' he answered, wondering how on earth she knew.

'Are you looking for Gemma?'

'Yes, I am.'

'Please find her,' the little girl said, clutching his sleeve tighter. 'Bring her back. She's my friend.'

'I'll do my best,' said Banks. He turned to Peggy Graham. She blushed.

'I'm afraid I told them a policeman was coming,' she said. 'Sorry.'

'It's all right. Look, can I talk to this girl?'

'Elizabeth? Well . . . I suppose so. Though I don't know what . . . Come this way.' And she led both Banks and Elizabeth into the empty classroom.

'Now, Elizabeth,' she said. 'The nice policeman wants to talk to you about Gemma, to help him to find her. Just answer his questions. I'll stay here with you.' She glanced at Banks to ask if he minded, and he nodded his agreement. Elizabeth took hold of Peggy Graham's hand and stood beside her.

Banks crouched, hearing his knees crack as he did so, and rested his elbows on his thighs. 'You know we're trying to find Gemma,' he said. 'Did she ever say anything to you about going away?'

Elizabeth shook her head.

'Or about anyone wanting to take her away?'

Another shake.

'Did she have any older friends, big girls or big boys?'

'No.'

'Did she ever talk about her mummy and daddy?'

'It wasn't her daddy.'

'Mr Poole?'

Elizabeth nodded. 'She wouldn't call him Daddy.'

'What did she say about him?'

'I don't know.'

'Did she like him?'

'No.'

'Did he ever hurt Gemma?'

'She cried.'

'Why did she cry?'

'Don't know.'

'Did he ever hurt her, Elizabeth?'

'I don't know. She didn't like him. She said he smelled and he always told her to go away.'

'When did he tell her to go away?'

'He said she was a sp . . . sp . . . a spilled cat.'

'A spilled cat? Do you mean "spoiled brat"?'

'Yes.'

'When did he say this?'

'He wouldn't let her have the book.'

'What book?'

'She wanted a book and he wouldn't let her have it. He threw her other books away.'

'Why?'

'She spilled some paint on his newspaper. It too dirty. He was angry. He threw her books away and he wouldn't let her have any more.'

'What was too dirty, Elizabeth?'

'No. It too dirty.'

Banks looked at Peggy Graham. 'I think she's trying to say "at two-thirty",' she said, frowning.

'Is that right?' Banks asked Elizabeth. 'She spilled paint on his newspaper at two-thirty, so he threw her books away?'

She nodded.

'What were the books?'

'Storybooks. With pictures. Gemma likes reading. She reads to me. I'm not very good. Please find her.' Elizabeth started crying. Peggy Graham put an arm around her. 'It's all right, dear. The nice policeman will find Gemma. Don't cry.'

Elizabeth sniffled a few moments longer, then wiped her nose on her sleeve and left the room. Banks sighed.

'What was all that about?' Peggy asked.

'I wish I knew. Thanks for letting me talk to her anyway. I hope she doesn't stay upset.'

'Don't worry. Elizabeth's tough enough.'

Banks walked through the playground full of children. They were skipping, playing hopscotch, running around as usual, but like the ones coming out of the classroom they seemed much quieter, more subdued than children usually are.

He looked at his watch. Close to noon. Time to write up his notes before lunch with Jenny. Not that he had learned much from the teacher that he hadn't known or suspected already. Gemma kept herself to herself, perhaps suffered neglect at home, but was probably not physically abused. Still, there was the business of the bruise. How had she got it? And what had Elizabeth meant about 'at two-thirty' and Gemma's books? Banks walked past the tower block with JESUS SAVES written in red on the wall and back to the unmarked car he had parked by the mobile unit.

THREE

Damn it, cursed Jenny Fuller. She had pulled up at the lights just in time and all the essays on the back seat had slid off onto the floor. So few of the students bothered with paper clips or staples; it would be a hell of a job reshuffling them. If she hadn't been in such a hurry to meet Banks it would never have happened. She was on the south-eastern edge of Eastvale, coming up to the roundabout by the Red Lion, and she only had five minutes to park and get to Le Bistro. Still, Alan would wait.

The lights changed and the car lurched off again. To hell with the papers. She shouldn't be teaching until October anyway, and if it hadn't been for those American students – those American students with odd ideas of academic timetables and thousands of dollars to spend on an English education – then she could have been relaxing on a beach somewhere.

She smiled to herself, imagining Alan Banks sitting at one of Le Bistro's wobbly little tables, no doubt feeling out of place among the yuppie lunch crowd with their Perriers and portable telephones. He would be far more comfortable in the Queen's Arms with a pie and a pint in front of him, not at a table covered in a coral cloth with a long-stemmed rose in a vase at its centre. But Jenny had been lecturing to the Americans all morning, and she was damned if she was going to be done out of the shrimp *provençale* and the glass of white wine she had promised to treat herself to.

Jenny remembered her surprise the first time the East-vale CID had brought her into a case, involving a peeping Tom, three years ago. She had guessed (correctly) that they wanted a visible female presence as a sop to Dorothy

Wycombe and the Eastvale feminist contingent, WEEF, Women of Eastvale for Emancipation and Freedom. Still, she had done a good job, and since then her professional field of interests had broadened to include a certain amount of criminal and deviant psychology. She had even attended a series of fascinating lectures on the psychological profiling of serial killers, given by a visiting American from the FBI Behavioral Sciences section.

She had also had a brief fling with the visitor, but she didn't care to remember that too clearly. Like most of her affairs, it was best forgotten. Still, that was eighteen months ago, when she had been still hurting over her split with Dennis Osmond. Since then she had not been involved with anyone. Instead, she had done a lot of thinking about her lousy relationships, and the reasons for them. She hadn't come up with any answers yet. Most often she ended up wondering why the hell her professional insights seemed to shed no light at all on her personal life.

The tyres screeched as she turned right at the market square and drove down by Castle Hill between the terraced river gardens and the formal gardens. People sat on the terraces and ate packed lunches on one side of the road, while on the other, mothers dragged bored children around the displays of fading flowers.

At last, she crossed the small bridge over the River Swain, turned right and pulled up outside the café.

Le Bistro was one of Eastvale's newest cafés. Tourism, the dale's main industry, had increased, and the many Americans drawn to do the 'James Herriot' tour wanted a little more than fish and chips and warm beer, quaint as they found such things. In addition, a more sophisticated, cosmopolitan crowd had moved up from London while property in the north was still a good deal cheaper than down south. Many of them commuted from Eastvale to York, Darlington, and even as far as Tyneside, Leeds and Bradford, and they naturally demanded a little more diversity in matters of dining.

Best of all, as far as Jenny was concerned, was that Le Bistro was actually situated in a converted Georgian semi only four houses south of her own. The new owners had, somehow, received planning permission to knock down the wall between the two houses and turn them into a café. For Jenny it was a godsend, as she often couldn't be bothered to cook after a hard day. The food was good and the prices were relatively reasonable.

She dashed through the door. The place was fairly busy, but she saw Banks immediately. There he was in a dark grey sports jacket, white shirt and tie. As usual, his top button was open and the tie loose and askew. Under close-cropped black hair, his dark blue eyes sparkled as he looked over at her. He was working on a crossword and holding what looked like a glass of mineral water. Jenny couldn't suppress a giggle as she sat down in a flurry of apologies. Le Bistro didn't serve pints.

'It's all right,' said Banks rather glumly, putting his newspaper away in his briefcase. 'I'm supposed to be cutting down on the ale anyway.'

'Since when?'

Banks patted his stomach. 'Since I turned forty and noticed this beginning to swell.'

'Nonsense. You're as lean as ever. You're just suffering from male menopause. Next you'll be having an affair with a twenty-one-year-old rookie policewoman.'

Banks laughed. 'Chance would be a fine thing. But don't joke about it. You never know. Anyway, how are you?'

Jenny shrugged and tossed back the thick mane of red

hair that cascaded over her shoulders. 'Okay, I suppose. I'm not sure I like teaching summer school though.'

'Working in summer?' mocked Banks. 'Tut-tut, what a terrible thing. What is the world coming to?'

Jenny thumped him on the arm. 'It's supposed to be one of the perks of the job, remember? Teachers get summers off. Not this year, though.'

'Never mind. You're looking well for it.'

'Why, thank you, kind sir.' Jenny inclined her head graciously. 'And you haven't changed. Honestly, Alan. You still don't look a day over thirty-nine. How's Sandra?'

'Busy.'

'Oh-oh. Feeling all neglected, are we?'

Banks grinned. 'Something like that. But we're not here to talk about me.'

'And how's Susan Gay?' Jenny had spent some time helping Susan adjust to her CID posting, on a semi-professional basis, and the two had become fairly close. They were different personalities, but Jenny saw something in Susan – a sense of determination, a single-mindedness – that both appealed to her and disturbed her. If she could persuade Susan to relax a little, she felt, then a more balanced and attractive personality might be permitted to emerge.

Banks told her Susan was doing well, though she still seemed a little tense and prickly, and the two chatted about family and mutual friends. 'Have you studied the menu yet?' Jenny asked him after a short silence.

'Mm. No sausage and chips, I noticed. How's the croque monsieur?'

'Good.'

'Then I'll have that. And by the way, I like the music.'

Jenny cocked an ear. Singing quietly in the background

was the unmistakable voice of Edith Piaf. Typical of him to notice that, she thought. Left to herself she would have ignored it as wallpaper music.

'Wine?' she asked.

'Not for me. It makes me sleep and I've a lot of paperwork to do this afternoon.'

'So, it's about little Gemma Scupham, is it?' Jenny said, unfolding a coral napkin and spreading it over her lap. 'That's why you've called me in?'

Banks nodded. 'Superintendent Gristhorpe thought you might be able to help.'

'At least I'm not the token feminist this time.'

'No. Seriously, Jenny, can you help?'

'Maybe. What do you want from me?'

'For the moment I'd just like grounding in a few basics. I can understand a lot about things most people don't even want to think about – robbery, murder, even rape – but I can't seem to grasp the motivation for something like this.'

Jenny took a deep breath and held it a moment. 'All right. I'll do what I can. Shall we order first, though?' She called over the waitress and gave their orders, asking for a glass of white wine for herself right now, and a coffee for Banks, then she sat back in her chair. 'First you'd better tell me the details so far,' she said.

Banks told her. Before he finished, the food arrived, and they both tucked in.

Jenny pushed her plate away and set the half-full wine glass in front of her. Banks ordered another coffee.

'I don't really know where to start,' she said. 'I mean, it's not really my field.'

'You do know something about sexual deviance, though.'

'Honestly, Alan, you make me sound like a real pervert.

Basically, nobody really knows what causes someone to be a paedophile or a rapist or a sadist. They don't necessarily realize they're doing anything wrong.'

'Are you telling me that a man who sexually assaults little children doesn't think he's doing anything wrong?'

'Depends what you mean by wrong. He would know he's breaking the law, of course, but . . . He's only satisfying desires he can't help feeling. He never *asked* to feel them in the first place. And many also feel tremendous guilt and remorse.'

'For doing something they don't even think is wrong? You make it sound almost legitimate.'

'You asked. I'm just telling you what little I know.'

'I'm sorry. Go on.'

'Look, you might think a person is simply born the way he or she is, but sexual behaviour isn't fixed from the start. There are theories that almost everything is biologically based, caused by chemicals, or by genes. For what it's worth, most studies indicate that sexual behaviour is mostly a matter of learning. At first, everything is diffuse, in a kind of flux – polymorphous perverse, I believe Freud called infant sexuality. It depends on a number of factors what preferences come to the fore.'

'Like what?'

'Experience. Learning. Family. They're probably the most important. You try something, and if you like it, you do it again. That's experience. Many people are given no information about sex, or such wrong-headed information that they become very confused. That's learning, or lack of it. Even what we call normal sexuality is a dark, murky thing at best. Look at the extremes of sexual jealousy, of how sex and desire can so easily turn to violence. There's loss of control. Then there's the association of orgasm with death. Did you know it used to be called the "little death"?'

'You don't make it sound like much fun.'

'That's the point,' Jenny said. 'For a lot of people, it isn't. Desire is a ball and chain they can't get rid of, or a ringmaster they don't dare disobey. Sexuality has lots of possible outcomes other than what we label "normal" or socially acceptable. It's *learned* behaviour. When you're prepubescent or adolescent, any object or situation *could* become stimulating. Remember the thrill you used to get looking at pictures of naked women? It's easy as an adolescent to get fixated on things like underwear, big breasts, the image rather than the real thing. Remember our peeping Tom? That was his particular fixation, a visual stimulation.

'It doesn't take long before most of us start to prefer certain stimuli to others. Pretty soon sexual excitement and satisfaction become limited to a certain fairly narrow range. That's what we call normal. Your good old, socially approved, heterosexual sex. The problem with most sexual deviants, though, is that they can't handle what we regard as normal personal relationships. Many try, but they fail. It's a lot more complicated than that, of course. It may not be apparent on the surface that they've failed, for example. They may become very good at faking it in order to cover up their real needs and actions.'

'So what kind of person are we talking about? You said it's someone who can't handle ordinary relationships.'

'I'll have to do some research and see what I can come up with, but your basic deviant is probably pretty much the chap-next-door type, with some very notable exceptions, of course. By the way, you don't have to look around so nervously, you can smoke if you want. Giselle will fetch an ashtray. Remember, it's a *French* restaurant. Everyone smokes over there.'

Banks lit up and Giselle duly brought the ashtray along with their bill. 'Go on,' he said. 'You were telling me about the chap next door.'

'It's just that most sex offenders become skilled at leading quite normal lives on the surface. They learn to play the game. They can hold down a job, keep a marriage going, even raise children—'

'Paedophiles?'

'Yes.'

'I must admit that's a surprise,' said Banks. 'I've come across psychopaths and deviants of various kinds before – I mean, I'm not entirely ignorant on the subject – and it *has* often amazed me how they keep their secrets. Look at Dennis Nilsen, for Christ's sake, chopping up kids and putting their heads on the ring to boil while he takes his dog for a walk, saying hello to the neighbours. Such a nice, quiet man.' Banks shook his head. 'I know the Boston Strangler was married, and Sutcliffe, the Yorkshire Ripper. But how the hell can a paedophile keep a thing like that hidden from his wife and kids?'

'People can become very adept at keeping secrets if they have to, Alan. You don't spend all your life in someone else's company, under someone's scrutiny, do you? Surely you managed to find time alone to masturbate when you were a kid? And you probably thought about it a fair bit, too, anticipated the picture you'd look at or the girl you'd imagine undressing. The whole thing takes on a kind of magical intensity, a ritualistic element, if you like. A sex offender will simply spend all his free time anticipating and planning his deviant acts.'

Banks loosened his tie a little more. Jenny noticed him look around the restaurant and smile at the three business-men at the next table, who seemed to have been listening with growing fascination and horror to the conversation. 'You seem to know a lot about adolescent male behaviour,' he said.

Jenny laughed. 'Alan, I've embarrassed you. Oh, don't look so uncomfortable. It *is* part of my field, after all. The things little boys and little girls get up to.'

'What's your prognosis?' Banks asked.

Jenny sighed. 'For you? I'm afraid there's no hope. No, really, I honestly haven't done enough research for anything like that yet.' She frowned, the lines crinkling her smooth forehead. 'You know what really puzzles me, though? Again, it's probably something you've already considered from your point of view, but psychologically it's interesting, too.'

'What's that?'

'The woman.'

'You mean why she was there?'

'Yes. What's her part in the whole business?'

'Well, her presence would certainly give credibility to the social worker story. I doubt that even someone as thick as Brenda Scupham would have trusted a man alone.'

'No. I realize that. But think about it, Alan.' Jenny leaned forward, her hands clasped on the table. 'She's a woman. Surely you're not telling me she didn't know what they were doing, taking the child?'

'They acted together, yes. But he may have conned her into it somehow, for the sake of credibility. She might not have known what his motives were, especially if, as you say, paedophiles are good at keeping secrets.'

'Except from themselves. But I still think it's a strange thing for a woman to do – help abduct another woman's child. It's an even stranger thing for a couple to do. What on earth would she want with Gemma?'

'Now don't tell me you're going to give me all that sisterhood crap, because I just don't accept it. Women are just as—'

Jenny held her hand up. 'All right. I won't. But there's no need to start getting all shirty. It's not sisterhood I'm talking about, it's a very practical thing. As far as I know, sexual deviants can be fat or thin, big or little, young or old, rich or poor, but they almost always act *alone*. To put it technically, we're talking about people who exhibit primary characteristics of social aversion.'

'Hmm. I'm not saying we haven't considered they might have simply wanted a child so badly that they took someone else's, that they're not paedophiles. We just don't know. But think of the risk involved.'

Jenny ran her fingers around the stem of her wine glass. 'Maybe it does seem far-fetched. But women have snatched babies from prams. It's not my job to evaluate that kind of information. All I'm saying is that the couple element is curious, in psychological terms. And the method is unusual. As you say, think of the risk involved. Maybe the risk was part of the thrill.'

A short silence followed. Banks lit another cigarette. Jenny pulled a face and waved the smoke away. She noticed that Edith Piaf had finished now, replaced by some innocuous accordion music meant to evoke the Gauloise atmosphere of Parisian cafés.

'The superintendent mentioned the Moors Murderers, Brady and Hindley,' said Banks. 'I know he's got a bee in his bonnet about that case, but you have to admit there are parallels.'

'Hmm.'

'What I'm saying', Banks went on, 'is it may be one way of explaining the couple aspect. Brady thought human beings were contemptible creatures and pleasure the only end worth pursuing. And Hindley was besotted with him. She was witnessing it all as a demonstration of some form of love for him. I know it sounds weird, but . . .'

'I've heard the theory,' said Jenny. 'It's all to do with dominance. And I've heard a lot weirder theories, too. Christ, Alan, you know as well as I do that most psychology is guesswork. We don't really *know* anything. But Superintendent Gristhorpe may be right. It *could* be something like that. I'll look into it.'

'So you'll help?'

'Of course I'll help, idiot. Did you think I'd say no?'

'Quickly, Jenny,' said Banks, taking money from his wallet and placing it on the bill. 'Especially if there's even the slightest chance that Gemma Scupham might still be alive.'

FOUR

'Have you found her yet?'

Nothing much had changed in Brenda Scupham's front room by Thursday afternoon. The doll still lay in the same position on the floor, and the peculiar smell remained. But Brenda looked more tired. Her eyes were red-rimmed and her hair hung limp and lifeless beside her pale cheeks. She was wearing a grubby pink tracksuit bottom and a loose green sweatshirt. Les Poole slouched in the armchair, feet up, smoking.

'What's wrong, Les?' Banks asked. 'Is the Barleycorn not on all-day opening?'

'Very funny. I don't *live* there, you know.'

Brenda Scupham shot him a mean look, then turned to

Banks. 'Leave him alone. He's not done anything. He might not be much, but he's all I've got. I asked you, have you found my Gemma yet?'

'No,' said Banks, turning from Poole. 'No, we haven't.'

'Well, what do you want? More questions?'

'I'm afraid so.'

Brenda Scupham sighed and sat down. 'I don't know where this is going to get us.'

'I need to know more about Gemma's habits, for a start.'

'What do you mean, habits?'

'Her routines. How did she get to school?'

'She walked. It's not far.'

'Alone?'

'No, she met up with the Ferris girl from over the street and the Bramhope kid from two houses down.'

'Did she come home with them, too?'

'Yes.'

Banks made a note of the names. 'What about lunchtime?'

'School dinners.'

'Why?'

'What do you mean, why?'

'The school's not far away. Surely it'd have saved you a penny or two if she came home for lunch?'

Brenda Scupham shrugged. 'She said she liked school dinners.'

'Did she ever say anything about anyone following her or stopping her in the street?'

'Never.'

'And she wasn't out on her own?'

'No. She was always with her friends, whether she was off to school or playing out. Why are you asking all these questions?'

'Brenda, I'm trying to figure out why Gemma's abductors came to the house rather than snatching her in the street. Surely she must have been alone out there at some time?'

'I dare say. She'd nip to the shop now and then. You can't keep your eyes on them every minute of the day. She is seven, you know. She knows to look right before left when she's crossing the street, and not to take sweets from strangers.' When she realized what she'd said, she put her hand to her mouth and her eyes filled with tears.

'I'm sorry if this is painful for you,' Banks said, 'but it is important.'

'I know.'

'Was Gemma a happy child, would you say?'

'I suppose so. They live in their own worlds, don't they?'

'Would she be given to exaggeration, to lying?'

'Not that I know of, no.'

'It's just that I heard a story about Les here throwing some of Gemma's books out. Does that mean anything to you?'

Les Poole sat up and turned to Banks. 'What?'

'You heard, Les. What's so important about her spilling paint on your paper at two-thirty?'

Poole looked puzzled for a few seconds, then he laughed out loud. 'Who told you that?'

'Never mind. What's it all about?'

He laughed again. 'It was *the* two-thirty. The two-thirty from Cheltenham. Silly little bugger spilled coloured water all over my racing form. You know, the jar she'd been dipping her bloody paintbrush in.'

'And for that you threw her books out?'

'Don't be daft. They were just some old colouring

books. She was painting in them on the other side of the table and she knocked her paint jar over and ruined my bloody paper. So I grabbed the books and tore them up.'

'How did she react?'

'Oh, she whined and sulked for a while.'

'Did you ever grab her hard by the arm?'

'No, I never touched her. Just the books. Look, what's all this—'

'Why wouldn't you get her the new book she wanted?'

Poole sat back in the chair and crossed his legs. 'Couldn't afford it, could we? You can't give kids everything they ask for. You ought to know that if you've got kids of your own. Look, get to the point, Mr Banks. I might not have had much time for the little beggar but *I* didn't run off with her, did I? We're the victims, not the criminals. I think it's about time you realized that.'

Banks looked at him, and Poole quickly averted his gaze. It made Banks think of his first lesson in police thinking. He had been involved in interviewing a petty thief about a burglary in Belsize Park, and he came away convinced that the man hadn't committed it. Surprised to see the charges being laid and the evidence gathered, he had mentioned his doubts to his commanding officer. The man, a twenty-year veteran called Bill Carstairs, had looked at Banks and shaken his head, then he said, 'He might not have done this job, but he sure as hell has done something he ought to be put away for.' Looking at Poole made Banks feel the same way. The man was guilty of something. If he had nothing to do with Gemma's disappearance, or even with the Fletcher's warehouse job, he was still guilty of *something*.

Banks turned back to Brenda Scupham.

'You think we abused Gemma, don't you?' she said.

'I don't know.'

'You've been listening to gossip. Probably gossip from kids, at that. Look, I'll admit I didn't want her. I was twenty-one, the last thing I wanted was to be lumbered with a kid, but I was brought up Catholic, and I couldn't get rid of her. I might not be the best mother on earth. I might be selfish, I might not be up to encouraging her in school and paying as much attention to her as I should. I'm not even a very good housekeeper. But all that . . . I mean, what I'm saying is I never abused her.'

It was an impassioned speech, but Banks got the feeling that she was protesting too much. 'What about Les?' he asked.

She glanced over at him. 'If he ever touched her he knows he'd be out of here before his feet could touch the floor.'

'So why did you give her up so easily?'

Brenda Scupham chewed on her lip and fought back the tears. 'Do you think I haven't had it on my mind night and day since? Do you think there's a moment goes by I don't ask myself the same question?' She shook her head. 'It all happened so fast.'

'But if you hadn't abused Gemma in any way, why didn't you just tell Mr Brown and Miss Peterson that and send them away?'

'Because they were the authorities. I mean, they looked like they were and everything. I suppose I thought if they'd had some information then they had to look into it, you know, like the police. And then when they found there was nothing in it, they'd bring Gemma back.'

'Did Gemma go willingly?'

'What?'

'When she left with them, did she cry, struggle?'

'No, she just seemed to accept it. She didn't say anything.'

Banks stood up. 'That's it for now,' he said. 'We'll keep you informed. If you remember anything, you can report it at the mobile unit at the end of the street.'

Brenda folded her arms and nodded. 'You make *me* feel like a criminal, Mr Banks,' she said. 'It's not right. I've tried to be a good mother. I'm not perfect, but who is?'

Banks paused at the door. 'Mrs Scupham,' he said, 'I'm not trying to prove any kind of case against you. Believe it or not, all the questions I ask you are to do with trying to find Gemma. I know it seems cruel, but I need to know the answers. And if you think about it for a while, considering how many other children there are on this estate, and all over Swainsdale, and how many of them really *are* abused, there's a very important question needs answering.'

Brenda Scupham's brow furrowed, and even Poole glanced over from his fireside seat.

'What's that?' she asked.

'Why Gemma?' Banks said, and left.

3

ONE

Marjorie Bingham lingered behind the others on the narrow track and kicked at small stones as she walked. She could hear her husband's muffled voice, carried back on the breeze, as he explained the history of Dales lead mining to Andrew and Jane.

'Most people think that lead mining here only goes back as far as Roman times. It doesn't, you know. It goes back much further than that. It might even go back as far as the Bronze Age – though there's no hard evidence for that, of course – but certainly the Brigantes . . .'

God, she thought, what a bloody bore Roger has become. Only six months up from Coventry after the company move and here he is, playing the country squire and rabbiting on about spalling hammers, knockstones, buckers and hotching tubs. And just look at him: pants tucked into the expensive hiking boots, walking stick, orange Gore-Tex anorak. All for a quarter-mile trek from the Range Rover to the old mine.

Knowing Andrew, Marjorie thought, he was probably thinking about opening time, and Jane was absorbed with her new baby, which she carried in a kind of makeshift sack on her back. Little Annette was asleep, one leg poking out each side of the central strap, her head lolling, oblivious to them all, and especially oblivious to the bloody lead mines.

'Of course, the Romans used lead in great quantities. You know how advanced their plumbing systems were for their time. I know you've been to the Roman Baths in Bath, Andrew, and I'm sure you'll agree . . .'

Young Megan capered ahead picking flowers, reciting, 'He loves me, he loves me not . . .' as she pulled off the petals and tossed them in the air. Then she spread her arms out and pretended to walk a tightrope. She didn't have a care in the world, either, Marjorie thought. Why do we lose that sense of wonder in nature? she asked herself. How does it happen? Where does it go? It wasn't that she didn't appreciate the countryside – there was no denying it was beautiful, not to mention healthy, especially on a lovely autumn morning like this – but she couldn't feel ecstatic about it. To be honest, she loved the shops and the busy hum of city life much more. Even Eastvale would have been preferable. But no: Roger said they had to seize their opportunity for a newer, better lifestyle when it came along. And so they had ended up in dull, sleepy Lyndgarth.

A weekend in the country now and again suited Marjorie perfectly – that was what it was there for, after all, unless you were a farmer, a painter or a poet – but this felt more like incarceration. She hadn't been able to find a job, and the new neighbours weren't particularly friendly, either. Someone told her you have to winter out two years before you are accepted, but she didn't think she could stand it that long. Nor the fact that Roger was in his element. She was bored stiff. She didn't have children to fill her days like Jane. Still, at least their visit had brought a welcome break to the routine. She should be grateful for that. She would have been if it hadn't been for Roger seizing his chance to pontificate.

'The Pennine mines are the only ones in Yorkshire. Know why? It's because the lead ore occurs in Carboniferous rocks – the Yoredale Series and Millstone Grit. The ores aren't exactly *part* of the rocks, you understand, but . . .'

At last they reached the old smelting mill, not much more than a pile of stones, really, and not much bigger than a detached house. Most of the roof had collapsed, leaving only the weatherworn beams. Inside, sunlight shone through the roof and through the gaps between the stones onto the ruined ore hearths and furnaces, and picked out the motes of dust they kicked up. Marjorie had never liked the old mill. It was a dry, smelly, spidery sort of place. Over in one corner, the dusty ground was darkened, as if some wandering drunk had been sick there.

'In the earlier mills,' Roger went on, 'they used to burn off the sulphur first, changing the lead to oxide. Of course, for that you need places to roast then reduce the ore. But by the time this mill was built, they'd invented vertical furnaces that used bellows . . .'

They all obediently followed his pointing stick and oohed and aahed. He should have been a bloody tour guide, Marjorie thought.

Suddenly, Jane looked nervously around the mill. 'Where's Megan?' she asked.

'Probably playing outside,' Marjorie said, noting the anxiety in her voice. 'Don't worry, I'll find her. I've heard this bit before, anyway.' Roger glared at her as she left.

Thankful to be out of the gloomy smelting mill and away from the droning echo of Roger's voice, Marjorie shielded her eyes and looked around. Megan was clambering over a pile of scree towards the opening of the flue. Marjorie knew all about the flue, because she'd heard Roger read her the relevant sections from the book several times out loud. 'Listen to this, darling . . .' But the only thing she needed to know right now was that it could be dangerous.

Built originally to extract and condense the fumes of the smelting process and carry them far away from the immediate area, the flue was a bricked hump about two hundred yards long. It looked very much like a tall factory chimney that had fallen on its side and half buried itself in the gentle slope of the hillside. Because it was old, sections of the arched roof had collapsed here and there, and more were liable to follow suit at any moment. It had originally ended at a vertical chimney on the hilltop, designed to carry the lead fumes away, but that had long since fallen down.

Megan was happily scrambling along over the scree to the dark entrance. Marjorie set off after her. 'Megan!' she shouted. 'Come away!' Behind, she noticed that the others had come out of the smelting mill and stood watching a few yards away. 'It's all right,' Marjorie said over her shoulder. 'I'll catch up with her before she gets inside. It's quite safe out here.'

Maybe she had underestimated the six-year-old's speed and nimbleness, she thought, as she struggled over the rocks, trying not to trip up. But she made it. Megan got to the verge of the flue just as Marjorie managed to grab her shoulder.

'It's not safe, Megan,' she said, sitting down to catch her breath. 'You mustn't go in there.' As she looked into the black hole, she shivered. Far up ahead, she could see the tiny coin of light where the flue ended. Its floor was scattered with bits of stone, most likely fallen from the arched roof. A few yards or so in, she noticed a large oddly-shaped hump. It was probably a collapsed section, but something about it made her curious. It looked somehow deliberate, not quite as random as the other scatterings. She packed Megan off down the rise to join her parents and crawled into the opening.

'Where do you think you're going?' she heard Roger calling. 'Marjorie! Come back!' But she ignored him. Just for a moment, the sunlight had flashed on something ahead.

It was dark inside the flue, despite the light from behind her, and she hurt her knees as she crawled over the bed of flinty stones. She tried to stand, back bent low. The place smelled dank and foisty, and she tried to keep her breathing to an absolute minimum. She remembered Roger saying that the poisonous fumes of the volatilized lead condensed on the flue walls, which boys were employed to scrape at regular intervals. What a job that would be, she thought, crawling through here day after day and scraping lead off the stone.

When she arrived about six feet away from the hump, she could still make out nothing clearly. If she edged to one side and moulded her back against the curve of the wall, some light passed her and provided a faint outline. Then Roger blocked the entrance and yelled for her to come back.

'Get out of the way,' she shouted. 'I can't see a bloody thing!'

Oddly enough, Roger did as she asked. A faint wash of light picked out some of the details in the heap of stones, and as soon as Marjorie saw the small hand sticking out of the pile, she screamed and started to turn. As she did so, she stumbled and kicked some small stones near the body.

A cloud of flies rose out of the heap and buzzed angrily up the flue.

TWO

'We've had three confessions already,' said Gristhorpe, as Banks took the Helmthorpe road out of Eastvale. Roger Bingham's message had been vague, and both avoided speculating whether the body of Gemma Scupham had been discovered. 'One of them told us at great length exactly what he'd done with Gemma and how much he enjoyed it. I tell you, Alan, sometimes it's a bloody shame you can't lock a man up for his thoughts.' He ran a hand through his unruly grey hair. 'Good God, did I really say that? Shows how much this business is getting to me. Anyway, we got him for wasting police time instead. He'll do six months with any luck.'

'The searchers turn up anything yet?' Banks asked.

Gristhorpe shook his head. 'They're doing the area east of the estate now, past the railway tracks. We've taken on a few civilian volunteers. And we've interviewed all the known local child-molesters. Nothing there.'

At Fortford, Banks turned left by the pub and passed between the Roman fort and the village green.

'Anything on the car?' Gristhorpe asked.

After his visit to Brenda Scupham the previous afternoon, Banks had caught up with his paperwork on the case, helped Susan with the house-to-house and Richmond check the garages and car-rental agencies.

'Not so far. We've got through most of the garages and agencies. Phil's still at it.'

'Well, maybe it was their own car, after all,' said

Gristhorpe. 'They've vanished into thin air, Alan. How can they do that?'

'Either very clever or very lucky, I suppose. No one on the estate was very communicative, either,' he went on. 'I only did a couple of streets with Susan, but she said the others were no different. And she had another chat with that Mr Carter at number sixteen. Waste of time, she said. He just wanted to talk about Dunkirk. People are scared, you know, even when we show them our warrant cards.'

'I don't blame them,' said Gristhorpe.

'But I reckon if it *had* happened to someone else around there, they'd speak up now.'

'You never know with people, Alan. Remember the old Yorkshire saying, "There's nowt so queer as folk".'

Banks laughed. At the junction in Relton, he turned right. A slow-moving tractor in front pulled over to the side and gave him just enough space to squeeze by. 'I've been on the phone to Belfast, too,' he added. 'The lads over there spent most of yesterday with Terry Garswood, Gemma's father, and they're certain he had nothing to do with it. For a start, he was on duty that day and couldn't have got away without someone noticing, and apparently he had neither the inclination nor the money to hire someone else to steal her for him.'

'Well, look on the bright side,' said Gristhorpe. 'At least that's one less lead to follow. There it is.' He pointed out of the car window. 'Pull in here.'

They were on Mortsett Lane, about halfway between Relton and Gratly, below the looming bulk of Tetchley Fell. Banks pulled up on the gravelled lay-by next to a Range Rover and looked at the narrow track. There was no way you could get a car up there, he thought. The stony path was only about three feet wide, and it was bordered by small boulders and chips of flint that would play havoc with tyres. Ahead, he could just make out the partially collapsed roof of the smelting mill over the rise.

He had seen the place before, but from a different perspective. Looking down from the Roman road that cut diagonally across the fell, he had been impressed by the range of colour, from pale yellow to dark green, purple and grey, and by the flue hugging the hillside like a long stone tunnel. Now, as they neared the mill, all he could see was the murky opening to his left and the group of people huddled together by the mill to his right.

'Which one of you is Mr Bingham?' Gristhorpe asked, after he had introduced Banks and himself.

'I am,' said a countryish type, in gear far too expensive and inappropriate for the short walk. 'My wife, Marjorie, found the . . . er . . . Well, I remembered there was a phonebox back down on the road.'

Gristhorpe nodded and turned to the woman. 'Did you disturb anything?'

She shook her head. 'No. I never touched . . . I . . . When I saw the hand I ran back. And the flies . . . Oh, my God . . . the flies . . .'

Her husband took her hand and she buried her face in his shoulder. The other couple looked on sadly, the man with a grim set to his mouth and the woman stroking her child's golden hair. Banks noticed a head over her shoulder, a sleeping baby in a backpack.

Gristhorpe turned to Banks. 'Shall we?'

Banks nodded and followed him over the scree. They had to walk carefully, as many of the stones wobbled under them. Finally, they managed to scrabble to the gloomy semicircle and peer inside. Gristhorpe brought the torch out of his pocket and shone it ahead. They could easily see the heap that Marjorie Bingham had mentioned, but couldn't pick out any details from so far away. Gristhorpe had to bend almost double to walk, which made it very difficult to negotiate a path through the rubble that littered the flue's floor. Banks, being a little shorter, found it easier. But he felt uncomfortable.

He had never liked caves; they always seemed to bring out a latent sense of claustrophobia. Once he and Sandra had visited Ingleton and gone in the caves there. When he had to stoop and almost crawl on his belly to get under a low overhang, he had felt the weight of the mountain pressing on his back and had to struggle to keep his breathing regular. The flue wasn't as bad as that, but he could still feel the heavy darkness pushing at him from all sides.

Gristhorpe walked a few feet behind him with the torch. Its beam danced over lead-stained stones, which glistened here and there as if snails had left their slimy tracks. They went as cautiously as they could in order not to destroy any forensic evidence, but it was impossible to pick a narrow path through the rubble of the flue. Finally, they stood close enough, and Gristhorpe's torch lit on a small hand raised from a heap of rocks. They could see nothing else of the body, as it had been entirely covered by stones.

As they stood and looked at the hand, a gust of wind blew and made a low moaning sound in the flue like someone blowing over the lip of a bottle. Gristhorpe turned off the torch and they headed back for the entrance. They had probably disturbed too much already, but they had to verify that there was indeed a body on the site. So often people simply *thought* they had found a corpse, and the truth turned out to be different. Now they had to follow procedure.

First they would call the police surgeon to ascertain that the body was indeed dead. No matter how obvious it might appear, no matter even if the body is decapitated or chopped into a dozen pieces, it is not dead until a qualified doctor says it is.

Then the SOCO team would arrive and mark off the area with their white plastic tape. It might not seem necessary in such an isolated place, but the searching of a crime scene was a very serious business, and there were guidelines to follow. With Vic Manson in charge, they would take photographs and search the area around the body, looking for hairs, fibres, anything that the killer might have left behind. And then, when the photographs had been taken, the doctor would take a closer look at the body. In this case, he might move aside a few stones and look for obvious causes of death. There was nothing more that Banks and Gristhorpe could do until they at least had some information on the identity of the victim.

Banks gulped in the fresh, bright air as they emerged into daylight. He felt as if he had just made an ascent from the bottom of a deep, dark ocean with only seconds to spare before his oxygen ran out. Gristhorpe stood beside him and stretched, rubbing his lower back and grimacing.

'I'll call it in,' said Banks.

Gristhorpe nodded. 'Aye. And I'll have another word with this lot over here.' He shook his head slowly. 'Looks like we've found her.'

There was nothing to do but wait after Banks had made the call over the police radio. Gristhorpe got Marjorie Bingham's story, then let the shocked group go home.

Banks leaned against the rough stone of the smelting mill and lit a cigarette as Gristhorpe walked carefully around the flue entrance looking down at the ground. It was quiet up there except for the occasional mournful call of a curlew gliding over the moorland, a cry that harmonized strangely with the deep sigh of the breeze blowing down the flue and ruffling the blades of grass on the hillside. The sky was the whitish blue of skimmed milk, and it set off the browns, greens and yellows of the desolate landscape. Beyond the mill, Banks could see the purple-grey cleft of a dried-up stream-bed cutting across the moorland.

Gristhorpe, kneeling to peer at the grass a few yards to the right of the flue entrance, beckoned Banks over. Banks knelt beside him and looked at the rusty smear on the grass.

'Blood?' he said.

'Looks like it. If so, maybe she was killed out here and they dragged her into the flue to hide the body.'

Banks looked at the blood again. 'It doesn't look like much, though, does it?' he said. 'And I'd say it's smeared rather than spilled.'

'Aye,' said Gristhorpe, standing. 'Like someone wiped off a knife or something. We'll leave it to the SOCOs.'

The first to arrive was Peter Darby, the photographer. He came bounding up the track, fresh-faced, two cameras slung around his neck and a square metal case at his side. If it's Gemma Scupham in there, Banks thought, he won't look so bloody cheerful when he comes out.

Darby went to take some preliminary photographs, starting with the stained grass, on Gristhorpe's suggestion, then the flue entrance, then carefully making his way inside. Banks could see the bulbs flash in the black hole as Darby took his pictures. When he'd finished in the flue, he took more photographs in and around the smelting mill.

About half an hour after Peter Darby, Dr Glendenning came huffing and puffing up the path.

'At least I didn't need a bloody truss to get here this

time,' he said, referring to the occasion when they had all been winched up the side of Rawley Force to get to a body in a hanging valley. He pointed towards the flue. 'In there, you said?'

Gristhorpe nodded.

'Hmphh. Why the bloody hell do you keep on finding bodies in awkward places, eh? I'm not getting any younger, you know. It's not even my job. You could get a bloody GP to pronounce the body dead at the scene.'

Banks shrugged. 'Sorry.' Glendenning was a Home Office pathologist, one of the best in the country, and both Banks and Gristhorpe knew he would be offended if they didn't call him to the scene first.

'Aye, well . . .' He turned towards the entrance.

They accompanied Glendenning as he picked his way over the scree, complaining all the way, and ducked to enter the flue. Banks held the torch this time. It didn't provide much light, but the SOCOs had been instructed to bring bottled-gas lamps as it would be impossible to get a van with a generator up the narrow track.

Glendenning knelt for a while, sniffing the air and glancing around the inside of the flue, then he touched the small hand and moved it, muttering to himself. Next he took out a mercury thermometer and held it close to the body, measuring the air temperature.

The entrance of the flue darkened and someone called out. It was Vic Manson, fingerprint expert and leader of the SOCO team. He came up the passage with a gas lamp and soon the place was full of light. It cast eerie shadows on the slimy stone walls and gave an unreal sheen to the heap of stones on the ground. Manson called back to one of his assistants and asked him to bring up some large plastic bags.

Then everyone stood silent, breath held, as the men started to lift the stones and place them in the bags for later forensic investigation. A few spiders scurried away and a couple of obstinate flies buzzed the man angrily, then zigzagged off.

Banks leaned against the wall, his back bent into its curve. One stone, two, three . . . Then a whole arm became visible.

Banks and Gristhorpe moved forward. They crouched over and looked at the small hand, then both saw the man's wristwatch and frayed sleeve of a grey bomber jacket. 'It's not her,' Gristhorpe whispered. 'Jesus Christ, it's not Gemma Scupham.'

Banks felt the relief, too. He had always clung to a vague hope that Gemma might still be alive, but the discovery of the body had seemed to wreck all that. Nobody else in the dale had been reported missing. And now, as Manson and his men picked stone after stone away, they looked down at what was obviously the body of a young man, complete with moustache. A young man with unusually small hands. But, Banks asked himself, if it isn't Gemma Scupham, then who the hell is it?

THREE

Jenny darted into the Eastvale Regional Headquarters at two o'clock, just in time for her appointment with Banks. She always seemed to be rushing these days, she thought, as if she were a watch a few minutes slow always trying to catch up. She wasn't even really late this time.

'Miss Fuller?'

Jenny walked over to the front desk. 'Yes?'

'Message from Detective Superintendent Gristhorpe, miss. Says he's on his way. You can wait in his office if you wish.'

Jenny frowned. 'But I thought I was to see Alan – Chief Inspector Banks?'

'He's at the scene.'

'What scene?'

'It looks like a murder scene. I'm sorry I can't say any more, miss. We don't really know anything yet.'

'That's all right,' Jenny said. 'I'll wait.'

'Very well. The superintendent's office—'

'I know where it is, thanks.'

Jenny poured herself some coffee from the machine at the bottom of the stairs, then went up to Gristhorpe's office. She had been there before, but never alone. It was larger than Alan's and much better appointed. She had heard that rank determines the level of luxury in policemen's offices, but she also knew that the department itself was hardly likely to supply such things as the large teak desk, or the matching bookcases that covered one wall. The cream-and-burgundy patterned carpet, perhaps – it was hardly an expensive one, Jenny noticed – but not the shaded desk lamp and the books that lined the shelves.

She glanced over the titles. They were mostly works of criminology and law – the essential *Archbold's Criminal Pleading, Evidence & Practice* and Glaister's *Medical Jurisprudence and Toxicology* in addition to several other technical and forensic texts – but there were also books on history, fishing, cricket, a few novels and Sir Arthur Quiller-Couch's edition of *The Oxford Book of English Verse*. What surprised Jenny most was the number of mystery paperbacks: about four feet of them, mostly Margery Allingham, Ngaio Marsh, Edmund Crispin and Michael Innes.

'That's just the overflow,' a voice said behind her, making her jump. 'The rest are at home.'

'I didn't hear you come in,' Jenny said, putting her hand to her chest. 'You startled me.'

'We coppers are a light-footed lot,' Gristhorpe said, with a twinkle in his baby-blue eyes. 'Have to be to catch the villains. Sit down.'

Jenny sat. 'This murder, I couldn't help thinking . . . It's not . . .?'

'No, it's not, thank God. It's bad enough, though. We don't know who the victim is yet. I left Alan at the scene. I decided to stick with the Gemma Scupham case and let him handle the murder.'

Jenny had never felt entirely at ease with Superintendent Gristhorpe, but she didn't know why. He seemed very much his own man – self-contained, strong, determined – and he projected a solid, comforting presence. But something made her feel awkward. Perhaps, she speculated, it was the underlying sense of isolation she sensed, the fortress he seemed to have built around his feelings. She knew about his wife's death from cancer several years ago, and guessed that perhaps a part of him had died with her. Susan Gay, she remembered, had said that she also felt uncomfortable with him, yet he had a reputation as a kind and compassionate man.

His physical presence was difficult to ignore, too. He was a big man – bulky, but not fat – with bushy eyebrows and an unruly thatch of grey hair. With his reddish, pock-marked complexion and the slightly hooked nose, he was very much the dalesman, she thought, if indeed there was such a creature, weathered and moulded by the landscape.

'I did a bit of preliminary research last night,' Jenny

began. 'I *can* probably give you a capsule version of the paedophile types.'

Gristhorpe nodded. As she spoke, Jenny somehow felt that he probably knew more than she did about the subject. After all, some of his books dealt with criminal psychology and forensic psychiatry, and he was reputed to be well read. But she didn't feel he was simply being polite when he let her speak. No, he was listening all right, listening for something he might not have come across or thought of himself. Watching her carefully with those deceptively innocent eyes.

She balanced her black-rimmed reading-glasses on her nose and took her notes out of her briefcase. 'Basically, there are four types of paedophile,' she began. 'And so far it doesn't seem like your couple fits any. The first kind is someone who hasn't really been able to establish satisfactory relationships with his peers. It's the most common type, and he only feels sexually comfortable with children. He usually *knows* his victim, maybe a family friend, or even a relation.'

Gristhorpe nodded. 'What about age, roughly?'

'Average age is about forty.'

'Hmm. Go on.'

'The second type is someone who seems to develop normally but finds it increasingly difficult to adjust to adult life – work, marriage, et cetera. Feels inadequate, often turns to drink. Usually the marriage, if there is one, breaks down. With this type, something sets things in motion. He reaches a kind of breaking-point. Maybe his wife or girlfriend is having an affair, intensifying his feelings of inadequacy. This kind doesn't usually know his victim. It may be someone he sees passing by in a car or something. Again, not much like the situation you described at Brenda Scupham's.'

'No,' agreed Gristhorpe. 'But we've got to keep an open mind at this point.'

'And I think we can dismiss the third type, too,' Jenny went on. 'This is someone who generally had his formative sexual experiences with young boys in an institution of some kind.'

'Ah,' said Gristhorpe. 'Public school?'

Jenny looked up at him and smiled. 'I suppose that would qualify.' She turned back to her notes. 'Anyway, this type is generally a homosexual paedophile, the type that cruises the streets for victims or uses male prostitutes.'

'And the last?'

'The wild card,' Jenny said. 'The psychopathic paedophile. It's hard to pin this type down. He's in search of new sexual thrills, and pain and fear are generally involved. He'll hurt his victims, introduce sharp objects into the sexual organs, that kind of thing. The more aggressive he gets, the more excited he becomes. A person like this usually has a history of antisocial behaviour.'

Gristhorpe held the bridge of his nose and grunted.

'I'm sorry I can't really be of any more help yet,' Jenny said, 'but I'm working on it. The really odd thing, as I told Alan, is that there were two of them, a man and a woman. I want to look a bit further into that aspect.'

Gristhorpe nodded, 'Go ahead. And please don't underestimate your usefulness.'

Jenny smiled at him and shuffled her notes back into the briefcase.

'This stuff the newspapers were on about,' Gristhorpe went on, 'organized gangs of paedophiles, what do you think of that?'

Jenny shook her head. 'It doesn't figure. Paedophiles are like other sexual deviants, essentially loners, solo operators. And most of the allegations of ritual abuse turned out to be social workers' fantasies. Of course, when you get abuse in families, people close ranks. They might look like organized gangs, but they're not really. Paedophiles simply aren't the types to form clubs, except . . .'

'Except what?'

'I was thinking of kiddie porn, child prostitution and the like. It's around, it happens, there's no denying it, and that takes a bit of organization.'

'Videos, magazines?'

'Yes. Even snuff films.'

'We're doing our best,' Gristhorpe said. 'I've been in touch with the paedophile squad. Those rings are hard to penetrate, but if anything concerning Gemma turns up, believe me, we'll know about it.'

Jenny stood up. 'I'll do a bit more research.'

'Thanks.' Gristhorpe walked over to open the door for her.

Jenny dashed back to her car, got in and turned her key in the ignition. Suddenly, she paused. She couldn't remember where she was supposed to go or why she was in such a hurry. She checked her appointment book and then racked her brains to see if she had forgotten anything. No. The truth was, she had nowhere to go and no reason at all to hurry.

FOUR

Banks breathed deeply, grateful for the fresh air outside the flue. Claustrophobia was bad enough, but what he had just seen made it even worse.

After Gristhorpe had gone to meet Jenny, the SOCOs

had slowly and carefully removed all the stones from the body of a man in his mid- to late-twenties. When they had finished, Dr Glendenning bent forward to see what he could find out. First, he opened the bomber jacket and cursed when he had to stop the tangle of greyish intestines from spilling out of the man's shirt. A couple more flies finally gave up the ghost and crawled out from under the tubing and took off indignantly. The wind moaned down the flue. Quickly, Banks had searched the dead man's pockets: all empty.

Banks lit a cigarette; fresh air wasn't enough to get the taste of the flue and of death out of his mouth. The smell was difficult to pin down. Sickly, sweet, with a slight metallic edge, it always seemed to linger around him like an aura for days after attending the scene of a murder.

Glendenning had been crouched in the flue alone for over half an hour now, and the SOCOs were still going over the ground inside the taped-off area: every blade of grass, every stone.

Banks wandered into the smelting mill and looked at the ruins of the furnace and the ore hearth while he waited, trying to put the first shocking glimpse of those spilled intestines out of his mind. He had seen the same thing once before, back in London, and it wasn't something even the most hardened policeman forgot easily. He stared at the dullish brown patch in the corner, marked off by the SOCOs as blood. The murder, they said, had probably taken place in the mill.

At last, Glendenning emerged from the flue, red in the face. He stood upright and dusted his jacket where it had come into contact with the stones. A cigarette dangled from his mouth.

'I suppose you want to know it all right away, don't

you?' he said to Banks, sitting on a boulder outside the smelting mill. 'Time of death, cause of death, what he had for breakfast?'

Banks grinned. 'As much as you can tell me.'

'Aye, well, that might be a bit more than usual in this case. Given the temperature, I'd say rigor mortis went basically according to the norm. It was just after two o'clock when I got the chance to have a really good look at him. Allowing, say, two or three hours for rigor to start, then about ten or twelve to spread, I'd say he was killed sometime after dark last night, but not much later than ten o'clock. His body temperature confirms it, too. Is that good enough for you?'

Banks said it was, thank you very much, doctor, and mentioned the blood in the smelting mill.

'You're probably right about that,' Glendenning said. 'I'll check post-mortem lividity later when I get him on the table, but as far as I could tell there was no blood around the body, and there would be, given a wound like that.'

'What about cause of death?'

'That's not difficult. Looks like he was gutted. You saw that for yourself.' Glendenning lit a new cigarette from the stub of his old one. 'It's an especially vicious crime,' he went on. 'In the first place, to do something like that you have to get very close.'

'Would it take a lot of strength?'

'Aye, a fair bit to drag the knife up when it's stuck so deeply in. But not a superman. Given a sharp enough knife. What are you getting at? Man or woman?'

'Something like that.'

'You know how I hate guesswork, laddie, but I'd go for a moderately strong man or an exceptionally strong woman.'

'Thanks. First we'll check all the female bodybuilders in Yorkshire. Left-handed or right?'

'I should be able to tell you later when I get a good look at the entry point and the direction of the slit.'

'What about the weapon?'

'Again, you'll have to wait. All I can say now is it looks like a typical upthrust knife wound. Have you made arrangements for the removal?'

Banks nodded.

'Good. I'll get to it as soon as I can.' Glendenning stood up and headed down the track to his car. Banks looked at his watch: almost three o'clock and he hadn't had lunch yet. Maybe an hour or so more up here and he'd be able to leave the scene for a local constable to guard. He called Vic Manson over.

'Any sign of the murder weapon?'

'Not so far. I don't think it's around here. The lads have almost finished the third grid search, and they'd have found it by now.'

Banks walked back over to the smelting mill and leaned against the wall watching the men examine the scree outside the flue entrance. 'An especially vicious crime,' Dr Glendenning had said. Indeed it was. It was hard to believe, thought Banks, that in such beautiful countryside on such a fine autumn evening, one human being had got so close to another that he could watch, and perhaps even savour, the look in his victim's eyes as he thrust a sharp knife in his groin and slowly dragged it up through the stomach to the chest.

●

FIVE

Brenda Scupham lay alone in bed that night. Les was out at the pub. Not that she really cared. These days he was practically worse than useless. He mostly kept out of her way, and that suited her fine. The only thing was, she didn't really want to be alone tonight. A nice warm body to love her and hold her would help take her mind off the bad things she couldn't seem to stop herself from feeling.

She hadn't wanted Gemma, it was true. But things like that happened. She had done her best. At first, there always seemed to be so much to do: changing nappies, feeding, scraping and saving for new clothes. And the sleepless nights she had listened to Gemma cry from her cot, leaving her till she cried herself to sleep because her own mother had said you shouldn't make a habit of being at a baby's beck and call. Well, she should know all about that, Brenda thought.

Even as she got older, Gemma had got in the way, too. Every time Brenda had a man over, she had to explain the child. Nobody stayed with her when they found out she had a kid. One night was the best she could expect from most, then a hasty exit, usually well before dawn, and Gemma there wailing away.

Brenda understood women who had beaten or killed their children. It happened all the time. They could drive you to that. One night, she remembered with shame, she had wrapped three-month-old Gemma in blankets and left her on the steps of the Catholic church. She hadn't been home five minutes before guilt sent her racing back to reclaim the bundle. Luckily, nobody else had got there first.

But no matter what those policemen tried to say, she had never abused Gemma. Some mothers sat their children on the elements of electric cookers, poured boiling water on them, locked them in the cellar without food or drink until they died of dehydration. Brenda would never have done anything like that. She put up with Gemma and took her pleasure when she could. True, she had left the child alone for visits to the pub. But nothing had ever happened to her. Also true, she never had much time to spend with her, what with the odd bit of waitressing she did on the sly to eke out her social. Meals had occasionally been forgotten, old clothes left unwashed too long. Gemma herself, like most kids, was not overfond of bathtime, and she had never complained about going without a bath for a couple of weeks.

What upset Brenda most as she lay there alone in the dark was accepting that she had never really *liked* her child. Oh, she had got used to her, all right, but there was something secretive and isolated about Gemma, something alien that Brenda felt she could never reach. And there was something creepy about the way she skulked around the place. Many a time Brenda had felt Gemma's accusing, woebegone eyes on her. Even now, alone in the dark, she could feel Gemma's eyes looking at her in that way. Still, you didn't *choose* your child, no more than she chose to be born. She wasn't made to order.

But now Gemma was gone, Brenda felt guilty for feeling relieved when Miss Peterson and Mr Brown took her away. Why did it have to be so complicated? Why couldn't they have been real social workers like they said they were? Then she wouldn't have to feel so guilty for being relieved. Now she couldn't even bear to think about what they might have done to Gemma. She shivered. Gemma must be dead. Brenda only hoped it had happened quickly and painlessly and that soon the police would find out everything and leave her alone to get her grieving done.

Again she replayed what she could remember of the social workers' visit. Maybe she had been a fool for believing them, but they *had* looked so real, and they *had* been so convincing. She knew she had neglected Gemma and that she was wrong to do so, however much she couldn't help herself. She knew she was guilty, especially after what happened the week before. But they surely couldn't have known about that? No, they were right. She had to let them take the child. She found herself hoping, after the door closed, that they would decide to keep her or find her a good home. It would be best for everyone that way.

And then there was Les. She remembered defending him to the police that morning, saying he wasn't much but he was better than nothing. She wasn't even sure that was true any longer. Mostly, she'd been thinking of sex. He used to do it three, four times a night, if he hadn't had a skinful of ale, and she couldn't get enough of him. He had made her laugh, too. But lately all the passion had gone. It happened, she knew, and you became nothing more than a maid, your home no more than a hotel room.

She turned on her side and put her hand between her legs, then began gently stroking herself with her fingers. It would help her forget, she thought, rubbing harder. Forget her foolishness, forget her guilt, forget Gemma. Gemma, precious stone, name stolen from an old school-friend whose serene beauty she had always envied.

Just before the climax flooded her, an image of Gemma going out of the door with Mr Brown and Miss Peterson appeared in her mind's eye. As she came, it receded, like someone waving goodbye from a train window.

4

ONE

At ten past eleven on Saturday morning, Banks stood at his office window, coffee in hand, and looked down on the market square. It was another beautiful day – the fifth in a row – with a pale-blue sky and high wispy clouds. It was also four days since Gemma Scupham's abduction.

Down in the cobbled square, the market was in full swing. Tourists and locals browsed the stalls, where vendors dealt in everything from clothes and used books to car accessories and small electrical gadgets. As Banks watched them unload new stock from the vans, he speculated how much of the goods were stolen, fallen off the back of a lorry. Most of the things for sale were legitimate, of course – over-production or sub-standard stuff rejected by a company's quality control and sold at slightly above cost – but a busy market was an ideal place for getting rid of hot property.

There would be nothing from the Fletcher's warehouse job, though; televisions and stereos attracted too much attention at outdoor markets. Mostly, they would be sold by word of mouth, through pubs and video retailers.

Banks thought again about how smooth the operation had been. The burglars had cut through a chain-link fence, drugged a guard dog, and disabled the alarm system. They had then loaded a van up with electrical goods, taken off into the night and never been seen since. It would have taken at least three men, he speculated, and Les Poole was probably one of them. But there were far more serious things to think about now. At least Poole was under surveillance, and any step he made out of line would soon come to Banks's attention.

The traffic along Market Street slowed almost to a standstill as yet more tourists poured into town. Because it was market day, parking was a problem. Drivers would spend an extra half-hour cruising around the narrow streets looking for a parking space. It would be a busy day for the traffic police.

Banks opened the window a couple of inches. He could hear the honking horns and the babble of voices down in the square, and the smell of fresh bread drifted up from the bakery on Market Street, mingled with exhaust fumes.

At their morning conference, Gristhorpe had assigned Banks and DC Susan Gay to the lead-mine murder; Gristhorpe himself, along with DS Richmond, would pursue the Gemma Scupham investigation, with Jenny Fuller acting as consultant. With each day that went by, the pressure increased. Parents were scared; they were keeping their children home from school. Ever since Gemma had disappeared, police forces county-wide had been knocking on doors and conducting searches of wasteland and out-of-the-way areas. The surprising thing was that nothing had come to light so far. The way it seemed, Gemma had disappeared from the face of the earth. Despite his reassignment, Banks knew he would have to keep up to date on the case. He couldn't forget Gemma Scupham that easily.

For a moment, he found himself wondering if the two cases could be connected in some way. It was rare that two serious crimes should happen in Swainsdale at about the same time. Could it be more than mere coincidence? He didn't see how, but it was something worth bearing in mind.

His first task was to identify the body they had found. Certainly a photograph could be published; clothing labels sometimes helped; then there were medical features – an operation scar, birthmark – and dental charts. It would be easy enough to track down such information if the man were local, but practically impossible if he were a stranger to the area. Banks had already sent DC Gay to make inquiries in Gratly and Relton, the nearest villages to the mine, but he didn't expect much to come of that. At best, someone might have seen a car heading towards the mine.

A red van had got itself wedged into the junction of Market Street and the square, just in front of the Queen's Arms, and irate motorists started honking. The van's owner kept on unloading boxes of tights and women's underwear, oblivious to the angry tourists. One man got out and headed towards him.

Banks turned away from the window and went over the lead-mine scene in his mind. The victim had probably been murdered in the smelting mill, an out-of-the-way place. His pockets had been emptied and his body had been hidden in the flue, which few people ever entered due to the danger of falling stones. Safe to assume, Banks thought, that the killer didn't want the body found for a while. That made sense, as most leads in an investigation occur in the first twenty-four hours. But the body *had* been found much sooner than the killer expected, and that might just give Banks an edge.

Just as Banks was about to leave his office in search of

more coffee, the phone rang. It was Vic Manson from the forensic lab near Wetherby.

'You've been quick,' Banks said. 'What have you got?'

'Lucky. You want to know who he is?'

'You're sure?'

'Uh-huh. I'd like to claim brilliant deduction, but it was routine.'

'Fingerprints?' Banks guessed. It was the first thing they would check, and while most people's prints weren't on file anywhere, a lot were. Another break.

'Got it. Seems he did a stretch in Armley Jail. Tried to con an old lady out of her life's savings, but she turned out to be smarter than him. Name's Carl Johnson. He's from Bradford, but he's been living in your neck of the woods for a year or so. Flat 6, 59 Calvin Street.'

Banks knew the street. It was in the north-eastern part of Eastvale, where a few of the large old houses had been converted into cheap flats.

'You can get your man to pull his file from the computer,' Manson said.

'Thanks, Vic. I'll do that. Keep at it.'

'Have I any bloody choice? We're snowed under. Anyway, I'll get back to you as soon as we find out any more.'

Banks hurried over to Richmond's office. Richmond sat over his keyboard, tapping away, and Banks waited until he reached a point when he could pause. Then he explained what Vic Manson had said.

'No problem,' said Richmond. 'Just let me finish entering this report in the database and I'll get you a printout.'

'Thanks, Phil.'

Banks grabbed a coffee and went back to his office to wait. The market square was teeming with people now, lingering at stalls, feeling the goods, listening to the vendors' pitches, watching the man who juggled plates as if he were a circus performer.

Carl Johnson. The name didn't ring a bell. If he had been in London, Banks would have got out on the street to question informers and meet with undercover officers. Someone would have heard a whisper, a boast, a rumour. But in Eastvale no real criminal underbelly existed. And he certainly knew of no one capable of killing in the way Carl Johnson had been killed. There were low-lifes like Les Poole, of course, but Poole was a coward at heart, and whatever he was, he wasn't a murderer. Still, it might be worth mentioning Johnson's name to him, just to see the reaction.

Had the killer not known about Johnson's record, that he would be easy to identify? Certainly whoever it was had gone to great lengths to hide the body, but he hadn't tried to destroy the fingerprints, as some killers did. Perhaps he was squeamish – unlikely, given the way he'd killed Johnson – or he was careless. Careless or cocky. Whatever the reason, Banks at least had something to go on: Flat 6, 59 Calvin Street. That was the place to start.

TWO

If Gristhorpe had expected inverted crosses, black candles, pentagrams and ceremonial robes, he couldn't have been more mistaken. Melville Westman's Helmthorpe cottage was as ordinary as could be: teal wallpaper with white curlicue patterns, beige three-piece suite, television, music centre. Sunlight poured through the windows past the white lace curtains and gave the place a bright, airy feel.

The only clues to Westman's interests were to be found in the bookcase: Eliphas Levi's *Le Dogme et le Rituel de la Haute Magie*, Mather's translation of *The Key of Solomon*, Crowley's *Magick in Theory and Practice*, *Malleus Maleficarum* and a few other books on astrology, cabbala, the tarot, witchcraft and ritual magic. In addition, a sampler over the fireplace bore the motto, 'Do what thou wilt shall be the whole of the law' in the same kind of embroidery one would expect to find such ancient saws as, 'A house is built of bricks; a home is built on love.'

Similarly, if Gristhorpe had expected a bedraggled, wild-eyed Charles Manson lookalike, he would have been disappointed. Westman was a dapper, middle-aged man with sparse mousy hair, dressed in a grey V-neck pullover over a white shirt, wearing equally grey pants with sharp creases. He was a short, portly man, but he had presence. It was partly in the slightly flared nostrils that gave his face a constant expression of arrogant sneering, and partly in the controlled intensity of his cold eyes.

'It took you long enough,' he said to Gristhorpe, gesturing towards an armchair.

Gristhorpe sat down. 'What do you mean?'

'Oh, come on, Superintendent! Let's not play games. The girl, the missing girl. I read about it in the paper.'

'What's that got to do with you?'

Westman sat opposite Gristhorpe and leaned forward in his chair, linking his hands on his lap. 'Nothing, of course. But you have to ask, don't you?'

'And?'

Westman smiled and shook his head slowly. 'And nothing.'

'Mr Westman,' Gristhorpe said. 'In cases like this we have to consider every possibility. If you know anything about the child's disappearance, it'd be best if you told me.'

'I told you. I know nothing. Why should I?'

'We both know about your involvement in witchcraft and Satanism. Don't be naive.'

'Involvement? Witchcraft? Satanism? Superintendent, just because I practise a different religion from you, don't assume I'm some kind of monster. I'm not a Satanist, and I'm not a witch, either. Most people you would call witches are silly dabblers who appropriate the old ways and practices as an excuse for sexual excess. Ex-hippies and New Agers.'

'Whatever you call yourself,' Gristhorpe said, 'there's a history of people like you being involved in sacrifice.'

'Sacrificial virgins? Really! Again, you're confusing me with the psychopathic Satanists who use the ancient ways as an excuse. People who read too much Aleister Crowley – he *did* exaggerate, you know – and found he appealed to their sick fantasies. You find a few bloody pentagrams daubed on a wall and a bit of gibberish in Latin and you think you're dealing with the real thing. You're not.'

Gristhorpe pointed towards the bookcase. 'I notice you have a few Aleister Crowley books yourself. Does that make you a psychopathic Satanist?'

Westman's lips curled at the edges like an old sandwich. 'Crowley has things to teach to those who understand. Do you know the purpose of magic, Superintendent?'

'Power,' said Gristhorpe.

Westman sniffed. 'Typical. It comes from the same root as "magi", wise man. The purpose of the "Great Work" is to become God, and you dismiss it as mere human hunger for power.'

Gristhorpe sighed and tried to hold onto his temper.

The man's sanctimonious tone was grating on his nerves. 'Mr Westman, I don't really give a damn what illusions you cling to. That's not the purpose—'

'Illusions! Superintendent, believe me, the work of the magician is far from an illusion. It's a matter of will, courage, intense study of—'

'I don't want a lecture, Mr Westman. I know enough about the subject already. I know, for example, that sacrifice is important because you regard living creatures as storehouses of energy. When you kill them, when you spill their blood, you release this energy and concentrate it. I also know it's as much a matter of blood-lust, of murderous frenzy, as it is of any practical purpose. The incense, incantations, and finally the gushing of blood. It's orgasmic, a sexual kick.'

Westman waved his hand. 'I can see you know nothing, Superintendent. Again, you're talking about the deviants, the charlatans.'

'And', Gristhorpe went on, 'a human sacrifice is the most effective of all, gives you the biggest kick. Especially the sacrifice of a pure child.'

Westman pursed his lips and put his forefinger to them. He stared at Gristhorpe for a few moments, then shrugged and sat back in the chair. 'Human sacrifice is rare in true magic,' he said. 'It's difficult enough for those who practise such arts to simply exist in such a narrow-minded world as the one we inhabit; we are hardly likely to make things worse by kidnapping children and slaughtering them.'

'So you know nothing at all about Gemma Scupham?'

'Only what I read in the newspapers. And though I expected a visit, given my notoriety, as far as I can gather, I bear no resemblance to either of the suspects.'

'True, but that doesn't mean you're not associated with them in some way. A lot of people don't do their own dirty work.'

'Insults, is it now? Well, maybe you're right. Maybe I prepared a couple of zombies to do the job. Do you remember the Rochdale scandal, Superintendent? Ten children were taken from their parents and put into care by child-workers who believed a few wild tales about ritualistic, satanic abuse. And what happened? They were sent home. There was no evidence. Children have over-active imaginations. If some six-year-old tells you he's eaten a cat, the odds are it was a chocolate one, or some kind of animal-shaped breakfast cereal.'

'I know about the Rochdale affair,' Gristhorpe said, 'and about what happened in Nottingham. It didn't come out at the trial, but we found out later there *was* ritual abuse involved. These kids were tortured, starved, humiliated and used as sex objects.'

'But they weren't sacrificed to the devil, or any such nonsense. All these tales about organized satanic abuse were discredited. Most such abuse takes place in extended families, between family members.'

'That's not the issue.' Gristhorpe leaned forward. 'Gemma Scupham was abducted from her home and we can't find hide nor hair of her. If she'd been killed and dumped somewhere in the dale, we'd most likely have found her by now. We haven't. What does that imply to you?'

'I don't know. You're supposed to be the detective. You tell me.'

'One of two things. Either she's dead and her body has been very well hidden, perhaps somewhere other than Swainsdale, or someone is keeping her alive somewhere, maybe for a part she's due to play in some ritual. That's why I'm here talking to you. And, believe me, I'd rather be elsewhere.'

'I applaud your deductive abilities, Superintendent, but you'd be making better use of your time if you *were* somewhere else. I know nothing.'

Gristhorpe looked around the room. 'What if I were to arrange for a search warrant?'

Westman stood up. 'You don't need to do that. Be my guest.'

Gristhorpe did. It was a small cottage, and it didn't take him long. Upstairs was a bedroom and an office, where a computer hummed on a messy desk and a printer pushed out sheets of paper.

'I'm a systems consultant,' Westman said. 'It means I get to do most of my work at home. It also means I have to work weekends sometimes, too.'

Gristhorpe nodded. They went downstairs and looked at the kitchen, then into the cellar, a dark, chill place with whitewashed walls, mostly used for storing coal and the various bits and pieces of an old Vincent motorcycle.

'A hobby,' Westman explained. 'Are you satisfied now?'

They climbed back up to the living room. 'Do you know of anyone who might be involved?' Gristhorpe asked. 'For any reason?'

Westman raised his eyebrows. 'Asking for help now, are you? I'd be happy to oblige, but I told you, I've no idea. I do not, have not, and never will sacrifice children, or any other human beings for that matter. I told you, I'm not a dabbler. It would take too long to explain to you about my beliefs, and you'd probably be too prejudiced to understand anyway. It's certainly not tabloid Satanism.'

'But you must know people who do know about these

things. These dabblers you mentioned – these Satanists, thrill-seekers – any of them around these parts?'

'Not that I know of. There are a couple of witches' covens, but they're pretty tame, and you probably know about them, anyway. Amateurs. You'd never find them sacrificing a fly, let alone a child. Their get-togethers are a bit like a church social. No, Superintendent, I think you're on the wrong track.'

Gristhorpe stood up. 'Maybe, Mr Westman, but I like to keep an open mind. Don't trouble yourself, I'll see myself out.'

In the street, Gristhorpe breathed in the fresh air. He didn't know why he felt such distaste for Westman and his kind. After all, he had read a fair bit about the black arts and he knew there was nothing necessarily *evil* about an interest in magic. Perhaps it was his Methodist background. He had given up going to chapel years ago, but there was still an innate sense that such desire for Godlike power, whether mumbo-jumbo or not, was a sacrilege, a blasphemy against reason and common sense as much as against God.

The limestone face of Crow Scar towered over the village to the north. Today it was bright in the autumn sun, and the higher pastures were already turning pale brown. The dry-stone walls that criss-crossed the daleside shone like the ribs and vertebrae of a giant poking through the earth.

Gristhorpe walked along High Street, busy with tourists window-shopping for walking gear and local crafts, or ramblers sitting at the wooden picnic-tables outside the Dog and Gun and the Hare and Hounds, sipping pints of Theakston's and nibbling at sandwiches. It was tempting to join them, but Gristhorpe decided to wait until he got back to Eastvale before eating a late lunch.

He turned at the fork and headed for the Helmthorpe station. It was a converted terrace house, built of local greyish limestone, and was staffed by a sergeant and two constables. Constable Weaver sat pecking away at an old manual typewriter when Gristhorpe entered. Gristhorpe remembered him from the Steadman case, the first murder they'd had in Helmthorpe in a hundred years.

Weaver looked up, blushed and walked over. 'I can't seem to get used to the computer, sir,' he said. 'Keep giving the wrong commands.'

Gristhorpe smiled. 'I know what you mean. I can't help but feel like an incompetent idiot when I have to deal with the things. Still, they have their uses. Look, lad, do you know Melville Westman?'

'Yes.'

'Anything on him? I'm not asking for anything that might be on record, you understand, just rumours, suspicions?'

Weaver shook his head. 'Not really, sir. I mean, we know he's one of those black magicians, but he's not stepped out of line in any real way. Can't say I believe in it myself, curses and whatnot.'

'What about the sheep?'

'Aye, well, we suspected him, all right – still do, for that matter – but there was nowt we could prove. Why, sir?'

'It might be nothing, but I'd like you to keep a discreet eye on him, if you can. And keep your ears open for gossip.'

'Is this about the young lass, sir?'

'Yes. But for Christ's sake don't spread it around.'

Weaver looked hurt. 'Of course not, sir.'

'Good. Let me know if you see or hear anything out of the ordinary, and try not to let him know you're watching. He's a canny bugger, that one is.'

'Yes, sir.'

Gristhorpe walked outside and headed for his car. Westman was probably telling the truth, he thought, but there had been so many revelations about the links between child abuse and satanic rituals in the past few years that he had to check out the possibility. It couldn't happen here, everyone said. But it did. His stomach rumbled. Definitely time to head back to Eastvale.

THREE

Banks believed you could tell a lot about people from their homes. It wasn't infallible. For example, a normally fastidious person might let things go under pressure. On the whole, though, it had always worked well for him.

When he stood in the tiny living room of Flat 6, 59 Calvin Street and tried to figure out Carl Johnson, he found very little to go on. First, he sniffed the air: stale, dusty, with an underlying hint of rotting vegetables. It was just what one would expect of a place unoccupied for a couple of days. Then he listened. He didn't expect to hear ghosts or echoes of the dead man's thoughts, but homes had their voices, too, that sometimes whispered of past evils or remembered laughter. Nothing. His immediate impression was of a temporary resting-place, somewhere to eat and sleep. What furniture there was looked second-hand, OXFAM or jumble-sale stuff. The carpet was worn so thin he could hardly make out its pattern. There were no photos or prints on the cream-painted walls; nor was there any evidence of books, not even a tattered bestseller.

The kitchen was simply a curtained-off portion of the room, with a hotplate, toaster and a little storage space.

Banks found a couple of dirty pans and plates in the sink. The cupboards offered nothing more than tea bags, instant coffee, sugar, margarine and a few cans of baked beans. There was no refrigerator, and a curdled bottle of milk stood by the sink next to some mouldy white bread and three cans of McEwan's lager.

The bedroom, painted the same drab cream as the living room, was furnished with a single bed, the covers in disarray, pillow greasy and stained with sweat or hair-cream. Discarded clothes lay in an untidy heap on the floor. The dresser held socks and underwear, and apart from a couple of checked shirts, sneakers, one pair of Hush Puppies, jeans and a blouson jacket, there was little else in the wardrobe. Banks could spot no evidence of Johnson having shared his flat or bed with anyone.

Banks had never seen a place that told so little about its occupier. Of course, that in itself indicated a number of things: Johnson clearly didn't care about a neat, clean, permanent home; he wasn't sentimental about posses-sions or interested in art and literature. But these were all negatives. What *did* he care about? There was no indi-cation. He didn't even seem to own a television or a radio. What did a man do, coming home to such surroundings? What did he think about as he sat in the creaky winged armchair with the threadbare arms and guzzled his baked beans on toast? Did he spend every evening out? At the pub? With a girlfriend?

From what Banks knew of his criminal record, Carl Johnson was thirty years old and, after a bit of trouble over 'Paki-bashing' and soccer hooliganism in Bradford as a lad, he had spent three years of his adult life in prison for attempted fraud. It wasn't a distinguished life, and it seemed to have left nothing of distinction to posterity.

Banks felt oppressed by the place. He levered open a window and let some fresh air in. He could hear a baby crying in a room across the street.

Next, he had to do a more thorough search. He had found no letters, no passport, no bills, not even a birth certificate. Surely nobody could live a life so free of bureaucracy in this day and age? Banks searched under the sofa cushions, under the mattress, over the tops of the doors, deep in the back of the kitchen and bedroom cupboards. Nothing. There aren't many hiding places in a flat, as he had discovered in his days on the drug squad, and most of them are well known to the police.

Carl Johnson's flat was no exception. Banks found the thick legal-sized envelope taped to the underside of the cistern lid – a fairly obvious place – and took it into the front room. He had been careful to handle only the edges. Now he placed it on the card table by the window and slit a corner with his penknife to see what was inside. Twenty-pound notes. A lot of them, by the looks of it. Using the knife, he tried to peel each one at a time back and add it up. It was too awkward, and he kept losing his place. Patience. He took an evidence bag from his pocket, dropped the money in and took one last look around the room.

The whole place had a smell of petty greed about it, but petty criminals of Johnson's kind didn't usually end up gutted like a fish in old lead mines. What was different about Johnson? What had he been up to? Blackmail? Banks could read nothing more from the flat, so he locked up and left.

Across the hallway, he noticed a head peeping out of Flat 4 and walked over. The head retreated and its owner tried to close the door, but Banks got a foot in.

'I didn't see anything, honest, mister,' the woman said. She was about twenty-five, with straight red hair and a pasty, freckled complexion.

'What do you mean?'

'I didn't see you. You weren't here. I've got nothing. Please—'

Banks took out his warrant card. The woman put her hand to her heart. 'Thank God,' she said. 'You just never know what might happen these days, the things you read in the papers.'

'True,' Banks agreed. 'Why were you watching?'

'I heard you in there, that's all. It's been quiet for a while.'

'How long?'

'I'm not sure. Two or three days, anyway.'

'Do you know Carl Johnson?' Johnson's identity hadn't been revealed in the press yet, so the woman couldn't know he was dead.

'No, I wouldn't say I knew him. We chatted on the stairs now and then if we bumped into each other. He seemed a pleasant enough type, always a smile and a hello. What are you after, anyway? What were you doing in there? Has he done a moonlight flit?'

'Something like that.'

'He didn't look like a criminal type to me.' She hugged herself and shuddered. 'You just can't tell, can you?'

'What did you talk about, when you met on the stairs?'

'Oh, this and that. How expensive things are getting, the weather . . . you know, just ordinary stuff.'

'Did you ever meet any of his friends?'

'No. I don't really think he had any. He was a bit of a loner. I did hear voices a couple of times, but that's all.'

'When? Recently?'

'Last couple of weeks, anyway.'

'How many people do you think were talking?'

'Only two, I'd say.'

'Could you describe the other voice?'

'I'm sorry, I wasn't really listening. I mean, it's muffled anyway, you couldn't actually hear what anyone was saying. And I had the telly on. I could only hear them in the quiet bits.'

'Was it a man?'

'Oh, yes, it was another man. I'm certain about that. At least, he had a sort of deep voice.'

'Thank you, Mrs . . .?'

'Gerrard. Miss.'

'Thank you, Miss Gerrard. Do you know if Mr Johnson owned a car?'

'I don't think he did. I never saw him in one, anyway.'

'Do you have any idea what he did for a living?'

She looked away. 'Well, he . . .'

'Look, Miss Gerrard, I don't care if he was cheating on the social or the taxman. That's not what I'm interested in.'

She chewed her lower lip a few seconds, then smiled. 'Well, we all do it a bit, don't we? I suppose even coppers cheat on their income tax, don't they?'

Banks smiled back and put a finger to the side of his nose.

'And an important detective like yourself wouldn't be interested in something as petty as that, would he?'

Banks shook his head.

'Right,' she said. 'I only know because he mentioned the weather once, how nice it was to have outdoor work.'

'Outdoor work?'

'Yes.'

'Like what? Road work, construction?'

'Oh, no, he weren't no ditch-digger. He was a gardener, Mr Johnson was, had real green fingers.'

It was amazing the skills one could learn in prison these days, Banks thought. 'Where did he work?'

'Like I say, I only know because we got talking about it, how some people are so filthy rich and the rest of us just manage to scrape by. He wasn't no communist, mind you, he—'

'Miss Gerrard, do you know who he worked for?'

'Oh, yes. I do go on a bit, don't I? It was Mr Harkness, lives in that nice old house out Fortford way. Paid quite well, Mr Johnson said. But then, he could afford to, couldn't he?'

The name rang a bell. There had been a feature about him in the local rag a year or two ago. Adam Harkness, Banks remembered, had come from a local family that had emigrated to South Africa and made a fortune in diamonds. Harkness had followed in his father's footsteps, and after living for a while in Amsterdam had come back to Swainsdale in semi-retirement.

'Thank you,' Banks said. 'You've been very helpful.'

'Have I?' She shrugged. 'Oh well, always a pleasure to oblige.'

Banks walked out into the street and mulled over what he had learned from Miss Gerrard. Johnson had been working for Adam Harkness, probably for cash in hand, no questions asked. That might explain the thousand or so pounds in the envelope. On the other hand, surely gardening didn't pay *that* much? And why did he hide the money? To guard against thieves, perhaps? Having sticky fingers himself, Johnson would probably be all too aware of the danger of leaving large sums of money lying around the place. Maybe he didn't have a bank account, was the kind who hid his fortune in a mattress or, in this case, under the cistern lid. But it still didn't ring true. Banks looked at his watch. Almost four in the afternoon. Time to pay Adam Harkness a visit before dinner.

FOUR

Detective Sergeant Philip Richmond's eyes were beginning to ache. He saved his data, then stood up and stretched, rubbing the small of his back. He'd been at it for four hours, much too long to sit staring at a screen. Probably get cancer of the eyeballs from all the radiation it emitted. They were all very well, these computers, he mused, but you had to be careful not to get carried away with them. These days, though, the more courses he took, the more he learned about computers, the better his chances of promotion were.

He walked over to the window. Luckily, the new computer room faced the market square, like Banks's office, but the window was tiny, as the place was nothing but a converted storage room for cleaners' materials. Anyway, the doctor had told him to look away from the screen into the distance occasionally to exercise his eye muscles, so he did.

Already many of the tourists were walking back to their cars – no doubt jamming up many of Eastvale's side streets and collecting a healthy amount in tickets – and some of the market stalls were closing.

He'd knock off soon, and then get himself ready for his date with Rachel Pierce. He had met her last Christmas in Barnard Castle, at the toy shop where she worked, while checking an alibi on a murder case, and they had been going steady ever since. There was still no talk of wedding bells, but if things continued going as well as they had been for much longer, Richmond knew he would seriously consider tying the knot. He had never met anyone quite as warm and as funny as Rachel before. They even shared a taste for science fiction; they both loved Philip K. Dick and Roger Zelazny. Tonight they would go and see that new horror film at the Crown – new for Eastvale, anyway, which was usually a good few months behind the rest of the country. Rachel loved scary films, and Richmond loved the way they made her cling to him. He looked at his watch. Barring emergencies, he would be with her in a couple of hours.

The phone rang.

Richmond cursed and answered it. The switchboard operator told him it was someone calling for Superintendent Gristhorpe, who was out, so she had put the call through to Richmond.

'Hello?' a woman's voice came on the line.

Richmond introduced himself. 'What can I do for you?'

'Well,' she said hesitantly, 'I really wanted the man in charge. I called that temporary number, you know, the one you mentioned in the paper, and the constable there told me to call this number if I wanted to talk to Superintendent Gristhorpe.'

Richmond explained the situation. 'I'm sure I can help you,' he added. 'What's it about?'

'All right,' she said. 'The reason I'm calling you so late is that I've only just heard it from the woman who does the cleaning. She does it once a week, you see, on Saturday mornings.'

'Heard what?'

'They've gone. Lock, stock and barrel. Both of them. Oh, don't get me wrong, it's not as if they aren't fully paid up or anything, and I wouldn't say they looked exactly like the couple the papers described, but it is funny, isn't it? People don't usually just take off like that without so much as a by-your-leave, not when they've paid cash in advance.'

Richmond held the receiver away from his ear for a moment and frowned. Why didn't this make any sense? Was he going insane? Had the computer radiation finally eaten its way into his frontal lobes?

'Where are you calling from?' he asked.

She sounded surprised. 'Eastvale, of course. My office. I'm working late.'

'Your name?'

'Patricia. Patricia Cummings. But—'

'One thing at a time. You said your office. What kind of office?'

'I'm an estate agent. Randall and Palmer's, just across the square from the police station. Now—'

'All right,' Richmond said. 'I know the place. What are you calling about?'

'I thought I'd made myself perfectly clear, but apparently you need it spelled out.'

Richmond grinned. 'Yes, please. Spell it out.'

'It's about that girl who disappeared, Gemma Scupham. At least it might be. That's why I wanted to speak to the man in charge. I think I might know something about the couple you're looking for, the ones who did it.'

'I'll be right over,' Richmond said, and hung up. He left a message at the front desk for Gristhorpe and dashed out into the market square.

5

ONE

As Banks drove west towards Fortford again, the low sun silhouetted the trees ahead. Some of them, stripped bare by Dutch elm disease, looked like skeletal hands clawing their way out of the earth. An evening haze hung over Fortford and softened the edges of the hills beyond the village. It muted the vibrant greens of the ryegrass on the lower dalesides and washed out the browns and greys of the upper pastures.

Banks drove into the village and passed the green, to his left, where a group of elderly locals sat gossiping and passing the time on a bench below the partially excavated Roman fort on the round hillock opposite. Smoke from their pipes drifted slowly on the hazy evening air.

It felt like a summer evening, Banks thought, and wondered just how long the fine weather would last; not long, if you believed the forecasters. Still, at least for now he could drive with his window down and enjoy the fresh air, except when it was permeated by the overripe tang of manure. Sometimes, though, a different smell would drift in, a garden bonfire, burning vegetation acrid on the air. He listened to Gurney's 'Preludes' and felt that the piano music possessed the same starkly beautiful quality as the songs, unmistakably Gurney, heart-rending in the way it snatched moments of order from chaos.

At the corner, by the whitewashed sixteenth-century pub, he turned right onto the Lyndgarth road. Way ahead, about halfway up the daleside, he could see Lyndgarth itself, limestone cottages clustered around a small green, and the stubby, square tower of St Mary's. About half a mile north of the village, he could make out Gristhorpe's old grey farmhouse. Just to the left of Lyndgarth, a little lower down the hillside, stood the dark ruin of Devraulx Abbey, partially hidden by trees, looking eerie and haunted in the smoky evening light.

Banks drove only as far as the small stone bridge over the River Swain and turned left into a gravelled drive. Sheltered on all sides but the water by poplars, 'Leasholme' was an ideal, secluded spot for a reclusive millionaire to retire to. Banks had phoned Adam Harkness earlier and been invited that very evening. He doubted he would find out much from Carl Johnson's employer, but he had to try.

He parked at the end of the drive beside Harkness's Jaguar. The house itself was a mix of Elizabethan and seventeenth-century styles, built mostly of limestone, with grit-stone lintels and cornerstones and a flagged roof. It was, however, larger than most, and had clearly belonged to a wealthy landowner. Over the door, the date read 1617, but Banks guessed the original structure had been there earlier. The large garden had little to show but roses at this time of year, but it looked well designed and cared for. Carl Johnson's green fingers, no doubt.

Finally, irritated by the cloud of gnats that hung over him, Banks rang the bell.

Harkness opened the door a few moments later and beckoned him inside, then led him along a cavernous hallway into a room at the back of the house, which turned out to be the library. Bookcases, made of dark wood, covered three walls, flanking a heavy door in one and a stone hearth in another. A white wicker armchair faced the fourth wall, where french windows opened into the garden. The well-kept lawn sloped down to the riverbank, fringed with rushes, and just to the left, a large copper beech framed a view of the Leas, with Lyndgarth and Aldington Edge beyond, just obscuring Devraulx Abbey behind its thick foliage. The river possessed a magical quality in the fading light; slow-moving, mirror-like, it presented a perfect reflection of the reeds that grew by its banks.

'It is spectacular, isn't it?' Harkness said. 'It's one of the reasons I bought the place. It's much too big for me, of course. I don't even use half the rooms.'

Banks had noticed the dust in the hall and a certain mustiness to the atmosphere. Even the library was untidy, with a large desk littered with papers, pens, rubber bands and a few books placed in small piles on the floor beneath the shelves.

'How long have you been here?' Banks asked.

'Two years. I still travel a fair bit. I'm not retired yet, you know, still got a lot of life in me. But I thought it was time I deserved to take things easy, put in a bit more golf.'

Harkness looked about fifty-five. He was Banks's height, with silver hair and that brick-red, lined complexion peculiar to the Englishmen who have spent years in warmer climates. He wore a white short-sleeved shirt and navy-blue trousers. The pot belly and sagging breasts showed he wasn't a man who took much exercise off the golf course.

'Drink?'

'A small Scotch, please,' Banks said.

'Sit down.' Harkness offered Banks the wicker chair and pulled a swivel chair for himself from behind the desk.

Banks sat. Music played softly in the background: the Radio Three Dvořák concert, by the sound of it. He glanced at the books on the shelves and, for some reason, got the impression they were more for show than use, bought by the yard. A full set of the *Encyclopaedia Britannica*, some Book Club editions of Jane Austen and Dickens, a mail-order 'Great Writers' series.

Harkness passed Banks the drink in a heavy crystal glass then joined him, carefully tugging up the creases of his trousers before he sat. 'You didn't tell me very much on the telephone,' he said. 'How can I help you?'

'I'd just like to ask you a few questions about Carl Johnson.'

Harkness shook his head slowly. 'I still find it hard to believe such a thing could happen. We live in dangerous times.' His accent was an odd mix of South African and public-school English, his manner relaxed. A man used to being in charge, Banks guessed.

'Did you know much about Mr Johnson? About his life, his background?'

Harkness shook his head. 'I rarely saw him. He would come and put in his hours whether I was here or not. That was our arrangement. I'm afraid I know nothing at all about his personal life.'

'Did you know he had a criminal record?'

Harkness raised an eyebrow and looked at Banks over the top of his glass. 'I know he'd been in jail, if that's what you mean.'

'How did you find out?'

'He told me when he came for the interview.' Harkness allowed a brief smile. 'In fact, he told me that's where he learned the job.'

'And that didn't bother you?'

'The man had served his time. He was obviously honest enough to let me know about his past right from the start. Besides, I believe in giving everyone another chance. Everyone's capable of change, given the right conditions. Carl was a good, hard worker. And he was always very open and honest in his dealings with me. Anyway, I'm not an easy man to defraud.'

'I thought you hardly ever talked to him.'

'We had to discuss his work occasionally.'

'How much did you pay him?'

'Five pounds an hour. I know that's not very much for a skilled worker, but he seemed grateful enough. And it was . . . how shall I say? . . . cash in hand.'

'How long had he been working for you?'

'Since March.'

'How did you make contact with him?'

'My previous gardener left. I placed an advertisement in the local paper and Carl Johnson replied. He seemed to know his stuff, and I was impressed with his frankness, so I took him on. I never regretted it.' He pointed towards the windows. 'As you can see, he did a fine job.'

Banks put his glass down. Harkness offered him another, but he refused. The light had almost gone now, and the river seemed to hoard its last rays and glow from deep within. Harkness turned on the desk lamp.

'Do you know any reason', Banks asked, 'why someone might want to kill him?'

'None. But as I said, I knew nothing about his personal life.'

'When did you last see him?'

'Monday.'

'Did he seem worried about anything?'

'Not that I could tell. We had a brief conversation about

the lawn and the roses, as far as I can remember, and that's all. As I said, he didn't confide in me.'

'He didn't seem different in any way?'

'No.'

'Did he ever mention any of his friends or acquaintances, a girlfriend, perhaps?'

'No. I assumed he acted like any normal young man on his own time.'

'Ever heard of a bloke called Les Poole?'

'No.'

Banks scratched the scar by his right eye and crossed his legs. 'Mr Harkness,' he said, 'can you think of any reason why Johnson had over a thousand pounds hidden in his flat?'

'A thousand pounds, you say? Well . . . no. I certainly didn't pay him that much. Perhaps he saved up.'

'Perhaps.'

'He may have worked for others, too. We didn't have an exclusive contract.'

'You never asked?'

'Why should I? He was always available when I needed him.'

'Where were you on Thursday evening?'

'Really, Chief Inspector! You can't believe I had anything to do with the man's death?'

'Just a matter of elimination, sir.'

'Oh, very well.' Harkness rubbed his chin. 'Let me see . . . Well, Thursday, I'd have been at the Golf Club. I played that afternoon with Martin Lambert, and after the game we had dinner at the club.'

'What time did you leave?'

'Not until well after eleven. The others will vouch for me.'

Banks nodded. He felt that Harkness was enjoying the game, one he knew he could win. There was a kind of smugness and arrogance about him that irked Banks. He had come across it before in powerful and wealthy people and had never been able to accept it.

'I understand you were born around these parts?' he asked.

'Yes. Lyndgarth, as a matter of fact. We emigrated when I was four.'

'South Africa?'

'Yes. Johannesburg. My father saw opportunities there. He liked to take risks, and this one paid off. Why do you ask?'

'Out of interest. You took over the business?'

'When he died. And, I might add, I succeeded him out of ability, not nepotism. I worked with him for years. He taught me all he knew.'

'Is the company still in existence?'

'Very much so. And our mines are still productive. But I've had very little to do with that part of the operation of late. I moved to Amsterdam over ten years ago to handle the sales end of the business.' He looked down, swirled the amber liquid in his crystal snifter, then looked Banks in the eye. 'Quite frankly, I couldn't stomach the politics over there. Apartheid disgusted me, and I lacked the courage to become a revolutionary. Who wants another white liberal, anyway?'

'So you moved to Amsterdam?'

'Yes.'

'But you kept your business interests in South Africa?'

'I said I couldn't stand living with the politics, Chief Inspector. I didn't say I was a fool. I also don't believe in sanctions. But that's not what you came to hear about.'

'Still, it is fascinating. Are you married?'

'Divorced, back in Amsterdam.' He shifted in his chair. 'If you don't mind—'

'I'm sorry.' Banks put down his empty glass and stood up. 'It's just a copper's instinct. Curiosity.'

'It's also what killed the cat.'

Harkness said it with a smile, but Banks could hardly miss the cutting edge. He ignored it and walked to the library door.

As they walked down the gloomy hall with its waist-high wainscoting, Banks turned to one of the doors. 'What's in here?' he asked.

Harkness opened the door and turned on a light. 'Living room.'

It was a spacious, high-ceilinged room with wall-to-wall thick pile carpeting and a burgundy three-piece suite. Next to the fireplace stood a tall bookcase stacked with old *National Geographic* magazines. A couple of landscapes hung on the walls: original oils, by the look of them. Banks couldn't tell who the artists were, but Sandra would probably know. Again, Banks noticed how untidy the room was and how dusty the fixtures. Beside the sofa was a long, low table, and at its centre stood a tarnished silver goblet encrusted with dirt. Banks picked it up. 'What's this?' he asked.

Harkness shrugged. 'Carl found it when he was digging the garden one day and he brought it to me. It looks old. I keep meaning to get it cleaned up and valued. He thought it might be worth something. I suppose,' he went on, 'you could take that as another example of his honesty. He could have kept it.'

Banks examined the goblet. It had some kind of design engraved on it, but he couldn't make out what it was through the grime. It looked like a coat of arms. He put it back down on the table. It was something Tracy would be interested in, he thought. Would have been, he corrected himself.

Harkness noticed him looking around. 'It's a bit of a mess, I'm afraid. But as I said, the house is too big and I don't use all of it anyway.'

'Don't you have a cleaning lady?'

'Can't abide maids. Ever since I was a child in South Africa we had them, and I never could stand them. Always fussing around you. And I suppose as much as anything I couldn't stand the idea of anyone having to clean up after anyone else. It seemed so undignified, somehow.'

Banks, whose mother had charred at a Peterborough office block to bring in a bit of extra money, said, 'Yet you employed a gardener?'

Harkness led the way to the front door. 'That's different, don't you think? A gardener is a kind of artist in a way, and I've no objection to being a patron of the arts. I always thought of the grounds as very much Carl's creation.'

'I suppose you're right,' Banks said at the door. 'Just one more question: did he ever mention the old lead mine near Relton?'

'No. Why?'

'I just wondered if it was special to him for some reason. Can you think of any reason he might have been there?'

Harkness shook his head. 'None at all. Digging for hidden treasure, perhaps?' His eyes twinkled.

'Perhaps,' Banks said. 'Thank you for your time.'

'My pleasure.'

Harkness closed the door slowly but firmly and Banks

got into his car. As he drove back to Eastvale in the blue-grey twilight with the haunting piano music playing, he wondered about Harkness. Many business dealings don't bear close scrutiny, of course, and you don't get as rich as Harkness without skirting the law and stepping on a few toes here and there. Is that what Harkness was getting at with his remark about curiosity killing the cat? If that was so, where did Johnson fit in? It might be useful having a criminal for a gardener if you wanted other kinds of dirty business done. On the other hand, it might also, after a while, turn out to be very inconvenient. At least, Banks concluded, it might be worthwhile asking a few questions about Mr Adam Harkness.

TWO

'This must be it, sir,' said DS Richmond as he pulled in behind Patricia Cummings outside the last cottage in a terrace of four, right on the north-western edge of Eastvale, where the road curved by the side of the River Swain into the dale. It was a pleasant spot, handy for both the town life, with its cinemas, shops and pubs, and for getting out into the more rural reaches of the dale itself. The holiday cottages were small – just right for a couple – and the view of the entry into the dale proper was magnificent. Of course, the slopes there were not as dramatic as they became beyond Fortford and Helmthorpe, but looking down the valley even in the fading light one could make out the grey, looming shapes of the higher fells and peaks massed in the distance, and the nearer, gentler slopes with their drystone walls and grazing sheep showed a promise of what was to come.

Patricia Cummings opened the door, and Richmond entered the living room with Gristhorpe, who had returned to the station just a few minutes after Richmond had been to see Patricia. She turned on the light, and they looked around the small room that the estate agent would probably describe as cosy, with its two little armchairs arranged by the fireplace. Gristhorpe felt he had to stoop under the low ceiling, even though a few inches remained. He felt like Alice must have done before she took the shrinking potion.

What struck Gristhorpe immediately was the absolute cleanliness of the place. It reminded him of his grandmother's cottage, a similarly tiny place in Lyndgarth, in which he had never seen a speck of dust nor a thing out of place. The dominant smell was pine-scented furniture polish, and the gleaming dark surfaces of wood stood testament to its thorough application. They glanced in the kitchen. There, too, everything shone: the sink, the small fridge, the mini-washer and dryer unit under the counter.

'Did the cleaner do the place?' Gristhorpe asked.

Patricia Cummings shook her head. 'No. It was like this when she found it. Spotless. She phoned me because she was sure they were supposed to be staying another two weeks.'

'And were they?'

'Yes.'

'They'd already paid the rent?'

'For a month, altogether. Cash in advance.'

'I see.'

Mrs Cummings shifted from one foot to the other. She was a middle-aged woman, neatly dressed in a grey suit with a pearl blouse and ruff. She had a small lipsticked mouth and pouchy rouged cheeks that wobbled as she spoke. Gristhorpe noticed a gold band with a big diamond cluster, biting into the flesh of her plump ring finger.

'They said they were responding to an advertisement we placed in *The Dalesman*,' she said.

'What names did they give?'

'Manley. Mr and Mrs Manley.'

'Did you see any identification?'

'Well, no . . . I mean, they paid cash.'

'Is that unusual?'

'Not really. Not normal, but it happens.'

'I see.' Gristhorpe looked over towards Richmond, who seemed similarly constrained by the tininess of the place. 'Let's have a look around, shall we, Phil?'

Richmond nodded.

'I'll show you,' Patricia Cummings said.

'If you don't mind,' Gristhorpe told her, 'it would be best if you waited here. It would give forensics one less person to eliminate, if it comes to that.'

'Very well. Is it all right if I sit down?'

'By all means.'

The stone staircase was narrow and its whitewashed ceiling low. Both men had to stoop as they went up. Upstairs were two small bedrooms and a bathroom-toilet. Everywhere was just as spotless as the living room, ceramic surfaces gleaming.

'Someone's really done a job on this, sir,' Richmond said as they entered the first bedroom. 'Look, they've even washed the sheets and folded them.' It was true; a small pile of neatly folded sheets lay on the mattress, and the oak chest of drawers shone with recent polish. The same pine scent hung in the air. The second bedroom was a little shabbier, but it was easy to see why. From the neatly made bed and the thin patina of dust that covered the wardrobe, it was clear the room hadn't been used by the cottage's most recent occupants.

'I can't imagine why there'd even be two bedrooms,' Richmond said. 'I mean, it'd feel crowded enough in this place with two people, let alone children as well.'

'Aye,' said Gristhorpe. 'It's old-world rustic charm all right.'

Both the sink and the bathtub had been thoroughly cleaned out, and shelves and medicine cabinet emptied.

'Come on,' said Gristhorpe. 'There's nothing for us here.'

They went back downstairs and found Patricia Cummings painting her nails. The sickly smell of the polish pervaded the small room. She raised her eyebrows when they entered.

'Are all the cottages rented out?' Gristhorpe asked.

'All four,' she said.

They went outside. The row reminded Gristhorpe of Gallows View, a similar terrace not too far away, where he and Banks had investigated a case some years ago. The light of the cottage next door was on, and Gristhorpe thought he saw the curtains twitch as they walked towards it. Gristhorpe knocked, and a few moments later a skinny young man with long, greasy hair answered.

Gristhorpe introduced himself and Richmond, and the young man let them in. The place was furnished exactly the same as next door: sideboard along one wall, a small television on a stand, two armchairs, an open fireplace, wall-to-wall dark carpets and wallpaper patterned with grapevines against an off-white background. Job lot, no doubt. The young man had made his mark by arranging a row of books along the sideboard, using wine bottles as bookends. They were mostly poetry, Gristhorpe noticed, and a couple of local wildlife guides.

'This won't take long,' he said to the youth, who had introduced himself as Tony Roper. 'I'd just like to know if you can tell me anything about your neighbours.'

'Not really,' said Tony, leaning against the sideboard. 'I mean, I came here mostly for the isolation, so I didn't do much mixing.' He had a Scottish accent, Gristhorpe noticed, leaning more towards Glasgow than Edinburgh.

'Did you meet them?'

'Just in passing.'

'Did they introduce themselves?'

'The Manleys. Chris and Connie. That's what they said. They seemed pleasant enough. Always had a smile and a hello whenever we bumped into one another. Look, what's wrong? Nothing's happened to them, has it?'

'When did you last see them?'

Tony frowned. 'Let me see . . . It was a couple of days ago. Thursday, I think. Thursday morning. They were going off in the car.'

'Did they say where?'

'No. I didn't ask.'

'Had they packed all their stuff, as if they were leaving?'

'I'm afraid I didn't notice. Sorry. I was out walking most of the time.'

'It's all right,' Gristhorpe said. 'Just try and remember what you can. Did you see or hear them after that time?'

'Come to think of it, I don't reckon I did. But they never made much noise anyway. Maybe a bit of telly in the evenings. That's about all.'

'Did they ever have any visitors?'

'Not that I know of.'

'You never heard them arguing or talking with anyone?'

'No.'

'Were they out a lot?'

'A fair bit, I'd say. But so was I. I've been doing a lot of walking, meditating, writing. I'm really sorry, but I honestly didn't pay them a lot of attention. I've been pretty much lost in my own world.'

'That's all right,' Gristhorpe said. 'You're doing fine. What did they look like?'

'Well, he . . . Chris . . . was about medium height, with light, sandy-coloured hair brushed back. Receding a bit. He looked quite fit, wiry, you know, and he had a pleasant, open kind of smile. The kind you could trust.'

'Any distinctive features?'

'You mean scars, tattoos, that kind of thing?'

'Anything.'

Tony shook his head. 'No. He was quite ordinary looking, really. I just noticed the smile, that's all.'

'How old would you say he was?'

'Hard to say. I'd guess he was in his late twenties.'

'What about the woman?'

'Connie?' Tony blushed a little. 'Well, Connie's a blonde. I don't know if it's real or not. Maybe a year or two younger than him. Very pretty. A real looker. She's got lovely blue eyes, a really smooth complexion, a bit pale . . .'

'How tall?'

'An inch or two shorter than him.'

'What about her figure?'

Tony blushed again. 'Nice. I mean, nice so's you'd notice in the street, especially in those tight jeans she wore, and the white T-shirt.'

Gristhorpe smiled and nodded. 'Did you notice what kind of car they drove?'

'Yes. It was parked outside often enough. It was a Fiesta.'

'What colour?'

'White.'

'Did they always dress casually?'

'I suppose so. I never paid much attention, except to her, of course. Now I think of it, Chris was a bit more formal. He usually wore a jacket and a tie. You don't think anything's happened to them, do you?'

'Don't worry, Tony,' Gristhorpe said. 'I'm sure they're fine. Just one more thing. Did you ever hear sounds of a child there at all?'

Tony frowned. 'No.'

'Are you sure?'

'I'd have noticed. Yes, I'm sure. They didn't have any children.'

'Fine. Thanks very much, Tony,' Gristhorpe said. 'We'll leave you to enjoy the rest of your holiday in peace.'

Tony nodded and accompanied them to the door.

'You'll let me know, will you, if they're all right? I mean, I didn't really know them, but they were neighbours, in a way.'

'We'll let you know,' said Gristhorpe, and followed Richmond to the car.

'Will you be needing me any more?' asked Patricia Cummings.

Gristhorpe smiled at her. 'No, thanks very much, Mrs Cummings. You can go home now. Just one thing, could you leave that set of keys with us?'

'Why?'

'So we can let the Scene-of-Crime team in.'

'But—'

'This is important, Mrs Cummings, believe me. I wouldn't ask it otherwise. And don't rent the place out again until we give the OK.'

Her cheeks quivered a bit, then she dropped the keys into Gristhorpe's outstretched hand, climbed into her car and drove off with a screech of rubber. Gristhorpe got into the police Rover beside Richmond. 'Well, Phil,' he said, 'what do you think?'

'I'm not sure, sir. The description doesn't fit.'

'But it would if they dyed their hair and got dressed up in business clothes, wouldn't it? Both descriptions were vague enough – Brenda Scupham's and Tony Roper's.'

'That's true. But what about the car?'

'They could have stolen one for the abduction, or rented one.'

'A bit risky, isn't it? And we've checked all the rental agencies.'

'But we used the descriptions Brenda Scupham gave us.' Gristhorpe scratched his ear. 'Better get back to the rental agencies and find out about any couples their general age and appearance. Mention the man's smile. That seems to be a common factor. And the woman is clearly attractive. Someone might remember them.'

Richmond nodded. 'You think it was this Manley couple, sir?'

'I'm not saying that, but I think we'd better treat them as serious contenders for the moment.'

'It certainly seems odd the way they left the place in such a hurry.'

'Yes,' Gristhorpe muttered. 'And that cleaning job. Why?'

'Just a fastidious couple, maybe?'

'Maybe. But *why* did they leave in a hurry?'

'Could be any number of reasons,' Richmond said. 'A family emergency, perhaps?'

'Did you notice a phone in the cottage?'

'No. I suppose that's part of the rustic peace.'

'Mm. There is one thing.'

'Sir?'

'Let's say, for the sake of argument, that they did have to leave because of a family emergency. Nobody could have phoned them, but they could have used the nearest phonebox if they had to keep checking on someone who was ill.'

'You mean they wouldn't have stayed behind to clean up the place, sir?'

'There's that, aye. But there's something odder. The money. They paid cash in advance. How much do these places go for?'

'I don't know, sir. I forgot to ask.'

'It doesn't matter, but it must be a fair whack. Say a hundred and fifty a week.'

'Something like that. And probably a deposit, too.'

'Then why didn't they ask for some of their money back?'

'They might have had a hard time getting it.'

'Perhaps. But they didn't even try. That's three hundred quid we're talking about, Phil. Plus deposit.'

'Maybe they were loaded.'

Gristhorpe fixed Richmond with the closest his benign features could get to a look of contempt. 'Phil, if they were loaded, the *first* thing they would do is ask for their money back. That's how the rich get that way, and that's how they stay that way.'

'I suppose so,' Richmond mumbled. 'What do we do now?'

'We get the forensic team in, that's what we do,' Gristhorpe said, and reached for the radio.

THREE

The house was in darkness when Banks got home from the station around ten o'clock that Saturday evening. Tracy, he remembered, was at a dance in Relton with her friends. Banks had grilled her thoroughly about who was going and who was driving. He had been undecided, loath to let her go, but Sandra had tipped the balance. She was probably right, Banks admitted. Barring a punch-up between the Eastvale lads and the Relton lads, a fairly regular feature of these local dances, it ought to be a harmless enough affair. And Tracy was a big girl now.

So where was Sandra? Banks turned the lights on, then went into the kitchen thinking he might find a note. Nothing. Feeling anxious and irritated, he sat down, turned on the television and started switching channels: an American cop show, a documentary on Africa, a pirate film, a quiz show. He turned it off. The silence in the house closed in on him. This was absurd. Normally he would change into jeans and a sports shirt, pour a drink, put some music on, perhaps even smoke a cigarette if both Sandra and Tracy were out. Now all he could do was sit down and tap his fingers on the chair arm. It was no good. He couldn't stay home.

Grabbing his jacket against the evening chill, he walked along Market Street past the closed shops and the Golden Grill and the Queen's Arms. The light through the red and amber coloured windows beckoned, and he could see people at tables through the small clear panes, but instead of dropping in, he continued along North Market Street, quiet under its old-fashioned gas lamps, window displays of gourmet teas, expensive hiking gear, imported shoes and special blends of tobacco.

The front doors of the community centre stood open. From the hall, Banks could hear a soprano struggling through Schubert's 'Die Junge Nonne' to a hesitant piano accompaniment. It was Saturday, amateur recital night. He took the broad staircase to his left and walked up to the first floor. He could hear voices from some of the rooms, mostly used for the meetings of local hobby clubs or for committees of various kinds. The double glass doors of the gallery were closed, but a faint light shone from behind the partition at the far end of the room.

Banks walked softly down the carpeted gallery, its walls bare of pictures at the moment, and stopped outside the cramped office at the end. He had already heard Sandra's voice, but she was unaware of his presence.

'But you can't *do* that,' she was pleading. 'You've already agreed—'

'What? You don't give a . . . Now look—' She moved the receiver away from her ear and swore before slamming it down in its cradle. Then she took two deep breaths, tucked loose strands of blonde hair behind her ears, and picked up the phone again.

'Sandra,' Banks said as gently as he could.

She turned round and put her hand to her chest. Banks could see the angry tears burning in her eyes. 'Alan, it's you. What are you doing here? You scared me.'

'Sorry.'

'Look, it's not a good time. I've got so damn much to do.'

'Let's go for a drink.'

She started dialling. 'I'd love to, but I—'

Banks broke the connection.

Sandra stood up and faced him, eyes blazing. 'What the hell do you think you're doing?'

He took her arm. 'Come on. Let's go.'

She shook him off. 'What are you playing at?'

Banks sighed and sat on the edge of the desk. 'Look at you,' he said. 'You're frustrated as hell.' He smiled. 'You look pretty close to murder, too. I think it's time you took a break, that's all. God knows, you've helped take my mind off my problems often enough when you've watched me beating my head against a brick wall. I'm just trying to return the favour.'

Sandra bit her lower lip. Some of the anger left her eyes, but the tears still burned there. 'It's just that bloody Morton Ganning,' she said. 'He's only pulled out of the show, that's all.'

'Well, bugger him,' Banks said.

'But you don't understand.'

Banks took her coat from the rack by the office door. 'Come on. You can tell me over a drink.'

Sandra glared at him for a moment, then smoothed her skirt and walked over. Before she could put her coat on, Banks put his arms around her and held her close. At first she stood limp, then slowly, she raised her arms and linked them behind him. She buried her head in his shoulder, then broke free, gave him a playful thump on the arm and that cheeky smile he loved so much. 'All right, then,' she said. 'But you're buying.'

Ten minutes later, they managed to squeeze into a small corner table in the Queen's Arms. The place was busy and loud with the jokes and laughter of the Saturday night crowd, so they had to put their heads close together to talk. Soon, though, the noise became a background buzz and they no longer had to strain to hear one another.

'He's the most famous of the lot,' Sandra was saying. 'He's got paintings in galleries all over the country. It was going to be a hell of a coup to get him, but now he's backed out. He's a real bastard.'

'I thought the idea was to give locals a chance, the lesser-known ones?'

'It is. But Ganning would have drawn a damn good crowd. Indirectly, he'd have got them all more publicity, given them more chance of making a sale.'

'For the right reasons?'

'That doesn't matter. So what if they come to see his work? They'd see the others too.'

'I suppose so.'

Sandra sipped her gin and tonic. 'I'm sorry to go on about it, Alan, really I am. It's just that I've been so involved. I've put in so much bloody work it makes me boil.'

'I know.'

'What's that supposed to mean?'

'Nothing.'

Her blue eyes hardened. 'Yes it is. I can tell by your tone. You're not complaining, are you? That I haven't been doing my little wifely duties – cooking your meals, washing your clothes?'

Banks laughed. 'I didn't marry you for your "little wifely duties" as you call them. I can look after myself. No. If I am complaining at all, it's about hardly seeing you over these past few weeks.'

'Like I hardly see you when you're on a case?'

'*Touché.*'

'So what do you mean? You expect me to be there whenever you decide to come home?'

'No, it's not that.'

'What is it then?'

Banks lit a cigarette, playing for time. 'It's . . . well, just that the house seems so empty. You're never there, Tracy's never there. I feel like I'm living alone.'

Sandra leaned back in her chair. She reached out and grabbed one of Banks's cigarettes. 'Hey,' he said, putting his hand over hers. 'You've stopped.'

She broke free. 'And I'll stop again tomorrow. What's really bothering you, Alan?'

'What I said. The empty house.'

'So it's not just me, what I'm doing?'

'No, I don't suppose it is.'

'But you take it out on me?'

'I'm not taking anything out on you. I'm trying to explain what the problem is. For Christ's sake, you asked me.'

'Okay, okay. Keep your shirt on. Maybe you need another pint.'

'Wouldn't mind.'

Sandra held out her hand. 'Money, then.'

Banks looked gloomily into the last quarter-inch of deep gold liquid in his glass while Sandra threaded her way to the bar. She was right. It wasn't just her at all. It was the whole damn situation at home. He felt as if his children had suddenly become different people overnight, and his wife hadn't even noticed. He watched her coming back. She walked slowly, concentrating on not spilling the drinks. It was absurd, he felt, but even after all these years just seeing her made his heart speed up.

Sandra placed the glass carefully on the beer mat in front of him and he thanked her.

'Look,' she said, 'I know what you mean, but you have to accept things. Brian's gone. He's got his own life to lead. When did you leave home?'

'But that's not the same.'

'Yes it is.'

'It was stifling in Peterborough, with Dad always on at me and Mum just taking it all. It wasn't the same at all.'

'Perhaps the circumstances weren't,' Sandra allowed. 'But the impulse certainly is.'

'He's got a perfectly good home with us. I don't see why he'd want to go as far as bloody Portsmouth. I mean, he could have gone to Leeds, or York, or Bradford and come home on weekends.'

Sandra sighed. 'Sometimes you can be damned obtuse, Alan Banks, do you know that?'

'What do you mean?'

'He's left the nest, flown the coop. For him it's a matter of the farther the better. It doesn't mean he doesn't love us any more. It's just part of growing up. You did it yourself. That's what I mean.'

'But I told you, that was different.'

'Not all that much. Didn't you used to get on at him all the time about his music?'

'I never interfered with what he wanted. I even bought him a guitar.'

'Yes. In the hope he'd start playing classical or jazz or something other than what he did.'

'Don't tell me you liked that bloody racket any more than I did?'

'That doesn't matter. Oh, what's the use. What I'm trying to say is that we didn't drive him away, no more than your parents drove you away, not really. He wants to be independent like you did. He wants his own life.'

'I know that, but—'

'But nothing. We still have Tracy. Enjoy her while you can.'

'But she's never home. She's always out with that Harrison boy, getting up to God knows what.'

'She's not getting up to anything. She's sensible.'

'She doesn't seem interested in anything else any more. Her schoolwork's slipping.'

'Not much,' Sandra said. 'And I'll bet yours slipped a bit when you got your first girlfriend.'

Banks said nothing.

'Alan, you're jealous, that's all.'

'Jealous? Of my own daughter?'

'Oh, come on. You know she was the apple of your eye. You never were as close to Brian as you were to her. Now she seems to have no time for you, you resent it.'

Banks rubbed his cheek. 'Do I?'

'Of course you do. If only you could bring as much perception to your own family as you do to your cases you wouldn't have these problems.'

'Knowing is one thing, feeling all right about it is quite another.'

'I realize that. But you have to start with knowing.'

'How do you cope?' Banks asked. 'You've been like a stranger to me these past few months.'

'I didn't say I'd been coping very well either, only that I've been doing a lot of thinking about things.'

'And?'

'It's not easy, but we've reached that time when our children are no longer children. They can no longer keep us together.'

Banks felt a chill run through him. 'What do you mean they can't keep us together?'

'What I say. Oh, for God's sake don't look so worried. I didn't mean it *that* way. Maybe I didn't choose the best words. The kids gave us a lot in common, shared pleasures, anxieties. They'll still do that, of course, though I'm sure more on the anxieties side, but we can't relate to them the same way. They're not just children to be seen and not heard. You can't just order them not to do things. They'll only rebel and do worse. Remember your own childhood? You were a bit of a shit-disturber even when I met you. Still are, if truth be known. See Brian and Tracy for what they are, for what they're becoming.'

'But what did you mean about them keeping us together? It sounded ominous to me.'

'Only that we won't have them to gather around for much longer. We'll have to find other things, discover one another in other ways.'

'It could be fun.'

Sandra nodded. 'It could be. But we've both been avoiding it so far.'

'You too?'

'Of course. How many times have we spent an evening in the house alone together these past eighteen years?'

'There's been times.'

'Oh yes, but you can count them on the fingers of one hand. Besides, we knew Brian would be back from Boys' Brigade or Tracy from the Guides, or they were up in their rooms. We're not old, Alan. We married young and we've got a lot ahead of us.'

Banks looked at Sandra. Not old, certainly. The earnest face, her eyes shining with emotion, black eyebrows contrasting with the blonde hair that hung down over her shoulders. A lump came to his throat. If I walked into the pub right this moment, he thought, and saw her sitting there, I'd be over like a shot.

'Where do we start?' he asked.

Sandra tossed back her head and laughed. People turned to look at her but she paid them no attention. 'Well,

I've got this bloody show to organize still, and it's not all been a matter of staying late at the gallery to avoid facing things. I *do* have a lot of hours to put in.'

'I know that,' Banks said. 'And so do I.'

Sandra frowned. 'There's still nothing on that missing child, is there?'

Banks shook his head. 'No. It's been five days now since she was abducted.'

'Just imagine what her poor mother must be going through. Have you given up hope?'

'We don't expect miracles.' He paused. 'You know something? She reminds me of Tracy when she was that age. The blonde hair, the serious expression. Tracy always did take after you.'

'You're being sentimental, Alan. From the photo I saw in the paper she didn't look a bit like Tracy.'

Banks smiled. 'Maybe not. But I'm on another case now. That reminds me. Have you ever heard of a bloke called Adam Harkness?'

'Harkness? Of course I have. He's pretty well known locally as a patron of the arts.'

'Yes, he mentioned something like that. Has he given your lot any money?'

'We weren't as needy as some. Remember that bumper grant we got?'

'The oversight?'

'They still haven't asked for it back. Anyway, he's given money to the Amateur Operatic Society and a couple of other groups.' She frowned.

'What is it?'

'Well, some of the arts groups are a bit, you know, leftish. They tend to get blinkered. It's the old package deal: if you're against this, you have to be against that too.

You know, you have to be pro-abortion, anti-apartheid and green to boot.'

'Well?'

'Some of them wouldn't take Harkness's money because of the way he makes it.'

'South Africa?'

'Yes.'

'But he's anti-apartheid. He just told me. That's partly why he left. Besides, things have changed over there. Apartheid's fallen to pieces.'

Sandra shrugged. 'Maybe. And I wouldn't know about his personal beliefs. All I know is that Linda Fish – you know, that woman who runs the Writers' Circle – wouldn't take any money towards engaging visiting speakers and readers.'

'Linda Fish, the champagne socialist?'

'Well, yes.'

'What does she know about him?'

'Oh, she's got contacts among South African writers, or so she claims. All this anti-apartheid stuff is a load of bunk, she thinks. She's got a point. I mean, after all, whatever he professes to believe he's *still* earning his fortune by exploiting the system, isn't he?'

'I'd better have a talk with her.'

'Well,' Sandra said, 'you don't make his kind of money by being square and above-board, do you? Let's drop it anyway. I'm sure Linda will be delighted to see you. I think she's secretly fancied you ever since she found out you'd read Thomas Hardy.'

Banks gave a mock shudder. 'Look,' he said, 'I've just had an idea.'

Sandra raised her eyebrows.

'Not that kind of idea. Well . . . Anyway, when all this

is over – the show, the case – let's go on holiday, just you and me. Somewhere exotic.'

'Can we afford it?'

'No. But we'll manage somehow. Tracy can stay with your mum and dad. I'm sure they won't mind.'

'No. They're always glad to see her. I bet she'll mind this time, though. To be separated from the first boyfriend for even a day is a pretty traumatic experience, you know.'

'We'll deal with that problem when we get to it. What about the holiday?'

'You're on. I'll start thinking of suitably exotic places.'

'And . . . er . . . about that other idea . . .'

'What other idea?'

'You know. *Erotic* places.'

'Oh, *that* one.'

'Yes. Well?'

Sandra looked at her watch. 'It's ten past eleven. Tracy said she'd be home at twelve.'

'When has she ever been on time?'

'Still,' Sandra said, finishing her drink and grabbing Banks's arm. 'I think we'd better hurry.'

FOUR

The tea was cold. Wearily, Brenda Scupham picked up her cup and carried it to the microwave. When she had reheated it, she went back into the living room, flopped down on the sofa and lit a cigarette.

She had been watching television. That was how she had let the tea get cold. Not even watching it really, just sitting there and letting the images and sounds tumble over her and deaden the thoughts that she couldn't keep at bay. It had been a documentary about some obscure African tribe. That much she remembered. Now the news was on and someone had blown up a jumbo jet over a jungle somewhere. Images of the strewn wreckage taken from a helicopter washed over her.

Brenda sipped her tea. Too hot now. It wasn't tea she needed, anyway, it was a drink. The pill she had taken had some effect, but it would work better with a gin and tonic. Getting up, she went and poured herself a stiff one, then sat down again.

It was that man from the newspaper who had got her thinking such terrible thoughts. Mostly the police did a good job of keeping the press away from her, but this one she had agreed to talk to. For one thing, he was from the *Yorkshire Post*, and for another, she liked the look of him. He had been kind and gentle in his questioning, too, sensitive to her feelings, but had nevertheless probed areas Brenda hadn't even known existed. And somehow, talking about her grief over the loss of her 'poor Gemma' had actually made her feel it more, just as speculating about what might have happened to the child had made her imagine awful things happening, fears she couldn't shut out even now, long after the man had gone, after she had taken the tranquillizer, and after the images of Africa had numbed her. It was like being at the dentist's when the anaesthetic numbs your gums but you can still feel a shadow of pain in the background when he probes with his drill.

Now she found herself drifting way back to when she first got pregnant. Right from the start she knew instinctively that she didn't want the child growing inside her. Some days, she hoped to fall and induce a miscarriage, and other, worse days, she wished she would get run over by a bus. The odd thing was, though, that she couldn't actually bring herself to do any of these things – throw herself down the stairs, get rid of the foetus, jump out of a window. Maybe it was because she had been brought up Catholic and believed in a sort of elemental way that both suicide and abortion were sins. She couldn't even sit in a bathtub and drink gin like that dateless June Williams had done when Billy Jackson had got her in the family way (not that it had worked anyway; all June had got out of it was wrinkled skin and a nasty hangover). No, whatever happened just had to happen; it had to be God's will, even though Brenda didn't think now that she really believed in God.

Later, still stunned by the pain of childbirth, when she saw Gemma for the first time, she remembered wondering even back then how such a strange child could possibly be hers. And she turned her back. Oh, she had done the necessaries, of course. She could no more neglect to feed the child and keep her warm than she could have thrown herself under a bus. But that was where it stopped. She had been unable to feel love for Gemma, which is why it felt so strange, after talking about her loss to the reporter, that she should actually *feel* it now. And she felt guilty, too, guilty for the way she had neglected and abandoned Gemma. She knew she might never get a chance to make it up to her.

She poured another gin. Maybe this would do the trick. The thing was, it had been guilt made her hand Gemma over in the first place. Guilt and fear. The social workers, real or not, had been right when they talked about abuse; it was their timing that seemed uncanny, for though Brenda might have neglected her daughter, she had never, *ever* hit her until a few days before they called. Even then, she hadn't really hit Gemma, but when the man and the woman with their posh accents and their well-cut clothes called at her door, she somehow felt they had arrived in answer to a call; they were her retribution or her salvation, she didn't really know which.

Gemma had angered Les. When she spilled the paint on the racing page of his paper, he retaliated, as he usually did, not by violence, but by hitting her where it hurt, tearing up and throwing out some of her colouring books. Afterwards, he had been in a terrible mood all through teatime, needling Brenda, complaining, arguing. And to cap it all, Gemma had been sitting there giving them the evil eye. She hadn't said a word, nor shed a tear, but the accusation and the hurt in those eyes had been too much. Finally, Brenda grabbed her by the arm and shook her until she did start to cry, then let go of her and watched her run up to her room, no doubt to throw herself on her bed and cry herself to sleep. She had shaken Gemma so hard there were bruises on her arm. And when the social workers came, it was as if they knew not only how Brenda had lost her temper that day, but that if it happened again she might keep on shaking Gemma until she killed her. It was silly, she knew that – of course they couldn't *know* – but that had been how she felt.

And that was why she had given up Gemma so easily, to save her. Or was it to get rid of her? Brenda still couldn't be sure; the complexity of her feelings about the whole business knotted deep in her breast and she couldn't, try as she might, sort it all out and analyze it like she assumed most people did. She couldn't help not being smart, and most of the time it never really bothered her that other people knew more about the world than she did, or that they were able to talk about things she couldn't understand, or look at a situation and break it down into all its parts. It never really bothered her, but sometimes she thought it was bloody unfair.

She finished her gin and lit another cigarette. Now she had talked to the reporter she thought she might like to go on television. They had asked her on the second day, but she had been too scared. Maybe, though, in her best outfit, with the right make-up, she might not look too bad. She could make an appeal to the kidnapper, and if Gemma was still alive . . . Still alive . . . no, she couldn't think about that again. But it might help.

She heard a key in the door. Les back from the pub. Her expression hardened. Over these past few days, she realized, she had come to hate him. The door opened. She went and poured herself another gin and tonic. She would have to do something about Les soon. She couldn't go on like this.

FIVE

Later that Saturday night, after closing time, a car weaved its way over a desolate stretch of the North York Moors some thirty miles east of Eastvale. Its occupants – Mark Hudson and Mandy Vernon – could hardly keep their hands off one another. They had been for a slap-up dinner and drinks at the White Horse Farm Hotel, in Rosedale, and were now on their way back to Helmsley.

As Mark tried to concentrate on the narrow, unfenced road, the rabbits running away from the headlights' beam, his hand kept straying to Mandy's thigh, where her short skirt exposed a long stretch of delectable nylon-encased warm flesh. Finally, he pulled into a lay-by. All around them lay darkness, not even a farmhouse light in sight.

First they kissed, but the gear-stick and steering wheel got in the way. Metros weren't built for passion. Then Mark suggested they get in the back. They did so, but when he got his hand up her skirt and started tugging at her tights, she banged her knee on the back of the seat and cursed.

'There's not enough room,' she said. 'I'll break my bloody leg.'

'Let's get out, then,' Mark suggested.

'What? Do it in the open air?'

'Yes. Why not?'

'But it's cold.'

'It's not that cold. Don't worry, I'll keep you warm. I've got a blanket in the back.'

Mandy considered it for a moment. His hand found her left breast inside her blouse and he started rubbing her nipple between his thumb and forefinger.

'All right,' she said. 'We've not got much choice, have we?'

And indeed they hadn't. They couldn't take a room at the hotel because Mark was married, supposed to be at a company do, and Mandy still lived with her mother and brother, who expected her home from her girlfriend's by midnight. He had bought her an expensive five-course dinner, and they had drunk Chateauneuf-du-Pape. Going home, he had even negotiated the winding one-in-three hill that led over the open moors because it was more isolated up there than on the valley road. This might be one of the last warm evenings of the year; he might never get another chance.

Using the torch, they made their way over the heather

and found a shaded knoll surrounded by rocks and boulders about fifty yards from the road. Mark spread the blanket and Mandy lay down. Open moorland stretched for miles all around, and a half-moon frosted the heather and gave the place the eerie look of a moonscape. It *was* cold, but they soon ceased to notice as they warmed each other with caresses. Finally, Mark got Mandy's tights and knickers down around her ankles, pushed her knees apart and lay on top of her.

Mandy stretched out her arms and snatched at the heather as the waves of pleasure swept through her. Soon, Mark speeded up and began to make grunting sounds deep in his throat. Mandy knew the end was close. She could smell the port and Stilton on his breath and feel his stubble against her shoulder. The more he groaned, the more she snatched at the heather by the nearest rock, but even as he came and she encouraged him with cries of ecstasy, she was aware that what she clutched in her right hand wasn't grass or heather, but something softer, some kind of material, more like an article of clothing.

6

ONE

That Sunday morning in Eastvale passed as most Sundays did. The locals read the papers, washed their cars, put the roast in, went to church, messed about in the garden. Some took walks in the dale or went to visit nearby relatives. The fine weather held, and tourists came, of course, jamming the market square with their cars, posing by the ancient cross or the façade of the Norman church for photographs, perhaps enjoying a pub lunch at the Queen's Arms or tea and sandwiches at the Golden Grill, then driving on to the craft show at Helmthorpe, the sheep fair at Relton, or the big car-boot sale in Hoggett's field near Fortford. And out in the dale, around massive Witch Fell between Skield and Swainshead, the search for seven-year-old Gemma Scupham went into its fourth full day.

Back in Eastvale, at eleven-thirty that morning, a very nervous and hungover Mark Hudson walked into the police station carrying a Marks and Spencer's bag. He quickly placed it on the front desk, mumbling, 'You might be interested in this,' then tried to make a casual exit.

It was not to be. The desk sergeant caught a glimpse of yellow cotton in the bag, and before he knew it Mark Hudson was whisked politely upstairs to the CID.

Gristhorpe, aware that his office was far too comfortable for the interrogation of suspects, had Hudson taken to an interview room with a metal desk and chairs bolted to the floor and a small window covered by a metal grille. It smelled of Dettol and stale cigarette smoke.

With Richmond along to take notes, Gristhorpe planted himself firmly opposite a sweating Mark Hudson and began.

'Where did you find the clothes?'

'On the moors.'

'More precisely?'

'On the road between Rosedale Abbey and Hutton-le-Hole. I don't remember exactly where.'

'When?'

'Last night. Look, I just—'

'What were you doing out there?'

Hudson paused and licked his lips. He looked around the room and Gristhorpe could tell he didn't like what he saw. 'I . . . well, I'd been to a company do at the White Horse. I was on my way home.'

'Where do you live?'

'Helmsley.'

'What company do you work for?'

Hudson looked surprised at the question. 'Burton's. You know, the rag trade. I'm a sales rep.'

'And this do you were at, what was it in honour of?'

'Well, it wasn't really . . . I mean, it was just an informal affair, some of the lads getting together for a meal and a chat.'

'I see.' Gristhorpe eased back in his chair. 'And what made you stop in such a godforsaken place?'

'I needed to . . . you know, call of nature.'

'Were you by yourself?'

'Yes.'

Gristhorpe sniffed a lie, but he left it alone.

'Why did you wait so long before coming here? You must have known what you'd found. It's been in all the papers.'

'I know. I just thought . . . It was very late. And I didn't want to get involved.' He leaned forward. 'And I was right, wasn't I? I decided to help, and here I am being interrogated like a suspect.'

'Mr Hudson,' said Gristhorpe, 'in the first place, you're not being interrogated, you're simply being questioned, and in the second place, a child is missing, perhaps dead. How would you treat someone who walks in here, drops a bundle of what looks like the child's clothes and then tries to scarper?'

'I didn't try to scarper. I just wanted you to have the clothes, in case there was a clue. As I said, I didn't want to get involved. I thought of putting them in the post, but I knew that would take too long. I know how important time is in things like this, so I finally decided to come forward.'

'Well, thank you very much, Mr Hudson.'

'Look, if I really had done anything to that child, I'd hardly have come in here at all, would I?'

Gristhorpe fixed Hudson with his baby-blue eyes. 'Psychopaths are unpredictable, Mark,' he said. 'We never know what they'll do next, or why they do it.'

'For God's sake!'

'Where's the girl, Mark?'

Hudson hesitated, looked away. 'What girl?'

'Come on, Mark. You know who I mean. The girl who was with you. Your accomplice.'

'Accomplice?'

'Miss Peterson. Where is she?'

'I've never heard of anyone called Peterson.'

Gristhorpe gave that one a 'maybe'. 'Where's Gemma Scupham?'

'Please, you've got to believe me. I don't know anything. I had nothing to do with it. I'm just trying to do my civic duty.'

Gristhorpe let the staring match continue until Hudson looked down at the stained metal desk, then he asked, 'Can you remember exactly where you found the bundle of clothing?'

Hudson rubbed his damp forehead. 'I was thinking about that on my way here,' he said. 'That you might want to know.'

'It could be useful. We still haven't found the girl's body.'

'Yes, well . . . I could try. I mean, I think I might remember if I saw the spot again. But it was dark and it's pretty bleak up there. I must admit after I found the clothes I didn't want to hang around.'

'And you were no doubt under the influence of Bacchus?'

'What?'

'You'd been drinking?'

'I'd had a little wine, yes. But I wasn't over the limit, if that's what you mean.'

'I don't care how much you had to drink,' said Gristhorpe, standing up. 'Although judging by your eyes this morning I'd say you're concerned about it. What I want you to do is to take me to the spot where you found the clothes. I'll go with you in your car and DS Richmond here will follow. All right?'

'I don't have much choice, do I?'

'No,' said Gristhorpe. 'No, you don't.'

TWO

Gristhorpe said nothing during the journey. They crawled up Sutton Bank into the Hambleton Hills, passed through Helmsley, then turned off the main road into Hutton-le-Hole. On the broad village green, split by Hutton Beck, the sides connected by a small white bridge, tourists ate picnics. Several sheep also picnicked from the grass itself, keeping their distance from the humans. It was a marvel of work-saving, Gristhorpe thought, letting the sheep wander the village and keep the green well cropped.

Beyond Hutton, they turned north onto a narrow, unfenced road over the desolate moors.

'I'd have more chance if we were going the other way,' Hudson said. 'I mean, that was the way I was driving, and it was very dark.'

'Don't worry,' said Gristhorpe, 'you'll get your chance.'

They had no luck on the way to Rosedale, so Gristhorpe turned in the car park and set off back again, up the one-in-three hill, with Richmond still behind. The moorland stretched for miles on all sides, a dark sea of purple heather, just past its prime. Hudson seemed to be concentrating as they drove, screwing up his eyes and looking into the distance, trying to remember how long he had been driving before he stopped. Finally, he pointed to a small outcrop of rocks among the heather about fifty yards from the roadside. 'This is it!' he shouted. 'This is the place.'

Gristhorpe turned into the lay-by and waited for Richmond to pull in behind. 'Are you sure?' he asked.

'Well, I can't be hundred per cent, but I'd been driving about this long, and I remember those rocks over there. There aren't many spots like that around here.'

Gristhorpe opened the door. 'By the roadside here, then? Let's take a look.'

'Well, actually,' Hudson said, 'it was further from the road, closer to the rocks.'

Richmond had joined them, and Gristhorpe gave him a puzzled look before he said, 'Phil. If you stopped for a piss on this road at half past twelve at night, would you walk fifty yards or so away from your car to do it?'

Richmond shook his head. 'No way, sir.'

'I thought not.' He fixed Hudson with his innocent gaze again. 'But you did, right?'

'Yes.'

'Why?'

'I don't know. I wasn't really thinking about it, I suppose I didn't want to be seen.'

Gristhorpe looked around the desolate landscape in disbelief. 'Didn't want to be seen?'

'That's right.'

'You had a torch, I assume?'

'Yes.'

Gristhorpe raised his bushy eyebrows and shook his head. 'Come on, then, show us where.'

Hudson led them over the rough, springy heather towards the outcrop, a natural shelter, and pointed. Gristhorpe didn't want to ruin any more evidence there might be, so he stood at the entrance and looked. It was a small area, maybe three or four yards square, surrounded on all sides but one with rocks, some as high as Gristhorpe's chest, but most of them no more than knee-high stones. In the centre, a small area of heather looked as if it had been flattened recently. There had been some blood on the yellow dungarees, he recalled. In all likelihood, there would be more blood around here, and perhaps other valuable trace evidence.

'Where exactly did you find the bundle of clothes?' Gristhorpe asked.

Hudson thought for a moment, then pointed towards one of the smaller rocks near a corner of the flattened heather. 'There. Stuffed under there. I think.'

'What made you look there?'

He shrugged. 'I don't know. Maybe I saw something out of the corner of my eye.'

Gristhorpe stood for a few moments taking in the scene, then turned to go back to the car.

'Can I go home now?' Hudson asked when they arrived. 'My wife. She'll be wondering where I am.'

'You can phone her when we get back to the station.'

'Station?'

'Yes. Phil?' Gristhorpe ignored Hudson's protests. 'Radio in and get the SOCO team, if you can raise any of them on a Sunday afternoon.'

'Will do, sir.' Richmond went to his car.

'But I don't understand,' Hudson went on as Gristhorpe took him by the arm and gently guided him into the passenger seat.

'Don't you? It's simple really. I don't believe you. First off, I don't believe anyone would walk this far for a piss on a dark night in a place like this, and second I don't like the fact that you didn't show up at the station till nearly noon and then tried to leave as soon as you'd dumped the bag.'

'But I've explained all that.'

Gristhorpe started the car. 'Not to my satisfaction, you haven't. Not by a long chalk. I don't like it at all. Besides, there's another thing.'

'What?'

'I don't like *you*.'

THREE

When Jenny Fuller pulled up outside Superintendent Gristhorpe's house above Lyndgarth at about seven o'clock that evening, lights shone a welcome from the lower windows. She hadn't phoned to say she was coming, but Phil Richmond had told her at the station that the superintendent had finally abandoned his camp bed and gone home.

She knocked at the heavy door and waited. When Gristhorpe opened it, he was clearly surprised to see her there but didn't hesitate to invite her in.

'I've just finished doing a bit of work on the wall,' he said as they stood in the hall. 'Until it got too dark. Fancy a cup of tea?'

'Mm, yes please,' Jenny said.

'I can offer you something stronger if you'd like?'

'No. No, tea will be fine. I was just on my way to visit a colleague in Lyndgarth and I thought I'd drop by. I don't have much, I'm afraid, but I can give you a sketch of what I've dug up so far. It might be some help.'

Gristhorpe directed her to the study while he went to the kitchen. Jenny stood and gazed at the books, the clearly divided sections on military and naval history, general history, Yorkshire, then the novels, philosophy, poetry. On the small table by the armchair lay a paperback copy of *The Way of All Flesh*. Jenny had always loved the title but had never read it. Her background in English was distinctly weak, she realized.

Somehow the house and this room in particular spoke of a solitary, meditative, serious man, perhaps ill at ease in company. All that was missing was a pipe lying in an ashtray on the table, and perhaps a pipe-rack over the hearth. But Gristhorpe had a gregarious side to his character, too, she knew. He enjoyed telling tales with his mates and colleagues over a pint; he wasn't at all uneasy in groups. A man's man, perhaps?

Gristhorpe came back bearing a tray with a teapot and two mugs, a little jug of milk and a bowl of sugar. Jenny moved the book from the table and he set the tray down. He bade her sit in the leather armchair that she knew instinctively was 'his' and pulled up a smaller chair for himself.

'That camp bed was beginning to make me feel like an old man,' he said. 'Besides, they know where I am if anything breaks.'

'No progress?'

'I wouldn't say that. We've talked to the neighbours again, and to Gemma's school-friends, the kids she played with, and none of them saw anyone hanging about or heard Gemma mention anyone they didn't know. So that's a blank. But . . .' Gristhorpe went on to tell her about the Manleys' deserted cottage and his outing to the moors with Mark Hudson.

'What's happened to him?' she asked.

'I sent him home when I finally got the truth out of him. He led us on a merry dance, but he's got nothing to do with Gemma. He was out for a bit of extramarital activity. He'd settled on the spot in advance because it was some distance from the road and the rocks offered protection. He just stumbled across the clothing. We've got the woman's name. Of course, we'll talk to her and have another chat with him, just for procedure's sake.'

'So the clothing *is* Gemma Scupham's?'

'Yes. The mother identified it. And there's a bit of blood

on it – at least, it looks like blood. But we won't know much more till tomorrow, when the forensic team gets its job done.'

'Still . . .' Jenny shivered.

'Cold?'

'Oh, no. I'm fine, really.' Jenny was wearing jeans and a fuzzy russet jumper that matched the colour of her hair, a warm enough outfit for a mild night. 'Someone walked over my grave, that's all.' She sipped some soothing tea. 'I've been looking at instances of pairs of sexual deviants, and quite frankly there's hardly any. Often you'll find a couple who might commit crimes for gain, like Bonnie and Clyde, I suppose, but deviants usually act solo.'

'What about the ones who don't?' Gristhorpe asked.

'There are *some* case studies. Usually you get a dominant leader and an accomplice, and usually they're both male. Leopold and Loeb, for example.'

Gristhorpe nodded.

'Have you read *Compulsion*?' Jenny asked.

'Yes. It was one of Ian Brady's favourite books, you know.'

'There are some parallels. The way your couple seem to have coldly planned and executed the crime, for a start,' Jenny said. 'But there's another thing: mixed pairs are very rare. Brady and Hindley come to mind, of course.'

'Aye,' said Gristhorpe. 'Maybe Alan's told you I've got what you might call an unhealthy preoccupation with that case. But I was involved in the search. And I heard the tape of young Lesley Ann Downey pleading for her life.' He shook his head and let the silence hang.

'Is that why you're getting so actively involved in this case? I mean, you don't usually.'

Gristhorpe smiled. 'Partly, I suppose. And maybe I'm

trying to prove there's life in the old dog yet. I'm getting near retiring age, you know. But mostly I want to stop them before they do it again. We spend most of our time making cases against people we think have broken the law. Oh, we talk about prevention – we have coppers on the beat, keeping their eyes open – but mostly we come on the scene after the fact. That's also true this time, I realize. Gemma Scupham may be lost to us, but I'm damned if I'm going to let it happen to another child on my patch. Make sense?'

Jenny nodded.

'So what do you think?' he asked.

'From what little I know so far,' Jenny said, 'I'd say it's certainly possible we could be dealing with a Brady–Hindley pair. And they may not be paedophiles, as such. Paedophiles have a genuine sexual attraction to children, and they don't usually go in for murder unless they panic, but children also make good victims just because they're very vulnerable, like women. Brady's last victim was a seventeen-year-old male homosexual, I gather. Hardly a child.'

'You've obviously done your research,' Gristhorpe said. 'Owt else?'

'I'd look more closely at why they did it the way they did, and why they chose Gemma Scupham. It's also come out from a few studies lately that more women are involved in paedophilia than we'd ever thought before, so I wouldn't discount that possibility altogether. Maybe she wasn't along just for the ride.'

'Could *he* have been the one along for the ride?' Gristhorpe asked.

'I doubt it. Not according to the statistics, at least.'

'Any good news?'

Jenny shook her head. 'What it comes down to', she said, leaning forward, 'is that in my opinion – and remember it's still all basically guesswork – you're probably dealing with a psychopath, most likely the male, and a woman who's become fixated on him, who'll do anything he says. There's something odd about them, though, something odd about the whole business. The psychology doesn't quite add up.' She frowned. 'Anyway, I'd concentrate on him. He might not be a paedophile in particular, so I wouldn't depend on criminal records. I think it's more likely that he just likes to act out sadistic fantasies in front of an adoring audience. I – Oh, God, what am I saying? The poor damn kid.' Jenny flopped back in the chair and put her hand to her forehead. 'I'm sorry,' she said. 'I'm behaving like a silly girl.'

'Nay, lass,' said Gristhorpe. 'When they played that tape there wasn't a dry eye in the courtroom – and they were hardened coppers all.'

'Still,' said Jenny, 'if I'm to be any help I have to try to remain calm and objective.'

'Aye,' said Gristhorpe, sitting down again. 'Aye, you can try. But I don't imagine it's easy for any of us with a possible psychopath on the loose, is it? Another cup of tea?'

Jenny looked at her watch. No, she didn't have to hurry; she had plenty of time. 'Yes,' she said. 'That'd be very nice. I think I will.'

7

ONE

'**Don't tell me** you've been burning the midnight oil?' Gristhorpe said, when Vic Manson phoned at nine o'clock Monday morning.

Manson laughed. 'Afraid so.'

'Anything?'

'Where do you want me to start?'

'Start with the search of the moorland.'

'The lads haven't finished yet. They're still out there. No sign of a body so far.'

'What about the clothes?'

'I've got Frank's report in front of me. He's our blood expert. It was a dry stain, so we can't tell as much as we'd like – the presence of certain drugs, for example – but it *is* blood, it's human, and it's group A, one of the most common, unfortunately, and the same as Gemma's, according to our files. We're doing more tests.'

'Anything else?'

'Well, we can tell a fair bit about how it came to be there and – this is the interesting part – first, there wasn't very much, nowhere near enough to cause loss of life. It was restricted to the bib area of the T-shirt and the dungarees, which might make you think on first sight that someone cut her throat, but no way, according to Frank. At least not while she was wearing them.'

'Then how did it get to be there?'

'It didn't drip. It was smeared, as if you cut your finger and wiped it on your shirt.'

'But you surely wouldn't wipe it on a white T-shirt and yellow dungarees?'

'I wouldn't, no. That'd be grounds for divorce. But Gemma was only seven, remember. How careful were you about getting your clothes dirty when you were seven? Someone else washed them for you.'

'Still . . . And less of your cheek, Vic. What kind of injury could have caused it?'

'We can't say for certain, but most likely a scratch, a small cut, something like that.'

'Any idea how long the clothes had been out there?'

'Sorry.'

'Anything else at all?'

'Yes. In addition to the items I've mentioned, we received a pair of white cotton socks and child's sneakers. There was no underwear. You might care to consider that.'

'I will.'

'And there was some whitish powder or dust on the dungarees. It's being analysed.'

'What about the cottage?'

'Very interesting. Whoever cleaned that place up really did a good job. They even took the vacuum bag with them and combed out all the fibres from the brushes.'

'As if they had something to hide?'

'Either that or they were a right pair of oddballs. Maybe house-cleaning in the nude got them all excited.'

'Aye, and maybe pigs can fly. But we've got nothing to tie them in to the missing lass?'

'No prints, no bloodstains, no bodily fluids. Just hair. It's practically impossible to get rid of every hair from a scene.'

'And it's also practically impossible to pin it down to any one person,' said Gristhorpe.

'There's still the DNA typing. It takes a bloody long time, though, and it's not as reliable as people think.'

'Was there anything that might have indicated the child's presence?'

'No. The hairs were definitely adult. Some sandy coloured, fairly short, probably a man's, and the others we found were long and blonde. A woman's, I'd say. A child's hairs are usually finer in pigment, with a much more rudimentary character. We found some fibres, too, mostly from clothes you can buy anywhere – lamb's wool, rayon, that kind of thing. No white or yellow cotton. There was something else, though, and I think this will interest you.'

'Yes.'

'Well, you know we took the drains apart?'

'Will Patricia Cummings ever let me forget?'

'There's a fair bit of dark sludge in there.'

'Could it be blood?'

'Let me finish. No, it's not blood. We haven't run the final tests yet, but we think it's hair-dye, the kind you can wash out easily.'

'Well, well, well,' said Gristhorpe. 'That *is* interesting. Just one more thing, Vic.'

'Yes.'

'I think you'd better get the lads digging up the cottage gardens, front and back. I know it's a long shot – most likely somebody would have seen them burying anything out there – but we can't overlook it.'

'I suppose not.' Manson sighed. 'Your estate agent's going to love us for this.'

'Can't be helped, Vic.'

'Okay. I'll be in touch later.'

Gristhorpe sat at his desk for a moment running his palm over his chin and frowning. This was the first positive link between Mr Brown and Miss Peterson, who had abducted Gemma Scupham on Tuesday afternoon, and Chris and Connie Manley, who had abandoned a pre-paid holiday cottage in spotless condition on the Thursday of that same week. Coincidence wasn't enough; nor was the fact that Manson's men had found traces of hair-dye in the drains, but it was a bloody good start. His phone buzzed.

'Gristhorpe,' he grunted.

'Sir,' said Sergeant Rowe, 'I think there's someone here you'd better see.'

'Yes? Who is it?'

'A Mr Bruce Parkinson, sir. From what he tells me, I think he might know something about the car. You know, the one they used to take that young lass away.'

Christ, it was coming in thick and fast now, the way it usually did after days of hard slog leading nowhere. 'Hang onto him, Geoff,' said Gristhorpe. 'I'll be right down.'

TWO

Dark satanic mills, indeed, thought DC Susan Gay as she approached Bradford. Even on a fine autumn day like this, even with most of the mills closed down or turned into craft shops or business centres, the tall, dark chimneys down in the valley still had a gloomy aspect.

Bradford had been cleaned up. It now advertised itself as the gateway to Brontë country and boasted such tourist attractions as Bolling Hall, the National Museum of Photography and even Undercliffe Cemetery. But as Susan navigated her way through the one-way streets of the city centre, past the gothic Victorian Wool Exchange and the Town Hall, with its huge campanile tower, Bradford still felt to her like a nineteenth-century city in fancy dress.

After driving around in circles for what seemed like ages, she finally turned past St George's Hall and drove by the enormous Metro Travel Interchange onto Wakefield Road. The next time she had to stop for a red light, she consulted her street map again and found Hawthorne Terrace. It didn't seem too far away: a right, a left and a right again. Soon she found herself in an area of terrace back-to-backs, with washing hanging across rundown tarmac streets. The car bumped in potholes as she looked for the street name. There it was.

An old man in a turban and a long white beard hobbled across the street on his walking stick. Despite the chill that had crept into the air that morning, people sat out on their doorsteps. Children played hand-cricket against wickets chalked on walls and she had to drive very slowly in case one of the less cautious players ran out in front of her chasing a catch. Some of the corner shops had posters in Hindi in their windows. One showed a golden-skinned woman apparently swooning in a rajah's arms – a new video release, by the look of it. She noticed the smells in the air, too: cumin, coriander, cardamom.

At last she bumped to a halt outside number six, watched by a group of children over the street. There were no gardens, just a cracked pavement beyond the kerb, then the houses themselves in an unbroken row. The red bricks had darkened over the years, and these places hadn't been sandblasted clean like the Town Hall. Like any other northern city, Bradford had its share of new housing, both council and private, but the Johnsons' part of town was pre-war, and here, old didn't mean charming, as it often did out in the country. Still, it was no real slum, no indication of abject poverty. As she locked her car door and looked around, Susan noticed the individualizing touches to some of the houses: an ornate brass door-knocker on one bright red door; a dormer window atop one house; double-glazing in another.

Taking a deep breath, Susan knocked. She knew that, even though the Johnsons had agreed to her coming, she would be intruding on their grief. No matter what the late Carl's police record said, to them he was a son who had been brutally murdered. At least she wasn't the one to break the news. The Bradford police had already done that. The upstairs curtains, she noticed, were drawn, a sign that there had been a death in the family.

A woman opened the door. In her late fifties, Susan guessed, she looked well preserved, with a trim figure, dyed red hair nicely permed and just the right amount of make-up to hide a few wrinkles. She was wearing a black skirt and a white blouse tucked in the waistband. A pair of glasses dangled on a cord around her neck.

'Come in, dearie,' she said, after Susan had introduced herself. 'Make yourself at home.'

The front door led straight into a small living room. The furniture was old and worn, but everything was clean and well cared for. A framed print of a white flower in a jar standing in front of a range of mountains in varying shades of blue brightened the wall opposite the window, which admitted enough sunlight to make the wooden surfaces of the sideboard gleam. Mrs Johnson noticed Susan looking at it.

'It's a Hockney print,' she said proudly. 'We bought it at the photography museum when we went to see his exhibition. It brightens up the place a bit, doesn't it? He's a local lad, you know, Hockney.' Her accent sounded vaguely posh and wholly put on.

'Yes,' said Susan. She remembered Sandra Banks telling her about David Hockney once. A local lad he might be, but he lived near the sea now in southern California, a far cry from Bradford. 'It's very nice,' she added.

'I think so,' said Mrs Johnson. 'I've always had an eye for a good painting, you know. Sometimes I think if I'd stuck at it and not . . .' She looked around. 'Well . . . it's too late for that now, isn't it? Cup of tea?'

'Yes, please.'

'Sit down, dearie, there you go. Won't be a minute. Mr Johnson's just gone to the corner shop. He won't be long.'

Susan sat in one of the dark blue armchairs. It was upholstered in some velvety kind of material, and she didn't like the feel of it against her fingertips, so she folded her hands in her lap. A clock ticked on the mantelpiece. Beside it stood a couple of postcards from sunny beaches, and three cards of condolence, from neighbours no doubt. Below was a brown tiled hearth and fireplace, its grate covered by a gas-fire with fake glowing coals. Even though it was still warm enough indoors, Susan could make out a faint glow and hear the hiss of the gas supply. The Johnsons obviously didn't want her to think they were stingy.

Before Mrs Johnson returned with the tea, the front door opened and a tall, thin man in baggy jeans and a red short-sleeved jumper over a white shirt walked in. When he saw Susan, he smiled and held out his hand. He had a narrow, lined face, a long nose, and a few fluffy grey hairs around the edges of his predominantly bald head. The corners of his thin lips were perpetually upturned as if on the verge of a conspiratorial smile.

'You must be from the police?' he said. 'Pleased to see you.'

It was an odd greeting, certainly not the kind Susan was used to, but she shook his hand and mumbled her condolences.

'Fox's Custard Creams,' he said.

'Pardon?'

'That's what Mother sent me out for. Fox's Custard Creams.' He shook his head. 'She thought they'd go nice with a cup of tea.' Unlike his wife's, Mr Johnson's accent was clearly and unashamedly West Riding. 'You think I could get any, though? Could I hell-as-like.'

At that moment, Mrs Johnson came in with a tray bearing cups and saucers, her best china, by the look of it, delicate pieces with rose patterns and gold around the rims, and a teapot covered by a quilted pink cosy. She set this down on the low polished-wood table in front of the settee.

'What's wrong?' she asked her husband.

He glanced at Susan. 'Everything's changed, that's what. Oh, it's been going on for years, I know, but I just can't seem to get used to it, especially as I'm home most of the time now.'

'He got made redundant,' said Mrs Johnson, whispering as if she were telling someone a neighbour had cancer. 'Had a good job as a clerk in the accounts department at British Home Stores, but they had staff cutbacks. I ask you, after nearly thirty years' loyal service. And how's a man to get a job at his age? It's young 'uns they want these days.' Her accent slipped as she expressed her disgust.

'Now that's enough of that, Edie,' he said, then looked at Susan again. 'I'm as tolerant as the next man – I don't want you to think I'm not – but I'd say things have come to a pretty pass when you can buy all the poppadoms and samosas you want at the corner shop but you can't get a packet of Fox's blooming Custard Creams. What'll it be next? that's what I ask myself. Baked beans? Milk? Butter? *Tea?*'

'Well, you'll have to go to Taylor's in future, won't you?'

'Taylor's! Taylor's was bought out by Gandhi's or some such lot months back, woman. Shows how much shopping you do.'

'I go to the supermarket down on the main road.' She looked at Susan. 'It's a Sainsbury's, you know, very nice.'

'Anyway,' said Mr Johnson, 'the lass doesn't want to hear about our problems, does she? She's got a job to do.' He sat down and they all waited quietly as Mrs Johnson poured the tea.

'We do have some ginger biscuits,' she said to Susan, 'if you'd like one.'

'No thanks. Tea'll be fine, Mrs Johnson, honest.'

'Where do you come from, lass?' asked Mr Johnson.

'Sheffield.'

'I thought it were Yorkshire, but I couldn't quite place it. Sheffield, eh.' He nodded, and kept on nodding, as if he couldn't think of anything else to say.

'I'm sorry to be calling at a time like this,' Susan said, accepting her cup and saucer from Mrs Johnson, 'but it's important we get as much information as we can as soon as possible.' She placed the tea carefully at the edge of the low table and took out her notebook. In a crucial inter-rogation, either she would have someone along to do that, or she would be taking the notes while Banks asked the questions, but the Johnsons were hardly suspects, and all she hoped to get was a few names of their son's friends and acquaintances. 'When did you last see Carl?' she asked first.

'Now then, when was it, love?' Mr Johnson asked his wife. 'Seven years? Eight?'

'More like nine or ten, I'd say.'

'Nine years?' Susan gasped at the number. 'You hadn't seen him in all that time?'

'Broke his mother's heart, Carl did,' said Mr Johnson, with the incongruous smile hovering as he spoke. 'He never had no time for us.'

'Now that's not true,' said Mrs Johnson. 'He fell in with bad company, that's what happened. He was always too easily led, our Carl.'

'Aye, and look where it got him.'

'Stop it, Bert, don't talk like that. You know I don't like it when you talk like that.'

Susan coughed and they both looked at her shame-facedly. 'Sorry,' said Mrs Johnson. 'I know we weren't close, but he *was* our son.'

'Yes,' said Susan. 'What I was wondering was if you could tell me anything about him, his friends, what he liked to do.'

'We don't really know,' said Mrs Johnson, 'do we, Bert?' Her husband shook his head. 'It was nine years ago, I remember now. His twenty-first birthday. That was the last time we saw him.'

'What happened?'

'There was a local lass,' Mr Johnson explained. 'Our Carl got her . . . well, you know. Anyway, instead of doing the honourable thing, he said it was her problem. She came round, right at his birthday party, and told us. We had a barney and Carl stormed out. We never saw him again. He sent us a postcard about a year later, just to let us know he was all right.'

'Where was it from?'

'London. It was a picture of Tower Bridge.'

'Always did have a temper, did Carl,' Mrs Johnson said.

'What was the girl's name?' Susan asked.

Mr Johnson frowned. 'Beryl, if I remember correctly,' he said. 'I think she moved away years back, though.'

'Her mum and dad still live round the corner,' said Mrs Johnson. Susan got their address and made a note to call on them later.

'Did Carl keep in touch at all?'

'No. He wasn't even in much after he turned sixteen, but there's not been a dicky-bird since that postcard. He'd be thirty when he . . . when he . . . wouldn't he?'

'Yes,' Susan said.

'It's awful young to die,' Mrs Johnson muttered. 'I blame bad company. Even when he was at school, whenever he got in trouble it was because somebody put him up to it, got him to do the dirty work. When he got caught shoplifting that time, it was that what's-his-name, you know, Bert, the lad with the spotty face.'

'They all had spotty faces,' said Mr Johnson, grinning at Susan.

'You know who I mean. Robert Naylor, that's the one. He was behind it all. He always looked up to the wrong people did our Carl. Always trusted the wrong ones. I'm sure he wasn't *bad* in himself, just too easily led. He always seemed to have this . . . this *fascination* for bad 'uns. He liked to watch those old James Cagney films on telly. Just loved them, he did. What was his favourite, Bert? You know, that one where James Cagney keeps getting these headaches, the one where he loves his mother.'

'*White Heat.*' Mr Johnson looked at Susan. 'You know the one. "Top of the world, Ma!"'

Susan didn't, but she nodded anyway.

'That's the one,' said Mrs Johnson. 'Loved that film, our Carl did. I blame the telly myself for a lot of the violence that goes on these days, I really do. They can get away with anything now.'

'Did you know any of his other friends?' Susan asked her.

'Only when he was at school. He just wasn't home much after he left school.'

'You don't know the names of anyone else he went around with?'

'Sorry, dearie, no. It's so long ago I just can't remember. It's a miracle Robert Naylor came back to me, and that's only because of the shoplifting. Had the police round then, we did.'

'What about this Robert Naylor? Where does he live?'

Mrs Johnson shook her head. Susan made a note of the name anyway. It might be worth trying to track him down. If he was such a 'bad 'un' he might even have a record by now. There didn't seem anything else to be gained from talking to the Johnsons, Susan thought. Best nip round the corner and find out about the girl Carl got pregnant, then head back to Eastvale. She finished her tea and stood up to leave.

'Nay, lass,' said Mr Johnson. 'Have another cup.'

'No, I really must be going. Thank you very much.'

'Well,' he said, 'I suppose you've got your job to do.'

'Thank you for your time,' Susan said, and opened the door.

'You can be sure of one thing, you mark my words,' said Mrs Johnson.

Susan paused in the doorway. 'Yes?'

'There'll be someone behind this had an influence on our Carl. Put him up to things. A bad 'un. A *real* bad 'un, with no conscience.' And she nodded, as if to emphasize her words.

'I'll remember that,' said Susan, then walked out into the cobbled street where bed-sheets, shirts and under-clothes flapped on a breeze that carried the fragrances of the east.

THREE

The man sitting under a graphic poster about the perils of drunken driving had the irritated, purse-lipped look of an accountant whose figures won't add up right. When he saw Gristhorpe coming, he got to his feet sharply.

'What are you going to do about it, then?' he asked.

Gristhorpe looked over to Sergeant Rowe, who raised his eyebrows and shook his head, then he led the man to one of the downstairs interview rooms. He was in his mid-thirties, Gristhorpe guessed, dressed neatly in a grey suit, white shirt and blue-and-red-striped tie, fair hair combed back, wire-framed glasses, and his chin thrust out. His complexion had a scrubbed and faintly ruddy look that Gristhorpe always, rightly or wrongly, asso-ciated with the church crowd, and he smelled of Pears soap. When they sat down, Gristhorpe asked him what the problem was.

'My car's been stolen, that's what. Didn't the sergeant tell you?'

'You're here about a stolen car?'

'That's right. It's outside.'

Gristhorpe rubbed his brow. 'I'm afraid I don't understand. Can you explain it from the beginning?'

The man sighed and looked at his watch. 'Look,' he said, 'I've been here twenty-two minutes already, first waiting to see the sergeant back there, then explaining everything to him. Are you telling me I have to go through it all again? Because if you are, you've got a nerve. I had trouble enough getting this time off from the office in the first place. Why don't you ask the other policeman what happened?'

Gristhorpe kept his silence throughout the tirade. He was used to impatient, precise and fastidious people like Mr Parkinson and found it best to let them carry on until they ran out of steam. 'I'd rather hear it from you, sir,' he replied.

'Oh, very well. I've been away for a while. When I—'

'Since when?'

'When what?'

'When did you go away?'

'Last Monday morning, a week ago. As I was saying, I left my car in the garage as usual, then I—'

'What do you mean, "as usual"?'

'Exactly what I say. Now if—'

'You mean you were in the habit of doing this?'

'I think that's what "as usual" means, don't you, Inspector?'

'Carry on.' Gristhorpe didn't bother to correct him over rank. If the car turned out to be a useful lead, it would be important to find out how many people knew about Parkinson's habit of leaving his car for days at a time, and why he did so, but for now it was best to let him finish.

'When I returned this morning, it was exactly as I had left it, except for one thing.'

'Yes?'

'The mileage. I always keep a careful record of how many miles I've done on each journey. I find it's important these days, with the price of petrol the way it is. Anyway, when I left, the milometer stood at 7655. I know this for a fact because I wrote it down in the log I keep. When I got back it read 7782. Now, that's a difference of one hundred and twenty-seven miles, Inspector. Someone has driven my car one hundred and twenty-seven miles in my absence. How do you explain that?'

Gristhorpe scratched his bristly chin. 'It certainly sounds as if someone borrowed it. If you—'

'*Borrowed?*' echoed Parkinson. 'That implies I gave someone permission. I did no such thing. Someone stole my car, Inspector. *Stole* it. The fact that they returned it is irrelevant.'

'Mm, you've got a point,' said Gristhorpe. 'Were there any signs of forced entry? Scratches around the door, that kind of thing?'

'There were scratches at the bottom of the chassis I'm positive weren't there before, but none at all around the door or windows. I imagine that today's criminal has more sophisticated means of entry than the wire coat hanger some fools are reduced to when they lock themselves out of their cars?'

'You imagine right,' said Gristhorpe. 'Keys aren't hard to come by. And garages are easy to get into. What make is the car?'

'Make. I don't see—'

'For our records.'

'Very well. It's a Toyota. I find the Japanese perfectly reliable when it comes to cars.'

'Of course. And what colour?'

'Dark blue. Look, you can save us both a lot of time if you come and have a look yourself. It's parked right outside.'

'Fine,' Gristhorpe stood up. 'Let's go.'

Parkinson led. As he walked, he stuck his hands in his pockets and jingled keys and loose change. Outside the station, opposite the market square, Gristhorpe sniffed the air. His experienced dalesman's nose smelled rain. Already, clouds were blowing in from the north-west. He also smelled pub grub from the Queen's Arms, steak-and-kidney pie if he was right, and he realized he was getting hungry.

Parkinson's car was, indeed, a dark blue Toyota, illegally parked right in front of the police station.

'Look at that,' Parkinson said, pointing to scratched paintwork on the bottom of the chassis, just behind the left front wheel. 'Careless driving that is. Must have caught against a stone or something. Well? Aren't you going to have a look inside?'

'The fewer people do that, the better, sir,' said Gristhorpe, looking to see what stones and dirt were trapped in the tread of the tyres.

Parkinson frowned. 'What on earth do you mean by that?'

Gristhorpe turned to face him. 'You say you left last Monday?'

'Yes.'

'What time?'

'I took the eight-thirty flight from Leeds and Bradford.'

'To where?'

'I don't see as it's any of your business, but Brussels. EEC business.'

Gristhorpe nodded. They were standing in the middle

of the pavement and passers-by had to get around them somehow. A woman with a pram asked Parkinson to step out of the way so she could get by. A teenager with cropped hair and a tattoo on his cheek swore at him. Parkinson was clearly uncomfortable talking in the street. A mark of his middle-class background, Gristhorpe thought. The working classes – both urban and rural – had always felt quite comfortable standing and chatting in the street. But Parkinson hopped from foot to foot, glancing irritably from the corners of his eyes as people brushed and jostled past them to get by. His glasses had slipped down his nose, and a stray lock of hair fell over his right eye.

'How did you get to the airport?' Gristhorpe pressed on.

'A friend drove me. A business colleague. It's no mystery, Inspector, believe me. Long-term parking at the airport is expensive. My colleague drives a company car, and the company pays. It's as simple as that.' He pushed his glasses back up to the bridge of his nose. 'It's not that I'm overly concerned about saving money, of course. But why pay when you don't have to?'

'Indeed. Do you always do it that way?'

'What way?'

'Don't you ever take it in turns?'

'I told you. He has a company car. Look, I don't see—'

'Please bear with me. Did nobody notice the car was gone?'

'How could they? It was in the garage, and the garage door was locked.'

'Have you asked if anyone heard anything?'

'That's your job. That's why—'

'Where do you live, sir?'

'Bartlett Drive. Just off the Helmthorpe road.'

'I know it.' If Gristhorpe remembered correctly, Bartlett Drive was close to the holiday cottage the Manleys had so suddenly deserted. 'And the car was replaced as if it had never been gone?'

'That's right. Only they didn't bargain for my record-keeping.'

'Quite. Look, I'll get someone to drive you home and take a full statement, then—'

'What? You'll do what?' A couple walking by stopped and stared. Parkinson blushed and lowered his voice. 'I've already told you I've given up enough time already. Now why don't you—'

Gristhorpe held his hand up, palm out, and his innocent gaze silenced Parkinson just as it had put the fear of God into many a villain. 'I can understand your feelings,' Gristhorpe said, 'but please listen to me for a minute. There's a chance, a very good chance, that your car was used to abduct a little girl from her home last Tuesday afternoon. If that's the case, it's essential that we get a forensic team to go over the car thoroughly. Do you understand?'

Parkinson nodded, mouth open.

'Now, this may mean some inconvenience to you. You'll get your car back in the same condition it's in now, but I can't say exactly when. Of course, we'll try to help you in any way we can, but basically, you're acting like the true public-spirited citizen that you are. You're generously helping us try to get to the bottom of a particularly nasty bit of business, right?'

'Well,' said Parkinson. 'Seeing as you put it *that* way.' And the first drops of rain fell on their heads.

FOUR

Banks and Susan stood at the bar in the Queen's Arms that Monday lunchtime, wedged between two farmers and a family of tourists, and munched cheese-and-onion sandwiches with their drinks. Banks had a pint of Theakston's bitter, Susan a Slimline Tonic Water. A song about a broken love affair was playing on the jukebox in the background, and somewhere by the door to the toilets, a video game beeped as aliens went down in flames. From what he could overhear, Banks gathered that the farmers were talking about money and the tourists were arguing about whether to go home because of the rain or carry on to the Bowes Museum.

'So you found the girl's parents?' Banks asked.

'Uh-uh.' Susan put her hand to her mouth and wiped away some crumbs, then swallowed. 'Sorry, sir. Yes, they were home. Seems like everyone except the Pakistanis around there is unemployed or retired.'

'Get anything?'

Susan shook her head. Tight blonde curls danced over her ears. Banks noticed the dangling earrings, stylized, elongated Egyptian cats in light gold. Susan had certainly brightened up her appearance a bit lately. 'Dead end,' she said. 'Oh, it happened all right. Right charmer Carl Johnson was, from what I can gather. But the girl, Beryl's her name, she's been living in America for the past five years.'

'What happened?'

'Just what his folks said. He got her in the family way, then dumped her. She came around to make a fuss, embarrass him like, at his twenty-first birthday party. He was still living at home then, off and on, and his parents invited a few close relatives over. There was a big row and he stormed out. Didn't even take any of his clothes with him. They never saw him again.'

Banks sipped at his pint and thought for a moment. 'So they've no idea who he hung around with, or where he went?'

'No.' Susan frowned. 'They know he went to London, but that's all. There was a chap called Robert Naylor. Mrs Johnson saw him as a bad influence.'

'Has he got form?'

'Yes, sir. I checked. Just minor vandalism, drunk and disorderly. But he's dead. Nothing suspicious. He was riding his motorbike too fast. He lost control and skidded into a lorry on the M1.'

'So that's that.'

'I'm afraid so, sir. From what I can gather, Johnson was the type to fall in with bad company.'

'That's obvious enough.'

'What I mean, sir, is that both his parents and Beryl's mother said he looked up to tough guys. He wasn't much in himself, they said, but he liked to be around dangerous people.'

Banks took another sip of beer. One of the tourists bumped his elbow and he spilled a little on the bar. The woman apologized. 'Sounds like the kind that hero-worships psychos and terrorists,' Banks said. 'He'd probably have been happy working for the Krays or someone like that back in the old days.'

'That's it, sir. He was a weakling himself, but he liked to boast about the rough company he kept.'

'It fits. Small-time con-man, wants to be in with the big boys. So you're thinking that might give us somewhere to look for his killer?'

'Well, there *could* be a connection, couldn't there?' Susan said, pushing her empty plate away.

Banks lit a cigarette, taking care that the smoke didn't drift directly into Susan's face. 'You mean he might have been playing out of his league, tried a double-cross or something?'

'It's possible,' said Susan.

'True. At least it's an angle to work on, and there don't seem very many. I dropped by the Barleycorn last night and found Les Poole. I just thought I'd mention Johnson to him, seeing as they're both in the same business, so to speak.'

'And?'

'Nothing. Poole denied knowing him – well, of course he would – and he's not a bad liar. No signs in his voice or his body language that he wasn't telling the truth. But . . .' Banks shook his head. 'I don't know. There was something there. The only way I can describe it is as a whiff of fear. It came and went in a second, and I'm not sure even Les was aware of it, but it was there. Anyway, no good chasing will-o'-the-wisps. Adam Harkness's Golf Club alibi checks out. I still think we might bring South Africa up whenever we question someone, though. Johnson *could* have been blackmailing Harkness, and Harkness could afford to pay someone to get rid of him. Have you had time to ask around the other flats?'

'Last night, sir. I meant to tell you, but I set off for Bradford so early. There's a student on the ground floor called Edwina Whixley. She heard male voices occasionally from Johnson's room. And she saw someone coming down the stairs one day she thought *might* have been visiting him.'

'Did you get a description?'

'Yes.' Susan fished for her notebook and found the page. 'About five foot five, mid-thirties, cropped black hair and squarish head. He was wearing a suede zip-up jacket and jeans.'

'That's all?'

'Yes, sir.'

'Ring a bell?'

Susan shook her head.

'Me, neither. Maybe you can get her to come and look at some mugshots. And you might as well check into Johnson's form, his prison mates, that kind of thing. See if you can come up with any local names, anyone fitting the description.'

'Yes, sir.' Susan picked up her bag and left.

She had a very purposeful, no-nonsense walk, Banks noticed. He remembered the trouble she had had not so long ago and decided it had actually done her good. Susan Gay wasn't the kind to throw her hands up in the air and surrender. Adversity strengthened her; she learned from her mistakes. Maybe that hardened her a bit, made her more cynical and less trusting, but perhaps they weren't such bad qualities for a detective. It was hard not to be cynical when you saw so much villainy and human misery, but in many cases the cynicism was just a shell, as the sick jokes at crime scenes and post-mortems were ways of coping with the horror and the gruesomeness of death, and perhaps, too, with the fact that it comes to us all at one time. The best coppers, Banks thought, are the ones who hang onto their humanity against all odds. He hoped he had managed to do that; he knew Gristhorpe had; and he hoped that Susan would. She was young yet.

The tourists decided to go home, partly because their youngest child was making a fearful racket, and the farmers had moved on to discuss the prospects for the three-forty at Newmarket. Banks drained his pint, then headed back to the office. There was paperwork to be done. And he would make an appointment to meet with Linda Fish, from the Writers' Circle, tomorrow, much as the thought made him wince, and see what light she could shed on Mr Adam Harkness.

FIVE

The strange woman called on Brenda Scupham shortly after Les had left for the pub that Monday evening. She was washing the dishes and lip-synching to a Patsy Cline record when the doorbell rang. Drying her hands with the tea towel, she walked through and opened the door.

'Mrs Scupham? Brenda Scupham?'

The woman stood there in the rain, a navy-blue raincoat buttoned up to her neck and a dark scarf fastened over her head. Wind tugged at the black umbrella she held. Beyond her, Brenda could see the nosy woman from number eleven across the street peeking through her curtains.

Brenda hugged herself against the cold and frowned. 'Yes. What do you want?'

'I'm Lenora Carlyle,' the woman said. 'You might have heard of me?'

'Are you a reporter?'

'No. Can I come in?'

Brenda stood back, and the woman let down her umbrella and entered. Brenda noticed immediately in the hall light her intense dark eyes and Romany complexion. She unfastened her scarf and shook out her head of luxuriant, coal-black hair.

'I don't want anything,' Brenda went on, suddenly nervous.

'I'm not a reporter, Brenda, and I'm not selling anything,' the woman said in soft, hypnotic tones. 'I'm a psychic. I'm here because of your daughter, Gemma. I want to help you.'

Brenda just gaped and stood back as the woman unbuttoned her raincoat. Numbly, she took the umbrella and stood it on the rubber mat with the shoes, then she took the woman's coat and hung it up.

Lenora Carlyle was heavy-set, wearing a chunky-knit black cardigan covered with red and yellow roses, black slacks, and a religious symbol of some kind on a chain around her neck. Or so the odd-looking cross with the loop at the top seemed to Brenda. Lenora straightened her cardigan and smiled, revealing stained and crooked teeth.

Brenda led her into the living room and turned off the music. She still felt a little frightened. The supernatural always made her feel that way. She wasn't sure if she believed in it or not, but she'd heard of enough strange things happening to people to make her wonder – like the time her old friend Laurie Burton dreamed about her father for the first time in years the very night he died.

After they had sat down, Brenda lit a cigarette and asked, 'What do you mean, help? How can you help?'

'I don't know yet,' Lenora said, 'but I'm sure I can. If you'll let me.'

'How much do you want?'

'I don't want anything.'

Brenda felt suspicious, but you couldn't argue with that. 'What do you want me to do?' she asked.

Lenora put a friendly hand on her knee. 'Nothing, dear, except relax and be open. Are you a believer?'

'I . . . I don't know.'

'It's all right. The Lord knows His own. Do you have something of Gemma's? Something personal.'

'Like what?'

'Well, hair would be best, but perhaps an article of clothing, a favourite toy. Something she felt strongly about, touched a lot.'

Brenda thought of the teddy bear one of her ex-boyfriends – Bob? Ken? – had bought Gemma some years ago. Even now she was older, Gemma never slept without it. Brenda felt a pang of guilt as she thought about it. If there were any chance that Gemma *was* alive, she would miss her teddy bear terribly. Being without it would make her so miserable. But no. Gemma was dead; she had to be.

She went upstairs to Gemma's room and Lenora Carlyle followed her. While Brenda walked to the tiny bed to pick up the bear, Lenora stood on the threshold and seemed to take several deep breaths.

'What is it?' Brenda asked.

Lenora didn't answer. Instead, she walked forward, reached out for the bear, and sat down on the bed with it. The bedspread had Walt Disney characters printed all over it: Mickey Mouse, Donald Duck, Bambi, Dumbo. How Gemma loved cartoons. They were the only things that made her smile, Brenda remembered. But it was an odd, inward smile, not one to be shared.

Lenora clutched the bear to her breast and rocked slowly, eyes closed. Brenda felt a shiver go up her spine. It was as if the atmosphere of the room had subtly changed, somehow become thicker, deeper and colder. For what seemed like ages, Lenora hung onto the bear and rocked silently. Brenda clutched her blouse at her throat.

Then finally, Lenora opened her eyes. They were glazed and unfocused. She began to speak.

'Gemma is alive,' she said. 'Alive. But, oh, she's so alone, so frightened. So much suffering. She wants you. She wants her mother. She *needs* you, Brenda. You must find her.'

Brenda felt light-headed. 'She can't be,' she whispered. 'They've found her clothes . . . I've seen them.'

'She's alive, Brenda.' Lenora turned and grasped Brenda's wrist. Her grip was tight.

Brenda steadied herself on the back of the small chair by Gemma's desk. She felt dizzy, her skin cold and clammy, as if she had had too much to drink and the world was spinning fast. 'Where can I find her?' she asked. 'Where do I look? Tell me, where do I look?'

8

ONE

By Tuesday morning, the searchers had turned up
nothing buried in the garden of the holiday cottage; nor
had anything of interest been discovered on the moors
where Gemma's clothing had been found. Gristhorpe sat
in his office going over the paperwork, waiting to hear
from forensics about Parkinson's car. Outside, mucky
clouds, like balls of black wool, started to attack from the
west.

It was close to twelve when Vic Manson called.

'What did you find?' Gristhorpe asked.

'Plenty. The girl was in there all right. We found her
prints. Windows, back of the front seat, all over. I checked
them with the ones on file, and they match.'

'Good work, Vic.'

'And we found yellow fibres.'

'The dungarees?'

'Looks like it. I'm still waiting for the confirmation.'

'Anything else?'

'A bit of black hair-dye smeared on the driver's
headrest. Soil and gravel in the wheels, could have come
from just about anywhere locally. Lay-by, track, drive,
quarry.'

'No particular kind of limestone deposit you only find
on Aldington Edge, or anything like that?'

Manson laughed. 'Sorry, no. Look, remember that whitish powder I told you about on the kid's dungarees? It's a lime solution, most likely whitewash.'

'Where from?'

'Same as the soil and gravel, it could have come from anywhere, really. A pub wall, a cellar, outhouse.'

'You can't be more specific?'

'Whitewash is whitewash. Now if you'll kindly get off the bloody phone and let me get on with the confirmations, we'll have a pile of stuff that just might stand up in court when you catch the bastards.'

'All right, all right. And Vic?'

'Yes.'

'I'm eternally grateful.'

'I'll remember that.'

Gristhorpe hung up. He no longer had to sit around waiting for the phone to ring. There were things to do: question Parkinson again, and his neighbours; get in touch with the press and television. They could run this on *Crimewatch*. And where had he seen whitewash recently? Calling for Richmond on his way, he swept down the corridor towards the stairs.

TWO

Why was it, Banks thought, as he sat in Corrigan's Bar and Grill on York Road near the bus station, that so many people gravitated towards these trendy, renovated pubs? What on earth was wrong with a down-to-earth, honest-to-goodness old pub? Just look at Le Bistro, that place where he had met Jenny last week. All coral-pink table-cloths, long-stemmed wine glasses and stiff napkins.

And now this: eighteenth-century Yorkshire translated almost overnight into twentieth-century New York, complete with booths, brass rails, square Formica-top tables and waitresses who might bustle in New York, but in Yorkshire moved at their normal couldn't-care-less pace. At least some things didn't change.

And then there was the menu: a large, thin laminated card of bold, handwritten items with outrageous prices. Burgers, of course, club sandwiches, corned beef on rye (and they didn't mean Fray Bentos), and such delights for dessert as raspberry cheesecake, pecan pie and frozen yoghurt. All to the accompaniment (not *too* loud, thank the Lord) of Euro-pop.

Maybe he was getting conservative since the move to Yorkshire, he wondered. Certainly in London, Sandra and he had happily embraced the changes that seemed to happen so fast from the 60s on, delighted in the varieties of food and ambience available. But somehow here, in a town with a cobbled market square, ancient cross, Norman church and excavated pre-Roman ruins, so close to the timeless, glacier-carved dales and towering fells with their jagged limestone edges and criss-cross drystone walls, the phoney American theme and fashionable food seemed an affront.

The beer was a problem, too, just as it was in Le Bistro. Here was no Theakston's bitter, no Old Peculier, no Tetley's, Marston's or Sam Smith's, just a choice of gassy keg beer and imported bottled lagers from Germany, Holland, Mexico and Spain, all ice-cold, of course. Funnily enough, he sat over a glass (they didn't serve pints, only tall heavy glasses that tapered towards their thick bases) of Labatt's, one of the less interesting lagers he remembered from his trip to Toronto.

Such were his thoughts as he puzzled over the menu waiting for Linda Fish, the champagne socialist, to show. Corrigan's had been *her* choice, and as he wanted information, he had thought it best to comply. The sacrifices a copper makes in the course of duty, he thought to himself, shaking his head. At least there was an ashtray on the table. He looked out of the window at the lunchtime shoppers darting in and out of the shopping centre opposite in the rain. Raincoats, waxed jackets, a chill in the air: it looked as if autumn had arrived at last.

Linda walked in after he had been musing gloomily for ten minutes or so. She packed up her telescope umbrella and looked around, then waved and came over to join him. She had always reminded Banks of an overgrown child. It was partly the way she dressed – today blue sweatpants and a matching sweatshirt with a pink teddy bear on its front – and partly the slightly unformed face, a kind of freckled, doughy blob on which had been stuck two watery eyes accentuated by blue shadow, a button nose and thin lips made fuller by lipstick. Her straw-coloured hair looked as if she had just cut it herself with blunt scissors in front of a funfair mirror. As always, she carried her oversized and scuffed leather shoulder bag, something she had picked up in Florence, she had once told him, and with great sentimental value. Whether it was stuffed with bricks and toiletries or unpublished manuscripts, he had no idea, but it certainly looked heavy.

Linda squeezed her bulk into the booth opposite Banks. 'I hope you don't mind meeting here,' she said conspiratorially, 'but I'm afraid I've become quite addicted to the chilli-burgers.'

'It's fine,' Banks lied. She wasn't from Yorkshire, and her slight lisp seemed to make the Home Counties accent sound even posher. Whatever you might say or think about Linda, though, Banks reminded himself, she was far from stupid. Not only did she run the local Writers' Circle with such energy and enthusiasm that left most bystanders gasping, but she was indeed a *published* writer, not a mere hopeful or dilettante. She had, in fact, published a short novel with a large firm only a year ago. Banks had read it, and admitted it was good. Very good, in fact. No, Linda Fish was no fool. If she wanted to look ridiculous, then that was her business.

'I'm afraid I won't be able to tell you very much, you know,' she said.

'Even a little will help.' Banks flapped the menu. 'Anything you'd recommend?'

Her blue eyes narrowed in a smile. 'I can see you're uncomfortable,' she said. 'I'm sorry I suggested we meet here. Men are obviously much happier in pubs.'

Banks laughed. 'You're right about that. But let's see what I can salvage from the situation. Who knows, I might even find something I like.'

'Good,' said Linda. 'Well, you know what I'm having. Are you not familiar with this kind of food?'

'American? Yes, I've never been to the States but I was in Toronto a couple of years ago. I think I can find my way around. I always found it was best to stick with the burgers.'

'I think you're right.'

A waitress ambled along, playing with her hair as she approached. 'Yes?' She stood beside the booth, weight balanced on her left hip, order pad in one hand and pencil in the other. She didn't even look at them. Linda ordered her chilli-burger and a bottle of San Miguel, and Banks went for the mushroom-and-cheese burger and another glass of Labatt's. He leaned back on the red vinyl banquette and lit a Silk Cut. The grill had filled up a bit since Linda arrived, most truant sixth-formers buzzing with conversation and laughter, and the Euro-pop droned on.

'Do you want to interrogate me before lunch or after?' Linda asked.

Banks smiled. 'I always find a full stomach helps. But if you're—'

She waved her hand. 'Oh no, I'm not in a hurry or anything. I'm just interested.' She stuck her hand deep in her bag and frowned, leaning slightly to the side, as she rummaged around in there like a kid at a fairground lucky dip. 'Ah, got them.' She pulled out a packet of menthol cigarettes.

'You know,' she said, lighting up, 'I'd never really thought about it before, but you could be useful to me.'

'Me? How?'

'I'm thinking of writing a detective story.'

'Good Lord,' said Banks, whose knowledge of detective fiction stopped at Sherlock Holmes.

'From what I've read,' Linda went on, 'it's clear that one can get away without knowing much police procedure, but a little realism does no harm. What I was thinking was—'

The waitress appeared with their food and drinks at that moment, and Linda's attention was diverted towards her chilli-burger. Feeling relieved at the interruption, Banks bit into his burger. It was good. But his reprieve was only temporary.

'What I was thinking,' Linda went on, wiping the chilli sauce from her chin with a paper napkin, 'was perhaps that you could advise me. You know, on police procedure. And maybe tell me a bit about some of your cases. Give me an insight into the criminal mind, so to speak.'

'Well,' said Banks, 'I'd be glad to help if you have any specific questions. But I don't really think I can just sit down and tell you all about it.'

Her eyes narrowed again, and she bit into her burger. When she had finished that mouthful, she went on, 'I suppose that's a compromise of sorts. I'm sure your time is too valuable to waste on writers of fiction. Though I *did* get the impression that you are fairly well read.'

Banks laughed. 'I like a good book, yes.'

'Well, then. Even Hardy and Dickens had to do their research, you know. They had to ask people about things.'

Banks held up his hands. 'All right, you've convinced me. Just give me specific questions and I'll do my best to answer them, OK?'

'OK. I haven't got that far yet, but when I do I'll take you up on it.'

'Now, what can you tell me about Adam Harkness?'

'Ah-hah, the interrogation at last. As I said, I can't tell you very much, really. But I don't believe all that phoney anti-apartheid rubbish, for a start.'

'Why not?'

'Because it doesn't square with what I've heard. Oh, I'm sure he probably even believes it himself now, and it's a trendy enough position for white South African expatriates to take. But how do you think his father made his money? You can't tell me he didn't exploit the blacks. Everybody did. And you won't see Adam Harkness giving his money away to support the ANC.'

'He told me he left South Africa because he didn't agree with the politics.'

'That's not what I heard.'

'What did you hear?'

'It's just rumours, but I've a friend lives there, a writer, and she said there was some kind of scandal about to break but the Harknesses hushed it up.'

'What kind of scandal?'

'Nobody really knows. My friend suspects he killed someone, a black mine-worker, but there's no proof.'

It was possible, Banks supposed, ten or more years ago to cover up the murder of a black by a rich and powerful white man in South Africa. For all he knew, despite the scrapping of racial classification, it probably still was. Attitudes don't change overnight, whatever politicians might decree.

'Have you ever heard of a man called Carl Johnson?' Banks asked.

'Only from the papers. He was the one killed, wasn't he, at the old lead mine?'

'That's right. He worked as a gardener for Harkness.'

'Did he now?' She leaned forward. 'And you think there might be some connection?'

'There might be.'

'You surely don't think Adam Harkness murdered him?'

'Harkness has an alibi. But a man like him can afford to have things done.'

Her eyes opened wide. They looked like oysters on a half-shell. 'Do you mean that kind of thing really goes on? In England? Hit men and contracts and all that?'

Banks smiled. 'It has been known.'

'Well . . . there's obviously more to this crime business than I realized. But I'm afraid I can't help you any further.'

'Could you get in touch with your friend? Ask her for more information?'

'I could try, but I got the impression they put a lid on it pretty securely. Still, if it might help . . .'

'It might.'

'I've just had a thought.'

'Yes?'

'If the rumour's true, about Harkness and the black miner, and if that Johnson person was killed at an old mine, there's a sort of symmetry to that, isn't there?'

'I suppose there is,' Banks agreed. Symmetry, for Christ's sake, he thought. Plenty of it in books, but not in real life. 'It's just a very isolated spot,' he said.

'So why would anyone go there to meet a killer?'

'Obviously it was someone he trusted. He didn't have a car, so someone must have picked him up, or met him somewhere, and taken him there. Perhaps he thought he was going to get money.'

'Oh, yes,' said Linda. 'I see. Well, I'd better leave the police work to you, hadn't I? But, you know, that's exactly the kind of thinking I'm interested in. Now, I'm going to have a chocolate sundae and you can tell me all about your most interesting case.'

THREE

Gristhorpe and Richmond stood in the rain outside Parkinson's house. Semi-detached, with a frosted-glass door and a pebble-dash façade, it was more modern than the row of tiny limestone cottages that faced it across the lopsided square of unkempt grass. Gristhorpe hadn't realized that Parkinson's house was *so* close to the abandoned cottage. This was the extreme north-western edge of Eastvale, and both the new and the old houses shared a superb view west along the valley bottom. Not today, though; everything was lost in the grey haze of rain.

Richmond wore a belted navy-blue Aquascutum over his suit, and Gristhorpe a rumpled fawn raincoat with the collar turned up. Neither wore a hat. It was the kind of rain that you felt inside rather than out, Gristhorpe thought, already registering the aches in his joints. Outside you merely got beaded in moisture, but inside you were damp and chilled to the marrow.

They had already tried the semis to the west, the last pair, with only the Helmthorpe road and a drystone wall between them and the open country, but found nobody home. In fact, as Gristhorpe stood there looking around, he noticed how quiet and secluded the area was. Given that Parkinson had kept his car in the garage at the back of his house, it wouldn't have been at all difficult for someone to 'borrow' it without being seen. Apart from a few cars and delivery vans on the main road, there was nothing else around.

They walked up the path and rang the bell of the semi adjoining Parkinson's. A few moments later a man answered and, after they had showed their identification, he invited them in.

'Come in out of the rain,' he said, taking their coats. 'I'll put the kettle on.'

He was about forty, small and thickset, with sparse fair hair and lively grey eyes. His right arm, encased in plaster, hung in a sling over the lower part of his chest.

They settled down in the cheerful living room, where the element of an electric fire took some of the chill out of their bones, and their host, Mr David Ackroyd, came in with mugs of tea and joined them. Two women were talking on the radio about the menopause. He turned it off and sat down. Richmond installed himself in the armchair opposite, long legs crossed, notebook and pen in hand.

'What happened?' Gristhorpe asked, indicating the arm.

'Broke it on Sunday. Doing a bit of climbing out Swainshead way.' He shook his head. 'Silly bugger I am. I ought to know I'm too old for that sort of thing.'

'So you're not usually home weekdays?'

'Good lord, no. I'm a civil servant . . . well, civil as I can be to some of the riff-raff we get in the job centre these days.' His eyes twinkled. 'And servant to the devil, according to some. I'll be back at work again in a couple of days. The doctor says I just need a bit of a rest to get over the shock.'

'Are you married?'

He frowned. 'Yes. Why do you ask?'

'Does your wife work?'

'She's an auditor with the tax office.'

'So she's usually out all day, too?'

'Yes. Most people around here are. Have to be to pay the mortgages, prices being the way they are. What's going on?'

'Just trying to feel out the lie of the land, so to speak,' Gristhorpe said. 'Did you know Mr Parkinson's car was stolen while he was away?'

'Yes. He came dashing in to tell me as soon as he checked the mileage. I told him to go to the police.'

'Did you notice anything at all?'

'No. Of course, I was out at work all the time until the weekend. Everything seemed quite normal.'

'Did he often make these trips?'

'Yes. Quite proud of himself he was about it too. He got a promotion in the company a short while ago. Exports. They do a bit of business with the Common Market countries. You know how it is, everything's Euro-this and Euro-that these days.'

'And he always left his car in the garage?'

'Yes. Look, between you and me, Bruce is a bit tight. Short arms and deep pockets, if you know what I mean. He hasn't quite got to the company-car level yet but his boss, the bloke who usually goes with him, has. He lives a few miles north of here, so it's easy for him to pick Bruce up.'

'How many people do you think knew about this arrangement?'

'I couldn't say.'

'But Mr Parkinson was the sort to talk about such things in public?'

'Well, I suppose so. I mean, it's nothing, is it, really? Just idle chatter, pub talk. He liked to let people know how important he was, how he got to travel to Europe on business and all that. I don't think he was worried that someone might overhear him and take off with his car.'

'Could that have happened?'

'Easily enough, I suppose.' He rubbed the plaster on his arm. Gristhorpe noticed that a couple of people had signed it in ballpoint just below the elbow. 'We ought to be more careful, oughtn't we?' Ackroyd went on. 'Lord knows, we hear enough about crime prevention on telly, we should know better than to go blabbing all our holiday and business plans in a pub. You just don't think, do you?'

'Which pub is this, Mr Ackroyd?'

'Pub? Well, I was speaking figuratively, really, but there's a local in the next street. It's called the Drayman's Rest. Nothing special really, but they do a decent pint and the company's all right.'

'Do you and Mr Parkinson go there regularly?'

'I suppose you could say that. Not that we're big drinkers, mind you.' He laughed. 'Bruce always drinks halves and makes them last. It's just the social thing, the local, isn't it? A chat and a few laughs with the lads after work, that sort of thing.'

'Do you know most of the regulars?'

'Oh, aye. Except we get a few strangers in from the holiday cottages over the road. They never cause any trouble, though, and we make them welcome enough.'

'Get friendly with them, do you?'

'Well, some are easier than others, if you know what I mean. Some just like to keep to themselves, grab a sandwich and a pint and sit in the corner reading the paper. But there's outgoing ones. I like talking to people. That's how you learn, isn't it?'

'Have you met any interesting strangers in there recently?'

'What?'

'The past couple of weeks. Anyone been especially friendly?'

Ackroyd rubbed his chin. 'Aye, well now you mention it, there was Chris and Connie.'

Gristhorpe looked over at Richmond. 'The Manleys?'

'That's it. I always thought it a bit odd that they liked to stand at the bar and talk to the locals.'

'Why?'

'Well, with a bird like her I wouldn't be in the pub in the first place,' Ackroyd said, and winked. 'But usually it's the couples tend to keep to themselves.'

'They didn't?'

'No. Oh, they weren't pushy or anything. Just always there with a hello and a chat. Nowt special. It might be the weather, the news . . . that kind of thing.'

'And Mr Parkinson's European business trips?'

'Well, he did go on a bit . . . Now wait a minute, you

can't be suggesting that Chris and Connie . . .? No, I don't believe it. Besides, they had a car of their own. I saw them in it.'

'A white Fiesta?'

'That's right.'

'What kind of impression did they give you, Mr Ackroyd?'

'They just seemed like regular folk. I mean, Chris liked to talk about cars. Bit of a know-it-all, maybe. You know, the kind that likes to dominate conversations. And she seemed happy enough to be there.'

'Did she say much?'

'No, but she didn't need to. I mean most of the men in that place would've given their right arms—' He stopped, looked at his cast and laughed. 'No, that wasn't how I got it, honest. But what I'm trying to say is that it wasn't just that she was a looker, though she was that all right. The long blonde hair, those lovely red lips and the blue eyes. And from what I could tell she had all her curves in the right places, too. No, it wasn't just that. She was sexy. She had a presence. Like she didn't have to do anything. Just walk in, smile, stand there leaning on the bar. There was something about her you could feel, like an electric charge. I am rambling on, aren't I? Do you know what I mean?'

'I think so, Mr Ackroyd.' Some women just gave out an aura of sex, Gristhorpe knew. That kind of sex appeal was common enough on screen – the way Marilyn Monroe's clothes always seemed to want to slip off her body, for example – but it also happened in real life. It was nothing to do with looks, though a combination of beauty and sex appeal could be deadly when it occurred, and some women didn't even realize they had it.

'How did Mr Manley act towards her?' he asked.

'No special way in particular. I mean, he wasn't much to look at himself. I got the impression he was sort of pleased that so many men obviously fancied her. You knew she was *his* and you could look but you couldn't touch. Now I think about it, he definitely seemed to be showing her off, like.'

'Nobody tried to chat her up?'

'No.' He scratched his cheek. 'And that's a funny thing, you know. Now you've got me talking I'm thinking things that never really entered my head at the time. They were just an interesting couple of holidaymakers, but the more I think about them . . .'

'Yes?'

'Well, the thing that really struck you about Chris was his smile. When he smiled at you, you immediately wanted to trust him. I suppose it worked with the women too. But there was something . . . I mean, I can't put my finger on it, but you just sort of *knew* that if you really did try it on with Connie, outside a bit of mild flirting, that is, then he'd be something to reckon with. That's the only way I can express it. I suppose everyone picked up on that because nobody tried it on. Not even Andy Lumsden, and he goes after anything in a skirt as a rule.'

'Where were they from?'

'Chris and Connie? Do you know, I couldn't tell you. He didn't have a Yorkshire accent, that's for certain. But it was hard to place. South, maybe. It was sort of character-less, like those television newsreaders.'

'They didn't say where they were from?'

'Come to think of it, no. Just said they were taking some time off and travelling around for a while, having a rest from the fast lane. They never really said anything about themselves. Funny that, isn't it?'

'They didn't even say what they were taking time off from?'

'No.'

Gristhorpe stood up and nodded to Richmond. He shook Mr Ackroyd's good hand and wished him well, then they walked back out into the drizzle.

'What now?' Richmond asked.

Gristhorpe looked at his watch. 'It's half past two,' he said. 'I reckon we've just got time for a pint and a sandwich at the Drayman's Rest, don't you?'

FOUR

Susan Gay parked her red Golf outside and went up to her flat. She had had a busy day going over mugshots with Edwina Whixley – to no avail – and questioning the other occupants of 59 Calvin Street again. She had also made an appointment to see the governor of Armley Jail, where Johnson had served his time, at four-thirty the following afternoon. She knew she could probably have asked him questions over the phone, but phone calls, she always felt, were too open to interruptions, and too limiting. If the governor needed to consult a warden for additional information, for example, that might prove difficult over the phone. Besides, she was old-fashioned; she liked to be able to watch people's eyes when she talked to them.

She put her briefcase by the door and dropped her keys on the hall table. She had made a lot of changes to the place since her promotion to CID. It had once been little more than a hotel suite, somewhere to sleep. But now she had plants and a growing collection of books and records.

Susan favoured the more traditional, romantic kind of classical music, the ones you remember bits from and find yourself humming along with now and then: Beethoven, Tchaikovsky, Chopin, bits of opera from films and TV adverts. Most of her records were 'greatest hits', so she didn't have their complete symphonies or anything, just the movements everyone remembered.

Her reading was still limited mostly to technical stuff, like forensics and criminology, but she made space on her shelves for the occasional Jeffrey Archer, Dick Francis and Robert Ludlum. Banks wouldn't approve of her tastes, she was sure, but at least now she knew she *had* tastes.

As usual, if she was in, she had *Calendar* on the television as she fussed around in the kitchen throwing together a salad. Normally, she would just be listening, as the TV set was in the living room, but this evening, an item caught her attention and she walked through, salad bowl in hand and stood and watched open-mouthed.

It was Brenda Scupham and a gypsyish-looking woman on the couch being interviewed. She hadn't caught the introduction, but they were talking about clairvoyance. Brenda, in a tight lemon chiffon blouse tucked into a black miniskirt much too short for a worried mother, sat staring blankly into the camera, while the other woman explained how objects dear to people bear psychic traces of them and act as conduits into the extrasensory world.

Brenda nodded in agreement occasionally. When Richard Whiteley turned to her and asked her what she thought, she said, 'I don't know. I really don't know,' then she looked over at the other woman. 'But I'm convinced my Gemma is still alive and I want to beg whoever knows where she is to let her come back to her mother, please. You won't be punished, I promise.'

'What about the police?' he asked. 'What do they think?'

Brenda shook her head. 'I don't know,' she said. 'I think they believe she's dead. Ever since they found her clothes, I think they've given up on her.'

Susan flopped into her armchair, salad forgotten for the moment. Bloody hell, she thought, Superintendent Gristhorpe's going to *love* this.

9

ONE

Gristhorpe was indeed furious when he heard about Brenda Scupham's television appearance. As he had no TV set of his own, though, he didn't find out until Wednesday morning.

'It's been over a week now since Gemma Scupham disappeared,' he said, shaking his head over coffee and toasted teacakes with Banks at the Golden Grill. 'I can't say I hold out much hope. Especially since we found the clothes.'

'I can't either,' Banks agreed. 'But Brenda Scupham's got some bloody psychic to convince her that Gemma's alive. Who would you rather listen to, if you were her?'

'I suppose you're right. Anyway, it all connects: the abandoned cottage, the borrowed car, the hair-dye. We've got descriptions of the Manleys out – both as themselves and as Peterson and Brown. Somebody, somewhere must know them. How about you?'

Banks sipped some hot black coffee. 'Not much. The lab finally came through with the scene analysis. The blood in the mill matched Johnson's, so we can be pretty certain that's where he was killed. Glendenning says it was a right-handed upthrust wound. Six-inch blade, single-edged. Probably some kind of sheath-knife, and you know how common those are. No handy footprints or tyre tracks, and no sign of the weapon. I'm off to see Harkness again, though I don't suppose it'll do much good.'

'You think he did it?'

'Apart from the mysterious stranger seen leaving Johnson's building, he's the only lead I've got. I keep telling myself that just because I didn't take to the man it doesn't mean he's a killer. But nobody gets that rich without making a few enemies. And Johnson was a crook. He *could* have been involved somewhere along the line.'

'Aye, maybe you're right. Be careful, though, the last thing I need right now is the ACC on my back.'

Banks laughed. 'You know me. Diplomacy personified.'

'Aye, well . . . I'd better be off to see Mrs Scupham. See if I can't talk some sense into her. I want a word with that bloody psychic, too. I've got Phil out looking for her.' He looked outside. A fine mist nuzzled the window.

'Hang on a minute, sir,' Banks said. 'You know, Brenda Scupham might be right.'

'What?'

'If Gemma *is* alive, a television appeal won't do any harm. It might even do some good.'

'I realize that. We can't have any idea what the woman's going through. All I want to do is reassure her that we *are* doing the best we can. If Gemma is alive, we've more chance of finding her than some bloody tea-leaf reader. There's a trail to follow somewhere in all this, and I think we're picking it up. But these people, the Manleys or whatever they call themselves now, they talked to enough people, got on well enough with the locals, but they gave nothing away. We don't even know where they come from, and we can't be sure what they look like, either. They're still two-dimensional.'

'What about the notes they used to pay for the cottage?'

'Patricia Cummings, the estate agent, said she paid the cash directly into the bank. Right now it's mixed up with all the rest of the money they've got in their vaults.'

'How did they hear about the cottage? Did they say?'

'Told her they'd read about it in *The Dalesman*.'

'You could get—'

'I know, I know – the list of subscribers. We're checking on it. But you can buy *The Dalesman* at almost any newsagent's, in this part of the country, anyway.'

'Just a thought.'

Gristhorpe finished his teacake and wiped his mouth with the paper serviette. 'At the moment it looks like our best bet lies with the descriptions – if that's what they really look like. Christ knows, maybe they're Hollywood special-effects people underneath it all. We've got the artist working with Ackroyd and the crowd in the Drayman's Rest. Should be ready for tomorrow's papers. And I was thinking about the whitewash they found on Gemma's clothes, too. I've seen it in two places recently: Melville Westman's, the Satanist, or whatever he calls himself, and the holiday cottage.'

'I suppose the Manleys could have kept Gemma there,' Banks said. 'Perhaps they drugged her. She's not very big. It wouldn't be difficult to get her out of the cottage after dark.'

'Aye, that's true enough. Still, I'm getting a warrant and sending a few lads to give Westman's place a good going-over.'

'You don't like him any better than I like Harkness, do you?'

Gristhorpe grinned. 'No,' he said. 'No, I don't.' He pushed his chair back. 'Must be off. See you later, Alan.' And he walked out into Market Street.

TWO

Adam Harkness's house clearly hadn't been vacuumed or tidied since Banks's last visit. At least a crackling fire took the chill out of the damp air in the library. The french windows were firmly closed. Beyond the streaked glass, drops of rain pitted the river's surface. Lyndgarth and Aldington Edge were shrouded in a veil of low grey cloud.

'Please, sit down,' Harkness said. 'Now what can I do for you, Chief Inspector? Have you found Carl's killer?'

Banks rubbed his hands in front of the fire, then sat. 'Not yet,' he said. 'There's a couple of points you might be able to help me clear up, though.'

Harkness raised a challenging eyebrow and sat in the chair opposite Banks. 'Yes?'

'We've learned that Johnson might have met with a certain individual on a couple of occasions shortly before his murder. Did he talk to you about any of his friends?'

'I've already told you. He was my gardener. He came a couple of times a week and kept the garden in trim. That's all.'

'Is it? Please think about it, Mr Harkness. Even if Johnson was only the hired help, it would be perfectly natural to have a bit of a chat now and then about innocuous stuff, wouldn't it?' He felt that he was giving Harkness a fair chance to come up with something he might have forgotten or chosen not to admit earlier, but it did no good.

Harkness folded his hands in his lap. 'I knew nothing whatsoever about Carl Johnson's private life. The moment he left my property, his life was his own, and I neither know nor care what he did.'

'Even if it was of a criminal nature?'

'You might believe he was irredeemably branded as a criminal. I do not. Besides, as I keep telling you, I have no knowledge of his activities, criminal or otherwise.'

Banks described the man Edwina Whixley had seen coming down the stairs of Johnson's building: thickset, medium height, short dark hair, squarish head. 'Ever see or hear about him?'

Harkness shook his head. 'Carl always came here alone. He never introduced me to any of his colleagues.'

'So you never saw this man?'

'No.'

'How did Johnson get here?'

'What?'

'Carl Johnson? How did he get here? He didn't have a car.'

'There are still buses, Chief Inspector, including a fairly regular service from Eastvale to Lyndgarth. There's a bus stop just by the bridge.'

'Of course. Did Johnson ever mention any of his old prison friends?'

'What? Not to me. It would hardly have been appropriate, would it?' Harkness picked up the poker and jabbed at the fire. 'Look, why don't you save us both a lot of wasted time and energy and accept that I'm telling the truth when I say I knew *nothing* about Carl's private life?'

'I don't know what gives you the impression I don't believe you.'

'Your attitude, for a start, and the questions you keep on asking over and over again.'

'Sir,' said Banks, 'you have to understand that this is a murder investigation. People forget things. Sometimes they don't realize the importance of what they know. All I'm doing is trying to jog your memory into giving up *something* that Johnson might have let slip in a moment of idle chatter. Anything. It might mean nothing at all to you – a name, a date, an opinion, whatever – but it might be vital to us.'

Harkness paused. 'Well . . . of course, yes . . . I suppose I see what you mean. The thing is, though, there really *is* nothing. I'm sure if he'd said anything I would have remembered it by now. The fact is we just didn't talk beyond discussing the garden and the weather. Basically, we had nothing else in common. He seemed a reticent sort of fellow, anyway, kept himself to himself, and that suited me fine. Also, remember, I'm often away on business.'

'Was there ever any evidence that Johnson had used the house in your absence?'

'What do you mean, "used the house"? For what purpose?'

'I don't know. I assume he had a key?'

'Yes. But . . .'

'Nothing was ever out of place?'

'No. Are you suggesting he might have been stealing things?'

'No. I don't think even Carl Johnson would have been that stupid. To be honest, I don't know what I'm getting at.' Banks scratched his head and glanced at the river and copper beech, leaves dripping, beyond the french windows. 'This is a fairly out-of-the-way place. It could be suitable for criminal activities in any number of ways.'

'I noticed nothing,' Harkness said, with a thin smile. 'Not even a muddy footprint on my carpet.'

'You see,' Banks went on, 'Johnson's life is a bit of a mystery to us. We've got his record, the bald facts. But how did he think? We don't seem to be able to find anyone who was close to him. And there are years missing. He may have been to Europe, Amsterdam perhaps. He may even have had friends from South Africa.'

Harkness sat bolt upright and gripped the arms of the chair. 'What are you insinuating?'

'I've heard rumours of some sort of a scandal. Something involving you back in South Africa. There was some sort of cover-up. Do you know what I'm talking about?'

Harkness snorted. 'There are always scandals surrounding the wealthy, Chief Inspector. You ought to know that. Usually they derive from envy. No, I can't say I do know what you're talking about.'

'But was there any such scandal involving you or your family out there?'

'No, nothing that stands out.'

Banks got that almost-infallible tingle that told him Harkness was holding back. He gave his man-of-the-world shrug. 'Of course, I'm not suggesting there was any truth in it, but we have to investigate everything that comes up.'

Harkness stood up. 'It seems to me that you are spending an unusual amount of time investigating *me* when you should be looking for Carl Johnson's killer. I suggest you look among his criminal cronies for your killer.'

'You've got a point, there. And, believe me, we're trying to track them down. Just out of interest, did Johnson ever mention South Africa to you?'

'No, he did not. And don't think I don't know what you're getting at. You're suggesting he was blackmailing me over some secret or other, aren't you, and that I killed him to silence him? Come on, is that what you're getting at?'

Banks stood up and spoke slowly. 'But you couldn't have killed him, could you, sir? You were dining at the Golf Club at the time of the murder. A number of very influential people saw you there.' He regarded Harkness, who maintained an expression of outraged dignity, then said, 'Thank you very much for your time,' and left.

As he drove down to the main road with the windscreen-wipers tapping time to Gurney's 'Sleep', he smiled to himself. He had got at least some of what he had wanted: a sure sense that Harkness was holding something back; and the satisfying knowledge that the man, rich, confident and powerful notwithstanding, could be rattled. Time now to make a few overseas phone calls, then perhaps have another chat with Mr Adam Harkness.

THREE

'You think I acted dishonestly, is that what you're saying?'

'Irresponsibly is the word I had in mind,' Gristhorpe replied. He was sitting opposite Lenora Carlyle in a small interview room at the station. A WPC sat by the window to take notes. With her wild black hair, her high, prominent cheekbones and blazing dark eyes, Lenora certainly looked dramatic. She seemed composed as she sat there, he noticed, arms folded across her jumper, a slightly superior smile revealing stained teeth. It was the kind of smile, Gristhorpe thought, that she probably reserved for the poor, lost believers with whom she no doubt had to deal now and then.

'I do my job, Superintendent,' she said, 'and you do yours.'

'And just what is your job? In this case it seems to consist of giving a poor woman false hope.' Gristhorpe had just been to see Brenda Scupham, and he had noticed the fervour in her eyes when she spoke of what Lenora had told her.

'I can tell there's no convincing you, but I don't happen to believe it's false. Look, are you upset because Brenda criticized you on television? Is that why you've got me in here?'

'What was the source of your information about Gemma Scupham?'

'I'm a psychic. You know that already.'

'So the "other side" is the source?'

'If you want to put it like that, yes.'

'Are you sure?'

'What are you getting at?'

Gristhorpe leaned back and rested his forearms on the table. 'Ms Carlyle, we're investigating the abduction of a child, a very serious crime, and one that happens to be especially odious to me. All of a sudden, you walk into Brenda Scupham's house and tell her you know the child is still alive. I'd be a bloody idiot if I didn't ask you *how* you know.'

'I've told you.'

'Aye. And, as you well know, I don't happen to believe in convenient messages from the other side.'

She smiled. 'It's stalemate, isn't it, then?'

'No, it isn't. Are you aware that I could hold you if I wanted?'

'What do you mean?'

'You profess to have information about a missing child, but you won't reveal your source. As far as I know, you could have something to do with Gemma Scupham's disappearance.'

'Now look here—'

'No. *You* look here. If that child *is* alive and you know

something that could help us find her, you'd better tell me, because I'm getting tired of this.'

'I only know what I told Brenda – that Gemma is alive, she's scared and she wants her mother. You know, you'd do much better with an open mind. The police *have* used psychics to help them in the past.'

And a fat lot of good it's done, thought Gristhorpe, feeling himself being manipulated into the position of doing exactly that. The woman might know something, after all, and he couldn't dismiss the possibility, even if it meant playing her game. 'All right.' He sighed. 'Did you get any impressions about where she is?'

Lenora shook her head.

'Any images, sounds, smells?'

'Nothing like that. Just an overwhelming emotional sense of her presence somewhere. Alive. And her fear.'

'Near or far?'

'I can't say.'

Gristhorpe scratched his chin. 'Not much to go on, is it?'

'I can't help that. I'm merely a medium for the messages. Do you want to consult me professionally? Do you want me to try and help you?'

Gristhorpe noticed the smile of triumph. 'Ms Carlyle,' he shot back, 'if you *fail* to help us, I'll make sure you're thrown in jail. Do you know Melville Westman?'

It was only fleeting, but he saw it, a split-second sign of recognition. It was second nature for him to notice the signs, the body language, the way eye-contact broke off. He could see her trying to decide how much to admit. 'Well?' he prodded.

'The name sounds vaguely familiar,' she said with a toss of her head. 'I might have come across him.'

'Let me fill you in. Melville Westman calls himself a magician. There have been incidents in the past few years of such groups using children in their rituals. Now, I don't know what you're up to, but if you and Westman have any involvement in Gemma's disappearance, direct or indirect, I'll find out about it.'

'This is ridiculous!' Lenora said. 'I've had enough of your accusations and insinuations.' She tried to push the chair back to get to her feet, but forgot it was bolted to the floor and she got stuck, half-standing, between it and the table.

'Sit down.' Gristhorpe waved his hand. 'I haven't finished yet. What's your connection with Westman?'

She sat down, chewed on her lower lip for a moment, and answered, 'I know him, that's all. We're acquaintances.'

'Met at the magician's circle, did you?'

'You don't have to be sarcastic. It's a small community for anyone interested in the occult. We've had discussions, loaned one another books, that's all.'

'I'm asking you if Westman has told you anything about Gemma Scupham's whereabouts. Are you some kind of messenger, some salve to the conscience come to spare the mother a little pain until you've finished with the child? Or are you just tormenting her?'

'Don't be absurd. What would Melville want with the child?'

'You tell me.'

'He wouldn't. He's not that kind.'

'What kind?'

'The kind that performs elaborate rituals, sacrifices animals and . . .'

'Children?'

'Look, I'm not denying there are lunatic fringes around, but Melville Westman doesn't belong to one.'

'Is there anyone in the area you would associate with a lunatic fringe?'

'No.'

'Ever heard of the Manleys? Chris and Connie. Or Miss Peterson and Mr Brown?'

'No.'

'Did Melville Westman send you?'

'No, he bloody well didn't. I came forward to help the mother of my own free will,' Lenora said through clenched teeth. 'And this is how you treat me. I thought the police would—'

'You know nothing about the way we work, or you'd hardly have had Brenda Scupham shooting her mouth off on television.'

'That wasn't my doing.'

'It doesn't matter whose doing it was. It happened. And if that child *is* dead, I want you to think of how much harm you've done her mother.'

Lenora put her fist to her heart. 'The child is alive, Superintendent. I'm convinced of it.'

For a moment, Gristhorpe was taken aback by the passion in her voice. After everything he had accused her of, she was still clinging to her original story. He let the silence stretch for a while longer, holding her intense gaze. He could feel something pass across the air between them. He couldn't put his finger on what it was, a tingling sensation, the hackles on his neck rising, and he certainly had no idea whether or not she was right about Gemma. He did know, though, that she was telling the truth as far as she knew it. The damn woman was genuine in her beliefs. He could see, now, how Brenda Scupham had been convinced.

'I want you to know', he said slowly, 'that I'll check and

double-check on everything you've told me.' Then he broke off the staring match and looked towards the bare wall. 'Now get out. Go on, get out before I change my mind.' And he didn't even turn to watch her go. He knew exactly the kind of smile he would see on her face.

FOUR

Armley Jail was built in 1847 by Perkin and Backhouse. Standing on a low hill to the west of the city centre, it looks like a structure from the Middle Ages, with its keep and battlements all in dark, solid stone – especially in the iron-grey sky and the rain that swept across the scene. Eastvale Castle seemed welcoming in comparison, Susan thought. Even the modern addition to the prison couldn't quite overcome the sense of dank medieval dungeons she felt as she approached the gates. The architects could hardly have come up with a place more likely to terrify the criminals and reassure the good citizens, she thought, giving a shiver as she got out of the car and felt the rain sting her cheek.

She showed her warrant card, and at four-thirty on that dreary September afternoon, the prison gates admitted her, and a uniformed attendant led her to a small office in the administrative block to meet Gerald Mackenzie. She had found herself wondering on her way what kind of person felt drawn to prison work. It must be a strange world, she thought, locked in with the malcontents. Like the police, the prison service probably attracted its share of bullies, but it also had an appeal, she guessed, for the reformers, for people who believed in rehabilitation. For many, perhaps, it was just a job, a source of income to pay the mortgage and help feed the wife and kids.

Mackenzie turned out to be a surprisingly young man with thin brown hair, matching suit, a crisp white shirt and what she took to be a regimental or club tie of some kind. The black-framed glasses he wore gave him the look of a middle-management man. He was polite, offered coffee, and seemed happy enough to give her the time and information she wanted.

'From what I can remember,' he said, placing a finger at the corner of his small mouth, 'Johnson was a fairly unassuming sort of fellow. Never caused any trouble. Never drew attention to himself.' He shook his head. 'In fact, I find it very hard to believe he ended up the way he did. Unless he was the victim of some random crime?'

'We don't think so,' Susan said. 'How did he spend his time?'

'He was a keen gardener, I remember. Never went in much for the more intellectual pursuits or the team games.'

'Was he much of a socializer in any way?'

'No. As I said, I got the impression he kept very much to himself. I must confess, it's hard to keep abreast of everyone we have in here – unless they're troublemakers of course. The well-behaved ones you tend to leave to themselves. It's like teaching, I suppose. I've done a bit of that, you know. You spend most of your energy on the difficult students and leave the good ones to fend for themselves. I mean, there's always far more to say about a wrong answer than a right one, isn't there?'

'I suppose so,' said Susan. The memory of an essay she wrote at police college came to mind. When the professor had handed it back to her, it had been covered in red ink. 'So Johnson was an exemplary prisoner?'

'Inmate. Well, yes. Yes, he was.'

'And you don't know a lot more about him, his routine, his contacts here?'

'No. I don't actually spend much time on the shop floor, so to speak. Administration, paperwork . . . it all seems to take up so much time these days. But look, I'll see if I can get Ollie Watson to come in. He worked Johnson's wing.'

'Would you?'

'No trouble.'

Mackenzie ducked out of the office for a moment and Susan examined a framed picture of a pretty dark-skinned woman, Indian perhaps, with three small children. Mackenzie's family, she assumed, judging by the way the children shared both his and the woman's features: a certain slant to the nose here, a dimple there.

A few minutes later, Mackenzie returned with Ollie Watson. As soon as she saw the fat, uniformed man with the small black moustache, Susan wondered if the 'Ollie' was a nickname because the man looked so much like Oliver Hardy. He pulled at the creases of his trousers and sat down on a chair, which creaked under him.

'Mr Watson,' Susan said after the introductions, 'Mr Mackenzie tells me you're in the best position to give me some information about Carl Johnson's time in here.'

Watson nodded. 'Yes, ma'm.' He shifted in his seat. It creaked again. 'No trouble, Carl wasn't. But you never felt you ever got to *know* him, like you do with some. Never seemed much interested in anything, 'cept the garden, I suppose.'

'Did he have friends?'

'Not close ones, no. He didn't mix much. And people left him alone. Not because they were scared of him or anything. Just . . . there was something remote about him. It was as if they hardly even noticed him most of the time.'

'What about his cell-mates? Did he share?'

'Most of the time, yes.' He smiled. 'As you probably know, it gets a bit overcrowded in here. Must be because you lot are doing such a good job.'

Susan laughed. 'Us or the courts. Was there anyone in particular?'

'Let me see . . .' Watson held out his hand and counted them off on his fingers. 'There was Addison, that's one. Basically harmless, I'd say. Business fraud. Then there was Rodgers. No real problems there, either. Just possession . . .'

'Johnson was brutally murdered,' Susan butted in on Watson's leisurely thought process. 'Did he meet anyone you think capable of doing that?'

'Good lord, no. Not in here,' said Watson, as if prison were the last place on earth where one would expect to find real evil-doers. 'He was never in with any of the really hard, serious lags. We keep them separate as best we can.'

'But someone could have involved him in a criminal scheme, something that went wrong? Drugs, perhaps?'

'I suppose it's possible. But Rodgers was only in for possession of marijuana. He wasn't a dealer.'

'What about the business fraud?'

'Like I said, he was harmless enough. Just the old purchasing scam.'

Susan nodded. She had come across that before. A purchasing officer for a large company simply rents some office space, a phone and headed stationery, then he 'supplies' his company with goods or services that don't exist and pockets the payment. He has to be careful to charge only small amounts, so the purchase orders don't have to go to higher management for signing. If it can be worked carefully and slowly over a number of years, the purchasing scam can prove extremely lucrative, but most practitioners get greedy and make mistakes.

'Could he have got Johnson involved in something more ambitious? After all, Johnson was a bit of a con-man himself.'

Watson shook his head. 'Prison took the life out of Addison. It does that to some people. You're on the job long enough you get to recognize the signs, who'll be back and who won't. Addison won't. He'll be straight as a die from now on. He was just a mild-mannered clerk fancied a crack at the high life.'

Susan nodded, but she had already noted Addison's name in her book. 'What about the others?'

'Aye,' Watson lifted his hand again. 'Who did we say . . . Addison, then the possession fellow, Rodgers. Then there was Poole. I wouldn't worry about him, either.'

'Poole?' said Susan, suddenly alert. 'What was his first name?'

'Leslie. But everyone called him Les. Funny-looking bloke, too. One of those old-fashioned Elvis Presley haircuts.' Watson laughed. 'Until the prison barber got to him, that is. From what he said, though, the women seemed—'

But Susan was no longer listening. She couldn't help but feel a sudden surge of joy. She had one-upped Richmond. With all his courses, caches and megabytes, he hadn't discovered what she had by sheer old-fashioned legwork. He was working on the Gemma Scupham case, of course, not the Johnson murder, but still . . .

'Sorry for interrupting,' she apologized to Watson, then looked at Mackenzie. 'May I use your phone, sir?'

10

ONE

In the evening beyond the venetian blinds in Banks's office, puddles gleamed between the cobbles, and water dripped from the crossbars of lamp-posts, from eaves and awnings. Muted light glowed behind the red and amber windows of the Queen's Arms, and he could hear the buzz of laughter and conversation from inside. The square itself was quiet except for the occasional click of high heels on cobbles as someone walked home from work late or went out on a date. An occasional gust of cool evening air wafted through his partly open window, bringing with it that peculiar fresh and sharp after-the-rain smell. It made him think of an old John Coltrane tune that captured in music just such a sense of an evening after rain. He could make out the gold hands against the blue face of the church clock: almost eight. He lit a cigarette. The gaslights around the square – an affectation for tourists – came on, dim at first, then brighter, reflecting in twisted sheets of incandescent light among the puddles. It was the time of day Banks loved most, not being much of a morning person, but his epiphany was interrupted by a knock at the office door, shortly followed by PC Tolliver and DC Susan Gay leading in an agitated Les Poole.

'Found him at the Crown and Anchor, sir,' explained Tolliver. 'Sorry it took so long. It's not one of his usual haunts.'

'Bit up-market for you, isn't it, Les?' Banks said. 'Come into some money lately?'

Poole just grunted and worked at his Elvis Presley sneer. Tolliver left and Susan Gay sat down in the chair beside the door getting out her notebook and pen. Banks gestured for Poole to sit opposite him at the desk. Poole was wearing jeans and a leather jacket over a turquoise T-shirt, taut over his bulging stomach. Even from across the desk, Banks could smell the beer on his breath.

'Now then, Les,' he said, 'you might be wondering why we've dragged you away from the pub this evening?'

Les Poole shifted in his chair and said nothing; his features settled in a sullen and hard-done-by expression.

'Well, Les?'

'Dunno.'

'Have a guess.'

'You found out something about Gemma?'

'Wrong. I'm working on another case now, Les. The super's taken that one over.'

Poole shrugged. 'Dunno then. Look, shouldn't I have a brief?'

'Up to you. We haven't charged you with anything yet. You're just helping us with our inquiries.'

'Still . . . what do you want?'

'Information.'

'About what?'

'Can you read, Les?'

'Course I can.'

'Read the papers?'

'Now and then. Sporting pages mostly. I mean, most of your actual news is bad, isn't it? Why bother depressing yourself, I always say.'

Banks scratched the thin scar beside his right eye.

'Quite. How about the telly? That nice new one you've got.'

Poole half rose. 'Now look, if this is about that—'

'Relax, Les. Sit down. It's not about the Fletcher's warehouse job, the one you were going to tell me you know nothing about. Though we might get back to that a bit later. No, this is much more serious.'

Poole sat down and folded his arms. 'I don't know what you're on about.'

'Then let me make it clear. I can do it in two words, Les: Carl Johnson. Remember, the bloke I asked you about a couple of days ago, the one you said you'd never heard of?'

'Who?'

'You heard.'

'So what. I still don't know no Ben Johnson.'

'It's Carl, Les. As in Carl Lewis. Better pay more attention to those sporting pages, hadn't you? And I think it was a bit too much of a slip to be convincing. Don't you, Susan?'

Banks looked over Poole's shoulder at Susan Gay, who sat by the door. She nodded. Poole glanced around and glared at her, then turned back, tilted his head to one side and pretended to examine the calendar on the office wall, a scene of the waterfalls at Aysgarth in full spate.

'According to the governor of Armley Jail,' Susan said, reading from her notes to give the statement authority, 'a Mr Leslie Poole shared a cell with a Mr Carl Johnson for six months about four years ago.'

'Bit of a coincidence, isn't it, Les?' Banks said.

Poole looked up defiantly. 'What if it is? I can't be expected to remember everyone I meet, can I?'

'Have we refreshed your memory?'

'Yeah, well . . . now you mention it. But it was a different bloke. Same name, all right, but a different bloke.'

'Different from whom?'

'The one you mean.'

'How do you know which one I mean?'

'Stands to reason, dunnit? The bloke who got killed.'

'Ah. That's better, Les. And here was me thinking you weren't up on current affairs. How did you hear about it?'

'Saw it on the telly, didn't I? On the news. Someone gets croaked around these parts you can't help but hear about it somewhere.'

'Good. Now seeing as this Carl Johnson you heard about on the news is the same Carl Johnson you shared a cell with in Armley Jail—'

'I told you, it was a different bloke!'

Banks sighed. 'Les, don't give me this crap. I'm tired and I'm hungry. I haven't eaten since elevenses, and here I am sticking around out of the goodness of my heart just to talk to you. I'm trying to be very civilized about this. That's why we're in my nice comfortable office just having a friendly chat instead of in some smelly interview room. Listen, Les, we've got prison records, we've got fingerprints, we've got warders who remember. Believe me, it was the same person.'

'Well, bugger me!' Les said, sitting up sharply. 'What a turn-up for the book. Poor old Carl, eh? And here was me hoping it must have been someone else.'

Banks sighed. 'Very touching, Les. When did you last see him?'

'Oh, years ago. How long was it you said? Four years.'

'You haven't seen him since you came out?'

'No. Why should I?'

'No reason, I suppose. Except maybe that you both live in the same town.'

'Eastvale ain't that small.'

'Still,' said Banks, 'it's a bit of a coincidence, isn't it? He's been in Eastvale a few months now. It strikes me that, given your records, the two of you might have got together to do a little creative thievery. Like the Fletcher's warehouse job, for example. I'm sure Carl was versatile enough for that.'

'Now there you go again, accusing me of that. I ain't done nothing.'

'Les, we could drive down to your house right now, pick up the television and the compact music centre, maybe even the video, too, and likely as not *prove* they came from that job.'

'Brenda bought those in good faith.'

'Bollocks, Les. What's it to be?'

Poole licked his lips. 'You wouldn't,' he said. 'You wouldn't dare go and take them away, not after what's happened to poor Brenda.' A sly smile came to his face. 'Think how bad it would look in the papers.'

'Don't push me, Les.' Banks spoke quietly, but the menace in his voice came through clearly. 'What we're dealing with here is a man who was gutted. Ever been fishing, Les? Ever cleaned a fish? You take one of those sharp knives and slit its gullet open to empty the entrails. Well, someone took a knife like that, someone who must have known Carl Johnson pretty well to get so close to him in such a remote spot, and stuck the knife in just above his balls and dragged it slowly up his guts, sliced his belly button in two, until it got stuck on the chest bone. And Carl's insides opened up and spilled like a bag of offal, Les. If his jacket hadn't been zipped up afterwards they'd have spilled all over the bloody dale.' He pointed at Poole's beer belly. 'Do you know how many yards of intestine you've got in there? Are you seriously telling me that I'll let a few stolen electrical goods get in the way of my finding out who did that?'

Poole held his stomach and paled. 'It wasn't me, Mr Banks. Honest, it wasn't. I've got to go to the toilet. I need a piss.'

Banks turned away. 'Go.'

Poole opened the door, and Banks asked the uniformed PC standing there to escort him to the gents.

Banks turned to Susan. 'What do you think?'

'I think he's close, sir,' she said.

'To what?'

'To telling us what he knows.'

'Mm,' said Banks. 'Some of it, maybe. He's a slippery bugger is Les.'

He lit a cigarette. A short while later, Poole returned and resumed his seat.

'You were saying, Les?'

'That I'd nothing to do with it.'

'No,' said Banks. 'I don't believe you had. For one thing, you haven't got the bottle. Just for the record, though, where were you last Thursday evening?'

'Thursday? . . . Let me see. I was helping my mate in his shop on Rampart Street.'

'You seem to spend a lot of time at this place, Les. I never took you for a hard worker before, maybe I was wrong. What do you do there?'

'This and that.'

'Be more specific, Les.'

'I help out, don't I? Make deliveries, serve customers, lug stuff around.'

'What's your mate's name again?'

'John.'

'John what.'

'John Fairley. It's just a junk shop. You know, old 78s, second-hand furniture, the odd antique. Nothing really valuable. We empty out old people's houses, when they snuff it, like.'

'Nothing new? No televisions, stereos, videos?'

'You're at it again. I told you I had nothing to do with that. Let it drop.'

'What's he look like, this John Fairley?'

'Pretty ordinary.'

'You can do better than that.'

'I'm not very good at this sort of thing. He's strong, you know, stocky, muscular. He's a nice bloke, John, decent as they come.'

'What colour's his hair?'

'Black. Like yours.'

But Banks could see the guilt and anxiety in Poole's eyes. John's shop was where they fenced the stuff, all right, and John Fairley's description matched that of the man Edwina Whixley had seen coming down from Carl Johnson's flat, vague as it was.

'Do we know him, Les?'

'Shouldn't think so. I told you, he's straight.'

'If I went to see this mate of yours, this John, he'd tell me you were in the shop all evening Thursday, would he?'

'Well, not *all* evening. We worked a bit late, unloading a van full of stuff from some old codger from the Leaview Estate who croaked a few weeks back.'

'What time did you finish?'

'About seven o'clock.'

'And where did you go after that?'

'Pub.'

'Of course. Which one?'

'Well, first we went to the Oak. That's the nearest to Rampart Street. Had a couple there, just to rinse the dust out of my mouth, like, then later we went down the local, the Barleycorn.'

'I assume you were seen at these places?'

'I suppose so. That's what I did. Cross my heart and hope to die.'

'I wouldn't do that, Les.'

'What?'

'Hope to die. Look what happened to Carl Johnson.'

Poole swallowed. 'That's got nothing to do with me.'

'But we don't know why he was killed, do we? Let's just take a hypothetical scenario, all right? A sort of falling out among thieves. Say Carl was involved in the Fletcher's warehouse job, and say there were two or three others in on it as well. Now, maybe Carl got too greedy, or maybe he tried to stick away a few pieces of merchandise for himself – like one of his accomplices might have done, too – you know, a nice new telly, and maybe a stereo. Follow my drift so far?'

Poole nodded.

'Good. So let's say one of these thieves doesn't have much regard for human life. He gets mad at Carl, arranges to meet him to discuss the problem, persuades him to go for a ride, then guts him. Now, what do you think this bloke, who's already killed once, might do if he gets wind there's a problem with *another* of his accomplices?'

Poole's jaw dropped.

'What's wrong, Les? Cat got your tongue?'

Poole shook his head. 'Nothing. I ain't done nothing.'

'So you keep saying. Say it often enough and *you* might

believe it, but I won't. Are you sure there's nothing you want to tell me, Les? Maybe you met this bloke, or maybe Carl talked about him. I'd hate to have to hang around some filthy old lead mine while the doc tried to stuff you into a body sack without spilling your guts all over the dirt.'

Poole put his hands over his ears. 'Stop it!' he yelled. 'It's not bloody fair. You can't do this to me!'

Banks slammed the desk. 'Yes, I bloody well can,' he said. 'And I'll go on doing it until I find out the truth. If I have to, I'll lock you up. More likely I'll just let you go and tell the press you were kind enough to give us a few tips on the warehouse job. What's it to be, Les? Your choice.'

Poole looked around the office like a caged animal. Seeing no way out, he sagged in his chair and muttered, 'All right. You're a bastard, you know.'

Banks glanced over at Susan Gay. She turned a page in her notebook.

'Look, about this 'ypo-whatsit story of yours,' Poole said.

'Hypothetical.'

'That's right. I mean, you can't pin owt on anyone for just telling an 'ypothetical story, can you?'

Banks grabbed his coffee mug, pushed his chair back, put his feet on the desk and lit a cigarette. 'Maybe, maybe not,' he said. 'Just tell us about the bloke, Les. Talk to me. I'm listening.'

'Yeah, well, I did bump into Carl a couple of times, accidental like. We had a jar or two now and then, talked about old times. There was this mate he mentioned. I didn't want to say before because I didn't want to get involved, not now that I'm going straight and all— What's up with you?'

'Sorry, Les,' Banks said. 'Just a bit of coffee went down the wrong way. Carry on. Tell me about this mate of Carl's.'

Poole scowled. 'Anyway, I remembered from the time inside, like, this bloke he used to talk about sometimes, like it was his hero or something. I never met him myself, but just hearing about him gave me the creeps. Funny that, like Carl seemed to get some kind of kick out of telling me about this bloke and what he did and all that, but to me it was a bit over the top. I mean, I'm no fucking angel, I'll admit that, but I've got my limits. I never hurt anyone. Remember, this is all 'ypothetical.'

'The man, Les.'

'Hold on, I'm getting to him. Anyways, as I was saying, Carl said he was here in Eastvale. Well, that's when I cut out. I didn't want nothing to do with them. I didn't want to get mixed up in anything.'

'What didn't you want to get mixed up in, Les?'

'You know, anything, like, criminal.'

'I see. Were they in on Fletcher's warehouse job? Johnson and this other bloke?'

'I think so. But like I said, I stayed well away after I heard this bloke was in town.'

'Tell me about him.'

'Not much to tell. Like I said, I never met him. According to Carl, he's never been inside, yet he's been up to more evil than many as have.'

'What kind of evil?'

'You name it. If what Carl says is right, this bloke worked with some of the London mobs, you know, peddling porn and hurting people who wouldn't pay up, but now he's gone freelance. Bit of a rover. Never stays in one place very long. Got lots of contacts.'

'And he's never been inside?'

'Not as anyone knows of.' Poole leaned forward. 'Look, Mr Banks,' he said, licking his lips. 'This bloke's really nasty, know what I mean? Carl told me he was in a fish-and-chip shop once and got arguing with the woman in front. She was carrying a dog with her, like, one of those Pekinese things, and this bloke just plucked it out of her arms and flung it in the frier then walked out cool as a cucumber. He's a nutter. I didn't want nothing to do with him.'

'Can't say I blame you,' said Banks. 'What's his name?'

'Dunno. Carl never said.'

'Les!'

'Look, I don't want anyone knowing I—'

'Just between you and me, Les. Off the record.'

'You promise?'

'I'm in the business of preventing crime, remember? It'd hardly be in my interests to have another murder on my patch, would it? And you've no idea how much I'd miss you.'

'Huh. Even so . . .'

'Les.'

Poole paused. 'All right, all right. I'll trust you – still 'ypothetical like. All I know is his name is Chivers. It's pronounced with a "sh", like in shivers. I don't know if it's his real name or a nickname.'

'What does he look like?'

'I don't know. I told you, I never met him.'

Banks wasn't convinced. For a start, he was certain that Poole *had* been connected with the Fletcher's warehouse job, and now it seemed a good bet that Johnson and this Chivers person had been involved, too, along with John Fairley, the junk-shop owner. He could understand Poole's not wishing to implicate himself, of course, especially as it was now a matter of murder.

The thing to remember about Les Poole was that he had spent time inside; he knew the value of information and of silence. He knew how to get as much slack as he could while giving as little as possible in return. Maybe he was a small-time crook, a coward and a bully, not too bright, but he knew the ropes; he knew how to duck and dodge to save his own neck, how to measure out exactly enough co-operation to get himself out of trouble. Banks sensed that he was holding back, that he *had* met this Chivers, but there was no percentage in pushing him yet. They needed more leverage, and Poole was right about one thing: impounding Brenda Scupham's television would look very bad indeed.

'Is he still in Eastvale?'

'Dunno. Don't think so.'

'Is there anything else you can tell me about him?'

'No. 'Cept I'd stay out of his way if I were you. Carl said he had this bird and—'

'What bird's this, Les?'

'This bird Chivers had with him. Some blonde bint. Apparently, he always has a bit of spare with him. The lasses like him. Must be his unpredictable, violent nature.'

They liked Les, too, Banks remembered, and wondered if there had been a spot of bother about this blonde. Maybe Les had made a pass and Chivers put a scare in him. Or maybe Carl Johnson had. It wasn't so difficult, he thought, to fill in the rest from the scraps Poole dished out.

'What did Carl say about Chivers's girlfriend?' he asked.

'Just that Chivers knifed a bloke once for looking at her the wrong way. Didn't kill him, like, just cut him up a bit.

Anyway, like I said, he never had any shortage of birds. Not scrubbers either, according to Carl. Quality goods. Maybe it was his smile,' Les added.

'What smile?'

'Nothing. Just that Carl said he had this really nice smile, like. Said his mates called him "Smiler" Chivers.'

When Banks heard Poole's last comment, the warning bells began to ring. 'Susan,' he said, looking over Poole's shoulder. 'Do you know if the super's still here?'

TWO

Brenda Scupham couldn't concentrate on the television programme. For a moment she thought of going out, maybe to the pub, but decided she couldn't stand the questions and the looks people would give her. She hadn't enjoyed going out much at all since Gemma had gone. For one thing, people had given her dirty looks when they saw her, as if they blamed her or she wasn't obeying the proper rules of mourning or something. Instead, she took another tranquillizer and poured herself a small measure of gin. Again she wondered what the hell was going on.

All she knew was that the police had called at her house earlier that evening looking for Les. He'd been out of course, and she hadn't known where, though she was sure the policeman hadn't believed her. When she asked what they wanted, they wouldn't tell her anything. Surely, she thought, if it had anything to do with Gemma, they should tell her?

She looked over at the television and video. Maybe that's what it was all about? She knew they were stolen. She wasn't *that* stupid. Les hadn't said so, of course, but then he wouldn't; he never gave away anything. He had dropped them off in John's van one afternoon and said they were bankrupt stock. All the time the police had been coming and going because of Gemma, Brenda had been worried they would spot the stolen goods and arrest her. But they hadn't. Perhaps now they had some more evidence and had decided to arrest Les after all.

How her life could have changed so much in just one week was beyond her. But it had, and even the tranquillizers did no real good. She had enjoyed going on television with Lenora Carlyle – that had been the high spot of the week – but nothing had come of it. Just as nothing had come of the police search, the *Crimewatch* reconstruction, or her appeals through the newspapers. And now, as she sat and thought about the police visit, she wondered if Les might have been involved in some way with Gemma's disappearance. She couldn't imagine how or why – except he hadn't got on very well with Gemma – but he *had* been acting strangely of late.

And the more she thought about it, the more she lost faith in Lenora's conviction that Gemma was still alive. She couldn't be. Not after all this time, not after the blood-stained clothing they had brought for her to identify. And apart from that one statement, Lenora had come up with nothing else, had she? Surely she ought to be able to picture where Gemma was if she was any good as a psychic? But no, nothing. And what if Gemma was alive somewhere? It didn't bear thinking about. She felt closer to her daughter now she was gone than she ever had while Gemma had been around.

Time after time her thoughts circled back to Mr Brown and Miss Peterson. Should she have known they weren't who they said they were? And if she hadn't felt so guilty about not loving Gemma the way a good mother should and about shaking her the week before, would she have let her go so easily? They had been so convincing, kind and understanding rather than accusing in their approach. They had looked so young, so official, so competent, but how was she to know what child-care workers were supposed to look like?

Again she thought of the police officers who had come to her house earlier. Maybe they had found Gemma and some clue had led them to Les. But still she couldn't imagine what he could possibly have to do with it. He had been out when the child-care workers called. Still, there was no denying the police were after him. If he had anything to do with Gemma's abduction, Brenda thought, she would kill him. Damn the consequences. It was all his fault anyway. Yes, she thought, reaching for the gin bottle again. She would kill the bastard. For now, though, she was sick of thinking and worrying.

The only thing that worked, that took away the pain, even though it lasted such a short time, was the video. Slowly, she got up and went over to the player. The cassette was still in. All she had to do was rewind and watch herself on television again. She had been nervous, but she was surprised when she watched the playback that it didn't show so much. And she had looked so pretty.

Brenda poured herself another generous measure, turned on one element of the fire and reclined on the sofa with her dressing gown wrapped around her. She had watched the video once and was rewinding for a second viewing when she heard Les's key in the door.

THREE

'You don't believe for a moment he told you everything, do you?' Gristhorpe asked Banks later in the Queen's Arms. It was a quiet Wednesday evening, a week since the first news of Gemma Scupham's disappearance – and despite the helicopters and search tactics learned from the North American Association of Search and Rescue, she still hadn't been found. Banks and Gristhorpe sat at a table near the window eating the roast beef sandwiches that they had persuaded Cyril, the landlord, to make for them.

Banks chewed and swallowed his mouthful, then said, 'No. For a start, I'm sure he's seen this Chivers bloke, but he couldn't really admit to it without implicating himself in the warehouse job. We let him walk. For now. Les won't stray far. He's got nowhere to go.'

'And then?'

Banks grinned. 'Just an idea, but I'd like to find out if Les really does know anything about Gemma's abduction. I had a phone call just after I'd finished with Poole. Jim Hatchley's coming into town. Seems his mother-in-law's commissioned him to install a shower—'

Gristhorpe slapped the table. One of the customers at the bar turned and looked. 'No, Alan. I'm not having any of Hatchley's interrogation methods on this one. If Gemma's abductors get off because we've bent the rules I'd never bloody forgive myself. Or Sergeant Hatchley, for that matter.'

'No,' said Banks, 'that's not what I had in mind.' He outlined his plan and both of them ended up laughing.

'Aye,' said Gristhorpe, nodding slowly. 'Aye, he'd be

the best man for *that* job, all right. And it might work, at that. Either way, we've nothing to lose.'

Banks washed his sandwich down with a swig of Theakston's bitter and lit a cigarette. 'So where do we go now?' he asked.

Gristhorpe leaned back in his chair and folded his hands in his lap. 'Let's start with a summary. I find it helps to get everything as clear as possible. In the first place, we know that a couple who called themselves Chris and Connie Manley rented a cottage and changed their appearance. Then they "borrowed" a dark blue Toyota from Bruce Parkinson, passed themselves off as social workers called Mr Brown and Miss Peterson, and conned Brenda Scupham into handing over her daughter on Tuesday afternoon. After that, they drove a hundred and twenty-seven miles before returning the car to its owner.

'As far as we know, they left the cottage on Thursday in a white Fiesta. We don't have the number, and Phil's already checked and rechecked with the rental outlets. Nothing. And it hasn't been reported stolen. We could check the ownership of every white Fiesta in the country, and we bloody well will if we have to, but that'll take us till doomsday. They might not be registered as owners, anyway. Nobody saw them with the child in Eastvale, and there was no evidence of a child's presence in the cottage, but she could have been there – the whitewash supports that – and we found her prints in Parkinson's car. Why they took her, we don't know. Or where. All we know is they most likely didn't bring her back, which to me indicates that she could well be lying dead and buried somewhere in a hundred-and-twenty-mile radius. And that includes the area of the North York Moors where we found the bloodstained clothes. Vic says there wasn't enough blood on them to cause death, but that doesn't mean the rest didn't spill elsewhere, or that she might not have died in some other way. Poole told you that this Chivers person was involved in the porn trade in London, so that's another ugly possibility to consider. I've been onto the paedophile squad again, but they've got nothing on anyone of that name or description.

'Anyway. Next we find Carl Johnson's body in the old lead mine on Friday morning. Dr Glendenning says he was probably killed sometime after dark on Thursday. You follow all the leads you can think of in the Johnson murder, and we arrive at this same man called Chivers with a smile that people notice, a blonde girlfriend and a nasty disposition. You think Poole knows a bit more. Maybe he does. There are too many coincidences for my liking. Chivers and the girl are the ones who took Gemma. Maybe one or both of them also killed Carl Johnson. Chivers, most likely, as it took a fair bit of strength to rip his guts open. But why? What's the connection?'

'Johnson could have double-crossed them on the warehouse job, or maybe he knew about Gemma and threatened to tell. Whatever Johnson was, he wasn't a paedophile.'

'Assuming he found out they'd taken her?'

'Yes.'

'That's probably our best bet. Makes more sense than killing over a bloody TV set, though stranger things have happened.'

'Or it could have been over the girlfriend,' Banks added. 'Especially after what Poole told me about the knifing.'

'Aye,' said Gristhorpe. 'That's another strong possibility. But let's imagine that Carl Johnson found out Chivers and his girlfriend had taken Gemma and . . . well, done whatever they did to her. Now Johnson's no angel, and he seems to have an unhealthy fascination with bad 'uns, from what you tell me, but somehow, they've gone too far for him. He doesn't like child-molesters. He becomes a threat. They lure him out to the mine. Maybe the girl does it with promises of sex, or Chivers with money, I don't know. But somehow they get him there and . . .' Gristhorpe paused. 'The mine might be a connection. I know the area's been thoroughly searched already, but I think we should go over it again tomorrow. There's plenty of spots around there a body could be hidden away. Maybe the clothes on the moors were just a decoy. What do you think, Alan?'

Banks frowned. 'It's all *possible*, but there are still too many uncertainties for my liking. I'd like to know more about the girl's part in all this, for a start. Who is she? What's in it for her? And we've no evidence that Chivers killed Johnson.'

'You're right, we don't have enough information to come to conclusions yet. But we're getting there. I thought you fancied Adam Harkness for the Johnson murder?'

'I did, though I'd no real reason to. Looks like I might have been wrong, doesn't it?'

Gristhorpe smiled. 'Happens to us all, Alan. You always did have a chip on your shoulder when it came to the rich and influential, didn't you?'

'What?'

'Nay, Alan, I'm not criticizing. You're a working-class lad. You got where you are through brains, ability and sheer hard slog. I'm not much different myself, just a poor farm-boy at heart. I've no great love for them as were born with silver spoons in their mouths. And I don't mind sticking up for you when Harkness complains to the ACC about police harassment. All I'm saying is be careful it doesn't blur your objectivity.'

Banks grinned. 'Fair enough,' he said. 'But I haven't finished with Mr Harkness yet. I called the Johannesburg police and set a few inquiries in motion. You never know, there might be something to that scandal yet. And I called Piet in Amsterdam to see if he can track down Harkness's ex-wife. There's still a chance Harkness might have been involved somewhere along the line. What about your black magician, Melville Westman?'

'Nothing,' said Gristhorpe. 'The lads did a thorough job. He looks clean. It's my bet that Gemma was in the Manleys' cottage at some point, and that's where the whitewash on her clothes came from. That's not to say I won't be having another word with Mr Westman, though.' Gristhorpe smiled. His own feelings about people like Melville Westman and Lenora Carlyle were not so different from Banks's feelings about the rich and powerful, he realized: different chip, different shoulder, but a prejudice, nonetheless.

'I'm going to call my old mate Barney Merritt at the Yard first thing in the morning,' Banks said. 'He ought to be able to get something out of Criminal Intelligence about Chivers a damn sight quicker than the formal channels. The more we know about him, the more likely we are to be able to guess at the way he thinks. The bastard might never have been nicked but I'll bet a pound to a penny he's on the books somewhere.'

Gristhorpe nodded. 'Oh, aye. No doubt about it. And it looks as if we're all working on the same case now. You'd better get up to date on the Gemma files, and we'd better let Phil know so he can access his databases or whatever he does. I want this bloke, Alan. I want him bad. I mean I want him in front of me. I want to see him sweat. Do you know what I mean?'

Banks nodded and finished his drink. From the bar, they heard Cyril call time. 'It's late,' he said quietly. 'Time we were off home.'

'Aye. Everything all right?'

'Fine,' said Banks. 'Just think yourself lucky you don't have daughters.'

Banks walked in the rain, coat buttoned tight, and listened to his Walkman. It was after eleven-thirty when he got home, and the house was in darkness. Sandra was already in bed, he assumed; Tracy, too. He knew he wouldn't be able to sleep just yet, after the conversation with Gristhorpe had got his mind working, and as he had drunk only two pints in the pub, he felt he could allow himself a small Scotch. What was it the medics said, three drinks a day is moderate? Some kind soul had brought him a bottle of Glen Garioch from a holiday in Scotland, so he poured himself a finger and sat down. Though he wasn't supposed to smoke in the house, he lit a cigarette anyway and put on a CD of Barenboim playing Chopin's Nocturnes. Even at low volume, the clarity of the sound was astonishing. He had hardly begun to let his mind roam freely over the image of Chivers he had created so far when he heard the front door open and close softly, then the creak of a stair.

He opened the living-room door and saw Tracy tiptoeing upstairs.

'Come down here a moment,' he whispered, careful not to wake Sandra.

Tracy hesitated, halfway up, then shrugged and followed him into the living room.

Banks held out his wristwatch towards her. 'Know what time it is?'

'Of course I do.'

'Where've you been?'

'Out with Keith.'

'Where to?'

'Oh, Dad! We went to the pictures, then after that we were hungry so we went for a burger.'

'A burger? At this time of night?'

'You know, that new McDonald's that's opened in the shopping centre. It's open till midnight.'

'How did you get home?'

'Keith walked me.'

'It's too late to be out on a weeknight. You've got school in the morning.'

'It's only midnight. I'll get plenty of sleep.'

There she stood, about seven stones of teenage rebellion, weight balanced on one hip, once long and beautiful blonde hair chopped short, wearing black leggings and a long, fawn cable-knit jumper, pale translucent skin glowing from the chill.

'You're too young to be out so late,' he said.

'Oh, don't be so old-fashioned. *Everyone* stays out until midnight these days.'

'I don't care what everyone else does. It's you I'm talking about.'

'It would be different if it was Brian, wouldn't it? He could always stay out as late as he wanted, couldn't he?'

'He had to live with the same rules as you.'

'Rules! I bet you've no idea what he's up to now, have you? Or what he got up to when he was still at home. It's all right for him. Honestly, it's not fair. Just because I'm a girl.'

'Tracy, love, it's not a safe world.'

Her cheeks blazed red and her eyes flashed

dangerously, just like Sandra's did when she was angry.
'I'm fed up of it,' she said. 'Living here, being interrogated
every time I come in. Sometimes it's just absolutely
fucking awful having a policeman for a father!'

And with that, she stormed out of the room and up the
stairs without giving Banks a chance to respond. He stood
there a moment, stunned by her language – not that she
knew such words, even five-year-olds knew them, but that
she would use them that way in front of him – then he felt
himself relax a little and he began to shake his head
slowly. By the time he had sat down again and picked up
his drink, he had started to smile. 'Kids . . .' he mused
aloud. 'What can you do?' But even as he said it, he knew
that Sandra had been right: the problem was that Tracy
wasn't a kid any more.

FOUR

Brenda had locked the door earlier, and slid the bolt and
put the chain on, too. When the key wouldn't work, she
could hear Les fumble around for a while, rattling it and
mumbling. Brenda could see his silhouette through the
frosted-glass panes in the door as she sat on the stairs and
listened. He tried the key again, then she heard him swear
in frustration and start knocking. She didn't answer.

'Brenda,' he said, 'I know you're in there. Come on,
love, and open up. There's something wrong with my key.'

She could tell by the way he slurred his words that he'd
been drinking. The police either hadn't found him, then,
or had let him go before closing time.

He rattled the door. 'Brenda! It's fucking cold out here.
Let me in.'

Still she ignored him, sitting on the staircase, arms wrapped around herself.

The letter box opened. 'I know you're in there,' he said. 'Have a heart, Brenda.'

She stood up and walked down the stairs to the door. 'Go away,' she said. 'I don't want you here any more. Go away.'

'Brenda!' He was still on his knees by the letter box. 'Don't be daft, love. Let me in. We'll talk about it.'

'There's nothing to talk about. Go away.'

'Where? This is my home. It's all I've got.'

'Go back to the police. I'm sure they'll give you a bed for the night.'

He was silent for a few moments. Then she heard shuffling outside. The letter box snapped shut, then opened again. 'It wasn't nothing, love,' he said. 'A mistake. It was some other bloke they were after.'

'Liar.'

'It was. Honest it was.'

'What have you done with my Gemma?'

Another pause, even longer this time, then, 'How could you think such a thing? It wasn't nothing to do with that. Look, let me in. It's raining. I'll catch cold. I'm freezing my goolies off out here.'

'Good.'

'Brenda! The neighbours are watching.'

'I couldn't care less.'

'What about my things?'

Brenda dashed up to the bedroom. Les's 'things', such as they were, shouldn't take up much space. She was a bit unsteady on her feet, but she managed to stand on a chair and get an old suitcase down from the top of the wardrobe. First, she emptied out his underwear drawer. Shirts and trousers followed, then she tossed in his old denim jacket. He was wearing the leather one, she remembered. She dropped a couple of pairs of shoes on the top, then went into the bathroom and picked up his razor, shaving cream, toothbrush. For some reason, she didn't know why, she also picked up a package of tampons and put them in the suitcase, too, smiling as she did so. And on further thought, she took his condoms from the bedside drawer and put them in as well.

Enjoying herself more than she had since her TV appearance, Brenda searched around for anything else that belonged to him. A comb. Brylcreem. Half a packet of cigarettes. No, she would keep them for herself. Nothing else.

As she struggled to fasten the suitcase, she could hear him outside in the street yelling up at her: 'Brenda! Come on, Brenda, let me in. Please. I'm freezing to death out here.'

She walked over to the window. Les stood by the gate at the bottom of the path, partly lit by a nearby street-lamp. Across the street, lights came on as people opened their doors or peered through curtains to see what was going on. This would give the neighbours something to talk about, Brenda thought, as she opened the window.

Les looked up at her. For a moment, she remembered a scene in a play they'd taken her to see with the school years ago, where some wally in tights down on the ground had been chatting up a bird on a balcony. She giggled and swayed, then got a hold on herself. After all, she had an audience. 'Bugger off, Les,' she yelled. 'I've had enough of you and your filthy ways. If it wasn't for you I'd still have my Gemma.'

'Open the fucking door, cow,' said Les, 'or I'll kick it down. You never liked the little bitch anyway.'

'I loved my daughter,' said Brenda. 'It was you used to upset her. Where is she, Les? What have you done with her?'

Another door opened down the street. 'Be quiet,' a woman shouted. 'My husband's got to get up to go to work at five o'clock in the morning.'

'Shut up, you stuck-up old bag,' shouted someone else. 'Your husband's never done a day's work in his life. This is the best show we've had in ages.' Bursts of laughter echoed down the street.

A window slid open. 'Give him hell, love!' a woman's voice encouraged Brenda.

'What's going on?' someone else asked. 'Has anyone called the police yet?'

'See what you've started,' Les said, looking around at the gathering of neighbours and trying to keep his voice down. 'Come on, love, let me in. We'll have a cuddle and talk about it. I've done nowt wrong.'

'And what about that telly?' Brenda taunted him. 'Where did that come from, eh? Have you noticed the way the police look at it every time they come here?'

'Must be fans of *The Bill*,' someone joked, and the neighbours laughed. 'Anyone got a bottle,' the joker continued. 'I could do with a wee nip.'

'Buy your own, you tight-fisted old bugger,' came the reply.

'Open the door,' Les pleaded. 'Brenda, come on, love, have mercy.'

'I'll not show no mercy for you, you snake. Where's my Gemma?'

'I'll do you for bloody slander, I will,' yelled Les. 'Making accusations like that in front of witnesses.' He

241

turned to the nearest neighbour, an old woman in a dressing gown. 'You heard her, didn't you?'

'Maybe she's right,' said the woman.

'Aye,' said the man next door.

'Hey,' said Les. 'Now, come on.' He looked up at the window again. 'Brenda, let me in. I don't like the look of this lot.'

'Too bad.' Brenda swung the suitcase behind her as far as she could, then let it fly out the window. It hit the gatepost and burst open, showering its contents over the garden and street. Les put his hands up to try and stop it from hitting him, but all he managed to catch was the packet of tampons. It spilled its contents on his shoes as he grasped it too tightly. One of the neighbours noticed and started laughing. Les stood there in the rain, half in shadow, surrounded by the flotsam and jetsam of his life and a packet of tampons spilled like cigarettes at his feet. He looked up at Brenda and shouted one last appeal. Brenda closed the window. Before she pulled the curtains on him, she noticed some of the neighbours edging forward in a semicircle towards Les, who was backing down the street, looking behind him for a clear escape route.

11

ONE

'**Les Poole's** done a bunk, sir.'

'Has he, now?' Banks looked up from his morning coffee at Susan Gay standing in his office door. She was wearing a cream skirt and jacket over a powder-blue blouse fastened at the neck with an antique jet brooch. Matching jet teardrops hung from her small ears. Her complexion looked fresh-scrubbed under the tight blonde curls that still glistened from her morning shower. Her eyes were lit with excitement.

'Come in and tell me about it,' Banks said.

Susan sat down opposite him. He noticed her glance at the morning papers spread out on his desk. There, on the front pages of all of them, the police artist's impression of Smiler Chivers and his blonde girlfriend stared out.

'There was a bit of a barney last night on the East Side Estate,' Susan began. 'According to PC Evans, who walks the beat down there, Les Poole was out in the street yelling at Brenda to let him in.'

'She locked him out?'

'Seems like it.'

'Why?'

'Well, that's where it gets interesting. PC Evans talked to some of the neighbours. Most of them were a bit tight-lipped, but he found one chap who'd been watching it all from his bedroom window down the street. He said it looked like the others had turned into a mob and were about to attack Poole. That's why he ran off.'

'Any idea why, apart from his sparkling personality?'

'While they were yelling at each other, Brenda apparently made some comment about Poole being responsible for Gemma's disappearance.'

'What?'

'That's all he heard, sir, the neighbour. Brenda kept asking Poole what he'd done with Gemma.'

Banks reached for a cigarette, his first of the day. 'What do you think?' he asked.

'About Poole?'

'Yes.'

'I don't know. I mean it could just have been something Brenda thought up on the spur of the moment to hit out at him, couldn't it?'

'I know Poole's been holding something back,' Banks said. 'That's just his nature. But I never really thought . . .' He stubbed out his unfinished cigarette and stood up. 'Come on. First, let's send some of the lads out looking for him. And then we'd better have another word with Brenda.' He picked up one of the newspapers. 'We'll see if she recognizes the artist's impression, too.'

They drove in silence to East Side Estate. It was a blustery morning, with occasional shafts of sunlight piercing the clouds and illuminating a bridge, a clump of trees or a block of maisonettes for a few seconds then disappearing. There ought to be a shimmering dramatic soundtrack, Banks thought, something to harmonize with the odd sense of revelation the fleeting rays of light conveyed.

Banks knocked on the frosted pane of Brenda's door,

but no one answered. He knocked harder. Across the street, a curtain twitched. Discarded cellophane wrapping and newspaper blew across the road, scraping against the tarmac.

'They'll be having the time of their lives,' Susan said, nodding towards the houses opposite. 'Twice in two days. A real bonanza.'

Banks renewed his efforts. Eventually he was rewarded by the sight of a blurry figure walking down the stairs.

'Who is it?' Brenda asked.

'Police.'

She fiddled with the bolts and chain and let them in.

'Sorry,' she said, rubbing the back of her hand over her eyes. 'I was fast asleep. Must have been those pills the doctor gave me.'

She looked dreadful, Banks thought: knotted and straggly hair in need of a good wash, puffy complexion, mottled skin, red eyes. She wore a white terry-cloth robe, and when she sat down in the living room under the gaze of Elvis, it was clear she wore nothing underneath. As she leaned forward to pick up a cigarette from the table, the bathrobe hung loose at the front, revealing her plump, round breasts. Unembarrassed, she pulled the lapels together and slouched back in the chair. Banks and Susan sat on the sofa opposite her.

'What is it?' Brenda asked after she had exhaled a lungful of smoke. 'Have you found Gemma?'

'No,' said Banks. 'It's about Les.'

She snorted. 'Oh, him. Well, he's gone, and good riddance, too.'

'So I heard. Any idea *where* he's gone?'

She shook her head.

'Why did you throw him out, Brenda?'

'You should know. It was you lot had him at the station last night, wasn't it?'

'Did you know the neighbours nearly lynched him?'

'So what?'

'Brenda, it's dangerous to make accusations like the one you did, especially in front of a crowd. You know from experience how people feel whenever children are involved. They can turn very nasty. There's records of people being torn apart by angry mobs.'

'Yes, I know. I know all about what people do to child-molesters. They deserve it.'

'Did Les molest Gemma? Is that it?'

Brenda blew out more smoke and sighed. 'No,' she said. 'No, he never did anything like that.'

'Maybe when you weren't around?'

'No. I'd have known. Gemma would have . . .' She paused and stared at the end of her cigarette.

'Perhaps Gemma wouldn't have mentioned it to you,' Banks suggested. 'You told us yourself she's a quiet, secretive child. And children are almost always afraid to speak out when things like that happen.'

'No,' Brenda said again. 'I would have known. Believe me.'

Whether he believed her or not, Banks felt that line of questioning had come to a dead end. 'What reason do you have to think Les was involved in her disappearance, then?' he asked.

Brenda frowned. 'You had him in for questioning, didn't you?'

'What made you think that had anything to do with Gemma?'

'What else would it be about?'

'So you just assumed. Is that it?'

'Of course. Unless . . .'

'Unless what?'

Brenda reddened, and Banks noticed her glance towards the television set.

'Did you think it was about the Fletcher's warehouse job?'

Brenda shook her head. 'I . . . I don't know.'

'Did Les ever mention an acquaintance named Carl Johnson to you?'

'No. He never talked about his pub mates. If I ever asked him where he'd been or who he'd been with, he just told me to mind my own business.'

'Look, this is important,' Banks said slowly. 'Think about it. When you accused Les out in the street, did you have any other basis for doing so apart from the fact that we'd taken him in for questioning?'

'What?'

Banks explained, Brenda leaned forward to put out her cigarette. She held her robe closed this time. 'That and the way he's been acting,' she said.

'What do you mean?'

'It's hard to put into words. Ever since Gemma . . . well, things haven't been the same between us. Do you know what I mean?'

Banks nodded.

'I don't know why, but they haven't. And he just looks so sheepish, the way he creeps around all the time, giving me guilty smiles. Mostly, though, he's been keeping out of my way.'

'In what way could he have been involved, Brenda?' Susan asked.

Brenda looked sideways towards her, as if seeing her for the first time. 'How should I know?' she said. 'I'm not the detective, am I?' She spoke more harshly than she had to Banks. Woman to woman, he thought, Brenda Scupham was uncomfortable.

Banks gently took the focus away from Susan. 'Brenda, have you any proof at all that Les had something to do with Gemma's disappearance?'

'No. Just a feeling.'

'Okay. I'm not dismissing that. What you told us, about this Mr Brown and Miss Peterson, that was all true, wasn't it?'

'Yes. That's how it happened.'

Banks showed her the newspaper pictures of Chivers and the blonde. 'Do you recognize these people?'

She squinted at the pictures. 'It could be him. The hair's sort of the same, but a different colour. I don't know about her, though. People look so different with their hair up. Him, though . . . I think . . . yes . . . I think it might be.'

Banks put the paper aside. 'You told us Les wasn't in when they came.'

'That's right. He was at the pub.'

'How did he react when you told him?'

'I don't know what you mean.'

'Did he seem shocked, upset, what?'

Tears came to Brenda's eyes. 'He said I was a stupid cow for letting them take her . . . but . . .'

'But what?'

She rubbed the backs of her hands across her eyes. 'I need a cup of tea. I can't really get started without my cup of tea in the morning. Do you want some?'

'All right,' said Banks. It wouldn't be a bad idea to give her a couple of minutes to mull over his question.

He and Susan waited silently while Brenda went into the kitchen and made tea. Outside, a car went by, a dog barked, and two laughing children kicked a tin can down the street. The wind shrilled at the ill-fitting windows, stirring the curtains in its draught. Banks studied the portrait of Elvis. It really was grotesque: a piece of kitsch dedicated to a bloated and gaudy idol.

As a teenager, he had been a keen Elvis fan. He had seen all those dreadful movies of the early 60s, where Elvis usually played a slightly podgy beach-bum, and he had bought all the new singles as soon as they came out. Somehow, though, after the Beatles, Bob Dylan, the Rolling Stones and the rest, Elvis had never seemed important again.

Still, he remembered how he had listened to 'They Remind Me Too Much of You' over and over again the night June Higgins chucked him for John Hill. He had been assembling a model Messerschmitt at the time, so maybe it was the glue fumes that had made his eyes water. Gluesniffing hadn't been invented back then. He had been thirteen; now Elvis was dead but lived on in garish oils on walls like this.

The whistle blew. When it stopped, Banks heard Brenda go upstairs. A few moments later she came in with the teapot and three mugs. She had taken the opportunity to get dressed, run a brush through her hair and put on a bit of make-up.

'Where were we?' she asked, pouring the tea. 'There's milk and sugar if you want it.' Susan helped herself to a splash of milk and two teaspoons of sugar. Both Banks and Brenda took theirs as it came.

'Les's reaction when you told him about Gemma.'

'Yes. I've been thinking about it while the tea was mashing,' Brenda said. 'He didn't believe me at first. I'd say more than anything he was surprised. It's just that . . .

well, he turned away from me, and I couldn't see his face, but it was like he knew something or he suspected something, like he was frowning and he didn't want me to see his expression. Do you know what I mean?'

'I think so.'

'I could just feel it. I know I've not got any proof or anything, but sometimes you can sense things about people, can't you? Lenora says she thinks I'm a bit psychic, too, so maybe that's it. But I never thought for a moment he had anything to do with it. I mean, how could I? What could Les have had to do with those two well-dressed people who came to the door? And we lived together. I know he didn't care for Gemma much, she got on his nerves, but he wouldn't hurt her. I mean he *was* surprised, shocked, I'm sure of that, but when it sank in, he seemed to be *thinking*, puzzling over something. I put it out of my mind, but it nagged. After that we never really got on well. I'm glad he's gone.' She paused, as if surprised at herself for saying so much, then reached for a second cigarette.

'What made you accuse him last night?' Banks asked.

'It's just something that had been at the back of my mind, that's all. Like I said, I never really believed he had anything to do with it. I just had this nagging feeling something wasn't right. I suppose I lashed out, just for the sake of it. I couldn't help myself.'

'What about now?'

'What?'

'You said you didn't think Les had anything to do with Gemma's disappearance at first. What do you think now?'

Brenda paused to blow on her hot tea, cradling the mug in her palms, then she turned her eyes up to Banks and shook her head. 'I don't know,' she whispered. 'I just don't know.'

TWO

Banks and Jenny dashed across the cobbles in the rain to the Queen's Arms. Once through the door, they shook their coats and hung them up.

'Double brandy, then?' Banks asked.

'No. No, really, Alan. I didn't mean it,' Jenny said. 'Just a small Scotch and water, please.'

Now she was embarrassed. She put her briefcase on the chair beside her and sat down at a table near the window. She had been in Banks's office going over all the material on the Carl Johnson murder – statements, forensic reports, the lot – and when she got to the photographs of his body, she had turned pale and said she needed a drink. She didn't know why they should affect her that way – she had seen similar images in textbooks – but suddenly she had felt dizzy and nauseated. Something about the way the belly gaped open like a huge fishmouth . . . no, she wouldn't think about it any more.

Banks returned with their drinks and reached for his cigarettes.

'I'm sorry,' she said. 'You must think I'm a real idiot.'

'Not at all. I just wasn't thinking. I should have prepared you.'

'Anyway, I'm fine now.' She raised her glass. 'Cheers.'

'Cheers.'

She could see Market Street through a clear, rain-streaked pane. Young mothers walked by pushing prams, plastic rainhats tied over their heads, and delivery vans blocked the traffic while men in white smocks carried boxes in and out of the shops, oblivious to the downpour. All the hurly and burly of commerce so essential to a thriving English market town. So normal. She shivered.

'I take it you're assuming the crimes are related now?' she asked.

Banks nodded. 'We are for the moment. I've read over the paperwork on the Gemma Scupham case, and I've filled the super in on Johnson. How are you getting on with him, by the way?'

Jenny smiled. 'Fine. He doesn't seem like such an ogre when you get to know him a bit.'

'True, he's not. Anyway, we know that the Manleys abducted Gemma, and that in all likelihood the man's real name is Chivers. We still don't know who the woman is.'

'But you don't know for sure that this Chivers killed Carl Johnson?'

'No. I realize it's a bit thin, but when you get connections like this between two major crimes you can't overlook them. Maybe in a big city you could, but not in Eastvale.'

'And even if he did it, you don't know if the woman was present?'

'No.'

'Then what do you want from me?'

'For a start, I want to know if you think it could be the same person, or same people, psychologically speaking.'

Jenny took a deep breath. 'The two crimes are so different. I can't really find a pattern.'

'Are there no elements in common?'

Jenny thought for a moment, and the images of Johnson's body came back. She sipped at her drink. 'From all I've seen and heard,' she said, 'I'd say that the two crimes at least demonstrate a complete lack of empathy on the criminal's part, which leans towards the theory of the psychopath. If that's the case, he probably wasn't sexually interested in Gemma, only in his power over her, which he may have been demonstrating to the woman, as I said to the superintendent last time we met.' She ran her hand through her hair. 'I just don't have anything more to go on.'

'Think about the Johnson murder.'

Jenny leaned forward and rested her hands on the table. 'All right. The couple who took Gemma showed no feeling for the mother at all. Whoever killed Johnson didn't feel his pain, or if he did, he enjoyed it. You know even better than I do that murder can take many forms – there's the heat of the moment, and there's at least some distancing, as when a gun's used. Even the classic poisoner often prefers to be far away when the poison takes effect. But here we have someone who, according to all the evidence you've shown me, must have stood very close indeed to his victim, looked him in the eye as he killed slowly. Could you do that? Could I? I don't think so. Most of us have at least some sensitivity to another's pain – we imagine what it would feel like if we suffered it ourselves. But one class of person doesn't – the psychopath. He can't relate to anyone else's pain, can't imagine it happening to him. He's so self-centred that he lacks empathy completely.'

'You keep saying "he".'

Jenny slapped his wrist playfully. 'You know as well as I do that, statistically speaking, most psychopaths are men. And it might be pretty interesting to try to find out why. But that's beside the point. That's what the two crimes, what I know of them, have in common. There are other elements that fit the psychopath profile, too: the apparent coolness and bravado with which Gemma was abducted; the charm Chivers must have exhibited to her

mother; the clever deceit he must have played to get
Johnson out to the mill, if that's what he did. And you can
add that he's also likely to be manipulative, impulsive,
egocentric and irresponsible. You're nursing your pint,
Alan. Anything wrong?'

'What? Oh, no. I'm just preserving my liver. I have to
meet Jim Hatchley for dinner in a couple of hours.'

'So he's in town again, is he?'

'Just for a little job.'

Jenny held her hand up. 'Say no more. I don't want to
know anything about it. I can't understand why you like
that man.'

Banks shrugged. 'Jim's all right. Anyway, back to
Chivers. What if he committed the Carl Johnson murder
out of self-preservation?'

'The method was still his choice.'

'Yes.' Banks lit another cigarette. 'Look, I'll tell you
what I'm getting at. Just before you arrived, I talked to my
old friend Barney Merritt at the Yard, and he told me that
Criminal Intelligence has got quite a file on Chivers.
They've never been able to put him away for anything, but
they've had reports of his suspected activities from time to
time, and they've usually had some connection with
organized crime. The closest they came to nabbing him
was four years ago. An outsider trying to muscle in on a
protection racket in Birmingham was found on a building
site with a bullet in his brain. The police knew Chivers was
connected with the local mob up there, and a couple of
witnesses placed him with the victim in a pub near the
site. Soon as things got serious, though, the witnesses
started to lose their memories.'

'What are you telling me, Alan, that he's a hit man or
something?'

Banks waved his hand. 'No, hold on, let me finish. Most of the information in the CI files concerns his suspected connection with criminal gangs in London and in Birmingham, doing hits, nobbling witnesses, enforcing debt-collection and the like. But word has it that when business is slack, Chivers is not averse to a bit of murder and mayhem on the side, just for the fun of it. And according to Barney, his employers started to get bad feelings about him about a year ago. They're keeping their distance. Again, there's nothing proven, just hearsay.'

'Interesting,' said Jenny. 'Is there any more?'

'Just a few details. He's prime suspect – without a scrap of proof – in three murders down south, one involving a fair amount of torture before death, and there are rumours of one or two fourteen-year-old girls he's treated roughly in bed.'

Jenny shook her head. 'If you're getting at some kind of connection between that and Gemma, I'd say it's highly unlikely.'

'But why? He likes his sex rough and strange. He likes them young. What happens when fourteen isn't enough of a kick any more?'

'The fact that he likes having sex with fourteen-year-old girls in no way indicates, psychologically, that he could be interested in seven-year-olds. Quite the opposite, really.'

Banks frowned. 'I don't understand.'

'It was something else I discovered in my research. According to statistics, the younger the child, the older the paedophile is likely to be. Your Chivers sounds about the right age for an unhealthy interest in fourteen-year-olds, but, you know, if you'd given me no information at all about Gemma's abduction, I'd say you should be looking for someone over forty, most likely someone who knew

Gemma – a family friend, neighbour or even a relative – who lives in the area, or not far away, and probably lives alone. I certainly wouldn't be looking for a young couple from Birmingham, or wherever.'

Banks shook his head. 'Okay, let's get back on track. Tell me what you think of this scenario. We know that plenty of psychopaths have found gainful employment in organized crime. They're good at frightening people, they're clever, and they make good killers. The problem is that they're hard to control. Now, what do you do with a psychopath when you find him more of a business liability than an asset? You try to cut him loose and hope to hell he doesn't bear a grudge. Or you have him killed, and so the cycle continues. His old bosses don't trust Chivers any more, Jenny. He's *persona non grata*. They're scared of him. He has to provide his own entertainment now.'

'Hmm.' Jenny swirled her glass and took another sip. 'It makes some sense, but I doubt that it's quite like that. In the first place, if he's hard to control, it's more likely to mean that he's losing control of himself. From what you told me, Chivers must have been a highly organized personality type at one time, exhibiting a great deal of control. But psychopaths are also highly unstable. They're prone to deterioration. His personality could be disintegrating towards the disorganized type, and right now he might be in the middle, the mixed type. Most serial killers, for example, keep on killing until they're caught or until they lose touch completely with reality. That's why you don't find many of them over forty. They've either been caught by then, or they're hopelessly insane.'

Banks stubbed out his cigarette. 'Are you suggesting that Chivers could be turning into a serial killer?'

Jenny shrugged. 'Not necessarily a serial killer, but

it's possible, isn't it? He doesn't fit the general profile of a paedophile, and he's certainly changing into *something*. Yes, it makes sense, Alan. I'm not saying it's true, but it's certainly consistent with the information you've got.'

'So what next?'

Jenny shuddered. 'Your guess is as good as mine. Whatever it is, you can be sure it won't be very pleasant. If he is experiencing loss of control, then he's probably at a very volatile and unpredictable stage.' She finished her drink. 'I'll give you one piece of advice, though.'

'What's that?'

'If it is true, be very careful. This man's a loose cannon on the deck. He's very dangerous. Maybe even more so than you realize.'

THREE

'Congratulations,' said Banks, 'I really mean it, Jim. I'm happy for you. Why the hell didn't you tell me before?'

'Aye, well . . . weren't sure.' Sergeant Hatchley blushed. A typical Yorkshireman, he wasn't comfortable with expressions of sentiment.

The two of them sat in the large oak-panelled dining room of the Red Lion Hotel, an enormous Victorian structure by the roundabout on the southern edge of Eastvale. Hatchley was looking a bit healthier than he had on his arrival that afternoon. Then the ravages of a hangover had still been apparent around his eyes and in his skin, but now he had regained his normal ruddy complexion and that tell-me-another-one look in his pale-blue eyes. Just for a few moments, though, his colour deepened even more and his eyes filled with pride. Banks was congratulating him on his wife's pregnancy. Their first.

'When's it due?' Banks asked.

'I don't know. Don't they usually take nine months?'

'I just wondered if the doctor had given you a date.'

'Mebbe Carol knows. She didn't say owt to me, though. This is a good bit of beef.' He cut into his prime-rib roast and washed it down with a draught of Theakston's bitter. 'Ah, it's good to be home again.'

Banks was eating lamb and drinking red wine. Not that he had become averse to Theakston's, but the Red Lion had a decent house claret and it seemed a shame to ignore it. 'You still think of Eastvale as home?' he asked.

'Grew up here,' replied Hatchley around a mouthful of Yorkshire pudding. 'Place gets in your blood.'

'How are you liking the coast?'

'It's all right. Been a good summer.' Sergeant Hatchley had been transferred to Saltby Bay, between Scarborough and Whitby, mostly in order to make way for Phil Richmond's boost up the promotion ladder. Hatchley was a good sergeant and always would be; Richmond, Banks suspected, would probably make at least Chief Inspector, his own rank, and might go even further if he kept on top of the latest computer technology and showed a bit more initiative and leadership quality. Susan Gay, their most recent DC, was certainly demonstrating plenty of initiative, though it didn't always lead where it should.

'Do I detect a note of nostalgia?' Banks asked.

Hatchley grinned. 'Let me put it this way. It's a bit like a holiday. Trouble is – and I never thought I'd be complaining about *this* – it's a holiday that never bloody ends. There's not much goes on for CID to deal with out there, save for a bit of organized pickpocketing in season, a few

B-and-Es, or a spot of trouble with the bookies now and then. It's mostly paperwork, a desk job.' Hatchley uttered those last two words with flat-vowelled Yorkshire contempt.

'Thought you'd be enjoying the rest.'

'I might be a bit of a lazy sod, but I'm not bloody retiring age yet. You know me, I like a bit of action now and then. Out there, half the time I think I've died and gone to Harrogate, only by the sea.'

'What are you getting at, Jim?'

Hatchley hesitated for a moment, then put his knife and fork down. 'I'll be blunt. We're all right for now, Carol and me, but after the baby's born, do you think there's any chance of us getting back to Eastvale?'

Banks sipped some wine and thought for a moment.

'Look,' Hatchley said, 'I know the super doesn't like me. Never has. I knew that even before you came on the scene.'

Three and a half years ago, Banks thought. Was that all? So much had happened. He raised his eyebrows.

'But we get on all right, don't we?' Hatchley went on. 'I mean, it took us a while, we didn't have the best of starts. But I know my faults. I've got strengths, too, is all I'm saying.'

'I know that,' Banks said. 'And you're right.' He remembered that it had taken him two years to call Sergeant Hatchley by his first name. By then he had developed a grudging respect for the man's tenacity. Hatchley might take the easy way out, act in unorthodox ways, cut corners, take risks, but he generally got what he set out to get. In other words, he was a bit of a maverick, like Banks himself, and he was neither as thick nor as thuggish as Banks had first thought.

Apart from Gristhorpe, Banks felt most comfortable with Hatchley. Phil Richmond was all right, pleasant enough, but he always seemed a bit remote and self-absorbed. For God's sake, Banks thought, what could you expect from a man who read science fiction, listened to New Age music and spent half his time playing computer games? Susan Gay was too prickly, too over-sensitive to feel really at ease with, though he admired her spunk and her common sense.

'It's not up to me,' Banks said finally. 'You know that. But the way Phil's going it wouldn't surprise me if he went in for a transfer to the Yard before long.'

'Aye, well, he always was an ambitious lad, was Phil.'

It was said without rancour, but Banks knew it must have hurt Hatchley to be shunted to a backwater so as not to impede a younger man's progress up the ranks. Transfer to CID was no more a 'promotion' *per se* than transfer to Traffic and Communications – a sergeant was a sergeant, whether he or she had the prefix 'detective' or not – though some, like Susan Gay, actually saw it that way, as a mark of recognition of special abilities. Some detectives were transferred back to uniform; some returned from choice. But Banks knew that Hatchley had no desire to walk the beat or drive the patrol cars again. What he wanted was to come back to Eastvale as a Detective Sergeant, and there simply wasn't room for him with Richmond at the same rank.

Banks shrugged. 'What can I say, Jim? Be patient.'

'Can I count on your support, if the situation arises?'

Banks nodded. 'You can.' He smiled to himself as the unbidden image of Jim Hatchley and Susan Gay working together came to mind. Oh, there would be fun and games ahead if Sergeant Hatchley came back to Eastvale.

Hatchley finished his pint and looked Banks in the eye. 'Aye, well that's all right then. How about a sweet?'

'Not for me.'

Hatchley caught the waiter's attention and ordered Black Forest gateau, a cup of coffee and another pint of Theakston's. Banks stayed with his glass of red wine, which was still half-full.

'Down to business, then,' Hatchley said, as he tucked into the dessert.

Banks gave him a summary of the case and its twists and turns so far, then explained what he wanted him to do.

'A pleasure,' said Hatchley, smiling.

'And in the meantime, you can concentrate on installing that shower or whatever it is. I can't say how long we'll be. It depends.'

Hatchley pulled a face. 'I hope it's sooner rather than later.'

'Problem?'

'Oh, not really. As you know, I've got a few days' leave. There's not a lot on in Saltby at the moment, anyway, and Carol will be all right. She's built up quite a gaggle of mates out there, and there'll be no keeping them away since we heard about the baby. You know how women get all gooey-eyed about things like that. You can almost hear the bloody knitting needles clacking from here. No, it's just that it might mean staying on longer than I have to at the in-laws', that's all.'

'You don't get on?'

'It's not that. We had them for two weeks in July. It's just . . . well, you know how it is with in-laws.'

Banks remembered Mr and Mrs Ellis from Hatchley's wedding the previous Christmas. Mrs Ellis in particular had seemed angry that Hatchley stayed at the reception too long and drank too much. But then, he thought, she had every right to be annoyed. 'They don't approve of your drinking?' he guessed.

'You make it sound as if I'm an alcoholic or something,' Hatchley said indignantly. 'Just because a bloke enjoys a pint or two of ale now and then . . . No, they're religious, Four Square Gospel,' he sighed, as if that explained it all. 'You know, Chapel on Sundays, the whole kit and caboodle. Never mind.' He sat up straight and puffed out his chest. 'A man's got to do what a man's got to do. Just hurry up and find the bugger. What about this Chivers bloke? Any leads?'

'According to Phil, we've already had sightings from St Austell, King's Lynn, Clitheroe and the Kyle of Lochalsh.'

Hatchley laughed. 'It was ever thus. Tell me about him. He sounds interesting.'

Banks told him what Barney Merritt had said and what he and Jenny had discussed late afternoon.

'Reckon he's done her, the kid?'

Banks nodded. 'It's been over a week, Jim. I just don't like to think about what probably happened *before* he killed her.'

Hatchley's eyes narrowed to slits. 'Know who the tart is? The blonde?'

'No idea. He picks them up and casts them off. They're fascinated by him, like flies to shit. According to what Barney could dig up, his full name's Jeremy Chivers, called Jem for short. He grew up in a nice middle-class home in Sevenoaks. No record of any trouble as a kid. No one can figure out how he got hooked up with the gangs. He had a good education, moved to work for an insurance company in London, then it all started.'

'It's not hard for rats to find the local sewer,' said Hatchley.

'No. Anyway, he's twenty-eight now, apparently looks even younger. And he's no fool. You've got to be pretty smart to keep on doing what he does and get away with it. It all satisfies whatever weird appetites he's developing.'

'If you ask me,' said Hatchley, 'we'd all be best off if he found himself at the end of a noose.'

Banks remembered his early feelings about Hatchley. That comment, so typical of him and so typical of the burned-out, cynical London coppers Banks had been trying to get away from at the time, brought them all back.

Once, Banks would have cheerfully echoed the sentiment. Sometimes, even now, he felt it. It was impossible to contemplate someone like Chivers and what he had done to Carl Johnson – if he had done it – and, perhaps, to Gemma Scupham, without wanting to see him dangling at the end of a rope, or worse, to make it personal, to squeeze the life out of him with one's own hands. Like everyone who had read about the case in the newspapers, like everyone who had children of his own, Banks could easily give voice to the outraged cliché that hanging was too good for the likes of Chivers. What was even worse was that Banks didn't know, could not predict for certain, what he would do if he ever did get Chivers within hurting distance.

The conflict was always there: on the one hand, pure atavistic rage for revenge, the gut feeling that someone who did what Chivers did no longer deserved to be a member of the human race, had somehow, through his monstrous acts, forfeited his humanity; and on the other hand, the feeling that such a reaction makes us no better than him, however we sugar-coat our socially sanctioned murders, and with it the idea that perhaps more insight is to be gained from the study of such a mind than from its destruction, and that knowledge like that may help prevent Chiverses of the future. There was no easy solution for him. The two sides of the argument struggled for ascendancy; some days sheer outrage won out, others a kind of noble humanism took supremacy.

Instead of responding to Hatchley's comment, Banks gestured for the bill and lit a cigarette. It was time to go home, perhaps listen to Mitsuko Uchida playing some Mozart piano sonatas and snuggle up to Sandra, if she was in.

'Ah well,' sighed Hatchley. 'Back to the in-laws, I suppose.' He reached into his pocket, pulled out a packet of extra-strong Trebor mints and popped one in his mouth. 'Once more unto the breach, dear friends . . .'

FOUR

The piece of luck that Banks had been hoping for came at about six-thirty in the morning. Like most police luck, it was more a result of hard slog and keen observation than any magnanimous gesture on the part of some almighty deity.

The telephone woke Banks from a disjointed dream full of anger and frustration. He groped for the receiver in the dark. Beside him, Sandra stirred and muttered in her sleep.

'Sir?' It was Susan Gay.

'Mmm,' Banks mumbled.

'Sorry to wake you, sir, but they've found him. Poole.'

'Where is he?'

'At the station.'

'What time is it?'

'Half past six.'

'All right. Phone Jim Hatchley at Carol's parents' place and get him down there, but keep him out of sight. And—'

'I've already phoned the super, sir. He's on his way in.'

'Good. I'll be there as soon as I can.'

Sandra turned over and sighed. Banks crept out of bed as quietly as he could, grabbed the clothes he had left folded on a chair and went into the bathroom. He still couldn't shake the feeling the dream had left him with. Probably something to do with the row he had with Tracy after he got back from dinner with Jim Hatchley. Not even a row, really. Trying to be more understanding towards her, he had simply made some comment about how nice it was to have her home with the family, and she had burst into tears and dashed up to her room. Sandra had shot him a nasty look and hurried up after her. It turned out her boyfriend had chucked her for someone else. Well, how was he supposed to know? It all changed so quickly. She never told him about anything these days.

As soon as he had showered and dressed, he went out to the car. The wind had dropped, but the pre-dawn sky was overcast, a dreary iron grey, except to the east where it was flushed deep red close to the horizon. For the first time that year, Banks could see his breath. Already, lights were on in some of the houses, and the woman in the newsagent's at the corner of Banks's street and Market Street was sorting the papers for the delivery kids.

Inside the station, an outsider would have had no idea it was so early in the morning. Activity went on under the fluorescent lights as usual, as it did twenty-four hours a day. Only a copper would sense that end-of-the-night-shift feel as constables changed back into civvies to go home and the day shift came in bright-eyed and bushy-tailed, shaved faces shining, or make-up freshly applied.

Upstairs, where the CID had their offices, was quieter. They hardly had a need for shift work, and their hours varied depending on what was going on. This past week, with a murder and a missing child, long hours had been taking their toll on everyone. Richmond was there, looking red-eyed from too much staring at the computer screen, and Susan Gay had dark blue smears under her eyes.

'What happened?' Banks asked her.

'I'd just come in,' she said. 'Couldn't sleep so I came in at six and thought I'd have another look at the forensic reports, then they brought him in. Found him sleeping in a ditch a mile or so down the Helmthorpe road.'

'Jesus Christ,' said Banks. 'It must have been cold. Where is he?'

'Interview room. PC Evans is with him.'

'Sergeant Hatchley?'

'Got here just before you. He's in position.'

Banks nodded. 'Let's wait for the super.'

Gristhorpe arrived fifteen minutes later, looking brighter than the rest of them. His hair was a mess, as usual, but his innocent blue eyes shone every bit as alert and probing as ever.

'Let's have at him, then,' he said, rubbing his hands. 'Alan, would you like to lead, seeing as you know him so well? Let me play monster in reserve.'

'All right.'

They headed for the small interview room. Before they went in, Banks asked Richmond if he would get them a large pot of tea.

The drab room seemed overcrowded with four of them, and the heat was turned too high. PC Evans went and sat in the corner by the window, ready to take notes, Banks sat opposite Poole, and Gristhorpe at right angles.

Poole licked his lips and looked around the room.

'You look like you've been dragged through a hedge backwards, Les,' Banks said. 'What happened?'

'Sleeping rough. Nowhere to go, had I?'

He was unshaven, his leather jacket was scuffed and stained with mud, his greasy hair bedraggled and matted. He also had a black eye and a split lip. The tea arrived. Banks played mother and passed a large steaming mug over to Les. 'Here, have a cuppa,' he said. 'You don't look like you've had your breakfast yet.'

'Thanks.' Poole grasped the mug with both hands.

'How'd you get the war wounds?'

'Bloody mob, wasn't it? I need protection, I do.'

'From your neighbours?'

'Bloody right.' He pointed to his face. 'They did this to me before I managed to run off. I'm a victim. I should press charges.' Poole slurped some tea.

'Be our guest,' said Banks. 'But later. There's a few other things to deal with first.'

Poole frowned. 'Oh? Like what?'

'Like why did you run?'

'That's a daft question. You'd bloody run if you had a mob like that after you.'

'Where were you heading?'

'Dunno. Anywhere. I'd got no money so I could hardly stay in a bleeding hotel, could I?'

'What about your mate at the shop?'

'Wasn't in.'

'What did the mob want with you, Les?'

'It was all that silly bitch Brenda's fault. Put on a right show, she did, chucking my stuff at me like that. And that's another thing. I'll bloody sue her for damage to property.'

'You do that, Les. She'd probably have to sell the telly and that nice little stereo system to pay her costs. Why did they turn on you?'

Les glanced nervously at Gristhorpe, then said to Banks, 'Is he going to stay here all the time?'

Banks nodded. 'If I can't get the truth out of you, he takes over. Believe me, you'll be a lot happier if that never happens. We were talking about your neighbours. Look at me.'

Poole turned back. 'Yeah, well, Brenda yelled some stupid things out the window. It was her fault. She could have got me killed.'

'What did she yell?'

Banks could see Poole weighing him up, gauging what he knew already. Finally, he said, 'Seeing as she's probably already told you, it doesn't matter, does it?' He kept glancing at Gristhorpe out of the corner of his eye.

'It matters a lot,' Banks said. 'It's a very serious allegation, that is, saying you were mixed up with Gemma's disappearance. They don't take kindly to child-molesters in prison, Les. This time it won't be as easy as your other stretches inside. Why don't you tell us what you know?'

Poole finished his tea and reached for the pot. Banks let him pour another large mug. 'Because I don't know anything,' he said. 'I told you, Brenda was out of line.'

'No smoke without fire, Les.'

'Come on, Mr Banks, you know me. Do I look like a child-molester?'

'How would I know? What do you think they look like? Ogres with hairs growing out of their noses and warts on their bald heads? Do you think they go around carrying signs?'

'She was trying to stir it, to wind me up. Honest. Ask her. Ask her if she *really* thinks I had anything to do with it.'

'I have, Les.'

'Yeah? And what did she say?'

'How did you feel when she told you Gemma had been abducted?'

'Feel?'

'Yes, Les. It's something people do. Part of what makes them human.'

'I know what it means. Don't think I don't have feelings.' He paused, and gulped down more tea. 'How did I feel? I dunno.'

'Were you upset?'

'Well, I was worried.'

'Were you surprised?'

'Course I was.'

'Did anything spring to mind, anything to make you wonder maybe about what had happened?'

'I don't know what you mean.'

'I think you do, Les.'

Banks looked over at Gristhorpe, who nodded grimly.

Poole licked his lips again. 'Look, what's going on here? You trying to fit me up?'

Banks let the silence stretch. Poole squirmed in his hard chair. 'I need a piss.'

Banks stood up. 'Come on, then.'

They walked down the corridor to the gents and Banks stood by the inside of the door while Poole went to the urinal.

'Tell us where Gemma is, Les,' Banks said, as Poole relieved himself. 'It'll save us all a lot of trouble.'

All of a sudden, the stall door burst open. Poole turned. A red-faced giant in a rumpled grey suit with short fair hair and hands like hams stood in front of him. Poole pissed all over his shoes and cursed, cringing back against the urinal, holding his arms out to ward off an attack.

'Is that him?' the giant said. 'Is that the fucking pervert who—'

Banks dashed over and held him back. 'Jim, don't. We're still questioning—'

'Is that the fucking pervert or isn't it?'

Hatchley strained to get past Banks, who was backing towards the door with Poole scrabbling behind him. 'Get out, Les,' Banks said. 'While you can. I'll keep him back. Go on. Hurry!'

They backed into the corridor and two uniformed constables came to hold Hatchley, still shouting obscenities. Banks put a protective arm around Poole and led him back to the interview room. On the way, they passed Susan Gay, who looked at Poole and blushed. Banks followed her gaze. 'Better zip it up, Les,' he said, 'or we'll have you for indecent exposure as well.'

Poole did as he was told and Banks ushered him back into the room, Hatchley cursing and shouting behind them, held back by the two men.

'What the hell's going on?' Gristhorpe asked.

'It's Jim,' Banks explained, sitting Poole down again. 'You know what he's been like since that bloke interfered with his little girl.'

'Aye,' said Gristhorpe, 'but can't we keep a leash on him?'

'Not easy, sir. He's a good man. Just a bit unhinged at the moment.'

Poole followed the exchange, paling.

'Look,' he said, 'I ain't no pervert. Tell him. Keep him away from me.'

'We'll try,' Banks said, 'but we might have a hard time getting him to believe us.'

Poole ran a hand through his greasy hair. 'All right,' he said. 'All right. I'll tell you all I know. OK? Just keep him off me.'

Banks stared at him.

'Then you can tell them all I'm not a pervert and I had nothing to do with it, all right?'

'If that's the way it turns out. If I believe you. And it's a big if, Les, after the bollocks you've been feeding us this past week.'

'I know, I know.' Poole licked his lips. 'Look, first off, you've got to believe me, I had nothing to do with what happened to Gemma. Nothing.'

'Convince me.'

Outside, they could hear Hatchley bellowing about what he would do to perverts if he had his way: 'I'd cut your balls off with a blunt penknife, I bloody would! And I'd feed them down your fucking throat!' He got close enough to thump at the door and rattle the handle before they could hear him being dragged off still yelling down the corridor. Banks could hardly keep from laughing. Jim and the uniforms sounded like they were having the time of their lives.

'Christ,' said Les, with a shudder. 'Just keep him off me, that's all.'

'So you had nothing to do with Gemma's disappearance?' Banks said.

'No. See, I used to talk about the kid down the pub, over a jar, like. I admit I wasn't very flattering, but she was a strange one was Gemma. She could irritate you just by looking at you that way she had, accusing like. Make you feel like dirt.'

'So you complained about your girlfriend's kid. Nothing odd in that, is there, Les?'

'Well, that's just it, isn't it? What I've been saying. It was just pub talk, that's all. Now, I never touched her, Mr Banks. Never. Not a word of a lie. But Brenda got pissed off that time after Gemma spilled her paints on my racing form and gave her a bloody good shaking. First time I seen her do it, and it scared me, honest it did. Left big bruises on the kid's arm. I felt sorry for her, but I'm not her fucking father, what am I supposed to do?'

'Get to the point, Les. Those lads out there can't hold Sergeant Hatchley down for ever.'

'Aye, well, I didn't exactly tell you the truth before. You see, I did meet this Chivers and his bird a couple of times, with Carl at the pub. Never took to him. She wasn't a bad-looking bint, mind you. A bit weird, but not bad. He thought I was coming on to her once and warned me, all quiet and civilized, like, that if I went so much as within a yard of her he'd cut off my balls and shove them up my arse.' Poole paused and swallowed. No doubt he was realizing, Banks thought, that threats to his privates were coming thick and fast from all sides. 'He gave me the creeps, Mr Banks. There was something not right about him. About the pair of them, if you ask me.'

'Did this Chivers seem interested when you talked about Gemma?'

'Well, yeah, about as interested as he seemed in anything. He was a cool one. Cold. Like a fucking reptile. There was just no reading him. He'd ask about her, yeah, over a few drinks, like, but I thought nothing of it. And once he told me about a case he'd read in the papers where some couple had pretended to be child-care workers and asked to examine a child. Thought that was funny, he did. Thought it showed bottle. I put it out of my mind. To be honest, soon as we'd done the Fl— soon as we'd finished our bit of business, I wouldn't go near him or her. I can't explain it. They seemed nice and normal enough on the surface, all charm and that nice smile of his, but inside he was hard and cold, and you never knew what he was going to do next. I suppose that's the kind of thing she liked. There's no figuring out some women's taste.'

'So Chivers showed some interest in Gemma and he told you about the newspaper story, right?'

'Right. And that's as far as it went.'

'Did Chivers give you any reason to believe he was interested in little children?'

'Well, no, not directly. I mean, Carl told me a few stories about him, how he'd been involved in the porn trade down The Smoke and how he wasn't averse to a bit of bondage and that. Just titillating stories, that's all. And when you saw him and his bird together, they were weird, like they had something going that no one could get in on. She hung on his every word and when he told her to do something, she did. I mean . . . it was . . . Once, we was in the car, like, plann— just talking, with them two in the front and me and Carl in the back, and he told her to suck him off. She got right down there and did it, and all the time he kept talking, just stopping once, like, to give a little sigh when he shot his load. Then she sat back up again as if nothing had happened.'

'But they never made any direct reference to children?'

'No. But you see what I mean, don't you, Mr Banks? I mean, as far as I'm concerned, them two was capable of anything.'

'I see what you mean. What did you do?'

'Well, I kept quiet, didn't I? I mean, there was no way of knowing it was them took Gemma. The descriptions weren't the same. And then when Carl turned up dead, I had a good idea who might have liked killing someone that way and . . . I was scared. I mean, wouldn't you be? Maybe Carl had made the same connection, too, and Chivers had offed him while the bint looked on and laughed. That's the kind of feeling they gave you.'

'Do you have any evidence that Chivers killed Carl?'

'Evidence? That's down to you lot, isn't it? No, I told you. I kept away from him. It just seemed like something he would do.'

'Where are they now, Les?'

'I've no idea, honest I don't. And you can turn your gorilla on me and I can't tell you any different. I haven't seen nor heard of them since last week. And I don't want to.'

'Do you think they're still in Eastvale, Les?'

'Be daft if they were, wouldn't they? But I don't mind saying I was scared shitless those two nights sleeping out. I kept thinking there was someone creeping up on me to cut my throat. You know what it's like out in the country, all those animal noises and the wind blowing barn doors.' He shuddered.

'Is that everything, Les?'

'Cross my heart.'

Banks noticed he didn't say 'hope to die' this time. 'It'd better be,' said Banks, standing and stretching. He walked over to the door and peered outside, then turned to Gristhorpe. 'Looks like they've got Jim away somewhere. What shall we do now?'

Gristhorpe assessed Poole with a steady gaze. 'I think

he's told us all he knows,' he said finally. 'We'd better take him to the charge room then lock him up.'

'Good idea,' Banks said. 'Give him a nice warm cell for the day. For his own safety.'

'Aye,' said Gristhorpe. 'What'll we charge him with?'

'We could start with indecent exposure.'

They spent another hour or so going over Poole's statement with him, and Poole made no objections as the constable finally led him down to the charge room. He just looked anxiously right and left to make sure Hatchley wasn't around. Banks wandered to his office for a cigarette and another cup of coffee. Gristhorpe joined him there, and a few minutes later Jim Hatchley walked in with a big grin on his face.

'Haven't had as much fun since the last rugby club trip,' he said. 'How did you know he'd be going for a piss anyway? I was getting a bit fed up stuck in there. I'd read the *Sport* twice already.'

'People want to urinate a lot when they're anxious,' Banks said. 'He did before. Besides, tea's a diuretic, didn't you know that?'

Hatchley shook his head.

'Anyway, he'd have wanted to go eventually. We'd just have kept him as long as necessary.'

'Aye,' said Hatchley, 'and me in the fucking shit-house.'

Banks smiled. 'Effective, though, wasn't it? More dramatic that way.'

'Very dramatic. Thinking of doing a bit of local theatre, are you?'

Banks laughed. 'Sometimes that's what I think I am doing already.' He walked over to the window and stretched. 'Christ, it's been a long morning,' he muttered.

The gold hands against the blue face of the church clock stood at ten-twenty. Susan Gay walked in and out with the latest developments. Not much. There had been more reports of Chivers, from Welshpool, Ramsgate and Llaneilian, and all had to be checked out by the locals. So far, they didn't have one clear lead. Just after eleven, the phone rang, and Banks picked it up.

'Detective Inspector Loder here. Dorset CID.'

Banks sighed. 'Not another report of Chivers?'

'More than that,' said Loder. 'In fact, I think you'd better get down to Weymouth if you can.'

Banks sat upright. 'You've got him?'

'Not exactly, but we've got a dead blonde in a hotel room, and she matches the description you put out.'

12

ONE

Gristhorpe sat in the passenger seat of the unmarked police car with a road map spread out on his knees. Banks drove. He would have preferred his own Cortina, mostly because of the stereo system, but Sandra needed it for all her gallery work. Besides, Gristhorpe was tone deaf; for all his learning, he couldn't appreciate music. Banks had packed his Walkman and a couple of tapes in his overnight bag; he knew it wouldn't be easy getting to sleep in a strange hotel room, especially after what awaited them in Weymouth, and music would help.

They were heading down the M1 past Sheffield with its huge cooling towers, shaped like giant whalebone corsets, and its wasteland of disused steel factories. It was almost one-thirty in the afternoon, and despite the intermittent rain they were making good time.

Gristhorpe, after much muttering to himself, decided it would be best to turn off the motorway just south of Northampton and go via Oxford, Swindon and Salisbury. Banks drove as fast as he could, and just over an hour later they reached the junction with the A43. They skirted Oxford in the late afternoon and didn't get held up until they hit Swindon at rush hour.

After Blandford Forum, they passed the time reading signposts and testing one another on Hardy's names for the places. They managed to keep abreast until Gristhorpe went ahead with Middleton Abbey for Milton Abbas.

After a traffic snarl-up in the centre of Dorchester, they approached Weymouth in the early evening. Loder had given clear directions to the hotel, and luckily it was easy to spot, one of the Georgian terraces on the Dorchester Road close to the point where it merged with the Esplanade.

A plump, curly-haired woman called Maureen greeted them in the small lobby and told them that Inspector Loder and his men had been gone for some time but had left a guard outside the room and requested she call them at the station as soon as Banks and Gristhorpe arrived. Their booking for the night had already been made: two singles on the third floor, one floor down from where the body had been discovered.

Out of courtesy, Banks and Gristhorpe waited for Loder to arrive before going up to the room. They had requested that, as far as possible, things should be left as they were when the chambermaid discovered the body that morning. Of course, Loder's Scene-of-Crime men had done their business, and the Home Office pathologist had examined the body *in situ*, but the corpse was still there, waiting for them, in the position she had been found.

Loder walked in fifteen minutes later. He was a painfully thin man with a hatchet face and a sparse fuzz of grey hair. Close to retirement, Banks guessed, and tired. His worn navy-blue suit hung on him, and his wire-rimmed glasses seemed precariously balanced near the end of his long, thin nose. As he spoke, his grey-green eyes peered over the tops of the lenses.

After the formalities were over, the three men headed up the thickly carpeted stairs to room 403.

'We tried to do as you asked,' Loder said as they climbed. 'You might see some traces of the SOCO team's presence, but otherwise . . .' He had a local accent, a kind of deep burr like a mist around his vowels, and he spoke slowly, pausing between thoughts.

The uniformed constable stepped aside at Loder's gesture, and they entered the room and turned on the light. They had no need to wear surgical gloves, as the forensic scientists had already been over the scene. What they were getting was part preservation, part re-creation.

First, Banks studied the room in general. It was unusually spacious for a seaside hotel room, with a high ceiling, ornate moulding and an oriel window overlooking the sea, now only a dim presence beyond the Esplanade lights. The window was open a fraction and Banks felt the pleasant chill of the breeze and heard the distant wash of waves on the beach. Gristhorpe stood beside him, similarly watchful. The wallpaper, a bright flower pattern, gave a cheerful aura, and a framed watercolour of Weymouth's seafront hung over the writing-desk. There was little other furniture: armchair, television, dressing table, wardrobe and bedside tables – and the large bed itself. Banks left that until last.

The shape of a woman's body was clearly defined by the twisted white sheet that covered it. At first glance, it looked like someone sprawled on her back in the morning just before stretching and getting up. But instead of her head resting on the pillow, the pillow was resting on her head.

'Is this how you found her?' Banks asked Loder.

He nodded. 'The doc did his stuff, of course, but he tried not to disturb her too much. We put the body back much as it was, as you requested.'

There was an implied criticism in his tone. Why on

earth, Loder seemed to be asking, did you want us to leave the body? But Banks ignored him. He always liked to get the feel of a scene; somehow it told him much more than photographs, drawings and reports. There was nothing morbid in his need to *see* the body where it lay; in fact, in many instances, this included, he would far rather not. But it did make a difference. Not only did it give him some sort of contact with the victim, the symbolism of having *touched* the corpse, something he needed to fuel him through a murder investigation, but it also sometimes enabled him to enter the criminal's and the victim's minds. He didn't think there was anything particularly psychic about this; it was more a Holmesian manner of working back from the little things one observed to the circumstances that created them. There was no denying, though, that sometimes he did get a true *feel* for the way the killer thought and what his next moves might be.

From the disapproval in his tone, Banks formed the impression that Loder was a highly moral man, outraged not only by the murder but by the delay in getting the corpse to its proper place. It was a woman's body, too, and that seemed to embarrass him.

Slowly, Banks walked over to the bed and picked up the pillow. Gristhorpe stood beside him. The woman's long blonde hair lay spread out on the undersheet. She had been beautiful, no doubt about that: fine bone structure, a clear complexion, full lips. Apart from her head, only her neck and shoulders were exposed, alabaster skin clouded with the bluish tinge of cyanosis.

Her left hand grasped the top of the sheet and bunched it up. She wore red nail polish, but Banks thought he could also detect traces of blood around the tips of her fingers and smeared on the white sheet. He lifted the sheet. She was naked underneath. Carefully, he replaced it, as if to avoid causing her further embarrassment. Loder wasn't the only sensitive one, no matter what he thought.

Gristhorpe opened one of her eyelids. 'See that,' he said pointing to the red pinpricks of blood in the once-blue eye.

Banks nodded. It was a petechial haemorrhage, one sign of asphyxiation, most likely in this case caused by the pillow.

Banks touched her right hand and shivered; it was cold and stiff with rigor.

'We've got the skin and blood samples, of course,' said Loder, when he saw Banks examining the nails. 'Looks like she put up a bit of a struggle. We should be able to type the killer, maybe even do a DNA profile.'

'We don't have time for that,' Gristhorpe said. 'This one's got to be stopped fast.'

'We-ell,' said Loder, in his slow burr, 'at least it'll come in useful in court. Is it her, the one you're looking for?'

'We didn't have a very good description,' Gristhorpe answered. 'Alan?'

'Couldn't say.' Banks turned to Loder. 'She was with the man, though, you said?'

'Yes. The one with the nice smile. You mentioned it specifically in the papers. That's why we called you boys in.'

'Any identification?' Gristhorpe asked.

Loder shook his head. 'Nothing. Whoever did it took everything. Clothes, handbag, the lot. We tried her fingerprints but they're not on file.' He paused. 'It looks as if she was killed here, and the doc says she certainly hasn't been moved since she died. He's anxious to get to the PM, of course, but ruling out drugs, his findings so far are consistent with asphyxiation.'

'Any idea of the time?'

'Doc puts it between six and nine in the morning.'

'Anything else we should know?'

Loder glanced towards the body and paused for a moment before speaking. 'Nothing else unusual about the body,' he said, 'unless you count the fact that she'd had sex around the time she was killed.'

'Forced?'

'Not so far as the doc could make out.' Loder walked towards the window, leaned on the sill and looked out over the Esplanade lights. 'But it probably wouldn't be, would it, if she was sleeping with the bloke. Now, if you gentlemen are through, could we possibly get out of here? I seem to have spent far too much time with her already today.' He sounded weary, and Banks wondered if he were not only tired but ill; he certainly seemed unusually thin and pale.

'Of course,' said Gristhorpe, looking over at Banks. 'Just a couple more questions first, while they're fresh in my mind.'

Loder sighed. 'All right.'

'I don't suppose the chambermaid actually cleaned the room, did she, given what she found here?'

'No,' said Loder, a thin smile on his lips. 'No, she didn't. I'm sure you'll want to talk to her yourselves, but the one odd thing – and I noticed it, too – was that the room looked as if it *had* just been cleaned. The SOCO team tried to disturb things as little as possible. They took their samples, dusted for prints and so on, but you can see what it was like.'

Indeed they could. The room looked spotless, clean and tidy. Under the thin patina of fingerprint powder, wood surfaces gleamed with recent polishing. Gristhorpe glanced in the small bathroom and toilet, and it was the same, as if the fixtures and fittings had been scrubbed with Ajax, the towels hung neatly on the racks. There wasn't a smear of toothpaste or a trace of stubble stuck to the sides of the sink.

'The cottage the Manleys left in Eastvale was just the same,' Gristhorpe said. 'What do you make of it, Alan?'

Banks shrugged 'Partly getting rid of evidence, I suppose,' he said. 'Though he kindly left us semen samples, not to mention blood and skin under her fingernails. Maybe he's got a pathological obsession with cleanliness and neatness. I've heard it's not uncommon among psychopaths. Something to ask Jenny about, anyway.' He pointed to two thin, glossy leaflets on the dressing table. 'Were those there when the chambermaid came in?'

'No,' said Loder. 'Sorry. One of the crime-scene boys found them and forgot to put them back.'

'Would you show us where?'

Loder opened one of the drawers, which was lined with plain paper, and slipped the brochures under. 'Like this,' he said. 'I thought maybe he'd forgotten them, or they slipped under the lining by accident. The chambermaid said she cleans out the drawers thoroughly between guests, so they can't have been there before. They're ferry timetables, see. For Cherbourg and the Channel Islands. We reckon that's where he must have gone.'

'What time do the ferries start?'

'Early enough.'

'Did he have a car?'

'Yes; parked out back. A white Fiesta. See, he wouldn't need it to get to the ferry dock, and once he gets over to the Channel Islands or France, well . . . Anyway, our lads have taken it to the police garage.'

'Is there anything else?' Gristhorpe asked.

Loder shook his head.

'All right, let's get out of here. Tell your boys they can get her to the mortuary. Will the pathologist be able to start the autopsy tonight?'

'I think so.' Loder closed the door behind them. 'As I said, he's been chomping at the bit all day as it is.' The police guard resumed his post and Loder led the way downstairs.

'Good,' said Gristhorpe. 'I think we can leave it till morning to talk to the hotel staff. I trust your lads have already taken statements?'

Loder nodded.

'We'll see what a good night's sleep does for their memories then. Anything else you can think of, Alan?'

Banks shook his head, but couldn't prevent his stomach from rumbling.

'Oh, aye,' said Gristhorpe. 'I forgot we hadn't eaten all day. Better see what we can rustle up.'

TWO

'Is this the place?' Susan Gay asked.

Richmond nodded. 'Looks like it.'

Rampart Street sounded as if it should have been situated near the castle, but instead, for reasons known only to town planners, it was a nondescript cul-de-sac running south of Elmet Street in Eastvale's west end. One side consisted of pre-war terrace houses without gardens. Mostly they seemed in a state of neglect and disrepair, but some tenants had attempted to brighten things up with window boxes and brass door-knockers.

The other side of the street, with a small Esso garage on the corner, consisted of several shops, including a greengrocer's with tables of fruit and vegetables out front; a betting shop; a newsagent-cum-video rental outlet; and the incongruously named Rampart Antiques. However one defines 'antique', whether it be some kind of intrinsic beauty or simply age, Rampart Antiques failed on both counts.

In the grimy window, Susan spotted a heap of cracked Sony Walkmans without headphones, two stringless acoustic guitars, and several dusty box-cameras, along with the occasional chipped souvenir plate with its 'hand-painted' scene of Blackpool tower or London Bridge wedged among them. One corner was devoted to old LPs – Frank Sinatra, the Black Dyke Mills Band, Bobby Vinton, Connie Francis – covers faded and curled at the edges after too long in the sun. An old Remington office typewriter, which looked as if it weighed a ton, stood next to a cracked Coronation mug and a bulbous, pink china lamp-stand.

Inside was no less messy, and the smell of dust, mildew and stale tobacco made Susan's nose itch.

'Can I help you?'

The man sat behind the counter, a copy of *Penthouse* open in front of him. It was hard to tell how tall he was, but he certainly had the short black hair, the squarish face and the broken nose that the woman in Johnson's building had mentioned.

'John Fairley?' Richmond asked.

'That's me.'

Richmond and Susan showed their warrant cards, then Richmond said, in his formal voice, 'We have received information which leads us to believe that there may be stolen property on these premises.' He handed over a copy of the search warrant they had spent all afternoon arranging. Fairley stared at it, open-mouthed.

By then, both Richmond and Susan were rummaging through the junk. They would find nothing on display, of course, but the search had to be as thorough as possible. Susan flipped through the stack of old 45s on wobbly tables – Ral Donner, B. Bumble and the Stingers, Karl Denver, Boots Randolph, the Surfaris, names she had never heard of. One table groaned under the whole of Verdi's *Rigoletto* on 78s. There were also several shelves of books along one wall: *Reader's Digest* condensed editions; old Enid Blytons with torn paper covers that said 2/6 on the front; books with stiff pages and covers warped and stained by water-damage, most by authors she had never heard of. She doubted whether even Banks or Gristhorpe would have heard of them, either. Who on earth would want to buy such useless and smelly junk?

When they were satisfied that there were no videos or stereos hidden among the cracked figurines and rusted treadle sewing machines, they asked Fairley if he would show them the rest of the premises. At first he hesitated, then he shrugged, locked the front door, turned the sign to read CLOSED, and led them through the moth-eaten curtain behind the counter. Silent so far, he seemed resigned to his fate.

The curtain led into a corridor with a filthy sink piled with cups growing mould from old tea leaves. Next to the sink was a metal counter-top streaked with rust on which stood, among the mouse droppings, a bottle of camp coffee, a quarter of Typhoo tea, some curdled milk and a bowl of sugar lumps.

The corridor ended in a toilet with a stained bowl and washbasin, flaking plaster and spider webs in the corners.

It was almost impossible to open the door to the other room on the ground floor, but slim Richmond managed to slip in and discover that it was packed mostly with collapsed cardboard boxes. There were also some books, video cassettes and magazines of a slightly suspect eroticism, though perhaps not the more prosecutable variety of pornography.

After he had finished there, Richmond pointed to the other door off the corridor. 'Where's that lead?' he asked.

Fairley tried to bluff his way out of opening it. He said it led nowhere, wasn't part of the premises, but Richmond persisted. They soon found themselves following Fairley down to a cellar with whitewashed walls. There, lit by a bare bulb, stood what looked like the remnants of the Fletcher's warehouse job. Two television sets, three videos and a compact-disc player.

'Bankrupt stock,' said Fairley. 'I was going to put them in the window when I've got room.'

Richmond ignored him and asked Susan to check the serial numbers on the cartons with the list that the manager of Fletcher's had supplied. They matched.

'Right,' said Richmond, leaning back against the stack of cartons. 'Before we go down to the nick, I'd like to ask you a few questions, John.'

'Aren't you going to charge me?'

'Later.'

'I mean, shouldn't I have a solicitor present or something?'

'If you want. But let's just forget the stolen goods for the moment, shall we? Have you got any form, John?'

Fairley shook his head.

'That's good,' Richmond said. 'First offence. It'll go better for you if you help us. We want to know about Carl Johnson.'

'Now look, I didn't have nothing to do with that. You can't pin that on me.'

It was interesting to watch Richmond at work, Susan thought. Cool, relaxed and looking as elegant as ever in the dingy room, careful not to lean against the wall for fear of marking his suit, he set Fairley at ease and led him gently through a series of preliminary questions about his relationship with Johnson and Poole before he got to Chivers. At the mention of the name, Fairley became obviously nervous.

'Carl brought him here,' he said, squatting miserably on a box. 'I never liked him, or that girlfriend of his. They were both a bit doolally, if you ask me.'

'What do you mean?'

'Just that look he got in his eyes sometimes. Oh, he could be pleasant enough on the surface, but when you saw what was underneath, it was scary. I couldn't look him in the eye without trembling.'

'When did you see him last?'

'Couple of weeks ago.'

'Did you ever think he might be concerned with Carl's death?'

'I . . . well, to be honest, it crossed my mind, I don't know why. Just the kind of person he seemed.'

'Yet you didn't come forward?'

'Do you think I'm crazy or something?'

'Did you know of any reason he might have had for killing Johnson?'

Fairley shook his head. 'No.'

'There was no falling out over the loot?'

'What loot?'

Richmond kicked a box. 'The alleged loot.'

'No.'

'What about the girl? Did Johnson make a play for her?'

'Not that I know of. She was sexy enough, and she knew it, but she was Chivers's property, no mistaking that. NO ENTRY signs on every orifice. Sorry, love.' He looked at Susan, who simply gave him a blank stare. 'No,' he went on, turning back to Richmond, 'I don't think Carl was daft enough to mess with her.'

'What about Gemma Scupham?'

Fairley looked surprised. 'The kid who was abducted?'

'That's her.'

'What about her?'

'You tell me, John.'

Fairley tensed. A vein throbbed at his temple. 'You can't think I had anything to do with that? Oh, come on! I don't go in for little girls. No way.'

'What about Chivers?'

'Nothing about him would surprise me.'

'Did he ever mention her?'

'No. I mean, I *had* heard of her. Les complained about her sometimes and Carl sympathized. Chivers just seemed to be standing back, sort of laughing at it all, as if such a problem could never happen to him. He always seemed above everything, arrogant like, as if we were all just petty people with petty concerns and he'd think no more about stepping on us if he had to than he would about swatting a fly. Look, why are you asking me about Gemma? I never even met the kid.'

'She was never in this shop?'

'No. Why should she have been?'

'Where is Chivers now?'

'I don't know and I don't want to know. He's bad news.'

Richmond sat down carefully on a box. 'Has it never

struck you', he said, 'that if he did kill Johnson, then you and Les might be in danger, too?'

'No. Why? We didn't do nothing. We always played square.'

'So did Carl, apparently. Unless there's something you're not telling me. It doesn't seem to matter with Chivers, does it? Why do you think he killed Carl, if he did?'

'I told you, I don't know. He's a nutter. He always seemed to me like he was on the edge, you know, ready to go off. People like him don't always need reasons. Maybe he did it for fun.'

'Maybe. So why not kill you, too? Might that not be fun?'

Fairley licked his lips. 'Look, if you're trying to scare me you're doing a damn good job. Are you trying to warn me I'm in danger or just trying to make me talk? I think it's about time I saw a solicitor.'

Richmond stood up and brushed off the seat of his pants with his palm. 'Are you sure you have no idea where Chivers went after he left Eastvale?'

'None.'

'Did he say anything about his plans?'

'Not to me.'

'Where did he come from?'

'Dunno. He never talked about himself. Honest. Look, are you winding me up about all this?' Fairley had started to sweat now.

'We need to find him, John,' said Richmond quietly. 'That's all. Then we'll all sleep a little easier in our beds.' He turned to Susan. 'Let's take him to the station now and make it formal, shall we?' He rubbed the wall and held up his forefinger. 'And we'd better get a SOCO team down here, too. Remember that whitewash on Gemma's clothing?'

Susan nodded. As they left, she noticed that John Fairley seemed far more willing to accompany them to the station than most villains they arrested.

'I'll tell you one thing for free,' he said as they got in the car.

'What's that?' said Richmond.

'He had a gun, Chivers did. I saw it once when he was showing off with it in front of his girlfriend.'

'What kind of gun?'

'How would I know? I don't know nothing about them.'

'Big, small, medium?'

'It wasn't that big. Like those toy guns you play with when you're a kid. But it weren't no toy.'

'A revolver?'

'What's the difference?'

'Never mind.'

'Isn't it enough just to know the bastard's got a gun?'

'Yes.' Richmond sighed, looking over at Susan. 'Yes, it is.'

THREE

Banks and Gristhorpe leaned on the railings above the beach and ate fish and chips out of cardboard cartons. The hotel didn't do evening meals, and, as in most seaside towns, all the cafés seemed to close at five or six.

'Not bad,' said Gristhorpe, 'but they do them better up north.'

'If you like them greasy.'

'Traitor. I keep forgetting you're still just a southerner underneath it all.'

Banks tossed his empty carton into a rubbish bin and looked out to sea. Close to shore, bright stars shone through gaps in the clouds and reflected in the dark water. Farther out, the cloud covering thickened and dimmed the quarter moon. The breeze that was slowly driving the clouds inland carried a chill, and Banks was glad he had put on a pullover under his sports jacket. He sniffed the bracing air, sharp with ozone. A few cars droned along the Esplanade, and the sound of people talking or laughing in the night drifted on the air occasionally, but mostly it was quiet. Banks lit a cigarette and drew deep. Silly, he thought, but it tasted better out here in the sea air pervaded with the smells of salt water and seaweed.

'Do you know,' said Banks finally, 'I think I'm developing a feel for Chivers. I *know* he's been here. I know he killed the girl.'

Gristhorpe gave him a steady, appraising look. 'Not turning psychic on me, are you, Alan?'

Banks laughed. 'Not me. Look, there's the white Fiesta, the smile, the blonde, the neatness of the hotel room. You'll agree the incidents have those things in common?'

'Aye. And tomorrow morning we'll have a word with the hotel staff and look over Loder's reports, see if we can't amass enough evidence to be *sure*. Maybe then we'll know what the next move is. If that bastard's slipped away abroad . . .' Gristhorpe crumpled up his cardboard box and tossed it in the bin.

'We'll get him.'

Gristhorpe raised an eyebrow. 'More intuition?'

'No. Just sheer dogged determination.'

Gristhorpe clapped Banks lightly on the shoulder. 'That I can understand. I think I'll turn in now. Coming?'

Banks sniffed the night air. He felt too restless to go to

bed so soon. 'Think I'll take a walk on the prom,' he said. 'Just to clear out the cobwebs.'

'Right. See you at breakfast.'

Banks watched Gristhorpe, a tall, powerful man in a chunky Swaledale sweater, cross the road, then he started walking along the promenade. A few couples, arms around one another, strolled by, but Weymouth at ten-thirty that Friday evening in late September was as dead as any out-of-season seaside resort. Over the road stood the tall Georgian terrace houses, most of them converted into hotels. Lights shone behind some curtains, but most of the rooms were dark.

When he got to the Jubilee Clock, an ornate structure built to commemorate Queen Victoria's Diamond Jubilee, Banks took the steps down to the beach. The tide hadn't been out long and the glistening sand was wet like a hardening gel under his feet. The footprints he made disappeared as soon as he moved on.

As he walked, it was of John Cowper Powys he thought, not Thomas Hardy. Somebody had mentioned *Weymouth Sands* to him around Christmas time and, intrigued, he had bought a copy. Now, as he actually trod Weymouth sands himself for the first time since he was a child, he thought of the opening scene where Magnus Muir stood meditating on the relationship between the all-consuming unity of the sea and the peculiar and individual character of each wave. The Esplanade lights reflected in the wet sand, which sucked in the remaining moisture with a hissing sound every time a wave retreated.

Heady thoughts for a lowly chief inspector. He stood for a moment and let the waves lick at his shoes. Farther south, the lights of the car ferry terminal seemed to hang suspended over the water. Loder was right, he thought:

Chivers would have been a fool to take his car. Much easier to mingle with the foot-passengers and rent one wherever he went. Or, even more anonymous, travel by train if he got to France.

Seeing the dead woman in the hotel had shaken Banks more than he realized. Wondering why, as he doubled back along the ribbed sand at the edge of the beach, he felt it was perhaps because of Sandra. There was only a superficial resemblance, of course, but it was enough to remind him of Sandra in her twenties. Though Sandra had ridiculed the idea, the photo of Gemma Scupham had also reminded him of a younger Tracy, albeit a less doleful-looking one. Tracy took after Sandra, whereas Brian, with his small, lean, dark-haired Celtic appearance, took after Banks. There were altogether too many resemblances for comfort in this case.

Banks thought about what he had said earlier, the *feel* he was developing for the way Chivers operated. Then he thought about what he *hadn't* told Gristhorpe. Standing in that room and looking down at the dead woman, Banks had known, as surely as he knew what happened at Johnson's murder, that Chivers had been making love to her, smiling down, and that as he was reaching his climax – that brief pause for a sigh that Les Poole had mentioned – he had taken the pillow and held it over her face. She had struggled, scratching and gouging his skin, but he had pushed it down and ejaculated as she died.

Was he really beginning to understand something of Chivers's psychopathic thought processes? It was a frightening notion, and for a moment he felt himself almost pull in his antennae and reject the insight. But he couldn't.

The blonde woman – he wished he knew her name – must somehow have started to become a liability. Perhaps she was having second thoughts about what they'd done to Gemma; maybe she was overcome by guilt and had threatened to go to the police. Perhaps Chivers had conned her into thinking they were taking the child for some other reason, and she had found out what really happened. She could have panicked when she saw the newspaper likenesses, and Chivers didn't feel he could trust her any longer. Or maybe he just grew tired of her. Whatever the reason, she ceased to be of use to him, and someone like Chivers would then start to think of an *interesting* way to get rid of her.

He must be easily bored, Banks thought, remembering what he and Jenny had talked about in the Queen's Arms. A creative intelligence, though clearly a warped one, he showed imagination and daring. For some years, he had been able to channel his urges into legitimate criminal activity – a contradiction in terms, Banks realized, but nonetheless true. Chivers had sought work from people who had logical, financial reasons for what they employed him to do, and however evil they were, whatever harm they did, there was no denying that at bottom they were essentially businessmen gone wrong, the other side of the coin, not much different from insider traders and the rest of the corporate crooks.

Now, though, perhaps because he was deteriorating, losing control, as Jenny had said, Chivers was starting to create his own opportunities for pleasure, financed by simple heists like the Fletcher's warehouse job. The money he got from such ventures would allow him the freedom to roam the country and follow his fancy wherever it led him. And by paying cash, he would leave no tell-tale credit-card traces.

Now, it seemed, Chivers was escalating, craving more

dangerous thrills to satiate his needs. He was like a drug addict; he always needed more to keep him at the same level. Gemma Scupham, Carl Johnson, the blonde. How quickly was he losing control? Was he starting to get careless?

A wave soaked one foot and the bottom of his trouser leg. He stepped back and did a little dance to shake the water off. Then he reached for a cigarette and, for some reason, thought of Brian, not more than seventy miles east of him, in Portsmouth. College had only just started, and he might be feeling lonely and alien in a strange city. It was so close, yet Banks wouldn't be able to visit.

He missed his son. Much as Tracy had always seemed the favourite, with her interests in history and literature, her curiosity and intelligence, and Brian always the outsider, the rebel, with his loud rock music and his lack of interest in school, Banks missed him. Certainly he felt the odd one out now that Tracy was only interested in boys and clothes.

Brian was eighteen, and Banks had turned forty in May. With a smile, he remembered the compact disc of Nigel Kennedy playing the Brahms violin concerto that Brian had bought him for his birthday. Well, at least the thought was there. And he also remembered his recent row with Tracy. In a way, she had been right: Brian *had* got away with a lot, especially that summer, before he had left for the polytechnic: late-night band practices; a week-long camping trip to Cornwall with his mates; coming in once or twice a little the worse for drink. But of one thing Banks was certain: Brian wasn't taking drugs. As an experienced detective, he knew the signs, physical and psychological, and had never observed them in his son.

He turned from the beach and found a phonebox on the

Esplanade. It was eleven o'clock. Would he be in? He put his phonecard in and punched in the number Brian shared with the other students in the house. It started to ring.

'Hello?'

A strange voice. He asked for Brian, said it was his father.

'Just a minute,' the voice mumbled.

He waited, tapping his fingers against the glass, and after a few moments Brian came on the line.

'Dad! What is it? What's wrong?' he asked.

'Nothing. I'm just down the coast from you and I wanted to say hello. How are you doing?' Banks felt choked, hearing Brian's voice. He wasn't sure his words came out right.

'I'm fine,' Brian answered.

'How's college?'

'Oh, you know. It's fine. Everything's fine. Look, are you sure there's nothing wrong? Mum's okay, isn't she?'

'I told you, everything's all right. It's just that I won't be able to make the time to drop by and I thought, well, being so close, I'd just give you a ring.'

'Is it a case?'

'Yes.'

Silence.

'Are you still there, Dad?'

'Of course I am. When are you coming up to visit us again?'

'I'll be up at Christmas. Hey, I've met some really great people down here. They play music and all. There's this one guy, we're going to form a band, and he's been playing some great blues for me. You ever heard of Robert Johnson? Muddy Waters?'

Banks smiled to himself and sighed. If Brian had ever

taken the trouble to examine his collection – and of course, no teenager would be seen dead sharing his father's taste in music – he would have found not only the afore-mentioned, but Little Walter, Bessie Smith and Big Bill Broonzy, among several dozen others.

'Yes, I've heard of them,' he said. 'I'm glad you're having a good time. Look, keep in touch. Your mother says you don't write often enough.'

'Sorry. There's really a lot of work to do. But I'll try to do better, promise.'

'You do. Look—'

His time ran out and he didn't have another card. Just a few more seconds to say hurried goodbyes, then the electronic insect sound of a dead line. When he put the phone down and started walking back to the hotel, Banks felt empty. Why was it always like that? he wondered. You call someone you love on the phone, and when you've finished talking, all you feel is the bloody distance between you. Time to try sleep, perhaps, after a little music. Sleep that knits up the ravell'd sleave of care. Some hope.

13

ONE

Hotel or bed and breakfast, it didn't seem to make much difference with regard to the traditional English breakfast, thought Gristhorpe the following morning. Of course, there was more choice at the Mellstock Hotel than there would be in a typical B and B, but no one in his right mind would want to start the day with a 'continental' breakfast – a stale croissant and a gob of strawberry jam in a plastic container. As it was, Banks sat struggling over a particularly bony kipper while Gristhorpe stuck to bacon and eggs and wished he hadn't. Between them, they shared a rack of cold toast and a pot of weak instant coffee.

Gristhorpe felt grumpy. He hadn't slept well; the mattress had been too soft, and his back was bothering him. The breakfast didn't help either, he realized, feeling the onset of heartburn.

'I dropped in at the hotel bar for a nightcap yesterday,' he said, pushing the plate aside and pouring more coffee. 'Thought I might be able to get something out of the regulars.'

'And?' asked Banks, pulling a bone from the corner of his mouth.

'Nothing much. There's a couple from Wolverhampton staying the week, and they said the Barlows, as they called themselves, were in once or twice. Always pleasant. You know, nodded and said hello, but never got into any conversations. The missis thought they were a honeymoon couple.'

'You know,' said Banks, 'he's really starting to get on my nerves, Chivers. He turns up somewhere, goes around smiling like Mr Clean, and people die.'

'What do you expect?'

'It's just his bloody nerve. It's as if he's challenging us, playing catch-me-if-you-can.'

'Aye, I know what you mean,' said Gristhorpe, with a scowl. 'And we won't catch him sitting here picking at this fine English cuisine. Come on.' He pushed his plate away and stood up abruptly, leaving Banks to follow suit.

The hotel manager had provided a small room on the ground floor for them to conduct interviews. First, they read over the statements that DI Loder and his men had taken from the hotel staff, then asked to see Meg Wayne, the chambermaid.

She looked no older than fourteen or fifteen, a frightened schoolgirl with her uniform and starched cap that couldn't quite contain her abundant golden hair. She had a pale, clear complexion, and with a couple of red spots on her cheeks, Gristhorpe thought, she could probably pass herself off as one of Tess's milkmaid friends in Hardy's book. Her Dorset burr was even more pronounced than Loder's, her voice soft and surprisingly low.

'Mr Ballard, the manager, said I could take the day off,' she said, 'but I don't see the point, do you? I mean, the rooms need doing every day no matter what happens, and I could certainly do with the money.'

'Still,' said Gristhorpe, 'it must have been a shock?'

'Oh yes. I've never seen a dead body before. Only on telly, like.'

'Tell us what you saw yesterday, Meg.'

'We-ell, I opens the door as usual, and as soon as I does I knows something's wrong.'

'Were the curtains open?'

'Part way. Enough to see by.'

'And the window?'

'Open a bit. It was chilly.' She fiddled with a set of room keys on her lap as she spoke.

'Did you go into the room?'

'Not right in. I just stood in the doorway, like, and I could see her there on the bed, with her head all covered up.'

'Tell me exactly what you saw,' said Gristhorpe. He knew that people tend to embellish on what they have observed. He also wanted to be certain that Loder and his SOCO team had restored the room to the way it had been when Meg opened the door. He grimaced and rubbed his stomach; the heartburn was getting worse.

'It looked like just twisted sheets at first,' she said, 'but then, when my eyes grew more accustomed, I could tell it was someone under there. A shape.' She blushed and looked down at her lap. 'A woman's shape. And the pillow was over her head, so I knew she was . . . dead.'

'It's all right, Meg,' said Gristhorpe. 'I know it's upsetting. We won't be much longer.'

Meg nodded and took a deep breath.

'Did you see the woman's face?'

'No. No, I just knew it was a woman by the outline of the sheets.'

'Did you disturb anything in the room?'

'Nothing. Like I told Mr Loder, I ran straight off to Mr Ballard and he sent for the police. That's God's honest truth, sir.'

'I believe you,' said Gristhorpe. 'We just have to make certain. You must have been upset. Maybe there's something you forgot?'

'No, sir.'

'All right. Did you ever see the people who were staying in that room?'

'Not as far as I know. I don't see many guests, sir. I have to do my job when they're out.'

'Of course. Now think, Meg, try to remember, was there anything else about the scene that struck you at the time?'

Meg squeezed her eyes shut and fiddled with the keys. Finally, she looked at Gristhorpe again. 'Just how tidy it was, sir. I mean, you wouldn't believe the mess some guests leave you to clean up. Not that I mind, like. I know they pay for the service and it's my job, but . . .'

'So this room was unusually tidy?'

'Yes.'

'Did you see anything at all on the table or the dresser?' She shook her head. 'Nothing. They were empty.'

'All right, Meg, we're just about finished now. Can you remember anything else at all?'

'Well, it's funny,' she said, 'but just now when I had my eyes closed I did remember something. I never really paid it any mind at the time, though I must have noticed it, but it stuck.'

'What is it?'

'I don't think it can be important, but it was the smell. I use Pledge Natural on the furniture. I'd know that smell anywhere. Very clean and . . . But this was something else . . . a sort of pine-scented polish . . . I don't know. Why would anybody want to polish furniture in a hotel room?'

'Thank you, Meg,' said Gristhorpe. 'You can go now. You've been a great help.'

'I have? Thank you.' She went to the door and turned, with her fingers touching the handle. 'I'm not looking forward to this, sir,' she said. 'Between you and me, I'm not looking forward to opening any doors in this hotel this morning.' And she left.

Gristhorpe reached into his side pocket, took out a pack of Rennies he carried for such emergencies as English breakfasts and southern fish and chips, and chewed two of them.

'All right?' Banks asked.

'Aye.' Gristhorpe pulled a face. 'Just ought to watch my diet, that's all.'

Next they saw the receptionist, Maureen, rather prickly at being called away from her domain. Gristhorpe basked in antacid relief and left Banks to do most of the questioning. She had very little to tell them save that the Barlows had checked in the evening of Wednesday, September 24, at about six o'clock with just one tan suitcase between them. She had told them about parking and got their car licence number, then he had signed the register Mr and Mrs Barlow and given an address in Lichfield. Loder had already checked this and found it didn't exist. No, Maureen hadn't asked for any identification. Why should she? And yes, of course he had skipped out on his bill. If you'd just murdered your lover, you'd hardly stop at the front desk and pay your hotel bill, would you? No, nobody had seen him leave. It wasn't a prison camp or one of those Russian gulags, you know. What did she think of them? Just ordinary, no one you'd look twice at if you saw them in the street. Her, maybe, but he was just a nondescript bloke with a nice smile. In fact, Maureen remembered wondering what an attractive, if rather stuck-up, girl like her was doing with the likes of him.

And that was it. They talked briefly with Mr Ballard, who didn't remember seeing the Barlows at all, and to the bellboy who had carried their suitcase to their room and remembered nothing but the pound tip the bloke had given him. Nobody knew what they did with their time. Went for walks, the cinema in the evening, or to a pub. Nothing unusual about them. Nothing much else to do in Weymouth.

By the time they had finished the interviews, it was eleven-thirty. DI Loder had said he would drop by that morning as soon as the autopsy results became available, and they met him walking into the lobby. He looked as if he had slept badly, too, Gristhorpe thought, with bags under his eyes and his long face pale and drawn. The three of them decided to take some fresh air on the prom while they discussed the results.

'Anything?' Gristhorpe asked as they leaned on the railings. A faint breeze ruffled his thick grey hair. The weather was overcast, but reasonably warm. Seagulls squawked overhead.

Loder shook his head slowly. 'First, we've made inquiries at the ferry dock and no one remembers anyone of his description. We can't really make too much of that, though, as it's very busy down there. And the autopsy findings bear out what the doc suspected. She died of asphyxiation, and the pillow fibres in her lungs indicate that's how it happened. No sign of drugs or anything, though it'll be a while before all the test results come back. We've sent the tissue for DNA testing – it looks like our man's Group O, by the way – but that'll take some time. She did have sex prior to death, and there were no signs of sexual assault, so we assume it was by consent. Otherwise healthy. Poor woman, we don't even know her name yet.

Only one surprise: she was eight weeks pregnant.'

'Hmm,' said Gristhorpe. 'I wonder if Chivers knew that.'

Loder shrugged. 'Hardly a motive for murder.'

'I don't think he needs much of a motive. It could have pushed him over the edge.'

'Or maybe it made her a liability,' Banks suggested. 'Not so much just because she was pregnant but because it softened her, brought out the guilt over what they'd done? If she found out she was going to have a child of her own . . .'

'There's no point in speculating,' said Gristhorpe. 'It's something we might never know. Anything else?'

'Nothing from the car,' Loder said. 'A few partials . . . fibres and the like, but you know as well as I do most stuff's mass-produced these days. Could have come from almost any blue cotton shirt. There's not a lot else to say. We've got men asking around about him, if anyone saw him after he left the hotel. Nothing so far. Oh, and I informed Interpol and the authorities on the Channel Islands.'

'Good,' said Gristhorpe. 'That seems to cover it all.'

'What next?' asked Loder.

'We can only wait, can't we?'

'Looks like it. I'd better be off back to the station, keep on top of it.'

'Thanks.' Gristhorpe shook his hand. 'Thanks a lot.'

They watched Loder walk off towards his car. 'He's got a point,' said Gristhorpe. 'What *do* we do next?'

Banks shrugged. 'I can only speculate.'

'Go ahead.'

Banks watched a ferry steam out of the dock. The flock of gulls swooped on a dead fish on the beach. 'I've been thinking about Chivers,' he said, lighting a cigarette and looking out to sea. 'Trying to fathom his thought processes.'

'And?'

'And I'm not sure, but . . . look, he must know we're after him by now. Surely he's seen the stuff in the newspapers. What does he do? He kills the woman, too much extra baggage, and he takes off. Now a normal criminal would certainly head for the continent and disappear. But we know Chivers isn't normal.'

'I think I follow your train, Alan. I've had the same thought myself. He's playing a game, isn't he? Laughing at us.'

Banks nodded. 'And he likes the attention. Jenny said he's likely to be egocentric, but he's also probably impulsive and irresponsible. I've thought about that a lot.'

'So where would he head, given the way he thinks?'

'Back to where it started, I think,' said Banks. 'I'll bet you a pound to a penny the bastard's back in Eastvale.'

TWO

It was late that Saturday evening when Banks and Gristhorpe arrived back in Eastvale. They were delayed by a six-car pile-up into a jackknifed lorry on the M1 just south of Leicester, and as they passed by Pontefract and Castleford on the A1, the rain fell in buckets, slowing traffic to a crawl.

So it was that on Sunday morning, as the bells rang in the church and people crossed the market square in their Sunday best for the morning service, the members of Eastvale CID sat in the conference room around the large oval table drinking coffee and pooling their findings.

Richmond and Susan brought the others up to date on John Fairley's information about Chivers and the fact that he owned a gun.

'Fairley seems the least involved of them all,' said Richmond. 'We had a good long chat when we brought him in. He's got no prior form. I'm sure he's dealt with stuff that fell off the back of a lorry before, but the Fletcher's warehouse job is his first big bit of fencing, we're sure of that. Susan?'

'I agree,' said Susan Gay, looking up from the notes in front of her. 'Seems it was Johnson's idea, and he recruited Les Poole easily. They were mates of Fairley's, genuinely helping out at the shop for a bit of under-the-counter pocket money. Chivers was the prime mover. Without him, I don't reckon the others would have had the guts to go through with it. It was Chivers drugged the guard dogs and cut through the chain-link fence. Poole drove the van, backed it up to the loading bay and away they went. The back of Fairley's shop is just a quiet backstreet, so they got unloaded without any trouble. It wasn't too hard to make a few sales through their pubmates, word of mouth, and they'd already got rid of most of the stuff by the time we called.'

'Was there any falling out over the loot?' Banks asked.

'No,' said Richmond. 'Not as far as we could tell. Everyone seemed happy with his share. Poole took the television and stereo as part of his cut. Johnson got a thousand in cash. Fairley's got no idea why Johnson was killed, though he said he wouldn't be surprised to hear that Chivers had done him. Chivers scared him, seemed the type who'd do it for fun.'

'And he's seen or heard nothing of him since?'

'No, sir. And doesn't want to.'

'What about Gemma?' Banks asked. 'Does Fairley know anything about what happened to her?'

'Just confirms what Poole told us, that's all,' said Richmond. 'After we spotted the whitewash in the cellar, we had the team do a thorough search last night, but they've turned up nothing to indicate Gemma was there.'

'Right,' said Gristhorpe, standing up and looking at his watch. 'I've told you what Alan thinks about Chivers being in the area, and I agree with him. What I propose is that we start trying to flush him out. Phil, I'd like you to muster as many men as you can and start knocking on doors, asking questions. Somebody must have seen the bastard. The station and the bus station are obvious places to start. He left his car in Weymouth and unless he stole one, the odds are that he took some other form of transport. The lads down there are doing their bit, too. We're co-ordinating with a DI Loder. I'll get in touch with the media and we'll see if we can't get something on the local news tonight. I want it all in the open. If he is here, I want him to know we're closing in on him. I want him to panic and make a run for it.

'Susan, get in touch with as many of those concerned citizens who helped in the search for Gemma and get them to ask around. Tell them to make sure they don't take any risks, though. This one's dangerous. You know the kind of thing to ask about. Smoke from a cottage that's supposed to be empty, odd noises, suspicious strangers, that kind of thing. Especially anyone who insists on paying cash in large amounts. We'd better put a watch on Fairley's shop, Brenda Scupham's place and the holiday cottage, too, just in case. And we'll ask around the pubs. He's not the type to lie low. He'll be wanting to see the effect he's having.

And remember, he may have altered his appearance a bit. He's done it before, so don't rely on hair colour. The one thing he can't change is that bloody smile. All right?'

Everyone nodded and dispersed. Banks returned to his office and looked out on the church-goers pouring into the market square: women in powder-blue suits holding onto their broad-brimmed hats in the wind, clutching hand-bags; husbands in dark suits at their sides, collars too tight, shifting from foot to foot as their wives chatted, thinking maybe now they'd done their duty they'd be able to sneak off to the Queen's Arms or the Crooked Billet for a quick one before dinner; restless children dreaming of an afternoon at Kinley Pond catching frogs, or climbing trees to collect birds' eggs in Brinely Woods – either that or sniffing glue under the railway bridge and planning a bit of recreational B and E. And somewhere, in the midst of all that quotidian human activity and aspiration, was Jeremy Chivers.

Banks didn't notice Susan in his doorway until she cleared her throat. He turned.

'Sorry, sir,' she said, 'it slipped my mind at the meeting, but you had a call from Piet Kuypers, Amsterdam police. Said to call him back, you'd know what it was about.'

'Did he leave a message?'

'No. Just said he had a few interesting speculations for you.' Susan handed him a piece of paper. 'The top's his work number,' she said, pointing, 'and that one's home.'

'Thank you.' Banks took the paper and sat down. In the excitement of the chase for Chivers, he realized, he had quite forgotten asking Piet to check up on Adam Harkness. He hadn't liked the man much, but as soon as it became clear that Chivers had more than likely killed Carl

Johnson, there had seemed no real reason to consider Harkness any longer.

Puzzled, he dialled Piet's home number. A child's voice answered. Banks couldn't speak Dutch, and the little girl didn't seem to understand English. The phone banged down on a hard surface and a moment later a man's voice came over the line, again in Dutch.

'Piet? It's me. Alan Banks in Eastvale?'

'Ah, Alan,' said Piet. 'That was my daughter, Eva. She only began to learn her English this year.' He laughed. 'How are you?'

'I'm fine, Piet. Hope I didn't disturb your lunch but I've been out of town and I got a message to call you.'

'Yes. You have a moment?'

'Yes, of course.'

Banks heard the receiver placed, more gently this time, on the hard surface, and he put his feet on the desk and lit a cigarette while he waited for Piet to come back. He realized he had been talking too loudly, as one does on the telephone to foreigners, and reminded himself that Piet's English was almost as good as his own.

'Sorry about that,' said Piet. 'Yes, I did a little snooping, as you call it, about that man Harkness.' His voice bore only traces of a Dutch accent.

'Anything interesting?'

'Interesting, yes, I think so. But nothing but rumours, you understand. Hearsay. I found his wife. She has since remarried, and she didn't want to talk about her relationship with Harkness, but she hinted that part of the reason they separated was that he had what she called filthy habits.'

'Filthy habits?'

'Yes. Like what, I thought? What do you English regard

as a filthy habit? Picking his nose in bed? But I couldn't get her to say any more. She is very religious. She had a strict Dutch Protestant upbringing in a small town in Friesland. I'm sorry, Alan, but I couldn't force her to talk if she did not want to.'

Banks sighed. 'No, of course not. What happened next?'

'I talked to some of my colleagues on drugs and vice, but they don't know him. Mostly they're new. You don't last that long working on drugs and vice, and Harkness has been gone, how long did you say, two years?'

'Something like that,' said Banks.

'So I had an idea,' Piet went on. 'I went to see Wim Kaspar. Now Wim is a strange man. Nobody really knows how far it all went, but he was, how do you English say, made to leave work early?'

'Fired?'

'No. I know that word. Not exactly fired.'

'Made redundant?'

Piet laughed. 'Yes, that's it. Such an odd phrase. Well, there was something of a cloud over Wim, you see. Nobody could prove anything, but it was suspected he took bribes and that he was involved with the drugs and girls in the Red Light district. But Wim worked many years in the Red Light district, ever since patrolman, and he knows more than anybody else what goes on there. And I don't care what people say – maybe it is true – but he is a good man in many ways. Do you understand?'

'I think so,' said Banks, remembering now that Piet was a nice bloke but took ages getting to the bloody point.

'Wim heard and saw many things that went no further. It's give and take in that world. You scratch my back and I'll scratch yours. Especially if what they say about him is true. So I talked to him and he remembers something. Now you must understand, Alan, that there is no proof of this. It's just rumours. And Wim will never repeat officially what he told me.'

'Tell me, Piet.'

'According to Wim's contacts, your Mr Harkness visited the Red Light district on several occasions.'

'Piet, who doesn't visit the Red Light district? It's one of your main tourist attractions.'

'No, wait. There's more. There are some places, very bad places. Not just the pretty women in the windows, you understand?'

'Yes?'

'And Wim told me that your Mr Harkness visited one of these places.'

'How did your source know who he was?'

'Alan, you must remember Mr Harkness is well known in Amsterdam, and not without influence. Do you want me to go on?'

'Yes, please.'

'It was a very bad place,' Piet continued. 'You understand prostitution is not illegal here, that there are many brothels?'

'Yes.'

'And the live sex shows and the whips and chains and all the rest. But this one brothel, Wim says, was a very special place. A place that caters for people who like little girls.'

'Jesus Christ!'

'It happens, Alan. What can I say? Girls disappear from the big cities, they turn up in these places. Sometimes they are used for snuff films. You know what they are?'

'I know. Why wasn't he arrested?'

'Sometimes it is better to leave the little fish. Also, Harkness was an important man and, how shall I say, perhaps pressure could be brought to bear. He could have been useful.'

Banks sighed. He knew the scenario. Get something on a man like Harkness and you've got him in your pocket: the police version of blackmail.

'Alan, in Amsterdam, just as, I suspect, in your London, you can get anything you want if you have the money to pay for it. Anything. If we can find these places and find evidence, we close them down and arrest the people responsible. But these men are very clever. And sometimes policemen can be bought, protection can be paid. Or blackmailed. We all have skeletons in our cupboards. Alan? Are you still there?'

'Yes. Yes, Piet, I know. I was thinking. Listen, I'd like you to do me a big favour. I assume places like this are still in existence?'

'There is one place now we are suspicious of. On the surface, it seems like an ordinary brothel, but rumour has it that young girls can be had there, for a price. Our undercover men are watching, but we have no proof yet.'

'I'd like you to find out if there are any new girls.' He gave Piet Gemma's description, praying he was wrong. At least it meant she might still be alive, if Harkness kept his connections in Amsterdam. He still couldn't work out the whys and the wherefores, how everything linked up, but he knew it would not have been so difficult for Harkness or someone else to smuggle Gemma out of the country, even during the search. The ferry from Immingham, for example, was always crowded; it would be easy enough to slip in among the other families with a sleeping child on the overnight journey, when everyone was tired. 'I don't care whether you get enough proof to lock them up or not. Rumours will do fine for me. Use your contacts, informers. Maybe even your friend Wim might be able to help?'

'Yes,' said Piet slowly. 'I understand. I'll try. What more can I say?'

'And Piet.'

'Yes?'

'Thanks. Thanks a lot. You did a great job.' Then Banks slammed down the receiver and rushed to find Gristhorpe.

THREE

It was about time the place had a good cleaning, Brenda thought, wielding the Hoover like a lawnmower. She knew she wasn't good at housekeeping, but now she had so much time on her hands and nothing but bad thoughts and terrifying dreams, she had to do something or she would fall apart. The ground-in dirt and the food stains wouldn't come out, of course, they would need shampooing, but the dust would. At least it was a start.

The vacuum was so noisy that she didn't hear the bell. It was only the steady thumping on her door that broke through. She turned off the machine and listened again. Another knock. For a moment she just stood there, worried it might be Les. She wasn't frightened of him – she knew he was a coward at heart – but she didn't feel like another public row and she was damned if she was going to let him in. On the other hand, it might be the police with news of Gemma. She glanced out of the window but couldn't see a police car. That didn't matter, she realized. The plain-clothes men drove ordinary cars.

She sighed and stood the Hoover in the corner. Well, if

it *was* Les, she'd just have to tell him to stay away and call the police if he insisted on pestering her. The blurred figure through the frosted glass wasn't Les, that was for certain, but she couldn't tell who it was until she opened the door and saw Lenora Carlyle standing there with her long black hair and penetrating eyes. She didn't want to let Lenora in. Somehow, she thought, that entire episode had been a weakness, a mistake. She had been grasping at straws. And look what she was left with: nothing but a video of herself, which was already beginning to feel like an embarrassment. But she stood aside politely. Lenora hung up her coat and followed her into the front room.

'Tea?' said Brenda, feeling like a cup herself.

'Yes, please, dear, if it's no trouble.' Lenora sat on the sofa and brushed down her skirt. 'Been cleaning, I see.'

'Yes.' Brenda shrugged and went to make the tea. When it was ready, she brought it in on a tray and poured, then lit a cigarette.

'I sense there's been some great change,' Lenora said, frowning with concentration. 'Some sort of upheaval.'

'If you mean I chucked Les out, I suppose you're right.'

Lenora looked disappointed at such a prosaic explanation. 'Any news?'

Brenda shook her head.

'Well, that's why I'm here, really. You remember what I said before?'

'That Gemma's still alive?'

'That's right.' Her eyes glittered. 'More than ever I'm convinced of it, Brenda.'

'I don't think so.' Brenda shook her head. 'Not after all this time.'

'But you must have faith. She's frightened and weak. But she's alive, Brenda.'

'Don't.'

'You must listen.' Lenora put her mug down and leaned forward, clasping her hands. 'I saw animals. Jungle animals, Brenda. Lions, tigers, leopards. They're connected with Gemma somehow.'

'What are you saying? She's been taken to Africa or something?'

Lenora flopped back on the sofa. 'I don't know. The message is very weak. That's all I see. Gemma and animals.'

'Look, I really don't—'

'They're not harming her, Brenda.'

'I don't believe you.'

'But you *must* believe!'

'Why must I believe? What good has it done me?'

'Don't you want to see your Gemma again?'

Brenda stood up. 'Of course I want to see Gemma again. But I can't. She's dead. Can't you understand? She's dead. She must be. If she's not dead by now she must be suffering so much. It's best that she's dead.' The tears and grief she had felt welling up for so long were breaking the dam.

'We must cling to the gift of life, Brenda.'

'No. I don't want to listen to this. You're frightening me. Go away. Leave me alone.'

'But Brenda, I—'

'Go on.' Brenda pointed at the door, tears burning her eyes. 'Go away. Get out!'

Lenora shook her head slowly, then, shoulders slumped, she got up and left the room. When Brenda heard the door close, she sank back into her chair. She was shaking now and tears burned down her cheeks. Dammit, why wouldn't they all leave her alone? And why couldn't she know for sure? Every day that Gemma stayed missing was more like hell. Why couldn't they find her body, then Brenda could get her grieving done with, organize the funeral, move on. But no. Just day after day of misery. And it was all her fault, all Brenda's fault for not loving her daughter enough, for losing control and shaking her so much she was terrified what she might do the next time.

She stared at the large TV screen and saw her own reflection distorted through her tears. She remembered the interview she had watched over and over again. Vanity. Madness. It had all been madness. In a sudden burst of rage, she drew back her arm and flung her mug as hard as she could at the screen.

FOUR

Just a few hours ago the wind had been cool, and there had been only enough blue sky to make baby a new bonnet. Now, as Banks and Susan drove to Harkness's, the wind had dropped, the sun had come out and the afternoon had turned out fine. Gristhorpe had been out when Banks went to find him, so he had left a message and found Susan, who happened to be in the corridor at the time.

Enjoying probably the last fine weekend of the season, families sat out on the green at Fortford eating picnics, even though it wasn't particularly warm and the grass must still be damp. Banks turned right on the Lyndgarth road, and as they approached the bridge, they saw even more people ambling along The Leas or sitting on the riverbank fishing.

Banks drove in silence, tense and angry over the

forthcoming confrontation. They turned in the drive just before the old pack-horse bridge, and the car flung up gravel as they stopped. They had no evidence, he reminded himself, only supposition, and everything depended on bluffing and scaring Harkness into blabbing. It wouldn't be easy; it never was with those so used to having things their own way. Piet's information wasn't anywhere near enough to get him in court. But Harkness *had* known Johnson, and Johnson had known Chivers. Jenny said the paedophile was likely to be over forty, lived alone, and probably knew Gemma. Well, Harkness hadn't known Gemma, but he could have heard of her through Johnson and Chivers. It made sense.

After the conversation, Banks had checked the time and, finding they were only two hours ahead, tried the South African police again. They still had nothing to report, and he got the impression they were dragging their feet. He could only speculate on the nature of the crime there, and on the depth of the cover-up. He had tried Linda Fish from the Writers' Circle again, too, but she had heard no more from her writer friend. He had felt too edgy simply to wait around for more information to come in.

Harkness answered the door at the first ring. He seemed nervous to see them, Banks thought, fidgety and too talkative as he led them this time into the living room and bade them sit.

'Have you found out who killed Carl?'

'We're looking for a man called Jeremy Chivers,' Banks said. 'Someone Johnson knew. Did he ever mention the name?'

'Let's not go through all that again.' Harkness walked over to the mantelpiece. 'Who is this Chivers?'

'A suspect.'

'So why have you come to pester me again?'

Banks scratched the little scar by his right eye. It wasn't always reliable, but it did have a tendency to itch in warning when he hadn't quite realized that something was wrong. 'Well, I'll tell you, Mr Harkness. I've just had a chat with a friend of mine on the Amsterdam police, and he told me some very odd things.'

'Oh?'

'Yes. You lived there for some time, didn't you?'

'Yes, you know I did. But I can assure you I never came into contact with the police.'

'Clever there, sir, weren't you?' said Susan suddenly.

Harkness looked from one to the other, reddening. 'Look, what is this?' he said. 'You can't just come in here—'

Banks waved him to silence, ready to make his accusation. But just before he opened his mouth to speak, he paused. Something was definitely bothering him. Even now, he didn't know what it was: tension in the air, a feeling of *déjà vu*, or that little shiver when someone steps on your grave. It would come. He went on, 'Everyone knows you can get anything you want in Amsterdam. If you know where to go. If you can pay for it.'

'So what? It's hardly different from any other city in that way, I should think.' Harkness paced, hands in his pockets.

'True,' said Banks, 'though it does have something of a reputation for sex in various forms, straight and other.'

'What are you suggesting? Get to the point.'

'That's just it. We have information leading us to believe that you frequented a brothel. A very special kind of brothel. One that made young children available to its customers.'

'What! This is monstrous. I've already told you the Assistant Chief Commissioner is a good friend of mine, the Commissioner, too. If you don't take back your slanderous allegations, I'll make sure you're out of the force before bedtime tonight. Damn it, I think I'll do it anyway.'

'I don't think so,' said Banks. 'The Commissioner is particularly upset about this case. He has grandchildren the same age as Gemma Scupham, so I don't think the fact that you belong to the same golf club will cut a lot of ice with him, sir.'

'But this is preposterous! You can't possibly be suggesting that I had anything to do with that?'

'Well, I—' Banks stopped, suddenly aware of what was bothering him. He shot Susan a quick glance and stood up. Looking puzzled, she followed suit. 'Probably not,' he said. 'But I had to find out. I'm sorry, Mr Harkness. I just wanted to test your reaction to the allegations.'

'You've got a damned nasty way of going about your business, Banks. I most certainly will be talking to your superior.'

'As you wish.' Banks followed Susan to the door. 'But please understand, we have to follow every lead, however incredible, however distasteful. I'm very sorry to have bothered you, sir. I think I can safely say we won't be troubling you again.'

'Well . . .' Harkness looked confused. He opened his mouth as if to complain more, then seemed to think better of it, realizing they were leaving, and stood there gulping like a fish. 'I should damn well think so,' he muttered finally. 'And don't think I don't mean it about talking to the Commissioner.'

'What is it?' Susan asked as they drove back onto the road. 'Sir? Why did you do that?'

Banks said nothing. When they were out of sight of the house, about half a mile down the road, hidden by the roadside trees, he pulled into a lay-by.

'What is it?' Susan asked again. 'I picked up the signal to get out, but why? You were rattling him. We could have had him.'

'This is the third time I've visited Harkness,' Banks said slowly, hands still gripping the wheel. 'Both times before the place has been a bit of a mess – dusty, untidy, a typical bachelor dwelling.'

'So?' said Susan. 'He's had the cleaning lady in.'

'I don't think so. He said he didn't employ one. Notice how clean the surfaces were, and that silver goblet on the coffee table?'

'Yes. Polished so you could see your face.'

'You weren't there,' Banks said, 'but it's the same polish smell as in the Weymouth hotel room, something with a strong scent of pine.'

'You can't be thinking . . . . surely?'

Banks nodded. 'That's just what I am thinking, Susan. We've got to radio for help.' He gestured with his thumb back towards the house. 'I think Chivers is in there somewhere, and he's armed.'

14

ONE

To the casual observer, nothing unusual occurred around The Leas and Devraulx Abbey that fine Sunday afternoon in late September. If one fisherman approached another, had a chat, then replaced him at the riverbank, or if a picnicking family, shortly after having a few words with a passing rambler complete with rucksack and stick, decided to pack up and leave because the wasps were bothering them, then what of it? The Abbey closed early, and there were a few more cars on the road than usual, but then it was such a surprisingly beautiful afternoon that everyone wanted to enjoy a bit of it before the rain and wind returned.

Still in the same position, about half a mile down the road, out of sight of the Harkness house, Banks and Susan waited. Birds called, insects hummed, a light breeze hissed through the trees. At last, another car joined them, and Superintendent Gristhorpe got out, along with DS Richmond, and strode purposefully over to Banks's Cortina. There wasn't much to say; everything had been taken care of on the radio. The replacement fishermen were policemen in plain clothes; the picnicking families had all been cleared from the area, and a tight circle had been drawn around Harkness's house and grounds.

'If he's in there,' Gristhorpe said, 'he won't get away.

Alan, let's you and I go back to the house, say we have a few more questions. Let's see if we can't defuse this mess before it blows up.'

'But sir,' said Susan. 'I think I should go, too.'

'No,' said Gristhorpe. 'Stay here with Phil.'

'But—'

'Look. I'm not doubting your competence, Susan. But what we need here is experience. Alan?'

'I agree,' said Banks.

Gristhorpe took a .38 Smith and Wesson from his pocket and handed it to Banks, who automatically checked it, though he knew Gristhorpe would have already done so. Susan's lips drew tight and Banks could feel the waves of humiliation flowing from her. He knew why – she had potential, but she was young, inexperienced, and she had made mistakes before – and he agreed completely with the superintendent's judgement. There was no room for error in dealing with someone like Chivers.

'Ready?' said Gristhorpe.

Banks nodded and joined him in the unmarked Rover, leaving Susan to fume and Richmond to console her in Banks's own Cortina.

'How do you read it?' Gristhorpe asked, as Banks drove slowly back towards the pack-horse bridge.

'Harkness is nervous, and I think he's shit-scared, too. And it's not just because of what I think he's done to Gemma Scupham. If I had to guess, I'd say Chivers is either in the house somewhere, or he's been there and he's hiding out nearby. And Harkness isn't harbouring him out of the kindness of his heart. He's damn close to being held hostage. There's nothing he can do, though, without incriminating himself.'

'All right,' said Gristhorpe. 'Let me do the talking. Keep your eyes peeled. We'll try and get Harkness out of there if we can.'

Banks nodded, turned into the driveway and crunched over the gravel. He felt a claw tighten at the pit of his stomach; the gun hung heavy in his pocket.

They rang the doorbell. Harkness flung the door open and growled, 'You again? What the bloody hell do you want this time?'

Gristhorpe introduced himself. 'I think it might be best if we did this at the station,' he said to Harkness.

'Am I under arrest? You can't be serious. This is nothing but a tissue of unsubstantiated lies.'

He was sweating.

'I think it would be best, sir,' said Gristhorpe. 'Of course, you have the right to consult your solicitor.'

'I'll sue the both of you for wrongful arrest. I'll have you off the force. I'll—'

Banks thought he noticed a flash of movement behind Harkness on the staircase, but it was hard to see into the house clearly. What followed next was so sudden and so unexpected, he realized in retrospect that there was nothing he could have done to prevent it.

They heard a sound like a dull pop and Harkness's eyes seemed to fill with blood. His forehead opened like a rose in time-lapse photography. Both Banks and Gristhorpe flung themselves out of the way by instinct. As Banks flattened himself against the wall of the house, he became aware of the blood and tissue on his face and chest. Harkness's. He wanted to be sick.

Time seemed to hang like overripe fruit ready to fall at any moment. Harkness lay half in and half out the door, only a small hole showing in the back of his closely cropped skull and a pool of dark blood thickening under his face around his head. Gristhorpe stood back, flat against the wall on one side of the door, Banks on the other. From inside, they heard nothing but silence. Then, it could have been minutes or just seconds after the shooting, they heard a crash from the far side of the house, followed by a curse and the sound of someone running.

They glanced quickly at one another, then Gristhorpe nodded and swung himself into the doorway first, gun sweeping the hall and stairwell. Nothing. Banks followed, adopting the stance he had learned in training: gun extended in one hand, other hand gripping the wrist. They got to the front room and found no one. But there, beyond the french windows, one of which had been smashed by a careless elbow as he dashed by, they saw Chivers running down the lawn towards the riverbank.

'Get on the radio, Alan,' said Gristhorpe. 'Tell them to close in. And tell them to be bloody careful. Get an ambulance here, too.'

Banks dashed to the car and gave the message to the plain-clothes watchers, all of whom carried police radios in their fishing boxes or picnic hampers. After he had radioed headquarters for an ambulance, he hurried through the house after Gristhorpe and Chivers.

Chivers was in the garden, heading for the river. As he ran, he turned around and fired several times. A window shattered, slate chips showered from the roof, then Gristhorpe went down. Banks took cover behind the copper beech and looked across at the superintendent's body sprawled on the lawn. He wanted to go to him, but he couldn't break cover. Carefully, he edged around the tree trunk and looked for Chivers.

There weren't many places Chivers could go. Fences

and thick hedges blocked off the riverbank to the east and west, enclosing Harkness's property, and ahead lay the water. With a quick glance right and left and a wild shot, Chivers charged into the water. Soon it was up to his hips, then his waist. He aimed towards the tree and fired again. The bullet thudded into the bark. When Banks looked around the trunk again, he saw the other police in a line across the river, all with guns, closing fast. Gristhorpe must have commandeered the whole bloody dale, he thought. Glancing back towards the house, he saw Susan Gay and Phil Richmond framed by the french window staring at Gristhorpe. He waved to them to take cover.

Chivers stopped when the water came up to his armpits and fired again, but the hammer fell with an empty click. He tried a few more times, but it was empty. Banks shouted for Richmond and Susan to see to the superintendent, then he walked down the slope.

'Come on,' he said. 'Look around you. It's over.'

Chivers looked and saw the men lining the opposite bank. They were in range now. He looked again at Banks. Then he shrugged, tossed the gun in the water, and smiled.

TWO

Everything had been done by the book; Banks saw to that. Thus, when they finally got to talk to Chivers, the custody record had been opened; he had been offered the right to legal advice, which he had repeatedly refused; offered the chance to inform a friend or relative of his arrest, at which he had laughed; and even offered a cup of tea, which he had accepted. The desk sergeant had managed to rustle up a disposable white boiler suit to replace his wet clothes, as according to the Police and Criminal Evidence Act, 'a person may not be interviewed unless adequate clothing has been offered to him'. And the interview room they sat in, while not especially large, was at least 'adequately heated, lit and ventilated' according to the letter of the law. If questioning went on for a long time, Chivers would be brought meals and allowed periods of rest.

In addition, Jenny Fuller had turned up at the station and asked if she could be present during the questioning. It was an unusual request, and at first Banks refused. Jenny persisted, claiming her presence might even help, as Chivers seemed to like to show off to women. Finally, Banks asked Chivers's permission, which galled him, and Chivers said, 'The more the merrier.'

Back at Harkness's house, Banks knew, the SOCO team would be collecting evidence, Glendenning poring over Harkness's body, a group of constables digging up the garden that Carl Johnson had so lovingly tended, and police frogmen searching the river.

Sometimes, thought Banks, the creaking machinery of the law was a welcome prophylactic on his desire to reach out and throttle someone. Hampered as he had often felt by the Act, today, ironically enough, he was glad of it as he sat across the table looking at the man who had murdered at least three people, wounded Superintendent Gristhorpe and abducted Gemma Scupham.

As he looked, he certainly felt the impulse to kill Chivers, simply to swat him as one would a troublesome wasp. But it wasn't an impulse he was proud of. All his life, both in spite of and because of his job, Banks had tried to cultivate his own version of compassion. If crime really was part of what made us human, he thought, then it merited deep study. If we simply kill off the pests that bother us, we make no progress at all. He knew that he could, in some strange way, *learn* from Chivers. It was a knowledge he might deeply wish to reject, but spiritual and intellectual cowardice had never been among his failings.

Banks sat opposite Chivers, Richmond stood behind him, by the door, and Jenny sat by the window, diagonally across from him.

Close up, the monster didn't look like much at all, Banks noted. About Banks's height, and with the same kind of lean, wiry strength, he sat erect, hands placed palms down on the table in front of him, their backs covered with ginger down. His skin was pale, his hair an undistinguished shade of sandy brown, and his general look could only be described as boyish – the kind of boy who pulled pranks and was amused to see their effects on the victims.

If there was anything outstanding about him at all, it was his eyes. They were the kind of green the sea looks sometimes, and when he wasn't smiling they looked just as cold, as deep and as unpredictable as the ocean itself. When he did smile, though, they lit up with such a bright, honest light you felt you could trust him with anything. At least, it was *almost* like that, Banks thought, if it weren't for that glint of madness in them; not quite insanity, but close enough to the edge. Not everyone would notice, but then not everyone was looking at him as a murderer.

Banks turned on the tape recorder, repeated the caution and reminded Chivers of his rights. 'Before we get onto the other charges against you,' he said, 'I'd like to ask you a few questions about Gemma Scupham.'

'Why not?' said Chivers. 'It was just a lark really.' His voice, a little more whiny and high-pitched than Banks had expected, bore no trace of regional accent; it was as bland and characterless as a BBC 2 announcer's.

'Whose idea was it?'

'Mr Harkness wanted a companion.'

'How did he get in touch with you?'

'Through Carl Johnson. We'd known each other for a while. Carl was . . . well, between you and me he wasn't too bright. Like that other chap, what's his name?'

'Poole?'

'That's right. Small-time, the two of them. Low-lifes.'

'How did you first meet Harkness?'

'Look, does any of this really matter? It's very dull stuff for me, you know.' He shifted in his chair, and Banks noticed him look over at Jenny.

'Humour us.'

Chivers sighed. 'Oh, very well. Harkness knew Carl was a gutless oaf, of course, but he had contacts. Harkness needed someone taken care of a couple of months ago.' He waved his hand dismissively. 'Someone had been stealing from him in the London office, apparently, and Harkness wanted him taught a lesson. Carl got in touch with me.'

'What happened?'

'I did the job, of course. Harkness paid well. I got an inkling from our little chats that this was a man with unusual tastes and plenty of money. I thought a nice little holiday in Yorkshire might turn out fruitful.' He smiled.

'And did it?'

'Of course.'

'How much?'

'Please. A gentleman never discusses money.'

'How much?'

Chivers shrugged. 'I asked for twenty thousand pounds. We compromised on seventeen-fifty.'

'So you abducted Gemma Scupham just for money?'

'No, no. Of course not. Not just for the money.' Chivers leaned forward. 'You don't understand, do you? It sounded like fun, too. It had to be interesting.'

'So you'd heard about Gemma through Les Poole and thought she would be the perfect candidate?'

'Oh, the fool was always moaning about her. Her mother sounded as thick as two short planks, and she clearly didn't care much about the child anyway. They didn't want her. Harkness did. It's a buyer's market. It was almost too easy. We picked her up, drove around for a while just to be on the safe side, then dropped her off at Harkness's after dark and returned the car.' He smiled. 'You should have seen his face light up. It was love at first sight.'

'Did either Johnson or Poole know about this?'

'I'm not stupid. I wouldn't have trusted either of them.'

'So what went wrong?'

'Nothing. It was the perfect crime,' Chivers mused. 'But Carl got foolish and greedy. Otherwise you'd never have gone anywhere near Harkness.'

'But we did.'

'Yes. Carl suspected something. Maybe he actually saw the child, I don't know. Or perhaps he caught Harkness drooling over his kiddie porn and put two and two together. That surprised me, that did. I never thought him capable of that. Putting two and two together and coming up with the right answer. I must admit I underestimated him.'

'What happened?'

Chivers made a steeple with his hands and his eyes glazed over. He seemed lost in his own world. Banks repeated the question. Chivers seemed to come back from a great distance.

'What? Oh.' He gave a dismissive wave of the hand. 'He tried to put the touch on Harkness. Harkness got worried and called me again. I said I'd take care of it.'

'For a fee?'

'Of course. I wouldn't say I'm in it for the money, but I need a fair bit to keep me in the style to which I'm accustomed. Harkness arranged to meet him at the old lead mine to pay him off and Chelsea and I gave him a lift there. Poor bastard, he never suspected a thing.'

'Chelsea?'

He stared at a spot above Banks's left shoulder. 'Yes. Silly name, isn't it? Fancy naming someone after a flower show, or a bun. Poor Chelsea. She just couldn't quite understand.'

'Understand what?'

'The beauty of it all.' Chivers's eyes turned suddenly back on Jenny. They looked like a dark-green whirlpool, Banks thought, with blackness at its centre, evil with a sense of humour. 'She liked it all the time, you know, the thrill. And she never liked poor Carl anyway. She said he was always undressing her with his eyes. You should have seen the look in *her* eyes when I killed him. She was standing right next to me and I could smell her sex. Needless to say, we had a *lot* of fun later that night. But she got jittery, read the newspapers, began to wonder, asked too many questions . . . As I said, she didn't fully comprehend the beauty of it all.'

'Did you know she was pregnant?'

He turned his eyes slowly back to Banks. 'Yes. That was the last straw. It turned her all weepy, the sentimental fool. I had to kill her then.'

'Why?'

'Wouldn't want another one like me in this universe,

would we?' He winked. 'Besides, it was what she wanted. I have a knack of knowing what people really *want*.'

'What did she want?'

'Death, of course. She enjoyed it. I know. I was there. It was glorious, the way she thrust and struggled.' He looked over at Jenny again. '*You* understand, don't you?'

'And Harkness?' Banks said.

'Oh, it was very easy to see into his dirty soul. Little children. Little kiddies. He'd had it easy before. South Africa, Amsterdam. He found it a bit difficult here. He was getting desperate, that's all. It's simply a matter of knowing the right people.'

Banks noticed that Chivers had dampened a part of his cuff and was rubbing at an old coffee ring on the desk. 'What happened to Gemma?' he asked.

He shrugged. 'No idea. I completed my side of the bargain. I suppose when the old pervert had finished with her he probably killed her and buried the body under the petunia patch or something. Isn't that what they do? Or maybe he sold her, tried to recoup what he'd spent. There's plenty in the market for that kind of thing, you know.'

'What about the clothing we found?'

'You want me to do your job for you? I don't know. I suppose as soon as things got too hot for him he wanted to put you off the scent. Does that sound about right?'

'Why did you come back to Eastvale? You could probably have got away, you know.'

Chivers's eyes dulled. 'Fatal flaw, I suppose. I can't bear to miss anything. Besides, you only caught me because I wanted you to, you know. I've never been on trial, never been in jail. It might be interesting. And, remember, I'm not there yet.' He shot Jenny a quick smile and began to rub harder at the coffee stain, still making no impression. He was clearly uncomfortable in the boiler suit they had found for him, too, scratching now and then where the rough material made his skin itch.

Banks walked over to the door and opened it to the two uniformed officers who stood outside and nodded for them to take Chivers down to the holding cells for the time being.

Chivers sat at the desk staring down at the stain he was rubbing and rubbing. Finally, he gave up and banged the table once, hard, with his fist.

THREE

Banks stood by his office window with the light off and looked down on the darkening market square again, a cigarette between his fingers. Like Phil and Jenny, he had felt as if he needed a long, hot bath after watching and listening to Chivers. It was odd how they had drifted away to scrub themselves free of the dirt: Jenny, pale and quiet, had gone home; Richmond had gone to the computer room. They all recognized one another's need for a little solitude, despite the work that remained.

Little people like Les Poole and others Banks had met in Eastvale sometimes made him despair of human intelligence; someone like Chivers made him wonder seriously about the human *soul*. Not that Banks was a religious man, but as he looked at the Norman church with its low square tower and the arched door with its carvings of the saints, he burned with unanswered questions.

They could wait, though. The hospital had called to tell him that Gristhorpe had a flesh wound in his thigh and was already proving to be a difficult patient. The SOCOs had called several times from The Leas area; no luck so far in finding Gemma's body, and it was getting dark. The frogmen had packed up and gone home. They had found Chivers's gun easily enough, but no trace of Gemma. They would be back tomorrow, though they didn't hold out much hope. The garden was in ruins, but so far the men had uncovered nothing but stones and roots.

Harkness's body lay in the mortuary now, and if anyone had to make him look presentable for the funeral, good luck to them. Banks shuddered at the memory. He had washed and washed his face, but he could still smell the blood, or so he thought. And he had tossed away his jacket and shirt, knowing he could never wear them again, and changed into the spares he always kept at the station.

And he thought of Chelsea. So that was her name, the poor twisted shape on the hotel bed in Weymouth. Why had she been so drawn to a monster like Chivers? Can't people *see* evil when it's staring them right in the face? Maybe not until it's too late, he thought. And the baby. Chivers knew his own evil, revelled in it. Chelsea. Who was she? Where did she come from? Who were her parents and what were they like? Bit by bit, he would find out.

He had been alone with his thoughts for about an hour, watching dusk fall slowly on the cobbled square and the people dribble into the church for the evening service. The glow from the coloured-glass windows of the Queen's Arms looked welcoming on the opposite corner. God, he could do with a drink to take the taste of blood out of his mouth, out of his soul.

The harsh ring of the telephone broke the silence. He picked it up and heard Gristhorpe say, 'The buggers wouldn't let me out to question Chivers. Have you done it? Did it go all right?'

Banks smiled to himself and assured Gristhorpe that all was well.

'Come and see me, Alan. There's a couple of things I want to talk about.'

Banks put on his coat and drove over to Eastvale General. He hated hospitals, the smell of disinfectant, the starched uniforms, the pale shadows with clear fluid dripping into them from plastic bags being pushed on trolleys down gloomy hallways. But Gristhorpe had a pleasant enough private room. Already, someone had sent flowers and Banks felt suddenly guilty that he had come empty-handed.

Gristhorpe looked a little pale and weak, mostly from shock and blood loss, but apart from that he seemed in fine enough fettle.

'Harkness never expected any trouble from the police over Gemma's abduction, did he?' he asked.

'No,' said Banks. 'As Chivers told us, why should he? It was almost the perfect crime. He'd managed to keep a very low profile in the area. Nobody knew how sick his tastes really were.'

'Aye, but everything changed, didn't it, after Johnson's murder?'

'Yes.'

'And you were a bit hard on Harkness, given that chip on your shoulder, weren't you?'

'I suppose so. What are you getting at?'

Gristhorpe tried to sit up in bed and grimaced. 'So much so that he might think we'd get onto him?' he said.

'Probably.' Banks rearranged the pillows. 'I think he felt quite certain I'd be back.' The superintendent was wearing striped pyjamas, he noticed.

'And he claimed harassment and threatened to call the

Commissioner and probably the Prime Minister for all I know.'

'Yes.' Banks looked puzzled. What was Gristhorpe getting at? It wasn't like him to beat about the bush. Had delirium set in?

'Let's assume that Chivers is telling the truth,' Gristhorpe went on, 'and he delivered Gemma to Harkness on Tuesday evening and killed Johnson on Thursday evening. Now Harkness *could* have spirited Gemma out of the house, say to Amsterdam, before Johnson's murder, but why should he? And if he hadn't done it by then, he'd probably be too nervous to make such a move later.'

'I suppose he would,' Banks admitted. 'And he could have taken her clothes up to the moors to put us off the scent on Thursday evening or Friday, whenever Chivers told him Johnson was dead and came to collect his fee. Harkness must have known we'd visit him then, given his connection with Johnson. But he could have buried her anywhere. It's a very isolated house, and pretty well sheltered by trees. I mean, even someone passing by on the road wouldn't notice him burying a body in the garden, would they?'

'But our men have found nothing so far.'

'You know it can take time. It's a big garden. If she's there, they'll find her. Then there's the river.'

'*If* she's there.'

Banks watched the blood drip slowly into Gristhorpe's veins. 'What do you mean?'

'This.' Gristhorpe rolled over carefully and took something out of his bedside cabinet. 'I got one of the lads to tag it as evidence and bring it here to me.'

Banks stared at the polished silver. 'The goblet?'

'Yes. It's a chalice actually, sixteenth-century, I think. Remember when Phil and Susan took me into Harkness's living room and laid me on the couch till the ambulance came? That's when I noticed it. I could hardly miss it, it was right at eye-level.'

'I still don't see what that's got to do with Gemma,' said Banks, who was beginning to worry that Gristhorpe was more seriously injured than he let on.

'Don't you?' Gristhorpe passed him the chalice. 'See those markings?'

Banks examined it. 'Yes.'

'It's the banner of the Pilgrimage of Grace. See where it shows the five wounds of Christ? I'll explain it, then you can go see if I'm right.'

Puzzled, Banks crossed his legs and leaned back in his chair.

FOUR

It was late twilight as Banks drove: the time of evening when the greens of the hillsides and the grey of the lime-stone houses and walls are all just shades of darkness. But the river seemed to glow with a light of its own, hoarded from the day, as it snaked through the wooded river meadows known as The Leas.

As he drove, Banks remembered Gristhorpe's words: 'In Yorkshire history, The Pilgrimage of Grace started as a religious uprising against Henry VIII, sparked by the closing of the monasteries in 1536. Harkness's house was built later, so this chalice would probably be a previous family heirloom and a powerful symbol to whoever owned it. In the seventeenth century, it was often dangerous to be a Roman Catholic in this part of the country, but they persisted. They didn't take unnecessary risks, though. So while they would invite some wandering incognito priest around to perform mass or take confession in their houses, they knew they might hear the soldiers hammering on the door at any moment, so they built priest holes, cavities in the walls where the priests could hide. Some were even more elaborate than that. They led to underground passages and escape routes.

'I grew up in Lyndgarth, just up the hill from Harkness's,' Gristhorpe had continued, 'and when we were kids there were always rumours about the old De Montfort house, as it was called then. We thought it was haunted, riddled with secret passages. You know how kids dream. We never went inside, of course, but we made up stories about it. I'd forgotten all about it until we went there tonight – and I must admit things happened quickly enough to put it right out of my mind again. Until I saw this chalice. It started me thinking. The date's right, the history, so it's worth a try, don't you think?'

Banks had agreed. He turned into the drive and stopped at the police tape. The man on duty came forward, and when he recognized Banks he let him through.

Banks nodded greetings as he passed the SOCO team at work in the garden, receiving shakes of the head to indicate that nothing new had been discovered. The grounds looked like a film set, with the bright arc-lights casting shadows of men digging, and it was loud with the sound of drills, the humming of the generator van and instructions shouted above the noise. Inside the house, men examined the corners of carpets and settees, sticking on pieces of Sellotape and lifting off fibres, or running over areas with compact hand-vacuums.

First, Banks checked the kitchen, behind the fridge and cooker, then the dining room, getting help to move out the huge antique cabinet that held cutlery and crystal glasses. Nothing.

The library yielded nothing either, so he went next to the living room where he had first noticed the grimy, tarnished chalice on the coffee table. It was partly seeing it again and noticing how clean it was that had first made him uneasy earlier that day, on his visit with Susan.

The bookcase opposite the fireplace looked promising, and Banks started pulling out the old *National Geographics*, looking for some kind of lever or button to press, and feeling, as he did so, more than a little foolish. It was like something out of Edgar Allan Poe, he thought.

Then he found it: a brass bolt sunk perfectly in the wood at the back of the central shelf, on the left. It slid back smoothly, as if recently oiled, and the whole bookcase swung away from the wall on hinges, just like a door. Before him loomed a dark opening with a flight of worn stone steps leading down.

Banks called for a torch, and when he had one, he stepped into the opening. On a hook to his left hung two keys on a ring. He plucked them off as he went by.

At the bottom of the stairs, a rough, dank passage led on, probably far away from the house to provide an escape for the itinerant priest. Banks shone his torch ahead and noticed that the passage was blocked by rubble after a few yards. But the two heavy wooden doors, one on either side of the passage, looked more interesting. Banks went to the one on his right and tried to open it. It was locked. Holding his breath, heart pounding, he tried the keys. The second one worked.

The hinges creaked a little as he slowly pushed the door open. Groping in the dark, he found a light switch, and a bare bulb came on, revealing a small, square room with whitewashed walls. At the centre of the room stood a leather armchair, the kind with a footrest that slides out as you sit in it, and in front of that stood a television set attached to a video. Banks doubted that priest holes had electricity, so Harkness must have gone to all the trouble of wiring his private den himself. In a rack beside the chair, Banks found a range of pornographic magazines, all of them featuring children being subjected to disgusting and degrading acts. In the cabinet under the video were a number of video cassettes of a similar nature.

Afraid of what he might find, Banks crossed the passage and fitted the other key in the lock. It opened easily. This time, he had no need to grope for a light switch. Beside the narrow bed stood a small orange-shaded table-lamp. Next to it sat a book of *Thomas the Tank Engine* stories and a bottle of pills. The walls were painted with the same white-wash as the other room, but a quilt decorated with stylized jungle animals – lions, tigers and leopards with friendly human expressions – covered the small, still shape on the bed.

It was Gemma Scupham, no doubt about it. From what Banks could see of her face between the dirty patches, it looked white, and she lay motionless on her back, her right arm raised above her head. The scar of a thin cut ran across the pale flesh of her inner arm.

Banks could sense no breath, no life. He bent over to look more closely. As he leaned over Gemma, he fancied he noticed one of her eyelids twitch. He froze. It happened again.

'My God,' he muttered to himself, and gazed down in awe as a tear formed and rolled out of the corner of Gemma's eye, leaving a clean and shining path through the grime.

DEAD RIGHT

For my Canadian family:
Gord & Shirley, John, Lynn & Bob,
Kate, Sarah, Pat & Brian, Alex,
Elizabeth, Brian & Amy

1

ONE

The boy's body sat propped against the graffiti-scarred wall in a ginnel off Market Street, head lolling forward, chin on chest, hands clutching his stomach. A bib of blood had spilled down the front of his white shirt.

Detective Chief Inspector Alan Banks stood in the rain and watched Peter Darby finish photographing the scene, bursts of electronic flash freezing the raindrops in mid-air as they fell. Banks was irritated. By rights, he shouldn't be there. Not in the rain at half past one on a Saturday night.

As if he didn't have enough problems already.

Banks had got the call the minute he walked in the door after an evening alone in Leeds at Opera North's *The Pearl Fishers*. Alone because his wife, Sandra, had realized on Wednesday that the benefit gala she was supposed to host for the Eastvale community centre clashed with their season tickets. They had argued – Sandra expecting Banks to forgo the opera in favour of her gala – so, stubbornly, Banks had gone alone. This sort of thing had been happening a lot lately – going their own ways – to such an extent that Banks could hardly remember the last time they had done anything together.

The limpid melody of the 'Au fond du temple saint' duet still echoed around his mind as he watched Dr Burns, the young police surgeon, start his *in situ* examination under the canvas tent the Scene of Crime officers had erected over the body.

PC Ford had come across the scene at eleven forty-seven while walking his beat, community policing being a big thing in Eastvale these days. At first, he said, he thought the victim was just a drunk too legless to get all the way home after the pubs closed. After all, there was a broken beer bottle on the ground beside the lad, he seemed to be holding his stomach, and in the light of Ford's torch, the dark blood could easily have passed for vomit.

Ford told Banks he didn't know quite what it was that finally alerted him this was no drunk sleeping it off; perhaps it was the unnatural stillness of the body. Or the silence: there was no snoring, no twitching or muttering, the way drunks often did, just silence inside the hiss and patter of the rain. When he knelt and looked more closely, well, of course, then he knew.

The ginnel was a passage no more than six feet wide between two blocks of terrace houses on Carlaw Place. It was often used as a short cut between Market Street and the western area of Eastvale. Now, onlookers gathered at its mouth, behind the police tape, most of them huddled under umbrellas, pyjama bottoms sticking out from under raincoats. Lights had come on in many houses along the street, despite the lateness of the hour. Several uniformed officers were circulating in the crowd and knocking on doors, seeking anyone who had seen or heard anything.

The ginnel walls offered some protection from the rain, but not much. Banks could feel the cold water trickling down the back of his neck. He pulled up his collar. It was mid-October, the time of year when the weather veered sharply between warm, misty, mellow days straight out of

Keats and piercing gale-force winds that drove stinging rain into your face like the showers of Blefuscuan arrows fired at Gulliver.

Banks watched Dr Burns turn the victim on his side, ease down his trousers and take the rectal temperature. He had already had a glance at the body, himself, and it looked as if someone had beaten or kicked the kid to death. The features were too severely damaged to reveal much except that he was a young white male. His wallet was missing, along with whatever keys and loose change he might have been carrying, and there was nothing else in his pockets to indicate who he was.

It had probably started as a pub fight, Banks guessed, or perhaps the victim had been flashing his money about. As he watched Dr Burns examine the boy's broken features, Banks imagined the scene as it might have happened. The kid scared, running perhaps, realizing that whatever had started innocently enough was quickly getting out of control. How many of them were after him? Two, probably, at least. Maybe three or four. He runs through the dark, deserted streets in the rain, splashing through puddles, oblivious to his wet feet. Does he know they're going to kill him? Or is he just afraid of taking a beating?

Either way, he sees the ginnel, thinks he can make it, slip away, get home free, but it's too late. Something hits him or trips him, knocks him down, and suddenly his face is crushed down against the rainy stone, the cigarette ends and chocolate wrappers. He can taste blood, grit, leaves, probe a broken tooth with his tongue. And then he feels a sharp pain in his side, another in his back, his stomach, his groin, then they're kicking his head as if it were a football. He's trying to speak, beg, plead, but he can't get the words out, his mouth is too full of blood. And finally he just slips away. No more pain. No more fear. No more anything.

Well, maybe it had happened like that. Or they could have been already lying in wait for him, blocking the ginnel at each end, trapping him inside. Some of Banks's bosses had said he had too much imagination for his own good, though he found it had always come in useful. People would be surprised if they knew how much of what they believed to be painstaking, logical police work actually came down to a guess, a hunch or a sudden intuition.

Banks shrugged off the line of thought and got back to the business at hand. Dr Burns was still kneeling, shining a penlight inside the boy's mouth. It looked like a pound of raw minced meat to Banks. He turned away.

A pub fight, then? Though they didn't usually end in death, fights were common enough on a Saturday night in Eastvale, especially when some of the lads came in from the outlying villages eager to demonstrate their physical superiority over the arrogant townies.

They would come early to watch Eastvale United or the rugby team in the afternoon, and by pub chucking-out time they were usually three sheets to the wind, jostling each other in the fish-and-chip-shop queues, slagging everyone in sight, just looking for trouble. It was a familiar pattern: 'What are you looking at?' 'Nothing.' 'You calling *me* nothing!' Get out of that if you can.

By midnight, though, most of the boozers had usually gone home, unless they had moved on to one of Eastvale's two nightclubs, where for a modest entrance fee you got membership, an inedible battered beefburger, a constant supply of ear-splitting music and, most important of all, the chance to swill back watery lager until three in the morning.

It wasn't that Banks had no sympathy for the victim – after all, the boy was *somebody's* son – but solving this case, he thought, would simply be a matter of canvassing the local pubs and finding out where mi-laddo had been drinking, whom he'd been upsetting. A job for Detective Sergeant Hatchley, perhaps; certainly not one for a wet Detective Chief Inspector with Bizet's melodies still caressing his inner ear; one whose only wish was to crawl into a nice warm bed beside a wife who probably still wasn't speaking to him.

Dr Burns finished his examination and walked over. He looked far too young and innocent for the job – in fact, he looked more like a farmer, with his round face, pleasant, rustic features and mop of chestnut hair – but he was quickly becoming conversant with the number of ways in which man could dispatch his fellow man to the hereafter.

'Well, it certainly looks like a boot job,' he said, putting his black notebook back in his pocket. 'I can't swear to it, of course – that'll be for Dr Glendenning to determine at the post-mortem – but it looks that way. From what I can make out on first examination, one eye's practically hanging out of its socket, the nose is pulped and there are several skull fractures. In some places the bone fragments might possibly have punctured the brain.' Burns sighed. 'In a way, the poor bugger's lucky he's dead. If he'd survived, he'd have been a one-eyed vegetable for the rest of his days.'

'No sign of any other injuries?'

'A few broken ribs. And I'd expect some severe damage to the internal organs. Other than that . . .' Burns glanced back at the body and shrugged. 'I'd guess he was kicked to death by someone wearing heavy shoes or boots. But don't quote me on that. It also looks as if he was hit on the back of the head – maybe by that bottle.'

'Just one person?'

Burns ran his hand over his wet hair and rubbed it dry on the side of his trousers. 'I'm sorry, I didn't mean to imply that. It was more likely two or three. A gang, perhaps.'

'But one person *could* have done it?'

'As soon as the victim was down on the ground, yes. Thing is, though, he looks pretty strong. It might have taken more than one person to *get* him down. Unless, of course, that was what the bottle was used for.'

'Any idea how long he's been there?'

'Not long.' Burns looked at his watch. 'Allowing for the weather conditions, I'd say maybe two hours. Two and a half at the outside.'

Banks made a quick back-calculation. It was twenty to two now. That meant the kid had probably been killed between ten past eleven and eleven forty-seven, when PC Ford found the body. A little over half an hour. And a half-hour that happened to coincide with pub closing-time. His theory was still looking good.

'Anyone know who he is?' Banks asked.

Dr Burns shook his head.

'Any chance of cleaning him up enough for an artist's impression?'

'Might be worth a try. But as I said, the nose is pulped, one eye's practically—'

'Yes. Yes, thank you, doctor.'

Burns nodded briskly and walked off.

The Coroner's Officer directed two ambulance attendants

to bag the body and take it to the mortuary, Peter Darby took more photographs and the SOCOs went on with their search. The rain kept falling.

Banks leaned back against the damp wall and lit a cigarette. It might help concentrate his mind. Besides, he liked the way cigarettes tasted in the rain.

There were things to be done, procedures to be set in motion. First of all, they had to find out who the victim was, where he had come from, where he belonged, and what he had been doing on the day of his death. Surely, Banks thought, someone, somewhere, must be missing him. Or was he a stranger in town, far from home?

Once they knew something about the victim, then it would simply be a matter of legwork. Eventually, they would track down the bastards who had done this. They would probably be kids, certainly no older than their victim, and they would, by turn, be contrite and arrogant. In the end, if they were old enough, they would probably get charged with manslaughter. Nine years, out in five.

Sometimes, it was all so bloody predictable, Banks thought, as he flicked his tab-end into the gutter and walked to his car, splashing through puddles that reflected the revolving lights of the police cars. And at that point, he could hardly be blamed for not knowing how wrong he was.

TWO

The telephone call at eight o'clock on Sunday morning woke Detective Constable Susan Gay from a pleasant dream about visiting Egypt with her father. They had never done anything of the kind, of course – her father was

a cool, remote man who had never taken her anywhere –
but the dream seemed real enough.

Eyes still closed, Susan groped until her fingers touched
the smooth plastic on her bedside table, then she juggled
the receiver beside her on the pillow.

'Mmm?' she mumbled.

'Susan?'

'Sir?' She recognized Banks's voice and tried to drag
herself out of the arms of Morpheus. But she couldn't get
very far. She frowned and rubbed sleep from her eyes.
Waking up had always been a slow process for Susan, ever
since she was a little girl.

'Sorry to wake you so early on a Sunday,' Banks said,
'but we got a suspicious death after closing time last
night.'

'Yes, sir.' Susan raised herself from the sheets and
propped herself against the pillows. *Suspicious death.* She
knew what that meant. Work. Now. The thin bedsheet
slipped from her shoulders and left her breasts bare. Her
nipples were hard from the morning chill in the bedroom.
For a moment, she felt exposed talking to Banks while she
was sitting up naked in bed. But he couldn't see her.
She told herself not to be so daft.

'We've got scant little to go on,' Banks went on. 'We
don't even know the victim's name yet. I need you down
here as soon as you can make it.'

'Yes, sir. I'll be right there.'

Susan replaced the receiver, ran her fingers through her
hair and got out of bed. She stood on her tiptoes and
stretched her arms towards the ceiling until she felt the
knots in her muscles crack, then she padded to the living
room, pausing to note the thickness of her waist and
thighs in the wardrobe mirror on her way. She would have

to start that diet again soon. Before she went to take a shower, she started the coffee-maker and put some old Rod Stewart on the CD player to help her wake up.

As the hot water played over her skin, she thought of last night's date with Gavin Richards, a DC from Regional Headquarters. He had taken her to the Georgian Theatre in Richmond to see an Alan Bennett play, and after that they had found a cosy pub just off Richmond market square, where she had eaten cheese-and-onion crisps and drunk a half-pint of cider.

Walking to her car, both of them huddled under her umbrella because it was raining fast and, like a typical man, Gavin hadn't bothered to carry one, she had felt his warmth, felt herself responding to it, and when he had asked her back to his house for a coffee she had almost said yes. Almost. But she wasn't ready yet. She wanted to. Oh, she wanted to. Especially when they kissed good night by her car. It had been too long. But they had only been out together three times, and that was too soon for Susan. She might have sacrificed her personal life for her career over the last few years, but she wasn't about to hop into bed with the first tasty bloke who happened to come along.

When she noticed she had been standing in the shower so long that her skin had started to glow, she got out, dried herself off briskly and threw on a pair of black jeans and a polo-neck jumper that matched her eyes. She was lucky that her curly blonde hair needed hardly any attention at all. She added a little gel to give it lustre, then she was ready to go. Rod Stewart sang 'Maggie Mae' as she sipped the last of her black, sugarless coffee and munched a slice of dry toast.

Still eating, she grabbed a light jacket from the hook

and dashed out the door. It was only a five-minute drive to the station, and on another occasion she might have walked for the exercise. Especially this morning. It was a perfect autumn day: scrubbed blue skies and only the slightest chill in the air. The recent winds had already blown some early lemon and russet leaves from the trees, and they squished under her feet as she walked to her car.

But today Susan paused only briefly to sniff the crisp air, then she got in her car and turned the key in the ignition. Her red Golf started on the first try. An auspicious beginning.

THREE

Banks leaned by his office window, his favourite spot, blew on the surface of his coffee and watched the steam rise as he looked out over the quiet market square. He was thinking about Sandra, about their marriage and the way it all seemed to be going wrong. Not so much wrong, just nowhere. She still hadn't spoken to him since the opera. Not that she'd had much chance, really, with him being out so late at the crime scene. And this morning she had barely been conscious by the time he left. But still, there was a discernible chill in the house.

Last night's rain had washed the excesses of Saturday night from the cobbles, just as the station cleaning-staff disinfected and mopped out the cells after the overnight drunk-and-disorderlies had been discharged. The square and the buildings around it glowed pale grey-gold in the early light.

Banks had his window open a couple of inches, and the sound of the church congregation singing 'We plough the fields, and scatter' drifted in. It took him back to the Harvest Festivals of his childhood, when his mum would give him a couple of apples and oranges to put in the church basket along with everyone else's. He often wondered what happened to all the fruit after the festival was over.

The *Dalesman* calendar on his wall showed Healaugh Church, near York, through a farm gate. It wasn't a particularly autumnal shot, Banks was thinking, as he heard the tap on his door.

It was Susan Gay, first to arrive after Detective Superintendent Gristhorpe, who was already busy co-ordinating with Regional HQ and arranging for local media coverage.

As usual, Susan looked fresh as a daisy, Banks thought. Just the right amount of make-up, blond curls still glistening from the shower. While no one would describe Susan Gay as an oil painting, with her small button nose and her serious, guarded expression, her clear, blue-grey eyes were intriguing, and she had a beautiful, smooth complexion.

Not for Susan, Banks thought, the wild, boozy Saturday nights favoured by Jim Hatchley, who followed hot on her heels looking like death warmed over, eyes bleary and bloodshot, lips dry and cracked, a shred of toilet paper stuck over a shaving cut, thinning straw hair unwashed and uncombed for a couple of days.

After the two of them had sat down, both nursing cups of coffee, Banks explained how the boy had been killed, then he walked over to the map of Eastvale on the wall by his filing cabinet and pointed to the ginnel where the body had been discovered.

'This is where PC Ford found him,' he began. 'There are no through roads leading west nearby, so people tend to cut through the residential streets, then take the Carlaw Place ginnel over the recreation ground to King Street and the Leaview Estate. Thing is, it works both ways, so he could have been heading in either direction. We don't know.'

'Sir,' said Susan, 'you told me on the telephone that he'd probably been killed shortly after closing time. If he'd been out drinking, isn't it more likely that he was heading *from* Market Street? I mean, that's quite a popular spot for young people on a Saturday night. There's a fair number of pubs, and some of them have live bands or karaoke.'

Karaoke. Banks felt himself shudder at the thought. The only other words that had a similar effect on him were *country-and-western music.* An oxymoron if ever there was one.

'Good point,' he said. 'So let's concentrate our survey on the Market Street pubs and the Leaview Estate to start with. If we draw a blank there, we can extend the area.'

'How much *do* we know, sir?' Sergeant Hatchley asked.

'Precious little. I've already had a look at the overnight logs, and there are no reports of any major shindigs. We've talked to the occupants of the terrace houses on both sides of the ginnel, as well as the people across the street. The only one with anything to say was watching television, so he didn't hear anything too clearly, but he was sure he did hear a fight or something outside during the Liverpool–Newcastle game on *Match of the Day.*'

'What exactly did he hear, sir?' Susan asked.

'Just some scuffling and grunting, then the sound of people running away. He thought more than one, but he couldn't say how many. Or which direction. He thought it was just the usual drunken yobs, and he certainly had no intention of going outside and finding out for himself.'

'You can hardly blame him, these days, can you?' said

Sergeant Hatchley, picking gingerly at the tissue over his shaving cut. It started to bleed again. 'Some of these yobs'd kill you as soon as look at you. Besides, it were a bloody good match.'

'Anyway,' Banks went on, 'you'd better check with Traffic, too. We don't know for certain whether the attackers ran home or drove off. Maybe they got a parking ticket or got stopped for speeding.'

'We should be so lucky,' muttered Hatchley.

Banks pulled two sheets of paper from a folder on his desk and passed one each to Susan and Hatchley. It showed an artist's impression of a young man, probably in his early twenties, with thin lips and a long, narrow nose. His hair was cut short and combed neatly back. Despite his youth, it seemed to be receding at the temples and looked very thin on top. There was nothing particularly distinctive about him, but Banks thought he could perceive a hint of arrogance in the expression. Of course, that was probably just artistic licence.

'The night-shift attendant at the mortuary came up with this,' he said. 'A few months back, he got bored with having no one to talk to on the job, so he started sketching corpses as a way of passing the time. *Still lifes*, he calls them. Obviously a man of hidden talents. Anyway, he told us this was mostly speculation, especially the nose, which had been badly broken. The cheekbones had been fractured, too, so he was guessing about how high and how prominent they might have been. But the hair's right, he says, and the general shape of the head. It'll have to do for now. The only things we know for certain are that the victim was a little over six foot tall, weighed eleven stone, was in fine physical shape – an athlete, perhaps – and he had blue eyes and blond hair. No birthmarks, scars, tattoos or other distinguishing features.' He tapped the folder. 'We'll try to get this on the local TV news today and in the papers tomorrow morning. For now, you can start with the house-to-house, then after opening time you can canvass the pubs. Uniform branch has detailed four officers to help. Our first priority is to find out who the poor bugger was, and the second is to discover who he was last seen with before he was killed. Okay?'

They both nodded and stood up to leave.

'And take your mobiles or personal radios and stay in touch with one another. I want the right hand to know what the left hand's doing. All right?'

'Yes, sir,' said Susan.

'As for me,' said Banks with a grim smile, 'Dr Glendenning has kindly offered to come in and do the post-mortem this morning, so I think one of us should pay him the courtesy of being present. Don't you?'

FOUR

A lot of detectives complained about house-to-house enquiries, much preferring to spend their time in scummy pubs with lowlife informers, getting the *real* feel of the Job, or so they thought. But Susan Gay had always enjoyed a good house-to-house. At the very least it was a good exercise in patience.

Of course, you got the occasional nutter, the boor, and the lecherous creep with his Hound of the Baskervilles straining at the end of its chain. Once, even, a naked child had toddled out to see what was happening and peed all over Susan's new shoes. The mother had thought it hilarious.

Then there were those endless hours in the rain, wind and snow, knocking at door after door, your feet aching, the damp and chill fast seeping right into the marrow of your bones, wishing you'd chosen some other career, thinking even marriage and kids would be better than this.

And, needless to say, every now and then some clever-arse pillock would tell her she was too pretty to be a police*man*, or would suggest she could put her handcuffs on him any time she wanted, *ha-ha-ha*. But that was all part of the game, and she didn't mind as much as she sometimes pretended she did to annoy Sergeant Hatchley. As far as Susan was concerned, the human race would always contain a large number of clever-arse pillocks, no matter what you thought. And the greatest percentage of them, in her experience, were likely to be men.

But on a fine morning like this, the valley sides beyond the town's western edge criss-crossed with limestone walls, slopes still lush green after the late-summer rains, and the purple heather coming into bloom up high where the wild moorland began, it was as good a way as any to be earning your daily crust. And there was nothing like a house-to-house for getting to know your patch.

The morning chill had quickly given way to warmth, and Susan guessed Eastvale might hit seventy before the day was over. Indian summer, indeed. She took her jacket off and slung it over her shoulder. At that time of year in the Dales, any good day was a bonus not to be wasted. Tomorrow might come rain, flood and famine, so seize the moment. Children played football in the streets, or rode around on bicycles and skateboards; men with their shirt-sleeves rolled up flung buckets of soapy water over their cars, then waxed them to perfection; groups of teenagers stood around street corners smoking, trying to look sullen and menacing, and failing on both counts; doors and windows stood open; some people even sat on their doorsteps reading the Sunday papers and drinking tea.

As Susan walked, she could smell meat roasting and cakes baking. She also heard snatches of just about every kind of music, from Crispian St Peters singing 'You Were on My Mind' to the opening of Elgar's cello concerto, which she only recognized because it was the same excerpt as the one on the CD she got free with her classical music magazine last month.

The Leaview Estate had been built just after the war. The houses, a mix of bungalows, semis and terraces, were solid, their style and materials in harmony with the rest of Swainsdale's limestone and gritstone architecture. No ugly maisonettes or blocks of flats spoiled the skyline the way they did across town on the newer East Side Estate. And on the Leaview Estate, many of the streets were named after flowers.

It was almost noon, and Susan had already covered the Primroses, the Laburnums and the Roses without any luck. Now she was about to move on to the Daffodils and Buttercups. She carried a clipboard with her, carefully ticking off all the houses she visited, putting question marks and notes beside any responses she found suspicious, keeping a keen eye open for bruised knuckles and any other signs of recent pugilism. If someone weren't home, she would circle the house number. After every street, she used her personal radio to report back to the station. If Hatchley or any of the uniformed officers got results first, then the communications centre would inform her.

A boy came speeding around the corner of Daffodil Rise on Rollerblades, and Susan managed to jump out of the way in the nick of time. He didn't stop. She held her hand to her chest until her heartbeat slowed to normal and thought about arresting him on a traffic offence. Then the adrenalin ebbed away and she got her breath back. She rang the bell of number two.

The woman who answered was probably in her late fifties, Susan guessed. Nicely turned out: hair recently permed, only a touch of lipstick, face-powder. Maybe just back from church. She wore a beige cardigan, despite the heat. As she spoke, she held it closed over her pale pink blouse.

'Yes, dearie?' she said.

Susan showed her warrant card and held out the mortuary attendant's sketch. 'We're trying to find out who this boy is,' she said. 'We think he might live locally, so we're asking around to find out if anyone knows him.'

The woman stared at the drawing, then tilted her head and scratched her chin.

'Well,' she said. 'It *could* be Jason Fox.'

'Jason Fox?' It sounded like a pop star's name to Susan.

'Yes. Mr and Mrs Fox's young lad.'

Well, Susan thought, tapping her pen against her clipboard, that's enlightening. 'Do they live around here?'

'Aye. Just over the street.' She pointed. 'Number seven. But I only said it *might* be. It's not a good likeness, you know, love. You ought to get a proper artist working for you. Like my lad, Laurence. Now there's an artist for you. He sells his prints at the craft centre in town, you know. I'm sure he—'

'Yes, Mrs . . .?'

'Ingram's the name. Laurence Ingram.'

'I'll bear him in mind, Mrs Ingram. Now, is there anything you can tell me about Jason Fox?'

'The nose isn't right. That's the main thing. Very good with noses, is my Laurence. Did Curly Watts from *Coronation Street* down to a tee, and that's not an easy one. Did you know he'd done Curly Watts? Right popular with the celebrities is my Laurence. Oh, yes, very—'

Susan took a deep breath, then went on. 'Mrs Ingram, could you tell me if you've seen Jason Fox around lately?'

'Not since yesterday. But then he's never around much. Lives in Leeds, I think.'

'How old is he?'

'I couldn't say for certain. He's left school, though. I know that.'

'Any trouble?'

'Jason? No. Quiet as a mouse. As I said, you hardly ever see him around. But it *does* look like him except for the nose. And it's easy to get noses wrong, as my Laurence says.'

'Thank you, Mrs Ingram,' said Susan, glancing over at number seven. 'Thank you very much.' And she hurried down the path.

'Wait a minute,' Mrs Ingram called after her. 'Aren't you going to tell me what's happened? After all the help I've given you. Has summat happened to young Jason? Has he been up to summat?'

If Jason's the one we're looking for, Susan thought, then you'll find out soon enough. As yet, he was only a 'possible', but she knew she had better inform Banks before barging in on her own. She went back to the corner of the street and spoke into her personal radio.

FIVE

Banks walked quickly through the narrow streets of tourist shops behind the police station, then down King Street towards Daffodil Rise. Beyond the Leaview Estate, the town gradually dissolved into countryside, the sides of the valley narrowing and growing steeper the further west they went.

Near Eastvale, Swainsdale was a broad valley, with plenty of room for villages and meadows, and for the River Swain to meander this way and that. But twenty or thirty miles in, around Swainshead, it was an area of high fells, much narrower and less hospitable to human settlements. One or two places, like Swainshead itself, and the remote Skield, managed to eke out an existence in the wild landscape around Witch Fell and Adam's Fell, but only just.

The last row of old cottages, Gallows View, pointed west like a crooked finger into the dale. Banks's first case in Eastvale had centred around those cottages, he remembered as he hurried on towards Daffodil Rise.

Graham Sharp, who had been an important figure in the case, had died of a heart attack over the summer, Banks had heard. He had sold his shop a few years ago, and it had been run since by the Mahmoods, whom Banks knew slightly through his son, Brian. He had seen them down at the station, too, recently; according to Susan, someone had lobbed a brick through their window a couple of weeks ago.

In what used to be empty fields around Gallows View, a new housing estate was under construction, scheduled for completion in a year's time. Banks could see the half-dug foundations scattered with puddles, the piles of bricks and boards, sun glinting on idle cranes and concrete-mixers. One or two streets had been partially built, but none of the houses had roofs yet.

Number seven Daffodil Rise really stood out from the rest of the houses on the street. Not only had the owners put up a little white fence around the garden and installed a panelled, natural-pine-look door, complete with a stained glass window-pane (lunacy, Banks thought, so easy to break and enter), they also had one of the few gardens in the street that lived up to the flower motif. And because it had been a long summer, many of the flowers usually gone by the end of September were still in bloom. Bees droned around the red and yellow roses that clung to their thorny bushes just under the front window, and the garden beds were a riot of chrysanthemums, dahlias, begonias and gladioli.

The front door was ajar. Banks tapped softly before walking in. He had told Susan Gay over the radio that she should talk to the parents and try to confirm whether the drawing might be of their son before he arrived, but not to tell them anything until he got there.

When Banks walked in, Mrs Fox was just bringing a tea-tray through from the kitchen into the bright, airy living room. Cut flowers in crystal vases adorned the dining table and the polished wood top of the fake-coal electric fire. Roses climbed trellises on the cream wall-paper. Over the fireplace hung a framed antique map of Yorkshire, the kind you can buy in tourist shops for a couple of quid. Along the narrowest wall stood floor-to-ceiling wooden shelving that seemed to be full of long-playing records.

Mrs Fox was about forty, Banks guessed. Sandra's age. She wore a loose white top and black leggings that outlined her finely tapered legs, with well-toned calves and shapely thighs – the kind you only got at that age from regular exercise. She had a narrow face, and her features seemed cramped just a little too close together. Her hair was simply parted in the middle and hung down as far as her shoulders on each side, curling under just a little at the bottom. The roots were only a slightly darker shade of blonde.

Mr Fox stood up to shake hands with Banks. Bald except for a couple of black chevrons above his ears, with a thin, bony face, he wore black-rimmed glasses, jeans and a green sweatshirt. He was exceptionally skinny, which made him appear tall, and he looked as if he had the kind of metabolism that allowed him to eat as much as he wanted without putting on a pound. Banks wasn't quite as skinny himself, but he never seemed to put on much weight either, despite the ale and the junk food.

Tea poured, Mrs Fox sat down on the sofa with her husband and crossed her long legs. Husband and wife left enough space for another person to sit between them, but Banks took a chair from the dining table, turned it around and sat, resting his arms on the back.

'Mr and Mrs Fox were just telling me,' Susan Gay said, getting her notebook out, 'that Jason looks like the lad in the drawing, and he didn't sleep here last night.'

'She won't tell us anything.' Mrs Fox appealed to Banks with her small, glittering eyes. 'Is our Jason in any trouble?'

'Has he ever been in trouble before?' Banks asked.

She shook her head. 'Never. He's a good boy. He never caused us any problems, has he, Steven? That's why I can't understand you coming here. We've never had the police here before.'

'Weren't you worried when Jason didn't sleep here last night?'

Mrs Fox looked surprised. 'No. Why should I be?'

'Weren't you expecting him?'

'Look, what's happened? What's going on?'

'Jason lives in Leeds, Chief Inspector,' Steven Fox cut in. 'He just uses our house when it suits him, a bit like a hotel.'

'Oh, come on, Steven,' his wife said. 'You know that's not fair. Jason's grown up. He's got his own life to live. But he's still our son.'

'When it suits him.'

'What does he do in Leeds?' Banks cut in.

'He's got a good job,' said Steven Fox. 'And there's not many as can say that these days. An office job at a factory out in Stourton.'

'I assume he's also got a flat or a house in Leeds, too?'

'Yes. A flat.'

'Can you give DC Gay the address, please? And the name and address of the factory?'

'Of course.' Steven Fox gave Susan the information.

'Do either of you know where Jason was last night?' Banks asked. 'Or who he was with?'

Mrs Fox answered. 'No,' she said. 'Look, Chief Inspector, can't you please tell us what's going on? I'm worried. Is my Jason in trouble? Has something happened to him?'

'I understand that you're worried,' Banks said, 'and I'll do everything I can to hurry things up. Please bear with me, though, and answer just a few more short questions. Just a few more minutes. Okay?'

They both nodded reluctantly.

'Do you have a recent photograph of Jason?'

Mrs Fox got up and brought a small framed photo from the sideboard. 'Only this,' she said. 'He was seventeen when it was taken.'

The boy in the photo looked similar to the victim, but it was impossible to make a positive identification. Teenagers can change a lot in three or four years, and heavy boots do a great deal of damage to facial features.

'Do you know what Jason did yesterday? Where he went?'

Mrs Fox bit her lip. 'Yesterday,' she said. 'He got home about twelve o'clock. We had sandwiches for lunch, then he went off to play football, like he usually does.'

'Where?'

'He plays for Eastvale United,' Steven Fox said.

Banks knew the team; they were only amateur players, but he'd taken Brian to see them once or twice, and they had demonstrated the triumph of enthusiasm over talent. Their matches had become quite popular with the locals, and they sometimes managed to draw two or three hundred to their bumpy field on a few acres of waste ground between York Road and Market Street.

'He's a striker,' said Mrs Fox, with pride. 'Top goal scorer in North Yorkshire last season. Amateur leagues, that is.'

'Impressive,' said Banks. 'Did you see him after the game?'

'Yes. He came home for his tea after he'd had a quick drink with his mates from the team, then he went out about seven o'clock, didn't he, Steven?'

Mr Fox nodded.

'Did he say whether he'd be back?'

'No.'

'Does he normally stop here on weekends?'

'Sometimes,' Mrs Fox answered. 'But not always. Sometimes he drives back to Leeds. And sometimes he doesn't come up at all.'

'Does he have his own key?'

Mrs Fox nodded.

'What kind of car does he drive?'

'Oh, my God, it's not a car crash, is it?' Mrs Fox put her hands to her face. 'Oh, please don't tell me our Jason's been killed in a car crash.'

At least Banks could assure her of that honestly.

'It's one of those little Renaults,' said Steven Fox. 'A Clio. Bloody awful colour, it is, too. Shiny green, like the back of some sort of insect.'

'Where does he park when he's here?'

Mr Fox jerked his head. 'There's a double garage round the back. He usually parks it there, next to ours.'

'Have you looked to see if the car's still there?'

'No. I'd no call to.'

'Did you hear it last night?'

He shook his head. 'No. We usually go to bed early. Before Jason gets back, if he's stopping the night. He tries to be quiet, and we're both pretty heavy sleepers.'

'Would you be kind enough to show DC Gay where the garage is?' Banks asked Steven Fox. 'And, Susan, if the car's there, see if he left the keys in it.'

Steven Fox led Susan out through the back door.

'Does Jason have a girlfriend?' Banks asked Mrs Fox while they were gone.

She shook her head. 'I don't think so. He might have someone in Leeds, I suppose, but . . .'

'He never mentioned her or brought her here?'

'No. I don't think he had anyone steady.'

'Do you think he would have told you if he had?'

'I can't see any reason why he wouldn't.'

'How do you and Jason get along?'

She turned away. 'We get along just fine.'

Susan and Steven Fox came back from the garage. 'It's there all right,' Susan said. 'A green Clio. I took the number. And no keys.'

'What is it?' Mrs Fox asked. 'If Jason wasn't in a car crash, did he hit someone? Was there an accident?'

'No,' said Banks. 'He didn't hit anyone.' He sighed and looked at the map over the fireplace. He couldn't really hold back telling them any longer. The best he could do was play up the uncertainty aspect. 'I don't want to alarm you,' he said, 'but a boy was killed last night, probably in a fight. DC Gay showed you the artist's impression, and someone suggested it might resemble Jason. That's why we need to know his movements and whereabouts.'

Banks waited for the outburst, but it didn't come. Instead, Mrs Fox shook her head and said, 'It *can't* be our Jason. He wouldn't get into fights or anything like that. And you can't really tell from the picture, can you?'

Banks agreed. 'I'm sure you're right,' he said. 'He's probably gone off somewhere with his mates for the weekend without telling you. Kids. No consideration sometimes, have they? Would Jason do something like that?'

Mrs Fox nodded. 'Oh, yes. Never tells us owt, our Jason, does he, Steven?'

'That's right,' Mr Fox agreed. But Banks could tell from his tone that he wasn't quite as convinced as his wife about Jason's not being the victim. In his experience, mothers often held more illusions about their sons than fathers did.

'Does Jason have any friends on the estate he might have gone out with?' Banks asked. 'Anyone local?'

Mrs Fox looked at her husband before answering. 'No,' she said. 'See, we've only been living in Eastvale for three years. Since we moved from Halifax. Besides, Jason doesn't drink. Well, not hardly.'

'When did he get this job in Leeds?'

'Just before we moved.'

'I see,' said Banks. 'So he hasn't really spent much time here, had time to settle in and make friends?'

'That's right,' said Mrs Fox.

'Does he have any other relations in the area he might have gone to visit? An uncle, perhaps, someone like that?'

'Only my dad,' said Mrs Fox. 'That's why we moved here, really, to be nearer my dad. My mam died two years ago, and he's not getting any younger.'

'Where does he live?'

'Up in Lyndgarth, so he's not far away, in case of emergencies, like. Eastvale was the closest town Steven could get a transfer.'

'What kind of work do you do, Mr Fox?'

'Building society. Abbey National. That big branch on York Road, just north of the market square.'

Banks nodded. 'I know the one. Look, it's just a thought, but does Jason spend much time with his grandfather? Might he be stopping with him?'

Mrs Fox shook her head. 'He'd have let us know, Dad would. He's got a telephone. Didn't want one, but we insisted. Besides, Jason would've needed the car.'

'Would your father know anything more about Jason's friends and his habits?'

'I don't think so,' said Mrs Fox, fidgeting with her wedding ring. 'They used to be close when Jason were a young lad, but you know what it's like when kids grow up.' She shrugged.

Banks did. He well remembered preferring the company of his grandparents to that of his mother and father when he was young. They were more indulgent with him, for a start, and would often give him a tanner for sweets – which he'd usually spend on sherbet, gobstoppers and a threepenny lucky bag. He also liked his grandfather's pipe rack, the smell of tobacco around the dark-panelled house, the tarnished silver cigarette case with the dint where a German bullet had hit it, saving his grandfather's life – or so his grandfather had told him. He had loved the stories about the war – not the second, but the first – and his grandfather had even let him wear his old gas mask, which smelled of rubber and dust. They had spent days walking by the River Nene, standing by the railway tracks to watch the sleek, streamlined *Flying Scotsman* go by. But all that had changed when Banks entered his teens, and he felt especially guilty about not seeing his granddad for a whole year before the old man died, while Banks was at college in London.

'Are there any other family members?' he asked. 'Brothers or sisters?'

'Only Maureen, my daughter. She's just turned eighteen.'

'Where is she?'

'Nurses' training school, up in Newcastle.'

'Would she be able to help us with any of Jason's friends?'

'No. They're not particularly close. Never were. Different as chalk and cheese.'

Banks glanced over at Susan and indicated she should put her notebook away. 'Would you mind if we had a quick look at Jason's room?' he asked. 'Just to see if there's anything there that might help us find out what he was doing last night?'

Steven Fox stood up and walked towards the stairs. 'I'll show you.'

The tidiness of the room surprised Banks. He didn't know why – stereotyping! no doubt – but he'd been expecting the typical teenager's room, like that of his son, Brian, which usually looked as if it had just been hit by a tornado. But Jason's bed was made, sheets so tightly stretched across the mattress you could bounce a coin on them, and if he had dirty washing lying around, as Brian always had, then Banks couldn't see it.

Against one of the walls stood shelving similar to that downstairs, also stacked with long-playing records and several rows of 45s.

'Jason likes music, I see,' Banks said.

'Actually, they're mine,' said Steven Fox, walking over and running his long fingers over a row of LPs. 'My collection. Jason says it's okay to use the wall space because he's not here that often. It's mostly sixties stuff. I started collecting in 1962, when "Love Me Do" came out. I've got everything The Beatles ever recorded, all originals, all in mint condition. And not only The Beatles. I've got all The Rolling Stones, Grateful Dead, Doors, Cream, Jimi Hendrix, The Searchers. . . . If you can get it on vinyl, I've got it. But I don't suppose you're interested in all that.'

Banks *was* interested in Mr Fox's record collection, and on another occasion he would have been more than happy to look over the titles. Just because he loved opera and classical music in general didn't mean he looked down on rock, jazz or blues – only on country-and-western and brass bands. This latter opinion was regarded as a serious lapse of taste in Yorkshire, Banks was well aware, but he felt that anyone who had had to endure an evening of brass-band renditions of Mozart arias, as he once had, was more than entitled to it.

Apart from Steven Fox's record collection, the room was strangely Spartan, almost an ascetic's cell, and even on such a warm day it seemed to emanate the chill of a cloister. There was only one framed print on the wall, and it showed a group of three naked women. According to the title, they were supposed to be Norse goddesses, but they looked more like bored housewives to Banks. There was no television or video, no stereo and no books. Maybe he kept most of his things in his flat in Leeds.

Steven Fox stood in the doorway as Banks and Susan started poking around the spotless corners. The dresser drawers were full of underclothes and casual wear – jeans, sweatshirts, T-shirts. By the side of the bed lay a set of weights. Banks could just about lift them, but he didn't fancy doing fifty bench-presses.

In the wardrobe, he found Jason's football strip, a couple of very conservative suits, both navy blue, and some white dress shirts and sober ties. And that was it. So much for any clues about Jason Fox's life and friends.

Back downstairs, Mrs Fox was pacing the living room, gnawing at her knuckles. Banks could tell she was no longer able to keep at bay the terrible realization that something bad might have happened to her son. After all, Jason hadn't come home, his car was still in the garage, and now the police were in her house. A part of him hoped, for her sake, that the victim wasn't Jason. But there was only one way to find out for certain.

2

ONE

Frank Hepplethwaite reached for his inhaler, aimed it at the back of his throat and let off a blast of nitro. Within seconds the pain in his chest began to abate, along with that suffocating sense of panic that always came with it.

Frank sat completely still in his favourite armchair, the one that Edna had been constantly nagging him to get rid of. True, the seat cushion was worn, and it bulged like a hernia through the support slats underneath; and true, the frayed upholstery had long since lost whatever pattern it might have had and faded to a sort of dull brown with a worn, greasy spot where he had rested the back of his head year after year. But he had never found anywhere else quite so comfortable to sit and read in all his seventy-six years – and though he was seventy-six, his eyes were as good as they'd ever been. Well, almost, if he put his reading glasses on. Better than his teeth and his heart, at any rate.

When he felt steady enough again, he rested his palms on the threadbare patches of fabric and pushed himself up, slowly, to standing position. Five foot ten in his stockinged feet, and he still weighed no more than ten stone.

Face it, though, Frank, he told himself as he wrapped his scarf around his neck and reached for his tweed jacket on the hook behind the door, you won't be able to go on like this by yourself much longer. Even now, Mrs Weston came in once or twice a week to tidy up and make his meals. And his daughter, Josie, came over from Eastvale to do his washing and to vacuum.

He could still manage the little domestic tasks, like boiling an egg, washing what few dishes he used, and making his bed in the morning – but he couldn't change the sheets, and any sort of elaborate meal was well beyond him. Not that he lacked the ability – he had been a passable cook in his time – he merely lacked the stamina. And for how much longer would he be able to manage even the little necessities? How long would it be before a simple visit to the toilet was beyond him, a bowel movement too much of a strain on his heart?

Best not think about that, he told himself, sensing the abyss that awaited him. Beyond this point be monsters. At least Edna had gone first, bless her soul, and while he missed her every minute he continued to live, at least he wouldn't have to worry about her coping after he'd gone.

Frank went into the hall and paused at the front door. He rarely got any letters these days, so he was surprised to see one lying on the carpet. It must have arrived yesterday, Saturday. He hadn't been out since Friday, hadn't even had cause to go into the hall, so it was no wonder he hadn't noticed it. Bending carefully, knees creaking, he picked it up and slipped it into his inside pocket. It could wait. It wasn't a bill. At least, it didn't look official; it didn't have one of those windows.

He opened the door, sniffed the air and smiled. Well, well, another taste of summer, with just a hint of peat smoke from the village. What strange weather the dale had been having these past few years. Global warming, the papers said, damage to the ozone layer, greenhouse effect. Whatever all that was. Bloody grand, anyway.

He decided to be devil-may-care today and took off his scarf, then he walked down the road towards the green, pausing by the whitewashed façade of The Swainsdale Heifer to watch out for traffic hurtling across the blind corner, the way it did despite the warning signs. Then he walked on the broad cobbled area in front of the gift shop, the small Barclay's Bank branch and the estate agent's office, past The King's Head to the third pub in the village, The Black Bull.

It would have to be the bloody farthest pub from his house, he always grumbled to himself, but The Black Bull had been his local for over forty years, and he was damned if he was going to change it now, even if the walk did sometimes put him out of breath. And even if the new landlord didn't seem to give a toss for anyone but tourists with plenty of readies to flash around.

Frank had seen a dozen landlords come and go. He was all right in his way, was old Jacob – a London Jew born of one of the few families lucky enough to escape to England from Germany just before the war – and he had his living to make, but he was a tight old skinflint. A drink or two on the house now and then would make an old man's pension go a lot further. The last landlord had understood that. Not Jacob. He was as close with his brass as old Len Metcalfe had been over ten years back.

Frank pushed the heavy door, which creaked as it opened, and walked across the worn stone flagging to the bar. 'Double Bell's, please,' he said.

'Hello, there, Frank,' said Jacob. 'How are you today?'

Frank touched his chest. 'Just a twinge or two, Jacob,' he said. 'Just a twinge. Other than that I'm right as rain.'

He took his drink and wandered over to his usual small table to the left of the bar, where he could see down the corridor to the machines and the billiard table on the raised area at the far end. As usual, he said hello to Mike and Ken, who were sitting on stools at the bar agonizing over a crossword puzzle, and to that poncy southern windbag, Clive, who was sitting a stool or two down from them puffing on his bloody pipe and pontificating about sheep breeding, as if he knew a bloody thing about it. A few of the other tables were occupied by tourists, some of them kitted out for a day's walking or climbing. It was Sunday, after all. And a fine one, at that.

Frank took a sip of Bell's, winced at the sharpness and hoped the burning he felt as it went down was just the whisky, not the final heart attack. Then he remembered the letter he had put in his pocket. He put on his reading glasses, reached his hand in and slipped it out.

The address was handwritten, and there was no indication of who had sent it. He didn't recognize the writing, but then he hardly ever saw handwriting these days. Everything you got was typed or done on computers. He couldn't make out the postmark clearly, either, but it looked like Brighouse, or maybe Bradford. It could even be Brighton or Bristol, for all he knew. Posted on Thursday.

Carefully, he tore the envelope open and slid out the single sheet of paper. It had type on both sides, in columns, and a large bold heading across the top. At first he thought it was a flyer for a jumble sale or something, but as he read, he realized how wrong he was.

Confused at first, then angry, he read the printed words. Long before he had finished, tears came to his eyes. He told himself they were Scotch tears, just the burning of the whisky, but he knew they weren't. He also knew who had sent him the flyer. And why.

TWO

Some of the more modern mortuaries were equipped with video cameras and monitor screens to make it easier for relatives to identify accident or murder victims from a comfortable distance. Not in Eastvale, though. There, the attendant still slid the body out of the refrigerated unit and slipped back the sheet from the face.

Which was odd, Banks thought, as the mortuary was certainly the most recently renovated part of that draughty old pile of stone known as Eastvale General Infirmary.

Steven and Josie Fox had been unwilling at first to come and view the body. Banks could see their point. If it *were* Jason, they would have to face up to his death; and if it *weren't*, then they would have gone through all the unpleasantness of looking at a badly beaten corpse for nothing.

Reluctantly, though, they had agreed, but refused Banks's offer of a police car and chose to walk instead. Susan Gay had returned to the station.

Because the hospital was small, old and too close to the tourist shops, another, much larger, establishment was under construction on the northern edge of the town. But, for now, Eastvale General was all there was. Every time he walked up the front steps, Banks shuddered. There was something about the dark, rough stone, even on a fine day, that made him think of operations without anaesthetic, of unsterilized surgical instruments, of plague and death.

He led the Foxes through the maze of high corridors and down the stairs to the basement, where the mortuary was. Banks identified himself to one of the attendants, who nodded, checked his files and touched Mrs Fox lightly on the arm. 'Please, follow me,' he said.

They did. Along a white-tiled corridor into a chilled room. There, the attendant checked his papers again before sliding out the tray on which the body lay.

Banks watched the Foxes. They weren't touching one another at all, not holding hands or clutching arms the way many couples did when faced with such a situation. Could there really be such distance between them that even the possibility of seeing their son dead at any second couldn't bridge it? It was remarkable, Banks had often thought, how people who no longer have any feelings for one another can keep on going through the motions, afraid of change, of loneliness, of rejection. He thought of Sandra, then pushed the thought aside. He and Sandra were nothing like the Foxes. They weren't so much separate as *independent*; they gave one another space. Besides, they had too much in common, had shared too much joy and pain over the years to simply go through the motions of a failed marriage, hadn't they?

The attendant pulled back the white sheet to reveal the corpse's face. Josie Fox put her hand to her mouth and started to sob. Steven Fox, pale as the sheet that covered his son, simply nodded and said, 'It's him. It's our Jason.'

Banks was surprised at what a good job the mortuary had done on the boy's face. While it was clear that he had been severely beaten, the nose was straight, the cheek-bones aligned, the mouth shut tight to cover the shattered teeth. The only wrong note was the way that one eye stared straight up at the ceiling and the other a little to the left, at Mr and Mrs Fox.

Banks could never get over the strange effect looking at dead people had on him. Not bodies at the crime scene, so much. They sometimes churned his guts, especially if the injuries were severe, but they were essentially *work* to him; they were human beings robbed of something precious, an insult to the sanctity of life.

On the other hand, when he saw bodies laid out in the mortuary or in a funeral parlour, they had a sort of calming effect on him. He couldn't explain it, but as he looked down at the shell of what had once been Jason Fox, he knew there was nobody home. The pale corpse resembled nothing more than a fragile eggshell, and if you tapped it hard enough, it would crack open revealing nothing but darkness inside. Somehow, the effect of all this was to relieve him, just for a few welcome moments, of his own growing fear of death.

Banks led the dazed Foxes out into the open air. They stood on the steps of the hospital for a moment, silently watching the people come out of the small congregationalist church.

Banks lit a cigarette. 'Is there anything I can do?' he asked.

After a few moments, Steven Fox looked at him. 'What? Oh, sorry,' he said. Then he shook his head. 'No, there's nothing. I'll take Josie home now. Make her a nice cup of tea.'

His wife said nothing.

They walked down King Street, still not touching. Banks sighed and turned up towards the station. At least he knew who the victim was now; first, he would let his team know, and then they could begin the investigation proper.

THREE

Detective Sergeant Jim Hatchley would normally have enjoyed nothing more than a pub crawl any day of the week, any hour of the day or night, but that Sunday, all he wanted to do as he walked into his fifth pub, The Jubilee, at the corner of Market Street and Waterloo Road, was go home, crawl into bed and sleep for a week, a month, nay, a bloody year.

For the past two weeks, his daughter, April, named after the month she was born because neither Hatchley nor his wife, Carol, could agree on any other name, had kept him awake all night, every night, as those bloody inconvenient lumps of calcium called teeth bored their way through the tender flesh of her gums with flagrant disregard for the wee bairn's comfort. Or for his. And he hadn't been well enough prepared for it. In fact, he hadn't been prepared for it at all.

The first year and a bit of April's life, you would never have known she was there, so quiet was she. At worst, she'd cry out a couple of times when she was hungry, but as soon as Carol's tit was in her mouth she was happy as a pig in clover. And why not, thought Hatchley, who felt exactly the same way about Carol's tit himself, not that he'd been getting much of *that* lately, either.

But now April had suddenly turned into a raging monster and put paid to his sleep. He knew he looked like he'd been on the piss every morning he went into work – he could see the way they were all looking at him – but if truth be told, he hadn't had a drink in weeks. A real drink in a pub, that was.

He remembered some story, an old wives' tale probably,

about rubbing whisky on a teething baby's gums to quieten it down. Well, Carol wouldn't let him do that – she said she had enough on her plate with one boozer in the family – so he had rubbed it on his own gums, so to speak, or rather let it caress them briefly and gently on its way down to his stomach. Sometimes that helped him get a ten-minute nap between screaming sessions. But he never had more than two or three glasses a night. He hadn't had a hangover in so long that not only had he almost forgotten what they felt like, he was actually beginning to miss them.

So it was with both a sense of nostalgia and a feeling that he'd rather be anywhere else, especially asleep in bed, that Sergeant Hatchley entered The Jubilee that Sunday lunchtime.

Contrary to rumours around the station, Hatchley didn't know the landlord of every pub in Eastvale. Apart from The Queen's Arms, the station's local, he tended to avoid the pubs near the town centre, especially those on Market Street, which always seemed to be full of yobs. If there were trouble on a Saturday night, which there often was these days, you could bet it would be on York Road or Market Street.

The Jubilee was also a chain pub: all fruit machines, theme nights, trivia and overpriced food. Overpriced ale, too. Rock bands played there on Friday and Saturday nights, and it had a reputation for getting some of the best up-and-coming bands in Yorkshire. Not that Hatchley gave a toss about rock music, being a brass-band man himself. The Jubilee was also reputed to be a fertile hunting ground for birds and drugs.

On Sunday lunchtimes, though, it became a family pub, and each family seemed to have about six children in tow. All of them screaming at once.

Hatchley leaned over the bar and presented his warrant card to the barmaid as she pulled someone a pint.

'Any trouble here Saturday night, love?' he asked.

She jerked her head without looking up at him. 'Better ask His Nibs over there. I weren't working.'

Hatchley edged down the bar and shoved his way through the drinkers standing there, getting a few dirty looks on the way. He finally caught the barman's attention and asked for a word. 'Can't you see I'm rushed off my feet?' the man protested. 'What is it you want?' Like everyone else behind the bar, he wore black trousers and a blue-and-white striped shirt with THE JUBILEE stitched across the left breast.

When Hatchley showed his card, the man stopped protesting that he was too busy and called one of the other bar staff to stand in for him. Then he gestured Hatchley down to the far end of the bar, where it was quiet.

'Sorry about that,' he said. 'I hate bloody Sunday lunchtimes, especially after working a Saturday night.' He scratched his thinning hair and a shower of dandruff fell on his shoulders. How bloody hygienic, Hatchley thought. 'My name's Ted, by the way.'

'Aye well, Ted, lad,' Hatchley said slowly, 'I'm sorry to disturb you, but we all have our crosses to bear. First off, was there any trouble in here on Saturday night?'

'What do you mean, trouble?'

'Fights, barneys, slanging matches, hair-pulling, that sort of thing.'

Ted frowned. 'Nowt out of the ordinary,' he said. 'I mean, we were busy as buggery, so there was no way I could see what were going on everywhere at once, especially with the bloody racket that band were making.'

'I appreciate that,' said Hatchley, who had had the

same conversation five times already that morning and was getting steadily sick of it. He slipped the sketch from his briefcase. 'Recognize him?' he asked.

The barman squinted at the drawing then passed it back to Hatchley. 'Could be any number of people, couldn't it?'

Hatchley wasn't sure why, but he felt the back of his scalp prickle. Always a sign something wasn't quite right. 'Aye, but it's not,' he said. 'It's an amateur artist's reconstruction of a lad's face, a face that were booted to a bloody pulp after closing time last night. So any help you could give us would be much appreciated, Ted.'

Ted turned pale and averted his eyes before answering. 'Well, seeing as you put it like that . . . But I'm telling you the truth. Nothing happened.'

Hatchley shook his head. 'Why don't I find myself believing you, Ted? Can you answer me that?'

'Look.' Ted held his hand up, palm out. 'I don't want any trouble.'

Hatchley smiled, showing stained and crooked teeth. 'And I'm not here to give you any.'

'It's just . . .'

'Frightened of something?'

'No. It's not that.' Ted licked his lips. 'I mean, I wouldn't want to swear to owt, but there were a lad looked a bit like that in last night. It could've been him.'

'What was he doing?'

'Having a drink with a mate.'

'What did this mate look like?'

'About my height. That's five foot six. Stocky build. Tough-looking customer, you know, like he lifted weights or summat. Short fair hair, almost skinhead, but not quite. And an earring. One of them loops, like pirates used to have in old films.'

'Had you seen them before?'

'Only the one in the drawing, if it is him. Sometimes comes in on a weekend after a match, like, just for a quick one with the lads. Plays for United.'

'Aye, so I've heard. Troublemaker?'

'No. Not at all. Not even much of a boozer. He's usually gone early. It's just . . .' Ted scratched his head again, sending more flakes of dandruff onto the polished bar. 'There was a bit of a scuffle Saturday night, that's all.'

'No punches?'

He shook his head. 'Far as I can tell, the lad in the picture bumped into another lad and spilled some of his drink. The other lad said something and this one replied, like, and gave him a bit of a shove for good measure. That's all that happened. Honest. Pushing and shoving. It were all over before it began. Nobody got beat up.'

'Could it have continued outside?'

'I suppose it could have. As I said, though, it seemed like summat and nowt to me.'

'This other lad, the one whose drink got spilled, did he have any mates with him?'

'There were three of them.'

Hatchley pointed to the sketch again. 'Did you see this lad and his mate leave?'

'Aye. I remember them because I had to remind them more than once to drink up.'

'Were they drunk?'

'Mebbe. A bit. They weren't arse over tit, if that's what you mean. They could still walk in a straight line and speak without slurring. Like I said, I'd seen the one in the picture a few times before, and he weren't much of a drinker. He might have had a jar more than usual, but who hasn't had by closing time on a Saturday night?'

'And it wasn't till after eleven o'clock that you got rid of them, right?'

'Aye. About quarter past. I know some places are a bit lax, but there's no extension of drinking-up time in The Jubilee. The manager makes that clear.'

'What about the other three?'

'They'd gone by then.'

'Were they drunk, too?'

'No. At least they didn't act it.'

'Anything else you can tell me about them?'

Ted looked away.

'Why do I get the impression you're still holding something back, Ted?'

'I don't know, do I?'

'I think you do. Is it drugs? Worried we'll close the place down and you'll lose your job?'

'No way. Look, like I said . . . I don't want to cause any bother.'

'What makes you think you'd be causing bother by telling me the truth, Ted? All right. Let me guess. If it's not drugs, then you're probably frightened these three hooligans are going to come back and wreck your pub if they find out you ratted on them. Is that it?'

'Partly, I suppose. But they weren't hooligans.'

'Oh? Who were they, then? Did you recognize them?'

'Aye. I recognized them. Two of them, anyroad.'

'Names?'

'I don't know their names, but one of them's that lad from the shop off Cardigan Road. You know, the one opposite the bottom of the Leaview Estate. And the other one's dad owns that new restaurant in the market square. The Himalaya.'

Hatchley raised his eyebrows.

'See what I mean?' Ted went on. 'See what I'm worried about, now? I don't want to get stuck in the middle of some bloody racial incident, do I? The lad in your picture called one of them a "Paki bastard" and told him to get out of the fucking way. That's what happened.'

FOUR

Gallows View, *déjà vu*, Banks thought, as he pulled up outside the Mahmoods' shop. Of course, the street had changed a lot in six years, and the wire mesh that covered the display windows was one of the changes. Inside, the smell of cumin and coriander was another.

The Mahmoods were one of three Asian families in Eastvale. In these parts of Yorkshire north of Leeds and Bradford you saw very few visible minorities, even in the larger cities like York and Harrogate.

Mahmood had enlarged the shop, Banks noticed. Originally, it had occupied the ground floor of only one cottage, and the Sharps had used the other as their living-room. But now the shop had been extended to take up the frontage of both cottages, complete with extra plate-glass window and a new freezer section. The Mahmoods sold a whole range of products, from bread, eggs, cigarettes, milk and beer to washing-up liquid, tights, magazines, lipstick, stationery and tooth-paste. They also rented out videos. Pretty soon, when the new estate was finished, the shop would be a little gold mine.

Unlike most people the racist bigots refer to as 'Pakis', Charles Mahmood actually did hail from Pakistan. Or rather, his father, Wasim Mahmood, did. Wasim and family emigrated to England in 1948, shortly after partition.

Charles was born in Bradford in 1953, around the time of Queen Elizabeth's coronation, and he was, naturally, given the name of her only male child because the Mahmoods were proud of their new country and its royal heritage.

Unfortunately for Charles, when his own son was born in 1976, the Prince of Wales had yet to marry and produce offspring. To name his child, Charles had to take the devious route of stealing one of the prince's middle names. He chose George. Why he didn't choose Philip, which might have been easier on the lad at school, nobody knew. As for George himself, he said he was only glad his dad hadn't called him Arthur, which would have seemed even more old-fashioned than George to his classmates.

Banks knew all this because George had been a contemporary of his own son, Brian, at Eastvale Comprehensive, and the two had become good friends during their last couple of years there. George had spent quite a bit of time at the Banks household, and Banks remembered his love of music, his instinctive curiosity about things and his sense of humour. They had all laughed at the story of the family names, for example.

Now the kids seemed to have lost touch, drifted apart as people do, and Banks hadn't seen George for a while. Brian had just started his third year at college in Portsmouth, and George was still in Eastvale, pretty much unemployed, as far as Banks knew, apart from helping his dad out at the shop. Even though they hadn't seen one another in a while, Banks still felt a little uneasy about interviewing George in connection with a criminal matter.

Charles Mahmood greeted Banks with a smile of recognition; his wife, Shazia, waved from the other side of the shop, where she was stacking shelves with jars of instant coffee.

'Is it about that brick-chucking?' asked Charles in his broad West Yorkshire accent.

Banks told him it wasn't, but assured him that the matter was still under investigation.

'What's up, then?' Charles asked.

'George in?'

'George?' He flicked his head. 'Upstairs. Why, what's happened?' Banks didn't think she could have heard, but Shazia Mahmood had stopped putting jars on shelves and seemed to be trying to eavesdrop.

'We don't know yet,' Banks said. 'There's nothing to worry about. I'd just like to talk to him. Okay?'

Charles Mahmood shrugged. 'Fine with me.'

'How's he doing these days?'

Charles nodded towards the stairs. 'You'd better ask him. See for yourself. He's in his room.'

'Problems?'

'Not really. Just a phase he's going through. Another seven-day wonder.'

Banks smiled, remembering the way his father used to say that about every hobby he took up, from Meccano to stamp-collecting. He'd been right, too. Banks still felt that he lurched restlessly from interest to interest. 'What particular phase is this one?' he asked.

'You'll find out soon enough.'

'I'd better go talk to him, then,' said Banks. 'The curiosity's killing me.'

He walked upstairs, aware of Shazia Mahmood's eyes drilling into his back, and didn't realize until he got to the top that he didn't know *which* room was George's. But it didn't matter by then. At the end of the hallway, beside the bathroom, a door stood slightly ajar and from inside the room, Banks could smell sandalwood incense and hear piano music.

It was jazz, certainly, but not Monk, Bill Evans or Bud Powell. No one like that. It didn't even resemble the wild flights of Cecil Taylor, one of whose records Banks had made the mistake of buying years ago on the strength of a review from a usually reliable critic. This music was repetitive and rhythmic, a sort of catchy, jangling melodic riff played over and over again with very few changes. It was vaguely familiar.

He tapped on the door and George Mahmood opened it. George was a good-looking boy with thick black hair, long eyelashes and loam-brown eyes. He looked at Banks for a moment, then said, 'You're Brian's dad, aren't you? The copper.'

It wasn't exactly the warm welcome Banks had hoped for; he had thought George might have remembered him with more affection. Still, attitudes change a lot in three years, especially when you're young. He smiled. 'Right. That's me. The copper. Mind if I come in?'

'Is this a social call?'

'Not exactly.'

'I didn't think so.' George stood aside. 'Better come in, anyway. I don't suppose I could stop you even if I wanted to.'

Banks entered the bedroom and sat on a hardback chair at the desk. George slouched in an armchair. But not before he turned down the music a couple of notches. He was wearing baggy black trousers and a white top with a Nehru collar.

'Who is that playing?' Banks asked.

'Why?'

'I like it.'

'It's Abdullah Ibrahim. He's a South African pianist.'

Now that George mentioned the name, Banks realized

he had heard of Ibrahim and his music before. 'Didn't he used to be called Dollar Brand?' he asked.

'That's right. Just like Muhammad Ali used to be called Cassius Clay.'

Banks hadn't heard of Cassius Clay in years, and he was surprised that someone as young as George had ever heard Ali's old name at all. They made a little uneasy small talk about Brian, then Banks got quickly to the point he had come for. 'George,' he said, 'I've come to ask you about Saturday night.'

'What about it?' George looked away towards the window. 'And my name's not George any more. That's a stupid name, just my father's post-colonial genuflection. My name's Mohammed Mahmood.'

As he spoke, George turned to look at Banks again and his eyes shone with defiant pride. Now Banks saw what Charles Mahmood meant. Now it made sense: Dollar Brand/Abdullah Ibrahim, the Koran lying on the bedside table. George was exploring his Islamic roots.

Well, Banks told himself, be tolerant. Not all Muslims support death threats against writers. He didn't know much about the religion, but he supposed there must be as many forms of Islam as there are of Christianity, which runs a pretty broad spectrum if you include the Sande-manians, the Methodists, the Quakers and the Spanish Inquisition.

Why, then, did he feel so uncomfortable, as if he had lost someone he had known? Not a close friend, certainly, but a person he had liked and had shared things with. Now he was excluded – he could see it in George's eyes – he was the enemy. There would be no more music, laughter or understanding. Ideology had come between them, and it would rewrite history and deny that the music, laughter and understanding had ever happened in the first place. Banks had been through it once before with an old school friend who had become a born-again Christian. They no longer spoke to one another. Or, more accurately, Banks no longer spoke to *him*.

'Okay, Mohammed,' he said, 'did you go to The Jubilee with a couple of mates on Saturday night?'

'What if I did?'

'I thought Muslims weren't supposed to drink?'

Banks could swear he saw George blush. 'I don't,' he answered. 'Well, not much. I'm stopping.'

'Who were you with?'

'Why?'

'Is there any reason you don't want to tell me?'

George shrugged. 'No. It doesn't matter. I was with Asim and Kobir.'

'Are they from around here?'

'Asim is. Asim Nazur. His dad owns the Himalaya. They live in the flat above it.'

'I know the place,' said Banks, who had eaten there on more than one occasion. He also knew that Asim Nazur's father was some sort of bigwig in the Yorkshire Muslim community. 'And the other lad?'

'Kobir. He's Asim's cousin from Bradford. He was just visiting, so we took him out to listen to some music, that's all. Look, why are—'

'What time did you leave the pub?'

'I wasn't looking at my watch.'

'Before closing time?'

'Yes.'

'Where did you go?'

'We bought some fish and chips at Sweaty Betty's, just down Market Street, then we ate them in a shop doorway because it were pissing down. After that we went home. Why?'

'You went your separate ways?'

'Course we went separate ways. You'd have to do, wouldn't you, if you lived in opposite directions?'

'Which way did you walk home?'

'Same way I always do from up there. Cut through the Carlaw Place ginnel over the rec.'

'What time would this be?'

'I'm not sure. Probably elevenish by then.'

'Not later?'

'No. A bit before, if anything. The pubs hadn't come out.'

'Mum and dad still up?'

'No, they were asleep when I got back. They close the shop at ten on a Saturday. They'd been up since before dawn.'

'Did you see anyone on your way?'

'Not that I remember.'

'Doesn't it worry you, walking alone across the rec at night?'

'Not particularly. I can handle myself.'

'Against how many?'

'I've been taking lessons. Martial arts.'

'Since when?'

'Since some bastard chucked a brick through our window and cut me mum. *They* might accept what's going on, but I won't.'

'What do you mean, "what's going on"?'

There was scorn in his voice. 'Racism. Pure and simple. We live in a racist society. It doesn't matter that I was born here, and my mum and dad before me, it's the colour of your skin people judge you on.'

'Not everyone.'

'Shows how much you know. The police are part of it, anyway.'

'Geor— Sorry, Mohammed, I didn't come here to argue the politics of racism with you. I came to find out about your movements on Saturday.'

'So what's happened? Why are you picking on me?'

'I understand there was an altercation in The Jubilee?'

'Altercation?'

'Yes. A disagreement.'

'I know what it means. I'm not just some ignorant wog just got off the boat, you know. I'm trying to remember. Do you mean that stupid pillock who bumped into me and called me a Paki bastard?'

'That's right.'

'So what?'

'What do you mean, "so what"? You're telling me you just let it go at that? You? With all your martial-arts training?'

George puffed up his chest. 'Well, I was all for doing the pair of them over, but Asim and Kobir didn't want any trouble.'

'So you just let it go by, a racial slur like that?'

'When you look like I do, you get used to it.'

'But you were angry?'

George leaned forward and rested his palms on his knees. 'Of course I were bloody angry. Every time you hear something like that said about you, you just get filled with anger and indignation. You feel dehumanized.' He shrugged. 'It's not something you'd understand.'

'Because I'm white?'

George slumped back in his chair. 'You said it.'

'But you listened to your friends this time?'

'Yes. Besides, we were in a crowded pub. Just about everyone else in the place was white, apart from a couple of Rastas selling drugs. And the last thing those bastards would do was come to our aid if anything happened. They'd probably join in with the whiteys.'

'What made you think they were selling drugs?'

'That's what they do, isn't it?'

Talk about racism, Banks thought. He moved on. 'Did you know the lad who insulted you?'

'I've seen him around once or twice. Arrogant-looking pillock, always looked down his nose at me. Lives on the Leaview Estate, I think. Why? You going to arrest him for racism?'

'Not exactly,' said Banks. 'He's dead.'

George's jaw dropped. 'He's wha . . .?'

'He's dead, Mohammed. His name was Jason Fox. Someone unknown, or several someones unknown, kicked seven shades of shit out of him in the Carlaw Place ginnel sometime after eleven o'clock last night.'

'Well it wasn't me.'

'Are you sure? Are you sure you weren't so upset by what Jason called you that you and your friends waited in the ginnel? You just admitted you knew Jason lived on the Leaview Estate, so it would be a pretty good guess that he'd take the same short cut home as you, wouldn't it? You waited there, the three of you, and when Jason came along, you gave him what for. I'm not saying you intended to kill him, just teach him a lesson. But he *is* dead, George, and there's no remedy for that.'

George looked so stunned he didn't even bother correcting Banks over his name. 'I'm not saying owt more,' he said. 'I want a solicitor. This is a fit-up.'

'Come on, George. It doesn't have to be like this.'

'Like hell it doesn't. If you're accusing me and my mates of killing someone, then you'd better arrest us. *And* get us a lawyer. And I told you, my name's Mohammed, not George.'

'Look, Mohammed, if I do what you're asking, I'll have to take you down to the station. And your mates.'

George stood up. 'Do it then. I'm not afraid. If you think I'm a killer you'd be taking me anyway, wouldn't you?'

Oh, bloody hell, Banks thought. He didn't want to do this, but the silly bugger had left him no choice. He stood up. 'Come on, then,' he said. 'And we'd better take the shoes and clothes you wore last night along with us too.'

3

ONE

The crosswinds on the A1 just south of Aberford almost blew Banks off the road. He felt relieved at last when he was able to edge out from between the two juggernauts that had him sandwiched and exit onto Wakefield Road.

It was another of those changeable days, with gale-force winds blowing a series of storms from the west. Between the bouts of rain, the sky would brighten, and Banks had even seen a double rainbow near the Ripon turn-off.

Even though Wakefield Road was busy, Banks still felt able to relax a little after the ordeal of the A1. He had been playing a Clifford Brown tape, finding the sound of the trumpet suited the weather, but he had hardly been able to listen for concentrating on the road. 'The Ride of the Valkyries' would have been more apt for his drive so far, with the big vans and lorries spraying up dirty rain all over his windscreen. Now, however, he found 'Gertrude's Bounce' a fine accompaniment for the wind blowing the leaves off the distant trees.

It was Monday morning, and Banks was on his way to Leeds to talk to Jason Fox's employer. George Mahmood and his friends were in custody at Eastvale station, where they could be kept for another six or seven hours. They all claimed racial discrimination and refused to say anything.

Though Banks felt sorry for them, especially for George, he was also bloody irritated by their attitude. And it was Jason Fox who deserved his pity, he reminded himself, not the cowardly bastards who had booted him to death. *If* they had done it. Banks couldn't see George Mahmood as a killer, but then he had to admit he was prejudiced. And George had changed. Nevertheless, he was willing to keep an open mind until an eyewitness or forensic evidence tipped the balance one way or the other. In the meantime, he needed to know more about Jason Fox's life, starting with where he worked and where he lived. He could have phoned the factory, but he really wanted a face-to-face chat with someone who knew something about Jason.

Banks entered the industrial landscape of south-east Leeds. He turned down Clifford Brown and concentrated on traffic lights and directions as he headed towards Stourton.

Just off Pontefract Road, he found the long, fenced laneway that led to the plastics factory where Jason had worked. Ahead, the horizon was a jumble of factory buildings and warehouses. A row of power-station cooling towers, the hour-glass shape of which always reminded Banks of old corsets adverts, spewed out grey smoke into the already grey air. Between the factories and the power station ran the sluggish River Aire, delivering its load of industrial effluent to the Humber estuary and the North Sea beyond.

Banks identified himself to the guard at the gate and asked where he could find the Personnel Department. 'Human Resources,' the guard told him, pointing. 'Over there.'

He should have known. Everyone used to call it Personnel a few years back, but now even the North Yorkshire police had their Human Resources Department. Why the change? Had 'personnel' suddenly become insulting to some pressure group or other, and therefore exiled to the icy wastes of the politically incorrect?

A hundred yards or so further on, Banks pulled up in front of the three-storey office block.

The Human Resources office was much like any other – untidy desks, computers, filing cabinets and constantly ringing telephones. A dark-haired young woman looked up and smiled as Banks walked in.

'Can I help you?' she asked.

'Hope so.' Banks showed her his card.

If she was surprised, she didn't show it. 'What is it?' she asked. 'My name's Mary, by the way. Mary Mason.'

'I've come about one of your employees. A lad called Jason Fox. I'd like to speak to his boss and workmates, if I can.'

Mary Mason frowned. 'I don't believe I know the name. Still, there's a lot of people work here, and I'm quite new to the job.' She smiled. 'Do you know what department he's in?'

The Foxes hadn't been that specific, Banks remembered. All he knew was that Jason worked in an office.

'Well,' Mary said, 'at least that lets out the shop floor, doesn't it? Just a minute.' She tapped away at her computer. A few moments later, she swivelled away from the screen and said, 'No. It's not just me. We don't have a Jason Fox working here.'

Banks raised his eyebrows in disbelief. 'Are you sure?'

'According to payroll records.'

'Computers make mistakes sometimes.'

Mary laughed. 'Don't I know it. Every once in a while my mouse starts running wild, all over the place. Nobody's managed to work out why yet, but they call it "mad mouse disease". In this case, though, I'd tend to believe the computer. Are you sure he was on the clerical staff?'

Banks scratched the scar beside his right eye. He wasn't sure of anything now. 'That's what I was told. Would it be too difficult to check all your employees?'

Mary shook her head. 'No. It'll take just a little longer. One of the benefits of computers. They do things fast, then you can spend the rest of your time varnishing your finger-nails.'

'I'll bet.'

Mary tapped a few keys and did the Ouija-board thing with her mouse, which wasn't running wild today as far as Banks could tell, then clicked the buttons a few times and squinted at the screen.

'Nope,' she said, shaking her head. 'No Jason Fox any-where in the company. Maybe he worked for another branch?'

'You have other branches?'

'Rochdale. Coventry. Middlesbrough.'

'No. His parents definitely said he lived and worked in Leeds. Look, are there any back records you can check, just in case?' It was probably pointless, but it was worth a look while he was here.

'I can search the files for the past few years, if you've got a bit of patience left.'

Banks smiled. 'If you would, please. I've got plenty of patience.'

Mary returned to her computer. Banks found himself tapping his foot on the floor as he waited. He wanted a cigarette. No chance in here; you just had to sniff the air.

Finally, with a frown creasing her brow, Mary whistled and said, 'Well, what do you know . . .?'

'You've found him?'

'I have indeed.'

'And?'

'Jason Fox. Can't be two, I don't suppose?'

'I doubt it.'

'Well, according to our records, he left the company two years ago after working for us for only one year.'

Now it was Banks's turn to frown. 'He left? I don't understand. Why?'

Mary stared at the screen and pressed her lips together in thought, then she looked at Banks with her warm, dark eyes, smiled and said, 'Look, I appreciate that you're a policeman, and a pretty senior one at that. I also appreciate this might be important, even though you haven't told me a thing. But personnel records are private. I'm afraid I can't just go around giving people any information they want at the drop of a hat, or a warrant card. I'm sure you could get a court order, if you really want to know. But I'm only doing my job. I'm sorry. I couldn't tell you any more, even if I knew.'

'I appreciate that,' said Banks. 'Can you tell me anything at all about his time here, about his friends?'

She shook her head. 'As I said, it was before my time. I've never heard of him.' She turned to face the others in the office. 'Anyone remember a Jason Fox used to work here?'

All she got in return was blank stares and shaking heads. Apart from one woman, who said, 'The name sounds familiar.'

'You're thinking of Jason Donovan,' someone else said, and they laughed.

'Can you at least tell me what department he worked in?' Banks asked.

'That I can tell you,' Mary said. 'He was in sales. Domestic. You'll find them in the old office building, across the yard. And,' she said, smiling, 'you should also find some of the people he worked with are still there. Try David Wayne first. He's one of the regional sales managers now.'

'Just a minute,' came the voice from the back of the office. 'Jason Fox, you said? Now I remember. It was a couple of years back. I'd just started here. There was some trouble, some sort of scandal. Something hushed up.'

TWO

The sound of the car pulling up woke Frank from his afternoon nap. Slowly, he groped his way back to consciousness – it seemed to take longer every time, as if consciousness itself were slowly moving further and further away from him – and walked over to the window. There they were: the three of them, struggling up the path against the wind. Well, he supposed they would have to come some time; Josie had already telephoned and told him what had happened to Jason.

He answered the knock, let them in and told them to make themselves comfortable while he went to put the kettle on. The good old English custom of a nice cup of tea, he thought, had helped people avoid many an embarrassing moment. Not that they should be embarrassed about what had happened, of course, but Yorkshire folk, especially, often fell short of words when it came to strong emotions.

Josie gave him a silent hug when he came through from the kitchen, then she sat down. Grief suited her in a way, he thought; she had always looked a bit pinched to him. These days, she had also started to look more like mutton dressed as lamb, too, with that make-up, her roots showing and those figure-hugging outfits she wore. At her age. Her mother would have been ashamed of her.

Steven looked as lacklustre as ever. Couldn't Josie, he wished again, have chosen someone with a bit of spunk in him?

Then there was Maureen. Good-natured, bustling, hard-working, no-nonsense Maureen. The best of the lot of them, in his book. A proper bonny lass, too; she'd break a few hearts in her time, with her laughing eyes and smiling lips and hair like spun gold all the way down to her waist. Well, not today. But that was how he remembered her. She had cut her hair short just after she started nurses' training. A real shame, that, he thought.

'When's the funeral?' he asked.

'Thursday,' Josie answered. 'Oh, you should have seen what they'd done to him, Dad.' She sniffled. 'Our poor Jason.'

Frank nodded. 'Nay, lass . . . Police getting anywhere?'

'Even if they were,' Josie sniffed, 'they wouldn't tell us, would they?'

The kettle boiled. Frank moved to rise, but Maureen sprang to her feet. 'I'll get it, Granddad. Stay where you are.'

'Thanks, lass,' he said gratefully, and sank back into his armchair. 'What *have* they told you?'

'They've got some lads helping them with their enquiries,' Josie said. 'Pakistanis.' She sniffed. 'They think it might have started as an argument in a pub, and that these lads followed our Jason, or waited for him in the ginnel and beat him up. The police think they probably didn't mean to kill him.'

'What do *you* think?' Frank asked.

Maureen came back with the teapot and raised her eyebrows at the question. 'We haven't really had much time to think about it at all yet, Granddad,' she said. 'But I'm sure the police know their business.'

'Aye.'

'What is it?' Steven Fox said, speaking for the first time. 'You don't think they'll do a good job?'

'I wouldn't know about that,' Frank said.

'Well what is it, then?' Josie Fox repeated her husband's question. Maureen started pouring milk and tea into mugs, spooning in sugar.

'Nowt,' said Frank. He fingered the folded, creased sheet of paper in his top shirt pocket and pulled it out.

'What's that, Granddad?' Maureen asked.

'Just something I got in the post.'

Maureen frowned. 'But what . . . I don't . . .'

'Oh, for crying out loud,' said Frank, his patience with them finally snapping. 'Don't you know what happened? Don't you know anything? Did you all turn your bloody backs?' He turned towards Maureen. 'What about you?' he snapped. 'I'd have expected more of you.'

Maureen started to cry. Frank felt the familiar pain, almost an old friend now, grip his chest. Hand shaking, he tossed the sheet towards Josie. 'Go on,' he said. 'Read it.'

THREE

Banks crossed the factory yard, dodging puddles rainbowed with oil. Crates and chunks of old machinery were stacked up by the sides of long, one-storey buildings with rusty corrugated iron roofs. Machine noises buzzed and roared from inside. Forklifts beetled back and forth across the uneven yard, carrying boxes on pallets. The place smelled of diesel oil and burnt plastic.

He soon found the old office building, which had probably been adequate in the early days, before the company grew. There was no receptionist, just a large open area with desks, computers, telephones and people. Filing cabinets stood against the walls. At the far end of the room, several small offices had been partitioned off, their lower parts wood and the upper parts, above waist height, glass.

A woman dashed by Banks on her way to the door, a couple of file folders stuffed under her arm. When he asked her if David Wayne was around, she nodded and pointed to the middle office. Banks walked between the rows of desks, attracting no attention at all, then knocked on the door that bore the nameplate 'David C. Wayne.'

The man who invited him in was younger than Banks had expected. Late twenties, early thirties at the most. He wore a white shirt with a garish tie, wavy brown hair falling over his collar. He had one of those high foreheads with little shiny red bumps at each side that made his hairline seem to be prematurely receding, and he smelled of Old Spice. A dark sports jacket hung over the back of his chair.

He frowned as he studied Banks's warrant card, then gestured to the spare chair and said, 'How can I help you?'

Banks sat down. 'I'm making enquiries about Jason Fox,' he said. 'I understand he used to work here?'

Wayne's frown deepened. 'That's going back a bit.'

'But you *do* remember him?'

'Oh, yes. I remember Jason all right.' Wayne leaned back in his chair and put his feet on the desk. The telephone rang; he ignored it. In the background, Banks could hear the hubbub of the office through the flimsy partition. 'Why do you want to know?' Wayne asked.

Much as Banks hated parting with information, it would do no harm in this case, he thought, and it might get Wayne to open up more quickly. He could already sense that something was not quite right, and the woman in the Human Resources Department had implied some sort of cover-up. So he told Wayne that Jason had been found dead, and that his parents had said he was working for this company.

'After all this time.' Wayne shook his head slowly. 'Amazing.'

'Why did he leave?'

'He didn't leave. Not exactly.'

'He was fired?'

'No.'

'Made redundant?'

'No.'

Banks sighed and shifted position. 'Look, Mr Wayne,' he said, 'I didn't come here to play a guessing game. I came to get information that might be important in a serious police investigation.'

'I'm sorry,' said Wayne, scratching his head. 'It's all still a bit embarrassing, you see.'

'Embarrassing? In what way?'

'I wasn't in management back then. I was just one of Jason's co-workers. I had more experience, though. In fact, I was the one who trained him.'

'Was he a poor worker?'

'On the contrary. He was very good at his job. Bright, energetic, quick to learn. Showed an extraordinary apti-tude for computers, considering he'd had no formal training in that area. Still, that's often the case.'

'Then what—'

'The job isn't everything, Chief Inspector,' Wayne went on quickly. 'Oh, it's important, I'll grant you that. You can put up with a lot of idiosyncrasies if someone's as good as Jason was. We've had our share of arseholes in our time and, by and large, if they're competent, hard-working arseholes, you just tend to put up with them.'

'But it was different with Jason?'

'Yes.'

'In what way?'

'It was his *attitude*,' Wayne explained. 'I suppose you'd call it his political beliefs.'

'Which were?'

'To put it in a nutshell, Jason was a racist. White power and all that. And it didn't take a lot to get him on his hobby-horse. Just some item in the newspaper, some new opinion poll or crime statistics.'

'What exactly did he say?'

'You name it. Asians and West Indians were his chief targets. According to Jason, if something wasn't done soon the immigrants would take over the country and run it into the ground. Anarchy would follow. Chaos. The law of the jungle. He said you only had to look around you to see what damage they'd done already. AIDS. Drugs. Unemployment. He put them all down to immigrants.' Wayne shook his head again. 'It was disgusting, really sick, some of the things he came out with.'

'Is that why he left?'

Wayne nodded. 'As I said, he didn't exactly leave. It was more of a mutual parting of the ways, maybe a little more desired on our side than his. But the company paid him off adequately and got rid of him. No blemish on his references, either. I suppose whoever employed him next found out what the bugger was like soon enough. I mean, it's all very well to crack the odd . . . you know . . . off-colour joke, have a bit of a laugh. We all do that, don't we? But Jason was serious. He didn't have a sense of humour about these things. Just hatred. A palpable hatred. You could feel it burning out of him when he spoke, see it in his eyes.' Wayne gave a little shudder.

'Do you know where he got it from?'

'No idea. Where *do* people get these things from? Are they born like that? Do we blame the parents? Peers at school? The recession? Society?' He shrugged. 'I don't know. Probably a bit of everything. But I do know that it was always there with Jason, always just beneath the surface, if it wasn't actually showing. And, of course, we have a number of Asian and West Indian employees here.'

'Did he ever insult anyone to their face?'

Wayne rubbed his forehead and glanced away from Banks, out at the bustling business activity through his window. 'Mostly he just made them feel uncomfortable,' he said, 'but once he went too far. That was enough. One of the secretaries. Milly. Nice woman. From Barbados. Jason usually kept her at arm's length. Anyway, she got pregnant, and at some point – so she said – when it started to show, Jason made some remark to her about all her kind could do was procreate, and there were too many of them already. Milly was upset, understandably, and she threatened to report him to the Race Relations Board. Well, the directors didn't want that . . . you know . . . the whole operation under the microscope, racism in the work-place and all that . . . so they asked Jason to leave.'

'They offered him money?'

'A fair settlement. Just what he would have got if he'd been made redundant.'

'And he went quietly?'

Wayne nodded.

'Could I speak to Milly?'

'She's no longer with the company.'

'Do you have her address?'

'I suppose I can tell you. I shouldn't, but given the circumstances.' He got up, pulled out a file from one of the cabinets against his wall, and told Banks the address. Then he sat down again.

'Do you know where Jason went after he left here?' Banks asked.

Wayne shook his head. 'Not a clue. He never got in touch again, and I can't say I was exactly eager to seek him out.'

'So when he left here he disappeared from your life?'

'Yes.'

'Did he have any close friends here?'

'Not really. I wasn't even particularly close to him myself. He was a bit of a loner. Never talked about his outside interests, family, girlfriends, that sort of thing. He had no patience with the usual office chit-chat. Except football. He loved to talk about football. Mad about it. On a Monday morning he'd talk about the weekend games for so long it was sometimes hard to get him working at all.'

'People listened, then? The same ones who were sickened by his racism?'

Wayne spread his hands. 'What can I say? There's nothing like an enthusiasm for sports to make a person seem more human. And we seem able to overlook an awful lot in our sports heroes, don't we? I mean, look at Gazza. The bugger beats up his wife and he's still a national hero.'

'What about enemies?'

Wayne raised his eyebrows. 'Probably just about every

immigrant in the country. At least the ones who knew what he was.'

'Anyone in particular?'

'Not that I can think of.'

'What was he like as a person? How would you describe him?'

Wayne put a pencil against his lips and thought for a moment, then he said, 'Jason was one of those people who can frighten you with their intensity. I mean, mostly he was withdrawn, quiet, in his own world. On first impression, he seemed rather shy, but when he did come out, whether to talk about a football game or comment on some political article in the paper, then he became very passionate, very fervent. He had charisma. You could imagine him speaking to groups, swaying their opinions.'

'A budding Hitler, then? Interesting.' Banks closed his notebook and stood up. He could think of nothing more to ask. 'Thanks for your time,' he said, holding out his hand. 'I might want to talk to you about this again.'

Wayne shook hands and nodded. 'I'll be here.'

And Banks walked through the busy office, back out into the bleak factory yard, the oil smell, the machinery noise, overflowing skips, the rainbowed puddles. Just as he got to the car, his mobile beeped.

FOUR

'No, Gavin, I can't possibly go out for a drink with you tonight. We're very busy.'

'The boy wonder got you working overtime, then?'

'I wish you wouldn't call him that.'

Susan heard Gavin chuckle over the line. 'Who's he got

pegged for this one, then? Our local MP? Leader of the hunt?' He laughed again.

Susan felt herself flush. 'That's not very funny.' She hated it when Gavin made fun of Banks.

'How about Saturday? We can go—'

'Maybe,' Susan said. 'Maybe Saturday. I'll have to see. Got to go now, Gavin. Work to do.'

'Okay. See you Saturday.'

'I said *maybe*. Just a minute . . . What's that?' Susan could hear sounds of shouting and scuffling, and they seemed to be coming from downstairs. 'Got to go, Gavin,' she said. 'I'll ring you back.'

'Susan, what's—'

Susan dropped the receiver on its cradle and walked to the top of the stairs. The scene below was utter chaos. Every Asian in Eastvale – all nine or ten of them – seemed to be pushing through the front doors: George Mahmood's parents, Ibrahim Nazur, owner of the Himalaya, and a handful of students from Eastvale College. A number of uniformed officers were holding them back, but they wanted to see the detectives, and Susan was the only CID officer in the station.

'Would you *please* not all shout at once!' Susan yelled from halfway down the stairs.

'What are you going to do about our children?' asked an angry Charles Mahmood. 'You can't just lock them up for nothing. This is racism, pure and simple. We're British citizens, you know.'

'Please believe me, Mr Mahmood,' said Susan, advancing down the stairs. 'We're only keeping them until we get—'

'No!' yelled Ibrahim Nazur. 'It's not fair. One law for whites and another law for us.'

That met a chorus of agreement and they surged forward again.

Suddenly, the front doors opened and a loud voice bellowed, 'What in God's name is going on here?' It had enough authority to command silence. Then Susan saw over the crowd the shiny, bald head of Chief Constable Jeremiah 'Jimmy' Riddle, and for the first time ever, she was grateful for the sight.

'Sergeant Rowe,' she heard Riddle say, 'would you please order your officers to remove these people from the police station? Tell them if they'll kindly wait outside we'll have some news for them in just a few minutes.' Then Riddle made his way through the silent crowd, cutting a swath rather like Moses parting the Red Sea.

Behind him, Sergeant Rowe muttered, 'Yes, sir,' and ordered three constables to usher the group out onto the street. They went without putting up a fight.

'That's better,' said Riddle, approaching Susan. 'It's DC Gay, isn't it?'

'Yes, sir.'

'Where's DCI Banks?'

'Leeds, sir. Pursuing inquiries.'

'"Pursuing inquiries", is he? Shopping, more bloody like. That Classical Record Shop of his. Anyone else here?'

'No, sir. Just me.'

Riddle jerked his head. 'Right, you. Upstairs.'

Susan turned and started walking up the stairs, feeling, she imagined, somewhat like a prisoner being sent down by the judge.

It could hardly be a worse time to piss off Jimmy Riddle.

Susan had passed the first parts of her sergeant's exam, the written, almost a year ago. But police promotion is a long drawn-out process. The last stage consisted of an appearance before the promotion board – presided over by an Assistant Chief Constable and a Chief Superintendent from Regional HQ.

That was six months ago now, but Susan still broke into a cold sweat every time she remembered the day of her board.

She had spent weeks reading up on policy, national guidelines and equal opportunities, but none of it prepared her for what lay behind the door. Of course, they kept her waiting in the corridor for about half an hour, just to make her extra nervous, then the Chief Superintendent came out, shook her hand and led her in. She could have sworn there was a smirk on his face.

First they asked her a few personal questions to get some idea of her overall bearing, confidence and articulateness. She thought she managed to answer clearly, without mumbling or stuttering, except when they asked what her parents thought of her choice of career. She was sure that she flushed, but rather than flounder around trying to explain, she simply paused to collect herself and said, 'They didn't approve, sir.'

Next came the scenarios. And her interviewers added complications, changed circumstances and generally did everything they could to confuse her or get her to change her mind.

'One of the men on your shift is regularly late in the morning,' the ACC began, 'putting extra pressure on his mates. What do you do?'

'Have a private word with him, sir, ask him why he's being late all the time.'

The ACC nodded. 'His mother's dying and she needs expensive care. He can't afford it on a copper's salary, so he's playing in a jazz band until the wee hours to make a bit extra.'

'Then I'd tell him he needs permission to work outside the force and advise him to get help and support from our Welfare Department, sir.'

'He thanks you for your concern, but he keeps on playing with the band and turning up late.'

'Then I'd think some disciplinary action would be in order, sir.'

The ACC raised his eyebrows. 'Really? But his mother is dying of cancer. He needs the extra income. Surely this is a reasonable way of earning it? After all, it's not as if he's taking bribes or engaging in other criminal acts.'

Susan stuck to her guns. 'He's causing problems for his fellow officers on the shift, sir, and he's disobeying police regulations. I think disciplinary action is called for if all other avenues have been exhausted.'

And she passed. Now she was due to go up before the chief next week for her *official* promotion. And that 'Chief', of course, was Chief Constable Riddle.

Still, she reminded herself as she walked into the small office she shared with Sergeant Hatchley, there was nothing Riddle could do now to block her promotion. She had already earned it, and the next step was purely a formality, a bit of pomp and circumstance. Unless, of course, she *really* screwed up. Then, she supposed, he could do whatever he wanted. He was, after all, the chief constable. And, if nothing else, he could certainly make her life uncomfortable.

The office seemed crowded with Riddle in it. The man's restless, pent-up energy consumed space and burned up the oxygen like a blazing fire. Susan sat in her chair and Riddle perched on the edge of Hatchley's desk. He was a tall man, and he seemed to tower over her.

'Who authorized the arrest?' he asked.

'They're not exactly under arrest, sir,' Susan said. 'Just detained for questioning.'

'Very well. Who authorized their detention?'

Susan paused, then said softly, 'I think it was DCI Banks, sir.'

'Banks. I knew it.' Riddle got up and started to pace, until he found out there was not enough room to do so, then he sat down again, his pate a little redder. Banks always said you could tell how angry Riddle was by the shade of his bald head, and Susan found herself stifling a giggle as she thought she could see it glow. It was like one of those mood rings that were a fad when she was a child, only Riddle's mood never softened to a peaceful green or calm, cool blue.

'On what evidence?' Riddle continued.

'There'd been some trouble earlier in the pub, sir. The Jubilee. It involved the Mahmood boy and the victim, Jason Fox. When DCI Banks questioned George Mahmood about it, he refused to co-operate. So did his friends. They asked for a lawyer.'

'And did they get one?'

'No, sir. Well, not until this morning. It was Sunday.'

'Any rough stuff?'

'No, sir.'

Riddle slid his hand across his head. 'Well, let's at least be thankful for small mercies. Have you any idea who Ibrahim Nazur *is*?'

'Owner of the Himalaya, sir.'

'More than that. He owns a whole bloody chain of restaurants, all over Yorkshire, and the Himalaya's just the latest. He's also a highly respected member of the Muslim community and one of the prime movers in that new mosque project down Bradford way.'

'Ah,' said Susan.

'"Ah", indeed. Anything from forensics?'

'Nothing conclusive, sir. Not yet.'

'Witnesses?'

'None, sir. Not so far. We're still looking.'

Riddle stood up. 'Right. I want the three of them out of here. Now. Do you understand?'

Susan stood too. 'Yes, sir,' she said.

'And tell Banks I'll be seeing him very soon.'

Susan nodded. 'Yes, sir.'

And with that, Jimmy Riddle straightened his uniform and marched downstairs to face his public.

FIVE

Late that afternoon, Banks walked up to the bar of The Black Bull in Lyndgarth and ordered a double Bell's for Frank Hepplethwaite and a half of Theakston's XB for himself.

According to Susan, who had phoned Banks earlier, Hepplethwaite was Jason Fox's granddad, and he said he had some information about Jason. He insisted on talking to the 'man in charge'. Banks had phoned Frank and, finding out that he didn't own a car, agreed to meet him in The Black Bull.

Before setting off back for Swainsdale, though, Banks had called at the Leeds address Jason Fox's parents had given him and found that Jason hadn't lived there for at least eighteen months. The flat was now occupied by a student called Jackie Kitson, and she had never heard of Jason Fox. There, the trail ended.

The barman of The Black Bull was a skinny, hunched, crooked-shouldered fellow in a moth-eaten, ill-fitting pullover. His greasy black hair and beard obscured most of his face, except the eyes that stared out in a way reminiscent of photos of Charles Manson. He served the drinks without a word, then took down Banks's order for one chicken-and-mushroom pie and one Old Peculier casserole. The Black Bull was one of those rare exceptions to the no-food-after-two-o'clock rule that blights most pubs.

Banks took the drinks and joined Frank at a round table by the door. At the bar, one man started telling the barman how much more cosy it was now most of the tourists had gone. He had a whiny, southern accent, and actually lowered his voice when he said 'tourists'. The barman, who clearly knew it was the tourist business that kept the place going, grunted 'Aye' without looking up from the glass he was drying.

Two other bar-stool regulars working at a crossword puzzle seemed overjoyed to discover that 'episcopal' was an anagram of 'Pepsi-Cola.' To the left, down the far end where the billiard tables were, two American couples were stuffing coins into the fruit machine, shifting occasionally to the video trivia game opposite.

'You must know Mr Gristhorpe, young lad?' said Frank after thanking Banks for the drink.

Banks nodded. 'He's my boss.'

'Lives here in Lyndgarth, he does. Well, I suppose you know that. Can't say I know him well, mind you. I'm a fair bit older, myself, and he's been away a lot. Good family, though, the Gristhorpes. Got a good reputation around these parts, anyroad.' He nodded to himself and sipped his Bell's.

Frank Hepplethwaite was a compact man with a thin, lined face, all the lines running vertically, and a fine head of grey hair. His skin was pale and his eyes a dull bottle-green. He looked as if he had once had quite a bit more flesh on his bones but had recently lost weight due to illness.

'Anyway,' he said, 'thank you for coming all the way out here. I don't get around so well these days.' He tapped his chest. 'Angina.'

Banks nodded. 'I'm sorry. No problem, Mr Hepplethwaite.'

'Call me Frank. Of course,' he went on, tapping his glass, 'I shouldn't be indulging in this.' He pulled a face. 'But there's limits to what a sick man will put up with.' He glanced at the table, where Banks had unconsciously rested his cigarettes and lighter. 'Smoke if you like, lad. I like the smell of tobacco. And second-hand smoke be buggered.'

Banks smiled and lit up.

'Nice state of affairs, isn't it,' said Hepplethwaite, 'when a man has to indulge his vices by proxy.'

Banks raised his eyebrows. The words sounded familiar, but he couldn't place them.

'Raymond Chandler,' said Hepplethwaite with a sly grin. 'General Sternwood at the beginning of *The Big Sleep*. One of my favourite films. Bogey as Philip Marlowe. Must have seen it about twenty times. Know it by heart.'

So that was it. Banks had seen the film on television just a few months ago, but he had never read the book. Ah well, another one for the lengthening list. As a rule, he didn't read detective fiction, apart from Sherlock Holmes, but he'd heard that Chandler was good. 'I'm sorry about what happened to your grandson,' he said.

The old man's eyes misted over. 'Aye, well . . . nobody

deserves to die like that. He must have suffered like hell.'
He took a folded sheet of paper from his pocket and passed
it to Banks. 'This is why I asked you to come.'

Banks nodded. He took the sheet, opened it and spread
it on the table in front of him. It looked professionally
printed, but most things did these days, with all the laser
printers and desktop publishing packages around. Banks
could remember the time – not so long ago – when all the
copying in a police station was done from 'spirit masters'
on one of those old machines that made your fingers all
purple. Even now, as he remembered it, he fancied he
could smell the acrid spirit again.

The masthead, in very large, bold capitals, read THE
ALBION LEAGUE and underneath that, it said in italics,
'*Fighting the good fight for you and your country.*'

Banks drew on his Silk Cut and started to read.

Friends, have you ever looked around you at the state of
our once-great nation today and wondered just how such
terrible degradation could have come about? Can you
believe this nation was once called *Great* Britain? And
what are we now? Our weak politicians have allowed this
once-great land to be overrun by parasites. You see them
everywhere – in the schools, in the factories and even in
the government, sapping our strength, undermining the
fabric of our society. How could this be allowed to happen? Many years ago, Enoch Powell foresaw the signs, saw
the rivers of blood in our future. But did anyone listen?
No . . .

And so it went on, column-inch after column-inch of
racist drivel. It ended,

And so we ask you, the true English people, heirs to King
Arthur and St George, to join us in our struggle, to help us

rid this great land of the parasite immigrant who crawls and breeds his filth in the bellies of our cities, of the vile and traitorous Jew who uses our economy for his own purposes, of the homosexual deviants who seek to corrupt our children, and of the deformed and the insane who have no place in the new order of the Strong and the Righteous. To purify our race and re-establish the new Albion in the land that is rightfully ours and make it truly our 'homeland' once again.

Banks put it down. Even a long draught of Theakston's couldn't get the vile taste out of his mouth. Reluctantly, he turned back to the pamphlet, but he could find no sign of an address, no mention of a meeting-place. Obviously, whoever wanted to join the Albion League would first have to find it. At the bottom of the pamphlet, however, in tiny print in the far right-hand corner, he could make out the letters *http://www.alblgue.com/index.html*. A website address. Everyone had them these days. Next, he examined the envelope and saw that it had been posted in Bradford last Thursday.

Their food arrived and they continued to speak between mouthfuls.

'What makes you think Jason sent you this?' Banks asked.

Frank Hepplethwaite turned away to face the dark wood partition between their table and the door. One of the Americans complained loudly that too many of the trivia questions dealt with English sports. 'I mean, how the hell am I supposed to know which player transferred from Tottenham Hotspurs to Sheffield Wednesday in 1976? What game do they play, anyway? And what kinda name is that for a sports team? Sheffield *Wednesday*.' He shook his head. 'These Brits.'

Frank turned back to Banks and said, 'Because it arrived only a couple of days after I let something slip. For which may God forgive me.'

'What did you let slip?'

'First you have to understand,' Frank went on, 'that when Jason was just a wee lad, we were very close. They used to come up here for summer holidays sometimes, him, Maureen and my daughter, Josie. Jason and I would go for long walks, looking for wild flowers on the riverbanks, listening for curlews over Fremlington Edge. Sometimes we'd go fishing up the reservoir, or visit one of the nearby farmers and help out around the yard for an afternoon, collecting eggs or feeding the pigs. We always used to go and watch the sheep-shearing. He used to love his times up here, did little Jason.'

'You mentioned his mother and his sister. What about his father?'

Frank took a mouthful of casserole, chewed, swallowed and scowled. 'That long streak of piss? To be honest, lad, I never had much time for him, and he never had much time for Jason. Do you know he never listens to those records he collects. Never listens to them! Still wrapped in plastic. I bloody ask you, what are you supposed to think of a bloke who buys records and doesn't even listen to them?'

Not much, Banks thought, chewing on a particularly stringy piece of chicken. Frank was obviously going to tell his story in his own time, his own way. 'Sorry to interrupt,' he said. 'What happened?'

Frank paused for breath before continuing. 'Time, mostly. That's all. I got old. Too old to walk very far. And Jason got interested in other things, stopped visiting.'

'Did he still come and see you occasionally?'

'Oh aye. Now and then. But it were only in passing, like, more of a duty.'

'When was the last time you saw him?'

'He drove out here the weekend before last. It'd be just a week before he died.'

'Did he ever talk about his life in Leeds? His job? Friends?'

'Not really, no. Once said he was learning about computers or summat. Of course, I know nowt about that, so we soon changed the subject.'

'Did he say *where* he was learning about computers?'

'No.'

'His parents told me he worked in an office.'

Frank shrugged. 'Could be. All I remember is him once saying he was learning about computers.'

'And in all his visits,' Banks went on, 'didn't he ever talk about this sort of thing?' He tapped the pamphlet with his knuckle.

Frank closed his eyes and shook his head. 'Never. That was why it came as such a shock.'

'Why do you think he never spoke to you about it?'

'I can't answer that one. Perhaps he thought I'd be against it, until I said what I did and gave him his opening? Perhaps he thought I was an old man and not worth converting? I *am* his granddad, after all, and we had a relationship of a kind. We didn't say much to each other when we did meet up these past few years. I'd no idea what he was up to. Mostly he'd just have time to drop by and buy me a drink and ask if I was doing all right before he was off to his football or whatever.'

Banks finished his pie. 'What makes you think you gave Jason an opening to send you this pamphlet?' he asked. 'What was it you said?'

'Aye, well . . . We were sitting in here one day, just like you and me are now.' Frank lowered his voice. 'The landlord here's called Jacob Bernstein. Not that fellow there. Jacob's not in right now. Anyway, I made a remark about Jacob being a bit of a tight-fisted old Jew.'

'What did Jason say?'

'Nowt. Not right away. He just had this funny sort of smile on his face. Partly a smile, partly a sort of sneer. As soon as I said it, I felt I'd done wrong, but these things slip out, don't they, like saying Jews and Scotsmen have short arms and deep pockets. You don't think about it being offensive, do you? You don't really mean any harm by it. Anyways, after a minute or so, Jason says he thinks he might have something to interest me, and a few days later, this piece of filth turns up in the post. Who else could have sent it?'

'Who else, indeed?' said Banks, remembering what David Wayne had told him that morning in Leeds. 'Did you ever meet any of Jason's circle?'

'No.'

'So there's no way you can help us try and find out who killed him?'

'I thought you already had the lads who did it?'

Banks shook his head. 'We don't know if it was them. Not for sure. At the moment, I'd say we're keeping our options open.'

'Sorry, lad,' said Frank. 'It doesn't look like I can help, then, does it?' He paused and looked down into his glass. 'It were a real shock,' he said, 'when I read that thing and knew our Jason were responsible. I fought in the war, you know. I never made a fuss about it, and I don't want to now. It were my duty, and I did it. I'd do it again.'

'What service?'

'RAF. Tailgunner.'

Banks whistled between his teeth. His father had been a radio operator in the RAF, so he had heard what a dangerous task tailgunner was, and how many had died doing it.

'Aye,' said Frank. 'Anyroad, like I said, I don't want to make a fuss about it. I said something terribly wrong about someone I consider a friend, and it shames me, but it shames me even more when my grandson thinks I'd have the time of day for this sort of rubbish. I fought the bloody Nazis, for crying out loud. And for what? So my own grandson could become one of them?'

There were tears in his eyes and Banks feared for his heart. 'Calm down, Mr Hepplethwaite,' he said, putting his hand on Frank's skinny wrist.

Frank looked at him through the film of tears, then gave a small nod and took a sip of Bell's. He coughed, patted his chest and forced a smile. 'Don't worry, lad,' he said. 'It's not quite "time, gentlemen, please" for this old codger yet.'

SIX

An emergency meeting of the Albion League had been called for that Monday evening. Not everyone was invited, of course, just the cell leaders and one or two of Neville Motcombe's current favourites, like Craig. About fifteen in all, they came from Leeds and Bradford, from Halifax, Keighley, Cleckheaton, Heckmondwike, Batley, Dewsbury, Brighouse and Elland. Skinheads, for the most part, aged between sixteen and twenty-four, racists all.

And these fifteen were the pick of the crop, Craig knew.

Each cell had between five and twelve members. They were the drones – football hooligans and otherwise violent skins – and Motcombe hardly ever came into contact with them except at rallies and at other large gatherings, when he addressed them from a distance. Mostly, he relied on his cell leaders to make sure his orders were communicated and carried out, and, maybe more important still, to make sure the cash kept trickling in. After all, the League was an expensive operation to run.

They met in the upstairs room of a pub in Bingley, and as he sat sipping his lager, Craig wondered if the landlord knew exactly what was going on up there. If he had, he might not have been so quick to let them use it. On the other hand, the prospect of selling a few extra pints on a slow Monday night might tempt even the best of us to leave our ethics and politics at the door. Nothing much surprised Craig any more. Not after what Motcombe had drawn him into.

Even though the window was half open, the place was still full of smoke. Craig could hear rain falling in the street outside. A pale streetlight halo glowed through the gauze of moisture. Occasionally, a car sloshed through the gathering puddles.

Meanwhile, Nev himself, erstwhile leader of the League, clad in his usual shiny leather jacket, was on his feet whipping his members into a frenzy. He didn't need to shout and wave his arms around like Hitler; there was enough power and conviction in his regular speaking voice. Mostly it was the eyes, though; they were the kind that trapped you and wouldn't let you go unless they were certain of your loyalty. They'd even made Craig tremble once or twice in the early days, but he was too good at his job to let it get to him.

'*Murdered*,' Motcombe repeated, disgust and disbelief in his tone. He slapped the table. 'One of us. Three of them. Three to one. They say one of his eyes was hanging out of its socket by the time the Paki bastards had finished with him.'

Stirrings and mumblings came from the crowd. One skin started rattling his glass on the table. Motcombe shushed him with an economic hand gesture, then pulled a slip of paper out of his pocket and started to read.

'George Mahmood,' he began, with the accent on *mood*. 'Asim Nazur.' This time, the name sounded like a sneer. People began to snigger. 'And Kobir Mukhtar. Sounds about right, that one, doesn't it? Mucky-tar?'

Sycophantic laughter came from the cell leaders.

'And do you know what happened?'

Several of them, Craig included, shook their heads.

'The police let them go. That's what.'

Howls of outrage.

'Oh, yes they did. This very afternoon. Our glorious warrior Jason is probably lying on some mortuary table, cut open from th'nave to th'chops as we speak, and the three bastards who put him there, the three *brown* bastards who put him there, are out walking the streets.' He slammed the table again. 'What do you think about that?'

'Ain't fair,' one of the cell leaders chimed in.

'Typical,' claimed another. 'Get away with bloody murder they do these days.'

'What we gonna do?' asked another.

Craig lit a cigarette and leaned forward. This promised to be interesting. As far as he was concerned, Jason Fox was an evil little pillock who deserved all he got.

'First off,' said Motcombe, 'I want a special edition of

the newsletter out pronto. Black border, the lot. And I want to see some oomph in it. Ray?'

One of the Leeds cell leaders looked up from his pint and nodded.

'You see to that,' Motcombe went on. 'Now Jason's no longer with us, I'm afraid we're left to rely on your rather more pedestrian prose style. But you can do it, Ray, I'm sure you can. You know the kind of thing I want. Outrage, yes, but make sure you emphasize the reason this all happened, the underlying causes, what we're all about. And make sure you mention the Pakis' names. We'll send each of them a copy. If they know that the entire National Socialist Alliance knows who they are, that should give them a fucking sleepless night or two. Okay?'

Ray smiled and nodded.

'And print extra copies. Next, I'd like Geoff and Keith to start working on a memorial concert for Jason. A big bash. You've got the contacts, so pick some appropriate bands, four or five of them, rent a large space and make arrangements. Soon as you can, okay?'

Geoff and Keith nodded and scribbled some notes.

'Now, as soon as I find out the details about the funeral,' Motcombe went on, 'I'll be contacting several members to accompany me in a tribute of honour for our fallen hero. For make no mistake about it, Jason Fox is a *martyr*, and his murder should provide us with a rallying point. We've got a chance to turn adversity into fortune here, if we choose to seize it. By all means let us grieve and mourn our lost comrade – indeed, grieve we *must* – but let us also, as *he* would have wished, use his death to spur us on to greater things, to faster growth. You all knew Jason. You know what he stood for. Let's do credit to his memory.'

A few of them nodded and muttered their agreement, then the Brighouse cell leader asked, 'Are we gonna crack some heads open, then?'

A number of 'ayes' went up, but Motcombe shushed them again. 'Don't worry,' he said. 'That'll be taken care of. In time. But for the moment, we'll just publish their names and leave it at that. Let's think of the long-term mission, and let's use our golden opportunity to gain a bit of public sympathy. Think of the hundreds of blokes at home just sitting on the fence right now. They know we're right, but they don't want to make that final move and admit it. Something like this could increase our membership tenfold. Nice, pure, Aryan lad, with his whole future ahead of him, murdered by Paki immigrant scum. That'll turn a few fence-sitters in our direction.'

Several members murmured in agreement. 'But we can't leave Jason's murder unavenged, can we?' one of them said. 'They'll think we're weak.'

'Sometimes you have to postpone your vengeance for the greater good, Mick. That's all I am saying. And there's strength in that, not weakness. Believe me. There'll be plenty of time for revenge down the road. Remember, the bastards who killed Jason got away with it because our corrupt legal system is on their side. But what would happen if one of us got picked up for clobbering a Paki right now? Eh? Answer me that one.' No one did. They all looked as if they knew the answer already. Motcombe looked at his watch. 'Now, I'll have to be on my way soon, I've got a lot to attend to, but there's no reason why you lot can't stay and enjoy a wake for Jason if you like. You've all got your orders. Meeting adjourned.'

Then Motcombe tossed back the rest of his orange juice. Unlike the others, Craig had noticed, he never drank alcohol or smoked. People got up and moved around the room, some of them heading down to the bar to buy more pints. The last Craig saw of Motcombe, he was walking out of the room with two Bradford cell leaders, an arm draped over each one's shoulder, deep in quiet conversation.

Liked his private meetings, did Nev, keeping the left hand and the right hand separate. Whatever he was talking to them about or asking them to do, you could bet it would have nothing to do with what he and Craig had been talking about over the past few weeks.

Craig tossed his cigarette out of the window into the rainy night, took a deep breath and went over to mourn Jason's death with Ray from Leeds and Dogface Russell from Horsforth.

SEVEN

It was late when Banks got home that evening, after stopping off at the station on his way from Lyndgarth, and he was tired.

Sandra was sitting at a table at the back of the living room sorting through some transparencies, holding them up to the desk light, scrutinizing each one in turn, her long blonde hair tucked behind her ears.

'Drink?' Banks asked.

She didn't look up. 'No, thanks.'

Fine. Banks went to the cocktail cabinet and poured himself a finger of Laphroaig, thought about it for a moment, then added another finger. He picked up the evening paper from the coffee-table and sat on the settee.

'Hard day?' he asked.

'Not bad,' Sandra said, without looking away from the transparency she was holding. 'Busy.'

Banks looked at the paper for a few minutes without taking anything in, then went over to the stereo. He chose a CD of arias by Angela Gheorghiu. A few seconds into the first one, Sandra looked over and raised a dark eyebrow. 'Must you?'

'What's wrong?'

'Do we really *have* to listen to this?'

'What harm is it doing?'

Sandra sighed and turned back to her transparency.

'Really,' Banks pressed on. 'I want to know. What harm is it doing? Is it too loud?'

'No, it's not too loud.'

'Then what's the problem?'

Sandra dropped the transparency on the table a little harder than necessary. 'It's bloody opera, is the problem.'

It was true that Sandra had once taken a magnet to one of his *Götterdämmerung* tapes. But that was Wagner, an acquired taste at the best of times. Who could possibly object to Angela Gheorghiu singing Verdi? Sandra had even been with him to see *La Traviata* on their season tickets last month, and she said she enjoyed it. But that was before last Saturday.

'I didn't think you found it *that* offensive,' Banks said, walking back to the stereo.

'No, leave it,' Sandra said. 'You've put it on. You've made your point. Just leave it.'

'What point?'

'What point? You know what point.'

'No, I don't. Enlighten me.'

Sandra snorted. 'Opera. Bloody opera. The most important thing on your agenda. In your life, for all I know.'

Banks sat down and reached for his Scotch. 'Oh, we're back to that again, are we?'

'Yes, we're back to that again.'

'Well, go on, then.'

'Go on, what?'

'Get it off your chest.'

'Oh, you'd like that, wouldn't you?'

'What do you mean?'

'You'd like me to get it off my chest. Let the little lady yell at you for a couple of minutes so you can tell your mates what a bloody fishwife she is. Pretend to listen, be all contrite, then just carry on as if nothing had happened.'

'It's not like that,' Banks protested. 'If you've got a problem, tell me. Let's talk about it.'

Sandra picked up another transparency and pushed a few loose strands of hair back behind her ears. 'I don't want to talk about it. There's nothing to talk about.'

Angela Gheorghiu had moved on to the 'Aubade' from *Chérubin* now, but its beauty was lost on Banks.

'Look, I'm sorry,' he said. 'I didn't realize it was *that* important to you.'

Sandra glanced sideways at him. 'That's just it, isn't it?' she said.

'What is?'

'You never do. You never do consider how important something might be to me. It's always your needs that come first. Like bloody opera. You never bother asking me what I might want to listen to, do you? You just go straight to your bloody opera without even thinking.'

Banks stood up again. 'Look, I said I'm sorry. Okay? I'll take it off if it bothers you so much.'

'I told you to leave it. It doesn't matter now. It's too late.'

'Too late for what?'

'Oh, Alan, give it a rest. Can't you see I've got work to do.' She gestured at the transparencies spread out across the table.

'Fine,' said Banks. 'Fine. You're pissed off, but you don't want to talk about it. You hate opera, but you want me to leave it on. I'm the one who never considers your needs or feelings, but right now you've got work to do. Well, just bloody fine.'

Banks tossed back the rest of his Laphroaig, grabbed his coat from the hall stand and slammed the front door behind him.

4

ONE

Banks was first to arrive at Tuesday morning's CID meeting in the 'boardroom' of Eastvale Divisional Police HQ shortly followed by DC Susan Gay, Superintendent Gristhorpe and, finally, Sergeant Hatchley.

Having been warned by Susan, Banks was dreading that Jimmy Riddle himself would show up. Riddle was a notoriously early riser, and the thirty miles or so of country roads from Regional HQ to Eastvale at such an hour would mean nothing to him. Especially if it gave him an opportunity to cause Banks grief.

Banks knew he would have to face the CC before long – Gristhorpe said he had already received *his* bollocking for letting his DCI too far off the leash – but he just didn't want it first thing in the morning, never his favourite time of day. Especially since he'd gone down to the Queen's Arms in a huff after his argument with Sandra the previous evening and had a jar too many.

He hadn't handled that situation well, he knew. He hadn't been at all reasonable. He had lived with Sandra long enough to know that when she lashed out like that – which was rare – it meant she had something important on her mind. And he hadn't bothered to find out what it was. Instead, he had stormed out like a petulant teenager.

As luck would have it, Jimmy Riddle hadn't turned up

by the time coffee and biscuits were served. That probably meant he wouldn't come, Banks thought with relief; usually Riddle liked to be first there, sparkling and spotless, to get a jump on everyone.

'Right,' said Gristhorpe. 'What have we got so far? Alan, have you talked to the lab?'

Banks nodded. 'Nothing yet. They're still trying, but they haven't found anything on the shoes or clothes we sent over for analysis. There's a lot of mud on George Mahmood's shoes, consistent with walking over the rec in the rain, and some sort of substance that looks a bit suspicious. But the lad was wearing trainers, for Christ's sake. Hardly what you'd choose if you were intending to kick someone's head in.'

'But we don't know that he was *intending* to do anything, do we?' Gristhorpe pointed out.

'True. Still, it'd be difficult to kick someone to death wearing trainers. Dr Glendenning specified heavy boots. Or Doc Martens, something like that.'

'Wouldn't the rain have washed any traces of blood away?' Susan asked.

'Lab says not. If there's enough of it, which there was, and if it gets in the stitching and seeps between the sole and upper they say it's damn near impossible to get rid of.'

Susan nodded.

'Vic Manson's working on fingerprints, too,' Banks said to Gristhorpe, 'but he doesn't hold out a lot of hope.'

'Fingerprints from where?'

'The broken bottle. According to the post-mortem, there were fragments of broken glass embedded in the back of Jason Fox's skull, and they match the fragments we found near the body. It looks as if he was hit with a bottle and then kicked. Anyway, Vic says the rain has probably buggered up his chances, but he's busy spraying SuperGlue into aquariums and lord knows what else.'

'What did you find out yesterday?' Gristhorpe asked.

'Quite a lot.' Banks told them in detail about Jason Fox's losing his job, his false address in Leeds, and the Albion League. 'I also checked out this Milly and her boyfriend,' he went on. 'The West Indian woman Jason insulted at work. Seems she's gone back to live with her family in Barbados.'

'Chalk up one victory to Jason Fox, then,' said Gristhorpe. 'Any idea where Jason lived when he wasn't at his parents' house?'

Banks smiled and produced an address in Rawdon.

'How did you find out?'

'Telephone directory. It doesn't seem as if Jason was making any particular secret out of where he lived. He just neglected to let his parents know he'd moved.'

'For eighteen months?'

Banks shrugged. 'Jason's relationship with his parents obviously wasn't close. There's a lot they don't know about him. I'm not entirely sure whether they didn't want to know, or whether he didn't want them to. From what I've seen so far, the Foxes aren't a particularly close family.'

'How did he make his living these past two years?' Gristhorpe asked. 'Do we know that?'

Banks shook his head. 'No. But according to the DSS he wasn't on the dole. His grandfather mentioned something about him studying computers, too, so that might be something he's got into more recently. I've asked Ken Blackstone to give us a hand down there, checking the local college courses. And we can check tax records, see if he got another job somewhere.'

Gristhorpe nodded. 'Know anything about this Albion League?'

Banks's only experience with neo-Nazis was with the National Front in the seventies, when he was a young copper on the Met. He had read about the more recent, smaller and tougher groups, like Combat 18 and Blood and Honour, with all their concomitant white-power rock bands and magazines, but he hadn't actually come across any of them in the line of duty. 'Not yet,' he said. 'And nobody else around here seems to have heard of them, either. Anyway, I faxed the Yard. They've got a special squad dealing with neo-Nazi groups.'

'Let's keep our fingers crossed. Have you got anything to add, Sergeant Hatchley?'

'The uniformed lads canvassed the whole Market Street area again yesterday,' said Hatchley. 'Pubs, cafés, fish and chip shops, bed and breakfasts, the lot. Some people remember Georgie Mahmood and his two mates in the fish and chip shop, all right, but no one saw them heading for the ginnel. And no one remembers seeing Jason and his mate. We've managed to get an artist's impression of the lad who was with Jason, but I wouldn't expect too much.' Hatchley scratched his nose. 'I'm wondering if it was something to do with drugs, sir, The Jubilee being the sort of place it is. A deal gone wrong, maybe?'

'Have we got anything from the Drugs Squad on the victim or suspects?'

Hatchley shook his head. 'No, sir. I've already checked with records. But still . . .'

'Well, we'll bear it in mind, anyway. Anything else?'

'Aye, sir. I had a chat with a couple of Jason's team-mates from Eastvale United. He had a jar with them after the game, right enough, but none of them admit to seeing him Saturday night, and none of them recognize the lad in the artist's impression.'

'Why hasn't Jason's mate come forward?' Gristhorpe mused aloud. 'Does he even know what's happened?'

'It's possible he doesn't, sir,' said Hatchley. 'If he lives far off, like, doesn't watch much telly or read the papers.'

Gristhorpe nodded and turned to face everyone. 'Either that or he did it. Let's dig a little deeper into the background here. First off, find out if George Mahmood and Jason Fox really did know each other better than George is letting on. Maybe they'd crossed swords before. Let's also find out what we can about Asim Nazur and that cousin of his, Kobir . . . what's his name . . .?'

'Mukhtar, sir,' said Susan.

'Right. Someone get in touch with Bradford CID and find out if they've got anything on Kobir Mukhtar.'

'I've already done that, sir,' said Susan. 'There was nothing on the computer, so I put in a request for information while we still had them in custody, just before . . . before the CC came round yesterday, sir.'

'And?'

'Nothing, sir. Seems clean.'

'All right.' Gristhorpe frowned. 'Susan, don't I recollect something about an incident involving the Mahmoods recently?'

'Yes, sir. About a month ago. Someone stole a brick from the building site by Gallows View and lobbed it through the Mahmoods' window. They'd covered the shop windows with wire mesh a while back after a previous incident, so the yob responsible chucked this brick through the bedroom window.'

'Anyone hurt?'

'Mrs Mahmood, sir. She was undressing for bed at the

time. The brick missed her head by several inches, but a long sliver of glass broke free and sliced into her upper arm. She was bleeding pretty badly when her husband hurried her to Eastvale General. It took fourteen stitches, and the doctor insisted they call the police.'

'They weren't going to?'

'They were reluctant, sir,' Susan said. 'Her husband said it would only cost them time and trouble, and they didn't expect any results in return. Apparently, this kind of thing had happened before, when they ran the shop in Bradford, and nobody ever did anything about it.'

'Well, this isn't bloody Bradford,' said Gristhorpe. 'Any leads?'

'They'd had a customer, a teenage girl, earlier in the day who complained about getting the wrong change. When Mrs Mahmood insisted she was right, the girl swept the newspapers and sweets off the counter and stalked out. We finally tracked her down, but she was in Penrith by the time of the incident. After that, nothing.'

'Could it have been Jason Fox, given his views on immigrants?'

'I suppose so,' Susan said. 'It happened about half past ten on a Saturday night, and we know Jason came to Eastvale on weekends. But we didn't know that then. I mean, we'd no reason to suspect him. And George Mahmood couldn't have known it was him.'

'Couldn't he? Maybe he had his suspicions. Maybe he even *saw* him. But you're right, we should avoid too much speculation at this point. Perhaps you should have another word with Jason's family, Susan, see if they're a bit more forthcoming. After that, you can try the Mahmoods again, then the Nazurs at the Himalaya, see if they can tell you anything else about what happened on Saturday night.' He looked at his watch, then smiled at Susan. 'Time it right, lass, and you might be at the Himalaya just around lunch-time.'

Hatchley laughed, and Susan blushed.

'That just about covers it.' Gristhorpe rubbed his bristly chin. 'But wherever we go,' he said, 'we tread carefully. On eggs. Remember that. Chief Constable Riddle is taking a personal interest in this case.' He cleared his throat. 'By the way, he apologized for not being with us this morning.'

Banks overheard Hatchley whisper to Susan Gay, 'Breakfast television.'

Gristhorpe ignored them. 'What we've all got to bear in mind at this point,' he said, 'is that while this case looked simple at first, things have changed. It's got a lot more complicated. And however odious a character Jason Fox is beginning to sound, remember, he didn't get a chance to fight back. That's voluntary manslaughter, at the very least, and more than likely it's murder. And don't forget, we've got all the ingredients of a racial incident here, too: white victim; handy Asian suspects picked up, interro-gated and locked in the cells overnight. When you add to that the fact that Jason Fox was a racist, George Mahmood is busy exploring his Muslim roots and Asim Nazur's dad is a pillar of the community, then you've got a powder-keg, and I don't want it going off on my patch, Jimmy Riddle or no Jimmy Riddle. Now let's get to it.'

TWO

It was quicker to walk to the Leaview Estate than to drive around Eastvale's confusing one-way system, so Susan nipped out of the fire-exit and took the winding cobbled streets behind the police station down to King Street. She passed the infirmary, then the Gothic pile of Eastvale Comprehensive on the right, with its turrets, clock and bell tower, and the weedy, overgrown rec on her left before entering the Leaview Estate. The weather was overcast today, windy, too, with occasional drizzle, but at least it wasn't cold.

The Foxes' garden looked less impressive in the dull light, Susan thought as she rang the doorbell, yet the roses still seemed to burn with an inner glow of their own. She felt like picking one to take home, but she didn't. That wouldn't look good at all. She could just see the headlines: POLICE WOMAN STEALS PRIZE ROSES FROM GRIEVING FAMILY. Jimmy Riddle would just love that. His pate would turn scarlet. And bang would go her promotion.

Josie Fox had her hair tied back today, and her face looked pale and drawn, lips bloodless without make-up. She was wearing a baggy olive jumper and black jeans.

'Oh, it's you. Come in,' she said listlessly, standing aside.

'I'm sorry to intrude,' Susan said, following her into the living room. 'But I have a few more questions.'

'Of course. Sit down.'

Susan sat. Josie Fox followed suit, folding her long legs under her. She massaged the bridge of her nose with her thumb and forefinger.

'Where's your husband today?' Susan asked.

She sighed. 'Steven's at work. I told him not to go in, but he said he'd be better off with something to do rather than just being stuck in the house all day. I can't say I'm not glad to see the back of him for a few hours. I couldn't face going in, myself. My daughter's come down from Newcastle to stay with us, so I'm not alone.'

'Is she in at the moment?'

'Upstairs, yes. Why?'

'Will you call her down, please?'

Josie Fox frowned, then shrugged and went to the bottom of the stairs to call. A minute or so later, Maureen Fox joined them. Susan's first impression was of a rather bossy, probably very fastidious sort of girl. She was attractive, too, in a sort of bouncy blonde, healthy, athletic way, with a trim figure that looked good in the tight jeans she wore, and symmetrical features, plump red lips, a creamy complexion.

Though Maureen Fox was obviously grieving, there was still a kind of energy emanating from her that she couldn't hide; it showed itself in the way her foot kept tapping on the floor, or one leg jerked when she crossed them; in her constant shifts of position, as if she were uncomfortable no matter how she sat. Susan wondered if Jason had been at all like her. Probably not, if Susan's own family were anything to go by: her brother the stock-broker, who could do no wrong, and her sister the solicitor, apple of her father's eye. Susan had nothing in common with either of them, and sometimes she thought she must have been a changeling.

'Why did you let them go?' Josie asked. 'You had them in jail, the ones who did it, and you let them go.'

'We don't know that they did it,' Susan said. 'And we can't just keep people locked up indefinitely without evidence.'

'It's because they're coloured, isn't it? That's why you had to let them go. It would've been different if you thought Jason had killed one of *them*, wouldn't it?'

'Mother!' Maureen cut in.

'Oh, Maureen. Don't be so naïve. Everybody knows

what it's like these days. The authorities bend over back-wards to help immigrants. You ought to know that, being in nursing. It's all opportunities for ethnics, not for decent, hard-working white folks. Look what happened to your dad.'

'What did happen to Mr Fox?' Susan asked.

'Oh,' said Maureen, with a flick of her head, 'Dad got passed over for promotion. Blamed it on some Asian bloke.'

'I see. Well, you're right in a way, Mrs Fox,' Susan went on, looking at Josie. 'The police *do* have to be very careful about how they treat people these days, especially visible minorities. We try to handle everyone the same way, no matter what colour they are.' She knew it was eyewash. In the overall scheme of things, racism, along with sexism, was alive and thriving in the police forces of the nation. But, damn it, that was what *she* tried to do. 'In this case, though,' she went on, 'we simply have no evidence yet to connect the suspects to the crime. No witnesses. No physical evidence. Nothing.'

'Does that mean they didn't do it?' Josie asked.

'It raises doubts,' said Susan. 'That's all. I'm afraid I can't say any more about it at the moment.'

'You haven't given up, have you?'

'Certainly not. We're investigating a number of leads. That's why I'm here.' She paused. 'I'm afraid we turned up a couple of disturbing facts about your son.'

Josie Fox frowned. 'Disturbing? Like what?'

'Did you know about Jason's racist views?'

'What do you mean?'

'Did he never talk about his opinions to you?'

'He never really talked about anything much,' she said. 'Especially not these past few years.'

'Were you aware of what he thought about Asians and blacks?'

'Well,' said Josie Fox, 'let's put it this way. I knew he had some opinions that might be unpopular, you know, about foreigners, immigrants and such, but I wouldn't say they were particularly extreme. Lots of people think the way Jason does and it doesn't make them racists.'

That was a new one on Susan: having racist views doesn't make you a racist? 'Did Jason ever mention belonging to any sort of an organization?' she asked. 'A group of like-minded people?'

It was Maureen Fox who broke the silence. 'No. Jason never mentioned it, but he did. Belong to a group, that is. We only found out about it yesterday.'

'Maureen!'

'Oh, Mother. Jason was a creep and you know it. That's why he could never keep a girlfriend. I don't care if I am speaking ill of the dead. I could never stomach him even when he was at school back in Halifax. All his talk about bloody racial purity making the country great again. It made me want to puke. It was those skins he hung around with at school, you know, them and their masters, the ones who prey on schoolkids in depressed areas. You should have done something, you and Dad.'

'Like what?' Josie Fox beseeched her. 'What could we have done to change him?'

'How do I know what you should have done? But you're his parents. You should have done *something*.' She turned to Susan. 'Yesterday we went to visit my granddad,' she said. 'He showed us a pamphlet he thought Jason had sent him in the post. He was very upset about it.'

'The Albion League?'

'You know?'

Susan nodded. 'Your grandfather told DCI Banks yesterday evening.'

Maureen looked at her mother. 'There. I told you Granddad wouldn't be able to keep it to himself.' She turned to Susan. 'Mum thought we should keep it in the family, to protect the family name, but . . .' She shrugged. 'Well, the cat's out of the bag now, isn't it?'

'I still don't see what this has to do with anything,' Josie Fox protested. 'Now you're making out my Jason was the villain, but he was the victim. Are you suggesting those boys might have killed him because of his beliefs?'

'Could they have known?'

'What do you mean?'

Susan paused for a moment, then continued softly, 'Jason wasn't here very often, Mrs Fox. He didn't put down roots, didn't get to know people. Could those boys have known about him, about what he . . . believed?'

'They could have found out somehow, I suppose. They're Asians, so I suppose they have their own gangs, their own networks, don't they? Maybe he did talk to one of them, that one in the shop.'

'Do you know if he ever shopped there?'

'I don't know, but he might have done. It's not far away, especially if you go to the bus stop down on Cardigan Drive.'

'But Jason had a car.'

'Doesn't mean he never took the bus, does it? Anyway, all I'm saying is he *might* have gone in the shop. It wasn't far away. That's all.'

'Do you remember about a month ago, when someone threw a brick—'

'Now, wait a minute,' said Josie. 'You're not going to blame that on our Jason. Oh, no. Be nice and easy for you, that, wouldn't it, blaming a crime on someone who can't answer for himself, just so you can make your crime figures look better, write it off your books.'

Susan took a deep breath. 'That's not my intention, Mrs Fox. I'm trying to establish a link between Jason and George Mahmood, if there is one. Given Jason's feelings about Asians, it doesn't seem entirely beyond the realm of possibility that he chucked the brick and George knew about it.'

'Well, you'll never know, will you?'

Susan sighed. 'Perhaps not. Do you know if Jason gave out any of those pamphlets to anyone on the estate?'

Josie Fox shook her head. 'I shouldn't think so. No, I'm fairly certain he didn't. I'd have heard about it.'

I'll bet you would, Susan thought. 'Did any of Jason's colleagues ever call here?'

'I told you the other day. No. We didn't know his friends.' For a moment, Susan had imagined a scene like the one in the Krays' east London home, the boys upstairs planning murder and mayhem while good old mum comes in with a tray of tea and biscuits, beaming at them. Obviously not. 'You'd almost think he was ashamed of us,' Josie Fox added.

'Or of them,' said Susan. 'Look, he was seen drinking with this lad in The Jubilee on Saturday night.' She turned to face Maureen again and showed her the picture. 'We're trying to trace him. He might be able to help us find out what happened. Have you ever seen Jason with anyone like that?'

Maureen shook her head. 'No.'

'Mrs Fox?'

'No.'

'You told us Jason was working at a plastics factory in

Leeds. Did you know that he left there two years ago, that he was asked to leave because of his racist views?'

Josie Fox's jaw dropped and she could only shake her head slowly, eyes disbelieving. Even Maureen paled.

'Do you know where he went after that?' Susan pressed on.

'No,' said Mrs Fox, her voice flat, defeated. 'As far as we knew that's where he worked.'

'Did he ever mention anything about studying computers?'

'Not to me, no.'

'Do you know where Jason lived in Leeds?'

'I gave you the address.'

Susan shook her head. 'He hasn't been living there in eighteen months. He moved to Rawdon. Did you never visit him?'

Again, she shook her head. 'No. How could we? We were both working during the week. Jason, too. Besides, he came to visit us at weekends.'

'Did you never telephone him?'

'No. He said it was a shared telephone, out on the landing, and the people in the other flats didn't like to be disturbed. He'd usually ring us if he wanted to tell us he was coming up.'

'What about at work?'

'No. His boss didn't like it. Jason would always ring us. I don't understand. This is all . . . Why didn't he tell us?'

'I don't know, Mrs Fox,' said Susan.

Tears welled in Josie Fox's eyes. 'How could he? I mean, where did it come from, him joining such a group, not telling us anything? We used to be such a close family. We always tried to bring him up properly, decently. Where did we go wrong?'

Maureen raised her eyes and sat rigidly, arms folded over her chest, staring at a spot high on the wall, as if she were both embarrassed and disgusted by her mother's display of emotion. *Where did we go wrong?* It was a question Susan had heard many times, both in the course of her work and from her own parents when they complained about her chosen career. She knew better than to try to answer it.

A lot of prejudices were inherited. Her father, for example: to all outside appearances, he was a decent and intelligent man, a regular churchgoer, a respected member of the community, yet he would never eat in an Indian restaurant because he thought he was being served horse-meat, dog or cat, and that the hot spices were used to mask the taste of decay.

Susan had inherited some of his attitudes, she knew, but she also knew she could fight against them; she didn't have to be stuck with them forever. So she went to lots of Indian restaurants and got to love the food. That was why Superintendent Gristhorpe's crack about having lunch at the Himalaya had made her blush. It was exactly what she had been thinking at the time: onion bhaji and vegetable samosas. *Mmmm.*

Whatever she did, though, it was always there, at the back of her mind: that feeling, inherited from her father, that these people weren't *quite like us*; that their customs and religious beliefs were barbaric and primitive, not Christian.

Where did we go wrong? Who knew the answer to that one? Giving up on the Foxes for now, Susan closed her notebook and walked back out onto Daffodil Rise. It had started to rain again.

THREE

The traffic on the Leeds ring road wasn't too bad, and Banks made it to Rawdon by eleven o'clock. Number seven Rudmore Terrace was an uninspiring, stone-clad semi just off the main road to Leeds and Bradford Airport. It had a small bay window, frosted-glass panes in the door and an overgrown garden.

First, Banks headed for number nine, where he noticed the lace curtains twitch as he walked up the path. Of course, when he knocked and a woman answered, she made a great pretence of being surprised to receive a caller, and left the chain on as she checked his warrant card and invited him in.

'You can't be too careful, these days,' she said as she put the kettle on. 'A woman in the next street was attacked just two weeks ago. Raped.' She mouthed the word rather than speaking it aloud, as if that somehow lessened its power. 'In the middle of the day, no less. I'm Liza Williams, by the way.'

Liza was an attractive woman in her early thirties, with short black hair, a smooth, olive complexion and light blue eyes. She led Banks through to the living-room, the carpet of which was covered with children's toys. The room smelled vaguely of Plasticine and warm milk.

'Jamie's taken the twins over to their grannie's for the morning,' she said, surveying the mess. 'To give me a breather, like. Two two-and-a-half-year-olds can be a bit of a handful, Mr Banks, in case you didn't know that already.'

Banks smiled. 'I didn't know. There's a couple of years between my boy and girl. But believe me, *one* two-and-a-half-year-old was bad enough. I can't imagine two.'

Liza Williams smiled. 'Oh, it's not so bad really. I complain but . . . I wouldn't want to be without them. Now, I don't suppose you came here to talk about children. Is it about that woman in the next street?'

'No. I'm North Yorkshire CID,' said Banks. 'That'd be West Yorkshire.'

'Yes, of course. I should have noticed the card.' She frowned. 'That just makes me even more puzzled.'

'It's about next door, Mrs Williams.'

She paused, then her eyes widened. 'Oh, I see. Yes, that's so sad, isn't it? And him so young.'

'I'm sorry?'

'You mean about the boy who was killed, don't you? Jason. In Eastvale. That's North Yorkshire, isn't it?'

'You knew?'

'Well we *were* neighbours, even if we weren't especially close ones. They say good fences make good neighbours, Mr Banks, and you need a big one to keep that ugly garden of his out of view. But fair's fair. He was quiet and considerate and he never complained about the twins.'

'Look, do you think we could just back up for a minute and get a few things straight?'

'Of course.'

'Jason Fox lived next door, at number seven, right?'

'Yes. That's what I was telling you.'

'Okay. And you read in the paper that Jason was killed in Eastvale on Saturday night?'

'Saw it on telly, actually. How else would I know? Soon as I heard it was him you could have knocked me over with a feather.'

'How did you know it wasn't some other Jason Fox?'

'Well, it's not that common a name, is it, and even if the

sketch they showed on the news wasn't very good, I could still recognize him from it.'

The kettle boiled and Liza Williams excused herself to make tea. She came back with a tray, a pot and two mugs.

'Why didn't you call the police?' Banks asked.

She frowned. 'Police? But why should I? Did I do something wrong?'

'No. I'm not accusing you of anything. Just curious.'

'Well, I never thought. Why would I? I didn't really know anything about Jason. Anyway, I was really very sorry to hear about what happened, but it didn't have anything to do with me, did it? It's none of *my* business. I mean, I've never even *been* to Eastvale.'

'But didn't you think the police might want to have a look around the house where Jason lived, maybe ask you a few questions about him?'

'Well . . . I . . . I don't know what to say. I'm sorry. I just assumed if the police wanted to ask me anything, they'd have asked me when they were round earlier. I thought you'd done what you had to do. I don't know what happens to people's houses after—'

'Just a minute,' said Banks, sitting on the edge of his seat. 'Did you say the police have already been around?'

'Yes. Plainclothes. Didn't you know?'

'Obviously not, or I wouldn't be asking you all these questions.'

Liza Williams didn't look or sound like a stupid woman. What could she be thinking of? 'When was this?'

'Sunday morning. Before I'd even heard what happened. Why? Is something wrong?'

'No. No. It's all right.' Banks scratched the scar beside his right eye. Liza poured the tea, meeting his eyes as she did so and splashing a little tea on the tray. She handed

Banks a steaming mugful. 'Did they talk to you?' he asked.

'No. They just went into Jason's house. Two of them. They seemed to have a key, seemed to know what they were doing.'

'How did you know they were police?'

'I didn't. I just assumed, the way they seemed so purposeful. Then, later that night, when I saw about Jason on the telly . . . It seemed to make sense.'

'What time was this, when they came?'

'Must have been about ten o'clock. Jamie had just come back from the newsagent's with the papers. We don't have them delivered bec—'

Banks tuned her out. At first he had considered the possibility, however remote, that West Yorkshire had been playing left hand to North Yorkshire's right. But Susan Gay hadn't even discovered Jason Fox's identity until lunchtime on Sunday, and the Foxes hadn't officially identified him until after that. So who had known who the victim was before the police did? And how had they found out?

Banks blew on his tea, took a sip, then leaned forward again. 'This is very important, Mrs Williams,' he said. 'Can you tell me anything about these men?'

FOUR

Steven Fox clearly wasn't expecting Susan, and his face showed surprise and suspicion when she turned up in his office at the building society.

'Time for a word?' she asked, smiling.

He looked at his watch. 'I suppose so. It's almost lunchtime anyway.'

'My treat,' said Susan. She sighed inwardly, realizing she'd have to forgo the Himalaya.

Steven Fox put on his raincoat, and they walked along York Road to the El Toro coffee bar on the opposite side of the market square from the police station. The El Toro, with its dim lighting, castanet-clicking muzak, bullfight posters and smell of espresso, wasn't renowned for its food, but the sandwiches were decent enough: Susan treated herself to prawn and tomato and Steven Fox settled for ham and cheese.

Once they had taken a bite or two and sipped some coffee, Susan began: 'Would you be surprised to hear that Jason was no longer working where you told us he was?'

Steven Fox paused and rubbed his glasses, steamed up by the coffee. 'To be honest,' he said, 'nothing much would surprise me about Jason. He was a law unto himself.'

'His mother was surprised.'

'Maybe she had more illusions.'

That might explain, Susan thought, why Steven Fox had seemed quicker to accept that Jason might have met a violent end than Josie had been.

'And you?' she asked.

'Jason was a peculiar lad. We never had a very close relationship. I don't know why.'

'Did you know anything about his affiliation with the Albion League?'

'Not until yesterday, no.' Steven Fox shook his head slowly. 'When Jason left home,' he said, 'that was it. We never really knew what he was up to after then. Still, I don't suppose it's the kind of thing you do tell your parents, is it? I mean, can you imagine your son sitting down at the dinner table one night and saying, "Guess what, Mum, Dad, I joined a neo-Nazi party today"?'

'Not unless he thought you shared his views.'

Steven banged his coffee cup down on the saucer, spilling some. 'Now, hold on a minute, that's quite an allegation. I resent that. I'm not a racist.'

Susan held her hand up. 'I'm not alleging anything, Mr Fox. I simply want to know.'

'Well, he didn't get it from me or his mother.'

'Do you have any ideas as to where he did get it from?'

'Well, that kind of thing . . . Do you really think it's as simple as . . . you know, just picking up or imitating someone's mannerisms or figures of speech?'

'No, I don't. But he had to start somewhere. What about this promotion business?'

'Josie told you about that?'

'Maureen, actually.'

Steven Fox shrugged. 'Back in Halifax, I lost out on a promotion to a fellow from Bengal. Nice chap, but . . . It was that, what do you call it . . .?'

'Positive discrimination?'

'Aye, only giving jobs to immigrants and women. Sorry. But I had more experience. And I'd put in more years. Anyway, it gave us some hard times, not enough money coming in, that sort of thing. I think Jason took it more to heart than I did, maybe because he already had some problems of his own at school. There were a lot of Asians there, recent immigrants for the most part, some of them with poor language skills, and Jason got into trouble once for suggesting to a teacher that they were holding back the rest and ought to be put together in a special class.'

'How long ago was that?'

'In his last year there. Just before we moved.'

'Didn't that concern you?'

'Well it . . . I mean, in a way, I suppose, he was right,

wasn't he? Maybe he should have put it more diplomatically. Lord knows, as I said, I'm no racist, but it seems to me that if you keep on catering for the demands of foreign cultures and other religions over your own, then you do sort of . . . weaken . . . your own, don't you? For crying out loud, they don't even sing a hymn and say the Lord's Prayer at morning assembly any more.'

Susan moved on quickly. 'Do you know the people who run the shop on Gallows View? The Mahmoods?'

'I know who you mean – I've nipped in there for a tin of soup from time to time – but I can't say I *know* them.'

'Remember about a month ago when someone chucked a brick though their window?'

'I read about it in the local paper. Why?'

'Was Jason up that weekend?'

'Oh, come on,' said Steven. 'Surely you can't imagine he'd do something like that?'

'Why not?'

'He wasn't a hooligan.'

'But he was a racist.'

'Still . . . anyway, I don't remember if he was here or not. And aren't you supposed to be looking for his killers?'

'Every little bit helps, Mr Fox. He wasn't living at the address you gave us in Leeds. Did you know that?'

'Not living there?' Steven Fox shook his head. 'Bloody hell, no. I just assumed . . . I mean, why would he lie about that?'

'I don't think he lied. He just omitted to let you know. Maybe he thought you weren't interested.'

Steven Fox frowned. 'You must think us terribly neglectful parents.'

Susan said nothing.

'But Jason was over eighteen,' he went on. 'He led his own life.'

'So you said. He still visited home, though.'

'He came home on weekends to get his washing done and get a free meal, like lots of kids do.'

'You said earlier that you and Jason were never close. Why was that?'

'I don't know really. When he was younger, he was always more of a mother's boy. Then, in his teens, he got involved in football. I've never been much interested in sports, myself. I was never very good at games at school. Always the last one to be picked, that sort of thing. I suppose I should have gone to watch him play, you know, shown more support . . . enthusiasm. It's not that I wasn't proud of him.' He shook his head. 'Maybe I was selfish. I had my record collection to catalogue. Jason had his football. We just didn't seem to have anything in common. But I couldn't see where any of it was leading. How could I know?' He looked at his watch. 'Look, I really do have to get back. I can't tell you anything more, honestly. If those boys really did kill Jason, you know, those immigrants you had to let go, I hope you find some evidence against them. If there's anything else I can do . . . ?'

And he got up to leave. Susan nodded, more than happy to see the back of him. For the second time that day she'd had to restrain herself from screaming that George, Asim and Kobir weren't immigrants, that they'd been bloody well born here, and their fathers before them. But she didn't. What was the point?

And now she had to go to the Himalaya and talk to Asim Nazur and his parents. They would certainly be thrilled to see her. Still, wicked though it sounded, maybe she still had room for a small samosa, after all. Just the one. For a simple pub fight gone wrong, she thought, this case was turning into a hell of a confusing affair.

FIVE

The little pane of glass in the front door smashed easily enough when Banks applied his elbow. He stuck his hand through carefully and turned the lock. He had a warrant to search the place and, as Jason's pockets had been emptied of everything, including his house keys, this seemed the easiest way to get in.

Inside, the house was so quiet that all he could hear was the hissing of blood in his ears. There wasn't even a clock ticking. He imagined it wasn't always like that, not with the twins next door.

He started in the living room, to his right. Three-piece suite, upholstered in tan corduroy, wallpaper with thin green and brown stripes, mirror over the mantelpiece, fake-coal electric fire. Television and video. Selection of tapes, mostly science fiction and horror by the look of them. A few paperbacks: Ayn Rand, Tom Clancy, Michael Crichton. And that was it. There was a sideboard against one wall and in one of the drawers Banks found a couple of bills addressed to Jason Fox. Nothing else.

The kitchen was spotless, dishes all in cupboards, mugs hanging from hooks over the counter. Very little in the fridge: a tub of *I Can't Believe It's Not Butter*; Cheddar cheese turning blue at the edges, sliced white bread, boiled ham, limp celery, lettuce, tomatoes. More the kind of stuff for sandwiches than hot meals. Maybe Jason did most of his eating out.

There were three bedrooms, one no bigger than a cupboard really. That one was completely empty, the other two showed some signs of occupation. Just as at the house in Eastvale, Jason's bed was tightly made, and a similar selection of clothes hung in the wardrobe. The dresser drawers were full of socks, underwear and T-shirts, along with an unopened box of condoms and a bottle of aspirin. The third bedroom looked like a guest room, with a single bed, empty drawers and not much else.

Except the computer.

But Banks didn't trust himself not to screw something up if he started messing around with that, so he made a note to get someone else in to give it the once-over.

Back in the hall, Banks could only marvel at the sheer *emptiness* of the place. There was no personality. You'd expect, if Jason were a member of a white-power organization, at least a few Skrewdriver CDs and maybe one or two copies of *The Order* strewn around the place. But it was as if someone had been there and stripped away all signs of character, if there had been any. And maybe someone had.

Two men, Liza Williams had said, and they had left with some cardboard boxes. Unfortunately, it had been raining in Leeds that Sunday morning, and they had both been wearing flat hats. Black or navy blue. One of them wore a black leather jacket and jeans, the other a donkey jacket. The one in the leather jacket was taller than the other.

No, Liza admitted, they weren't particularly well dressed, but then she watched a lot of police programmes on telly, so she didn't expect real policemen to be any better dressed than their fictional counterparts. No, she couldn't say how old they were, hadn't seen their faces, but she got the impression by the way they moved that they were probably fairly young and fit.

And that was about all she could say, she was sorry. She had, after all, only glimpsed them, and as she noticed they used a key to get in, she didn't worry about them being burglars or rapists. She first thought they were friends of Jason's – he sometimes had friends to stay – and then, after she heard of his death, she just assumed they'd been policemen come to return his belongings to his family or something. No, her husband hadn't seen them; he had already settled down with the Sunday papers, and once he did that . . .

The only thing she *had* noticed was a blue car parked outside, which she thought belonged to the men. But she didn't know what make it was, let alone the number. She did say it was clean, though.

Banks sighed as he closed the door behind him. He would have to get someone from West Yorkshire to fix the pane of glass he'd broken, and perhaps to question some of the other people in the street. Whatever they'd noticed, he hoped it would be more than Liza Williams.

SIX

By mid-afternoon, Susan was wet, tired and no further ahead than she had been in the morning. The Nazurs and the Mahmoods had been sullen and uncommunicative, as expected, and she had flinched at the clear accusations of racism in their eyes. No, Jason Fox had never been in the Mahmoods' shop, as far as they knew, and the Nazurs had never seen him in their restaurant. And they knew nothing about any Albion League.

Sergeant Hatchley was still out pounding the streets, so at least she got the opportunity to warm herself up with a cup of coffee and take a little quiet time for herself.

She had just put her cold wet feet on the radiator to warm them when one of the staff from the murder room came in bearing a fax. 'Just arrived,' he said.

Susan thanked him and looked at the single sheet. All it said was:

THE ALBION LEAGUE

along with a telephone number. A London number.

Curious, Susan picked up the phone and dialled. She remembered that Banks had faxed a request for information about the Albion League to Scotland Yard, so she wasn't surprised when someone there answered. After a bit of shuttling around and a lot of waiting, she finally got to someone who knew what she was talking about when she mentioned the Albion League. His name, he said, was Crawley.

'Is your boss there, love?' he asked.

Susan bristled, gripping the receiver tightly, but she said nothing.

'Well?' Crawley repeated.

'I'm afraid Detective Superintendent Gristhorpe is out of the office at the moment,' Susan finally managed, between gritted teeth.

'And you're DC Gay?'

'Yes.' At least he didn't make any cracks about her name.

'I suppose you'll have to do then.'

Not her day. 'Thanks a lot,' she said.

'Don't take offence, love.'

'I'll try not to, sweetie pie. Now how about the Albion League?'

She heard Crawley laugh at the end of the line, then he cleared his throat. 'Yeah, well, it's a neo-Nazi organization, white power. That's why we're interested, see, in why you want to know.'

'I'd have thought it was a simple enough enquiry,' Susan said.

'True enough, love, but nothing to do with those bastards is simple. They're flagged.'

'Flagged?'

'Any time their name comes up, certain people have to be informed.'

'That sounds very mysterious.'

'Does it?'

'Yes. Anyway, don't worry. I'm sure DCI Banks will send you a full report – he's heading the field investigation – but would you mind, just for the moment, humouring a poor DC? Could you give me some general idea of what this particular neo-Nazi organization is all about, what they want?'

She heard another brief chuckle down the line, then Crawley said, 'Want? That's easy. Same as all the rest of them, really. The usual things. Racial purity. Repatriation of immigrants and all ethnics. Keep Britain white. Oh, and they want the trains to run on time, too.'

'Some hope of that.'

'Tell me about it. Seriously, though, love, it's not so much what these people *want* – that's usually predictable enough – but what they're willing to do to get it – what means they'll use, how they're organized, what connections they have with other groups, whether they're armed, what international links they have, if any. That sort of thing. See what I mean?'

'Yes,' said Susan. 'And the Albion League, how do they fit into all that?'

There was a pause. Then Crawley said, 'I'm sorry, but I'm really not authorized to tell you any more than that. Have your boss give me a bell when he comes in, will you, love?'

And the line went dead.

SEVEN

By the time Banks had finished co-ordinating with West Yorkshire Police, it was late afternoon. He decided to drop by Tracy's residence and see what she was up to. She had only been at the University of Leeds for a little over two weeks, but already he missed her. Maybe he could take her for a spot of dinner or something. That way he would also avoid the rush-hour traffic on the way home.

And spending time with Tracy might also make him forget about his problems with Sandra for a short while.

When he got to the student residence building beside Woodhouse Moor, he was pleased to find that not just anyone could walk in. You had to know whom you wanted to see. Banks found a porter on duty, showed his identification and said he'd like to visit his daughter.

Impressed with Banks's credentials, the garrulous porter – who said he had been a policeman himself some years ago, before a leg injury forced him to retire – let him in.

As Banks walked up the two flights of stairs, he wondered if he should have announced himself first. What if Tracy were with a boy or something? Having sex? But he dismissed the idea. He couldn't imagine his daughter doing that. Either she'd be out at a lecture, or she'd be studying in her room.

When he got to her door, he knocked. He could hear music from down the hall, but not a sound from Tracy's room itself. He knocked again, more loudly this time. Nothing. He felt disappointed. She must be at a lecture.

Just as he was about to walk away, the adjacent door opened and a young tousle-haired girl stuck her head out. 'Oh, sorry,' she said in a husky voice. 'I thought you were knocking on *my* door. Sometimes you can't tell, if you've got some music on or something.' Then her eyes twinkled. 'Hey, you *weren't* knocking at my door, were you?'

'No,' said Banks.

She made a mock pout. 'Pity. You looking for Tracy, then?'

'I'm her father.'

'The detective. She's talked a lot about you.' The girl twisted a tendril of red hair around her index finger. 'I must say, though, she never told me you were quite so dishy. I'm Fiona, by the way. Pleased to meet you.'

She held out her hand and Banks shook it. He felt himself blush. 'Any idea where Tracy might be?'

Fiona looked at her watch. 'Probably in The Pack Horse with the others, by now,' she said, with a sigh. 'I'd be there myself, 'cept I'm on antibiotics for my throat, and I'm not supposed to drink. And it's no fun if you can't have a real drink.' She wrinkled her nose and smiled. 'It's just up the road. You can't miss it.'

Banks thanked her and, leaving the car parked where it was, set off on foot. He found The Pack Horse on Woodhouse Lane, close to the junction with Clarendon Road, not more than a couple of hundred yards away. He felt too formally dressed for the place, even though he had taken off his tie and was wearing casual trousers and a zippered suede jacket.

The pub had the polished wood, brass and glass look of a real Victorian ale house; it also seemed to be divided into a maze of rooms, most of them occupied by noisy groups of students. It wasn't until the third room that Banks found his daughter. She was sitting at a cluttered table with about six or seven other students, a pretty even mix of male and female. The jukebox was playing a Beatles oldie: 'Ticket to Ride'.

He could see Tracy in profile, chatting away over the music to a boy beside her. God, she looked so much like Sandra – the blonde hair tucked behind her small ears, black eyebrows, tilt of her nose and chin, the animated features as she talked. It made his heart ache.

Banks didn't like the look of the boy beside her. He had one of those expressions that always seem to be sneering at the world: something to do with the twist of the lip and the cast of the eyes. Either Tracy didn't notice, or it didn't bother her. Or, worse, she found it attractive.

As she spoke, she waved her hands about, stopping now and then to listen to his response and sip from a pint glass of pale amber liquid and nod in agreement from time to time. Her drink could have been lager, but Banks thought it was most likely cider. Tracy had always enjoyed non-alcoholic cider when they'd stopped for pub lunches during family holidays in Dorset or the Cotswolds.

But this glass of cider was probably alcoholic. And why not? he told himself. She was old enough. At least she wasn't smoking.

Then, as he stood there in the doorway, a strange emotion overwhelmed him. As he watched his daughter talk, laugh and drink, oblivious to her father's proximity, a lump came to his throat, and he realized he had lost her. He couldn't go over to the table and join the crowd –

simply couldn't do it. He didn't belong; his presence would only embarrass her. A line had been reached and crossed. Tracy was beyond him now, and things would never be the same. And he wondered if that was the only line that had been crossed lately.

Banks turned away and walked outside. The wind made his eyes water as he went in search of somewhere else to enjoy a quiet smoke and a drink before setting off back home.

EIGHT

That Tuesday night, the Albion League was holding one of its regular bashes in a small rented warehouse near Shipley. Dim and cavernous, it was the same kind of place people went to for raves, but without the Ecstasy. Here, Craig guessed, the only drugs were the lager that flowed from the kegs like water from a hosepipe, nicotine and, maybe, the odd tab of amphetamine.

But one way or another everyone was pumped up. Guitars, drums and bass crashed at breakneck pace, simple three-chord sequences, interrupted occasionally by a howl of unplanned feedback from the amps. The Albion League themselves were playing tonight, a makeshift white-power band consisting of whoever felt like picking up the instruments at the time. At the moment the lead singer was growling:

> White is white
> Black is black.
> We don't want 'em.
> Send 'em back.

Subtle. Craig wished he could wear earplugs.

From his table, Craig watched Motcombe work the room. He was good, no doubt about it. Slick. There must be at least a couple of hundred people in the place, Craig guessed, and Nev was walking around the tables patting a back here, leaning over for a smile and a word of encouragement there.

It was a miracle he managed to make himself heard with the band making so much bloody noise. Some of the older members, chronically unemployed factory workers and ageing skins, had settled into a far corner, as far away from the source of the racket as possible. What did they expect, Craig wondered, the Black Dyke Mills Band playing *Deutschland über Alles* or Wagner's *Ring* cycle? It was the rock bands that got the kids in, *and* got the message across through sheer volume and repetition.

The real trouble with this gig, Craig thought as he looked around, was that there was no chance of a bit of nooky. For some reason, girls didn't have much to do with white-power freaks, and most of the kids, in turn, seemed content enough with a celibate existence, fuelled by sheer race hatred alone.

The only females Craig could see tonight were a few peroxide scrubbers, like superannuated biker-girls, hanging out with the older crowd, and a table of skinny birds with shaved heads and rings through their noses. He sighed and drank some lager. Can't have everything. A job's a job.

The music stopped and the singer said they were going to take a short break. Thank God for that, thought Craig. Trying to keep one eye on Motcombe, he turned to the three skins at the table with him.

Christ, he thought, they couldn't be more than sixteen.

One of the Leeds cell leaders had spotted them causing a bit of aggro to a telephone box on their way home from a football match. He had joined in with them, then invited them to the show. Thick as two short planks, all three of them.

'What did you think of that, then?' Craig asked, lighting up.

'Not bad,' said the spotty one, who went by the name of Billy. 'I've heard better guitar players, mind you.'

'Yeah, well,' Craig said, with a shrug, 'they're pretty new, need a bit more practice, I'll admit. See, with this lot, though, it's the words that count most. Trouble is, most rock bands don't really pay any attention to what they're saying, know what I mean? I'm talking about the message.'

'What message?' the slack-jawed one asked.

'Well, see, if you were listening,' Craig went on, 'you'd have heard what they were saying about that we should send all the Pakis and niggers back home and get this country on its feet again.'

'Oh, yeah,' said Billy. '"White's white, black's black, we don't want 'em, send 'em back."'

'That's right.' Craig smiled. 'So you *were* listening. Great. That's what I mean, Billy. Most rock music is self-indulgent crap, but this is real music, music with a purpose. It's truth-telling music, this is. It tells it like it is.'

'Yeah,' said slackjaw. 'I think I see what you mean.'

In your fucking dreams, thought Craig. From the corner of his eye, he saw Motcombe about five tables away whispering in someone's ear. He couldn't make out who it was. How many irons did this one have in the fire? Even though the band had stopped playing, music still blared out of a sound system and the level of conversation was loud.

'So what do you think?' he asked. 'The message?'

'Well, yeah,' said pointy-head, speaking up for the first time. 'It sounds all right. Send 'em all back, like. I mean, it sounds good to me.' He grinned, showing bad teeth, and looked around at his friends. 'I mean, kick the fuckers out, right? Eh? Send the black bastards back to the jungle. Kick the fuckers out.'

'Right,' said Craig. 'You've got it. Thing is, there's not much a person can do by himself, all alone, if you see what I mean.'

'Except wank,' grinned slack-jaw.

Ah, a true wit. Craig laughed. 'Yeah, except wank. And you don't want to be wankers, do you? Anyway, see, if you get organized, like with others who feel the same way, then there's a lot more you can achieve. Right?'

'Right,' said Billy. 'Stands to reason, don't it?'

'Okay,' Craig went on, noticing the band picking up their instruments again. 'Think about it, then.'

'About what?' Billy asked.

'What I've just been saying. About joining the League. Where you get a chance to *act* on your beliefs. We have a lot of fun, too.'

A screech of feedback came from the amp. Billy put his hands over his ears. 'Yeah, I can see,' he said.

He was clearly the leader of the three, Craig thought, the Alex of the group; the others were just his droogs. If Billy decided it was a good idea, they'd go along with him. Craig noticed Motcombe glance around the room then walk out of the fire exit at the back with one of the Leeds cell leaders. He stood up and leaned over the three skins. 'Keep in touch, then,' he said, as the music started again. He pointed. 'See that bloke at the table there, over by the door?'

Billy nodded.

'If you decide you want to sign up tonight, he's the man to talk to.'

'Right.'

He patted Billy on the back. 'Got to go for a piss. See you later.'

Casually, he walked towards the toilets near the front door. The band had started their tribute to Ian Stuart, late leader of Skrewdriver who, Blood and Honour claimed, had been murdered by the secret service. And now the Albion League had a martyr on their hands. He wondered how quickly someone would write a song about Jason Fox.

Anyway, the toilets were empty, and most people were either talking loudly or listening to the band, so no one saw Craig nip out the front door. Not that it mattered, anyway; the room was so hot and smoky that no one could be suspect for going out for a breath of fresh air.

Instead of just standing there and enjoying the smell of the cool, damp night, he walked around the back of the building towards the big car park. Glancing around the corner, he saw Motcombe and the Leeds skin standing by Motcombe's black van talking. The car park was badly lit, so Craig found it easy enough to crouch down and scoot closer, hiding behind a rusty old Metro, watching them through the windows.

It didn't take long to figure out that they were talking about money. As Craig watched, the Leeds skin handed Motcombe a fistful of notes. Motcombe took a box out of his van and opened it. Then he placed the bills inside. The skin said something Craig couldn't catch, then they shook hands and he went back inside.

Motcombe stood for a moment, glancing around, sniffing the air. Craig felt a twinge of fear, as if Motcombe had twitched his antenna, sensed a presence.

But it passed. Motcombe opened the box, took out a handful of notes and stuffed them in his inside pocket. Then he squared his shoulders and strutted back in to work the crowd again.

5

ONE

'**The Albion League,**' said Gristhorpe in the boardroom on Wednesday morning, his game leg resting on the polished oval table, thatch of grey hair uncombed. Banks, Hatchley and Susan Gay sat listening, cups of coffee steaming in front of them. 'I've been on the phone to this bugger Crawley for about half an hour, but somehow I feel I know less than when I started. Know what I mean?'

Banks nodded. He'd spoken to people like that. Still, some had said the same thing about him, too.

'Anyway,' Gristhorpe went on, 'they're exactly what they sound like in their pamphlet – a neo-Nazi fringe group. Albion's an old, poetic name for the British Isles. You find it in Chaucer, Shakespeare, Spenser and a lot of other poets. Anyway, according to Crawley, this lot took it from William Blake, who elevated Albion into some sort of mythical spirit of the race.'

'Is this Blake a Nazi, then, sir?' Sergeant Hatchley asked.

'No, Sergeant,' Gristhorpe answered patiently. 'William Blake was an English poet. He lived from 1757 to 1827. You'd probably know him best as the bloke who wrote "Jerusalem" and "Tyger, Tyger".'

'"Tyger tyger, burning bright"?' said Hatchley. 'Aye, sir, I think we did that one at school.'

'Most likely you did.'

'And we sometimes used to sing the other one on the coach home after a rugby match. But isn't Jerusalem in Israel, sir? Was this Blake Jewish, then?'

'Again, Sergeant, no. I'll admit it sounds an ironic sort of symbol for a neo-Nazi organization. But, as I said, Blake liked to mythologize things. To him, Jerusalem was a sort of image of the ideal city, a spiritual city, a perfect society, if you like – of which London was a pale, fallen shadow – and he wanted to establish a *new* Jerusalem "in England's green and pleasant land".'

'Was he green, then, sir, one of them environmentalists?'

'No, he wasn't.'

Banks could see Gristhorpe gritting his teeth in frustration. He felt like kicking Hatchley under the table, but he couldn't reach.

The sergeant was trying it on, of course, but Hatchley and Gristhorpe always seemed to misunderstand one another. You wouldn't have thought they were both Yorkshiremen under the skin.

'Blake's Albion was a powerful figure, ruler of this ideal kingdom,' Gristhorpe went on. 'A figure of which even the heroes of the Arthurian legends were mere shadows.'

'How long have they been around?' Banks asked.

Gristhorpe turned to him, clearly with some relief. 'About a year,' he said. 'They started as a splinter group of the British National Party, which turned out to be too soft for them. And they think they're a cut above Combat 18, who they regard as nowt but a bunch of thugs.'

'Well, they're right on that count,' Banks said. 'Who's the grand Pooh-Bah?'

'Bloke called Neville Motcombe. Aged thirty-five. You'd

think he'd be old enough to know better, wouldn't you?'

'Any form?'

'One arrest for assaulting a police officer during a BNP rally years back, and another for receiving stolen goods.'

'Any connection with George Mahmood and his friends?' Banks asked.

Gristhorpe shook his head. 'Other than the obvious, none.'

'Surely the Albion League isn't based in Eastvale, sir?' Susan Gay asked.

Gristhorpe laughed. 'No. That's just where Jason Fox's parents happen to live. Luck of the draw, as far as we're concerned. Their headquarters are in Leeds – an old green-grocer's shop in Holbeck – but they've got cells all over West Yorkshire, especially in places where there's a high percentage of immigrants. As I said before, they're not above using the yobs, but there's also that element of a more intellectual appeal to disaffected white middle-class kids with chips on their shoulders – lads like Jason Fox, with a few bob's worth of brains and nobbut an 'a'porth of common sense.'

'How strong are they?' Banks asked.

'Hard to say. According to Crawley there's about fifteen cells, give or take a couple. One each in smaller places like Batley and Liversedge, but two or three in a larger city like Leeds. We don't really know how many members in each cell, but as a rough estimate let's say maybe eighty to a hundred members in all.'

'Not a lot, is it? Where does this Motcombe bloke live?'

'Pudsey, down by Fulneck way. Apparently he's got a nice detached house there.'

Banks raised his eyebrows. 'La-de-dah. Any idea how they're financed – apart from receiving stolen goods?'

'Crawley says he doesn't know.'

'Do you believe him?'

Gristhorpe sniffed and scratched his hooked nose. 'I smell politics in this one, Alan,' he said. 'And when I smell politics I don't believe anything I see or hear.'

'Do you want Jim and me to have a poke around in Leeds?' Banks asked.

'Just what I was thinking. You could pay the shop a visit, for a start. See if there's anyone around. Clear it with Ken Blackstone first, make sure you're not treading on anyone's toes.'

Banks nodded. 'What about Motcombe?'

Gristhorpe paused before answering. 'I got the impression that Crawley didn't want us bothering Mr Motcombe,' he said slowly. 'In fact, I think Crawley was only detailed to answer our request for information because they knew down there that we'd simply blunder ahead and find out anyway. The bull-in-a-china-shop approach. He was very vague indeed. And he asked us to proceed with caution.'

'So what do we do?'

A wicked grin creased Gristhorpe's face. 'Well,' he said, tugging his plump earlobe, 'I'd pay him a visit, if I were you. Rattle his chain a bit. I mean, it's not as if we've been officially warned off.'

Banks smiled. 'Right.'

'One more thing before you all go. These letters at the bottom of the Albion League's flyer.' Gristhorpe lifted the pamphlet from the table and pointed. '*Http://www.alblgue.com/index.html.* Now you all know I'm a bloody Luddite when it comes to computers, but even I know that's a web page address. Don't ask me what a web page looks like, mind you. Question is, can we do anything with it? Is it likely to get us anywhere? Susan?'

'It might do,' said Susan Gay. 'Unfortunately, we don't have access to the Internet over the station computers.'

'Oh. Why not?'

'I don't know, sir. Just slow, I suppose. South Yorkshire's even got their own web page. And West Mercia.'

Gristhorpe frowned. 'What do they do with them?'

Susan shrugged. 'Put out information. Community relations. Crimestoppers. Chief Constable's opinion on the state of the county. That sort of thing. It's an interface with the community.'

'Is it, indeed?' Gristhorpe grunted. 'Sounds like a complete bloody waste of time to me. Still, if this Albion League thing's worth a try, is there some way you could have a peek? Or should I say surf?'

Susan smiled. 'Browse, actually, sir. You surf the Net, but you browse the Web.'

'And is there any wonder I've no patience with the bloody machines?' Gristhorpe muttered. 'Whatever you call it, can you get a look at it?'

Susan nodded. 'I've got a hook-up from home,' she said. 'I can certainly give it a try.'

'Then do it, and let us know what you find. Alan, did those lads from West Yorkshire find anything on Jason Fox's computer?'

Banks shook his head. 'Clean as a whistle.'

'Clean as in somebody washed it?'

'That's what they said.'

Gristhorpe grimaced as he shifted his bad leg and shook it to improve the circulation before standing up. 'Right then,' he said. 'That's about it for now. Let's get cracking.'

TWO

Susan enjoyed the unexpected surprise of being able to go home during working hours, even though she knew she was there to work.

First, she kicked off her shoes and put on the kettle. Then she looked through her collection of different tea varieties and settled on Autumn, a black tea dotted with small pieces of apple, perfect for the drizzly, blustery day. On impulse, she put a pinch of cinnamon in the pot, too. While the tea was brewing, she put on her CD of Andrew Lloyd Webber's greatest hits, smiling as she thought how much Banks would hate it, then she poured herself a cup of tea and got down to work.

The computer was in her bedroom because her flat was so small. It was the one room where she never received visitors. At least not yet. But she wasn't going to allow herself to think about DC Gavin Richards right now.

Cup of apple-and-cinnamon-scented tea steaming beside her and 'Don't Cry for Me, Argentina' drifting in from the living room, Susan curled her feet under her on the office chair and logged in. Then she typed in the address from the flyer and clicked her mouse.

The screen remained blank for a long time as the various bits and pieces of the document coming in over the telephone line added up, then suddenly it turned black.

Next, a multicoloured image began to appear, line by line from the top of the screen down, and soon the Albion League's emblem, a swastika made out of burning golden arrows, appeared in full. Probably, Susan thought, remembering Superintendent Gristhorpe's words and the Blake song, it was some sort of image of Blake's 'arrows of desire'.

Around the top of the swastika, the words THE ALBION LEAGUE curled in a semi-circle of bold Gothic script.

It took a couple of minutes for the rest of the document to transfer. When it was complete, Susan started browsing through it. 'Memory' floated in from the living room.

Unlike pages in a book, web pages have an extra dimension provided by hypertext links, highlighted words or icons you can click on to go to another, related site. At first, Susan ignored these links and concentrated on reading the text. It was much the same as the pamphlet she had seen, only there was more of it.

The first paragraph welcomed the reader to the page and explained that the Albion League was a fast-growing group of concerned citizens dedicated to ethnic purity, freedom of speech, law and order, and the establishment of the true English 'homeland'.

After that came a number of links. Some were closely related sites, such as the British National Party's home page or Combat 18, and some were American or Canadian, such as Stormfront, Aryan Nation and the Heritage Front. They varied from the fairly literate to the downright unreadable, but some of the graphics were imaginatively conceived. Susan had never thought members of white-power groups to be particularly creative or intelligent. She had to remind herself that, these days, you didn't have to be an Einstein to work a computer. Almost any kid could do it.

She opted for the League's 'News' icon and was soon treated to a number of recent stories from the unique perspective of the Albion League.

The first item concerned the amount of public money being channelled towards the huge new mosque under construction between Leeds and Bradford, and contrasted it with the shocking state of disrepair of most of Britain's churches.

The second contended that a leading academic had 'proved' humans were actually descended from pale-skinned northern tribes rather than from 'hairy Africans'.

And so it went on: a Tory MP known for his stand on morality and family values had been surprised by a police raid on a homosexual brothel in Sheffield, wearing only a blonde wig and a tutu; Leeds City Council had voted to rename one of the city's streets after a black revolutionary 'scum' . . . example after example of government hypocrisy, just deserts and cultural decay.

One story concerned a white schoolboy who had been stabbed just outside the gates of a Bradford comprehensive school by three members of an Asian gang. It was a sad enough tale – and Susan remembered reading about it in the *Yorkshire Post* only a couple of weeks ago – but according to the Albion League, the tragic stabbing had occurred because the local council was dominated by 'ethnics' and by their brainwashed, politically correct white lackeys, who had all known about the school's problems for years but had never done anything. The victim could, therefore, be seen as 'a sacrifice to the multiracial society'. Susan wondered what they would make of Jason Fox's death.

She paused and took a sip of cold tea to soothe her stomach. The Lloyd Webber had finished ages ago and she had been too absorbed to go into the living room and put something else on. Though she hadn't actually learned much more about the Albion League and its members from the web page, she had learned enough to make her question how she felt about freedom of speech. These people would claim all attempts to silence them violated their basic democratic freedom. Yet given any power at all, they would silence everyone but straight white males.

At the end of the League's page, Susan found, as with many sites, a hypertext link to the page's designers. In this case, the name was *FoxWood Designs*.

Curious, Susan clicked on the name. Again she was disappointed. She had expected names and addresses, but all she got was a stylized graphic image of a fox peering out from some dark trees, along with an e-mail address.

Still, she thought, as she made a note of the address, there was a slight chance that if one half of the team was Mr Fox, then the other half was Mr Wood. And if she could track down Mr Wood, then she might just find *one* person who knew something about Jason Fox's life. And his death.

As soon as Susan hung up her modem, the telephone rang.

It was Gavin.

'Susan? Where've you been? I've been trying to phone you all morning. I bumped into Jim Hatchley in the station and he told me you were working at home.'

'That's right,' Susan said. 'What do you want?'

'Charming. And I was going to invite you to lunch.'

'Lunch?'

'Yes. You know, that stuff you eat to keep you alive.'

'I don't know . . .' said Susan.

'Oh, come on. Even a hard-working DC needs a spot of lunch now and then, surely?'

Come to think of it, Susan *was* hungry. 'Half an hour?'

'If that's all you can spare me.'

'It is.'

'Then I'll take it.'

'And you're paying?'

'I'm paying.'

Susan grinned to herself. 'Right. See you at The Hope and Anchor in ten minutes.'

THREE

The old greengrocer's turned out to be a former corner shop at the end of a street of back-to-backs between Holbeck Moor and Elland Road. The windows were boarded up with plywood, on which various obscenities, swastikas and racist slogans had been spray-painted. Drizzle suited the scene perfectly, streaking the soot-covered red brick and the faded sign over the door that read 'Arthur Gelderd: Greengrocer.'

Banks wondered what Arthur Gelderd, Greengrocer, would have thought if he knew what had become of his shop. Like Frank Hepplethwaite, Arthur Gelderd had probably fought against Hitler in the war. And forty or more years ago, before the supermarkets, this place would have been one of the local neighbourhood meeting places, and a centre of gossip; it would also have provided Gelderd and his family with a modest living. Now it was the headquarters of the Albion League.

Banks and Hatchley looked the building over in the slanting drizzle for a moment. Cars hissed by on Ingram Road, splashing up dirty rainwater from the gutters. The window in the shop door was protected by wire mesh, and the glass itself was covered with old adverts for Omo and Lucozade, so you couldn't see inside. In the centre was a cardboard clockface to show the time the shop would next be open. It was set at nine o'clock, and it would probably be set at that time forever.

Sergeant Hatchley knocked with his hamlike fist; the door rattled in its frame, but no one answered. He tried the handle, but the place was locked. In the silence after the knocking, Banks thought he heard a sound inside.

'What do we do?' Hatchley asked.

'Knock again.'

Hatchley did so. Harder this time.

It did the trick. A voice from behind the door shouted, 'What do you want?'

'Police,' said Banks. 'Open up.'

They heard someone remove a chain and turn a key in a lock, then the door opened.

For some reason, the new occupants hadn't removed the bell that hung on its pliant arc of metal at the back of the door, and it jangled as Banks and Hatchley walked in. The sound reminded Banks of childhood errands to his local corner shop, the way he used to watch, hypnotized, as Mrs Bray turned the handle on the machine and the bacon swung back and forth in the slicer, making a whooshing sound every time the whirling wheel-blade carved off a slice; he remembered the smoky smell of the cured meat in the air, mingled with fresh bread and apples.

What he smelled when he walked in now soon put such nostalgia out of his mind – burned carbon from the photo-copier and laser printer, recent paint, smoke and fresh-cut paper.

The place didn't even resemble a shop any more. What must have been the counter was covered with stacks of paper – more copies of the flyer, by the looks of it – and a computer hummed on a desk beside a telephone. On the walls were a framed poster of Adolf Hitler in full spate, addressing one of the Nuremberg rallies, by the look of it, and a large image of a swastika made out of burning arrows.

A short young man with lank black hair, antique National Health glasses and a spotty face shut the door behind them. 'Always happy to help the local police,' he said with a stupid grin. 'We're on the same side, we are.'

'Fuck off, sonny,' said Banks. 'What's your name?'

The young man blinked at the insult and stepped back a pace. 'There's no need—'

'Name?' Banks repeated as he and Hatchley advanced, backing the young man up against the counter.

The kid held his hands up. 'All right, all right. Don't hit me. It's Des. Des Parker.'

'We're just going to have a little look around, Des, if that's all right with you,' Banks said.

Des frowned. 'Don't you need a search warrant? I mean, I know my rights.'

Banks stopped and raised his eyebrows. He looked at Hatchley. 'Hear that, Jim? Des here knows his rights.'

'Aye,' said Hatchley, walking towards the telephone and picking up the receiver. 'Shall I do the honours, sir?'

Des looked puzzled. 'What honours? What's he doing?'

'Getting a search warrant,' Banks explained. 'In about half an hour we'll have fifty flatfoots going over the place with a fine-tooth comb. Sergeant Hatchley and I will stay here with you until they arrive. Maybe you'd like to inform the building's owner – if it's not you – while we wait. He might want to be here to make sure *his* rights aren't violated.'

Des gulped. 'Mr Motcombe . . . He wouldn't like that.'

'So what?'

'What's going on, Des? Who the fuck is this? Is there a problem?'

The new speaker came out of the back room, zipping

up his fly, accompanied by the sound of a toilet flushing. This one looked a few years older than Des Parker and at least fifty brain cells brighter. Tall and skinny, he was wearing black T-shirt, jeans and red braces, and his dyed blond hair was cut very close to his skull. He also wore a diamond stud in one ear and spoke with a strong Geordie accent. Definitely not the lad who'd been in The Jubilee with Jason Fox last Saturday.

'No problem at all,' Banks said, showing his warrant card again. 'We'd just like a quick shufty around, if that's all right with you. And you are?'

The newcomer smiled. 'Of course. We've got nothing to hide. I'm Ray. Ray Knott.'

'But, Ray!' Des Parker protested. 'Mr Motcombe . . . We can't just let—'

'Shut it, Des, there's a good lad,' said Ray with another smile. 'As I said, we've nothing to hide.' He turned to Banks. 'Sorry about my mate,' he said, pointing to his temple. 'He's none too bright, isn't Des. Few bricks short of a load.'

Banks picked up a copy of the flyer. 'What's this, then, Ray? The Albion League? A new football league, perhaps? Out to rival the Premier, are you?'

'Very funny,' said Ray. But he wasn't laughing.

'Tell us about Jason Fox,' Banks prompted.

'Jason? What about him? He's dead. Kicked to death by Pakis. You lot let them go.'

Hatchley, still poking around, brushed against the huge stack of pamphlets on the counter. They fell to the floor, scattering all over the place. Ray and Des said nothing.

'Sorry,' said Hatchley. 'Clumsy of me.'

Banks marvelled at him. Full of contradictions and surprises was Jim Hatchley. While he'd pin photos of half-naked women on his corkboard – at least he did before Susan moved in – he hated pornographers; and while he'd join in with lads laughing at racist jokes, and was certainly a casual bigot himself, he didn't like neo-Nazis, either. Of course, none of it seemed like a contradiction to him. The way he put it, he wasn't prejudiced, he hated everyone.

'We're not sure who killed him yet,' said Banks. 'Where were the two of you at that time?'

Ray laughed. 'You can't be serious. Me? Us? Kill Jason? No way. He was one of us.'

'So it won't do you any harm to tell me where you were, would it?'

'I were at home,' Des said.

'By yourself?'

'No. I live with me mum.'

'And I'm sure she's really proud of you, Des. Address?'

Des, stuttering, told him.

'What about you, Ray?'

Ray folded his arms and leaned against the counter, one leg crossed over the other, big grin on his face. 'Drinking in my local.'

'Which is?'

'The Oakwood. Up Gipton way.'

'Witnesses?'

Ray grinned. 'Six or seven at least. Local darts championship. I won.'

'Congratulations. What about Sunday morning?'

'Sleeping it off. Why?'

'Alone?'

'Yes.'

Banks made some notes, then said, 'There was no

contact address on your flyer. You're not a secret society, are you?'

'No. But we have to be careful. We have a position we want to get across, and we know it's not popular with a lot of people. So we don't exactly go around shouting about our existence to everyone.'

'I'll bet you don't.'

'Not everyone understands.'

'I'm sure they don't. How does a person join, then?'

'Why? You interested?'

'Just answer the fucking question.'

'All right. All right. No need to get shirty. Just my little joke. We recruit people.'

'Where?'

Ray shrugged. 'Wherever we can find them. It's no secret. Schools, youth clubs, football matches, rock concerts, the Internet. We vet them pretty thoroughly, too, of course, if they express any interest.'

'Tell me, Ray, what are *your* duties?' Banks asked, pacing around the small room as he talked. 'How high up the totem pole are *you*?'

Ray grinned. 'Me? Not very high. Mostly, I hand out pamphlets. And I'll be doing some of the writing now Jason's dead.'

'Propaganda? Was that his job?'

'One of them.'

'The Goebbels of the group, eh?'

'Come again?'

'Never mind, Ray. Before your time. Anything else?'

'I do some training.'

'What sort of training?'

'Country weekends. You know, survival skills, camping, hiking, physical fitness, that sort of thing.'

'Real Duke of Edinburgh's Award stuff?'

'If you like.'

'Weapons?'

Ray folded his arms. 'Now, you *know* that would be illegal.'

'Right. How silly of me to ask. Anyway, Ray, back to Jason Fox. How well did you know him?'

'Not very.'

'You mean the two of you didn't share your ideas on immigration policy and sing the occasional verse of the Horst Wessel song together after a couple of jars?'

'No,' said Ray. 'And you can sneer all you like. I'm getting fed up of this. Look, why don't you go get your search warrant and call in your bully boys. Either that or get the fuck off our property.'

Banks said nothing.

'I mean it,' Ray went on. 'I'm calling your bluff. Either bring in the bluebottles or bugger off.'

Banks thought for a moment as he engaged Ray in a staring match. He decided that there was nothing more to be learned here. Besides, he was getting hungry. 'All right, Ray,' he said. 'We've finished with you for the time being. Jim?'

'What? Oh, sorry.' Sergeant Hatchley managed to knock over a half-full mug of tea on the counter. Banks turned and watched as the dark stain spread around the bottom few pamphlets and began to rise up as the paper absorbed it. Then, with Hatchley behind him, he opened the door and they headed out to the car. The drizzle had stopped now and a brisk wind had sprung up, allowing the occasional shaft of sunlight to slant through puffy grey clouds.

'We didn't *have* to leave, sir,' Hatchley said as they got in the car. 'We could have leaned on them a bit more.'

'I know that. We can always go back if we need to, but I don't think we'll find any answers there.'

'Think they had anything to do with Jason's death?'

'I don't know yet. I can't honestly see why they would.'

'Me neither. What next?'

Banks lit a cigarette and slid the window down a couple of inches. 'We'll have a word with Neville Motcombe this afternoon,' he said, 'but before that, how do you fancy lunch with Ken Blackstone? There was something young Adolf said back there gave me an idea.'

FOUR

When Susan got to The Hope and Anchor, just around the corner on York Road, Gavin was already looking over the menu, a full pint beside him. Susan waved, stopped at the bar for her usual St Clement's and went over to join him. She put the copy of *Classic CD* that she'd bought at the newsagent's on the bench beside her.

'What brings you to town, then?' she asked.

'I had a couple of boxes of stuff to deliver to your records officer. It's not all computers, you know.'

The place was fairly quiet, and soon they had both ordered the lasagna-and-chips special. Gavin raised his glass. 'Cheers.'

'Cheers.' Susan smiled at him. A little over six foot, and only a couple of years older than her, Gavin was a good-looking fellow with a strong chin, soulful eyes and a mop of shaggy chestnut hair. He played fullback for the police rugby team.

'So,' Gavin said, 'you are the sergeant when a call is received that there is a small nuclear device in the

Swainsdale Centre. A validated code word has been given, it is a busy time of day, and you have twenty minutes to hand over every packet of Rice Crispies in Eastvale at a designated spot. What do you do?'

Susan laughed. 'Get in my car and drive like hell out of there.'

'Sorry, DC Gay, you fail.'

It was a running joke between them. They had met just after doing their boards, and since then they had been coming up with progressively more absurd versions of the scenarios they had been given to solve.

'What's that?' Gavin asked, pointing at the magazine.

'Just a music magazine.'

'I can see that. Bring it along in case the conversation gets boring, did you?'

'Idiot.' Susan grinned. 'I picked it up on the way. I thought I might have to wait for you.'

Gavin picked up the magazine. 'Classical music? With a free compact disc? Cecilia Bartoli. Sir Simon Rattle. I say. Alan Bennett plays are one thing, but I didn't know you were such a culture vulture.'

Susan snatched the magazine back. 'It's something I picked up from DCI Banks,' she said. 'I get to hear a lot of classical stuff travelling in the car with him and I thought . . . well, some of it's really interesting. This is just an easy way of finding out more about it, that's all. You get snippets of things on the disc, and if I like them, sometimes I'll go and buy the whole thing.'

'Ah, the ubiquitous DCI Banks. I should have known his hand would be in this somewhere. And where might golden boy be today?'

'He's gone to Leeds. And I told you not to call him that.'

'Leeds? Again? Know what I think?' Gavin leaned

forward and narrowed his eyes. 'I think he's got a fancy woman down there. That's what I think.'

'Don't be absurd. He's married.'

Gavin laughed. 'Well, I've never known that to stop a bloke before. What about this violinist you told me about? Is Banks bonking her?'

'You're disgusting. Her name's Pamela Jeffreys, and she's a violist not a violinist. For your information, DCI Banks is a decent bloke. He's got an absolutely gorgeous wife. She runs the art gallery at the community centre. I'm certain he's faithful to her. He wouldn't do anything like that.'

Gavin held his hand up. 'All right, all right. I know when I'm beaten. If you say so. He's a saint.'

'I didn't say that, either,' Susan said through gritted teeth. Then she glared at him.

Their food came, and they both tucked in. Susan concentrated on her lasagna and tried to ignore the chips. Not entirely successfully.

'I'll tell you one thing, though,' Gavin said, 'your Banks is definitely not a saint in Chief Constable Riddle's books.'

'Jimmy Riddle's a pillock.'

'That's as may be. But he's also Chief Constable Pillock, and your golden boy has been pissing him off mightily of late. Just a friendly word of warning, that's all.'

'Are you talking about those Asian kids we brought in?'

Gavin nodded. 'Could be something to do with them, yes. That and near causing a race riot.'

'A race riot? In Eastvale?' She laughed. 'It was a storm in a teacup, Gavin. I was there. And we'd good reason to detain those three kids. They're still not off the hook, you know. The lab found something suspicious on George Mahmood's shoe. They're still working on it.'

'Probably dog shit. I think you'll need a lot more than that to convince the CC.'

'They think it might be blood. Anyway, you know as well as I do that Jimmy Riddle only ordered their release because of political pressure.'

'Don't underestimate political pressure, Susan. It can be a powerful motivator. Especially in a person's career. Even so, you're probably right about his reasons.' Gavin pushed his empty plate aside. 'To be honest, I can't say I've ever heard the CC have a good word to say for darkies in private. But the public face is another matter. Sure they only got off because they're coloured. This time. And because Mustapha Camel, or whatever his name is, is some big wallah in the Muslim community. But there's a large section of the public – especially some of the more liberal members of the press – who say that they were only arrested in the first place because they were coloured. Take your pick. You can't win. Anyway, you might just want to warn DCI Banks that the CC is on the warpath.'

Susan laughed. 'What's new? I think he already knows that.' She glanced at her watch.

'Maybe *that's* why he's gone to Leeds?'

'DCI Banks isn't scared of Jimmy Riddle.'

'Well, maybe he should be.'

Susan wasn't certain from his expression whether Gavin was being serious or not. It was often difficult to tell with him. 'I've got to go,' she said, standing up.

'You can't. You haven't finished your chips.'

'They're fattening.'

'But I've not had my full half-hour yet.'

'Isn't life unfair,' Susan said, smiling as she pecked him on the cheek and turned to leave.

'Saturday?' he called out after her.

'Maybe,' she said.

6

ONE

DI Ken Blackstone, West Yorkshire CID, was already waiting when Banks and Hatchley arrived at the pub he'd suggested over the telephone, a seedy-looking dive near Kirkgate Market, at the back of the Millgarth police headquarters.

Most days there was an open-air market near the bus station, behind the huge Edwardian market hall, and today in the drizzle a few lost souls in macs wandered around the covered stalls, fingering samples of fabric and fruit, thumbing through tattered paperback romances and considering the virtues of buying that 'genuine antique' brass door-knocker.

But no one showed much enthusiasm, not even the vendors, who were usually keen to sing out the praises of their wares and draw customers to their stalls. Today most of them stood to the side, wearing flat caps and waxed jackets, drawing on cigarettes and shuffling from foot to foot.

The pub wasn't very busy inside, either. Blackstone had assured them the cook did a decent Yorkshire pudding and gravy, and luckily it turned out to be true. In deference to duty, Banks and Blackstone drank halves. Hatchley, unwilling to miss what was a rare opportunity these days, had a full pint of Tetley's bitter. A giant jukebox stood in one corner of the lounge bar, but it was silent at the moment, so they didn't have to shout.

'Well, Alan,' said Blackstone, echoing Gavin Richards's sentiments, 'you've been spending so much time down here this past year or two I'm surprised you're not thinking of moving.'

Banks smiled. 'I won't say it hasn't crossed my mind. Oh, not seriously. Well, maybe just a little bit seriously. With both Brian and Tracy gone, the house just seems too big, and much as I love Eastvale . . . I think Sandra misses big-city life. And I wouldn't mind being a bit nearer Opera North.' When he mentioned Sandra, he felt a pang. They hadn't talked since their argument the other night, and Opera North had certainly played its part in that.

Blackstone smiled. 'It's not such a bad place. You could do a lot worse.'

Banks looked at Hatchley, who had done a stint on the West Yorkshire force several years ago. 'Jim?'

'He's right,' Hatchley agreed. 'And it might not be a bad career move.' He winked. 'It's a long way from Jimmy Riddle. We'd miss you, of course.'

'Stop it, you'll make me cry,' Banks said, pretending to reach for a handkerchief.

'All right,' said Hatchley. 'We won't miss you, then.'

'Anyway,' Banks asked, 'how's crime?'

'Much the same as usual,' said Blackstone. 'We've had a spate of "steamings" lately. Five or six young lads will go into a shop, then, when the shopkeeper's got his cash register open, they rush into action, create chaos all around while they grab what they want from customers and till alike. Kids for the most part. Fifteen and under, most of them. They've also taken to doing building societies and post offices the same way.'

Banks shook his head. 'Sounds American to me.'

'You know how it goes, Alan. First America, then London, then the rest of the country. What else . . .? We've had a few too many muggings at cash dispensers, too. And to cap it all, it looks like we're heading for another drug war in Chapeltown.'

Banks raised his eyebrows.

Blackstone sighed. 'Bloke goes by the name of *Deevaughan*. Spelled like the county: Devon. Anyway, Devon came up from London about a month ago and sussed out the scene pretty quickly. Already it looks like we can put down one murder to him.'

'Can't prove anything, of course?'

'Course not. He was in a pub with twenty mates when it happened. This one's bad, Alan. Crack, cocaine, the usual stuff, of course. But word also has it he's a big heroin fan. He spent the last few years in New York and Toronto, and there's rumours of death follow him around wherever he goes. Still want to move here?'

Banks laughed. 'I'll think about it.'

'Anyway, you didn't come to talk about my problems. How can I help you this time?'

Banks lit a cigarette. 'Know anything about Neville Motcombe? Runs a white-power group called the Albion League. Lives out Pudsey way. Offices in Holbeck.'

Blackstone shook his head. 'I've heard of him, but I can't really say I know much, not off the cuff. Bit out of my bailiwick, to be honest.'

'What is? Neo-Nazis or Pudsey?'

Blackstone laughed. 'Both, I suppose.' With his thinning sandy hair, still enough left to curl around his ears, wire-rimmed glasses, long, pale face and Cupid's bow lips, Blackstone reminded Banks more of an academic than a copper. Except that he was always well dressed. Today, he wore a dazzling white shirt, its brightness outdone only by his gaudy tie, and a pinstripe suit that looked tailor-made, not off the peg, with a silk handkerchief poking out of the top pocket. Banks didn't even wear a suit and tie unless he had to, and he always kept the top button of his shirt undone. Today he was wearing his favourite suede jacket again, and his tie hung askew.

'How did you come to hear about him?' Banks asked.

Blackstone laughed. 'Bit of a joke around the station, actually. Seems he tried to flog a stolen stereo to one of our off-duty PCs at a car-boot sale last year. Luckily for us, it was one of our honest PCs, and he traced it to a Curry's break-in a couple of months earlier.'

'What happened?'

'Nothing. Motcombe swore blind he'd bought it at the market and we couldn't prove otherwise. Got a light rap on the knuckles, and that's the lot.'

'Did you know about the Albion League?'

'I've heard of it, yes. I try at least to stay abreast of possible troublemakers.'

'And you think they're likely ones?'

Blackstone pursed his lips. 'Mmm. I'd say they've got potential, yes. We've had a few unattributed racial incidents this past year or so. We can't tie them in to him and his group yet, but I have my suspicions.'

'Anything in particular?'

'Know that big mosque they're putting up out Bradford way?'

Banks nodded.

'There's been a few small acts of sabotage. Nothing much. Stolen building materials, spray-painted racist slogans, slashed tyres, scratched paintwork. That sort of thing.'

'And you suspect Motcombe's lot?'

'Well, it'd be surprising if there weren't some sort of organized group behind it. What really worries me is what level of violence they're likely to rise to.'

'A bomb? Something like that?'

Blackstone shrugged. 'Well, if the IRA can do it . . . Anyway, it's just speculation at the moment. Want me to dig around a bit more?'

Banks nodded. 'I'd appreciate it, Ken. Right now anything is better than nothing. We're getting nowhere fast.'

'What about those Asian lads you had in custody?'

'They're not off my list yet.'

'You said earlier you had an idea,' Sergeant Hatchley prompted Banks.

'Ah, yes.' Banks stubbed out his cigarette and looked at Blackstone. 'It's probably just a minor thing, really. We talked to two of Motcombe's cronies in Holbeck. Ray Knott and Des Parker.'

Blackstone nodded. 'We know Ray Knott,' he said. 'Used to be a dab hand at taking and driving away.'

'Used to be?'

Blackstone shrugged.

'Anyway,' Banks went on. 'At one point, Knott let slip that the Albion League, or Motcombe himself, actually owned the property. I'm wondering if that's true or whether it was simply some sort of figure of speech. You know, the way someone might say "Get off my property" even if it's only rented?'

'And you'd like me to check it out?'

'If you would.'

'May I ask why?'

'Because I'd like to know if money's involved. If

Motcombe owns property and lives in a nice house in Pudsey, maybe there's some scam involved.'

Blackstone nodded. 'Hmmm. Good thinking. I'll do what I can. As a matter of fact, I've got a couple of mates in the town hall, and they owe me a favour or two.'

Banks raised his eyebrows. 'What's this, Ken? Have you been tipping them off when their brothel's going to be raided?'

Blackstone laughed. 'Not exactly.'

'There's an address in Rawdon I'd like you to check, too, if it's not too much trouble. Jason Fox lived there. As far as we know, he hasn't been employed this past couple of years, so we'd like to know how he could afford it.'

'Will do,' said Blackstone. He looked at his watch. 'Look, I should get back to the station. I can make a couple of phone calls, get working on it pretty much straight away.'

'We should be moving along, too,' said Banks, looking at Hatchley, who started swigging the last of his ale in expectation of an imminent departure. 'We're going to pay Mr Motcombe a visit. And there's another thing, Ken.'

Blackstone raised his eyebrows.

'We still haven't been able to track down the lad Jason Fox was drinking with the night he was killed. If the Albion League, or Neville Motcombe himself, does actually own the Holbeck building, or the Rawdon house, do you think you could check and see if he owns any other property in the city? Who knows, it might lead us to Jason's mystery pal.'

'Who may or may not know something?'

Banks smiled and nudged Hatchley. 'Ever the optimist, our Ken, isn't he, Jim?'

Hatchley laughed. 'West Yorkshire does that to you.'

'Can do,' said Blackstone, standing up. 'I'll call you soon as I get anything.'

'Appreciate it,' said Banks. 'I owe you one.'

'I'll remember that if you ever transfer here.'

TWO

After lunch, Susan's Wednesday afternoon was becoming every bit as frustrating as Tuesday. She had telephoned the service provider that gave Internet and Web access to FoxWood Designs, but she couldn't get a name and address out of them over the phone. A court order would see to that, of course, but what grounds had she to seek one? A vague hunch that it might lead her to someone who might know something about a mysterious death?

Every once in a while she left her computer terminal, stretched, and paced around the flat for a while. She put on the disc that came with her magazine, and arias followed solo piano pieces, which in turn followed symphonic movements, from Monteverdi to Maxwell Davies. It was all very confusing.

Like Banks, she wondered about George Mahmood and his mates. Had they done it? They certainly could have. And maybe not many people would blame them. The reporters had been around the station in droves, of course, and there was sure to be an article on police racism in the weekly *Eastvale Gazette*, due out on Friday.

Susan turned back to her desk. Still working on the assumption that if 'Fox' was Jason Fox, then 'Wood' might turn out to be a real person, too, she phoned directory assistance and discovered, as she suspected, that in Leeds alone there were pages of 'Woods'.

Well, she supposed, she *could* try them all. And what would she say? Ask each one if he knew Jason Fox? If this Wood person didn't want the police to know he knew Jason, he would hardly be likely to tell her over the telephone, would he?

There had to be an easier way. Tax records? Business registries? Maybe FoxWood Designs was incorporated, or had registered their design as a trademark.

Suddenly she realized there might be an even easier way than that. Subterfuge.

She hurried back to the computer, where she typed away for a few minutes, then sat back to survey her handiwork. Not bad. She made one or two small changes, correcting a typo here and an awkward phrase there. When she had finished, the message read:

TO: FoxWood Designs
FROM: Gayline Fashions

I have just started my own fashion-design business and I'm looking for ways to find a wider audience for my products. I noticed your work recently on a Web page and was very impressed by what I saw. I realized that the Web is an ideal way to achieve my aims and from what I saw I realized your company would be more than capable of handling the graphics necessary for the sort of page I have in mind. I would really like to talk to you about this as soon as possible. Do you think you could supply me with your address so that I could come around and discuss the possibility of our working together? I would much appreciate the opportunity to get myself established on the World Wide Web without delay.

Susan Gay.
Sole Proprietor: Gayline Fashions.

Susan read it over. It wasn't perfect – English had never been her strong point at school – but it would do.

She saved the message and logged in again. Then, when all the preliminaries were done with, she took a deep breath, pressed enter, and sent her message bouncing around the world's computer systems to the e-mail address she had taken from the bottom of the FoxWood Designs page.

THREE

Before Banks and Hatchley even had time to ring Motcombe's doorbell, they saw the figure approaching through the frosted glass.

'Mr Motcombe?' said Banks, showing his identification.

'That's me,' said Motcombe. 'I'm surprised it took you so long. Please. Come in.'

They followed him through to the living room.

'You've been expecting us?' Banks asked.

'Ever since Jason's tragic demise.'

'But you didn't bother to call us?'

Motcombe smiled. 'Why should I have? I don't know anything that can help you. But that doesn't keep *you* away from *me*, does it? Sit down. Please.'

Hatchley sat in one of the deep armchairs and took out his notebook. Banks walked over to the window at the far end of the room. The house was perched on a hillside; the back window looked over towards the village of Tong, not much more than a mile away, past Park Wood. The smoking chimneys of Bradford stood to the right and Leeds sprawled to the left.

'Yes, it's impressive, isn't it?' Banks heard Motcombe

say behind him. 'It's one of the things that helps me remember what we're fighting for. That all isn't lost.' Motcombe was standing so close that Banks could smell peppermint toothpaste on his breath.

Banks turned and walked past him, glancing around at the rest of the room. The furniture looked solid and well crafted – a table, chairs, sideboard and a glass-fronted cabinet, all dark, shiny wood. While there were no posters of Hitler or swastikas on the bright floral wallpaper, inside the cabinet was obviously Motcombe's collection of Nazi memorabilia: armband, bayonet, German officer's cap – all bearing the swastika – a series of dog-eared photographs of Hitler, and what was probably a wartime edition of *Mein Kampf*, again with the swastika on the front.

'Hitler was an inspiration, don't you think?' Motcombe said. 'He made mistakes, perhaps, but he had the right ideas, the right intentions. We should have joined forces *with* him instead of sending our forces against him. Then we would have a strong, united *Europe* as a bulwark against the corruption and impurity of the rest of the world, instead of the moth-eaten rag-bag we do have.'

Banks looked at him. He supposed Motcombe was imposing enough. Tall and gaunt, wearing a black polo-neck jumper tucked into matching black trousers with sharp creases, and a broad belt with a plain, square silver buckle, he had closely cropped black hair – shorter even than Banks's own – a sharp nose and lobeless ears flat against his skull. His eyes were brown, and there was a gleam in them like the winter sun in a frozen mud puddle. A constant, sly smile twitched at the corners of his thin, dry lips, as if he knew something no one else did, and as if that knowledge made him somehow superior. He reminded Banks of a younger Norman Tebbit.

'That's all very interesting,' Banks said at last, resting the backs of his thighs against the table. 'But, if you don't mind, we've got some questions for you.'

'Why should I mind? As far as I'm concerned, we're on the same side.' Motcombe sat, crossed his legs and put his hands together in front of him, fingertips touching, as if in prayer.

'How do you work that one out?' Banks asked, thinking it odd that was the second time he'd heard that today.

'Easy. Jason Fox was killed on your patch. You did your job as best you could under the circumstances. You found his killers quickly. But you had to let them go.'

He narrowed his eyes and gazed at Banks. Just for a moment Banks fancied he saw a gleam of something in them. Conspiracy? Condescension? Whatever it was, he didn't like it.

'How that must have sickened you,' Motcombe went on, his voice a low, hypnotic monotone. 'Having to bow to political pressure like that. Believe me, I *know* how your hands are tied. I *know* about the conspiracy that renders our police ineffective. You have my every sympathy.'

Banks took a deep breath. It smelled like a non-smoking room, but at this point he didn't care. He lit up anyway. Motcombe didn't complain.

'Look,' said Banks, after he blew out his first mouthful. 'Let's get something straight from the start. I don't want your sympathy. Or your opinions. Let's stick to the facts. Jason Fox.'

Motcombe shook his head slowly. 'You know, I half-expected something like that. Deep down, most people agree with us. Just listen to the way they talk in pubs, the jokes they tell about Chinks, Pakis, Niggers and Yids. Listen to the way *you* talk when you let your politically correct guard down.' He pointed towards the window. 'There's a whole silent nation out there who want what we want but are afraid to act. We aren't. Most people just don't have the courage of their convictions. We do. All I want to do is make it possible for people to look into their hearts and see what's really there, to know that there are others who feel the same way, then to give them a way they can act on it, a goal to aim for.'

'A white England?'

'Is that such a bad thing? If you put your prejudices aside for just a few moments and *really think* about it, is that such a terrible dream to pursue? Look at what's happened to our schools, our culture, our religious trad—'

'Didn't you hear me the first time?' Banks asked, his voice calm but hard. 'Let's stick to the facts.'

Motcombe favoured him with that conspiratorial, condescending smile, as if he were regarding a wayward child. 'Of course,' he said, inclining his head slightly. 'Please, Chief Inspector, go ahead. Ask your questions. And there's an ashtray on the sideboard just behind you. I don't smoke myself, but my guests occasionally do. Second-hand smoke doesn't bother me.'

Banks picked up the ashtray and held it in his left hand while he spoke. 'Tell me about Jason Fox.'

Motcombe shrugged. 'What is there to say? Jason was a valued member of the Albion League and we will miss him dearly.'

'How long had you known him?'

'Let me see, now . . . about a year. Perhaps a little less.'

'How did you meet?'

'At a rally in London. Jason was flirting with the British National Party. I had already left them, as they didn't adequately serve my vision. We talked. At the time, I was just about to start setting up the League, making contacts. A few months later, when we got going, Jason and I met again at a conference. I asked him, and he joined us.'

'Were you close?'

Motcombe tilted his head again. 'I wouldn't say close, no. Not in the personal sense, you understand. In ideas, yes.' He tapped the side of his head. 'After all, that's where it counts.'

'So you didn't socialize with him?'

'No.'

'What was Jason's speciality? I heard he was your Minister of Propaganda.'

Motcombe laughed. 'Very good. Yes, I suppose you could put it like that. He wrote most of the pamphlets. He also handled the computer. An essential tool in this day and age, I fear.'

Banks showed him the vague drawing of the boy Jason had been drinking with the night he was killed. 'Do you know him?' he asked. 'Is he one of yours?'

'I don't think so,' Motcombe said. 'It's almost impossible to tell, but I don't recognize him.'

'Where were you on Saturday night?'

Motcombe's black eyebrows shot up and he laughed again. 'Me? Do you mean I'm a suspect, too? How exciting. I'm almost sorry to disappoint you, but as a matter of fact I was in Bradford, at a tenants' meeting. In a block of council flats where some people are becoming very concerned about who, or should I say *what* they're getting for neighbours. Crime is—'

'You can prove this, I suppose?'

'If I have to. Here.' He got up and took a slip of paper from the sideboard drawer. 'This is the address of the block where the meeting was held. Check up on it, if you want. Any number of people will vouch for me.'

Banks pocketed the slip. 'What time did the meeting end?'

'About ten o'clock. Actually, a couple of us went on to a pub and carried on our discussion until closing time.'

'In Bradford?'

'Yes.'

'Have you ever been to Eastvale?'

Motcombe laughed. 'Yes. I've been there on a number of occasions. Purely as a tourist, you understand, and not for about a year. It's a rather pretty little town. I'm a great lover of walking the unspoiled English countryside. What's left of it.'

'Have you ever heard of George Mahmood?'

'What a ridiculous name.'

'Have you ever heard of him?'

'As a matter of fact, I have. He's one of the youths responsible for Jason's death.'

'We don't know that.'

'Oh, come on, Chief Inspector.' Motcombe winked. 'There's a big difference between what you can prove and what you *know*. You don't have to soft-soap me.'

'Wouldn't think of it. Did Jason ever mention any racial problems in Eastvale?'

'No. You know, you're lucky to live there, Chief Inspector. As I understand it, these Mahmoods are about the only darkies in the place. I envy you.'

'Then why don't you move?'

'Too much work to be done here first. One day, perhaps.'

'Did Jason ever mention George?'

'Once or twice, yes.'

'In what context?'

'I honestly don't remember.'

'But you'd remember if he said he chucked a brick through their window?'

Motcombe smiled. 'Oh, yes. But Jason wouldn't have done a thing like that.'

For what it was worth, it was probably the first positive link between Jason Fox and George Mahmood that Banks had come across so far. But what *was* it worth? So Jason had noticed George in Eastvale and mentioned him to Motcombe. That didn't mean George knew Jason was a neo-Nazi.

And everything Motcombe said could have come from the newspapers or television. There had been plenty of local coverage of the detainment and release of the three Asian suspects. Ibrahim Nazur had even appeared on a local breakfast-television programme complaining about systemic racism.

'What about Asim Nazur?' he asked.

Motcombe shook his head. 'Doesn't sound familiar.'

'Kobir Mukhtar?'

Motcombe sighed and shook his head. 'Chief Inspector, you have to understand, these do not sound like the kind of people I mix with. I told you I remember Jason mentioned a certain George Mahmood once or twice. That's all I know.'

'By name?'

'Yes. By name.'

The Mahmood part, Jason might have known from the shop sign. But George? How could he have known that? Perhaps from the report in the *Eastvale Gazette* after the brick-throwing incident. As Banks recollected, George had been mentioned by name then.

If Motcombe were lying, then he was playing it very

cautiously, careful not to own to knowing *too* much, just enough. Obviously a story of a full-blown conspiracy among the three Asians to attack Jason Fox would be even better for propaganda purposes, but it would be much more suspicious. A jet flew across the valley, a bright flash of grey against the grey clouds. Suddenly, someone else walked into the room. 'Nev, have you got— Sorry, didn't know you'd got company. Who's this?'

'This,' said Motcombe, 'is Detective Chief Inspector Banks and Detective Sergeant Hatchley.'

'And now we've got that out of the way,' said Banks, 'maybe you'd care to tell us who you are?'

'This is Rupert,' said Motcombe. 'Rupert Francis. Come in, Rupert. Don't be shy.'

Rupert came in. He was wearing a khaki apron, the kind Banks had to wear for woodwork classes at school. His hair was cut short, but that was where his resemblance to Jason's mystery friend ended. In his mid to late twenties, Banks guessed, Rupert was at least six feet tall, and thin rather than stocky. Also, there was no sign of an earring and, as far as Banks could make out, no hole to hang one from.

'I'm a carpenter, a cabinet-maker,' said Motcombe. 'Though it's more in the form of a hobby than a true occupation, I'm afraid. Anyway, I've converted the cellar into a workshop and Rupert helps me out every now and then. He's very good. I think the traditional values of the craftsman are very important indeed in our society, don't you?'

Rupert smiled and nodded at Banks and Hatchley. 'Pleased to meet you,' he said. 'What's it about?'

'It's about Jason Fox,' said Banks. 'Didn't happen to know him, did you?'

'Vaguely. I mean, I saw him around. We weren't mates or anything.'

'Saw him around here?'

'Down the office. Holbeck. On the computer.'

Banks slipped the drawing from his briefcase again. 'Know this lad?'

Rupert shook his head. 'Never seen him before. Can I go now? I'm halfway through finishing a surface.'

'Go on,' said Banks, turning to Motcombe again.

'You really must try believing us, Chief Inspector,' he said. 'You see—'

Banks stood up. 'Are you sure there's nothing else you can tell us? About Jason? About his problem with George Mahmood?'

'No,' said Motcombe. 'I'm sorry, but that just about covers it. I told you when you first came that I couldn't tell you anything that would help.'

'Oh, I wouldn't say you haven't helped us, Mr Motcombe,' said Banks. 'I wouldn't say that at all. Sergeant.'

Hatchley put his notebook away and got to his feet.

'Well,' said Motcombe at the door, 'I suppose I'll see you at the funeral?'

Banks turned. 'What funeral?'

Motcombe raised his eyebrows. 'Why, Jason's, of course. Tomorrow.' He smiled. 'Don't the police always attend the funerals of murder victims, just in case the killer turns up?'

'Who said anything about murder?'

'I just assumed.'

'You make a lot of assumptions, Mr Motcombe. As far as we know, it could have been manslaughter. Why are you going?'

'To show support for a fallen colleague. Fallen in the course of our common struggle. And we hope to gain some media coverage. As you said yourself, why waste a golden opportunity to publicize our ideas? There'll be a small, representative presence at the grave-side, and we'll be preparing a special, black-border pamphlet for the event.' He smiled. 'Don't you realize it yet, Chief Inspector? Jason is a martyr.'

'Bollocks,' said Banks, turning to leave. 'Jason's just another dead Nazi, that's all.'

Motcombe tut-tutted. 'Really, Chief Inspector.'

At the door, Banks did his Columbo impersonation. 'Just one more question, Mr Motcombe.'

Motcombe sighed and leaned on the doorpost, folding his arms. 'Fire away, then, if you must.'

'Where were you on Sunday morning?'

'Sunday morning? Why?'

'Where were you?'

'Here. At home.'

'Alone?'

'Yes.'

'Can you prove it?'

'Is there any reason I have to?'

'Just pursuing enquiries.'

'I'm sorry. I'm afraid I can't prove it. I was alone. Sadly, my wife and I separated some years ago.'

'Are you sure you didn't visit number seven Rudmore Terrace in Rawdon?'

'Of course I'm sure. Why should I?'

'Because that was where Jason Fox lived. We have information that two men went there on Sunday morning and cleaned the place out. I was just wondering if one of them happened to be you.'

'I didn't go there,' Motcombe repeated. 'And even if I had done, I wouldn't have broken any law.'

'These men had a key, Mr Motcombe. A key, in all likelihood, taken from Jason Fox's body.'

'I know nothing about that. I have a key, too, though.' He grinned at Banks. 'As a matter of fact, I happen to own the house.'

Well, Banks thought, that was one question answered. Motcombe *did* own property. 'But you didn't go there on Sunday morning?' he said.

'No.'

'Did you give or lend a key to anyone?'

'No.'

'I think you did. I think you sent some of your lads over there to clean up after Jason's death. I think he had stuff there you didn't want the police to find.'

'Interesting theory. Such as what?'

'Files, perhaps, membership lists, notes on upcoming projects. And the computer had been tampered with.'

'Well, even if I did what you say,' said Motcombe, 'I'm sure you can understand how I would be well within my rights to go to a house I own to pick up property that, essentially, belongs to me, in my capacity as leader of the Albion League.'

'Oh, I can understand that completely,' Banks said.

Motcombe frowned. 'Then what . . .? I'm sorry, I don't understand.'

'Well, then,' Banks said slowly. 'Let me explain. The thing that bothers me is that whoever went there went before anyone knew that the victim was Jason Fox. Anyone except his killers, of course. Bye for now, Mr Motcombe. No doubt we'll be seeing you again soon.'

7

ONE

It was a long time since Frank had worn a suit, and the tie seemed to be choking him. Trust the weather to brighten up for a funeral, too. It was Indian summer again, warm air tinged with that sweet, smoky hint of autumn's decay, sun shining, hardly a breeze, and here he was in the back of the car, sweat beading on his brow despite the open window, sitting next to Josie, who was dressed all in black.

The drive to Halifax from Lyndgarth, where Steven had picked him up, was a long one. And a bloody ugly one once you got past Skipton, too, Frank thought as they drove through Keighley. Talk about your 'dark Satanic mills'.

He had wondered why they couldn't just bury the lad in Eastvale and have done with it, but Josie explained Steven's family connections with St Luke's Church, where his forebears were buried going back centuries. Bugger yon streak of piss and his forebears, Frank thought, but he kept his mouth shut.

Nobody said very much on the journey. Josie sobbed softly every now and then, putting a white handkerchief to her nose, Steven – who for all his sins was a good driver – kept his eyes on the road, and Maureen sat stiffly, arms folded, beside him, looking out the window.

Frank found himself drifting down memory lane: Jason, aged four or five, down by The Leas one spring afternoon, excited as he caught his first stickleback in a net made out of an old lace curtain and a thin strip of cane; the two of them stopping for ice-cream one hot, still summer day at the small shop in the middle of nowhere, halfway up Fremlington Hill, melting ice-cream dripping over his knuckles; an autumn walk down a lane near Richmond, Jason running ahead kicking up sheaves of autumn leaves, which made a dry soughing sound as he ploughed through them; standing freezing in the snow in Ben Rhydding watching the skiers glide down Ilkley Moor.

Whatever Jason had become, Frank thought, he had once been an innocent child, as awestruck by the wonders of man and nature as any other kid. Hang onto that, he told himself, not the twisted, misguided person Jason had become.

They arrived at the funeral home on the outskirts of Halifax with time to spare. Frank stayed outside watching the traffic rush by because he could never stand the rarefied air of funeral homes, or the thought of all those corpses in caskets, make-up on their faces and formaldehyde in their veins. Jason, he suspected, would have needed a lot of cosmetic attention to *his* face.

Finally, the cortège was ready. The four of them piled into the sleek black limousine the home provided and followed the hearse through streets of dark millstone grit houses to the cemetery. In the distance, tall mill chimneys poked out between the hills.

After a short service, they all trooped outside for the graveside ceremony. Frank loosened his tie so he could breathe more easily. The vicar droned on: 'In the midst of life we are in death: of whom may we seek for succour, but of thee, O Lord, who for our sins are justly displeased? Thou knowest, Lord, the secrets of our hearts . . .' A fly that must have been conned into thinking it was still summer buzzed by his face. He brushed it away.

Steven stepped forward to cast a clod of earth down on the coffin. The vicar read on: 'For as much as it hath pleased Almighty God of his great mercy to receive unto himself the soul of our dear brother here departed . . .' It should have been Josie dropping the earth, Frank thought. Steven never did get on with the kid. At least Josie had loved her son once, before they grew apart, and she must still feel a mother's love for him, a love which surely passeth all understanding and forgives a multitude of sins.

All of a sudden, Frank noticed Josie look beyond his shoulder and frown through her tears. He turned to see what it was. There, by the line of trees, stood about ten people, all wearing black polo-necks made of some shiny material, belts with silver buckles and black leather jackets, despite the warmth of the day. Over half had skinhead haircuts. Some wore sunglasses. The tall, gaunt one looked older than the rest, and Frank immediately guessed him to be the leader.

They didn't have to announce themselves. Frank knew who they were. As sure as he knew Jason was dead and in his grave. He had read the tract. As the vicar drew close to the end of his service, the leader raised his arm in a Nazi salute, and the others followed suit.

Frank couldn't help himself. Before he could even think about what he was doing, he hurried over and grabbed the leader. The man just laughed and brushed him off. Then, as Frank attempted to get at least one punch in, he was surrounded by them, jostling, pushing, shoving him between one another as if he were a ball, or as if they were playing 'pass the parcel' at some long-ago children's party. And they were laughing as they pushed him, calling him 'granddad' and 'old man'.

Frank flailed out, but he couldn't break away. All he saw was a whirl of grinning faces, shorn heads and his own reflection in the dark glasses. The world was spinning too fast, out of control. He was too hot. His tie felt tight again, even though he had loosened it, and the pain in his chest came on fast, like a vice gripping his heart and squeezing.

He stumbled away from the group, clutching his chest, the pain spreading like burning needles down his left arm. He thought he could see Maureen laying into one of the youths with a piece of wood. He could just hear her through the ringing and buzzing in his ears. 'Leave him alone, you bullies! Leave him alone, you fascist bastards! Can't you see he's an old man? Can't you see he's poorly?'

Then something strange happened. Frank was lying on the ground now, and gently, slowly, he felt himself begin to float above the pain, or away from it, more like, deeper into himself, detached and light as air. Yes, that was it, deeper into himself. He wasn't hovering above the scene looking down on the chaos, but far inside, seeing pictures of himself in years long gone.

A number of memories flashed through his mind: flak bursting all around the bomber like bright flowers blooming in the night, as Frank seemed to hang suspended above it all in his gun turret; the day he proposed to Edna on their long walk home in the rain after the Helmthorpe spring fair; the night his only daughter, Josie, was born in Eastvale General Infirmary while Frank was stuck in Lyndgarth, without even a telephone then, cut off from the world by a vicious snowstorm.

But his final memory was one he had not thought of in decades. He was five years old. He had trapped his finger in the front door, and he sat on the freshly scoured stone step crying, watching the black blood gather under the fingernail. He could feel the warmth of the step against the backs of his thighs and the heat of his tears on his cheeks.

Then the door opened. He couldn't see much more than a silhouette because of the bright sunlight, but as he shaded his eyes and looked up, he *knew* it was the loving, compassionate, all-healing figure of his mother bending over to sweep him up into her arms and kiss away the pain.

Then everything went black.

TWO

'Ah, Banks. Here you are at last.'

As soon as he heard the voice behind him on his way back to his office from the coffee machine, Banks experienced that sinking feeling. Still, he thought, it had to happen sometime. Might as well get it over with. Gird his loins. At least he was on his own turf.

Their enmity went back for some time; in fact, Banks thought it probably started the moment they met. Riddle was one of the youngest chief constables in the country, and he had come up the fast way, 'accelerated promotion' right from the start. Banks had made DCI fairly young, true, but he had made it the hard way: sheer hard slog, a good case-clearance record and a natural talent for detective work. He didn't belong to any clubs or have any wealthy contacts; nor did he have a university degree. All he had was a diploma in business studies from a poly-technic – and that from the days before they were all turned into second-string universities.

For Riddle, it was all a matter of making the right contacts, mouthing the correct buzzwords; he was a bean-counter, at his happiest looking over budget proposals or putting a positive spin on crime figures on 'Look North' or 'Calendar'. As far as Banks was concerned, Jimmy Riddle hadn't done a day's real policing in his life.

Hand on the doorknob, Banks turned. 'Sir?'

Riddle kept advancing on him. 'You know what I'm talking about, Banks. Where the hell do you think you've been these past few days? Trying to avoid me?'

'Wouldn't think of such a thing, sir.' Banks opened the door and stood aside to let Riddle in first. The chief con-stable hesitated for a moment, surprised at the courtesy, then stalked in. As usual, he didn't sit but started prowling about, touching things, straightening the calendar, eyeing the untidy pile of papers on top of the filing cabinet, looking at everything in that prissy, disapproving way of his.

He was immaculately turned out. He must have a clean uniform for each day, Banks thought, sitting behind his rickety metal desk and reaching for a cigarette. However strict the anti-smoking laws had become lately, they still hadn't stretched as far as a chief inspector's own office, where not even the chief constable could stop him.

To his credit, Riddle didn't try. He didn't even make his usual protest. Instead, he launched straight into the assault that must have been building pressure inside him since Monday. 'What on earth did you think you were doing bringing in those Asian kids and throwing them in the cells?'

'You mean George Mahmood and his mates?'

'You know damn well who I mean.'

'Well, sir,' said Banks, 'I had good reason to suspect they were involved in the death of Jason Fox. They'd been seen to have an altercation with him and his pal earlier in the evening at The Jubilee, and when I started to question George Mahmood about what happened, he asked for a solicitor and clammed up.'

Riddle ran his hand over his shiny head. 'Did you have to lock all three of them up?'

'I think so, sir. I simply detained them within the strict limits of the PACE directive. None of them would talk to us. As I said, they were reasonable suspects, and I wanted them where I could see them while forensic tests on their clothing were being carried out. At the same time, Detective Sergeant Hatchley was trying to locate any witnesses to the assault.'

'But didn't you realize what trouble your actions would cause? Didn't you *think*, man?'

Banks sipped some coffee and looked up. 'Trouble, sir?'

Riddle sighed and leaned against the filing cabinet, elbow on the stack of papers. 'You've alienated the entire Yorkshire Asian community, Banks. Had you never heard of Ibrahim Nazur? Don't you realize that harmony of race relations is prioritized in today's force?'

'Funny, that, sir,' said Banks. 'And I thought we were supposed to catch criminals.'

Riddle levered himself away from the cabinet with his elbow and leaned forward, palms flat on the desk, facing Banks. His pate seemed to be pulsing on red alert. 'Don't be bloody clever with me, man. I've got my eye on you. One false move, one more slip, the slightest error of judgement, and you're finished, understand? I'll have you back in Traffic.'

'Very well, sir,' said Banks. 'Does that mean you want me off the case?'

Riddle moved back to the filing cabinet and smiled, flicking a piece of imaginary fluff from his lapel. 'Off the case? You should be so lucky. No, Banks, I'm going to leave your chestnuts in the fire a bit longer.'

'So what exactly is it that you want, sir?'

'For a start, I want you to start behaving like a DCI instead of a bloody probational DC. And I want to be informed before you make any move that's likely to . . . to embarrass the force in any way. *Any* move. Is that clear?'

'The last bit is, sir, but—'

'What I mean,' Riddle said, pacing and poking at things again, 'is that as an experienced senior police officer, your input might be useful. But let your underlings do the legwork. Let them go gallivanting off to Leeds chasing wild geese. Don't think I don't know why you grab every opportunity to bugger off to Leeds.'

Banks looked Riddle in the eye. 'And why is that, sir?'

'That woman. The musician. And don't tell me you don't know who I'm talking about.'

'I know exactly who you're talking about, sir. Her name's Pamela Jeffreys and she plays viola in the English Northern Philharmonia.'

Riddle waved his hand impatiently. 'Whatever. I'm sure you think your private life is none of my business, but it is when you use the force's time to live it.'

Banks thought for a moment before answering. This was way out of order. Riddle was practically accusing him of having an affair with Pamela Jeffreys and of driving to Leeds during working hours for assignations with her. It was untrue, of course, but any denial at this point would only strengthen Riddle's conviction. Banks wasn't sure of the actual guidelines, but he felt this sort of behaviour far exceeded the chief constable's authority. It was a personal attack, despite the cavil about abusing the force's time.

But what could he do? It was his word against Riddle's. And Riddle was the CC. So he took it, filed it away, said nothing and determined to get his own back on the bastard one day.

'What *would* you like me to do, then, sir?' he asked.

'Sit in your office, smoke yourself silly and read reports, the way you're supposed to. And stay away from the media. Leave them to Superintendent Gristhorpe and myself.'

Banks cringed. He hated it when people used 'myself' instead of plain old 'me'. He stubbed out his cigarette. 'I haven't been anywhere near the media, sir.'

'Well, make sure you don't.'

'You want me to sit and read reports? That's it?'

Riddle stopped prowling a moment and faced Banks. 'For Heaven's sake, man! You're a DCI. You're not supposed to be gadding off all over the place interviewing people. Co-ordinate. There are plenty more important tasks for you to carry out right here, in your office.'

'Sir?'

'What about the new budget, for a start? You know these days we've got to be accountable for every penny we spend. And it's about time the Annual Policing Plan was prepared for next year. Then there's the crime statistics. Why is it that when the rest of the country's experiencing a drop, North Yorkshire's on the rise? Hey? These are the sort of questions you should be addressing, not driving off to Leeds and treading on people's toes.'

'Wait a minute, sir,' said Banks. 'Whose toes? Don't tell me Neville Motcombe's in the lodge as well?'

As soon as the words were out, Banks regretted them. It was all very well to want his own back on Riddle, but this wasn't the way to do it. He was surprised when Riddle simply stopped his tirade and asked, 'Who the hell's Neville Motcombe when he's at home?'

Banks hesitated. Having put his foot in his mouth, how could he avoid not shoving it down as far as his lower intestine? And did he care? 'He's an associate of Jason Fox's. One of the people I was talking to in Leeds yesterday.'

'What does this Motcombe have to do with the lad's death, if anything?'

Banks shook his head. 'I don't know that he does. It's just that his name came up in the course of our enquiries and—'

Riddle began pacing again. 'Don't flannel me, Banks. I understand this Jason Fox belonged to some right-wing, racist movement? Is that true?'

'Yes, sir. The Albion League.'

Riddle stopped and narrowed his eyes. 'Would this Neville Motcombe have anything to do with the Albion League?'

No flies on Jimmy Riddle. 'Actually,' Banks said, 'he's their leader.'

Riddle said nothing for a moment, then he went back and resumed his pose at the filing cabinet. 'Does this have anything to do with the Jason Fox case at all, or are you just tilting at windmills as usual?'

'I honestly don't know,' Banks said. 'It's what I'm trying to find out. It might have given George and his pals a motive to attack Jason.'

'Have you any proof at all that the three Asians knew Jason Fox belonged to this Albion League?'

'No. But I did find out that Jason knew George Mahmood. It's a start.'

'It's bloody nothing is what it is.'

'We're still digging.'

Riddle sighed. 'Have you got *any* real suspects at all?'

'The Asians are still our best bet. The lab hasn't identified the stuff on George's trainers yet because there are so many contaminating factors, but they still haven't discounted its being blood.'

'Hmm. What about the other lad, the one who was supposed to be with Jason Fox in the pub?'

'We're still looking for him.'

'Any idea who he is yet?'

'No, sir. That was another thing I—'

'Well, bloody well find out. And quickly.' Riddle strode towards the door. 'And remember what I said.'

'Which bit would that be, sir?'

'About tending to your duties as a DCI.'

'So you want me to find out who Jason's pal was at the same time as I'm reading reports on budgets and crime statistics?'

'You know what I mean, Banks. Don't be so bloody literal. Delegate.'

And he walked out, slamming the door behind him.

Banks breathed a sigh of relief. Too soon. The door opened again. Riddle put his head round, pointed his finger at Banks, wagged it and said, 'And whatever you might think of me, Banks, don't you ever dare imply again that I or any of my fellow Masons fraternize with fascists. Is that clear?'

'Yes, sir,' said Banks as the door closed again. *Fraternize with fascists*, indeed. He had to admit it had a nice ring to it. Must be the alliteration.

In the peace and silence following Riddle's withdrawal, Banks sipped his coffee and mulled over what he'd been told. He knew Riddle had a point about the way he did his job, and that certainly didn't make him feel any better. As a DCI, he should be more involved in the administrative and managerial aspects of policing. He *should* spend more time at his desk.

Except that wasn't what he wanted.

When he had been a DI on the Met and got promoted to DCI on transferring to Eastvale, it was on the understanding – given by both Detective Superintendent Gristhorpe *and* Chief Constable Hemmings, Jimmy Riddle's predecessor – that he was to take an active part as investigating officer in important cases. Even the Assistant Chief Constable (Crime), also since retired, had agreed to that.

Recently, when the powers that be had considered abolishing the rank of Chief Inspector, Banks was ready to revert to Inspector at the same pay, rather than try for Superintendent, where he was far more likely to be desk-bound. But it had never happened; the only rank to be abolished was that of Deputy Chief Constable.

Now Jimmy Riddle wanted to tie him to his desk anyway.

What could he do? Was it really time for another move?

But he didn't have time to think about these matters for very long. Not more than two minutes after Riddle had left, the phone rang.

THREE

Susan arrived ten minutes late for lunch at the Queen's Arms, where the object was to discuss leads and feelings about the Jason Fox case over a drink and a pub lunch. An informal brainstorming session.

Banks and Hatchley were already ensconced at a dimpled, copper-topped table between the fireplace and the window when Susan hurried in. They were both looking particularly glum, she noticed.

She stopped at the bar and ordered a St Clement's and a salad sandwich, then joined the others at the table. Hatchley had an almost-empty pint glass in front of him, while Banks was staring gloomily into a half. They scraped their chairs aside to make room for her.

'Sorry I'm late, sir,' she said.

Banks shrugged. 'No problem. We went ahead and ordered without you. If you want something . . .'

'It's all right, sir. They're doing me a sandwich.' Susan glanced from one to the other. 'Excuse me if I'm being thick or something, but it can't be the weather that's making your faces as long as a wet Sunday afternoon. Is something wrong? I feel as if I've walked in on a wake.'

'In a way, you have,' said Banks. He lit a cigarette. 'You know Frank Hepplethwaite, Jason's granddad?'

'Yes. At least I know who he is.'

'Was. I just got a call from the Halifax police. He dropped dead at Jason's funeral.'

'What of?'

'Heart attack.'

'Oh no,' said Susan. She had never met the old man but she knew Banks had been impressed with him, and that was enough for her. 'What happened?'

'Motcombe took nine or ten of his blackshirts to the grave side and Frank took umbrage. Made a run at them. He was dead before his granddaughter could get them to back off.'

'So they killed him?'

'You *could* say that.' Banks glanced sideways at Hatchley, who drained his pint, shook his head slowly and went to the bar for another. Banks declined his offer of a second half. Smoke from his cigarette drifted perilously close to Susan's nose; she waved her hand in the air to waft it away.

'Sorry,' said Banks.

'It doesn't matter. Look, sir, I'm having a bit of trouble understanding all this. It sounds like manslaughter to me. Are we pressing charges against Motcombe or not?'

Banks shook his head. 'It's West Yorkshire's patch. And they're not.'

'Why not?'

'Because Frank Hepplethwaite attacked Motcombe, and his lot were merely defending themselves.'

'Ten of them? Against an old man with a bad heart? That's not on, sir.'

'I know,' said Banks. 'But apparently they didn't punch or kick him. They just pushed him away. They were protecting themselves from him.'

'It still sounds like manslaughter.'

'West Yorkshire don't think they can get the CPS to prosecute.'

The Crown Prosecution Service, as Susan knew, were well known for their conservative attitude towards pursuing criminal cases through the courts. 'So Motcombe and his bully boys just walk away scot-free? That's it?'

Hatchley returned from the bar. At almost the same time, Glenys, the landlord's wife, appeared with the food: Susan's sandwich, plaice and chips for Hatchley and a thick wedge of game pie for Banks.

'Not exactly,' said Banks, stubbing out his cigarette. 'At

least not immediately. They were taken in for questioning. Their argument was that they were simply attending the funeral of a fallen comrade when this madman started attacking them and they were forced to push him away to protect themselves. The fact that Frank was an old man didn't make a lot of difference to the charges, or lack of them. Some old men are pretty tough. And they didn't know he had a bad heart.'

'Isn't there *anything* we can do?' Susan turned to Hatchley.

He shook his head, piece of breaded plaice on his fork in mid-air. 'It doesn't look like it.' Then he glanced at Banks, who looked up from his pie and nodded. 'It gets worse,' Hatchley went on. 'We're in no position to charge Motcombe, it seems, but Motcombe has brought assault charges against Maureen Fox, Jason's sister. It seems she attacked him and his mates with a heavy plank she picked up from the grave side and cracked a couple of heads open, including Motcombe's.'

Susan's jaw dropped. 'And *they're* charging *her*?'

'Aye,' said Hatchley. 'I shouldn't imagine much will come of it, but it's exactly the kind of insult Motcombe and his sort like to throw at people.'

'And at the justice system,' Banks added.

There were times, Susan had to admit, when she hadn't much stomach for the *justice system*, even though she knew it was probably the best in the world. Justice is always imperfect and it was a lot more imperfect in many other countries. Even so, once in a while something came along to outrage even what she thought was her seasoned copper's view. All she could do was shake her head and bite on her salad sandwich.

In the background, the cash register chinked and a

couple of shop-workers on their lunch-break laughed at a joke. Someone won a few tokens on the fruit machine.

'Any more good news?' Susan asked.

'Aye,' said Hatchley. 'The lab finally got back to us on that stuff they found on George Mahmood's trainers.'

'And?'

'Animal blood. Must have stepped on a dead spuggy or summat while he was crossing the rec.'

'Well,' Susan said, 'this is all very depressing, but I think I've got at least one piece of good news.'

Banks raised his eyebrows.

Susan explained about the message she had left with the FoxWood Designs page. 'That's why I was late,' she said. 'When I first checked, the reply hadn't come through, so I thought I'd give it just a few minutes more and try again.'

'And?' said Banks.

'And we're in luck. Well, it's a start, anyway.'

Susan brought the folded sheet of paper out of her briefcase and laid it on the table. Banks and Hatchley leaned forward to read the black-edged message:

Dear Valued Customer,

Many thanks for your interest in the work of FoxWood Designs. Unfortunately, we have had to suspend business for the time being due to bereavement. We hope you will be patient and bring your business to us in the near future, and we apologize for any inconvenience this may have caused you.

Yours sincerely,
Mark Wood

'Mark Wood. So we've got a name,' said Banks.

Susan nodded. 'As I said, it's not much, but it's a place

to start. This *could* be the lad who was with Jason in The Jubilee. At the very least, he's Jason's business partner. He ought to know something.'

'Maybe,' said Banks. 'But he still might prove to have nothing to do with the case at all.'

'But don't you think it's a bit fishy that he hasn't come forward yet, no matter who he is?'

'Yes,' said Banks. 'But Liza Williams didn't come forward, either. Jason's neighbour in Rawdon. She didn't see any reason to. Nor did Motcombe.'

'Well, sir,' Susan went on, 'I still think we should try and find him as soon as possible.'

'Oh, I agree.' Banks reached for his briefcase. 'Don't mind me, Susan. I'm just a bit down in the dumps about what happened to Frank Hepplethwaite.'

Susan nodded. 'I understand.'

'Anyway,' Banks went on, 'there's one thing we can check, for a start. I got a fax from Ken Blackstone listing Motcombe's properties and tenants. I haven't had time to have a good look at it yet.' He pulled the sheets of paper out and glanced over them. 'Seems Motcombe owns a fair bit of property,' he said after a few moments. 'Four houses in addition to his own, two of them divided into flats and bedsits, the semi where Jason Fox lived, and a shop with a flat above it in Bramley. He also owns the old grocer's shop where the Albion League operates from, as we thought.' Finally, a few seconds later, he shook his head in disappointment. 'There's no Mark Wood listed among the tenants. Maybe that would have been *too* easy.'

'I wonder where Motcombe got his money from,' Susan said.

'Members' dues?' Hatchley chipped in.

'Hardly likely,' said Banks, with a grim smile. 'Maybe

he inherited it? I'll get in touch with Ken again, see if he can work up some more background on Mr Motcombe for us.'

'You don't really think he did it, do you?' Susan asked.

'Kill Jason? Honestly? No. For a start, he doesn't seem to have a motive. And even if he did have something to do with it, he certainly didn't do it himself. I doubt he's got the bottle. Or the strength. Remember, Jason was a pretty tough customer. But let's have a closer look at him anyway. I don't like the bastard, or what he stands for, so any grief we can give him is fine with me. Even a traffic offence. Besides, I'd look a right prat if we overlooked something obvious, wouldn't I? And that's the last thing I need right now.'

'The chief constable?' Susan ventured.

Banks nodded. 'Himself. In the flesh. So I'd better get back to my desk and *co-ordinate*.'

FOUR

Banks felt bone-weary when he arrived home that evening shortly after six o'clock. He was still upset about Frank Hepplethwaite's senseless death, his run-in with Jimmy Riddle was still niggling him, and the lack of progress in the Jason Fox case was sapping his confidence. Well, he'd done the best he could so far. If only the lab boys or Vic Manson could come through with something.

Sandra wasn't home. In a way, that made him feel relieved. He didn't think he could deal with another argument right now. Or the cold shoulder.

He made himself a cheese omelette. There wasn't any real cheese in the fridge, so he used a processed slice. It tasted fine. Shortly after eight, when Banks was relaxing with *Così Fan Tutte* and a small Laphroaig, Sandra got back. Anxious to avoid another scene, Banks turned the volume on the stereo very low.

But Sandra didn't seem to notice the opera playing softly in the background. At least she didn't say anything. She seemed distracted, Banks thought, as he tried to engage her in conversation about the day.

When he offered to take her out for a bite to eat – the omelette not having filled him up nearly as much as he'd hoped – she said she'd already eaten with a couple of friends after the arts committee meeting and she wasn't hungry. All Banks's conversational gambits fell on deaf ears. Even his story of Jimmy Riddle's bollocking failed to gain an ounce of sympathy. Finally, he turned to her and said, 'What's wrong? Is this because of the other night? Are you still pissed off at me about that?'

Sandra shook her head. The blonde tresses danced over her shoulders. 'I'm not pissed off,' she said. 'That kind of thing is always happening with us. *That's* the real problem. Don't tell me you haven't noticed how little we see of one another these days? How we both seem to go our separate ways, have our separate interests? How little we seem to have in common? Especially now Tracy's gone.'

Banks shrugged. 'It's only been a couple of weeks,' he said. 'I've been busy. So have you. Give it time.'

'I know. But that's not it. We're always busy.'

'What do you mean?'

'Work. Yours. Mine. Oh, that's not the real problem. We've always been able to deal with that before. You've never expected a dutiful little wife staying at home all day cooking and cleaning, ironing, sewing buttons on, and I thank you for that. But even that's not it.' She took one of his cigarettes, something she did so rarely these days that the gesture worried him. 'I've been thinking a lot since the other night, and I suppose what I'm saying is that I feel alone. I mean in the relationship. I just don't feel I'm part of your life any more. Or that you're part of mine.'

'But that's absurd.'

'Is it? Is it, really?' She looked at him, frowning, black eyebrows crooked in the furrow of her brow. Then she shook her head slowly. 'I don't think it is, Alan. What was Saturday all about, then? And the other night? I think if you're honest with yourself, you'll agree. This house feels empty. Cold. It doesn't feel like a home. It feels like the kind of place that two people living separate lives use to sleep and eat in, occasionally passing one another on the landing and saying hello. Maybe stopping for a quick fuck if they've got time.'

'That's not fair, and you know it. I think you're just feeling depressed because both the kids have grown up and flown the coop. It'll take time to get used to.'

'Next thing, you'll be saying I'm feeling this way because it's that time of the month,' said Sandra. 'But you're wrong. It's not that, either.' She thumped her fist on the arm of the chair. 'You're not listening to me. You never really *listen* to me.'

'I *am* listening, but I'm not sure I understand what I'm hearing. Are you sure this isn't still about last Saturday?'

'No, it's not about last bloody Saturday. Yes, all right, I admit I was angry. I thought for once you might just forsake your sacred bloody opera to do something that *I* thought was important. Something for *my* career. But you didn't. Fine. And then the other night you go and put your opera on the stereo. But you've always been selfish. Selfishness I can deal with. This is something else.'

'What?'

'What I've been trying to tell you. We're both independent people. Always. That's why our marriage worked so well. I wasn't waiting and fretting at home for you to come back from work. Worrying that your dinner might get cold. Worrying that something might have happened to you. Though, Lord knows, that was something I never could put out of my mind, even though I tried not to let on to you too much. And if I was out and there was no dinner, if your shirt wasn't ironed, you never complained. You did it yourself. Not very well, maybe, but you did it.'

'I still don't complain when dinner's not ready. I made a bloody processed-cheese omel—'

Sandra held her hand up. 'Let me finish, Alan. Can't you see what's happened? What used to be our strength – our independence – now it's driving us apart. We've led separate lives for so long we take it for granted that's how a relationship should be. As long as you've got your work, your music, your books and the occasional evening with the lads at the Queen's Arms, then you're perfectly happy.'

'And what about you? Are you happy with your gallery, your photography, your committee meetings, your social evenings?'

Sandra paused a long time, long enough for Banks to pour them both a stiff Laphroaig, before she answered. 'Yes,' she said finally, in a soft voice. 'That's just it. Yes. Maybe I am. For a while I've been thinking they're all I do have. You just haven't been here, Alan. Not as a real factor.'

Banks felt as if a hand made of ice had slid across his heart. It was such a palpable sensation that he put his hand to his chest. 'Is there someone else?' he asked. On the stereo, Fiordiligi was singing quietly about being as firm as a rock.

Suddenly Sandra smiled, reached out and ran her hand over his hair. 'Oh, you sweet, silly man,' she said. 'No, there's no one else.' Then her eyes clouded and turned distant. 'There could have been . . . perhaps . . . but there isn't.' She shrugged, as if to cast off a painful memory.

Banks swallowed. 'Then what?'

She paused. 'As I said, I've been thinking about it a lot lately, and I've come to the conclusion that we should go our separate ways. At least for a while.' She reached forward and held his hand as she spoke, which seemed to him, like the smile, an out-of-place gesture. What the hell *was* wrong?

Banks snatched his hand back. 'You can't be serious,' he said. 'We've been married over twenty years and all of a sudden you just decide to up and walk out.'

'But I *am* serious. And it's not all of a sudden. Think about it. You'll agree. This has been building up for a long time, Alan. We hardly ever see one another anyway. Why continue living a lie? You know I'm right.'

Banks shook his head. 'No. I don't. I still think you're overreacting to Tracy's leaving and to Saturday night. Give it a little time. Maybe a holiday?' He sat forward and took her hand now. It felt limp and clammy. 'When this case is over, let's take a holiday, just you and me. We could go to Paris for a few days. Or somewhere warm. Back to Rhodes, maybe?'

He could see tears in her eyes. 'Alan, you're not listening to me. You're making this really difficult, you know. I've been trying to pluck up courage to say this for weeks now. It's not something I've just come up with on the spur of the moment. A holiday's not going to solve our problems.' She sniffled and ran the back of her hand under her nose. 'Oh, bugger,' she said. 'Look at me, now. I didn't want this to happen.' She grabbed his hand and gripped it tightly again. This time he didn't snatch it away. He didn't know what to say. The icy touch was back, and now it seemed to be creeping into his bones and inner organs.

'I'm going away for a while,' Sandra said. 'It's the only way. The only way both of us can get a chance to think things over.'

'Where are you going?'

'My parents'. Mum's arthritis is playing her up again, and she'll appreciate an extra pair of hands around the place. But that's not the reason. We need time apart, Alan. Time to decide whether there's anything left to salvage or not.'

'So this is just a temporary separation you have in mind?'

'I don't know. A few weeks, anyway. I just know I need to get away. From the house. From Eastvale. From you.'

'What about the community centre, your work?'

'Jane can take over for a while, till I decide what to do.'

'Then you might not come back?'

'Alan, I'm telling you I don't know. I don't know what to do. Don't make it harder for me. I'm at my wits' end already. The only sensible thing is for me to get away. Then . . . after a while . . . we can talk about it. Decide where we want to go next.'

'Why can't we talk now?'

'Because it's all too *close* here. That's why. Pressing in on me. Please believe me, I don't want to hurt you. I'm scared. But we've got to do it. It's the only chance we've got. We can't go on like this. For crying out loud, we're both still young. Too bloody young to settle for anything less than the best.'

Banks sipped more Laphroaig, but it failed to warm the

icy hand now busy caressing the inside of his spine. 'When are you going?' he asked, his voice curiously flat.

Sandra avoided his eyes. 'As soon as possible. Tomorrow.'

Banks sighed. In the silence, he heard the letterbox open and close. Odd, at that time of night. It seemed like a good excuse to get out of the room for a moment, before he started crying himself or said things he would regret, so he went to see what it was. On the mat lay an envelope with his name typed on the front. He opened the door, but it was quiet outside in the street, and there was no one in sight.

He opened the envelope. Inside he found a plane ticket from Leeds and Bradford Airport to Amsterdam Schiphol, leaving late the following morning, a reservation for a hotel on Keizersgracht, and a single sheet of paper on which were typed the words: 'JASON FOX: SHHHHH.'

8

ONE

The Dutch coast came into view: first the dull brown sandbars where the grey sea ended in a long white thread; then the dykes, marking off the reclaimed land, protecting it from the water level.

Banks turned off his Walkman in the middle of 'Stop Breaking Down'. He always listened to loud music when flying – which wasn't very often – because it was the only thing he could hear over the roar of the engines. And he hadn't played *Exile on Main Street* in so long he'd forgotten just how good it was. The Rolling Stones' raucous rhythm and blues, he found, also had the added advantage of blocking out depressing thoughts.

The plane banked lower over the patchwork of green and brown fields, and Banks could soon make out cars on the long straight roads, rooftops glinting in the midday sun. It was as lovely an autumn day in the Netherlands as it had been in Yorkshire.

Banks rubbed his eyes. He had spent a sleepless night in Brian's room because Sandra had insisted it would only have made things more difficult if they'd slept together. She was right, he knew, but still it rankled. It wasn't even a matter of sex. Somehow it seemed so unfair, when threatened with the loss of someone you had loved for over twenty years, that you didn't even get that one last night of warmth and companionship together to remember and cherish. It felt like all the things you had left unsaid when someone died.

No matter how long Sandra said that she had been grappling with the problem, her decision had come as a shock to Banks. Perhaps, as she had argued, that was a measure of how much he had turned his back, drifted away from the relationship, but somehow her words didn't soften the blow. Now, more than anything, he felt numb, a pathetic figure floating around in zero gravity.

When he thought of Sandra, he thought mostly of the early days in London, where they lived together for about a year before they got married. It was the mid-seventies. Banks was just finishing his business diploma, already thinking about joining the police, and Sandra was taking a secretarial course. Every Sunday, if he didn't have to work, they went on long walks around the city and its parks, Sandra practising her photography and Banks developing his copper's eye for suspicious characters. Somehow, in his memory, it was always autumn on these walks: sunny but cool, with the leaves crackling underfoot. And when they got back to the tiny Notting Hill flat, they'd play music, laugh, talk, drink wine and make love.

Then came marriage, children, financial responsibilities and a career that demanded more and more of Banks's time and energy. Most of his friends on the force were divorced before the seventies were over, and they all asked in wonder and envy how he and Sandra managed to survive. He didn't really know, but he put a lot of it down to his wife's independent spirit. Sandra was right about that. She wasn't the kind of person who simply hung around the house and waited for him to turn up, fretting and getting angrier by the minute as the dinner was ruined and the kids screamed for bedtime stories from daddy. Sandra went her own way; she had her own interests and her own circle of friends. Naturally, more responsibility for the children fell on her shoulders, because Banks was hardly ever home, but she never complained. And for a long time, it worked.

After Banks's near burn-out on the Met and a long rocky patch in the marriage, they moved to Eastvale, where Banks thought things would settle down and the two of them would enjoy a rural, peaceful and loving drift into middle age together; the kind of thing experienced by most couples married as long as they had been.

Wrong.

He looked at his watch. Sandra would be on the train to Croydon now, and whatever happened, whatever she finally decided, things would never be the same between them again. And there was nothing he could do about it. Not a damn thing.

He picked up that morning's *Yorkshire Post* from the empty seat beside him and looked at the headline again: 'WORLD WAR TWO HERO DIES AT GRANDSON'S FUNERAL: Neo-Nazis responsible, says granddaughter.' There was no photograph, but the basic facts were there: the Nazi salute; Frank Hepplethwaite's attack; Maureen Fox's spirited defence. All in all, it made depressing reading. And then there was the brief sidebar interview with Motcombe himself.

Motcombe deeply regretted the 'pointless death' of 'war hero' Frank Hepplethwaite, he began, while pointing out how ironic it was that the poor man had died attacking the only people who dared demand justice for his grandson's killers. Naturally, on further thought, neither he nor any member of his organization had any intention of pursuing charges against Maureen Fox, even though the head wound she gave him required five stitches; things had just got out of hand in the heat of the moment, and he could quite understand her attacking him and his friends with a plank. Grief makes people behave irrationally, he allowed.

Of course, Motcombe went on, everyone knew who had killed Jason Fox, and everyone also knew why the police were powerless to act. That was just the state of things these days. He was sympathetic, but unless the government finally decided to act and do something about immigration, then . . .

Jason was a martyr of the struggle. Every true Englishman should honour him. If more people listened to Motcombe's ideas, then things could only change for the better. The reporter, to give her due credit, had managed to stop Motcombe turning the entire interview into propaganda. Either that or the copy editor had made extensive cuts. Even so, it made Banks want to puke. If anyone was the martyr in this, it was Frank Hepplethwaite.

Frank reminded Banks of his own father in many ways. Both had fought in the war, and neither spoke very much about it. Their racial attitudes were much the same, too. Banks's father might complain about immigrants taking over the country, changing the world he had known all his life, making it suddenly alien and unfamiliar, threatening even. And in the same way, Frank might have let slip a remark about a tight-fisted Jew. But when it came down to it, if anyone needed help, black or Jewish, Banks's dad would be first in line, with Frank Hepplethwaite probably a close second.

As unacceptable as even these racial attitudes were, Banks thought, they were a hell of a long way from those held by Neville Motcombe and his like. Banks's dad's view, like Frank's, was based on ignorance and anxiety, on fear of change, not on hatred. Perhaps in Motcombe's case the hatred sprang from an initial fear, but in most people it never went that far. Just like a lot of people have bad childhoods but they don't all become serial murderers.

The wheels bumped on the runway, and soon Banks was drifting into the arrivals hall with the crowds. He was travelling light, with only one holdall, so he didn't have to wait at the baggage claim. The place was like a small city, bustling with commerce, complete with its shops, bank, post office and tourist information desk. A colleague had told him a while ago that even pornography was on sale openly at Schiphol. He had neither the time nor the inclination to look for it.

The first thing Banks needed when he got off an aeroplane alive was a cigarette. He followed the signs to the bus stop and found he had a fifteen-minute wait. Perfect. He enjoyed a leisurely smoke, then got on the bus. Soon it was speeding along the motorway under grids of electrical wires and tall streetlamps.

The excitement of arrival pushed Banks's problems into the background for the moment, and he began to take some pleasure in his rebellion, his little act of irresponsibility. So that no one would feel he had disappeared completely into thin air, he had rung Susan Gay and told her he was taking the weekend off to go to Amsterdam and should be back sometime Monday. Susan had sounded puzzled and surprised, but she had made no comment. What could she say, anyway? Banks was her boss. Now, as the bus sped towards the city centre, he began to savour the coming hours, whatever they might bring. It could hardly be worse than life in Eastvale right now.

He had been to Amsterdam once before, with Sandra, one summer when they were both between college and jobs. He remembered the bicycles, canals, trams and houseboats. The place was full of leftover sixties spirit back then, and they had tried it all while they could: the Paradiso, the Milky Way, the Vondelpark, the drugs – well, marijuana, at least – as well as taking in all the museums and the tourist sights.

Stationsplein looked much the same. The air was warm, tinged only faintly with the bad-drains smell from the canals. Trams clanked about in all directions. A Perspex-covered boat set off on its canal tour. Arrows of ripples hit the stone quay.

Mixed with the late-season tourists and ordinary folk were all the post-hippie youth styles: punk spikes, a green Mohican, studded leather vests, short bleached hair, earrings, nose-rings, pierced eyebrows.

Banks found the taxi rank nearby. He would have preferred to walk after being cooped up on the plane and the bus, but he hadn't got his bearings yet. He didn't even know how to get to the hotel, or how far it was.

The taxi was clean and the driver seemed to recognize the name of the hotel. Soon, he had negotiated his way out of the square and they were heading along a broad, busy street lined with trees, arcades, shops and cafés. The pavements were crowded with tourists, even in early October, and Banks noticed that some of the cafés and restaurants had tables out on the street. He opened the window a little and the smell of fresh-brewed coffee came in. God, it was like a summer's day.

The driver turned, crossed a picturesque bridge, then continued along one of the canals. Finally, after a few more turns, he pulled up in front of the hotel on Keizersgracht.

Banks paid what seemed like an exorbitant amount of guilders for such a short trip, then hefted his holdall out of the boot.

He looked up at the unbroken row of buildings in front of him. The hotel was small and narrow, about six floors high, with a yellow sandstone façade and a gabled roof. It was wedged in a long terrace of uneven seventeenth- and eighteenth-century buildings that had once, Banks guessed, probably been merchants' houses. Some were built of red brick, some of stone; some had been painted black or grey; some had gables, some had flat roofs. All of them seemed to have plenty of windows.

Banks dodged a couple of cyclists and walked into the hotel lobby. The man at the desk spoke good English. Banks remembered from his previous trip that most people spoke good English in Amsterdam. They had to do. After all, how many English people bothered to learn Dutch?

Yes, the man said, his room was ready, and he was delighted to be able to offer a canal view. Breakfast would be served in the ground-floor lounge between seven o'clock and nine. He was sorry that the hotel had no bar of its own, but there were plenty of fine establishments within a short walking distance. He hoped Mr Banks would be comfortable.

When Banks pulled out his credit card, the clerk waved it away, telling him the room was fully paid for until Monday morning. Banks tried to discover who had paid for it, but the clerk became extremely coy, and his English went downhill fast. Banks gave up.

Then the clerk handed him a message: a single sheet of paper bearing a typed message that read 'De Kuyper's: 16:00hr.'

Banks asked what 'De Kuyper's' meant and was told it

was a 'brown café' – a sort of Dutch local pub – about a hundred metres to his left along the canal. It was on a quiet street corner and would probably have a few tables outside. A very nice place. He couldn't miss it.

The room was a gabled attic up five flights of narrow stairs. When Banks got there, he was panting and beads of sweat had broken out on his forehead.

Though there was hardly room to swing a dead cat, and the bed was tiny, the room was clean, with black timber beams and pale blue wallpaper. It smelled pleasantly of lemon air-freshener. A blue ashtray stood on the bedside table, beside the reading light and telephone. There was also a small television set and *en suite* facilities.

The canal view more than made up for any inadequacies. Banks particularly liked the way the ceiling and the black-painted beams sloped down towards the gabled window, drawing the eye to its perspective. And sure enough, he looked down on Keizersgracht and the tall, elegant façades of the buildings opposite. If anything, the room was a little too warm and stuffy, so he opened the window, letting in hints of distant street sounds. He looked at his watch. Just after two. Plenty of time for a shower and a nap before the mystery meeting. But first, he headed for the telephone. There was always a chance that Sandra had changed her mind.

TWO

Susan Gay was worried about Banks. Kicking her heels back in her office with black coffee and a so-very-sinful KitKat, she thought about the brief, puzzling phone call. What the hell did he think he was doing, taking a few days off in the middle of a major investigation? Just when they were getting close to tracking down Mark Wood. All right, so it was the weekend. Or almost. But didn't he know that Jimmy Riddle would go spare if he found out? Even Superintendent Gristhorpe would be annoyed.

There had to be more to it. The way he had sounded on the phone bothered her. Abrupt. Distracted. Not like him at all.

Was it the Amsterdam thing? Is that what had him so worried? Was there some danger involved, or something illegal? Banks didn't often act outside the law, not like some coppers Susan had known, but he did sometimes – they all did – if he felt there was no other way. Was he up to something?

Well, she concluded, she didn't know, and there was probably no way of finding out until he got back and revealed all, if he did. Until then, the best thing to do was get on with her work and stop behaving like a mother hen.

She hadn't had a lot of luck so far tracking down Mark Wood. It would take her forever to check out all the listings in the telephone directory. Even then, he might not live in the Leeds area, or have a telephone. Sergeant Hatchley was in Leeds today with one of his old cronies from Millgarth, visiting the properties Motcombe owned. Maybe they would turn up something, but she doubted it.

She was just about to pick up the phone and start dialling down her list when it rang.

'Is that DC Gay?' the voice said. 'Susan?'

'Yes.' She didn't know who it was.

'It's Vic here, Vic Manson, from Fingerprints.'

'Ah, of course. Sorry, I didn't recognize your voice for a moment. How's it going?'

'I was trying to call Alan, but apparently he's not in his

office and all I could get at home was his answering machine. Do you know where he is?'

'I'm afraid he won't be in at all today.'

'Not ill, I trust?'

'Can I help, Vic?'

'Yes. Yes, of course. Do you know much about finger-prints?'

'Not a lot, I'm afraid. Have you got some news?'

'Well, yes, in a way. Though it's not very good. Not as good as I'd hoped for.'

'I'm listening.'

'Right. Well, when I talked to Alan earlier in the week I was testing the glass from the broken bottle found near Jason Fox's body.'

'I remember,' Susan said. 'He said something about spraying it with SuperGlue in an aquarium.'

Manson laughed. 'Yes. Cyanoacrylate fuming, as a matter of fact.'

'I'll take your word for it.'

'Yes . . . well, I'm sorry, but it didn't work. We found nothing on the glass. Probably because of the rain.'

'And that's it?'

'Not entirely. Do you know anything at all about ninhydrin?'

'Isn't it a chemical for getting prints from paper?'

'Sort of, yes. What ninhydrin does is it makes visible the amino acids you deposit with sweaty fingers, especially on paper.'

'I see. But I thought we were concerned with *glass* here, Vic, not paper?'

'Ah, yes,' said Manson. 'We were. That is until it got us nowhere. But I found a couple of fragments of glass that were also covered by part of the *label* and, luckily, two of them were under the body, label side up, but not touching the victim's clothing, quite protected from the rain. Amino acids are water soluble, you see. Anyway, I don't want to get too technical about it, but it took a long time, and I destroyed one fragment completely, but after I brought a smudge or two out with ninhydrin treatment, I was able to get much better ridge detail under laser light.'

'You got a fingerprint?'

'Now, hold on. Wait a minute,' said Manson. 'I told you from the start it's not a major breakthrough. What I got was a partial fingerprint. *Very* partial. Even with computer enhancement I couldn't do a hell of a lot more with it. And, remember, any number of people could have handled that bottle. The cellarman, the landlord, the bartender. Anyone.'

'So you're saying it's worthless?'

'Not completely. Oh, it certainly wouldn't stand up in a court of law. Not enough points of comparison. I mean, it could almost be mine, at a pinch. Well, I exaggerate, but you see what I mean.'

'Yes,' said Susan, disappointed. She began to feel impatient. 'Has this got us anywhere at all?'

'Well,' Manson went on, 'I ran it through the new computerized matching system and I got a list of possibles. I confined the search to Yorkshire and, of course, it only applies to people whose prints we have on file.'

'And the print could belong to any person on the list?'

'Technically, yes. At least, as far as court evidence is concerned. I'm sorry. I can send it over, anyway, if you'd like?'

'Just a minute,' said Susan, feeling her pulse quicken a little. 'Do you have it in front of you? The list?'

'Yes.'

'Let's try a hunch. Could you check for a name?'

'Of course.'

'Try *Wood*. Mark Wood.'

It was worth a try. Susan could hear her heart beating fast in the silence that followed. Finally, after what seemed like a millennium, Manson said, 'Yes. Yes, there is a Mark Wood. I don't have all the details here, of course, but West Yorkshire have probably got a file on him.'

'West Yorkshire?'

'Yes. That's where he lives. Castleford area. If he's still at the same address, that is.'

'You've got the address?'

'Yes.' He read it out to her.

'And let me guess,' Susan said. 'He was convicted for football hooliganism or some sort of racial incident?'

'Er . . . no, actually,' said Manson.

'What then?'

'Drugs.'

'Drugs?' Susan repeated. 'Interesting. Thanks a lot, Vic.'

'No problem. And tell Alan I called, will you?'

Susan smiled. 'Will do.'

Although Vic Manson said the evidence wouldn't stand up in court, that didn't matter to Susan at the moment. The link between the partial print on the beer bottle and Jason Fox's web-page design partner was just too strong to be coincidence.

At first, Susan had thought the other lad must have either run away or left Jason *before* the attack. Now, though, the picture looked very different indeed. Maybe they couldn't convict Mark Wood on the basis of the fingerprint, but they could try for a confession, or some sort of physical evidence. For a start, the people in The Jubilee should be able to identify him.

But first, Susan thought, reaching for her jacket and her mobile, they would have to find him. Already she was feeling tremors of excitement, the thrill of the chase, and she was damned if she was going to be stuck by herself in Eastvale while Sergeant Hatchley had all the fun and glory.

THREE

With his hair still damp, Banks stepped out into the late afternoon warmth. Sandra hadn't been home when he called, hadn't changed her mind. It was what he had expected, really, though he felt a tremendous sense of disappointment when all he got was his own voice on the answering machine.

After an hour or so spent listening to some Mozart wind quintets on the Walkman, though, followed by a long hot shower, he started to feel more optimistic than he had on the plane. Sandra would come back eventually. Give her a few days at her parents' to get over the tiff, and then things would soon return to normal. Well, almost. They'd have a lot of talking to do, a lot of sorting out, but they'd manage it. They always had.

As he walked onto Keizersgracht, he still had that disconnected feeling he had experienced on arriving, as if all this – canal, bicycles, houseboats – were somehow not quite real, not connected with his life at all. Could he be living some sort of parallel existence, he wondered, another life going on at the same time as he was back in Eastvale talking over the future with Sandra?

Or was he time-travelling? After feeling as if he'd been away for a year, would he suddenly find himself back in Eastvale only seconds after he had left? Or worse, would he land back right in the middle of that terrible conversation last night, moments before the magic envelope arrived?

He tried to shake off the feeling as he admired the façades of the old buildings along the canals. Rows of bicycles were parked on the stone quay, and a couple of small houseboats were moored nearby. That must be an interesting existence, Banks thought, living on the water. Maybe he'd try it. Now he was a free agent once again, he supposed he could do whatever he wanted, live where he pleased. As long as he had a source of income, of course. There was always Europol or Interpol.

The sun had disappeared behind a gauze of cloud, giving a slightly hazy, misty effect to the light. It was still warm, though, and he slung his jacket over his shoulder as he walked.

Two pretty young girls passed him by, students by the look of them, and the one with long hennaed hair smiled. Definitely a flirtatious smile. Banks felt absurdly flattered and pleased with himself. Here he was, in his early forties, and young girls were still giving him the eye.

He supposed he must look young enough, despite the hint of grey at the temples of his closely cropped black hair, and he knew he was in good shape for his age, still lean in physique, with the suggestion of wiry, compact strength. Casually dressed in jeans, trainers and a light-blue denim shirt, he probably seemed younger than he was. And while his rather long, sharply angled face was not handsome in any regular sense of the word, it was the kind of face women noticed and liked. Perhaps because of the lively and striking dark blue eyes.

He reached a small stone bridge with black iron railings. A flower vendor stood at the corner and the musky scent of roses filled the air. It took him back to a vivid memory, the way smells do, something to do with one of his walks with Sandra many years ago, but he cut it off. He stood for a moment, leaning on the railings and looking down into the murky water, with its floating chocolate wrappers and cigarette packets scattered among the rainbows of diesel oil, then took a deep breath and turned back to the street.

There was the pub, De Kuyper's, right on the corner, as the desk clerk had said. It had an exterior of dark brown wood and smoked plate-glass windows with the name painted in large white letters. A few small, round tables stood outside, all empty at the moment. Banks glanced inside the dark wood-panelled bar, saw no one he knew or who took any interest in him, then went out again. He patted his jacket pocket to make sure he had his cigarettes and wallet with him, then slung it over the back of a chair and sat down.

He was early for the meeting, as he had intended. While he didn't really expect any danger, not here, in the open, on a warm afternoon, he wanted to be able to cover as many angles as possible. His table was perfect for that. From where he sat, he could see all the way along the curving canal past the hotel he had walked from, and a fair distance in the other direction, too. He also had a clear view of the opposite bank. Somewhere, in the distance, he could hear an organ-grinder.

When the white-aproned waiter came by, Banks ordered a bottle of De Koninck, a dark Belgian beer he had tried and enjoyed once at Belgo, a London restaurant. With the beer in front of him, he lit a cigarette and settled back to wait, watching the people walk to and fro, laughing and talking, along the sides of the canal. He already had his suspicions about who would turn up.

As it happened, he didn't have long to wait. He had just lit his second cigarette and worked about halfway through the beer, when he noticed, out of the corner of his eye, someone coming down the narrow side street.

It was a familiar figure, and Banks congratulated himself for getting it right. None other than Detective Superintendent Richard 'Dirty Dick' Burgess in the flesh. A little more flesh than on their previous meeting, by the look of it, most of it on his gut. Burgess worked for Special Branch, or something very close to it, and whenever he appeared on the scene Banks knew there would be complications.

'Banks, me old cock sparrow,' said Burgess, putting on the Cockney accent Banks knew he'd lost years ago. Then he clapped Banks on the back and took a chair. 'Mind if I join you?'

FOUR

A steady drizzle had settled in by the time Susan passed the Garforth exit, and she had to switch on her windscreen wipers to clean off all the muck the lorries churned up. Castleford wasn't far, though, and soon the enormous cooling towers of Ferrybridge power station came into sight. She found the road to Ferry Fryston without much trouble and, pulling over into the car park of a large pub to consult her map, pinpointed the street she was looking for.

Mark Wood lived in a 'prefab' on one of the early postwar council estates. These were houses – mostly semis or short terrace blocks – built of concrete prefabricated in the factory then assembled on the site. In this area, they were built originally to house colliery workers, but since all the local pits had been closed during the Thatcher years, they were up for grabs, a source of cheap housing.

The houses themselves weren't up to much. They had no central heating, and the walls were damp. In the rain, Susan thought, the concrete looked like porridge.

Susan negotiated her way through the maze of 'avenues', 'rises', 'terraces' and 'drives' which curved and looped in great profusion, then she spotted Hatchley's dark-green Astra, just around the corner from Wood's house, as they had arranged over the phone.

Susan pulled up behind him, turned off her engine, then dashed over and jumped in beside him.

'Sorry if I kept you waiting, sarge,' she said. 'Three-car accident near the York junction.'

'That's all right,' said Hatchley, stubbing out a cigarette in the already overstuffed ashtray. 'Just got here myself. Bugger of a place to find. Bugger of a place to live, too, if you ask me.'

'How shall we play it?'

Hatchley squirmed in his seat and ran his pudgy fingers under the back of his collar, as if to loosen it. 'Why don't you start the questioning?' he said. 'It'll be good experience now you're going to be a sergeant. I'll jump in if I think it's necessary.'

'Fine,' said Susan, smiling to herself. She knew that Hatchley hated carrying out formal interviews unless he was talking either to an informant or a habitual criminal. With Wood, they just didn't know yet, so Hatchley would let her lead, then he would follow if she got somewhere interesting or fill in the gaps if she missed something.

As it turned out, Hatchley had even more reason for assigning the interview to Susan. When they knocked on the door, a young woman opened it, and Hatchley was useless at interviewing women. Susan finessed their way inside easily enough, showing her warrant card, after determining that Mark had just 'nipped out' to the shop for some cigarettes and would be back in a few minutes. Good, she thought; it gave her a chance to talk to the girlfriend alone first.

Inside, the house was clean and tidy enough, but Susan's sense of smell, always sensitive, reacted at once to the mingled baby odours – warm milk, mushy food and, of course, the whole mess when it all comes out transformed at the other end – and the kitty litter. Sure enough, a black-and-white cat prowled the room and a baby slept in its cot in the corner, occasionally emitting a tiny sniffle or cry, as if disturbed by dreams. One of the walls was damp, and the wallpaper was peeling off near the ceiling.

'What's it all about?' the woman asked. 'I'm Shirelle. Mark's wife.'

That was Susan's first shock. Shirelle was Afro-Caribbean. And she didn't look a day older than fourteen. She was small in stature, with a flat chest and slim hips, and her pale brown face was framed by long braided black hair that cascaded over her shoulders. Looking at her sitting there in the worn old armchair, it was hard to believe she was old enough to be a mother.

'We've just a few questions to ask your Mark, love,' said Susan, in as reassuring a tone as she could manage. When Shirelle didn't answer, she went on, 'Maybe you can help. Do you know Jason Fox?'

She frowned. 'No. I haven't met him. Mark mentioned him once or twice. They do some computer work together. But he never brings him here.'

I'm not surprised, Susan thought. 'Has Mark ever told you anything about him?'

'Like what?'

'What he's like, how they get on, that sort of thing.'

'Well, I don't think Mark likes him all that much. They haven't been working together for long, and I think Mark's going to break with him. Apparently, this Jason has some peculiar ideas about immigrants and stuff.'

You could say that again. 'Doesn't that bother you?'

'I'm not an immigrant. I was born here.'

'How long have they been working together?'

'A few months.'

'How did they meet?'

'They were both doing a computer course in Leeds at the same time, and neither of them could get a job after. I think this Jason had a bit of money to put into starting a business. Mark was top of the class, so Jason asked if he wanted to join him. Like I say, I don't think Mark's going to stick with him. It's just a start, that's all. It's hard to get started when you don't have the experience.'

'How's the business doing?' Susan asked.

Shirelle looked around her and snorted. 'What do *you* think? Hardly made enough to pay for this place and you can see what a dump it is.' Now she neither looked nor sounded like a fourteen-year-old.

The cat tried to climb on Susan's knee, but she pushed it away. 'It's not that I don't like cats, Shirelle,' she said. 'But I'm allergic to them.'

Shirelle nodded. 'Tina, come here!' she said.

But the cat, as cats do, gave her a you-must-be-joking look and ignored her. Finally, Shirelle shot forward, scooped up Tina and deposited her in the next room, closing the door.

'Thanks,' said Susan. 'Have you heard of the Albion League?'

Shirelle shook her head. 'What's that when it's at home?'

'Do you know where Mark was last Saturday night?'

Shirelle glanced away for just long enough that Susan knew she was going to tell a lie. Why? Had her husband told her to? Or did she want to avoid trouble with the police? With some people, it was habitual. Whatever the reason, as soon as she said, 'He was here. At home,' Susan asked her to think carefully about her answer.

'What time do you mean?' Shirelle asked, after a few moments' hesitation. 'Because he might, you know, have nipped down the pub for a jar or two with his mates.'

'Which pub would that be?'

'Hare and Hounds. At the corner. That's his local.' Shirelle seemed distracted by Sergeant Hatchley, who had said nothing so far, but just sat next to Susan on the sofa watching the whole proceedings, still as a statue, occasionally nodding encouragement and making a note in his black book. She kept looking at him, then turned her large, frightened eyes away, back to Susan.

'And if we were to ask there, at this Hare and Hounds,' Susan said, 'then they'd remember Mark from last Saturday night, would they?'

'I . . . I don't—'

At that moment the front door opened and a male voice called out, 'Sheri? Sheri?'

Then Mark Wood entered the room: stocky build, muscular, short hair, loop earring and all. Early twenties. The man in the picture.

'Hello, Mark,' said Susan. 'We've been wanting a word with you ever since last Saturday.'

When Mark saw Susan and Hatchley he stopped in his tracks and his jaw went slack. 'Who . . . ?' But it was obvious he knew who they were, even if he hadn't been expecting them. He put the packet of cigarettes on the table and sat in the other armchair. 'What about?' he asked.

'Jason. We'd have thought you might have got in touch with us, you know, since Jason died.'

'Jason what?' Shirelle burst in. She looked at Mark. 'Jason's *dead*? You never told me that.'

Mark shrugged.

'Well?' Susan asked.

'Well, what?'

'What do you have to say? Even if your wife didn't know, *you* knew Jason was dead, didn't you?'

'Read about it in the paper. But it's nothing to do with me, is it?'

'Isn't it? But you were there, Mark. You were in Eastvale drinking with Jason. You left The Jubilee with him shortly after closing time. What we want to know is what happened next.'

'I was never there,' Mark said. 'I was here. At home. Now we've got little Connor, I don't get out as much as I used to. I can't just leave Sheri alone with him all the time, can I? Besides, as you can probably tell, we're a bit short of the readies, too.'

'I'll bet you own a car, though, don't you?'

'Just an old banger. A van. I need it for the business.'

'Designing web pages?'

'That's not all we do. We do a bit of retail, refurbish systems, set up networks, troubleshoot, that sort of thing.'

'So you haven't been out dealing drugs for a while?'

'You know about that, do you?'

'We do our research. What do you expect?'

Mark shifted in his chair and shot a quick glance at

Shirelle. 'Yeah, well, it was years ago now. It's behind me. I've been clean ever since.'

'Were you selling drugs at The Jubilee last Saturday night?'

'No. I told you. I wasn't even there. Besides, I served my time.'

'You're right,' said Susan. 'Nine months, if I read the record right. It's nice to know there really is such a thing as rehabilitation. That's not what we're interested in anyway. All we care about is what happened to Jason Fox. What about the Albion League, Mark? Are you a member?'

Mark scoffed. 'That bunch of wankers? That was Jason's thing. Not mine.' He looked at Shirelle. 'Or isn't that obvious enough to you already?'

'Did Jason ever introduce you to their leader, Neville Motcombe, or any of the other members?'

'No. He kept asking me to go to meetings, but that's all. I think he picked up that I wasn't really interested.'

'But the two of you produced the web page for them.'

'Jason did that in his spare time. By himself. Thought it was a good idea to put the company's logo at the bottom. Said it could bring us more business.' He shrugged. 'Business is business, even if some of it does come from crackpots.'

'And did it?'

'Did it what?'

'Bring in more business?'

'Nah. Not much. To be honest I think hardly anyone even looked at it. I mean, would you?'

'But you were friends with Jason, too, weren't you?'

'I wouldn't really say that.'

'I understand he provided the capital to start the business?'

Mark looked at Shirelle. Susan guessed he was probably trying to work out exactly what his wife had told them already.

'Yes,' he said. 'I didn't have any money, but Jason put in a few hundred quid, just to get us going. Only a loan, mind you.'

'So you wouldn't say you were friends?'

'No. It's not as if we actually socialized together.'

'But you *were* socializing last Saturday night in Eastvale.'

'I told you, I wasn't there. I was here all evening.'

'Didn't you even nip out for a jar?' Susan asked. 'Shirelle here said she thought you might have done.'

Mark looked to his wife for guidance. 'I . . . I don't . . .' she said. 'They've been confusing me, Mark. *Was* it Saturday? I don't remember. I only said he might have gone out for a few minutes.'

'*Did* you go out, Mark?' Susan repeated.

'No,' said Mark. Then he turned to Shirelle. 'Don't you remember, love, when we went in town shopping in the afternoon, we picked up a couple of bottles at the offie then we rented that Steven Seagal video and we just stayed in and watched it. Don't you remember?'

'Oh, yes, that's right,' said Shirelle. 'Yes, I remember now. We stayed in and watched a video together.'

Susan ignored Shirelle; she was lying again. And she thought it interesting that no matter how poor people seemed, how short of the 'readies' they were, they always had enough money for booze, cigarettes, videos and pets. Cars, even. 'So you weren't in Eastvale at all last Saturday night, then, Mark?'

Mark shook his head. 'No.'

'I suppose the video rental shop will have a record?'

'I suppose so. They're computerized, all the latest gear, so they ought to. I never asked. I mean, I didn't think anyone would be interested.'

'But you could still be lying, couldn't you?' Susan went on. 'In fact, it doesn't matter at all whether you rented a video on Saturday afternoon or not, does it? You could have gone to Eastvale on Saturday evening, met Jason in The Jubilee and booted him to death. You could have watched the video after you got home.'

'I told you. I didn't do anything of the sort. I wasn't anywhere near there. Besides, why would I do a thing like that? I already told you, Jason was my business partner. Why would I kill the goose that lays the golden eggs?'

'You tell me. I understand you were going to dump him?'

Again, Mark looked at Shirelle, who stared into her lap.

'Look,' he said, 'I'm telling you, I didn't do anything. I wasn't anywhere near Eastvale. I've never even been there in my life.'

Suddenly, Hatchley lurched to his feet, making even Susan jump. 'Let's cut the bollocks, lad,' he said, putting his notebook back into his inside pocket. 'We know you were there. People *saw* you in the pub. And we've got a clear set of your fingerprints on the murder weapon. What have you got to say about that?'

Mark looked from side to side, as if seeking an escape route. Shirelle started to cry. 'Oh, Mark,' she wailed. 'What can we do?'

'Shut up blubbering,' he said, then turned back to Susan and Hatchley. 'I want a lawyer.'

'Later,' said Hatchley. 'First, we're going to fill a plastic bag with your shoes and clothes, then we're going to go back to Eastvale for a nice long chat in a proper police interview room. How do you feel about that?'

Mark said nothing.

Connor stirred in his cot and started to cry.

FIVE

'Tell me one thing,' Banks said. 'Why the hell have you dragged me all the way to Amsterdam?'

Burgess smiled, flipped open his tin of Tom Thumb cigars and selected one. 'Everything will be made clear in time. Shit, it's good to see you again, Banks,' he said. 'I knew I could rely on your curiosity to get you here. I can't think of a better man for a case like this.' He lit the small cigar and blew out a plume of smoke.

'What case would that be?' asked Banks, who had learned, over the years, to trust Burgess about as much as he would trust a politician in an election year.

'Oh, don't be coy. The Jason Fox case, of course.'

The waiter came out. Burgess asked Banks what he was drinking. Banks told him he'd have another De Koninck.

'Filthy stuff,' said Burgess. Then he turned to the waiter. 'Still, bring him another one, will you, mate, if that's what he wants. I'll have a lager. Whatever you've got on tap.'

Banks noticed that Burgess had his greying hair pulled back and tied in a ponytail. Bloody typical. The ageing stud look.

'Beautiful day, isn't it?' Burgess said when the waiter came back with their drinks. 'Aren't you glad I got you the ticket, Banks?'

'I'm overwhelmed with delight and gratitude,' said

Banks, 'but I wouldn't mind knowing what it's all about. Just a hint, maybe, to start with.'

'That's my Banks.' Burgess jerked forward – all his motions seemed jerky – and clapped him on the shoulder. 'Always anxious to get down to business. You know, you could have made super by now. Who knows, even chief super. If only you weren't such a Bolshie bastard. You never did learn to be nice to the right people, did you?'

Banks smiled. 'And *you* did?'

Burgess winked. 'I must've done something right, mustn't I? Anyway, enough about me. Some time earlier this week you – or someone in your division – set off an alarm bell I'd placed on a certain file.'

'The Albion League?'

'Who's a clever boy, then? Yes, the Albion League. I got a bloke called Crawley – good chap – to answer and instructed him to give away as little as possible. See, I wanted to know why *you* were so interested in the League. It's not as if they've got a big operation in North Yorkshire, after all. Then I found out about the Jason Fox killing, and things sort of fell into place.'

'You knew Jason was a member?'

'Of course I bloody did. He was Neville Motcombe's right-hand man. Hotly tipped for future Führerdom himself. Now Jason getting himself killed like that was a very bad thing, because it set off all kinds of warning bells all over the place. Which is why I'm here. You, too.'

A couple of young blonde girls walked by. One of them was wearing a tight T-shirt and high-cut turquoise shorts. She was pushing her bicycle as she chatted with her friend. 'Jesus Christ, would you look at that ass,' said Burgess, lapsing into his habitual American slang. 'Gives me such a hard-on I don't have enough skin left to close my eyes.' He gave a mock shudder. 'Anyway, where was I?'

'Warning bells.'

'Yes. I don't know how much you know about him, Banks, but Motcombe is a nasty piece of work. Just because he's a fucking fruitcake, it doesn't mean you should underestimate him.'

'I'd have thought that *you* would have had every sympathy with him,' Banks said. 'In fact, I'm surprised you're not a member of the Albion League yourself.'

Burgess laughed. 'Oh, what a cheap shot. You know what, Banks, you're so very predictable. That's one of the reasons I like you. I've been waiting for a remark like that ever since I sat down.' He settled back in his chair and puffed on his Tom Thumb. 'Do I think we're letting too many foreigners in? Yes. Do I think we've got a problem with our immigration policy? Damn right I do. But do I think a gang of goose-stepping football hooligans are the answer? No, I don't. Look at this lot.' He waved his arm around, as if to indicate the Dutch in general. 'Look at the problems they've had with their darkies. And they only have Dutch Guyana to worry about.'

'Surinam,' said Banks.

'Whatever.'

'And I think you'll find they also colonized a lot more of the world than just that.'

'Listen, Banks, stop being a bloody smart arse. That's not the point, and you know it. You can't convince me that England wouldn't be a damn sight more civilized and law-abiding if we hadn't let so many of the buggers in to start with.'

'Civilized and law-abiding as in football hooligans?'

'Oh, it's no fucking use arguing with you, is it? Got an

answer for everything, haven't you? Let me put it in a nutshell. While I think this Albion League might have some pretty good ideas, I don't like getting dressed up like an idiot and hanging around with skinheads and leather-fetishists without two brain cells to rub together between them. Credit me with a bit more sense than that, Banks. Whatever I am,' Burgess concluded, thrusting his thumb towards his chest, 'I am not a fucking loony.'

Burgess was actually wearing his trademark scuffed-up black leather jacket, but Banks let that one go by.

'Anyway,' Burgess went on after a long swig of generic lager, 'back to Neville Motcombe. We know he's got connections with other right-wing groups in Europe and America. Over the past four years, he's travelled exten-sively in Germany, France, Spain, Italy and Holland. He's also been to Greece and Turkey.'

'I wouldn't have thought a neo-Nazi would find much to interest him in Turkey,' Banks said.

'You'd be surprised. There are plenty of right-wing Turkish groups with access to arms. Get them cheap off the Russians in Azerbaijan or Armenia. Very strategically located for lots of nasty things, is Turkey. And don't forget, Johnny Turk's a slimy bastard. Anyway, Motcombe has also visited a number of Militia training camps in the south-western United States, and he's been spotted entering the Nazi party headquarters in Lincoln, Nebraska. That, for your information, is where most of the instructions on bombs and explosives come from. So this guy has talked to the sort of people who blew up that government building in Oklahoma City.' Burgess pointed his cigar at Banks. 'Whatever you do, Banks, don't underestimate Neville Motcombe. Besides, when you get right down to it, this isn't really about politics at all. There's something else.'

'What?'

'Money. One of the Turkish right-wingers Motcombe has been communicating with frequently of late, via the Internet, is a suspected international drug dealer. Heroin, mostly. And we happen to know he's looking for new outlets in England. They met when Motcombe was in Turkey during the summer, and electronic traffic between them has increased dramatically over the past three weeks. The wires are hot, you might say.'

'What do these messages say?'

'Ah, well, there's the problem. Our computer whizzes have been keeping an eye on these cyber-Nazis, as they're called. We know some of their passwords, so we can read a fair bit of the traffic. Until they get onto us and change the passwords, that is. Problem is, some of the really hot stuff is encrypted. They use PGP and even more advanced encryption programmes. I kid you not, Banks, these things make Enigma look like a fucking doddle.'

'So you can't decipher the messages?'

'Well, maybe they're just chatting away about Holocaust denial or some such rubbish – we can't exactly decipher their messages – but knowing the Turk, I doubt it. I'd say he's found the pipeline he was looking for.'

Banks shook his head. 'And Jason Fox?' he said. 'Do you think this could have something to do with his death?'

Burgess shrugged. 'Well, it's a bit of a coincidence, isn't it? And I know you don't like coincidences. I thought you should be filled in, that's all.'

'What a load of bollocks,' said Banks. 'And don't give me all this cloak-and-dagger shit. Encrypted e-mail. Vague suspicions. Is this what you dragged me all this way for?'

Burgess looked offended. 'No,' he said. 'Well, not

entirely. As it happens, I don't know much about it yet, myself.'

'So why *am* I here?'

'Because a very important person is here, *has* to be here for at least a week. Because it's essential you talk to this person before you go any further in your investigation. And because it wouldn't do for you to be seen together back home. Believe me, he'll be able to tell you a lot more than I can. Good enough?'

'What about the telephone?'

'Oh, give me a break, Banks. If they can eavesdrop on Charlie and Di, they can bloody well eavesdrop on you. Telephones aren't secure. Quit belly-aching and enjoy yourself. It won't be all work. I mean, what are you complaining about? You've got yourself a free weekend in one of the most exciting cities in the world. Okay?'

Banks thought for a moment, watching the bicycles and cars passing by along the canal. He lit a cigarette. 'So what happens next?' he said.

'Tomorrow afternoon, *I* get up to date on what's going on, then I'm off on my holidays, believe it or not. I think I'll just go out to Schiphol and take the first flight somewhere tropical. In the evening, *you* have a very important meeting.' Burgess told him to be at a bar near Sarphatipark at eight o'clock, but not whom he would find when he got there. 'And make sure you're not followed,' he added.

Banks shook his head at the melodrama. Burgess just loved this cloak-and-dagger crap.

Then Burgess clapped his hands, showering ash on the table. 'But until then, we're free agents. Two happy bachelors – and notice I didn't say "gay" – with the whole night ahead of us.' He lowered his voice. 'Now, what I suggest is that we find a nice little Indonesian restaurant, shovel down a plate or two of *rijsttafel* and swill that down with a few pints of lager. Then we'll see if we can find one of those little coffee shops where you can smoke hash.' He rested his arm over Banks's shoulder. 'And after that, I suggest we take a stroll to the red-light district and get us some nice, tight Dutch pussy. It's all perfectly legal and above board here, you know, and the girls have regular check-ups. Tried and tested, stamped prime grade A.' He turned to Banks and squinted. 'Now, I know you've got that lovely wife of yours waiting at home – Sandra, isn't it? – but there really is nothing quite like a little strange pussy once in a while. Take my word. And what she doesn't know won't hurt her. My lips will be eternally sealed, I can promise you that. How about it?'

As usual, Banks thought, the bastard showed his unerring instinct for finding the spot that hurt, like a dentist prodding at an exposed nerve. There was no way Burgess could know what had happened between Banks and Sandra the previous evening. Nobody knew but the two of them. Yet here he was, right on the mark. Well, to hell with him.

'Fine,' said Banks. 'You're on.' Then he raised his glass and finished his beer. 'But first, I think I'll have another one of these.'

9

ONE

'**I'm sorry we** had to take you away from your wife and child, Mark,' said Gristhorpe. 'Let's hope it won't be for long.'

Wood said nothing; he just looked sullen and defiant.

'Anyway,' Gristhorpe went on. 'I'd like to thank you for sparing us the time.' He balanced a pair of reading glasses on his hooked nose and flipped through some sheets of paper in front of him, glancing up over the top of his glasses from time to time. 'There's just a few points we'd like to get cleared up, and we think you can help us.'

'I've already told you,' Wood said. 'I don't know anything.'

Susan sat next to Gristhorpe in the interview room: faded institutional green walls, high, barred window, metal table and chairs bolted to the floor, pervading odour of smoke, sweat and urine. Susan was convinced they sprayed it in fresh every day. Two tape recorders were running, making a soft hissing sound in the background. It was dark outside by the time they actually got around to the interview. Gristhorpe had already given the caution. Wood had also phoned a solicitor in Leeds, Giles Varney, and got his answering machine. You'd be lucky to find a lawyer at home on a Friday evening, in Susan's experience. Still, he had left a message and steadfastly refused the duty solicitor. Hardly surprising, Susan thought, given that Giles Varney was one of the best-known solicitors in the county. She would have thought he was way out of Mark's league.

'Yes,' said Gristhorpe, taking off his glasses and fingering the papers in front of him. 'I know that. Thing is, though, that sometimes when people come into contact with the police, they lie.' He shrugged and held his hands out, palms up. 'Now, I can understand that, Mark. Maybe they do it to protect themselves, or maybe just because they're afraid. But they lie. And it makes our job just that little bit more difficult.'

'I'm sorry, I can't help you,' said Wood.

Good sign, Susan noted. Gristhorpe had the lad apologizing already.

'Now,' Gristhorpe went on, 'the last time you got into trouble, you told the police that you had no idea the van you were driving was used for carrying drugs, or that some of the people you were involved with were dealing drugs. Is that true?'

'Do you mean is that what I said?'

'Yes.'

Mark nodded. 'Yes.'

'And is the *statement* true?'

Mark grinned. 'Well, of course it is. It's what I told the court, isn't it? A matter of public record. It's hardly my fault if the magistrate didn't believe me.'

'Course not, Mark. Innocent people get convicted all the time. It's one of the problems with the system. Nothing's perfect. But with so many lies going around, you can understand why we might be just a bit wary, a little bit over-cautious, and perhaps not quite as trusting as you'd like, can't you?'

'I suppose so. Yes.'

Gristhorpe nodded. 'Good.'

The superintendent's interview technique, Susan noticed, was in direct contrast to that of Banks, with whose style she was more familiar. Banks would sometimes needle his interviewees, and when he'd got them confused and vulnerable, he would subtly suggest possible scenarios of how they had committed the crime, and why. He sometimes even went so far as to explain to them their feelings and state of mind while they were doing it. Then, if they were new to the world of crime, he would describe in graphic detail what kind of life they could expect in jail and after. Banks worked on his subjects' *imaginations*; he used words to paint images unbearable to the hearer.

Gristhorpe seemed to concentrate more on logic and reasoned argument; he was polite, soft-spoken and unrelenting. He seemed slower than Banks, too. As if he had all the time in the world. But Susan was keen to get it over with. She had already pulled a couple of favours to get the lab working overtime on Mark Wood's shoes and clothing, and if they came up with some solid forensic evidence, or if Gristhorpe got a confession, there was a good chance they could wrap things up before tonight. Jimmy Riddle would be pleased about that.

As a bonus, she would have the weekend free, for once, and she might get her Saturday night out with Gavin. She had considered phoning him earlier – even picked up the phone – but no, she told herself, it wouldn't do to seem *too* keen, *too* easily available. Let him cajole her. Seduce her. *Win* her.

'You see,' Gristhorpe went on, 'that's one of our main problems, sorting out the lies from the truth. That's why we have science to help us. Do you know what "forensic" means?'

Wood frowned and tugged on his earring. 'It means science, doesn't it? Like blood types, footprints, DNA and fingerprints?'

'That's a common error,' Gristhorpe said, toying with his glasses on the table. 'Actually, it means "for use in a court of law". It's from the Latin, related to the word *forum*. So one of the best systems we have to help us tell the lies from the truth is a complex and broad-ranging branch of science dedicated solely to presenting scientific evidence *in court*. Now, of course, before we get to court, we use this forensic evidence to help us identify the people who should be on trial. And in your case, I'm afraid the evidence tells us that you should be in court for the murder of Jason Fox. What do you have to say about that, Mark?'

'Nothing. What can I say? I've done nothing.'

Wood was taken aback by Gristhorpe's gentle and erudite logic, Susan could tell. But he was cool. She noticed that Gristhorpe let the silence stretch until Wood started squirming in his chair.

'Well, you must have something to say, lad,' Gristhorpe went on, putting on his glasses again and slipping a photograph from the file in front of him. 'This is an image of a fingerprint found on the label of a beer bottle,' he said, turning it around so Wood could see it clearly. 'It was developed by a very painstaking process. Forensic science doesn't produce miracles, Mark, but sometimes it seems to come close. Now, I'm sure you're an intelligent enough lad to know that fingerprints are unique. So far, no two fingers have been found to possess the same ridge characteristics. Isn't that amazing?'

Wood said nothing; his eyes were glued to the photo.

'Anyway,' Gristhorpe went on, 'what's particularly interesting about *that* fingerprint is that it came from a fragment of a broken bottle found at the scene of Jason Fox's murder. But perhaps I'm being precipitous in referring to it as a *murder* so soon, because that hasn't been proven yet. You do know that there's a big difference between homicide and manslaughter, don't you, Mark?'

Wood nodded. 'Yes.'

'Good. And there's also a big difference in jail sentences. But we won't let that detain us for the moment. Anyway, the point is that that is a close match for *your* fingerprint – one we already have on file – and that it was found in the ginnel by the rec, on a fragment of a broken beer bottle under Jason Fox's body. I'd like you to tell me how it got there.'

Wood licked his lips and glanced at Susan. She said nothing. He looked back into Gristhorpe's guileless blue eyes.

'Well, er . . . I suppose I must have touched it, mustn't I, if it's got my prints on it?' He smiled.

Gristhorpe nodded. 'Aye. I suppose so. When might that have happened, Mark?'

'I gave it to Jason,' Wood said finally.

'When?'

'When we came out of the pub. You see, I thought I wanted another beer, so I bought a bottle from out-sales as we were leaving, but then I remembered I had to drive back down the A1, so I just gave it to Jason. He said he was walking home.'

'Ah,' said Gristhorpe. 'So you *gave* the bottle of beer to Jason when you parted outside The Jubilee?'

'That's right. I was parked just down the street the pub was on. Market Street. Is that right?'

'That's the one.' Gristhorpe looked at Susan, who raised her eyebrows.

'What's wrong?' Wood asked.

Susan scratched the cleft of her chin. 'Nothing, really, Mark,' she said. 'It's just that you've confused me a bit. When I talked to you earlier you denied being in Eastvale at all last Saturday night. Don't you remember?' She pretended to read from the paper in front of her. 'You bought a couple of bottles of beer at the off-licence and rented a Steven Seagal video, which you and your wife watched that evening. You didn't even nip out to the Hare and Hounds for a quick one. That's what you said, Mark.'

'Yeah, well . . . it's like he said earlier, isn't it?' He looked at Gristhorpe.

'What would that be, Mark?' Gristhorpe asked.

'About people ly— About people not telling the exact truth sometimes when the police come after them.'

'So you didn't tell the truth?'

'Not exactly.'

'Why not?'

'I was scared, wasn't I?'

'What of?'

'That you'd fit me up for it because I've been in trouble before.'

'Ah, yes,' said Gristhorpe, shaking his head. 'The classic fit-up. That's another one of the problems we constantly have to fight against: the public's perception of the police, mostly formed by the media. Especially television. Well, I won't deny it, Mark, there *are* police officers who wouldn't stop at forging a notebook entry or altering a statement in order to convict someone. We're all embarrassed about the Birmingham Six, you know. That's why there are so many laws now to help people in your position. We can't beat you up. We can't force a confession out of you. We have to treat you well while you're in custody

– feed you, allow you exercise, give you access to a solicitor. That sort of thing. It's all covered in the PACE guidelines.' Gristhorpe spread his hands. 'You see, Mark, we're just humble public servants, really, gentle custodians here to see that your rights aren't abused in any way. By the way, you must be a bit hungry by now, aren't you? I know I am. How about I send out for some coffee and sandwiches?'

'Fine with me. Long as they're not salmon. I'm allergic to salmon.'

'No problem. Susan, would you ask one of the uniformed officers to nip over to the Queen's Arms and ask Cyril to do us two or three ham-and-cheese sandwiches? And have one of the lads up front bring us a pot of fresh coffee, please.'

'Of course, sir.'

Susan popped her head out of the door and made the request, then she went back to her chair.

'While we're waiting, though,' said Gristhorpe, 'and if you don't mind, Mark, let's get back to what happened last Saturday night, shall we? As I understand it, you've changed your original story – which, quite understandably, you now admit was a lie.'

'Because I was scared you'd fit me up.'

'Right. Because you were scared we'd fit you up. Well, I hope I've put your mind at rest about that.'

Wood leaned back in his chair and smiled. 'You're a lot nicer than those bastards from West Yorkshire who nabbed me on that drugs charge.'

Bloody hell, thought Susan, the old man's even getting compliments out of his suspects now, let alone mere apologies.

'Well,' said Gristhorpe, inclining his head modestly.

'West Yorkshire have a lot more problems than we do, being more urban and all. They sometimes have to cut corners a bit roughly.'

'You're telling me.'

'But that's all behind you now, Mark, isn't it? I see you've been a good lad since then. You took a course and then you went into business. Admirable. But now there's just this little spot of bother, and the sooner we get it cleared up, the sooner you can get back to leading a normal and productive life with your family. Did Jason ever try to interest you in the Albion League?'

'Sometimes. He'd spout a load of garbage about how the Holocaust didn't really happen – how most of the Jews died of typhoid and the showers were just ways of disinfecting them, like, not really death camps at all. I must admit, it made me a bit sick. Then I lost interest and didn't pay much attention after that. Half the time I thought he couldn't even be serious.'

'I understand your wife is Afro-Caribbean?'

'Her family's from Jamaica, yes.'

'How did you manage to reconcile this with doing business with a racist like Jason?'

'I never thought much about it, really, not at first. Like I said, I thought Jason spouted a load of silly rubbish. I figured he'd probably grow out of it.'

'You said "at first". What about after that?'

'Yeah, well, it started getting to me, Sheri being Jamaican and all. We had a couple of arguments. I was on the verge of ditching him when . . .'

'When what, Mark?'

'Well, you know, he died.'

'Ah, yes. Did you tell him you were married to a Jamaican woman?'

'Are you joking? And listen to him prattle on about that? He really had a bee in his bonnet about mixed marriages. No, I kept my private life and my business activities completely separate.'

Gristhorpe adjusted his glasses again and took a moment or two to look over some sheets of paper. Then he looked back at Wood, held his glasses in his hand and frowned. 'But you knew that Jason was doing this computer work for the League?'

The food came, and they took a moment's break to pass around sandwiches and pour coffee.

'Yes, I knew,' Wood answered. 'But what he did in his own time was up to him.'

'Even if you didn't agree? It bore the trademark of the business you ran together, didn't it?'

'We could use all the business we could get.'

'Right. So you let your name be used for neo-Nazi propaganda even though you found the idea loathsome. Your wife is black, for crying out loud, Mark. What do you think Jason Fox and his ilk would do with her if they got half a chance? What does that make you, Mark? Are you ashamed of her?'

'Now hold on a minute—'

Gristhorpe leaned forward. He didn't raise his voice at all, but he fixed Mark with his eyes. 'No, Mark, *you* hold on a minute. You were drinking with Jason Fox on the night he got killed. Now, you've already lied to us once or twice, but we'll let that go by for the moment. Your latest story is that you *were* with Jason, but the two of you parted outside The Jubilee, at which time you gave him the bottle of beer you'd bought from out-sales because you remembered you had to drive home. Is that right?'

'Yes.'

'And the two of you weren't close friends?'

'No. I've told you. We worked together. That's all.'

'So what were you doing pubbing with him in The Jubilee? Eastvale's a long way from your normal stamping ground, isn't it? Can you explain that?'

'He said he was going up to Eastvale to play football. I felt like a night out, that's all. Somewhere different. Just for a change. Sheri knew I'd been a bit down lately, like, about the business and all, and she said she didn't mind staying home with Connor. The Jubilee gets really good bands on a Saturday night, and I like live music.'

'So you drove all the way up from Castleford to spend a social evening with a business associate you didn't particularly like, someone who believed your wife and all her kind should be packed off in boats back to the Caribbean?'

Mark shrugged. 'I went to see the band. Jason said he'd come along, as he'd be in town anyway, that's all. I thought it might make a change from Razor's Edge and Celtic Warrior and all that other crap he listens to. Hear some decent music for once. The Jubilee's got a good reputation all over the north. Just ask anyone. And it's not that far. Straight up the A1. Doesn't take more than an hour and a half or so each way.'

'That's three hours' driving, Mark.'

'So? I like driving.'

'Where did you go after you left Jason?'

'I drove straight back home. I wasn't over the limit, if that's what you're thinking.'

'But you still came all this way knowing you'd be drinking and having to drive back?'

Wood shrugged. 'I'm not a big boozer. I can handle three or four pints over the course of an evening.'

'Are you sure you didn't have more than that, Mark?'

'I had three pints. Four at the most. If that put me over the limit, charge me.'

'Are you sure you didn't have too much to drink and ask Jason if you could stay at his house? Are you sure you didn't walk down—'

'No. I told you. I drove straight home.'

'All right, Mark. If you say so. I do, however, have one more question for you before I leave you to think over our little discussion.'

'What's that?'

'If you gave Jason the beer bottle, and he drank from it on his way home, then why didn't we find *his* fingerprints on it, too?'

TWO

The girl was incredibly beautiful, Banks thought. Part Oriental, she had long, sleek black hair, a golden complexion, a heart-shaped face with perfect, full lips and slightly hooded eyes. She couldn't have been more than nineteen or twenty years old.

At the moment, she was sitting on a chair bathed in the red neon glow, wearing dangling silver earrings and a black lace bra and panties. Nothing else. Her slender legs were parted slightly at the inner thighs so the plump mound of her pudendum was clear to see. She had a tiny tattoo – a butterfly, it looked like – on the inside of her left thigh.

And she was smiling at Banks.

'No,' said Burgess. 'Not that one. She's got no tits.'

Banks smiled to himself and came back to earth. Lovely

as the girl was, he could no more think of sleeping with her than he could with one of Tracy's friends. Though he was quite happy to wander around the red-light district window-shopping with Burgess, he had never intended to buy anything on offer there. Nor, he suspected, did Burgess, when it came right down to it. And after three or four *pils* with *jenever* chasers, it was doubtful whether either of them was even capable of much in that direction anyway.

Amsterdam was especially beautiful at night, Banks thought, with the necklaces of lights strung over the bridges mirrored in the canals, and the glowing, candle-lit interiors of glass-covered 'Lovers' tour boats spilling Mantovani violins as their wake made the reflections shimmer in the dark, oily water. He wished Sandra were with him, and not Burgess. They would wander the canals all night and get hopelessly lost again, just as they had done all those years ago.

At night the red-light district also had much more of an edge than during the day, when it was basically just another stop on a sightseeing tour. Most tourists stayed away at night, but as far as Banks could tell it wasn't any more dangerous than Soho. His wallet was safely zipped up in the inside pocket of his suede jacket, and he had nothing else of value. And if it came to violence, he could handle himself. Though he felt a bit light-headed, he wasn't drunk.

They wandered along, jostled by the crowds, stopping to look into the occasional window and surprised, more often than not, by the beauty and youth of the prostitutes on display. At one point someone bumped into Burgess and Banks had to step in and prevent a fight. Wouldn't go down well, that, he thought: SENIOR SCOTLAND YARD

DETECTIVE ARRESTED FOR ASSAULT IN AMSTER-
DAM'S RED LIGHT DISTRICT. Maybe, he thought with a
smile, he should have let it go on.

After a while the crowds began to feel claustrophobic,
and Banks was thinking of going back to his hotel when
Burgess said, 'Fuck it. You know what, Banks?'

'What?'

'Hate to admit it, but I probably couldn't even get it up
if I tried. Let's have another drink. A nightcap.'

That seemed like a good idea to Banks, who fancied
a sit-down and a smoke. So they nipped into a bar on a
street corner, and Burgess promptly ordered *pils* and
jenever again for both of them.

They chatted about mutual friends on the force over the
loud music – some sort of modern Europop, Banks thought
– and watched the punters come and go: sailors, punks,
prostitutes, the occasional dealer shifting some stuff.
When they'd finished their drinks, Burgess suggested
another round but Banks said they should find somewhere
nearer the hotel while he could still remember his way.

'Fuck the hotel. We can take a taxi anywhere we want,'
Burgess protested.

'I don't know where the nearest taxi rank is. Besides,
it's not far. The walk'll do you good.'

Burgess was truly over the top by now. He insisted on
just one more *jenever*, which he downed in one, and then,
after a bit more grumbling, he agreed to walk and stumbled
out after Banks into the street. They soon got out of the red-
light district and onto Damrak, which was still busy, with
Burgess meandering from side to side bumping into people.
Banks remembered that Dirty Dick's second nickname on
the Met was 'Bambi' on account of the way his physical co-
ordination went all to pieces when he was pissed.

'Got a joke,' Burgess said, nudging Banks in the ribs. 'This bloke goes into a pub with an octopus, and he says to the lads in the band, "I'll bet any of you a tenner my pet here can play any instrument you care to give him."'

They took one of the narrow streets that crossed the canals towards Keizersgracht. Banks found his attention wandering, Burgess's voice in the background. 'So one of the lads brings him a clarinet, and the bloody octopus plays it like he was Benny Goodman. Another bloke brings him a guitar and it's Django fucking Reinhardt.'

Banks fancied a coffee and wondered if he could get one at the hotel. If not, there was bound to be a café nearby. He looked at his watch. Only ten o'clock. Hard to believe they'd done so much in such a short time. A small café would actually be better than the hotel, he decided. He would dump Burgess, pick up his Graham Greene and find a place to sit, read and people-watch for a while.

'Anyway, this goes on for ages, instrument after instrument. Bongos, trombone, saxophone. You name it. Bring him a ukulele, and it's George Formby. The octopus plays them all like a virsh . . . a virsh . . . a virt-you-oh-so. Finally, one of the musicians says he's had enough and he goes out and finds a set of bagpipes. He gives them to the octopus and the octopus looks at them, frowns, turns them every which way then back again. "Looks like you're about to lose your tenner, mate," the musician says. Christ, I need a piss.'

Burgess tottered towards the quayside, hands working at his fly, head half-turned to look back at Banks, a crooked smile on his face. 'So the guy says, "Hang on a minute, mate. When he finds out he can't fuck it, he'll play it." Get it? Argh! Shi-it!'

It happened so quickly that Banks didn't even have a

chance to take half a step. One moment Burgess was pissing a long, noisy arc into the canal, the next, he had toppled forward with an almighty splash, followed by a string of garbled oaths.

10

ONE

By Saturday morning, Susan guessed, Mark Wood must be feeling like one of those mice that has wandered into a humane trap; it can't find its way back out, and it is just beginning to realize that it's in a trap. Even when the mice do get released, she realized, they generally find themselves a long way from home.

'Your solicitor, Mr Varney, rang,' said Gristhorpe. 'He's sorry, he was out last night. Anyway, he's on his way up from Leeds. What can we do for you in the meantime? Coffee? Danish?'

Wood reached forward and helped himself to a pastry. 'I don't have to talk to you until he gets here,' he said.

'True,' said Gristhorpe. 'But remember that caution I read you yesterday? If you don't say anything now, it could go very badly for you later when you try to change your story again.'

'What do you mean?'

'You know what I mean. You're a liar, Mark. You've already given us half a dozen old wives' tales. The more lies you tell, the lower your credibility rating falls. I'm offering you a chance to sweep the board clean, forget the lies and tell me the truth once and for all. What happened after you and Jason Fox left The Jubilee last Saturday night? Your solicitor will only give you the same advice. Tell the truth and I'll turn on the tape recorder.'

'But I've already told you.'

Gristhorpe shook his head. 'You lied. The bottle. The fingerprint, Mark. The fingerprint.'

Susan hoped to hell that Gristhorpe did get somewhere before Giles Varney arrived, because he'd milked that fingerprint for far more than it was worth already. They couldn't be certain it was Wood's, and Gristhorpe had framed his references to it with great care when the tapes were running, saying it was a 'close match' rather than an identical one.

Even 'close match' was pushing it a bit. One of the first things Varney would do was look at the forensic evidence and tell his client just how flimsy it was. Then Wood would clam up. Susan had phoned the lab just a few moments ago, and while they said they might get some results before the morning was out, it certainly wouldn't be within the hour.

Even then, she knew, these would only be preliminary results. But they might, at a pinch, at least be able to determine whether there was human blood on Wood's clothing and whether it matched Jason Fox's *general* type. For more specific and solid evidence, such as DNA analysis, they would have to wait much longer. Even a general grouping, Susan thought, along with an identification and statement from the landlord of The Jubilee, would be more than they had right now. And it might be enough to convince the magistrates to remand Wood for a while longer.

'Nobody touched that bottle but you, Mark,' Gristhorpe went on. 'The fingerprints prove that.'

'What about the bloke I bought if off? Why weren't his fingerprints on it?'

'That's not important, Mark. What matters is that *your*

fingeprints were on it and Jason's weren't. There's no getting away from that, solicitor or no solicitor. If you tell me the truth now, things will go well for you. If you don't . . . well, it'll be a jury you'll have to explain yourself to. And sometimes you can wait months for a trial. Years even.'

'So what? I'd be out on bail and you can't prove anything.'

True, Susan thought.

'Wrong,' Gristhorpe said. 'I don't think you'd get bail, Mark. Not for this. It was a vicious murder. Very nasty indeed.'

'You said it might not be murder.'

'That depends. The way things are looking now, you'd have to *confess* to make us believe it was manslaughter, Mark. You'd have to tell us how it really happened, *convince* us it wasn't murder. Otherwise we've got you on a murder charge. Concealing evidence, not coming forward, lying – it all looks bad to a jury.'

Wood chewed on his lower lip. Susan noticed the crumbs of pastry down the front of his shirt. He was sweating.

'You're a clever lad, aren't you, Mark?'

'What do you mean?'

'You know all about computers and the Internet and all that stuff?'

'So?'

'Now, me, I don't know a hard drive from a hole in the ground, but I *do* know you're lying, and I *do* know that your only way out of this tissue of lies you've got yourself well and truly stuck in is to tell me the truth. Now.'

Finally, Wood licked his lips and said, 'Look, I didn't kill anyone. All right, I was there. I admit it. I was there when it started. But I didn't kill Jason. You've got to believe me.'

'Why do I have to believe you, Mark?' Gristhorpe asked softly.

'Because you do. It's true.'

'Why don't you just tell me what happened?'

'Can I have a smoke?'

'No,' said Gristhorpe. 'After you've told me. If I believe you.' He turned on the dual cassette recorder and made the usual preamble about the time, date and who was present.

Wood sulked and chewed his lip for a moment, then began: 'We left The Jubilee just after closing-time, like I said. I had a bottle with me. Jason didn't. He didn't drink much. In fact, he had a thing about drink and drugs. Into health and fitness, was Jason. Anyway, we took the short cut – at least that's what he told me it was – through some streets across the road, and where the streets ended there's a ginnel that leads between two terrace blocks to some waste ground.'

'The rec,' said Gristhorpe.

'If you say so. I didn't know where the fuck we were.'

'Why were *you* also heading in that direction? I thought you said your car was parked on Market Street.'

'It was. Jason asked me back to his place for a drink. That's all. I know I shouldn't have been drinking so much when I was driving, but . . .' He grinned. 'Anyway, it was like you said yesterday. If I thought I'd had too much, I would've stopped the night.'

'At Jason's house?'

'His parents' house, yes.'

'Carry on.'

'Well, the ginnel looked a bit creepy to me, but Jason

went ahead. Then all of a sudden, they came at us, three of them, from where they'd been waiting at the other end. The rec end.'

'Three of them?'

'That's right. Asian lads. I recognized them. Jason had had a minor run-in with one of them earlier, in the pub.'

'What happened next?'

'I dropped the bottle and scarpered fast. I thought Jason was right behind me, but by the time I looked back he was nowhere in sight.'

'You didn't see what happened to him?'

'No.'

'And you didn't go back?'

'No way.'

'All right. What *did* you do next?'

'I kept going until I got to the car, then I drove home.'

'Why didn't you call the police?'

Wood scratched his neck and averted his eyes. 'I don't know. I suppose I didn't think of it, really. And I'd been drinking.'

'But your friend – sorry, your business associate – was in danger. He could at least expect a severe beating, and all you could do was scarper. Come on, Mark, you can't expect me to believe that. Surely you've got more bottle, a fit lad like you?'

'Believe what you want. I didn't know Jason was in danger, did I? For all I knew he'd run off in a different direction. I'd have been a proper wally to go back there and get my head kicked in.'

'Like Jason.'

'Yeah, well. I didn't know what happened, did I?'

'Did you really believe that Jason had got away too?'

'He could have done, couldn't he?'

'Okay. Now tell me, if you'd done nothing wrong, why didn't you come forward later, after you *knew* Jason had been killed?'

Mark scratched the side of his nose. 'I didn't know till I read it in the papers a couple of days later. By then I thought it would look funny if I came forward.'

Gristhorpe frowned. 'Look funny?'

'Yeah. Suspicious.'

'Why?'

'Because I hadn't said anything at the time. Isn't that something that makes you blokes suspicious?'

Gristhorpe spread his hands. 'Mark, we're simple souls, really. We're just thrilled to bits when someone decides to tell us the truth.'

'Yeah, well . . . I must admit I wasn't too proud of myself.'

'What for? Running away? Deserting your mate when he needed your help?'

Wood looked down at his hands clasped on his lap. 'Yes.'

'Any other reason you kept out of it?'

'Well, if they killed Jason, whether they meant to or not . . . I mean, I've got a wife and kid. Know what I mean? I wouldn't want to put any of us in danger by testifying if there were likely to be . . . you know . . . recriminations.'

'Recriminations? By the three attackers?'

'By them, yes. Or people like them.'

'Other Pakistani youths?'

'Well, yeah. I mean, they stick together, stand up for one another, don't they? I didn't want to put my wife and kid at risk.'

Gristhorpe shook his head slowly. 'This isn't making any sense to me, Mark. You look like a strong lad. Why didn't you stay and fight with Jason, give him a bit of support?'

'I told you, I was thinking of Sheri and Connor. I mean, how would they manage without me, if I got hurt, put in hospital?'

'Same way they'll have to manage without you when you get put in jail, I suppose,' said Gristhorpe. 'You're telling me you ran away out of concern for your wife and child?'

Wood's face reddened. 'I'm not saying that's what I thought straight off. It was instinctive. I didn't have much choice, did I? And like I said, I thought Jason was right behind me. It was three against two.'

'It was three against one after you ran off, Mark. What sort of choice did Jason have? The two of you could have taken those three easily. I'd have put *my* money on you.'

Wood shook his head.

'Are you telling me you're a coward, Mark? Strong-looking lad like you? Bet you lift weights, don't you? Yet when it comes to the crunch you bugger off and leave your mate to die alone.'

'Look, will you shut up about that?' Wood leaned forward and banged his fist down. The metal table rattled. 'The point is that I *didn't do anything*. It doesn't matter whether I ran away. Or why I ran away. All that matters is that I didn't kill Jason!'

'Calm down, Mark.' Gristhorpe raised his hand, palm out. 'What you're saying is true. Technically, at any rate.'

'What do you mean, technically?'

'Well, if what you're telling us is the truth at last—'

'It is.'

'—then you didn't kill Jason in any legal, criminal sense of the word. But I'd say you're morally responsible, wouldn't you? I mean, you could have saved him, but you didn't even try.'

'I told you to stop it with that. You can't prove it would have done any good if I'd stayed. Maybe I'd have got killed, too. What good would that have done anyone? I don't care about fucking *morality*. There's nothing you can charge me with.'

'How about leaving the scene?'

'That's crap, and you know it.'

'Maybe so,' Gristhorpe admitted. 'Nevertheless, deserting your mate the way you did . . . That's something you'll have to live with forever, isn't it, Mark?'

Gristhorpe went to the door and asked the two uniformed officers to come in and take Wood back to his cell, then he and Susan picked up their coffees and left the stuffy interview room for Gristhorpe's office. Up there, in a comfortable chair, with plenty of space and clean air to breathe, Susan felt herself relax.

'What do you think of his story?' Gristhorpe asked.

Susan shook her head. 'He's certainly a bit of a chameleon, isn't he? I hardly know what to think. I'll tell you one thing, though, sir, I think I caught him in at least one more lie.'

Gristhorpe raised his bushy eyebrows. 'Oh, aye? And which lie would that be?'

'Mark told us that when they left The Jubilee, Jason invited him back to his house for a drink, and maybe to stop overnight. Jason wouldn't have done that. His parents insisted he *never* brought his friends to their house.'

'Hmm. Maybe they're the ones who are lying?'

'I don't think so, sir. Why should they? If you think about it, Jason lived most of his life in Leeds. He only came home on weekends occasionally, mostly to play football for United, spend a little time with his parents, get his washing done, maybe visit his granddad. He never told any of them what he was up to in Leeds. It's easy to see why he wouldn't want to mention Neville Motcombe or explain how he got fired from the plastics factory. And that meant he couldn't mention the computer business either. He could have simply lied from the start, told them he'd left the factory of his own free will for something better, but he didn't. Didn't want to face the questions, I suppose. After that, all the lies became interconnected. Who knows what Mark might have let slip to Jason's parents?' She shook her head. 'Unless Mr and Mrs Fox are lying, which I doubt, then it's hardly likely Jason would suddenly decide to take one of his Leeds mates back to the Eastvale house on a whim. Too risky. And there's another thing. Jason didn't keep anything to drink at the Eastvale house. In fact, according to all accounts, he hardly drank at all.'

'Maybe he was intending to give Mark some of his dad's Scotch or something?'

'It's possible, sir,' Susan said. 'But as I say, I doubt it.'

'And maybe he would have bent the rules a bit if his mate had had too much to drink and needed somewhere to sleep it off? That might also explain why he didn't drive down from Market Street to Jason's place.'

'Again, sir,' said Susan, 'it's possible.'

'But you're not convinced. Do you think he did it?'

'I don't know, sir. I just don't trust his story.'

'Make that *stories*. All right, I'll bear your reservations in mind. I can't say I like them much, either.' He shook his head slowly. 'Anyway, we'd better arrange to bring in George Mahmood and his pals again.'

'Even though the forensic evidence supports George's story?'

'Even so.'

'Chief Constable Riddle will love that, sir.'

'The way I see it, Susan, we've got no choice. Mark Wood says he saw three Asian lads attack Jason Fox. Unless we can prove he's lying, it doesn't matter what we think. We *have* to bring them in.'

Susan nodded. 'I know, sir.'

'And give the lab another call. Ask them to get their fingers out. If all they can tell us is there's human blood on the clothes, I'd be satisfied for the time being. Because if we don't get something positive soon, Mark Wood is going to walk out of here in less than an hour and I'm still not happy with a word he's told us.'

TWO

Banks made it down to breakfast with just minutes to spare before the nine o'clock deadline, getting a frosty look from the stout waitress in the hotel lounge for his trouble. First, he helped himself to coffee from a table by the window, then he sat down and looked around. A large 'No Smoking' symbol hung over the lace-curtained window.

He doodled away at yesterday's *Yorkshire Post* crossword while he sipped the rich, black coffee and waited. Eventually, the waitress returned, and with a dour glance, she deposited a glass of orange juice and a plate in front of him. On the plate lay a few slices of cold ham, a chunk of Edam cheese, a hardboiled egg, a couple of rolls and some butter. The Dutch breakfast. Banks tucked in.

He felt fortunate in having only the mildest of hang-overs. The slight ache behind his eyes had been easily vanquished with the aid of two extra-strength paraceta-mols from his traveller's emergency kit, and he suspected that the minor sense-disorientation he felt was still more due to being in a foreign city than to the residual effects of alcohol. Whatever the reason, he felt fine. At least physically.

Only as he sipped the last of his coffee did he realize he hadn't thought of his domestic problems at all last night. Even now, in the morning's light, everything felt so distant, so disembodied. He could hardly believe that Sandra had really gone. Was it a question of not being there to see the tree fall in the woods, or was it what the psychologists of grief called denial? Maybe he would ask his psychologist friend Jenny Fuller when she got back from America. Jenny. Now, if Sandra really had gone, did that make him a free agent? What were the rules? Best not think about it too much. Maybe he would ring home again before going out, just to see if she had come back.

He was the only person sitting in the spotless lounge, with its dark wood smelling of polish, its lace doilies, ticking clock and knick-knacks stuffed in alcoves. As he had hoped, Burgess had either breakfasted earlier or hadn't even got out of bed yet. Banks suspected the latter.

Thank the Lord a passer-by had stopped to help him haul Burgess out of the canal last night. Dirty Dick had stood there dripping the foul water and complaining loudly about the canal-building Dutch engineers – most of whom, according to him, had only one parent, a mother, with whom they had indulged in unspeakable sexual relations.

Banks had finally managed to persuade him to calm down and walk back to the hotel before the police arrived and arrested them.

That, they succeeded in doing, and their arrival had attracted only a puzzled frown from the man on the desk as they traipsed through the lobby. Burgess had trailed dirty canal water as he went, his shoes squelching with every step. He had held his head high, like W.C. Fields trying to pretend he was sober, and walked with as much dignity as he could muster. After that, he had gone straight up to his room on the second floor, and that was the last Banks had seen or heard of him.

After breakfast, Banks went all the way back up to his room and phoned home again. Still nothing. Not that he had expected Sandra to get the *first* train back home, but one lives in hope. He didn't leave a message for himself.

As he trod carefully back down the steep, narrow stairs, tiptoeing over the landing near Burgess's room, he reflected on how he had enjoyed himself last night, how, against all expectations, he had enjoyed his night of freedom. He hadn't done anything he wouldn't normally have done, except perhaps drink too much and get silly, but he had *felt* differently about it.

For the first time, he found himself wondering if Sandra weren't, perhaps, right. Maybe they both did need a little time to manoeuvre and regroup after all the changes of the past few years, especially Sandra's new and more demanding work, and the loss of the children.

Not children now, Banks reminded himself. Grownups. He thought back to that evening in The Pack Horse only a few days ago, when he had watched Tracy with her friends and realized he couldn't cross the lounge to be with her; then he remembered a telephone call he had once made from Weymouth to his son in Portsmouth, realizing then for the first time how distant and independent Brian had become.

Well, there was nothing he could do about it. Any of it. Except to make damn sure he kept in touch with them, helped them the best he could, became a friend and not a meddlesome irritation to them. He wondered how they would take the news of their parents' separation. For that matter, who would tell them? Would Sandra? Should he?

He walked out onto Keizersgracht. The sun glinted on the parked bicycles on the quay and on the canal, making a rainbow out of a pool of oil. Reflections of trees shimmered gently in the ripples of a passing boat.

His mysterious meeting was set for eight o'clock tonight. Well, he thought, in the meantime, on a day like this, tourist map in hand, he could walk the city to his heart's content.

THREE

'You've got to admit, superintendent, that your evidence is pretty thin.'

Giles Varney, Mark Wood's solicitor, sat in Gristhorpe's office later that Saturday morning, staring out over the market square as he talked.

Outside, a sunny morning had brought plenty of tourists to the bustling open market, but now it was clouding over and, to Susan's well-trained nose, getting ready to pour down before the day was out. She had already seen the gusts of wind that would later bring the rain clouds billowing the canvas covers of the market stalls.

Varney wasn't a pinstripe lawyer like the one they'd had to deal with last year in the Deborah Harrison murder. He was casually dressed in jeans and a sports shirt, and his very expensive light wool jacket hung on a stand in the corner. He was young, probably not much older than Susan's own twenty-seven, in good shape, and handsome in a craggy, outdoorsy kind of way. He looked as if he were on his way to go hang-gliding.

There was something Susan didn't like about him, but she couldn't put her finger on it. An arrogance, perhaps, or overconfidence. Whatever it was, it put her on her guard.

'I realize that, Mr Varney,' said Gristhorpe, 'but I'm sure you can see our predicament.'

Varney smiled. 'With all due respect, it's not my job to see your predicament. It's my job to get my client out of jail.'

Supercilious prat, Susan thought.

'And it's our job,' countered Gristhorpe, 'to get to the bottom of Jason Fox's death. Your client admits he was at the scene.'

'Only *prior* to the crime. He couldn't have had any knowledge of what was going to happen.'

'Oh, come off it, Mr Varney. If three kids came at you in a dark alley, I think you'd have a pretty good idea what was about to take place, wouldn't you?'

'That's beside the point. And since when has saving your own skin been regarded as a criminal act? Technically, my client is not guilty of any crime. I expect you to release him immediately. I trust you have the real criminals in custody?'

'On their way. Again,' muttered Gristhorpe.

Varney raised an eyebrow. 'Yes, I understand you had these same chaps in custody once before and let them go?'

'Had to,' Gristhorpe said. 'No evidence. You'd have approved.'

Varney smiled again. 'Not having much luck with evidence these days, are you, superintendent?'

'There *is* one other small matter,' said Gristhorpe.

Varney glanced at his Rolex with irritation. 'Yes?'

'Your client has now become an important witness. I trust you'd have no objection to his remaining here in order to identify the suspects when we've brought them in?'

Varney narrowed his eyes. 'I don't know what you're up to, superintendent. But something smells. Still, how could I have any objection? And I'm sure my client will be more than willing to help sort out this mess for you. As long as he's released from his cell this very minute and treated as a witness rather than as a criminal. He also has to know that he's free to go home whenever he wants.'

Susan breathed a sigh of relief. She knew that Gristhorpe was playing for time, trying to find some reason to keep Mark Wood in Eastvale until the lab came up with something – or with nothing. This way, at least they might get another hour or so out of him, especially if they had him write another formal statement *after* the identification. Maybe a lot more time than that if they put together an identification parade, which would mean importing a few more Asians of similar build to George, Kobir and Asim.

As it turned out, they hardly had to wait at all. Just as Gristhorpe was about to leave the office and take Varney down to release Mark Wood, the phone rang. Gristhorpe excused himself, picked up the receiver, grunted a few times, then beamed at Susan. 'That's the lab,' he said. 'They've found traces of blood between the uppers and the soles of Mark Wood's Doc Martens, and it matches Jason Fox's blood group. I'm afraid, Mr Varney, we've got a few more questions for your client.'

Varney sniffed and sat down again. Gristhorpe picked

up his phone and called downstairs. 'Bert? Have young Mark Wood brought up from the cells, would you? Yes, the interview room.'

Giles Varney insisted on having a private talk with Mark Wood before the interview. Susan waited with Gristhorpe in his office, where they went over all Wood's previous statements, planning their strategy. The rags of cloud had drifted in from Scotland now and the air that blew in through the partially open window was beginning to smell like a wet dog. Susan walked over and watched some of the tourists looking at the sky, then heading for the pubs or for their cars.

'Hungry?' Gristhorpe asked.

'I can wait, sir,' said Susan. 'A few less calories won't do me any harm.'

'Me neither,' grinned Gristhorpe. 'But at my age you don't worry about it so much.'

There was a brisk tap at the door and Giles Varney walked in.

'Finished?' Gristhorpe asked.

Varney nodded. 'For the moment. My client wishes to make a statement.'

'Another one?'

'Look,' said Varney, with a thin smile, 'the blood evidence isn't much to write home about so far, you have to admit, and the fingerprint rubbish is even less. You should be grateful for what you can get.'

'In a few days,' Gristhorpe countered, 'we'll have DNA on the blood. And I suspect your client knows that will prove it's Jason Fox's. At the moment, I think we've got enough to hold him.'

Varney smiled. 'That's what I thought you'd say. What you hear might change your mind.'

'How?'

'After a certain amount of reflection, on the advice of his solicitor, my client is now willing to explain exactly what happened last Saturday night.'

'Right,' said Gristhorpe, getting up and glancing over at Susan. 'Let's get to it then.'

They went into the interview room where Mark Wood sat chewing his fingernails, went through the preliminaries and turned on the tape recorders.

'Right, lad,' said Gristhorpe. 'Mr Varney here says you wish to make a statement. I hope it's the truth this time. Now what have you got to say?'

Wood looked at Varney before opening his mouth. Varney nodded. 'I did it,' Wood said. 'I killed Jason. It was an accident. I didn't mean to.'

'Why don't you tell us what happened, Mark?' Gristhorpe coaxed him. 'Slowly. Take your time.'

Wood looked at Varney, who nodded. 'We were going back to his place, like I said before. Jason was going on about those Pakis back in The Jubilee, what he thought should be done with them. We started arguing. I told him I didn't like that racist crap. Jason was going on about how I was really a racist deep down, just like him, and why didn't I admit it, join the group. I laughed and told him I'd never join that band of wankers in a million years. I was pretty mad by then, so I told him that my wife was from Jamaica. Then he started insulting her, calling her a black bitch and a whore and calling little Connor a half-breed mutant. We were getting near the ginnel now and Jason was really laying into me. Really crude stuff. Like I'd betrayed the white race by marrying a nigger, and shit like that.' Mark paused and rubbed his temples. 'I'd had a few drinks, more than I admitted, and more than Jason at any rate, and sometimes I . . . well, I've got a bit of a temper when I'm pissed. I just lost it, that's all. He came at me. I had the bottle in my hand and I just lashed out with it and hit him.'

'What happened next?'

'He didn't go down. Just put his hand to the side of his head and swore, then he came at me again. He was strong, was Jason, but I reckon I'm probably stronger. Anyway, we started fighting, but I think the head wound had sort of weakened him and I managed to knock him down. I thought about what he'd said about Sheri and Connor and I just saw red. The next thing I knew, he wasn't moving, and I ran off.'

'And left him there?'

'Yes. I didn't know he was fucking dead. How could I? I thought I'd just put him out of action for a while.'

'Why did you empty his pockets?'

'I didn't. Why would I do that?'

'Because the whole thing was a lot more deliberate than you're saying? Because you wanted to make it look like a mugging? You tell me, Mark.'

'Superintendent,' Varney chipped in. 'My client is offering a voluntary statement. If he says he didn't empty the victim's pockets, then I suggest you believe him. He has no reason to lie at this point.'

'I'll be the judge of that, Mr Varney,' said Gristhorpe. He looked at Mark again.

Mark shook his head. 'I don't remember doing that. Honest.'

Gristhorpe sniffed and riffled through some sheets of paper in front of him. 'Mark,' he said finally. 'Jason Fox's injuries included a fractured skull and a ruptured spleen. Yet you say you only kicked him a couple of times?'

'That's how it happened. I admit I lost it, I was in a rage, but I didn't mean to kill him.'

'All right, Mark,' said Gristhorpe. 'Is this the statement you want to make?'

'Yes.'

'My client will be pleading to the charge of manslaughter, superintendent,' Varney said. 'And I think there might be some room for mitigating circumstances.'

'Plenty of time for charges later,' said Gristhorpe. 'Let's just go through the story again first.' Gristhorpe turned to Susan and sighed. 'Susan, go and make sure George Mahmood and his friends are released immediately. The poor sods won't know whether they're coming or going.'

Susan nodded and got up. As she left the interview room, she heard Gristhorpe say wearily, 'Right then, Mark, once more from the top.'

FOUR

Using a street map he'd bought that afternoon, Banks walked to the address Burgess had given him. Though he felt silly doing it, he had looked over his shoulder once in a while and taken a very circuitous route.

It was another brown café, this one on a street corner by Sarphatipark. The park itself was a dark rectangle wedged between blocks of tenements. It looked familiar. He was sure he had seen it before, with Sandra. It reminded him of the kind of square you'd find in Bloomsbury or Edinburgh. The café itself wasn't the kind of place listed in the tourist guides. The wood was dark and stained with years of tobacco smoke, and most of the

tables were scratched and blackened here and there where
cigarettes had been left to burn.

One or two locals sitting at the bar, working men by the
look of their clothes, turned and glanced at Banks as he
walked in and found a table in the far corner. One of them
said something to the man behind the bar, who shrugged
and laughed, then they paid him no further attention. Only
a few tables were taken, and only one of those by a young
man and a woman. It was pretty much of a men's pub by
the look of it. Accordion music was playing quietly behind
the bar. Welcome to hell.

The table wobbled. Banks took a beermat and placed it
under one leg. That helped. Not wanting a repeat of last
night, he decided he was going to stick with beer, and not
even drink many of those. That *jenever* could be deadly.
He ordered an Amstel, lit a cigarette and settled down to
wait, back to the wall, eyes on the door. After a day spent
walking around the city, stopping only at a café now and
then for a coffee and a cigarette, Banks was also glad of the
chance to rest his legs.

As he waited, he reflected on the curious and unsettling
experience he had had that afternoon. One of the places
he'd walked by was a canalside coffee house he remembered visiting with Sandra all those years ago. The kind of
place that also sold hash and grass. It didn't seem to have
changed at all. At first he had thought it couldn't possibly
be the same one, but it was. Curious, he had turned back
and wandered inside.

At the back, where it was darker, piles of cushions lay
scattered on the floor. You could lie back, smoke your
joint, look at the posters on the wall and listen to the
music. He had noticed a young couple there, in the far
corner, and for one spine-tingling moment, in the dim

light, he had felt he was looking down on himself and Sandra when they were young. And he hadn't even smoked any hash.

Shaken, he had walked out into the sunshine and gone on his way. It had been a good five or ten minutes before he could get rid of the spooky feeling. He and Sandra had smoked hash there with some Americans, he remembered. Dylan's *Blonde on Blonde* album had been playing, the long 'Sad-eyed Lady of the Lowlands'. Later, they had made love in their sleeping-bag in the Vondelpark, hidden away from other nighthawks by some bushes. Memories. Would he never escape them?

Just as he was lighting another cigarette, someone walked through the door. And for the second time that day Banks felt gobsmacked.

If he wasn't mistaken, it was the man he had last seen in Neville Motcombe's house: Rupert Francis, the tall, gangly woodworker.

He obviously noticed Banks's surprise. 'You can close your mouth now, sir,' he said. 'It really is me.'

Banks shook his head slowly. 'So I see. Rupert Francis, right? And what's with the "sir"?'

'Actually, I'm DS Craig McKeracher, sir,' he said, shaking hands. 'That makes you my senior officer. Pleasure to make your acquaintance.' He smiled sheepishly and sat down. 'I'm sorry about all the cloak-and-dagger stuff, sir, but if they found out who I really am they'd kill me.'

Banks shook hands and collected his thoughts. The waiter came over and Craig ordered a beer.

'I think we can drop the "sir",' said Banks.

Craig nodded. 'If you like. I must admit you gave me the shock of my bloody life when I saw you at Nev's place the other day. I thought the game was up right there and then.'

'You didn't have to show yourself.'

'I know. But I heard voices, so I thought up an excuse and came up to see what was going on. Part of my brief, after all, to keep my eyes and ears open. Just as well you'd never seen me before.'

'How long have you been undercover there?'

'About five months. Nev trusts me. "Rupert Francis" has an impeccable background with the neo-Nazi movement. BNP, fringe groups, the whole kit and caboodle. He's even been done on firearms and explosives charges. In addition to that, he's got a long and varied criminal record. Assault, burglary, drugs. You name it. That's something Nev also trusts.'

'How would he know about your record?'

Craig sipped some beer from the bottle before answering. His Adam's apple bobbed in his skinny throat. 'He's got a man on the inside somewhere. West Yorkshire. Some PC or DC sympathetic to the cause. Believe me, there are plenty of blokes on the Job who'd have no axe to grind with Neville Motcombe's ideas. However he does it, he has no problem checking out criminal records.'

'So it's you who wants me here, not Burgess?'

'Yes. After I'd seen you, I got in touch with Dirty – with Superintendent Burgess soon as I could. He's my controller, but with things getting so hot lately we've not had the chance for much more than minimal telephone contact. And you've got to be really careful over the phone. Anyway, I told him I wanted to talk to you as soon as possible, but I didn't want to risk doing it locally. Then I thought this would be a perfect opportunity. Know why I'm here?'

'Haven't a clue,' said Banks.

'I'm helping to organize an international conference on race and IQ, if you can swallow that. Anyway, Superintendent Burgess said not to worry, he'd make the arrangements.' Craig grinned. 'In fact, he said he'd enjoy it. You should have heard him when I told him you'd walked right into Nev's front room. I gather the two of you know each other? You and the super, that is?'

Banks stubbed out his cigarette and sipped some beer. 'You could say that.'

'He likes you. Honest, he does. Respects you. That's what he told me. I reckon he thinks you're a bit naïve, but he was glad to hear it was you on the Fox case and not someone else.'

'Maybe we should start a mutual admiration society.'

Craig laughed.

'Anyway,' Banks asked, 'why all this interest in the Albion League?'

'Because of Neville Motcombe and his contacts with known international terrorists. When he left the BNP and decided to start his own fringe group, we thought it'd be a good idea to keep an eye on him.'

Banks sipped some Amstel. 'And did he live up to your expectations?'

'In some ways, yes. In others, he exceeded them. The Albion League's nowhere near as politically active as we thought it would be. As Combat 18 are, for example. I'm not saying there haven't been violent incidents, there have, and I've even heard talk of a pipe bomb to sabotage the mosque opening. Now we know about that possibility, we can tighten security and make sure it doesn't happen. But mostly, as far as revolutionary action is concerned, they've been pretty tame so far. More like a fucking boys' club than anything else.'

'I wondered about that. What is it with Motcombe and these young boys? Is he gay or something?'

The waiter came over and they ordered two more beers. When he had gone again, Craig said, 'No. No, Nev's not gay. I'll confess I had my own suspicions when I first met him and he invited me down the cellar to help with his woodwork. Like, come and see my etchings. But he's not. If anything, I'd say he was asexual. His wife left him. If you ask me it was because he spent more time licking envelopes than licking her. He's that kind of person. Power is more important to him than romantic or sexual relationships. The youth thing is just part of his shtick. He actually used to be involved in church groups, youth clubs, that sort of thing. He was even a Boys' Brigade leader at one time. Always did like paramilitary organizations and uniforms.'

'What happened?'

'He got kicked out for trying to recruit kids to the BNP. Anyway, a big part of his thing is the emphasis on the old British values and virtues: war games in the Pennines, crafts, camping, hiking, survival techniques, a healthy mind and healthy body. That sort of thing.'

'Baden-Powell with swastikas?'

'If you like. He even throws in a bit of environmentalist stuff to hook the greenies. You know – preserve the traditional English village against pollution, that sort of thing. Thing is, to him pollution isn't only a matter of destroying the ozone layer and the rain forests or what have you, it includes most non-Aryan racial groups. Perhaps Nev's only saving grace as a human being is that his overriding trait is greed.'

'What do you mean?'

Craig rubbed his cheek and frowned. 'Just an observation of mine. Haven't you sometimes thought that people's vices are often the only things that make them interesting? As a pure neo-Nazi, Nev would simply be a bore. A sick and dangerous bore, perhaps, but a bore nonetheless. Predictable. It's the other stuff that's interesting, the stuff we didn't expect.'

'Burgess mentioned drugs. Is that right?'

Craig nodded, finished his beer and slid the bottle aside. 'Fancy walking?'

'Why not.'

They paid their bill and walked outside. There were still plenty of people on the streets, especially along Albert Cuypstraat, where they walked through the debris of that afternoon's market – wilted lettuce leaves, a squashed tomato, chicken bones, a piece of cardboard that said f4.50 on it. The smell of fish still infused the evening air. Now Banks knew why Sarphatipark had felt so familiar. He and Sandra had been there; they had spent an hour or two one afternoon wandering through the market stalls.

'Like I said,' Craig went on, 'Nev got to trust me, take me into his confidence. I think he liked the fact that according to my criminal record, I didn't mind doing anything as long as it was profitable. And it didn't take me long to work out that Nev likes profit more than anything.'

'So it's money with him, not politics?'

'Mmm, not entirely. Maybe it's both at the same time, if he can get it that way. If not, then I'd say money comes out distinctly on top. Like I said, Nev's a greedy bastard. Greedy for power and greedy for cash. First thing I found out when I got involved was that he was organizing some of his younger and thicker recruits into groups of thieves, turning their gains over to him, of course, for the good of the League.'

'And they did this?'

Craig snorted. 'Sure they did. Let's face it, most of these kids are pretty dense. Five or six of them would go into a shop, say, and as soon as—'

'Steaming?'

'You know about it?'

'I've heard the term. And I know it's been a problem for West Yorkshire CID recently. Along with muggings at cash dispensers. I didn't know Motcombe was behind it.'

'Some of it. I'm sure there are plenty of freelancers out there, too. But what Nev does is, he takes these kids' anger and channels it. He gives them someone to hate. He gives their rage some structure and provides them with real targets rather than nebulous ones. So they end up believing they're committing theft, assault and vandalism for a good cause. Isn't that what terrorism is basically all about, anyway? Add a few *olde worlde* patriotic values, a lot of guff about the "true English homeland" and a bit of green to the mix and it makes them feel like downright responsible and virtuous citizens, the only ones who really care about their country.'

'You make it sound easy.'

They turned right, towards the neo-Gothic mass of the Rijksmuseum, dark and solid against the night sky. Streetlights cast long shadows. A breeze stirred, wafting a smell of decay from the canal. Banks could hear music in the distance, see TV screens flickering through people's curtains.

Craig shrugged. 'It's not as hard as you think, that's the sad thing. Recruiting isn't, anyway. Take rock concerts, for example. Invitation only. Makes people feel privileged and exclusive right off the bat. Then the white-power bands get the kids all worked up with their rhythm and energy, and someone like me moves in to bring the message home. And they target schools, particularly schools that have a large number of immigrant pupils. They hang around outside in the street and pass out leaflets, then they hold meetings in different venues. They also hang out in the coffee bars where some of the kids go on their way home. You know, start chatting, give them a sympathetic shoulder for their problems with Ali or Winston. They get a surprising number of converts that way.'

'Some of whom Motcombe organizes into gangs of thieves?'

'Some, yes. But not all.' He laughed. 'One or two of the lads in the know have nicknamed him Fagin.'

Banks raised his eyebrows. '"You've got to pick a pocket or two,"' he sang, a passable imitation of Ron Moody in *Oliver*. 'I imagine he'd just love that.'

Craig smiled. 'I'll bet. Thing is, though, there's a lot of money to be made, one way or another. Steaming and mugging are just part of the bigger picture. These right-wing political groups finance themselves in any number of ways. Some deal in arms and explosives, for example. Then there's the rock angle. These bands record CDs. That means people produce, record, manufacture and distribute them. That can be big business. And where there's rock, there's drugs. There's a lot of money to be made out of that.'

'Motcombe has an arrest for receiving, doesn't he?'

'Yes. His one big mistake. A couple of his lads broke into a Curry's and ran off with a few videos and stereos under their arms. They didn't tell Nev where they'd got the stuff from. Anyway, since then, it's been cash only. And he skims off the top, too. I've seen him stuff the notes into his own pocket.' Craig shook his head. 'If there's one thing worse than a Nazi, it's a bent Nazi.'

'How does Jason Fox fit in? Was he one of the thieves?'

Craig paused and leaned on a bridge as they crossed to Hobbemakade, looking down at the reflections of the lights. Banks stood beside him and lit a cigarette. It was quiet now apart from a few cars and the whir of an occasional bicycle.

'No, Jason never went out steaming. Not his style. Too smart. Jason was a thinker. He was good at recruiting, at propaganda in general. The thing about Jason was, he was basically an honest kid. A straight, dedicated Nazi.'

'One of those boring fascists, without vices?'

Craig laughed. 'Almost. Not exactly boring, though. In some ways he was naïve in his sincerity, and that made him almost likeable. *Almost.* But he was also more dedicated, more driven, than most of the others. Frightening. See, when you come down to it, Nev's not much more than a petty crook with delusions of grandeur. Jason, on the other hand, was the genuine article. Real dyed-in-the-wool neo-Nazi. Probably even read *Mein Kampf.*'

'I thought even Hitler's most fanatical followers couldn't get through that.'

Craig laughed. 'True.'

'Have you any ideas as to why Jason was killed? Was he involved in this drug deal?'

They moved away from the bridge and headed down the street. Banks flicked his cigarette end in the water, immediately feeling guilty of pollution.

'No,' Craig said. 'Not at all. Jason was violently anti-drug. In fact, if you ask me, that's where you might want to start looking for your motive. Because he certainly knew about it.'

FIVE

'Another bottle of wine?'

'I shouldn't,' said Susan, placing her hand over her half-filled glass.

'Why not? You're not driving.'

'True.'

'And you've just wrapped up a case. You should be celebrating.'

'All right, all right, you silver-tongued devil. Go ahead.'

Gavin grinned, called the waiter and ordered a second bottle of Chablis. Susan felt her heart give a slight lurch the way it did when she first jumped The Strid at Bolton Abbey as a teenager. It happened the moment her feet left the ground and she found herself hurtling through space over the deep, rushing waters, because that was the moment she had committed herself to jumping, despite all the warnings. So what had she committed herself to by agreeing to a second bottle of wine?

She took another mouthful of filo pastry stuffed with Brie, walnuts and cranberries, and washed it down with the wine she had left in her glass. It hadn't even been there long enough to get lukewarm. Already, she was beginning to feel a little light-headed – but in a pleasant way, as if a great burden had been lifted from her.

They were in a new bistro on Castle Walk, looking west over the formal gardens and the river. A high moon silvered the swirling current of water far below and frosted the tips of the leaves on the trees. The restaurant itself was one of those hushed places where everyone seemed to be whispering, and food and drink suddenly appeared out of the silence as if by magic. White tablecloths. A floating candle in a glass jar on every table. It was also, she thought, far too expensive for a couple of mere DCs. Still, you had to push the boat out once in a while, didn't you, she told herself, just to see how far it would float.

She stole a glance at Gavin, busy finishing his venison. He caught her looking and smiled. She blushed. He really did have lovely brown eyes, she thought, and a nice mouth.

'So how does it feel?' Gavin asked, putting his knife and fork down. 'The success? I understand it was largely due to your initiative?'

'Oh, not really,' Susan said. 'It was teamwork.'

'How modest of you,' he teased. 'But seriously, Susan. It was you who found the killer's name. What was it . . . Mark something or other?'

'Mark Wood. Yes, but Superintendent Gristhorpe got him to confess.'

'I'd still say you get a big gold star for this one.'

Susan smiled. The waiter appeared with their wine, gave Gavin a sip to test, then poured for both of them and placed it in the ice bucket. Good God, Susan thought, an *ice* bucket. In Yorkshire! *What am I doing here? I must be mad.* She had finished her food now and concentrated on the wine while she studied the dessert menu. Sweets. Her weakness. Why she was a few inches too thick around the hips and thighs. But she didn't think she could resist nutty toffee pie. And she didn't.

'Chief Constable Riddle's pretty damn chuffed,' Gavin said later as they tucked into their desserts and coffee. 'Sunday or not, it's my guess he'll be down your neck of the woods again tomorrow dishing out trophies and giving a press statement. As far as he's concerned, this solution has gone a long way towards diffusing racial tensions.'

'Well, he was certainly keen to get everything signed, sealed and delivered this afternoon.'

'I'll tell you something else. Golden boy isn't exactly top of the pops as far as the CC is concerned.'

'What's new?' Susan said. 'And I told you, I wish you'd stop calling him that.'

'Where is he, by the way?' Gavin went on. 'Rumour has it he hasn't been much in evidence the last couple of days. Not like him to miss being in at the kill, is it?'

'He's taken some time off.'

'Pretty inconsiderate time to do that, isn't it?'

'I'm sure he has his reasons.' Susan pushed her empty dessert plate aside. 'Mmm. That pie was divine.'

'How very mysterious,' Gavin said. 'Is he often like that?'

'Sometimes. He can be a bit enigmatic when he wants, can the DCI. Anyway, I'm glad Jimmy Riddle's happy, but this just isn't the sort of solution that makes you feel exactly wonderful, you know.'

'Why not?'

'I can't help feeling a bit sorry for Mark Wood.'

'Sorry? I thought he was supposed to have kicked his mate to death?'

'Yes, I know.'

'Isn't that about as vicious as it gets?'

'I suppose so. But he *was* provoked. Anyway, I don't mean that. It's not so much *him* I feel sorry for, it's his family. He has a young wife and a baby. Poor devils. I can't help but wonder how they're going to manage without him.'

'He should have thought of that before he killed Jason Fox, shouldn't he?'

Susan drank some more wine. It tasted thin and acidic

after the sweetness of her dessert. 'I know,' she said. 'But you should have seen where they live, Gavin. It's a dump. Thin walls, peeling wallpaper, damp, cramped living-space. And it's a dangerous neighbourhood, especially for a young woman alone with her baby. Gangs, drugs . . . And it was partly because he was defending his wife, her race, that he ended up killing Jason.'

Gavin shook his head. 'I never took you for a bleeding heart, Susan. You can't allow yourself to start getting sentimental. It'll make you soft. He's a villain and you've done your job. Now let's just hope the court puts him away where he belongs. Poverty's no excuse. Plenty of people have it tough and they don't go around booting their pals to death. My dad was a miner, and more often out of work than in. But that doesn't give me an excuse to go around acting like a yob. If you want anything in this life, you go out and get it, you don't idle around moaning about what a bad hand you've been dealt.'

'I suppose so,' Susan said. She refilled her wine glass and smiled. 'Anyway, enough of that. Cheers.'

They clinked glasses.

'Cheers,' Gavin said. 'To success.'

'To success,' Susan echoed.

'Why don't we pay the bill and go,' Gavin said, leaning forward. His hand touched hers. She felt the tingle right down to her toes. 'I'll walk you home.'

Susan looked at him for a moment. Those soft, sexy brown eyes. Long lashes he had, too. 'All right,' she said, her hand turning to clasp his. 'Yes. I'd like that.'

SIX

No more than a few hundred miles away, over the North Sea, Banks and Craig McKeracher had passed the Rijksmuseum and were walking down the quiet streets towards Prinsengracht.

'Basically,' Craig was busy explaining, 'Nev met this right-wing loony in Turkey who had a load of heroin he wanted to shift, and he wondered if Nev could help. Nev couldn't, of course. He knows bugger all about dealing drugs. Doesn't know a fucking joint from a tab of acid. But he's always one to leave the door a little ajar, so he tells this bloke, hang on a while, let me see what I can do. Now there's only two people he knows with any brains who have ever had anything to do with drugs. One of them's yours truly, and the other's Mark Wood.'

Banks paused. 'Wait a minute. Motcombe knew Mark Wood?'

'Yes.'

'This is Jason's business partner?'

Craig snorted. 'Some partnership that'd be. There wasn't a lot of love lost between them, as far as I could see.'

'Is Mark a member of the League?'

Craig shook his head. 'No, he wouldn't have anything to do with them.'

'Then how . . .?'

'Mark and Jason met on this computer course, and they got on well enough at first. They were both good at it, too. Anyway, when they finished, Mark couldn't get a job. I understand he's got a wife and kid and lives in a shithole out Castleford way, so he was pretty desperate by then.

Nev finances Jason in the computer business – only because he knows it's something he'll be able to use to his advantage down the line – and Jason decides he'll take Mark on as partner, seeing as he came top of the class. Naturally, because Nev's putting money into the business, he's curious about Mark, so Jason arranges a meeting. I wasn't there, but I gather Nev had got details of his record by then and quizzed him about the drug arrest.'

'What were the details?'

'Mark used to be a roadie for a Leeds band, a mixed-race band, like UB40, and one of the Jamaicans, a Chapeltown bloke, was into dealing in a big way. Used the group van, and got Mark involved. They got caught. End of story. So Nev finds out that Mark has some contacts in Chapeltown who might know someone who'll be interested if the price is right.'

'This wouldn't involve a bloke called Devon, would it?'

Craig raised his eyebrows. 'Yeah. How'd you know about him?'

'Same source I heard about the steaming. Just a lucky guess. Carry on.'

'Right, well, like I said, living in this shithole with his wife and kid, Mark was definitely interested in making money, even though he didn't give a flying fuck for Nev's politics. But he made a perfect go-between. Devon and his mates probably wouldn't be any too happy if they knew their supplier was a fascist bastard who thought they should all be sent home to rot in the sun, at best. But Mark got on with the black community okay, and they seemed to accept him. And he wasn't a member of the League.'

Banks nodded. 'Okay. That makes sense.'

They spotted a vendor at the street corner, and as neither had eaten that evening, they bought bags of chips with mayonnaise, something Banks would never think of eating back in Eastvale. Here, they tasted wonderful.

'But how did Jason square all this with his politics?' Banks asked as they walked on. 'You said he was dedicated. Straight.'

'He didn't. That's the point. I'll get to it in a minute. See, in general, neo-Nazis aren't only racist, they're also anti-drug, same way they're anti-gay.'

'Even though many of Hitler's lot were homosexuals or junkies?'

Craig laughed. 'You can't expect logic or consistency from these buggers. I'll give Nev his due, though. Normally, he could make raping and murdering old ladies sound like a good thing to do for the cause. A true politician. A week or so later, when Mark's out of the way, he has another meeting with just me and Jason, and he tells us about this idea he came up with after travelling in America and talking to fellow strugglers there. What he thinks is that by providing a steady and cheap supply of heroin, you weaken and destroy the fabric of the black community, making them much poorer and more vulnerable when the big day comes, blah blah blah. It's his version of the smallpox blankets the whites gave the American Indians. Or, more recently, that newspaper story about the CIA financing the crack business in south-central Los Angeles. As a bonus, the blacks become complicit in their own destruction. That's the kind of irony Nev can't resist. And all the while he makes a tidy profit out of it, too. Couldn't be better.'

'Jason fell for this crap?'

Craig kicked at an empty cigarette packet in the street. 'Ah, not exactly. There's the rub. Motcombe needed one of us, someone *inside* the League, just to keep an eye on

Mark and make sure everything was going tickety-boo. He didn't fully trust Mark. Jason, being Mark's partner, seemed a natural choice. But Jason wasn't interested in profit; he'd have starved for the cause. Nev seriously underestimated his right-hand man's dedication. Jason didn't fall for all that rubbish about weakening the community from within. In fact, he saw the scheme for exactly what it was – a money-making venture on Nev's part. Apparently, he already suspected Nev of skimming for his own gain, and there was quite a little power struggle brewing between them. They argued. Jason said he knew the organization needed money, but this just wouldn't work, that there was no way they could limit the sale to blacks, that it would spread to the white community too and sap their spirit as well. He said drugs were a moral evil and a pure Aryan would have nothing to do with them. He also said heroin wouldn't encourage the immigrants to go back home, which is what the organization was supposed to be all about, and that they'd be better concentrating on making the buggers feel uncomfortable and unwelcome than plying them with opiates.'

'Impressive,' said Banks. 'But surely Motcombe must have suspected he'd react that way? Why did he even tell Jason in the first place?'

'I think Nev really did miscalculate the intensity of Jason's reaction. It would also have been pretty hard to keep anything like that from him. Nev fell in love with what he thought was his impeccable rhetoric, and he figured the best thing was to bring Jason in right from the start. No way, he thought, could anyone not see the absolute perfection of his logic and irony. At that point also, remember, he'd no idea how violently anti-drugs Jason was. It had simply never come up before.' Craig shook his head. 'I was there. Nev was absolutely stunned at Jason's negative reaction.'

'What happened next?'

'They argued. Nev couldn't convince him. In the end he said he'd abandon the idea.'

'But he didn't?'

'No way. Too much money in it. He just cut Jason out.'

'But Jason knew?'

'I think by then he was pretty certain Nev wouldn't give up potential profits that easily, yes.'

'Jason knew about the proposed drug deal and Motcombe was worried he'd go to the police.'

'That was always a possibility, yes. But even more of a threat was that he'd talk to other ranking neo-Nazis. Nev's peers and colleagues. Some of whom felt exactly the way Jason did about drugs. Think about it. If Jason could convince them Nev was nothing but a petty thief and a drug dealer, then Nev would never be able to hold his head up in the movement again. He'd be ostracized. Hypocrisy reigns in the far right every bit as much as it does in most other places. There's another thing, too.'

'What's that?'

'Jason had charisma. He was popular. Nev was coming to see him as a rival for power – and power meant money for Nev. So Nev was getting paranoid about Jason. It was Jason who made first contact with most of our members. It was Jason they went to when they had problems with the ideology of beating the crap out of some poor black or Asian kid. Jason who set them straight.'

'So Jason was making inroads on Motcombe's position?'

'Exactly.'

Banks nodded. He found a rubbish bin and dropped his

empty chip packet in it. They were near Keizersgracht now, not too far from the hotel.

'What was your role in all this?'

'Like I said, Nev wanted someone close, someone in the League to keep tabs on Mark. Obviously Jason wasn't going to do it, so I was the next logical choice. I hadn't been around as long as Jason, but I *did* have an impressive criminal record, including drugs charges.'

'So what it comes down to is that Motcombe had a pretty good motive for wanting Jason out of the way.'

Craig nodded. 'Exactly. That's why I needed to talk to you. To fill you in on it all. I don't know who killed Jason. I wasn't privy to that. Nev likes to keep his left hand and his right hand quite independent from one another. But I do know the background.'

They paused at a bridge. A young couple stood holding hands and looking into the reflections of lights in the water.

'Where do you want me to go with this?' Banks asked.

'Wherever it takes you. I didn't have you brought here to tell you to lay off, if that's what you think. And it's not a competition, or a race. Whatever we can get Motcombe for is fine with me. And with Superintendent Burgess. That's why he agreed to arrange this meeting. All I'm asking is that you hold off moving against Nev until you've got something you're certain will put him away for a long time.' He grinned. 'Oh, and I'd appreciate it if you don't blow my cover. I value my life, and I might need to stick around a while longer to see what he gets up to next.'

'When is this drug deal supposed to take place?'

'The heroin's already on its way.'

They reached the door of Banks's hotel. He thought for a moment, then said, 'All right.'

'Appreciate it, sir.'

'Coming in?'

'No. Got to go. I'm staying somewhere else.'

'Take care, then.'

'I will. Believe me.'

They shook hands, and Craig wandered off along the canal. Banks looked up at the hotel's façade. It was still early. He wasn't tired and didn't fancy sitting in a cramped room watching Dutch television. He also had a lot to think about. Zipping up his jacket against the chill, he wandered off in search of a quiet bar.

SEVEN

Susan put her hands behind her head, rested back on the pillow and sighed.

'Was that a sigh of contentment,' Gavin asked, 'or disappointment?'

She laughed and nudged him gently. 'You should know. You had something to do with it.'

'*I* did? Little old me?'

And to think that not more than an hour ago she had cold feet. When they had got back to her flat, she had asked Gavin in and one thing led to another, as she had known and hoped it would. She realized right from the start, though, that she had made her mind up when she agreed to the second bottle of wine. Committed. Like jumping The Strid. But when the crucial decision came out into the open, there was an embarrassing moment when it turned out that neither of them had any protection. Well, it was good in a way, Susan realized. It meant that he wouldn't think she was a slut, and she didn't think he had taken her out to dinner in the expectation of ending up in her bed. But it was bloody awkward, nonetheless.

Luckily, there was an all-night chemist's on York Road, not more than a couple of hundred yards away, and Gavin threw on his jacket and set off. While he was gone, Susan started to get nervous and have second thoughts. Instead of giving in to them, she busied herself tidying up the place, especially the bedroom, throwing clean sheets on the bed, and when he came back she found, after a little kissing and caressing, that her resolve was just as strong as before.

And now, as she basked in the afterglow, she was glad she had made the decision. One of Chopin's piano concertos – she didn't know which one – played softly from the living-room.

'Well, I couldn't think of a better way to celebrate,' said Gavin. His hand brushed Susan's thigh and started sliding up over her stomach.

'Mmm. Me neither.'

'And I'll tell you something else,' he whispered in her ear. 'I'll bet we're having a better victory celebration than anyone. Even golden boy, wherever he is.'

Something about the mention of Banks's name gave Susan a moment of uneasiness, the way she had felt naked talking on the telephone to him when the Jason Fox case started. But it passed. She smiled and stretched, feeling a little sleepy from the wine and sex. 'Oh, he's probably not having such a bad time,' she said. 'He does all right.'

'What makes you think that? You don't know where he is or what he's doing.'

'I do know where he is.'

Gavin's hand rested on her breast. He had soft hands, like silk brushing her warm skin. She felt her nipple harden. 'You know?' His hand moved again, downwards.

Susan gave a little gasp. 'Yes. Amsterdam. He's gone to Amsterdam.'

'Lucky devil,' said Gavin. Then he did something with his hand that made Susan realize she wasn't all that sleepy after all.

11

ONE

Finding Jimmy Riddle wearing out the carpet back at Eastvale Divisional HQ had about the same effect on Banks's stomach as the dodgy landing.

The plane had banked sharply and plunged into thick cloud. By the time Banks had seen the runway, they were practically on it, still at an awkward angle, and for one stomach-lurching moment he had been certain the pilot was coming in too steeply and would crash the plane, wing first. But it levelled out in time, and apart from a little more bouncing and swaying than usual, the landing had gone without incident.

And now, an hour and a half later, his stomach was going through the same cartwheels again.

It was late afternoon. Banks's flight had been delayed and he hadn't arrived at Leeds and Bradford until three o'clock; he hadn't even eaten lunch. Not much chance of a bite now. He hadn't intended calling at the station, but when he neared Eastvale, he couldn't face going back to the empty house immediately.

'Ah, Chief Inspector Banks,' said Riddle. 'I've been waiting for you. Nice of you to drop by.'

'Sorry, sir,' Banks mumbled, as Riddle followed him into his office.

Riddle tugged his trousers up at the knees to preserve

the creases and sat on the edge of the desk, looking down on Banks. Banks supposed he took that position because he thought it gave him a psychological edge. Little did he know.

'And take the bloody smirk off your face, man,' Riddle said. 'Have you any idea how much trouble you're in?'

'Trouble, sir?'

'Yes, Banks. Serious trouble this time. You bugger off for a weekend in Amsterdam in the middle of a major investigation and leave your underlings to do your work for you. And it so happens that while you're away, they solve the case.' He smiled. 'I must admit, that does give me more than a little satisfaction.'

'With due respect, sir—'

'With due *nothing*, Banks.' Riddle craned his neck forward. The tendons tautened and the skin around his throat flushed. 'What the bloody hell did you think you were up to? Can you answer me that?'

Banks had tried to prepare himself for a moment like this. If truth be told, though, he had expected it to come from Gristhorpe, not Riddle. And there was a big difference. It wasn't that he didn't trust Riddle. The man was squeaky clean. It wasn't even that he suspected Riddle of 'fraternizing with fascists'. That had only been a joke. A bad one, at that. But whereas Gristhorpe would accept Banks's explanation at face value and let things lie, Riddle was too much of an interfering bastard to do that.

If Banks told him what he had discovered from Craig McKeracher, Riddle would be on the phone to his cronies all over the place in a matter of moments. He wouldn't want to be left out. If there were any chance of glory to result from the situation, he would want his due share. And one wrong telephone call could have serious consequences for Craig. On the other hand, if Riddle could see nothing to be gained, then he would order Banks to pass on what he knew and leave it to West Yorkshire. Riddle hadn't got to be chief constable by pursuing the truth against all odds. The problem was, someone in West Yorkshire had already been leaking information to Motcombe.

A dilemma, then.

And Banks also knew that, as far as Riddle was concerned, the case was solved. Most satisfactorily solved.

So it was with carefully measured tones that he answered the question, aware even as he did so that it just wouldn't wash. 'I can't tell you everything, sir,' he said. 'At least, not just yet. It's very delicate. But I can assure you my trip was directly related to the Jason Fox case.'

Riddle shook his head. 'Delicate? Too delicate for the likes of me? No, Banks. That won't do. I've already told you, the Jason Fox case was solved in your absence.'

'I know, sir. I read about it in the morning paper.' Banks had picked up a copy of *The Independent* at Schiphol Airport and had seen a full report on the arrest and confession of Mark Wood for the murder of Jason Fox. Including a quote from Riddle to the effect that 'Fox was killed by a friend of his in a dispute after several drinks. While alcohol was certainly a factor, race was not, I am very pleased to say.' Banks didn't believe it for a moment. 'But I'm not sure that's how it happened,' he went on.

'Oh,' said Riddle. 'You're not sure that's how it happened, aren't you? Maybe if you'd been here doing your job you'd have a better idea about what's going on. Well, let me tell you Banks, that is *exactly* how it happened. Your fellow officers got a confession out of Mark Wood. While you were off cruising the red-light district, no doubt.'

Banks had to admit, that did hit a little too close to home. 'In all fairness, sir—'

Riddle stood up and went to lean on the filing cabinet, checking for dust first. 'Don't talk to me about fairness, Banks. I've been as fair with you as I can be. I've given you more latitude, more freedom to tilt at your own various windmills than I've allowed any man under my direct command. And what have you done with that freedom? You've abused it, that's what you've done. Day trips to Leeds to buy classical records and meet your bit on the side, and now a weekend in Amsterdam in the middle of a major investigation. What do you have to say?'

'If you'll allow me to get a word in, sir,' Banks said calmly. 'In the first place, my trip was *entirely* case related, and in the second case you haven't *solved* the Jason Fox case.'

Riddle's pate went on red alert. 'And I'm telling you the case is solved. *Telling* you, Banks.'

'But—'

'And who paid for this trip to Amsterdam, might I ask?'

Shit. If Banks told him it was the Met, Riddle either wouldn't believe him, or he'd be on the phone trying to find out exactly who was behind it, setting off alarms like a mad cow walking through a Cambodian minefield. Besides, Dirty Dick Burgess, the only one who could really vouch for him apart from Craig, was on holiday 'somewhere tropical'.

'I can't say, sir,' he said.

'I trust you didn't pay for it yourself, then, out of your own pocket?'

'No, sir.'

'I thought not. And your wife? Did she accompany you on this mysterious case-related mission?'

'No, sir.'

'Your mistress, perhaps? Or were you out there shagging the local girls?'

Banks stood up, his irritation growing. 'Look, sir, I'm beginning to resent these implications. You might be my senior officer, but I don't have to put up with personal abuse from you.'

Riddle stepped forward, chin jutting like the prow of a ship. 'You'll put up with whatever I dish out, laddie, and right now I'm dishing out a suspension.'

'You're what?'

'You heard me, Banks. I'm suspending you from your duties pending a disciplinary hearing into your activities.'

'You can't do that.'

'Yes, I bloody well can. Read the regulations. I think skiving off for a long weekend during an important investigation is grounds enough for an enquiry. Dereliction of duty. For crying out loud, man, you're a DCI. You're supposed to set an example.'

Banks sat down again, a leaden weight in his chest. 'I see. This is official, then?'

'Official as it gets.'

Banks could hardly believe what he was hearing. Anger burned inside him. Red behind his eyes. Everything was fucked. His marriage. Now his job. For some reason, this idiot had decided to persecute him. It just didn't matter to Riddle that there might still be unanswered questions in the Jason Fox case; he'd put his blinkers on and he wouldn't take them off. No doubt pleasing the Muslim community *and* the general populace simultaneously.

'So that's it, then?' he said. 'I'm free to go?'

'Yes. In fact, I order you to go.' Riddle grinned. 'You're suspended, Banks.'

'Right. I can tell you've been looking forward to saying those words for some time.'

Riddle nodded. 'Oh, yes.'

Banks got up, slipped his cigarettes in his top pocket and picked his jacket up from the coat rack. Next he picked up his briefcase but paused in front of Riddle and laid it down on the desk again on his way to the door. 'Is that your last word on the subject, sir?' he asked.

'Yes.'

Banks nodded. Then he swung his arm back as far as it would go and hit Riddle hard, right in the mouth. Riddle staggered back against the flimsy desk and slid to the floor. Which was where he lay, shaking his head and wiping blood from his mouth with the back of his hand as Banks said, 'And I've been looking forward to that, too, sir. Goodbye.' Then he left the station, his knuckles aching and bleeding.

TWO

The minute Susan heard raised voices arguing about Amsterdam, she tiptoed into the corridor like a sneaky schoolgirl to listen. Then she heard a loud crash, and saw Banks stalk out of his office and out of the building through the fire exit, without even glancing in her direction.

The chief constable hadn't left, though. Puzzled, Susan crossed the corridor and pushed Banks's office door open. Then she just stood there. Chief Constable Riddle was getting up from the floor, brushing dust from his uniform and dabbing his mouth with a bloodsoaked handkerchief.

He saw her standing in the doorway, pointed and said,

'Get back to your office, DC Gay. Nothing happened, you saw nothing, do you understand?'

'Yes, sir . . . Er . . . what about DCI Banks . . .?'

'DCI Banks is under suspension.'

Susan's jaw dropped.

'Back to your office,' Riddle said again. She noticed one of his front teeth was chipped. 'And remember: if word of this gets out, I'll know exactly where it came from, and your career won't be worth two penn'orth of shit, sergeant's exam or no sergeant's exam.'

'Yes, sir.'

Back in her office, Susan leaned on her desk, took a deep breath and tried to collect the thoughts that were suddenly spinning in her mind, out of control. Had she really just seen Jimmy Riddle getting up off the floor in Banks's office, wiping blood from his mouth? Yes, she had. Was that why Banks had got suspended?

But Riddle wanted her to keep it quiet, so there had to be another reason. He could have Banks kicked off the force for assaulting a senior officer, but it would have to be made public then.

She could understand Riddle's desire for silence easily enough – he would look like a real wimp if he publicly accused one of his DCIs of assault. After all, as Susan well knew, the police force was still very much a man's world, and physical prowess was important to men. Riddle would feel humiliated by what had just happened; it would be a blow to his macho ego. The last thing he'd want known was that Banks, four or five inches shorter than him and slighter in build, had knocked him down. If that got out, people all over the region would be sniggering at him behind his back even more than they did now.

So he must have suspended Banks for some other reason.

Amsterdam? Was that it?

And then she realized something. At first, it was just a vague sense of apprehension, then the tumblers fell into position, one inexorably after the other. Then came the final click, and the door opened.

Susan looked at her watch. Just after five.

First, she drove the short distance to Banks's house. As she drove, she chewed on her lip wondering if she were doing the right thing. She wished Superintendent Gristhorpe were here to advise her, but he'd gone off to teach a two-week course at Bramshill that morning. She didn't even know what she was going to say to Banks. After all, he was her senior officer. What could she, a mere DC, do to help?

But there were things she wanted to know. She had worked with Banks for several years now and had come to know his moods pretty well. She had seen him angry, sad, hurt and frustrated, but she had never seen him like this. Nor would she ever have thought him the kind of person to do something as stupid and impulsive as punching Jimmy Riddle.

Call it woman's intuition, a term she had a lot more respect for than she would ever care to admit in front of a roomful of male colleagues, but she felt something was seriously wrong. And it wasn't only to do with Riddle. All she could think of was that something had happened in Amsterdam. But what?

She walked up the front path to Banks's semi. Standing on the doorstep, she took a deep breath, counted to three, and rang the bell.

Nothing happened.

She rang again.

Still nothing.

She waited a few minutes more, tried knocking and ringing the bell. Still nothing. Where the hell was he? Looking around, she couldn't see his car.

She dashed down the path and jumped back in her Golf. She was starting to feel angry now, not a good emotional state for driving, but at least anger would sustain her all the way and help her do what she had to. She headed out of town through the darkening countryside at a dangerous speed, crossed over the A1 and headed south-east, then hurtled through the dark, through villages where families were just settling down to tea and an evening with the telly.

Soon she was on the outskirts of Northallerton, pulling up outside Gavin's modest terrace house.

Gavin answered on the first ring and smiled when he saw Susan. 'Come in,' he said, standing aside. 'This is an unexpected pleasure.'

Susan walked into the hall and Gavin leaned forward to plant a kiss on her cheek. She jerked back and slapped him hard across the face. Gavin staggered back a step or two. 'You bastard,' Susan said. 'You bastard. How could you do it?'

Gavin looked surprised. He held his hand to the reddening weal on his cheek. 'Do what? What the hell did you do that for?'

'You know why.'

'No, I don't. Look, take your coat off and come through. Then you can tell me what you're on about.'

Susan followed him into the living room but she didn't take her coat off. 'I won't be stopping,' she said. 'I'll just say what I have to say and go.'

Gavin nodded. He leaned against the wall with his arms folded. He was wearing tartan slippers, Susan noticed, and looked ridiculous. Somehow, that helped.

'All right,' he said. 'I'm listening. And it'd better be good after what you just did to me.'

'Oh, it's good all right,' Susan said. 'It took me a while. I don't know. Maybe I'm thick, maybe I'm a fool, but I worked it out in the end.'

'Well, you are supposed to be a detective after all. But, look, I still don't know what you're talking about. Will you back up a little and explain?'

Susan shook her head. 'You're so damn smooth, aren't you, Gavin? You used me. That's what I mean.'

'How did I use you? I thought you enjoyed—'

'I'm not talking about sex. I'm talking about information. All the time we were going out together, all the things I told you in private, all the station gossip. You passed it all on to Jimmy Riddle, didn't you? Even what I told you in bed on Saturday.'

'I don't know what you're talking about.'

But he looked away from her eyes, down at his slippers. Susan had seen that guilty gesture in enough criminals to know it meant Gavin was lying. 'Yes, you bloody well do,' she went on. 'How else could Riddle have known everything he did? I should have twigged much earlier, then maybe none of this would have happened.'

'What?'

'Riddle suspended Banks this afternoon. Don't tell me you didn't know.'

Gavin shrugged. 'Oh, that. Well, it's the chief constable's pre—'

'Don't give me that crap. You got me to talk about Banks in private. Shop talk. It was me who told you he liked to call at the Classical Record Shop whenever he had to go to Leeds. When Riddle mentioned that to me a few days ago, I didn't even think at the time about where he might have got it from. It was me who told you about Pamela Jeffreys, too, the violist involved in that case a couple of years ago, the one he felt guilty about. And on Saturday night, in bed, I told you Banks was in Amsterdam. My fault for being such a fool. Blame it on the wine. But you . . . you . . . You're beneath contempt.'

'Okay,' said Gavin, gazing at her coolly. 'So the chief constable wanted to be informed about what was going on at Eastvale. So what? He's like that. Unlike his predecessor, he likes to be in the know. Hands on. It's easy for you. *You* don't have to work close to him, day in, day out, do you?' He pointed his thumb at his chest. 'I do. And we all have our careers to consider, don't we? What's so wrong with that?'

Susan could hardly believe what she was hearing, even though it was exactly what she had expected. 'So you admit it? Just like that? You used me to spy on my colleagues?'

'Well, seeing as you have the evidence, there's not a lot else I can say, is there? I can hardly deny it. Yes. *Mea culpa.*'

'I don't understand, Gavin. How could you do that?'

Gavin shrugged. 'I never thought it would come to anything like this,' he said. 'It was only little titbits, nothing important. Like I said, Riddle just wanted to be kept informed. But that wasn't why I asked you out in the first place. That only came later. When he found out I was going out with you. And believe me, I didn't tell him. He's got quite a network, has Riddle.' He shrugged. 'I didn't really think it would do any harm.'

'Informed about Eastvale in general or DCI Banks in particular?'

Gavin shifted from foot to foot. 'Well, he *did* ask about Banks in particular. He never really approved of Banks, you know. Thought he was a bit of a maverick, if truth be told.'

'I know that,' said Susan. 'He never liked him. Right from the start. I remember the Deborah Harrison case, when Banks upset some of Riddle's important friends. Riddle was just looking for something to use against him. And you used me to get it for him. That's what I can't forgive.'

'Like I said, I didn't really think I was doing anything—'

'Oh, stuff it, Gavin. I'm not interested in your excuses. You used me to scupper Banks's career, and that's all I care about.'

'If that's how you want to see it.'

'Is there any other way?'

'I take it things are over between us, then?'

Susan could only look at him and shake her head. Then she turned to leave.

'What is it, Susan?' Gavin called after her. 'Fancy him yourself, do you? You should listen to the way you talk about him. Like a lovesick teenager. Believe me, it wasn't very difficult to get you talking about him. The hardest thing was getting you to stop. Even in bed.'

Susan slammed the door behind her and got back in her car. She couldn't move, couldn't even turn the key in the ignition. All she could do was sit there, hands gripping the steering wheel, shaking. She took deep breaths.

And then Susan did something she hardly ever did, something she always hated herself for when it happened. She started to cry. Bloody great convulsive sobs. Because, fuck it, she said to herself, Gavin was right. She had never admitted it, but she had known it for ages. It *was* Banks she cared about; it *was* Banks she fancied. And, dammit, he was a married man, he was her senior officer, and he wouldn't look at her that way in a month of Sundays. She was just another stupid girl in love with her boss and there was no way she could stay in Eastvale now, not after this.

THREE

It had long since turned dark when Banks got home. For hours, it seemed, he had driven around the Dales, hardly noticing where he was, or what music kept repeating on the cassette player. His knuckles still hurt, but the shaking inside had stopped. Had he really done it? Punched Jimmy Riddle? He realized he had, and he also realized that at the moment the anger had burst out of him, it was Sandra he had been thinking of, not the bloody job.

The house was quiet and empty. A different quality of silence and emptiness than he had ever felt there before. First, he had a look around to see if anything was missing. Sandra hadn't taken very much. Most of her clothes were still in the wardrobe, the scent of her hair still lingered on the pillows, and her photograph of the misty sunset above Hawes still hung over the fireplace in the living room.

It made him think how only on Sunday, yesterday, he had wandered the Amsterdam museums in the rain, a pilgrim marvelling at Rembrandt's *The Night Watch* in the Rijksmuseum, unsettled by *Crows in the Wheatfield* in the Van Gogh Museum, and, finally, elated by the bright, whimsical Chagalls in the Stedelijk Museum.

All the while thinking how Sandra would have loved it,

and how he would like to treat her to a visit one weekend in spring.

But Sandra was gone.

He noticed the red light blinking on the telephone answering machine. Thinking it might be Sandra, he got up and pressed the replay button. One call was Vic Manson, two were hang-ups, but the next four were from Tracy. On the last one, she said, 'Dad, are you there? It's Sunday now. I've been trying to ring you all weekend. I'm worried about you. If you *are* there, please answer. I talked to Mummy and she told me what happened. I'm so sorry. I love you, Daddy. Please give me a ring.'

Banks stood by the phone for a moment, head in his hands, tears burning in his eyes. Then he did what any reasonable man would do in his situation. He cranked Mozart's *Requiem* up as loud as he could bear it and got rat-arse drunk.

12

ONE

When Banks stirred on the sofa at about four o'clock in the morning, Mozart's *Requiem* was still playing on 'repeat'. And a more fitting piece of music he couldn't imagine. It was playing loudly, too, and he was surprised that none of his neighbours had called the police. Still, he *was* the police. Or used to be.

Wishing he were still unconscious, he groaned, rubbed his stubble, rolled off the sofa and put some coffee on, turning the volume down on the stereo as he went. Then he stumbled upstairs and swallowed a handful of aspirins, washed down with two glasses of water to irrigate his dehydrated cells.

Back downstairs, as the coffee dripped through the filter with frustrating slowness, he surveyed the damage: twelve cigarette ends in the ashtray; no burns on the sofa or carpet; about two fingers of Laphroaig left. If he were going to keep up this rate of drinking he would have to start buying cheaper Scotch. Still, it could have been a lot worse, he concluded, especially as he remembered the bottle had only been about three-quarters full when he started.

When the coffee was ready, he decided to switch from the *Requiem* to the C minor mass, something to bring a little more light and hope into his bleak world, then he tried to collect his thoughts.

He had punched Jimmy Riddle; that was the first memory to come back. And he had skinned knuckles to prove it. Well, that had been a stupid thing to do, he realized now, and it had also probably put the mockers on his career.

Jobless, then. Also wifeless and hung over. At least the hangover would go away. It *could* be worse, couldn't it? Yes it could, he realized. He could have been diagnosed with a terminal illness. He racked his brains to see if that had, in fact, happened, but could find no memory of it. It would probably happen today the way his lungs felt after all those cigarettes.

So what was he going to do? Become a private eye? Enter a monastery? Get a job with some security outfit? Or should he just carry on and solve the Jason Fox case on his own to show up the police, run rings around Jimmy Riddle, just like Sherlock Holmes did around Inspector Lestrade? Alan Banks, Consulting Detective. Had a nice ring to it.

He poured himself a cup of black coffee and flopped back on the sofa. Looking at the misty Hawes sunset over the fireplace, for some reason he remembered Sandra telling him on Thursday that there *might have been* somebody else, but there wasn't. Remembered the faraway look in her eyes when she said it.

And that made him angry. He pictured Sandra with some strapping, bearded young artist, standing in the wind on the moors doing a Cathy and Heathcliff, looking lovingly into each other's eyes and exercising restraint. 'No, my darling, we *mustn't*. There's too much at stake. Think of the children.' Grand passion collides with family values and moral responsibility. It was a scene from a cheap romance. But all the same, it made Banks clench his jaw. What *might* have been. And, come to think of it, he only had her word for it that she hadn't left him to run off with someone else, someone she would only take up with publicly after a 'decent' interval.

Well, two could play at that game. Banks had had his chances at infidelity in the past, too, but he hadn't taken them. He hadn't romanticized them, either. He thought especially of Jenny Fuller. There had been a time, some years ago, when something might have blossomed between them. Was it too late now? Probably. Jenny seemed to spend most of her time teaching in America these days, and she had a steady boyfriend over there. Then there was Pamela Jeffreys, the one Riddle thought was his mistress. Banks hadn't slept with Pamela, either, but it was an appealing thought.

So many choices. So many possibilities. Then why did he feel so bloody miserable and empty? Because, he concluded, none of them were what he wanted. What he wanted, when it came right down to it, was his job back, Sandra back and his hangover gone. Perhaps if he played a country-and-western song backwards . . .? He couldn't even do that, hating country and western the way he did. Still, taking stock of himself, he realized that, depressed as he was, he felt calmer now than when he was stuck at the airport yesterday contemplating his return home. Thumping Jimmy Riddle probably had something to do with that.

After the first cup of coffee, he realized he was hungry. He hadn't eaten anything since that snack on the plane, a million years ago now. Searching through the remnants in the fridge, he managed to throw together three rashers of streaky bacon and two eggs only a week past their sell-by date. That would have to do. The one remaining slice of bread was a little stale, but it hadn't turned green yet, and it would fry up nicely in the bacon fat. Cholesterol special. So what?

As he fried his breakfast, Banks remembered Tracy's messages. He would have to ring her today and put her mind at rest. Should he explain to her about losing his job, too? Best not, yet, he decided. It was bad enough his daughter should suddenly find herself the child of a broken marriage the minute she flew the coop, let alone the child of a disgraced copper. There would be time enough for that later. He would have to phone Brian in Portsmouth, too, and his own parents. They would all be upset.

Suddenly, the day ahead seemed full of things to do. None of them pleasant. The only bright spot was that he wouldn't have to worry about money for a while; the suspension was *with* pay. And Jimmy Riddle couldn't do a thing about that until *after* a disciplinary hearing.

He cursed as he broke an egg while lifting it onto the plate and yolk ran all over the counter. It would have to do. No more left. Carefully, he used the spatula to lift the one unbroken egg onto the fried bread, then patted the bacon with some kitchen roll to remove the excess grease and tucked in. When he'd finished, he poured another cup of coffee and lit a cigarette.

It was still just past five in the morning, and he hadn't a clue what to do to keep himself occupied until it was a decent time to start phoning people. Sleep was out of the question now, and he knew he couldn't possibly concentrate on reading a book or listening to music. He needed something completely mindless, something to keep his thoughts off his problems for a few hours. Like television.

But there was nothing on television at that time apart

from something educational on BBC2 and a studio discussion on ITV, so he started sorting through the video collection, odds and sods he'd picked up over the years. Finally, he found one that would do. It was still in its cellophane wrapper, so someone must have bought him it as a present and he'd forgotten he had it. *Bridge on the River Kwai*. Perfect. He remembered his dad taking him to see a revival of it at the Gaumont when he was about twelve. It would take him back to those days, when life was simple, and right at the moment he would have given anything on earth to be that innocent twelve-year-old again, grabbing his father's hand when Jack Hawkins burned leeches off with a cigarette, thrilling at the way all the birds flew up and the pool turned red with blood when they ambushed the Japanese patrol, and biting his nails to the quick as Alec Guinness made his final, dying, staggering way to the dynamite plunger. Yes, *The Bridge on the River Kwai* might just keep the dark hounds of depression at bay for another couple of hours, until daylight came.

TWO

Susan didn't know where she was going when she left the station around eleven o'clock that morning, only that she had to get out of the office for a while. Let Riddle suspend her, too, if he found out.

The next thing she knew she found herself on Castle Walk looking out over the formal gardens and the river, all framed in the branches of the beeches. It was the same view she'd had from the bistro with Gavin on Saturday night. Just thinking about that night made her burn with shame and rage.

Across the Swain, a belt of trees called The Green partially obscured the East Side Estate, but she could still make out a few of the light red brick terraces and maisonettes, and the three twelve-storey blocks of flats – a crime wave in themselves – poked their ugly heads way above the trees. Beyond the estate and the railway tracks were the chocolate factory and a few old warehouses, corrugated metal roofs glinting in the sun. A local diesel rattled by and blew its horn.

She would have to leave Eastvale; there was no doubt about that. Now that she had admitted her feelings to herself, she could no longer work with Banks. She couldn't trust herself not to act like a love-struck schoolgirl; nor could she go running off in tears every time she saw him, either. And she *would* have to see him. He might be suspended for the moment, but a disciplinary hearing would probably reinstate him, she thought.

It also hadn't taken her long to work out that, after what she had witnessed yesterday, Jimmy Riddle would want her as far away from North Yorkshire as possible. At least that could be easily accomplished without raising any eyebrows.

Although it *did* happen on occasion, it was rare for a DC to be promoted straight to the rank of detective sergeant within the same station. The most likely scenario was a transfer and at least a year back in uniform. This was supposed to be a safeguard against corruption: senior officers offering promotion in exchange for falsified evidence.

At first, Susan had hoped the chief constable would approve her request to stay. But being promoted within Eastvale CID didn't matter to her now. She had to leave. And the farther away, the better. Devon and Cornwall, maybe. She had fond memories of childhood holidays in that part of the world: St Ives, Torquay, Polperro.

How could she have been so stupid? she asked herself again. In cafés, pubs and in bed she had chatted away to Gavin about Banks and his idiosyncrasies, his love of music, his guilt over the injuries to Pamela Jeffreys, and Gavin had turned it over to Jimmy Riddle, who had twisted and perverted it beyond all recognition. If anyone deserved to be suspended, it was Riddle and Gavin. Fat chance.

An old woman walking a dog passed Susan on the path and said hello. After they had gone by, Susan paused a moment to sit on a bench. She was facing north now and to her left she could see the square Norman church tower, the bus station and the glass and concrete Swainsdale Centre. Straight ahead was the pre-Roman site in the distance, not much more than a couple of bumps in the grassland down by the river.

Even though there wasn't a great deal to do around the station in the aftermath of the Jason Fox case, Susan didn't think she could honestly stay away too long. After all, a call might come in, something important, and if she missed it she'd have to explain why.

And she remembered something else she had overheard yesterday: Banks expressing doubts about the solution. Though she couldn't quite put her finger on exactly what, there were things about Mark Wood's confession that rang false with her, too. Maybe she should have a look over the reports again. So with a sigh, she stood up and headed back around Castle Walk.

As she went up the stairs to CID, she told herself she would have to get a grip, lock up her feelings, keep them separate and behave like a professional. She could do it;

she'd done it before. On some level, being a woman in a man's world, she did it all the time. She would also have to work out how to deal with Banks's misplaced trust in her. Should she tell him about Gavin? Could she really do that?

THREE

Shortly after six o'clock that evening, Banks sat in Leeds Parish Church. Though not much to look at from the outside, the interior had recently been restored to all its Victorian Gothic glory, like the Town Hall, all stained glass, dark, polished wood and high arches.

He wasn't there because his troubles had driven him to religion. In fact, he was listening to a rehearsal of Vivaldi's *Gloria* by the St Peter's Singers and Chamber Orchestra. It certainly wasn't where he had expected to be, or what he had expected to be doing, when he woke up on the sofa that morning.

Tracy had rung him much earlier than he would have thought of ringing her. At least he was feeling a bit more human by then. She was full of concern, naturally, and he tried to assure her that he would be okay. Tracy told him she was going down to Croydon for a while to stay with her mother and grandparents, but she assured him she wasn't taking sides. He told her to go, take care of her mother; he'd see her when she came back. Reluctantly, she hung up. Maybe he hadn't lost Tracy after all.

He felt the need to get out of Eastvale around noon, so he phoned Pamela Jeffreys. As it turned out, she had a rehearsal that evening, but Banks was welcome to attend. She was surprised to hear from him and said she would be delighted to see him. Someone pleased to see him? Music to his ears.

He drove to Leeds in plenty of time to browse the city centre record shops first. A couple of CDs would be paltry compensation for the miserable time he'd had lately, but they would be better than nothing. Like the toy soldier his mother always used to buy him after he'd been to the dentist's.

By half past six, the conductor seemed frustrated by the soprano section's inability to enter on time, so he ended the rehearsal early. Pamela packed away her viola, grabbed her jacket and walked towards Banks. She was wearing black leggings and a baggy black velvet top, belted at the waist, with a scoop neckline which plunged just above the curve of her breasts. Her long raven hair hung over her shoulders and the diamond stud in her right nostril glittered in the side-lighting. Her skin was the colour of burnished gold, her eyes almond in shape and colour, and her finely drawn red lips revealed straight white teeth when she smiled. Many of them were crowned, Banks knew. Looking at her now, he found it hard to believe that only a couple of years ago she had been lying in a hospital bed covered in bandages wondering if she would ever be able to play again.

Banks gave her a peck on the cheek. She smelled of jasmine. 'Thank you for inviting me,' he said. 'Wouldn't have missed it for the world.'

She turned up her nose. 'We were terrible. But thanks anyway. And it's nice to see you, stranger.'

'Sorry I couldn't stick around after *The Pearl Fishers*,' Banks said.

'That's okay. I was knackered anyway. Long day. What did you think?'

'Wonderful.'

She grinned. 'For once, you're right. Everything seemed to fit together that night. Sometimes it just does that, you know, and nobody knows why.'

Banks gestured around the church. 'I'm surprised you have time for this.'

'St Peter's? Oh, if the schedules work out all right, I can do it. I need all the practice I can get. I've been recording the Walton viola concerto, too, with the orchestra. For Naxos. Finally the viola's getting some of the respect it deserves.'

'You were the soloist?'

She slapped his arm. 'No. Not me, you idiot. I'm not *that* good. The soloist was Lars Anders Tomter. He's *very* good.'

'I'm really glad it's all working out for you, anyway.'

Pamela smiled and made a mock curtsy. 'Thank you, kind sir. So, where now?'

Banks looked at his watch. 'I know it's a bit early, but how about dinner?'

'Fine with me. I'm starving.'

'Curry?'

Pamela laughed. 'Just because I'm Bangladeshi, it doesn't mean I eat nothing but curry, you know.'

Banks held his hands out. 'Whatever, then. Brasserie 44?'

'No, not there,' Pamela said. 'It's far too expensive. There's a new pizza place up Headingley, just off North Lane. I've heard it's pretty good.'

'Pizza it is, then. I'm parked just over in The Calls.'

'You can have curry if you really want.'

Banks shook his head, and they walked through the dimly lit, cobbled backstreets to the car. They were in the oldest part of Leeds, and the most recent to be redeveloped. Most of the eighteenth- and nineteenth-century warehouses by the River Aire had been derelict for years until the civic-pride restoration schemes of the eighties. Now that Leeds was a boom-town, they were tourist attractions, full of trendy new restaurants, usually located on something called a 'wharf', the kind of word nobody there would have used twenty years ago. Canary Wharf had a lot more to answer for than vanished fortunes, Banks thought.

'It's not that I think you eat curry all the time because you're Asian,' he said. 'It's just that there isn't a decent curry place in Eastvale. Well, there *is* one, but I think I might be *persona non grata* there at the moment. Anyway, pizza sounds great.'

'What did you get?' Pamela asked as she got into the Cavalier and picked up the HMV package from the passenger seat.

'Have a look,' said Banks, as he set off and negotiated the one-way streets of the city centre.

'*The Beatles Anthology?* I never would have taken you for a Beatles fan.'

Banks smiled. 'It's pure nostalgia. I used to listen to Brian Matthew do "Saturday Club" when I was a kid. If I remember rightly, it came on right after Uncle Mac's "Children's Favourites", and by the age of thirteen I'd got sick to death of "Sparky and the Magic Piano", "Little Green Man" and "Big Rock Candy Mountain".'

Pamela laughed. 'Before my time. Besides, my mum and dad wouldn't let me listen to pop music.'

'Didn't you rebel?'

'I did manage to sneak a little John Peel under the bedclothes once in a while.'

'I hope you're speaking metaphorically.' Banks drove past St Michael's church and The Original Oak, just opposite. The streetlights were on, and there were plenty of people about, students for the most part. A little further on, he came to the junction with North Lane, an enclave of cafés, pubs and bookshops.

'Here,' said Pamela, pointing. Banks managed to find a parking spot, and they walked around the corner into the restaurant. The familiar pizza smells of olive oil, tomato sauce, oregano and fresh-baked dough greeted them. The restaurant was lively and noisy, but they only had to wait at the bar for a couple of minutes before they got a tiny table for two in the back. It wasn't a great spot, too close to the toilets and the waiters' route to and from the kitchen, but at least it was in the smoking section. After a while, sipping the one glass of red wine he was allowing himself that evening, and smoking one of the duty-free Silk Cuts he'd picked up at Schiphol, Banks hardly noticed the bustle or the volume level any more.

'So, have you got a boyfriend yet?' he asked when they were settled.

Pamela frowned. 'Too busy,' she said. 'Besides, I'm not sure I trust myself to get involved again. Not just yet. How's your wife? Sandra, isn't it?'

'Yes. She's fine.'

After a while of small-talk, their pizzas came – Banks's marinara and Pamela's funghi.

'How's life at the cop shop?' Pamela asked between mouthfuls.

'I wouldn't know,' said Banks. 'I've been suspended from duty.'

He hadn't intended to tell her, certainly not with such abruptness, but it had come out before he could stop it. He couldn't seem to hold back *everything*. In a way, he was glad he'd said it because he had to confide in someone. Her eyes opened wide. As soon as she had swallowed her food, she said, 'What? Good Lord, why?'

As best he could, he told her about the Jason Fox case, and about thumping Jimmy Riddle.

'Aren't you still angry?' she asked when he'd finished.

Banks sipped some wine and watched Pamela wipe a little pizza sauce from her chin. The people at the next table left. The waiter picked up the money and began to clean up after them. 'Not really angry,' Banks said. 'A bit, perhaps, but not a lot. Not any more.'

'What, then?'

'Disappointed.'

'With what?'

'Myself mostly. For being too stupid not to see it coming. And for thumping Riddle.'

'I can't say I blame you, from what you've told me.'

'Oh, Riddle's an arsehole, no doubt about it. He even suggested that I took *you* to Amsterdam with me.'

'Me? But why?'

'He thinks you're my mistress.'

Pamela almost choked on a mouthful of pizza. Banks didn't feel particularly flattered. Afterwards, he couldn't tell if she were blushing or just red in the face from coughing. 'Come again,' she managed finally, patting her chest.

'It's true. He thinks I've got a mistress in Leeds and that's why I keep making up excuses to come here.'

'But how could he know? I mean . . .'

'I know what you mean. Don't ask me.' Banks smiled, felt his heart skip, but went on anyway, aiming for a light tone. 'It didn't seem like such a bad idea.'

Pamela looked down. He could see he'd embarrassed her. 'I'm sorry,' he said. 'That was supposed to be a compliment.'

'I know what it was supposed to be,' Pamela said. Then she smiled. 'Don't worry. I won't hold it against you.'

Please do, he almost said, but managed to stop himself in time. He wondered if she would take him home with her if he told her that he and Sandra had split up. They ate some more pizza in silence, then Pamela shook her head slowly and said, 'It just sounds so unfair.'

'Fairness has nothing to do with it.' Banks pushed his plate aside and lit a cigarette. 'Oh, sorry,' he said, looking at the small slice left on Pamela's plate.

'That's all right. I'm full.' She pushed hers aside, too. 'This Neville Motcombe you mentioned, isn't he the bloke who was interviewed in the *Yorkshire Post* this weekend? Something to do with neo-Nazis disrupting a funeral?'

'That's the one.'

'Didn't someone die there?'

'Yes,' said Banks. 'Frank Hepplethwaite. I knew him slightly.'

'Oh, I'm sorry.'

'It's okay. We weren't close friends or anything. It's just that I liked him, and I think, of anyone, he's the real victim in this whole mess. Tell me something, have you ever come across Motcombe in any other context?'

'What, you mean with me being the sort of person this Albion League might target?'

'Partly. Yes.'

She shook her head. 'Not really. I've been lucky, I suppose. Oh, I've been insulted in the street and stuff. You know, called a Paki bitch or a Paki slut. It's always "Paki". Can't they think of anything else but that?'

Banks smiled. 'That's part of their problem. Severely limited thinking. No originality.'

'I suppose so. I'm not saying it doesn't bother me when it happens. It does. It upsets me. But you get used to it. I mean, it starts not to surprise you as much, so you don't get shocked by it as easily. But it still hurts. Every time. Like hot needles being stuck through your skin. Sometimes it's just the way people look at you. Am I making any sense?'

'Perfect.'

'I remember once when I was a kid back in Shipley – oh, this must have been in the seventies, twenty years ago now – and I was walking back from my aunt's house with my mum and dad. We walked around this corner and there was a gang of skinheads. They surrounded us and started calling out racist insults and shoving us. There were about ten of them. There was nothing we could do. I was terrified. I think we all were. But my dad stood up to them, called them cowards and shoved them right back. At first they just laughed but then they started to get worked up and I could tell they were getting ready to really hurt us. My mother was screaming and I was crying and they got my dad on the ground and started kicking him . . .' She trailed off and shook her head at the memory.

'What happened?'

Pamela looked up and smiled through her tears. 'Would you believe it, a police car came by and they ran off? A bloody police car. About the only time the police have ever been there when I've needed them. Must have been a miracle.'

They both laughed. The waiter came by and took their plates.

'What now?' Pamela asked, after she'd wiped her eyes from the mingled tears of humiliation and laughter.

'Coffee? Dessert?'

She hit him on the arm again. 'I don't mean that, idiot. I mean, you. Your future.'

'Looks bleak. I'd rather concentrate on dessert.'

'Just a cappuccino for me.'

Banks ordered two cappuccinos and lit another cigarette.

'You're smoking too much,' Pamela said.

'I know. And just when I'd managed to cut down.'

'Anyway, you haven't answered my question.'

'What question was that?'

'You know quite well. Your future. What are you going to do?'

Banks shook his head. 'I don't know yet. It's too early to say.'

'Well surely when this chief constable person has done his investigation, he'll have to reinstate you?'

'I doubt it. Even if a disciplinary hearing really does reinstate me, it doesn't matter.'

'Why not?'

'Think about it,' said Banks. 'I hit the chief constable. Even if he does keep that just between the two of us, it still means I can't work with him any more. He'd find ways to make my life a living hell.'

'I understand it might make things difficult.'

'Difficult? It was *difficult* before all this. After . . .' He shrugged. 'Impossible, more like.'

The restaurant was full of students now. They looked like an artsy, literary crowd, all talking excitedly about the latest music, arguing loudly about books and philosophy. They made Banks feel old; made him feel he had wasted his life. A waiter passed by carrying plates, leaving a trail of garlic and basil smells.

'But you can get a job somewhere else,' Pamela said. 'I mean as a policeman. In a different region. Can't you?'

'I suppose so. I don't mean to be negative, Pamela, I just haven't thought that far ahead yet.'

'I understand.' She leaned forward and put her hand on his. Candlelight glittered in her diamond stud, made shadows of burnished gold and lit the soft down between her breasts.

Banks swallowed and felt his excitement rise. He wanted to take her home and lick every inch of her golden skin. Or did he? There would be consequences, confidences shared, a *relationship*. He didn't think he could handle anything like that right now.

Pamela sat back and flipped a long tress of hair over her shoulder with the back of her hand. 'What about this case you were working on?' she asked. 'You seemed to imply that it's not over.'

'Everyone thinks it is.'

'And you?'

Banks shrugged.

She toyed with a gold bracelet on her arm. 'Look, Alan, this person you talked about earlier. Mark Wood. *Did* he do it?'

'I don't know. He *might* have done. But not, I don't think, the way he said he did, or for the reason he claimed.'

'Does it matter?'

'Yes. It could mean the difference between manslaughter and murder. And if someone else was behind it, say Neville Motcombe, I'd hate to see him get away with it while Mark Wood takes the fall alone.'

'If you were still on the force, would you be working on this case?'

'Probably not. The chief constable's got his confession. Everybody's happy. Case closed.'

'But you're not on the force.'

'That's right.'

'So that means you *can* still work on it if you want.'

Banks smiled and shook his head. 'What impeccable logic. But I don't think so. I can't do it, Pamela. I'm sorry. It's over.'

Pamela sat back and studied him for a moment. He reached for another cigarette, thought twice about it, then lit up anyway.

'Remember when I was hurt?' she said.

'Yes.'

'And thought I might never play again?'

Banks nodded.

'Well, if I'd taken your negative attitude, I wouldn't have played again. And, believe me, there were times when giving up would have been the easiest thing in the world. But you helped me then. You encouraged me. You helped give me some strength and courage when I was at my lowest. I'd never had a friend like . . . someone who didn't want . . .' She turned away for a moment. When she looked back, her eyes were deeply serious and intense, glistening with tears. 'And now you're giving up. Just like that. I don't believe it. Not you.'

'What else can I do?'

'You can follow up on your ideas. On your own.'

'But how? I don't have the resources, for a start.'

'Someone will help you. You've still got friends there, in the department, haven't you?'

'I hope so.'

'Well, then?'

'I don't know. Maybe you're right.' Banks gestured for

the waiter and paid, waving aside all Pamela's attempts to contribute. 'My idea, my beat,' he said.

'So you *will* do something? You promise me you won't just sit around at home and mope?'

'Yes, I promise. I'll do something.' He scraped his chair back and smiled. 'Now, come on. Let me take you home.'

13

ONE

The first thing Banks needed to do, he realized in the cold light of Wednesday morning, was spend a few hours going over all the paperwork on the Jason Fox case – especially that which had been generated in his absence. He realized he had missed a lot over the weekend, and there were things he needed to know if he were to make any progress on his own. But how could he get hold of it? Nobody was going to kick him out of Eastvale station, he didn't think, but neither could they let him just walk in and take what he wanted.

There wasn't even a crust of bread left in the house, and he didn't fancy eating Sandra's leftover cottage cheese, so he made do with coffee and Vaughan Williams's 'Serenade to Music' for breakfast.

As he let the sensuous music flow over him, he thought about last night. When he had dropped Pamela at her flat, he had half-hoped she would invite him up for a drink, but she just thanked him for the lift, said she was tired and hoped she would see him again soon. He said he would call and drove off with a pang of disappointment about not getting to do something he probably wouldn't have done anyway, even if he had had the chance. But seeing her had been good for him. At least she had persuaded him to keep working on the case.

When the music finished, he picked up the phone and called Sandra in Croydon. He had been thinking of calling last night when he got in, but decided it was too late.

Her mother answered.

'Alan? How are you doing?'

'Oh, not so bad, considering. You?'

'About the same. Look, er, I'm really sorry about what's happened. Do you want to speak to Sandra?'

'Please.'

'Just a minute.'

She sounded embarrassed, Banks thought as he waited. Not surprising, really. What could she say? Her daughter had left her husband and come home to sort herself out. Banks had always got on well with his mother-in-law, and he didn't expect she was going to see him as a monster now, but neither was she going to chat with him about his feelings over the telephone.

'Alan?'

It was Sandra's voice. She sounded tired. He felt the icy hand squeeze his heart. Now he had her on the line, he didn't know what to say. 'Yes. I . . . er . . . I just wanted to know if you were okay.'

'Of course I'm okay. I wish you hadn't called.'

'But why?'

'Why do you think? I told you. I need time to work things out. This doesn't help.'

'It might help me.'

'I don't think so.'

'I spent the weekend in Amsterdam.'

'You did *what*?'

'In Amsterdam. It was strange. It brought back a lot of memories. Look, do you remember—'

'Alan, why are you telling me this? I don't want to

310

talk about it. Please. Don't do this to me. To us.'

'I'm only—'

'I'm going now.'

'Don't hang up.'

'Alan, I can't deal with this. I'm going now.'

'Can I speak to Tracy?'

There was silence for a while, then Tracy came on the phone. 'Dad, it's you. I was worried.'

'I'm okay, love. Your mother . . .?'

'She's upset, Dad. Honest, I don't understand what's happening any more than you do. All I know is Mum's confused and she says she needs some time away.'

Banks sighed. 'I know that. I shouldn't have called. She's right. Tell her I'm sorry. And tell her I . . .'

'Yes?'

'Never mind. Look, does Brian know about all this? I'm sorry, I haven't been very organized. Other than you, I haven't called anyone else.'

'It's all right, Dad. You don't have to apologize to me. I suppose it's hard to know what to do when something like this happens. I mean, it's not exactly something you can take a course on, is it?'

God, she sounded suddenly so mature, Banks thought. Much more mature than he felt right now. 'Does he?'

'Yes. We talked to him over the weekend.'

'How's he taking it?'

'Cool. You know Brian. He's okay.'

'When am I going to see you?'

'I'm staying the rest of the week down here. But I'll come up for the weekend if you want.'

'You will?' The icy hand relaxed its grip and Banks's heart warmed a little.

'Of course. You know I love you, Dad. I love you both. I

told you yesterday, I'm not taking sides. Please don't think because I came down here that I think any less of you.'

'I don't. Anyway, the weekend would be great.'

Tracy hesitated. 'You won't be at work all the time, will you?'

'I . . . er . . . no, I don't think so,' Banks answered. No point telling her about his suspension, he thought. The last thing he needed right now was his daughter feeling even more sorry for him from a distance. 'I'll pick you up at the train station. What time does your train get in?'

'It gets back to Leeds mid-afternoon. But I'll need to drop by the residence first. There might be messages. I shouldn't really have taken off like that. I've only just started there.'

'I'm sure they'll understand.'

'I hope so.'

'So why don't I come down to Leeds and pick you up at the student residence? Does that sound like a good idea?'

'That'd be great.'

'What time?'

'About six be okay?'

'Fine. And we'll stop at the King's Head in Masham for something to eat on the way back.'

'Great. And Dad.'

'What?'

'Take care of yourself.'

'I will. See you on Friday. Goodbye.'

'Goodbye.'

Banks hung onto the receiver for a while after the line went dead, then he swallowed, took a deep breath and dialled Brian's number in Portsmouth.

After six rings, a sleepy voice drawled, 'Uh. Yeah. Who is it?'

'Did I wake you?'

'Dad?'

'Yes.'

'Well, yeah, as a matter of fact you did. But it's all right. I should be getting up anyway. Next lecture's at ten. What's up?'

'I gather you've heard about your mother and me?'

'Yeah. It's too bad. Are you okay?'

'I'm doing fine.'

'And Mum?'

'I just talked to her. She's a bit confused right now, but she'll be okay.'

'Great. What's going to happen?'

'I don't know. She says she needs some time away.'

'She'll come back, Dad, you'll see.'

'I hope so.'

'Just wait and see. She's just having a mid-life crisis, that's all. She'll get over it.'

Kids. Banks couldn't help but smile. 'Right. And how are you?'

'Fine.'

'How's your classes?'

'All right. Hey, Dad, the band's got a couple of gigs coming up next weekend. Paying gigs.' Brian played in a local blues band. Banks thought he was a pretty good guitar player.

'That's great. Just don't let it get in the way of your studies.'

'I won't. Don't worry. Gotta go now, or I'll be late for the lecture.'

'When are you coming up?'

'I'll try to get up to see you before Christmas. Okay?'

'Fine. If money's a problem, I'll pay for your ticket.'

'Thanks, Dad, that'd be a great help. Gotta go.'

'Goodbye.'

'Bye, Dad. And hang in there.'

Hang in there. Like a kid from some American television programme. Banks smiled as he hung up. Well, that was enough family business for the moment, he thought. He knew he should phone his own parents and tell them what had happened, but he couldn't face them yet. They'd be really upset. All these years they had loved Sandra like the daughter they had never had. If anyone was likely to blame him for what had happened, it would be his own parents, not Sandra's, he thought ironically. No, best wait. Maybe Sandra would come up with Tracy at the weekend, then he wouldn't have to tell them anything.

He poured some more coffee and put on the Beatles CD that he'd bought in Leeds yesterday. It was the second of three anthologies, and he'd been thinking of buying it ever since it came out. He went straight to the second disc: outtakes of 'Strawberry Fields'. His favourite. Singing along, he tidied up a little, but soon started to feel restless and caged. Somehow, it didn't feel right to be home during the daytime, watching neighbours walk back and forth with shopping and the unemployed bank clerk over the street wash his car for the second time in a week.

It was time for action. He picked up the telephone, dialled the station and asked to be put through to DC Susan Gay's extension.

She answered on the second ring.

'Susan?' Banks said. 'It's me.'

'Sir? Are you . . . Is everything all right?'

He was sure she meant it, but her voice sounded tight and cool. 'I'm fine. Is Jim there?'

'No, he's out on the East Side Estate. Another break-in.'

'The super?'

'Away at Bramshill.'

'Good. Sorry, I didn't mean that to sound like it did. Look, I know I shouldn't ask you this, but do you think you could do me a favour?'

'Sir?'

'I need to look over the stuff on the Jason Fox case again. All of it – from the crime-scene photographs to Mark Wood's statements. Can you help?'

'Can I ask why you're still interested, sir?'

'Because I'm not satisfied. Will you help me?'

There was a long pause, then Susan said, 'Why don't you come to the station?'

'Is that a good idea?'

'It's pretty quiet here right now. The super's going to be away for a couple of weeks.'

'Well, if you're certain. I don't want to get you into trouble.' Banks heard a sound like a harsh cough or bark at the other end. 'Are you all right?'

'Fine. Frog in my throat. That's all. It's okay, sir. Really it is.'

'Are you sure? If Jimmy Riddle turns up—'

'If Jimmy Riddle turns up, I'm buggered. I know that. But there's far too much stuff to photocopy. And that would look suspicious, especially the way you have to account for every penny you spend around here these days. I'll take the risk if you will, sir.'

'All right.'

'But I'd still like to know why you're not satisfied.'

'I'll tell you about it when I know more myself. At the moment it's mostly just a feeling. That and a few bits of information about Mark Wood I picked up in Amsterdam.'

'Why don't you just come to the station as soon as you

can, then. I'll be waiting.' And she hung up hurriedly. Banks grabbed his coat and left the house. It was another sunny day, with a little high cloud and a slight chilly edge. The leaves had turned a little more than last week, and some were beginning to fall already.

He needed the exercise, so he decided to walk. When he plugged in his earphones and turned the Walkman on, the Roy Harper tape he'd been listening to on the plane home came on in the middle of 'McGoohan's Blues'. Protest with a mystical edge; pretentiousness with a wink. Well, that would do nicely.

He walked along Market Street past the roundabout, the zebra crossing, garage and school, the local shopping centre with its Safeway supermarket and collection of smaller shops and banks. There was a lot of traffic on Market Street today and the acrid smell of petrol and diesel fumes mingled with dry dusty air.

He paused across from The Jubilee, whose large stone and red-brick frontage curved around the junction of Market Street and Sebastopol Terrace. That was where Jason Fox had spent his last evening on earth before being dispatched to whatever circle of hell was reserved for racists. Why on earth did it matter who had killed him, or why? Banks wondered as he walked on. Wasn't it good enough that he was dead? Was it only Banks's insatiable bloody curiosity that made it so important, or was there some absolute standard of justice and truth to be served?

Banks had no answer. All he knew was that if he didn't get to spin it out until he thought it was all over, then it would stay with him like a sore that wouldn't heal. And he knew that, in some way, it was the murder of Frank Hepplethwaite he was out to avenge, not Jason Fox's.

One or two pairs of curious eyes followed him up the

stairs at the station, but nobody said anything. Susan was in her office waiting for him with a thick pile of papers in front of her.

'I feel like a schoolboy sneaking a look at naughty pictures,' Banks said. 'Can I take them to my office?'

'Of course,' said Susan. 'You don't have to ask my permission.' She stood up.

'Look, I appreciate this.'

'No problem.'

'Susan, is—'

'Sorry, sir. I've got to go.'

She dashed out and left him standing in her office. Well, he thought, it didn't take long to become a pariah around here, did it? But he could hardly blame Susan for wanting to put a bit of distance between them. Not after all that had happened. And she *had* put herself out to help him.

Checking to see that the coast was clear, he tiptoed across the corridor to his own office with the papers and shut the door behind him. Nothing had changed. Even the desk was still at the same odd angle after Riddle had fallen back on it. Embarrassed at the memory of what he'd done, Banks straightened it, sat down with the pile of paper, packet of cigarettes and ashtray beside him, window a couple of inches open, and settled down to read.

TWO

What the hell am I doing here? Susan wondered, as Banks stood aside and held the door of The Duck and Drake open for her. Why did I agree to this? *I must be insane*.

The Duck and Drake was a small hideaway in Skinner's

Yard, one of the many alleys off King Street. Wedged between an antiquarian bookshop and the Victoria wine shop, it had a narrow frontage and not much more room inside. One advantage was that it was one of the few pubs that still had a snug, a tiny room handy for private conversations. The doorway was so low that even Banks had to stoop. Inside, the snug was all dark wood beams and whitewashed stone walls hung with brass ornaments. An old black-leaded fireplace took up almost one entire wall. Above it ran a long wooden mantelpiece with a few tattered leatherbound books.

They had the snug to themselves. Banks bought the drinks and sat against the wall, opposite her, a small table between them.

Sipping her St Clement's, Susan could hear the occasional kerchunk of the fruit machine and chink of the cash register coming from the other rooms. If they wanted the barman's attention, they had to ring a little bell on the bar. It was an altogether too intimate and cosy set-up for Susan, but there was nothing she could do about it. Banks had been right in that The Queen's Arms was far too public a place for them to meet. And he was clearly oblivious to her discomfort, drinking his Sam Smith's Old Brewery Bitter and chewing on a cheese-and-onion sandwich. Susan had no appetite at all. Between mouthfuls, he told her about what he had discovered in Amsterdam.

Susan listened, frowning and biting her lower lip in concentration. When Banks had finished, she said, 'It makes sense, sir, but how does it change things? We already know Mark Wood killed Jason. He admitted it.'

Banks finished his sandwich, sipped some Sam Smith's and reached for his cigarettes.

'Yes,' he said. 'I've just read through his statements.

The kid's a pathological liar. He's confessed to manslaughter, but if I'm right it was murder. Premeditated murder.'

'I don't see how you can prove that.'

'There's the rub. According to the post-mortem report, Jason Fox was hit *on the back of the head* with the beer bottle, right?'

Susan nodded. 'That's where Dr Glendenning found the most damage to the skull, and the glass fragments.'

'But in his statement, Mark Wood said he hit Jason *on the side of the head.*'

'I noticed that,' said Susan, 'but, quite honestly, sir, I didn't think much of it. He was confused, under pressure. Basically, he was saying he just lashed out.'

'Yes, I understand that. The point is, that doesn't happen in a fight.'

'Sir?'

'Stand up.'

Banks edged out from the bench. The room itself was just about high enough for him to stand up in. There was no one else around. Susan got to her feet and stood close, facing him, almost close enough to feel the warmth of his body.

She concentrated on the demonstration, focusing on little details. He didn't look well, she noticed. He had dark bags under his eyes, and his face was pale. There was also a deep sadness in him that she had never noticed before.

'Pretend to hit me on the back of the head with an imaginary beer bottle,' he said.

'I can't, sir,' Susan said. 'Not from this angle. Jason must have had his back to Wood, walking either in front of or beside him. Or he must at least have been partly turned sideways.'

'Like this?' Banks turned sideways.

'Yes, sir.'

Banks went back to his seat and lit a cigarette. 'Been in many fights?' he asked.

'No, sir. But that—'

'Let me finish. I have. At school. And, believe me, you would never get your opponent to stand in that position. Not willingly. Not unless you'd hit him with your fist first and knocked him sideways.'

'Maybe that's what happened?'

Banks shook his head again. 'Listen to what you're saying, Susan. To do that, he'd have to have been holding the beer bottle in the same hand he punched Fox with and then swung back very quickly and hit him before he moved. Even if he had the beer bottle in the other hand and switched after he'd hit him, it still doesn't make sense. And remember, Jason was no slouch when it came to physical strength. You'd need every advantage to get the better of him. Let me ask you a question.'

'Yes, sir.'

'Was Mark Wood bruised in any way? Did he have a black eye or a cauliflower ear?'

'No.'

'You'd expect something like that, wouldn't you, if he'd been in an actual fight? Especially with as tough a customer as Jason Fox. Are you telling me Jason didn't even get one punch in?'

'I don't know, sir. Perhaps he hit Wood in the body, where it wouldn't show, and not in the face? I mean, we didn't do a strip search or anything.'

Banks shook his head. 'I'm sorry, but it's just not on. I had another good look at the crime-scene photographs as well, and I reread Dr Glendenning's post-mortem report. It just couldn't have happened the way Mark Wood said it did.'

'Well,' Susan said slowly, 'Superintendent Gristhorpe wasn't entirely convinced, either. But Mark said Jason Fox was goading him about his wife and kid. They needn't have faced off to start fighting. Mark probably just lashed out when he'd had enough. I suppose you saw it for yourself in the statement, but when we pushed Wood on exactly how and when it happened, he said it was all a blur, he couldn't remember.'

'How very convenient. He also denied emptying Jason Fox's pockets. Two loose ends.'

'That's the thing that bothered me most, sir. But we just assumed that either he lied because it would look bad for him, too deliberate, stopping to empty Jason's pockets instead of running off in a panic. Or maybe someone else came along later and robbed Fox while he was lying there.'

'I'd go for the first explanation, myself. It just didn't fit with the scenario he was painting for you. But why take his keys as well, unless they might have led to easier identification? I think whoever did this wanted to keep the victim's identity from us until they had a chance to clear out the Rawdon house of any dodgy files or notes he might have kept there, and they weren't taking any chances.'

'We just thought that if some opportunist came along and did it, he simply took everything. You know, just sort of scooped it all up quickly without pausing to separate the keys from the loose change.' Susan shrugged. 'Chief Constable Riddle didn't seem to be worried by any of this. And by then we had him breathing right down our necks.'

'It's still two loose ends too many for me.'

'Then I don't know where that leaves us, sir. What about motive?'

Banks told her about Mark's connection with Motcombe's drug deal, and Jason's disapproval.

'So you think Motcombe's behind it?' she said.

'I do. But proving it's another matter. Officially the case is closed. You got a confession. That pleased Jimmy Riddle. That and the opportunity to suspend me. I made a mistake there. I didn't expect you'd solve the case so quickly that he'd be buzzing round the station all weekend. To be honest, I didn't expect he'd find out where I'd gone.'

'Sir,' Susan blurted out, feeling her heart lurch into her throat. 'Can I tell you something?'

Banks frowned and lit another cigarette. 'Yes, of course. What is it?'

Susan chewed on her lip for a while, just looking at him, unsure now whether she dare speak out or not. Then she took a deep breath and told him all about Gavin's betrayal.

When she had finished, Banks just sat quietly staring down at the table. She was afraid of what he might say, especially as she could no longer deny to herself the way she felt about him. Please God, she prayed, let him never find out about *that*.

'I'm sorry, sir,' she said.

Banks looked at her, a sad, crooked smile on his face. 'Never mind. It wasn't your fault. How were you to know your boyfriend would run off and tell tales to Jimmy Riddle?'

'Whichever way you look at it, sir, I still betrayed a confidence.'

'Forget it.'

'How can I do that? Look how it's turned out.'

'It isn't over yet, Susan. I'm far from finished. It must have hurt you, this betrayal. I'm sorry.'

Susan looked down, into her empty glass.

'Fancy another drink?' Banks asked.

'No, sir. I'm fine. Really.'

'Well, I fancy another pint.'

Banks went to the bar and rang the bell. While he was waiting to get served, Susan sat, hunched in on herself, feeling miserable. No matter how bloody kind and forgiving Banks might be, she could never forgive herself for what she had done. It wasn't so much the betrayal itself, as the humiliation of letting herself be fooled and used by a bastard like Gavin.

'So what do you want to do?' she asked when he came back. 'I mean about Mark Wood.'

'I see from the paperwork that Wood's solicitor was called Giles Varney?'

'That's right. A real arrogant bastard. Expensive, too. It seemed a bit odd at the time, that he would get Varney to come all the way from Leeds.'

'Yes.'

'Wood also said something about him being Jason's solicitor, too – the one who helped them get the business set up. He didn't want a duty solicitor. He was adamant about that.'

'Interesting.' Banks sipped his pint, wiped his lips and said, 'And fishy. You know, I wouldn't be at all surprised if Varney is Motcombe's solicitor, too, or at least works for the same firm. I'll have to give Ken Blackstone a call and check. Now, according to the reports, it was only when the blood evidence came back that Wood confessed, right?'

'Yes, sir. It would have been pretty difficult to lie his way out of that one.'

'Did he have a private conference with Varney? Make phone calls?'

'Yes, sir. We did it all strictly according to PACE.'

Banks nodded. 'So Wood talked to Varney, then he made a telephone call, then he confessed.'

'Yes, sir.'

'Who did he call?'

'I don't know. It was made in private.'

'We should be able to find a record of the number. I'll bet you a pound to a penny it was Neville Motcombe. I'll bet he told Motcombe he was well and truly up the creek without a paddle and Motcombe talked to Varney, who then told him to plead manslaughter.'

'But why would he do that?'

'Isn't it obvious? You had him against the ropes. I mean, fine, early blood evidence doesn't necessarily mean a hell of a lot, but Wood *knew* he'd done it, and both he and Varney probably knew it was just a matter of time before we got results from DNA testing. And that they'd be positive. In the meantime, if Mark Wood admits to a lesser charge of manslaughter, denying that he's ever even met Motcombe, then the heat's off. It was just a fight that went wrong.

'And you can also bet that Varney will milk as much sympathy from the jury as he can from the fact that the fight started over Jason Fox making racist remarks about Mark Wood's wife and child. All Motcombe has to promise is that Wood will get a short sentence *and* that his family will be financially taken care of while he's inside. That and a nice bonus when he gets out. I think it's an offer I'd probably take if my balls were in the wringer like Wood's are.'

'*If* he pays a penny.'

'Yes. I suppose he could renege. And arrange for an accident in jail. I'm assuming he's not doing all this out of the kindness of his heart. He's doing it because Wood has something on him. Like the truth about what happened.'

'What can we do about it, if you're right?'

'*We* can't do anything, Susan. Remember, you're still on the job, but you're off the case. I, on the other hand, can do whatever I want.'

'But—'

Banks held his hand up. 'Susan, I appreciate what you've done so far, but I don't want to risk getting you into trouble again. Even Superintendent Gristhorpe wouldn't approve if he knew what I was up to.'

'He would if you told him, sir. I told you he had his doubts, too. But Jimmy Riddle just barged in and steam-rollered everything.'

'I know. But the super's not here. It's better this way for the time being. Believe me.'

'What next, then?'

Banks looked at his watch. 'Next, I think I'll get right back to basics and pay George Mahmood another visit. There's something missing from those statements. Some connection I'm missing, and it's starting to irritate me. It might be worth eating a mouthful or two of humble pie to find out what it is.'

THREE

Banks walked down King Street towards the Mahmoods' shop. As he passed School Lane, he could hear kids shouting on the rugby pitch and was almost tempted to go and watch. He had played rugby at school and when he first joined the Met. He'd been a pretty good winger, if he said so himself. Strong, slippery and fast.

Is this what private eyes feel like? he wondered as he cut down along Tulip Street, on the northern edge of the Leaview Estate. Walking the mean streets of Eastvale? He didn't even have a licence to validate what he was doing. How did you go about getting a private-eye licence in Yorkshire? Did you even need a licence?

He did, however, still have his warrant card. Riddle hadn't got the chance to ask for it, and Banks hadn't managed the cliché of slapping it down on the table. He supposed it would be an offence to use it while under suspension, but that was the least of his worries.

The builders were busy at work in the fields around Gallows View, mixing concrete, climbing ladders with hods resting on their shoulders, or just idling around chatting and smoking cigarettes. Soon, the row of old cottages would be swallowed up. Banks wondered if they'd change the name of the street and the fields when the new estate was finished. *Gallows Estate* probably wouldn't sit too well with the local council.

For Banks, approaching the Mahmoods' shop felt like coming full circle. Not only had the Jason Fox case led him there, but his first case in Eastvale had involved the previous owner. And the way things looked, this might be his last case.

George stood behind the counter, wearing his white shirt with its Nehru collar, serving a young woman with a baby strapped to her breast. When he saw Banks, he scowled. His mother, Shazia, came over from the freezer area, where she'd been stamping prices on packages of frozen pizza.

Though she only came up to Banks's shoulders, her eyes challenged him. 'What do you want this time, Mr Banks? Haven't you caused enough trouble around here?'

'As far as I know, I haven't caused any trouble, Mrs Mahmood. Not intentionally, at any rate. I have a job to do.' A small lie, he realized. *Had* a job would be more like it. 'I have a job to do, and it's sometimes difficult. I'm sorry if it caused you any pain.'

'Oh, are you? Such as throwing my son in a cell overnight, worrying his poor parents to death?'

'Mrs Mahmood, George wasn't *thrown* anywhere, and he exercised his right to make a telephone call. If he didn't ring you—'

She waved her hand impatiently. 'Oh, yes, he rang us, all right. But we still worried. A young boy being put in jail with all those criminals.'

'He was in a cell by himself. Look, I don't know where you've got this from—'

'And only because of his colour. Don't think we don't know that's why you pick on us.'

Banks took a deep breath. 'Look, Mrs Mahmood, I'm getting sick of this. We took your son in because he and his friends had an altercation with the victim's party on the night of the killing, because they live in pretty much the same area of town, because they refused to co-operate with us and because we found something suspicious on George's trainer.'

'Suspicious? Animal blood?'

'We didn't know that at the time. It *could* have been human blood.'

She shook her head. 'My son would never hurt anyone.'

'I'm sorry, but my business isn't always as trusting as it might be.'

'And what about the second time? Wasn't that persecution?'

'My colleagues turned up a witness who said he *saw* George and his two friends beat up Jason Fox. What could they do?'

'But he was lying.'

'Yes. But again, we didn't know that at the time.'

'So why have you come here pestering us all over again?'

'It's all right, Mother,' George said, walking over. The woman with the baby seemed torn between leaving and staying to eavesdrop on the conversation. She took a long time putting her change back in her purse, then Banks gave her a sharp glance and she scurried out murmuring comforting sounds to the baby, who had started to cry.

'Can we go somewhere and talk, Mohammed?' Banks asked.

George nodded towards the stockroom in the back of the shop.

'I'm going to call a solicitor,' Mrs Mahmood said.

'No need to, Mum,' said George. 'I can handle this.'

Banks followed him into the back. The stockroom was full of boxes and smelled of cumin and shoe polish. There were no windows, or if there were, they were covered by the stacks of boxes. A bare bulb shone in the centre of the room. Banks fancied it looked rather like a film-maker's idea of one of those interrogation rooms from the old days. He'd seen a film not too long ago in which two detectives had actually sat a woman in a chair with two bright desk lights pointed at her. He'd never tried that in interrogations himself; he wondered if it worked.

'What do you want?' George said. There wasn't a trace of friendliness in his voice. Whatever friendship there had ever been, through Brian, was gone now.

'I need your help.'

George snorted and leaned against a stack of crates, arms crossed. 'That's a laugh. Why should I help you?'

'To find out who really killed Jason Fox.'

'Who cares? From what I've heard, the racist bastard deserved everything he got. Besides, I read in the paper that his mate confessed. Isn't that good enough for you?'

'I'm not going to argue with you. Will you just answer a few straightforward questions, please?'

He shrugged. 'All right. No skin off my nose. But hurry up.'

'Cast your mind back to that Saturday night at The Jubilee. Why were you there?'

George frowned. 'Why? To listen to the band. Why else? Kobir was up visiting from Bradford, like I said, so Asim and me thought he'd enjoy it.'

'I understand The Jubilee has a good reputation for music?'

'Yeah.'

'Girls?'

'Yeah, it's a good place to meet girls.'

'And drugs?'

'If you're interested in that sort of thing. I'm not.'

'People come from miles around.'

'So?'

'And it was really busy that night?'

'Yeah. Well, Scattered Dreams are really popular. They're pretty new on the scene and they haven't got to the expensive venues yet. But they're already recording for an indie label. Pretty soon you'll be paying through the nose to go see them at Wembley or somewhere.'

'Okay. Now, apart from that little contretemps you had with Jason, did you notice anything else about him and his pal?'

'Never paid any attention, really. Except that they seemed to be talking pretty intensely a lot of the time.'

'Arguing?'

'Not loudly, not so's you'd notice. But they didn't look too happy with one another.'

'Did they try to chat up any girls?'

'Not that I saw.'

'They weren't listening to the music?'

'Not really. Some of the time. But they were sitting towards the back, closer to the bar. We were near the front, but the way the chairs were angled around the table, they were pretty much in my line of vision. When they weren't talking, the other one, the one that killed him, would seem to be listening, but the one that got killed even put his fingers in his ears every now and then.'

'What kind of music was it?'

George shifted position and put his hands in his pockets. 'Hard to describe, really. Sort of a mix between rap, reggae and acid rock. That's about the best I can do.'

No wonder Jason had put his fingers in his ears, Banks thought. He obviously hadn't known what kind of music to expect. But Mark Wood probably had.

'Did you see either of them talk to anyone else?'

George frowned. 'No. I was far more interested in the music than in those two pillocks.' The shop bell pinged. 'I'd better get back and help my mum. My dad's down at the cash and carry.'

'Just a couple more questions. Please.'

'Okay. But hurry up.'

'What about those Jamaicans selling drugs you mentioned when I first talked to you?'

'What about them?'

'Was that true?'

'Yes, of course it was. I suppose I should admit I don't know for certain they were from Jamaica, but they looked like Rastas, and one of them had dreadlocks.'

'And the drugs?'

'I saw a bit of money change hands now and then, then one of them would talk on his mobile. A while later he'd nip outside and bring back the Ecstasy or crack or hash or whatever from the person who was carrying it. They don't carry it on them. That's how they usually do it.'

'And you saw them doing that?'

'Sure. You think I should have reported it? You think the police don't know what's going on? You told me yourself The Jube has a reputation for drugs.'

'I'm sure the Drugs Squad are quite well aware of what's going on. It doesn't sound as if these lads are major dealers, though. Were they regulars?'

'I'd never seen them before.'

'Doing good business?'

'By the looks of it.' George sneered. 'Some of the white kids think it's cool to buy from spades.'

'Were they with anyone?'

'They were with the band as far as I could tell.'

A few connections started to form in Banks's mind. This was the link that had been eluding him. 'Were they actually playing with the band?'

George shrugged. 'No, maybe roadies or something. Hangers-on.' The bell pinged again. 'Look, I'd better get back. Really.'

'Right. Just one more thing. Did you see any contact at all between the Jamaicans and Jason, or Mark?'

'What? That would have been hardly likely, would it? I mean . . . wait a minute . . .'

'What?'

'Once, when I was going for a piss, I saw them pass one another in the corridor. Anyway, now I think of it, they sort of nodded at each other. Very quick, like, and expressionless. I thought it was a bit weird at the time, then I forgot about it.'

'Who nodded at whom?'

'The kid who confessed. He nodded at one of the Jamaicans. Like I said, I thought it was odd because he was with the bloke who called me a "Paki bastard" and there he was, on nodding terms with a Rasta.'

'So this was *after* your little conflict with Jason Fox?'

'Yes.'

'That makes sense,' Banks muttered, mostly to himself. 'You were very nicely set up.'

'Come again?'

'Oh, nothing. Just thinking out loud.' Banks followed George back into the shop. 'Thanks for your time, Mohammed.' He became aware of Shazia Mahmood glaring at him as he walked out onto the street.

For a moment, Banks just stood there on Gallows View as the chaotic thoughts settled into some sort of pattern, like iron filings when you hold a magnet under them. Motcombe's drug deal with the Turk and Devon, using Mark Wood as a go-between. Mark Wood's Jamaican wife, Mark's connection with a reggae band and with drug dealing. Scattered Dreams. That signal between Wood and the drug dealer. Jason's death warrant. There was a pattern all right, but now he had to come up with a way of *proving* it.

Banks set off towards King Street. A pneumatic drill from the building site broke the silence and sent a pack of scavenging sparrows spiralling off into the sky.

14

ONE

'**Ken, you're a mate,**' said Banks, 'so I want to let you know before you agree to anything that I'm under suspension.'

'Bloody hell!' Blackstone nearly spilled his drink. It was Thursday lunch-time, and they were in The City of Mabgate, near Millgarth, finishing bowls of chilli. 'What's it all about?' Blackstone asked when he'd recovered his equilibrium.

Banks told him.

Blackstone shook his head. 'They can't make it stick,' he said. 'It sounds like a personal vendetta to me.'

'It is. But don't underestimate personal vendettas, Ken. Especially when Chief Constable Jimmy Riddle's the one carrying them out. And for the record, I'd appreciate it if you didn't tell anyone else around here where I was over the weekend. It could mean real trouble for Craig McKeracher.'

Blackstone tilted his head and squinted at Banks. 'Are you hinting that one of our lads is bent?'

Banks sighed. 'Look, there's no evidence, but it seems clear that someone, most likely someone from West Yorkshire, is doing a few little favours for Neville Motcombe and his league of merry men.'

Blackstone's expression hardened. 'Are you certain?'

'No, not certain. It just seems to be the most obvious of things. As far as I know, so far it's just been a matter of accessing criminal records. If you use the PNC, you wouldn't have to be in West Yorkshire to do that, I'll admit, but that's where Motcombe lives. Logical deduction.'

'Brilliant, my dear Holmes,' said Blackstone. 'But *ve haff vays* of finding out who's been using the PNC, and what they've been looking for. I'll catch the bastard and have his bollocks for golf balls.'

'Maybe it's a "her"?'

'Maybe. But how many women do you find hanging around with these white-power groups? Not a lot. It inclines me to believe they've got more sense.'

'Well, not many of them like playing soldiers, that's for certain. I don't know what odds I'd take against how many of them actually *agree* with some of the stuff Motcombe's lot comes out with, though. Anyway, can I ask you one more favour, Ken?'

'Go ahead. You're doing pretty well for a suspended copper so far.'

'Thanks. Don't move on the mole until I've played out my hand.'

'Why not?'

'Same reason I asked you to keep quiet about Amsterdam. It could jeopardize Craig's cover as Rupert Francis. Or even his life. I don't think Motcombe's the forgiving sort.'

Blackstone squirmed and scratched the back of his neck. 'Okay. My lips are sealed. Want to tell me more?'

Banks told him about Motcombe's gangs of steamers and muggers, then about the Turkish connection and the possible heroin deal with Devon, the deal in which Mark Wood was to play such a big part. Blackstone listened without comment, shaking his head every now and then.

'That's quite a conspiracy,' he said finally. 'It makes me wonder about this suspension business. Do you think there's anything more to it?'

'Like what?'

Blackstone paused a moment. 'More sinister. Remember when John Stalker got taken off that investigation into the RUC's shoot-to-kill policy in Northern Ireland a few years back?'

'Yes.'

'I seem to remember they mocked up some story about him consorting with criminals just to shut him up and stop him embarrassing them. It was all political.'

Banks shook his head. 'A week or two ago I might have been paranoid enough to agree with you,' he said. 'The old conspiracy theory has its appeal. Especially when Dirty Dick Burgess appeared on the scene. And it wouldn't have surprised me if Jimmy Riddle had been in the BNP at the very least. But I don't think so. Whatever he is, Riddle isn't a card-carrying fascist. He's just a pushy, bull-headed arsehole, a frustrated headmaster with a mean streak. Put him on the inner-city streets where the real coppers work and he'd shit himself in five minutes.'

'Maybe so. But you're certain there's nothing more to it?'

'Pretty much. He's been looking for an excuse to nobble me ever since he took the job, and now he thinks he's found it.'

'Okay. So how can I help?'

'I'm going to ask you a couple more favours and I want to give you the chance to say no. I don't want you to stick your neck out for me. I'm giving you fair warning.'

Blackstone paused, then said, 'Go ahead. I'll tell you if I don't want to hear any more. Or when.'

'Fair enough.' Banks lit a cigarette. 'The way I see it, though, is that most of what's going on here is on *your* patch anyway, so you can regard me as informant, consultant, whatever the hell you like, as far as official records go.'

Blackstone laughed. 'Clever bugger. Thought it all out, haven't you? You'd have made a good lawyer. All right. I'm interested. I only hope you don't expect paying, that's all.'

Banks smiled. 'This is for free, Ken. First off, I'd like to know whether a solicitor called Giles Varney has ever acted for Neville Motcombe. There might be some record in the paperwork on that receiving charge. Or, better still, last Thursday, after that fracas at Frank Hepplethwaite's funeral. Someone got Motcombe out of Halifax nick pretty damn quickly.'

Blackstone got his notebook out. 'How d'you spell that?'

Banks spelled Varney for him.

Blackstone smiled. 'Well, that ought to be easy enough to do without compromising my career.'

'The next request might be a bit tougher, and I'll understand if you say no. There was a band from Leeds playing at The Jubilee in Eastvale on the Saturday Jason Fox was killed. They're called Scattered Dreams. Someone who was there told me that there were a couple of Jamaicans dealing small quantities of hash, crack and Ecstasy. Apparently, they might have been with the band in some capacity. Roadies, hangers-on, what have you.'

Blackstone nodded. 'A lot of small dealers are mobile now they've saturated the urban markets. And it makes sense they'd target places where there's loud music and lots of kids. I think I've heard of The Jubilee. Is that the one that advertises in the *Evening Post*?'

'That's the one. I suppose the Drugs Squad keeps tabs on these bands and their itinerant dealers?'

'I hope so,' said Blackstone. 'Though you never quite know what the DS is up to. They're a law unto themselves half the time.'

'Anyway,' Banks went on, ticking off on his fingers, 'Mark Wood had passing contact with one of these lads at The Jubilee. My thinking is that they might have been in this together. First off, I need to know if this band is the same one Mark Wood roadied for a couple of years back, when he was arrested on the drugs charge.'

Blackstone nodded.

'And then I'd like the names of the Jamaicans who were on the fringes of Scattered Dreams that night, if you can get them. I know that might be a bit more difficult.'

'I can only try,' said Blackstone. 'Actually, I know a bloke on the Drugs Squad who can keep his mouth shut. We did some courses at Bramshill together a few years back. Bloke called Richie Hall. He's a Jamaican himself, and he's done a fair bit of undercover work over the years. Anyway, the point is, he knows the music and drugs scene up north better than anyone I know. If he doesn't know who they are, nobody does.'

'Great. There might even be a short cut. Mark Wood's wife's Jamaican. Her maiden name is Shirelle Jade Campbell. They seem to have met up around the time Wood got involved with the band, and I'm wondering if there isn't maybe a family connection. A brother, cousin or something. At least that gives you a name to work on.'

'I'll pass it on to Richie. Like I said, if anyone knows, Richie does.'

'You sure you don't mind doing this, Ken?'

Blackstone shook his head. 'Nah. What are mates for.

I'll warn you, though, you'll be bloody lucky to get anything out of these lads even if we do track them down.'

'I know that. Actually, if I'm right, I was thinking of a slightly more devious approach to the truth. But let's wait and see, shall we?'

'Just as long as your expectations aren't too high. Who knows, there might even be a bit of glory in this for me.'

Banks smiled. 'Maybe. Whatever happens, there'll be no Brownie points for me from Jimmy Riddle. But I promise you, if there's any credit to be taken, it's yours. And lunch is on me.'

'Will you do *me* one small favour, Alan?'

'Name it.'

'Just be bloody careful, that's all.'

TWO

By nine o'clock on Friday morning, Banks felt edgy and restless alone in the house. He was pleased with himself, however, for avoiding the booze completely on Thursday evening, and for actually managing to finish *The Power and the Glory* as he listened to Beethoven's late quartets. So he felt full of energy when he woke up on Friday. There was nothing else he *could* do until he heard from Ken Blackstone, except pace the floor.

When his phone rang at about half past nine, he grabbed the receiver on the first ring. 'Yes? Banks here.'

'Alan, it's Ken.'

'What have you got?'

'Some answers for you. I hope. In answer to your first question, yes, Giles Varney is Neville Motcombe's solicitor and has acted for him on a number of occasions. Their professional relationship goes back to the time Motcombe started buying property in the Leeds area, about four years ago. It seems like they've been bosom buddies ever since.'

'Does Varney have any other known right-wing connections?'

'Yes. I checked around and he's pretty well known in some of the more extreme-right circles.'

'Great. That would seem to indicate that Mark Wood did a deal with Motcombe through Varney. Anything else?'

'This is where it gets a bit more complicated, I'm afraid. And you owe me. I had to spend yesterday evening in a pub with Richie Hall, and he drinks like a bloody fish. I'll be sending you the bill.'

Banks laughed. 'Find anything out?'

'Yes. The band Mark Wood worked with at the time of his first arrest was called Cloth Ears. They split up shortly after the drug bust. But this Scattered Dreams was formed partly from the ashes. Phoenix-like, you might say. Apparently the blokes you're interested in used to play with Cloth Ears but now they just hang around the fringes of Scattered Dreams and sell dope. Seems drugs have sapped whatever talents they might once have had, and most of the time they're too stoned to strum a chord. And you were right about the family connection. The one with the dreadlocks is Shirelle Wood's brother, Wesley Campbell, and the other's a mate of his called Francis Robertson. "Wes" and "Frankie", as they're known locally. Both of them have been seen to associate with Devon recently, according to Richie.'

'Low-level dealers?'

'Looks that way.'

'Excellent.'

'And in Shirelle Wood's favour, Richie says she's not

connected with any of this. In fact she stopped talking to her brother, Wes, as soon as she discovered he was involved in getting Mark busted the first time, and she hasn't talked to him since. Cut him off completely.'

Good for her, Banks thought. There were very few people he had come to have respect for in this whole business. Frank Hepplethwaite was one of them, and Shirelle Jade Wood was another. Pity about her husband. He should have followed her lead and cut off communications with Wesley Campbell, too. But no, Mark Wood thought he could make an easy fortune. And it was a sad thought that Shirelle and Connor would be the ones to suffer the most if the truth did come out.

'Thanks, Ken,' Banks said. 'You've done a great job.'

'No problem.'

'Now for the hard part.'

He heard Blackstone sigh. 'Somehow I had a feeling there might be more to it than this. I assume this is your "cunning plan" for getting to the truth?'

Banks laughed. 'Hear me out, Ken, then let me know if you think we can do it.'

THREE

About an hour later, Banks drove down to Leeds alone. There was no point involving Susan Gay or Jim Hatchley with his scheme. It was risky and could backfire, then he'd have their jobs on his conscience, too. Ken Blackstone would be fine; he was simply carrying out an investigation on his own patch, based on information received. The fact that Banks was along for the ride really didn't matter.

Banks lit a cigarette and turned up the volume on Bryn

Terfel's renditions of *Songs of Travel*. He looked at the digital clock. Eleven o'clock. Plenty of time to do what he had to and pick up Tracy at the residence by six o'clock.

As he pulled up behind Millgarth, he looked at his watch. Just after twelve. If Ken Blackstone had done his work, everything ought to be set up and ready to roll by now. He checked at the front desk and went straight up to Blackstone's office. In the corridor outside the CID offices, as arranged, sat Mark Wood, who had been brought in from Armley Jail shortly after Banks's nine-thirty talk with Ken Blackstone, just to answer a few more questions and help make the paperwork flow more smoothly.

Even though Wood had been sitting there for probably a couple of hours already, he hadn't asked for Giles Varney yet. If he did, they'd have to lie and tell him they couldn't get in touch. With Varney present, the plan would be useless.

Mark Wood didn't look much, Banks thought. Muscular, yes, but basically just another sullen, nervous kid chewing his fingernails in a police station.

Banks introduced himself. They hadn't met before, and it was important that Wood know *someone* from Eastvale was involved in all this. As expected, Wood looked puzzled and confused. When he asked Banks why he had come down all this way, Banks said it was nothing to worry about, he would find out in a while. He sounded like a doctor about to tell a patient he has a terminal illness.

Leaving Wood under guard in the corridor, they went into Ken Blackstone's office, where Wood could watch them through the glass partition if he wanted, though he couldn't hear what they were saying. That would make him even more nervous. Especially if they glanced his way once in a while as they spoke.

They had been standing behind the glass chatting for fifteen minutes about Leeds United's abysmal season and occasionally looking at Mark, when three large uniformed officers led Wesley Campbell and Francis Robertson along the corridor, as arranged. The two had been passive and compliant when picked up over an hour earlier, Ken said. That was either a mark of confidence that they'd be out again in two shakes of a lamb's tail, Banks thought, or they were too stoned to care. Both had been found in possession of small amounts of marijuana, and neither had time to flush it down the toilet, so they had been languishing in the charge room for a while. By now, they weren't quite as complacent.

As they passed Mark Wood, they glanced down at him, and Mark looked even more confused. His eyes widened with fear. Campbell actually struggled against his guards for a moment and tried to get closer to Wood, as if he wanted to warn or threaten him. But the guards held on. Campbell and Robertson were taken to separate interview rooms around the corner. Both seemed to know the PACE regulations by heart, and they asked to make their phone calls immediately.

At about two o'clock, after Banks and Blackstone had enjoyed a leisurely lunch across the road, it was time to start. They went back upstairs and took Mark into an interview room. It was agreed that Banks, being more familiar with the case, would do most of the questioning. Blackstone would give the occasional prod if things got slow. They weren't taping this one. There would be time for formalities later, with Banks well out of the way, if the plan worked. If it didn't, then all hell might break loose as far as disciplinary actions were concerned. Banks had already warned Ken and given him the option of staying well away, but Ken had insisted on being involved.

'Well, Mark,' said Banks, 'I know we haven't met until today, but I've had a great interest in you ever since I saw Jason Fox's body a couple of weeks ago.'

'I've told the police all about that,' Wood said. 'I've pleaded guilty to manslaughter. What's all this about?'

Banks raised an eyebrow. 'It's not quite settled yet,' he said. 'Not to *my* satisfaction, anyway.'

Wood folded his arms. 'I don't know what you mean. First you leave me hanging about in the corridor for hours, now you start interrogating me. I'm not saying anything. I want my solicitor.'

'Mr Varney? Well, we'll see what we can do. For the moment, though, I suggest you hold your horses, Mark, and listen to me. Certain new evidence has come to light that puts an entirely different complexion on the Jason Fox killing.'

'Oh? What's that, then?'

Banks jerked his head towards the door. 'We've just had a long chat with Mr Campbell and Mr Robertson, and they've told us some very interesting things.'

'Like what?'

'Like the truth about what you did to Jason Fox.'

'I don't know what you're talking about.'

'Oh, come on, Mark, surely you can do much better than that?'

'I'm not saying a word.'

'Listen to me, then. According to your brother-in-law Mr Campbell, an old mate of yours from the Cloth Ears days, the two of you were commissioned by Neville Motcombe to get rid of Jason Fox. Jason had become a major risk in a heroin deal you were planning, and a serious threat to Motcombe's power. Motcombe couldn't get any of his own members to do it because Jason was too popular with them. Instead, he got two of the people who were already involved in the drug deal – one from each side, so to speak – two people who also stood to gain a lot. I should imagine Devon wanted one or two of his own lads along just to make sure you did what you agreed, didn't he? From what I hear, he's not the kind of bloke to take undue risks. How am I doing so far?'

Wood's eyes widened. 'You know about Devon? Jesus Christ, does he know about this? Does he know I'm here? Have Wes and Frankie been talking to him? Shit, if Devon thinks I'm talking to the coppers, he'll fucking kill me.'

Banks ignored him. 'When Scattered Dreams played at The Jubilee, it gave you the perfect opportunity. Jason was going to be in Eastvale anyway – he had a football match in the afternoon – so you told him you were coming up and that the two of you could go see the band. Maybe it would be a chance to settle your differences and talk a bit of business, try to save the partnership somehow. I'd imagine you were compliant, more than willing to make compromises. You knew Scattered Dreams weren't Jason's cup of tea, but suggested he might like to broaden his horizons a bit. Who knows, maybe you promised to go to the next Celtic Warrior concert if he gave your lot a try. Jason had been to The Jubilee before, and he had mentioned that a couple of Pakistani youths went there on a fairly regular basis. I'm only guessing at this part, but I think he'd already chucked a brick through one of their windows, and he'd said he was looking for trouble with them. Perfect for you, if something like that happened in public, wasn't it? A bonus. As long as it was just a minor incident, enough to draw just a little attention.

'Anyway, according to Mr Campbell, you accompanied

Jason towards the ginnel, where he and Mr Robertson were waiting at the other end to render any necessary assistance. According to them, you whacked Jason on the back of the head with the bottle a couple of times, and he went down. After that, you managed to kick him to death all by yourself. They didn't have to do a thing. And that, Mark, with two eyewitnesses to testify against you, makes it murder.'

Wood turned pale. 'That's not true,' he said. 'It didn't happen like that at all. They're lying.'

Banks leaned forward. 'What didn't happen like what, Mark?'

'It was like I said. There was just me and Jason. We got into a fight. He slagged off Sheri and Connor. I didn't mean for him to die.'

Banks shook his head. 'I'm afraid that story's gone right down the toilet now, Mark, along with all your other stories. Let me see if I can get them right.' He began counting them off on his fingers, looking towards Ken Blackstone, who nodded at each one. 'First, you weren't anywhere near Eastvale the night Jason got killed. Second, you were at The Jubilee but you never went anywhere near the ginnel. Third, you *were* there and you saw George Mahmood and his mates kill Jason. And, fourth, you killed him yourself in a fair fight. How am I doing so far?'

Wood licked his lips and shifted in his chair.

'Problem is, Mark,' Banks went on, 'you're a liar. The only version we have any independent corroboration of is the one I just put to you, the one Mr Campbell told us about. So it looks as if that's the way it's going to go down now.' He paused, then went on. 'After this interview, DI Blackstone and I will be having a word with the Crown Prosecution Service about changing the charges from manslaughter to murder. That carries a much longer jail sentence, as I'm sure you know.'

'You can't be serious? You can't believe those bastards.'

'Why not? I certainly can't believe *you*. Look at your track record, Mark. No, I'm afraid this is the end of the line for you. You get charged with murder now, and you don't get out of jail for a long, long time. In fact, by the time you get out, your wife will have run off with another bloke long since, and your kid will have grown up and forgotten you. In the meantime, you'll be fending off the arse bandits in Wormwood Scrubs or Strangeways. And that's *if* you last that long. I suspect both Devon and Neville Motcombe have long reaches.'

Wood seemed to shrivel, to draw in on himself like a bank of ashes collapsing. Banks could tell Wood knew he was trapped. He knew lies wouldn't save him now, but he didn't know the best course of action. Time to tell him, time to give him a ray of hope. After pulling the carpet from under him, give him a foam mattress to land on.

'There's only one way out for you, Mark,' he said.

'What's that?' Mark's voice was no louder than a whisper.

'The truth. Right from the top.'

'How will that help?'

'I'm not saying it'll get you off scot-free. Nothing will do that. We don't have the power to make deals with criminals, reduce their sentences in exchange for information. That only happens on American TV shows. But I can guarantee it'll make things easier for you.'

Wood chewed on his knuckles for a few seconds, then said, 'I need protection. They'll kill me. My family, too.'

'We can help you with that, Mark. If you help us.'

Mark rubbed his nose with the back of his hand. 'I never meant to kill him,' he said. 'Honest I didn't. It was those two.' He was close to tears.

'Who?'

'Frankie and Wes.'

'What happened, Mark? Right from the beginning.'

Banks took out his cigarettes and offered Mark one. He took it with a shaking hand. 'All right,' he said. 'But what guarantee have I got that things will go easier for me if I tell you the truth? What are you offering me?'

'You've got my word,' said Banks.

'For what?'

'That you and your family will be protected and that your co-operation will be considered.'

'I want relocation for me and Sheri,' he said. 'And new identities. The Witness Protection Programme. That's what I want.'

'I've already told you, this isn't America, Mark. We don't do things that way in England. Look, like I said, I'm not telling you you're going to walk out of here a free man. You're not. One way or another, you'll serve some time. What I'm saying is that if you give us what we want, the charge can remain manslaughter, not murder.'

'It doesn't sound like that good a deal to me.'

'Well, it is,' Ken Blackstone chipped in. 'The difference is between, say, twenty-five years in a very nasty place – where you'll be vulnerable to anyone Devon or Motcombe care to send along – and maybe five in minimum security prison. Protected environment. Telly and conjugal visits thrown in.' He glanced at Banks, who nodded. 'Your choice, Mark. It's as simple as that.' Wood looked between the two of them and his gaze finally settled on Banks again. 'What about Sheri and Connor?'

347

'We'll take care of them, make sure they're safe,' said Banks. 'You have my word. What about it?'

Wood looked at Blackstone again, who assured him that Banks was right, then he rested back in his chair and said, 'All right. Okay. Neville Motcombe approached me several weeks ago and said he knew about my record for drugs offences. At first I didn't know what he was getting at, then it became clear that he'd made a contact for getting his hands on some pretty large amounts of heroin through Turkey at a rock-bottom price, and he hadn't a clue what to do about it. Drugs just weren't part of his gig, but he saw a way to make a lot of money and fuck up the "niggers" in the bargain, as he put it. He really does talk like that. Makes you sick. Anyway, he found out about my drug bust and decided I was to be the go-between.'

'What was in it for you?'

'Something in the region of fifty thousand quid over a period of a few months, if all went well. Maybe more in the future, if the supply didn't dry up.' He leaned forward and gripped the sides of the chair. 'Look, you can judge me all you like, but have you any idea what that would have meant to Sheri and me? It would have got us out of that fucking prefab, for a start, and it would have given me a good chance at expanding the business, buying some up-to-date equipment, making something out of it. And all I had to do was play go-between for Motcombe and Devon.' He laughed. 'It was a bit of a joke on Motcombe, too. He didn't know Sheri's Jamaican and that his money would actually be going to help one of the people he wanted to destroy.'

'Didn't that bother you, Mark? That he was intending to cause so much suffering in the West Indian community?'

'That was just a load of bollocks he came up with for

Jason's benefit. He was after profits, pure and simple.'

'Takes one to know one?'

'Something like that. Anyway, once you get heroin out on the streets, there's no telling what colour your buyers will be, is there? There's no colour bar on H. Even Jason knew that. Like I said, I thought it was funny that Sheri and Connor were going to get some benefit from this.'

Banks shook his head. 'So you agreed?'

Wood nodded. 'Under Motcombe's instructions, I met with Wes, then with Devon. They never met Motcombe, didn't know who he was. I called him Mr H. Anyway, we talked about prices, delivery schedules, methods of getting the stuff into the country, the lot. Then Devon said he'd think about it. A few days later he got in touch with me through Wes and told me to let Mr H know we were in business. I suppose Motcombe got in touch with his blokes in Turkey – I didn't have anything to do with that end of the operation – and they set things in motion. There were huge profits in it for everyone. Devon wouldn't stop at Leeds – he'd be shifting stuff to Bradford, Sheffield, Manchester, Birmingham, you name it. Somehow or other, that seemed to resolve the problems on both sides. Motcombe's about dealing with darkies and Devon's about dealing with a whitey like me.' Mark snorted. 'Great healer of race relations, greed, isn't it?'

'And where does Jason come in?'

'Motcombe made a big mistake there. I could have told him, but he didn't ask. He seemed to think Jason would just love the idea. I mean, I don't think they'd ever talked about drugs or anything other than League business before. But Jason was straight. Even with Motcombe's justification, he wouldn't go for it. Motcombe got worried that Jason would spread the word among his colleagues in the movement and they'd chuck him out and put Jason in charge instead. I suppose you know neo-Nazis aren't really supposed to be into drugs?'

Banks nodded.

'Then there was the matter of the money to be made. Anyway, Motcombe got paranoid, especially as Jason had gained a lot of respect in the movement and people looked up to him for guidance and leadership. Jason was fast becoming a loose cannon on the deck. So Motcombe decided things would be better all around with Jason out of the way. He knew I was desperate for the money, and he also knew me and Jason didn't get along, so he asked me if I could arrange for the Jamaicans to do away with him. That way, he said, if they happened to get caught, it'd only be two less "niggers" to worry about. You have to give the guy credit, at least he's consistent. I didn't want to do it. I mean, I'm no killer. I know Jason and me had our problems, but I didn't want to see him dead. You have to believe that. I had no choice.'

'What happened?' Banks asked.

Mark ran his hand over his head. 'Like Motcombe asked, I talked to Wes and I told him Jason was involved in the Turkish end of the deal and that he was planning to rip Devon off. I also said he turned out to be a racist bastard, a member of some loony fringe group. Well, I couldn't tell him the truth, could I? I had to make something up pretty quick, and it had to cover whatever publicity might come about when you found out who Jason was. Wes went back to Devon, who ordered it done. Just like that. No questions asked. And he also stipulated that I had to be in it with them. A sort of test of faith, I suppose. I didn't want to do it. I just didn't have any fucking choice.'

'There's always a choice, Mark.'

'Right. Sure. Easy for you to say that. It came down to me over Jason. Sheri and Connor over Jason. What would you have done? Like I said, Jason and me weren't close, and the bastard did get on my nerves with all that Nazi shit.'

'Who came up with the plan?'

'That was down to me. You know the rest. Motcombe wanted it done out of the way. I mean, he knew you'd find out who the victim was eventually, and what organization he belonged to, but he needed time to get his files out of Jason's house. He sent two of his blokes to do that. Anyway, Scattered Dreams were playing in Eastvale and Jason had mentioned possible trouble with some Pakistani kids who went there. Told me he'd already chucked a brick through one of their windows. It couldn't have been better.'

'What about the actual killing? How did it happen?'

Wood swallowed. 'Frankie and Wes were waiting at the other end of the ginnel, as we'd arranged, and when I hit Jason with the bottle they came forward and started booting him. I kicked him a couple of times, to make it look like I was with them all the way. But only a couple of times. And not very hard. He—' Wood stopped for a moment and put his head in his hands. 'Christ, he *begged* us to stop. I just thought about Connor and the damp walls and the yobs that taunt Sheri, call her a black bitch and threaten to gang-bang her every time she goes to the shops. I didn't think about Jason lying there till it was too late. You have to believe me, I didn't mean to kill him. It was Wes and Frankie. They're fucking maniacs. They'd been out in the van smoking crack.'

'All right, Mark,' said Banks. 'Calm down. Tell me,

what happened when we first arrested you? Why did you change your story?'

Mark shifted in his chair. 'Well, the evidence. It was getting pretty strong against me. I was up shit creek. So when Varney took me aside, I phoned Motcombe and basically explained the situation.'

'What did he say?'

'To tell you it was just a fight between the two of us, to leave him out of it, and he'd see I got the best legal help available. He'd also take care of Sheri and Connor financially while I was inside, if it came to that. What a laugh, Motcombe taking care of a black woman and a mixed-race kid.'

'But he didn't know that.'

'No. And I didn't tell him.'

'Have you had any contact with him since your arrest?'

Mark shook his head.

'What about Devon?'

'No. I phoned my fucking bastard of a brother-in-law, though, Wes.'

'What did you talk to him about?'

'I told him who Mr H was, where he lived. Just in case something went wrong and Motcombe didn't keep up his end of the bargain. You know, like maybe when he *did* find out Sheri's black and all, then he wouldn't help them. I needed some sort of insurance.'

'Okay, Mark, I need to know just one more thing before we start taking fresh statements and making this all official.'

'Yes?'

'Will you testify that Neville Motcombe instigated this conspiracy to murder Jason Fox?'

Wood's lips curled. 'Motcombe? Bloody right I will. No way that bastard's going to get away with it.'

'And Devon?'

Mark looked away. 'I don't know. That's different. I'd need some sort—'

'We'll see you and your family are protected, Mark, like I told you earlier.'

'I'll think about it. Okay?'

'Okay.' Banks smiled. 'I think that just about wraps it up for now. Thanks, Mark, you've been a great help.'

'What happens to me now?'

'You make your official statement, then you go back to Armley. Eventually, there'll be committal proceedings and a trial, but we'll cross those bridges when we get to them. In the meantime, we'll make sure your family is protected.' Banks looked at his watch. Just after three-thirty. Then he turned to Ken Blackstone. 'For the moment, though, I think it's about time we paid Mr Motcombe another visit.'

FOUR

Leaving one of Blackstone's most trusted DCs to take Mark Wood's official statement, Banks and Blackstone set off in the Cavalier for Motcombe's house. Most of the journey, they talked about getting enough evidence together for the CPS to take on Motcombe.

'I'm still not sure about this,' Banks said, driving along through Pudsey. 'I can't help feeling I'm jumping the gun. How bloody long's Motcombe likely to get for conspiracy to commit murder? That's assuming we can prove it. Giles Varney will whittle it down to conspiracy to assault, if he's got any brains. We might be better off leaving him to the Drugs Squad. He'd get longer for dealing heroin. And I promised Craig McKeracher I'd wait till I had something really solid before I moved in.'

Ken Blackstone shook his head. 'At this point, I don't think we have much choice. We've got evidence we have to act on. Mark Wood has actually *named* Motcombe as one of the blokes who requested Jason Fox's murder. Now Wood's blurted it all out, we *have* to go ahead. I don't think he'll get such a light sentence. Plus this way we also get Wes and Frankie in the bargain, and maybe even Devon, too. That'd be a real bonus.'

'Maybe so,' said Banks. 'I hope you're right.'

'Besides,' Blackstone added, 'I'd say we're best getting Motcombe off the streets as soon as possible. And none of what we're doing blows Craig McKeracher's cover. What we've got all came from Mark Wood.'

Banks turned down the hill to Motcombe's house and they got out of the car. The sky was clear and the countryside shone green and gold and silver. A chill wind from the valley whistled around their ears as they stood and knocked at the front door.

No answer.

'What's that noise?' Blackstone asked.

Straining his ears, Banks could detect a faint whining above the sound of the wind. 'Sounds like an electric drill or something. He must be down in the workshop. That's why he can't hear us.'

'Let's try the back.'

They walked around to the back of the house, which overlooked the valley and parkland. The sound of the drill was louder now.

Banks hammered on the back door. Still nothing. Just on the off chance, he tried the doorknob. It opened.

'Mr Motcombe!' he called out as the two of them

walked down the stairs to the workshop. 'We're coming in.' He began to feel a slight shiver of trepidation. It looked dark at the bottom, and they could be walking into a trap. Motcombe could have a Kalashnikov or an Uzi with him. He might be hiding away in a dark corner ready to start blasting away at them.

But still they advanced slowly towards where the sound was coming from. Then Banks noticed something odd. The high-pitched whine the drill was making hadn't changed the entire time they'd been there. Surely if Motcombe were working on something and really couldn't hear them, there would be variations in the pitch of the drill – when he stuck it into a piece of wood, for example. And if he were making so much noise when he worked, he would hardly leave the back door unlocked so that anyone could walk in, would he? Banks felt the back of his neck tingle.

At last, they approached the workroom and pushed the door open slowly on the brightly lit room.

Motcombe was there all right.

His body hung at an awkward angle, naked to the waist, his polo-neck tunic hanging in shreds around his hips as if it had been ripped or cut off. His left wrist had been wedged in a vice, which had been tightened until the bones cracked and poked through the flesh. Blood caked the oiled metal. The smell of blood and sweat mixed with iron filings, shaved wood and linseed oil. And cordite. The room felt crowded, claustrophobic, even with only the two of them there. Three, if you counted the dead man.

The drill lay on the workbench. Banks didn't want to touch it, but he wanted the sound to stop. He went over to the wall and pulled out the plug, using a handkerchief carefully, and hoping he wasn't smudging any valuable prints. Old habits die hard. Somehow, he doubted that there would be any. People who do things like this don't leave fingerprints.

The scene was a gruesome one. More so because of the unnaturally bright lights that Motcombe had rigged up so he could see clearly what he was working on. What Banks at first took to be bullet holes in Motcombe's chest and stomach turned out, on further examination, to be spots where the drill had been inserted. When the bit stopped spinning, he could see it was clogged with blood and tissue.

Motcombe's right arm was practically in shreds, striped with lacerations, patches of skin hanging off as if he'd been flayed. Someone had obviously shredded the flesh with a saw, cutting deep into the muscle and bone. Banks noticed the blood and chips of bone on the edge of a circular saw that lay on the floor beside the body.

The *coup de grâce* looked like two gunshot wounds to the head, one through the left eye and the other in the middle of the temple, both leaving large exit wounds.

'Well, Ken,' said Banks finally, backing away from the scene. 'I can't say I envy you sorting this little lot out.'

'Me neither,' said Blackstone, visibly pale. 'Let's get outside. I don't think I can stand being in here much longer.'

They stood outside the back door overlooking the valley and the peaceful village of Tong in the distance. Three large crows circled high in the blue air. Banks lit a cigarette to take the taste and smell of the workshop out of his mouth. 'Want to call it in?' he asked.

'Yes. Just give me a minute.'

'What do you think?'

Blackstone took a deep breath before answering. 'You

probably know as well as I do, Alan,' he said. 'Either Wes Campbell or Frankie Robertson phoned Devon the minute they saw Mark Wood at Millgarth. That was, what, over four hours ago now. This pisses Devon off mightily, and he sends a couple of lads over right away to help him vent his rage. You don't get far in Devon's business unless you're seen to act, and to act *fast*. He relies heavily on pure fear. Who knows, maybe he's even made a down payment to Motcombe and wants his money back, too? So they either torture him to find out where the money is, or they do it for fun, just to teach him a lesson. Then they execute him. Bang, bang.'

Banks nodded. 'Either that or they decided they didn't like Mr H's politics when Mark told them who he really was.'

'It's Devon's style, Alan,' Blackstone went on. 'Two head shots with a .38, by the looks of it. Remember those murders I told you about in New York, Toronto, Chapeltown?'

'Uh-huh.'

'Same MO. Torture and two head shots. It still doesn't help us prove anything. I don't suppose anyone can tie Devon to the scene. He'll have an alibi you can't break, and there'll never be any trace of a murder weapon.'

'We've still got Mark Wood to use against him.'

'If he doesn't suddenly lose his memory the minute he hears about what happened to Motcombe. I probably would if I were him.'

'And don't forget Campbell and Robertson. You've got them, too. They might not be quite as tough as they seem once you put the pressure on. Especially if they're deprived of their narcotic sustenance. And I'll bet you've got records of any telephone calls they made from Millgarth.'

Blackstone nodded and looked around, then he sighed. 'Well, we'd better set things in motion. Can I use your mobile?'

'Be my guest.'

They walked around to Banks's car at the front of the house and Banks handed him the phone. Blackstone tapped in the numbers, gave the details and requested more police, a murder van and a SOCO team.

'I'll tell you something,' he said when he'd finished. 'Your chief constable isn't going to like it, is he? Remember the song and dance he made in the paper about solving the murder, keeping race out of it?'

'Bugger Jimmy Riddle,' said Banks. 'This isn't a matter of race, it's drugs and greed. Anyway, they're West Yorkshire's Jamaicans, not ours. And I wasn't even here.'

'What do you think now?' Blackstone asked, handing Banks the phone. 'Still want to come and work for West Yorkshire?'

Banks stubbed out his cigarette on the wall and put the butt in his pocket to avoid contaminating the scene. 'I don't know, Ken. I really don't know. I might not have much choice, might I? Anyway, right now, I think I'd better make myself scarce before the troops arrive and all hell breaks loose. You'll be okay?'

'I'll be fine. I'll catch a lift back to Millgarth from one of the patrol cars. Go. Go.'

Banks shook Blackstone's hand. 'Thanks, Ken. I'd be interested to hear you tell them why you're here and how you got here, but I really can't stay.'

'I'll tell them I got the bus,' said Blackstone. 'Now be a good lad, Alan, and bugger off back to Eastvale. I think I hear the sound of sirens.'

Banks got in his car. He couldn't hear sirens, but the

sound of Neville Motcombe's electric drill still whined in his ears.

A mile or so down the road, the first patrol cars passed him, lights and sirens going. No hurry, Banks thought. No hurry at all. He lit another cigarette and switched on the tape player. Robert Louis Stevenson, sung by Bryn Terfel:

> Now when day dawns on the brow of the moorland,
> Lone stands the house, and the chimney-stone is cold.
> Lone let it stand, now the friends are all departed,
> The kind hearts, the true hearts, that loved the place of old.

Banks looked at his watch. Just gone half past four. Hard to believe, but they had hardly been half an hour at Motcombe's house. He still had plenty of time to go and pick up Tracy for the weekend, even with the rush-hour traffic. Plenty of time.